"Somewhere, I knew, was the one ideal love for whom I was intended, the one perfect love who would catch me up in my own wheel... a wheel whose high point intersected the arc of heaven; from its top I would see wonders of the human heart no one in North Chittendon ever suspected existed...."

THE MADNESS OF
A SEDUCED WOMAN

"Impossible to put down.... A richly textured, engrossing narrative.... Readers should find this Schaeffer's best book since ANYA."

—*Publishers Weekly*

"Almost hallucinatory clarity.... No contemporary author can write more vividly and more powerfully about the obsessive passion of a young woman than Susan Fromberg Schaeffer."

—Marge Piercy, author of VIDA

"Original and deeply serious.... A number of issues especially pertinent to our time shape the course of the narrative... the validity of the insanity plea; the doubtful merits of psychoanalysis; the conflict over abortion; as well as how society treats women, how men treat women and how women treat themselves.... Susan Schaeffer's powers of invention are prodigious."

—Lynne Sharon Schwartz,
The Chicago Tribune Book World

"Literature of the first magnitude.... Schaeffer has awesome imaginative and inventive powers.... Feelings come vibrantly—and often painfully—alive."

—*The Cleveland Plain Dealer*

THE MADNESS OF A SEDUCED WOMAN

The
MADNESS
of a
SEDUCED
WOMAN

Susan Fromberg Schaeffer

BANTAM BOOKS
TORONTO • NEW YORK • LONDON • SYDNEY • AUCKLAND

THE MADNESS OF A SEDUCED WOMAN
A Bantam Book / published by arrangement with E. P. Dutton, Inc.

PRINTING HISTORY
E. P. Dutton edition published April 1983
Bantam edition/August 1984

*Bantam Books are published by Bantam Books, Inc. Its trade-
mark, consisting of the words ''Bantam Books'' and the por-
trayal of a rooster, is Registered in U.S. Patent and Trademark
Office and in other countries. Marca Registrada. Bantam
Books, Inc., 666 Fifth Avenue, New York, New York 10103.*

For Neil

I would like to thank the following people: David Hewett, Valden Madsen, William Mundell, Miriam Andrews, Joseph Wise, Cathy Lowe, Evadne Lafayette, Leanne Domash, Timothy Seldes, and Karen Braziller, *multo altissima in orbe terrarum*.

"That we are the breath and similitude of God, it is indisputable, and upon record of holy scripture; but to call ourselves a microcosm, or little world, I thought it only a pleasant trope of rhetoric, till my near judgment and second thought told me there was a real truth therein. For first we are a rude mass, and in the rank of creatures which only are, and have a dull kind of being, not yet privileged with life, or preferred to sense or reason; next we live the life of plants, the life of animals, the life of men, and at last the life of spirits; running on, in one mysterious nature, those five kinds of existences which comprehend the creatures not only of the world, but of the universe. Thus is man that great and true amphibium, whose nature is disposed to live not only like other creatures in divers elements, but in divided and distinguished worlds; for though there be but one to sense, there are two to reason, the one visible, the other invisible."

— SIR THOMAS BROWNE

"I was driving the company of a stranger from Ragusa in Dalmatia to a place in Herzegovina: our conversation turned to the subject of travel in Italy, and I asked my companion whether he had ever been to Orvieto and looked at the famous frescoes there, painted by ..."

— SIGMUND FREUD

Contents

The
Upland
Pasture

1

It had been raining daily for almost two weeks, and so he had put off slaughtering the cow. She was more than ten years old and she no longer gave milk. If he waited any longer, the hired men would begin mumbling about how he threw out money feeding a cow who was good for nothing; they would complain about how she got loose more often than the other cows—and she did, because she followed members of the family right back to the house. She had an instinct for every hole in every hedge, every break in every fence, and there they would be, sitting in the library, he with his Plato, his daughter with her romances— he didn't know where she got them, he and his wife had given up trying to find out—his wife's nose buried in her fashion magazine (if her head wasn't buried under a pillow because she was suffering from one of her headaches), and they would hear the loud, familiar voice of Dierdre the cow, so named after one of his daughter's first fictional heroines, and then the steady bump, bump, bump of the cow's head against the pane of glass, and his wife would put down the book and start to complain, "She's going to break the window, when are you going to get rid of that cow!" And there would be the huge, wet nose prints on the windowpane; he would get up, avoiding his daughter's eyes. They both loved it when the cow nuzzled the windowpane and was puzzled each time by what kept her out. He would go outside and lead her back into the pasture or the barn, wherever the others were, while inside, his wife would be raving about him, what kind of farmer was he? Any other farmer worth his salt would have slaughtered that old cow long ago, not wasted tons of good feed fattening her up when her milk was too thin to churn and there wasn't enough of it to mention and she was more trouble than any animal could ever be worth. Then his daughter would get up, glowering at her mother, and go outside, wander-

3

ing aimlessly with her book under her arm, somehow ending up next to the cow. He had often come into the barn to find his daughter propped up against the golden tan side of the cow, reading her book—*Iris;* or, *Under the Shadow; Minerva,* or, *Once In a Life*—and he would always say the same thing: "Be careful, they're skittish, they kick, we've lost more than one man from a kick to the head," and she would say, "This cow won't kick me," and turn a page, and the cow never did, never kicked her, barely moved when she lay against her. The cow seemed to live in a half-dream while his daughter read against her, even slept against her. His wife and his daughter fought constantly now; from the day she was born they had not gotten along, but now it was worse. In the mornings, he often found his daughter asleep in Dierdre's stall, the cow stretched out next to her, her arm flung over the animal's neck or her hand on a hoof. "What if the cow should turn over on you?" he asked. "The cow won't turn over on me," she said. "Don't worry about it." "But if she should," he persisted. "Then she would turn over on me," said Agnes, his daughter. "Everything dies," she said; "you always say so. I wouldn't mind dying that way."

He didn't like it. If he had his way, Agnes could keep the cow for a pet forever. But he had long ago agreed that animals should be slaughtered when they were no longer useful because his wife had told him that the people of North Chittendon would laugh them out of the state if they treated their animals as pets. He had promised her that they would run their farm as if they were farmers, so it was too late now to go against his wife and say, no, this cow is not to be slaughtered, this cow should be treated like an old family friend, this cow belongs to our daughter. This cow stays alive because she means more to Agnes than either her mother or her father. A dumb animal with a big tongue, who could clean his daughter's face with one swipe and often did. He spied on Agnes, he hated to admit it. He saw how, when she finished her taffy, she stuck her face against the muzzle of the cow and the cow licked her face clean. He could never, if the truth were told, stand against his wife.

To this day, after twenty-one years of marriage, he did not know whether this was due to a weakness of his own or his sense of his wife's weakness. When things upset her, she began to have accidents. The iron would press against her arm rather than the arm of his shirt. She would bring a pail of berries out to the men who were stirring the huge cauldron of blackberry jam, and her foot would miss the last step, her ankle would turn, she

4

would fall down, and her eye would be black and blue for weeks. When she stopped having accidents, she would withdraw into her room and draw the curtains and complain of headache. Then she would begin to cry. It would be weeks before she would be up and around again. And he had noticed—it would have been impossible *not* to notice—that these spells came on after a disagreement between them. They came on for other reasons as well, but if he opposed her—well, then, he could see the bedroom darkening; he could see his wife moving away from him slowly, slowly folding herself into her bed while the rest of the world went on as usual, except that he was dreadfully lonely, and all around him, everyone behaved as if nothing were happening. They thought he would not want their sympathy or their pity, and he didn't, but he would have liked someone to talk to, and their exaggerated cheerfulness made him feel lonelier than ever. And in the midst of this was his daughter, Agnes, who moved through the rooms as if something had terrified her, who refused to talk about her mother, who, by the time she was ten, behaved exactly as did everyone else on the farm: She was cheerful, bright, as if everything were just as it should be, or better, she never asked about her mother, but she looked as if, at any moment, something might spring at her, and whatever it was, whatever it wanted, she would not be able to keep it off. And no one around her could help her. He understood that his daughter thought of him as weak, that she did not believe he could protect her from anything. She had her reasons.

For here he was, on the first sunny day in two weeks, not a cloud in the sky, leading Dierdre into one of the upland pastures where the sun would have dried out the ground so that neither he nor the animal would sink in up to their knees, and where, after he had slaughtered her, the wagon would come to fetch them back down to the barn. He had not fed the cow for twenty-four hours, believing that, before slaughter, the cow's bowels should be in an empty state, and he knew, from the way she ambled behind him, nudging him in the back every few feet, that she thought he was taking her out to pasture. He led the cow under the tree and took the rifle from his back. It was a 30.06 rifle. He placed the muzzle of the gun against the cow's forehead and fired. The cow's eyes rolled up and then down; her knees began bending. She looked, not as if she were dying, but as if she were folding herself up, preparing to lie down on the warm grass. Then suddenly she fell to one side. Even before he bent over her, he knew she was dead.

He was a very strong man. He tied her rear legs together and threw the rope over the thick branch of the cottonwood tree and he pulled her up until she was swinging from the branch, head down. She must have weighed more than three hundred pounds. He cut her throat with the sharp scythe-shaped knife he had carried up in his pack. The blood spilled onto the earth under the tree. He was about to gut the cow; he had the knife ready to make the incision from the rectum to the throat, but he thought he heard something. He turned and thought he saw someone farther down the pasture, but it was no one; it was just a huge weed. He heard the creak of the wagon wheels on the meadow road below him.

Let them do it, he thought; let them do it. They love it. They love to slaughter. They would laugh at him behind his back because he wasted a bullet on his cows whereas every other farmer they ever heard of put tongs through the nostrils of the cow and a rope through the loop on the tongs and pulled the cow's head down to the floor by the rope through his nose, and, where the cow's lower jaw touched the floor, they took a heavy iron mallet kept for the purpose, and by the second or third blow on the forehead, the bone was usually driven into the brain, and the animal was insensible or dead and the throat was cut and the job was well done. But he hated it. He hated the smell of the hot blood, the rich, thick smell which hit the back of the tongue and filled the nasal passages, exploding there; a rich smell, not sweet, but overpowering, sharp somehow, an iron tang, the smell like the taste of your own blood when you bit the inside of your mouth, steaming, rising in the air like a spirit if the day was cool. It was the only thing the men were superstitious about, some of them—the blood. Some of them would not use it; some of them objected if others collected it in buckets or tried running it into a wooden trough. No, they said, the blood can't be touched. The blood is life. It gives life. Let it go into the ground. A number of the men feared the spilled blood, but the rest of the men laughed at them. You don't know what you're missing, they'd say; you let it congeal; you cook it on the wood stove in an open pan; it gets thick, like liver. You slice it; you won't ever get sick if you eat the blood. The men who said the blood holds the life of the animal were horrified by the blood eaters; they watched them and waited. If, five years later, one of the blood eaters died violently, was thrown from a horse, fell from his roof repairing his gray slate shingles after the damage of the winter's ice, they'd say, it is because he ate the blood. That's what happens to people who eat blood.

The wagon wheels were creaking slowly along the meadow road. The axles needed grease. Unless he saw to it, nothing got done. He sat down in the shade of the cottonwood tree, and the shadow of the cow, swaying slightly in the wind, fell over his feet and withdrew, falling over his feet again. He knew he should get up and gut the animal. It was taking the others longer to get here than he thought it would, but he watched the cow sway back and forth and he was sleepy. He was remembering the first time he helped deliver a calf that would not come; he remembered how his arm disappeared inside the cow, how he finally felt the calf, how he drew it toward him, how, still inside the cow, he tied its front feet together with rope and lined its head up with its front hooves, how he pulled the calf in rhythm with the cow, how finally, the calf, slimy and dazed, slid into the bed of hay they had prepared for it. "You feel the calf near you now?" asked the old man who was teaching him; "you feel his spirit around you? He's close to you now, isn't he? You feel like he's inside your hide and you're in his?" This from a rough old man he would have believed incapable of feeling anything. The other hands said the old man was so tough he made a good breakfast of old horseshoes. "I feel him," he said. The old man put his arm around his shoulders.

The shadow of the cow passed back and forth across his legs. The shadow was flowing rhythmically, putting him to sleep. And then he could see it again, as if he were there, as if it were happening again, as if it had never stopped happening.

It is cool in the barn, and dark. Most of the doors and windows are shut to keep out the heat; outside, the heat is alive. Its intentions are not good. Rays of light cut through the greenish dusk of the farm; bits of chaff, of hay, of animal hair, float lazily in the long, sharp gold beams of light. He has come in here to sleep. He loves the odors of the animals, the odor of the hay, new cut and drying. He is high up in the hayloft when five of the men come in leading the old bull. They are all members of one family and they all work on his farm. From up here, at the top of the barn, they seem small, like players taking part in a ritual. "Well, let's get him," says one of the Bro\ s. "He sure ain't getting no one no more," says the youngest one; "hardly worth killing him. Thin hide." He slaps the bull on the side. The bull bellows and turns toward him, but the other men yank his head forward by the rope fastened to the tong in his nose. He watches

7

them prepare to pull the rope through the iron staple in the barn floor and watches them remember that the staple is rusted through and that they were supposed to replace it last week. The men shrug.

They go over to the horses' stalls and come back with leather thongs. They catch the bull's legs one at a time, tie the rear legs together, then the front legs. The bull falls heavily on his side. The youngest insists it's his turn to kill the bull and the others agree. He hits the bull with the iron mallet and the bull bellows. He hits him again and the bull begins to bleed from his ears. The bull lifts his head and bellows. The older men look at one another. "One more try," one of them says; "then one of us is coming in." The youngest Brown hits the bull again; there is the grating sound of a bone breaking. "Give it here," says Bill Brown. He picks up the iron mallet and brings it down on the bull's forehead. The bull's legs jerk and are still. They slit his throat. "You need practice with that thing," says Bill Brown; "once is enough. You can't get it up high enough." "*He* can't get it up?" says another of the men, and they burst out laughing. They are hauling the bull up; he is swinging, hanging by his rear legs, from a steel ring in the rafter. "You cut him," Bill Brown tells the youngest one; "you can do that." "Yeah, he can do that," says one of the other men; "the young ones know how to make the first cut." The young man's face flushes and he slits the bull open. The intestines fall out. They gut the bull. "I got the liver," Bill Brown calls out; "I get the first bite." He picks it up and smears his face with it. Then he takes a big bite of it. His mouth is raw and bloody. A raw and bloody animal seems to be disappearing into his mouth and down his throat. "Give it here, don't eat it all," his brother says. They pass the liver around. They smear their faces; they take a bite of it; they pass it back and forth until it is all eaten.

From his hayloft at the top of the barn, he cannot believe what he sees. Bill Brown beats his chest and roars. The others do the same. "Let's skin him and get it over with," says the youngest one. "Do it right," says Bill; "if we nick that hide, we'll catch it from Mrs. Dempster." "Here!" cries the youngest, and he throws something at one of his brothers. "What's this?" asks the brother; whatever it is drops down the front of his shirt. His younger brother collapses, helpless with laughter. "What the hell is it?" his brother demands, and fishes down the front of his shirt. When he pulls it out, the others explode with merriment. It

8

is the bull's testicles. They begin throwing the testicles back and forth at one another. Their hilarity knows no limits.

Up in the hayloft, he is trying to keep as still as he can. He wants to retch but he does not want to make a sound. He wants to fight down the disgust he feels toward these people he lives with and works with every day, but he cannot. He knows that they are only farmers; they are not criminals; they are not so bad; they are not bad at all, but they are utterly alien to him, alien and repugnant. If they were animals in his herd, he would slaughter them. Their faces are still smeared with the blood from the bull's liver, and when the sun touches them, their faces are like old battle masks, rusted iron, caked with earth. They are drinking deeply from the flasks they always carry with them: apple whiskey. Now that they have tired themselves out, they begin skinning the bull. He sees that they do not wrap their hands in towels, as he has asked them to do; they slide their hands between the hide and the meat without even rinsing them.

Drunk as they are, they use the sharp, scythelike knife to free the skin from the meat. Even from his perch in the hayloft, he can see that this hide will be free from cuts and nicks. Every now and then one of them stops, searches around in the hay, finds the bull's testicles and throws them at one of his brothers, and the skinning stops; the laughter starts up again. Eventually, they get through; they go out to get the wagon to take the meat to the ice house, to get the hired man who butchers the meat, cutting it into quarters, then the smaller cuts for Mrs. Dempster's kitchen. He comes down the long, long ladder as if he were climbing down to earth from another planet. Everything wavers in front of him. He goes out in back of the barn and throws himself on the cool rock under the apple tree. He knew how it was. He had to see for himself. He lies there for some time, as if dead. He does not see his daughter steal out of the barn's side door. Buried in the hay of a horse's stall, she has watched the whole thing.

Later—now—he seemed to know that. The sun had moved down the sky. The shadow of the cow covered him up to his breast. The creaking wagon was moving toward him and stopped as it reached the huge beech tree. "Well, here it is," he said, getting up. Just then, he saw someone walk out of the trees which bordered the far side of the pasture. He saw Agnes stop. He saw her raise her pail of berries and press it to her chest. She stared from him to the cow swinging from the tree. He could not see her face, but he knew the look of betrayal and contempt she turned on him. He waved to her as if there were nothing wrong. She did not wave back, but turned back into the woods.

He remembered his father talking about a cow, the best milk cow he had. But she had only male calves, he said; males were useless. All you needed was one for a whole herd. When he was young, he hated to hear talk like that. Now he saw it for himself. The farm was like a woman bearing hundreds and thousands of children, some growing in the womb of the earth, some in flesh and blood. He was responsible for everything on the farm. One bull might be enough for a herd. One man was not enough for even a small family. When he saw himself in his daughter's eyes, he knew he was weak. He did not approve of the nature of things, but he could not change it. What was worse, he could not accept things as they were. He pretended to accept it all—his wife, her headaches, her spells, her treatment of him, of their daughter—but he did not.

That night, before going to her room, Agnes paused before his chair in the library. "Mother told you to do it, didn't she?" she asked; "the two of you did it together, didn't you? You never cared about me!" He did not know what to say, but before he had a chance to catch his breath, she had disappeared upstairs. A moment later, he heard the bolt in her door slide shut.

North
Chittendon

2

You should see me here, Margaret, sitting on the open porch, looking out over the hills, listening for the whistle of the four-thirty train. I've been sick a lot this year and I'm not allowed to do much and one of the aides was looking through my records—they go so far back the old ones are on film—and she found out that once I wanted to write, so she presented me with a large box of white paper and a sizable collection of pens. But what do I have to write about and to whom am I to write? Even during all those years when everyone wanted me to tell them what happened, what I remembered, how I came to fire that shot, I never wanted to talk. Now I think I do. Maybe if I'd been willing to talk before, if I hadn't been so thoroughly convinced that talking to other people was the most futile pursuit in the world, things would have happened differently. By the time I met you and was willing to talk to you, it was too late. You know, yesterday I heard one of the nurses tell another that I was completely used up and I suppose she was right. At least it's true the years have worn me down and I'm not curious about much going on around me. And lately, I wonder if I ever was. Did I ever care what was happening around me? Did I know what was happening around me or was I busy watching the clouds move on the horizon of my own imagination?

I don't read books much anymore because I don't much care about how things turn out; they either turn out well or badly, and if the authors are at all truthful, they don't turn out very well *or* very badly. What interests me, I suppose, is how people get to where they find themselves in the end. I used to think I was interested in how lives turned out because curiosity was the last of the passions to die, but now I think there's more to it than that. I suppose I still want to know if my life had to turn out as it did. After all, I began life as the only child of a wealthy farmer.

The only person in the county wealthier than my father was my grandmother, who left me everything when she died. And everyone said I was so beautiful and intelligent, too. I had, as everyone used to say, all the advantages in life. Yet everything turned out so badly.

If my mother and my grandmother hadn't told me so many stories about their lives, would I have looked for and found different things when I left home? Family legends are dangerous, after all. Through the mists of time which separate you from those mysterious creatures, your young parents, you see legendary beings, and every act of theirs is mysterious, as mysterious and unreal as the acts of gods. You see them moving about, subject to inexorable laws, playing out their fates, determined so long ago, in a drama whose beginning you cannot know but in which you now play a part. And so you try to fit in, to find a place for yourself on the stage, and whatever you do, you do against the backdrop of their lives. I wonder now, if they had told me less, wouldn't I have felt more free? But I knew who I resembled in each of the four generations before me; they traced the genealogy of each of my traits backward, so that I knew my stubbornness was not mine but a hand-me-down from my grandmother and my mother. My intelligence belonged to four generations of my father's family, and my artistic talent to my grandmother and her grandmother before her. Nothing in the world was *mine*. Looking back now, it seems so clear. All I had to do was invent a new world. Not just a new continent, or a small island, but a new world. And that was what I tried to do. It was the only thing I ever wanted to do, and of course I failed. And have I ever found anything else I've wanted? I don't think I have. Oh, in spite of everything, little threads from this life and that life tangled with mine and I was knotted in to whatever life is, but I've never been part of it, not the way you've been all your life. I've never belonged.

You know, I'm not sure you're still alive, and if you get this letter, you'll be surprised I'm still kicking. Do you remember the first time you told me that you had a secret plan for your old age and that when all the storms were over, we would spend our last days rocking together on a porch? That was more than forty years ago, when you were my nurse, sharing that cell with me in the county jail. Well, I suppose your idea of a porch and my idea of a porch did not resemble one another much. I wanted to rock in a white wicker chair on the weathered porch of an old farmhouse, and you wanted to be in some modern thing made of stainless steel in front of a house in the city. But if these are my last days, then I wish you were here rocking with me or that I was there with you, and I wouldn't care what kind of porch I was rocking away on as long as you were there with me. I remember how astounded I was when you talked about us as two old ladies because I finally saw that I was important to you. It took me long enough to realize how important you were to me, but it took me forever to believe that *I* had any importance at all. I doubt if we will ever rock together on a porch again (as we did when I lived with you in Oregon, before I came back here to Highbury; I remember that time as if I had spent it in a strange sort of heaven), but I am going to pretend you are here and soon I will believe it. My imagination was always too strong; it's about time it did me some good.

And I keep going over it and over it. Was there anything they could have done to keep me safe? Suppose they hadn't told me so much about their lives? But, without words, their essential natures might have buffeted me even more brutally and I would not have had any chance, not even this one, to understand what I was. Oh, I believe that no matter what they had done, things would have turned out as they did. Unless they had locked me up. If they had kept me under lock and key from my fifteenth birthday until my twentieth, I might have escaped. I would have gained time. Time, at the very least, brings knowledge of one's nature, of the blindness and power of one's passions. Yes, if they had kept me under lock and key for five years, perhaps I wouldn't have been so willing to throw myself into the vicious cogs and wheels of passion. I might have thought twice before walking through the door marked *Love* into that new world I so wanted. But there was nothing they could do. If they refused to let me go on a picnic I was uncontrollable for weeks. Lock me up! I believed I had been locked up all my life, up there on that hill farm in North Chittenden.

And now that I've started to write to you, I see why I never tried writing before. Words! So many words! All the headlines, all the editorials, were about the bullet I fired from that gun, but I had been busy with words for so long. Words got me into trouble. They are the deadliest weapons of all, so that now the gun seems almost innocent by comparison. I fired the shot to stop the words; they were so busy eating everything up. You have no idea how I hate words, how I see them winding out of people's mouths like sticky strands of a web, infinitely elastic, linking the speaker to the listener forever, and finally weaving an impermeable cocoon around the mind and then the poor, fast-beating heart itself.

My grandmother, Eurydice Saltonstall, hated words. She said that was why she loved animals: because they didn't speak. At least not with words. I used to spend days with her while she sat on her brass bed talking to a pig. She used to look at the animals and say they felt pleasure and they felt pain and they didn't confuse the two. If their biological urges drove them forward, they didn't confuse themselves by wondering if they were in love, if they ought to get married, if they were sinning against the great god of the pigs. Do you remember her paintings? You brought one to my room in Highbury Asylum and you insisted on nailing it up even though they warned you that I was dangerous and might break it over your head. You were never afraid of me. Well, when we were in the room together, we were like two animals. I knew I was safe with you or I would never have let you stay in the cell or in the room at Highbury, and you knew you were safe with me even though the superintendent of the asylum, the jurors, the newspapers, everyone in the world, told you you weren't. In some ways, we were lucky. In some basic way, when we were together we were both deaf to words.

Usually, I was not so fortunate. Usually, when it came to words, I was like a savage. The words conjured up pictures of things in the world and the pictures escaped from their frames and ran free, and finally they covered the surface of reality like a hardened, lacquered mural. Would I have thought of love, eternal and perfect, if I had not been told of it first? And although when I was very young I rarely told anyone what I really thought, I clattered on interminably. I did not want to try and tell someone what I thought or felt and then see that blank, white, dead fisheye of incomprehension. I chattered. It was as if my mind, disconnected from my heart—or perhaps in collusion with it—incessantly created and recreated the reality I had chosen to believe in. And then when that reality chipped and flaked, it was repaired and replenished, given depth and context and dignity by words whose meaning I thought I knew. And so I walked around in a world swarming with emotions as if I knew what they were, and all the time I was a snake charmer teasing snakes into strange rhythms and shapes, unaware that these deadly creatures were not mine, and, because I didn't know they had a life apart from me, they would never be mine to live with peacefully and someday they would turn on me.

Well, in our day it was the fashion to neglect the mind and

16

fulfill one's biological destiny, and in every age there are rebels, and I was one. I didn't want children, or so I thought. But in the end, not having a child was the worst punishment life visited upon me. Today, some women are beginning to talk of the body as if it were a mousetrap waiting to spring shut on the mind, and I suppose the body *is* like that, but the mind is there, too, waiting to spring on the body. If I ever painted the inside of the human mind this is how I would paint it: two lions, equally strong, ready to spring at each other's throats and tear one another apart. And the background of this painting would be primeval because our minds are primeval, too. But I've said things like this before. What I want now is what I suppose I've always wanted. If I've had to stay alive so long, I want to know what my life has meant. I wish I had tried to find out earlier when everyone was so interested in the smallest thing I said or did. Even if I find out now, no one else will know what I find. But I am going to try and I am going to pretend I am talking to you, because, except for Doctor Train, you were the only person I could ever talk to. You could always hear the voice beneath the words. I am going to start talking now, listening as I speak to you for that voice beneath the words, and as I try to explain my life to you, perhaps I will explain it to myself. I am starting now, because, after all, it is my last chance.

3

When I was a child, a fortune-teller came once a year to North Chittendon and my mother and my grandmother and I would bounce down the mountain road to the field out past the common and there it would be, the gypsy wagon, painted black but adorned with streamers of red and yellow and orange. The gypsies themselves were more colorful than the trees in autumn, but the fortune-teller was different. She wore only black, and, unlike the others, whose hair was wild, she wore a tight black turban, so tight it seemed to have grown right on her head. There were always rumors that she had shaved her head because of something sinful she had done in her youth, although the more cynical women in the town said she was bald and that the talk about shaving of the head was all nonsense. When I was three, we went down to see the fortune-teller and she looked at my mother's hand and said she was sorry for her. My mother's eyes filled with tears, and she didn't ask for her fortune. I suppose she must have known it had already arrived. The fortune-teller looked at my grandmother's hand and said that she had a long lifeline and would be a wealthy woman, and my grandmother snorted. Everyone in or near North Chittendon knew she was already wealthy. Then she looked at my hand and said that I would be famous. Evidently, she repeated that prophecy for years, because I remember her saying the same thing when I was ten years old.

When I was sixteen, I decided I wanted nothing more to do with my family or their money and that I would support myself working as a clerk or a seamstress, and while I was looking for work in Montpelier, an old woman sat down next to me and told my fortune. She was no gypsy; she was dressed like any old lady in the town. She wore an old purple dress, and when she bent her head to look at my hand, the soft white flesh of her chin and throat bulged like white, rising dough. She told me I was going to be famous. I suppose fortune-tellers say that to many young women. When I was young, I wanted to be another Swedish Nightingale, a great writer, a great painter, a great dancer. And I did turn out to be famous, although not in the way I had expected. And it was too bad. I was utterly unsuited to fame. Even in my circumstances, disastrous as they were, another person might have been able to make something worthwhile, might have been able to make a life. But I did not like the spotlight. When a teacher asked for someone to give a dramatic reading of a poem, it was not I who volunteered. I was the one who came in early, who started the fire in the wood stove, who swept out the schoolroom before the others came, dusted the fine ash from yesterday's burned wood off the teacher's desk, and then sat down and waited for the others to come.

I sat there, rigid and nervous, until Louise, who was my only friend, came in and then I sighed and sat back in my seat. When she was there I felt safe. I don't know why, but I've never been able to have more than one friend at a time. I can see Louise standing in front of me now: a pale thin girl whose skin had, in winter, a greenish cast. She was the homeliest girl in the class, and the others used to comment on it, how odd we looked together. Then Sam, I think it was Sam, took to calling us Beauty and the Beast, and one afternoon, he came after us down the road to Mrs. Brown's house, where my father's wagon was waiting for me, and kept calling out, "Beauty and the Beast! Beauty and the Beast!" Louise started to cry. I didn't. I was incapable of crying in front of others. From the time I was old enough to understand such things, I prided myself on never crying at anything my mother said or did. I would not let her have the satisfaction of knowing I was hurt.

But I could not bear seeing Louise cry. I turned on Sam and told him to stop it now or I would get him in the eyes. He laughed at me. After all, he was two years older than I was, and he was a boy.

"Don't say it again," I warned him, looking down at my brown leather boots. Like all my shoes, they had a metal tip attached to their soles so that their toes would not wear down so fast; the heels, too, had metal plates attached to them. My father was an ingenious man. Shoes were expensive. Even if we were wealthy, he saw no reason for wasting money. If he couldn't put horseshoes on me, he could toughen the bottom of my shoes. Of course, Sam said it again and I ran at him and kicked him in the shins. He let out a shout and swung at me. His fist hit me in the eye and I fell down. I felt the pebbles of the dry road on my cheek and the dust tickled my nose. I went wild. I couldn't hear anything or see anything but Sam's face and all I wanted to do was tear it apart. Evidently, I almost did. Louise said I threw myself on him and clung onto him with all fours and he fell over backward, and I remember this: I remember crawling up toward his head, and when I got there I began raking at his face with my nails. I've always had long hard nails. They're more like talons. I remember Sam screaming. By then, I was crying with rage. I was crying because I had won. If I had won, I could afford to cry. "Say you're sorry," I insisted again and again, and over and over again, he said he was. I crawled off his body and sat down in the road, tears streaming down my face. He got up and ran into town as fast as a pig being chased by a farmer.

Louise was standing in the road, looking at me and crying. "Oh, Agnes," she said; "oh, Agnes." "Well, don't feel sorry for him," I said. I was looking down at my nails and my hands. They were bloody. I can still see Louise, standing there outlined against the deep green forest, the clear blue sky arching high over us both. "You shouldn't have," said Louise; "I know I'm ugly. What do I care what he says?" "You care," I said. "But I shouldn't!" she said; "I have to learn not to. There are worse things." "Do you believe that?" I asked her; "do you believe there are worse things?" She began to wail. No, she didn't believe there were worse things; she would never get married, never have a home of her own, never have children; she would never have anything because she had been born with her ugly face. "If I were a man, I'd marry you," I said. She started to smile through her tears and then she started to laugh, a hiccupy, choking laugh. "I tell you what," I said, "let's swear that if we never get married, we'll stay together forever." "Don't be silly," said Louise; "everyone says you're the most beautiful girl in the state. You'll get married, maybe even next year." "Let's swear," I insisted.

I remember it as if I were still standing there, streaked with blood and dust and tears, talking to her. I feel the cool breeze coming down the mountain. Spring was not far off. "Let's swear," she said. I remember how it felt when I pricked my finger with the pin I'd used to fasten my petticoat and how faint I felt when I saw the first little globe of red blood grow larger on the tip of my thumb. We swore. Do I have to tell you that Louise got married? That she married and moved away? Nevertheless, the oath held. We are still together. All I have to do is say her name, and there she is, standing in front of me in her handmade muslin dress with the lilac flowers printed on it, the cool wind from the mountain blowing her skirt forward toward me, drying the last of her tears. She is pushing her hair back from her forehead and threatening to put her hat back on and she is smiling at me. "You should see yourself," she said; "you're going to catch it when you get home." I said I didn't care.

Of course, when I got home, and my parents found out that I, a young lady of nine, had been fighting like a common hooligan, I was taken into the barn and my father gave me a good paddling. "You never cry," he said, when he was finished. "No," I said. He asked me if I wasn't afraid that Sam would lay for me the next day and I said no, I wasn't; I'd beaten him in a fair fight and he was two years older than I was, too. My father said that he guessed no boy worth much was going to admit that a little girl like me had taken him apart, and it was a good thing for me because, from what he'd heard, I'd almost taken out one of the boy's eyes, so if he'd wanted to come after me, I'd have something to worry about. I asked my father how he heard the news so fast and he said he'd met the doctor on the road when he was coming back up to the farm with bags of seed.

I remember everything about it, how later that night I woke up, terrified at what I'd done, crying because I'd hurt someone else, even if I'd hurt the horrible Sam. I looked at my nails and promised myself that, in the morning, I would cut them off. I didn't. Only those who feel unsafe in the world fight as furiously and savagely as I did, and I wasn't about to part with those nails. I remembered how his skin felt beneath my nails. It's always been a question, my memory, how well it worked, what I remembered, what I didn't. During the trial, during all those months, that was what everyone wanted to know: what I remembered. There's nothing like a trial to destroy one's memory. So many versions of an event are constructed and reconstructed, it's as if you take a train through many cities, and each one has the same town sign at each station, Montpelier, and when you're finished, someone asks you to describe Montpelier and you stare at them and don't know what to say. My memory of all my life is like that. Of course, I lived it myself and I ought to remember it as it really was, but I've heard so many versions of it, so many descriptions of my mind and character, so many interpretations of my motives that only now and then can I remember the original landscape.

I remember one other fight, and I know that the memory of it is my own, because I've told no one else about it. One afternoon, our teacher let us out early because it was harvest time and there were hardly any children in the school and I suppose there was something she wanted to do, too. Some of the girls asked Louise if she would like to come over to Harriet's house because she had baked some cookies and there was plenty of cider, and we could heat it up and stick in a toad, a floating cracker, and we'd have a good time. Louise said she would go if I would and I said we'd go. I suppose we both knew that by now the cider was hard and that the girls had a particular kind of fun in mind. But we rarely went anywhere with the other girls and we were curious about them and envious, too. The seven of us went through the town, past the town hall, the churches, Beatrice Brown's boardinghouse and on to Harriet's house, a tall, white wooden one. The other girls were giggling every step of the way. Louise and I were trying to look as if we belonged. Whenever one of the men of the town passed us, he would make a great show of jumping out of our way as if we were great ladies. The general hilarity began to infect me and I could see Louise catching it.

There was no one home at Harriet's house. The other girls, who lived in the town, didn't find that strange, but I, who lived on a farm where people were forever coming and going, often enough with an animal in their arms, found it odd, even frightening. Harriet gave us each a mug of hot cider with a toad floating in it and we went into the rear of the house and up a dark flight of stairs and then we were in the room over the shed. It was dark inside and Harriet pried a board loose from the back window so that we could see. "Hurry up. Finish your cider," she said. I was frightened. I drank mine down quickly; it burned. "Let's go," said Harriet; "she'll be back in an hour." The other girls began unbuttoning their shirtwaists. "What are you doing?" I asked. My voice was loud and echoing in the silent room. "We're taking off our clothes," one of them said; "just our outer clothes. You don't have to take anything else off." I looked at Louise and she looked at me. I began unbuttoning my blouse. Finally, I stood there with the others, all of us in our petticoats and camisoles. Harriet smiled and stretched her hands over her head and began to pull her camisole up and the next thing I knew, she was standing there naked from the waist up.

"No," I heard myself saying, "I'm not going to do that." The other girls had removed their camisoles and were starting on

22

their petticoats. "Oh, come *on*," Harriet said, coming over to me. She started to unbutton my camisole. I finished unbuttoning it and took it off. "Now your skirt," said Harriet. I let it drop to the floor. I took off all my petticoats until I was down to the last one and then I was grabbed by a panic which constricted my lungs and made my heart pound. "Take off your petticoat," said Harriet, impatient with me. She and the others were standing there absolutely naked. "No," I said; "it's not right." She came over to me as if she intended to tear my clothes off. "Leave me alone!" I cried; "leave me alone or I'll tell your mother!" The silence in the room was absolute. The girls looked at one another. Louise had started to cry. She had also stopped undressing. "You'll tell my mother?" Harriet hissed at me; "that's what you think! You prude! You queer thing!" She picked up my clothes and threw them at me. "Get out of here!" she said. She started pushing me across the room and then down the stairs. "Leave me alone," I warned her; "I have to get dressed." "Just get out," Harriet said. "If you touch me again," I said, "I'll claw your eyes out." They all knew about my nails. "Get dressed then," she said. I dressed as fast as I could and flew down the steps and burst out into the clear sunshine of the street. Louise was right behind me.

"Can you understand it?" I asked her. "*They* were the ones who were doing something wrong! They acted like I was the criminal!" Louise shook her head sadly. She must have known how useless it would be to explain anything to me when I was in such a state. "I'm going home," I said, "and I'm never going in one of their houses again." "They're not so bad," Louise whispered softly. "They are!" I said. I stared at her, amazed. We didn't agree. In the end, that was what was most shocking.

But, in a way, they were that bad. The girls, led by Harriet, came up in a buggy the next day and told my mother that I had asked them to take off all their clothes and when they didn't want to, I had called them filthy names. My grandmother held me by my arms while my mother listened. If my grandmother hadn't held me, I might have been arrested even earlier than I was. "Do you believe those girls?" my grandmother asked my mother. My mother, who in my opinion was always ready to think the worst of me, considered for some time. "No," she said at last; "her teacher says it's an agony for Agnes to stand at the board and write her sentences on the slate when she knows the others are watching her. She wouldn't want to get undressed in front of other people and she wouldn't want them undressing in front of

23

her, either." "Are you going to punish her?" my grandmother asked, and my mother said no, she wasn't. "If you ask me," said my grandmother, "they were up to something, undressing themselves most likely, and they thought Agnes would tell on them, so they decided to turn things around." "Is that how it was?" my father asked me. I nodded. "Well, don't worry about it," my mother said brusquely. Then I started to cry. I always cry when someone does or says something unexpectedly kind but, in my house, I rarely had occasion to burst into tears for that reason.

And now that I think of it, the whole business was probably innocent after all. One of the girls must have been peering into her looking glass and found a mole or a beauty mark or seen a bone jut out sharply when she turned her head, and, turning back, discovered that she really had a very bony shoulder. She must have wanted to compare her body with the other girls' and then she would have felt better about her own. It must have been something like that. We were all afraid, but I feared something no one else did and when my trap sprung, there was no one in it but me. And I must have been in that trap from the beginning. Everyone said I was born restless and too sensitive and intelligent for my own good. And I was relentlessly curious. I had to know everything that happened. And because so many people around me were unhappy, they told me everything I wanted to know. And I tried to take it all in, to make what I knew part of me, to make them part of me. I may have looked like a child, walking about like any other, but in reality I was like a plant choked by vines and weeds. When I saw the sky, I saw it through the flickering shadows that surmounted me.

To tell you my story is to tell you theirs. One summer, I planted morning glory seeds, and the trellis, which we had taken down to repaint, was not replaced in time; the seeds sprouted their thin, wiry vines, and the vines twisted over one another until they formed strands as thick as my finger. There was no unwinding them. So it was with us. In this composition I wrote when I was ten, you can see it: how we were twining over and over one another.

I hate my name. It is plain and ugly. If they had liked me better, they would not have named me Agnes. Agnes was the name of my father's mother. She was dead when I was born. They named me after a dead woman. My mother said it was all right with her because she didn't

24

want to name me after her mother and she said I should be named after someone in the family. My grandmother has a nice name. Her name is Eurydice. She says I must not go on about my name. It is a good and sensible name and it will make me a good and sensible child. I would rather have a pretty name and grow into a pretty child. My grandmother says I am a beautiful child and I look just like my mother. My mother says she cannot see how I look like her. She says we have the same color hair, that is all. I think my mother named me Agnes to punish me. She tells everyone that I was born having fits and that I have been having them ever since. She says I was a difficult child from the time I was born, always crying and spitting up my food. I do not think I was to blame for how I was then because I was just a baby. Grandmother does not blame the dog when it vomits up its food. Mother says I have headaches to punish her because when I have headaches I have to stay home from school and she is not free of me all day. She says I stay in my room and cry to make her unhappy. She says she knows that's what I'm doing because I have nothing to cry about. Mother says my trouble is I am a sensitive child. Sometimes she says it is not my fault because she was so upset before I was born, but she usually says it is not her fault and that I was born too sensitive for this world. She said a child named Agnes has no business being sensitive.

I have not been the same since they found the child in the woods. I guess that is true, because my mother always says that. Grandmother says all that is nonsense and hogwash. Grandmother is very peculiar, Mother always says so, so I don't know who to believe. One day, the men went out to look for timber and instead they found a little baby, all frozen. Our house was closest so they brought it in to us. The little child did not look dead at all. I thought he was sleeping. I picked him up and tried to warm him when everyone went out to talk about who could have left him in the woods near our house. Mother saw me with the child from the woods and she started screaming and pulled him away from me. She said I was peculiar after that. Grandmother says I was not peculiar until I went to Isaac Brown's funeral. I don't remember going to Isaac Brown's funeral. Grandmother says that is the trouble. If I could remember about it, I wouldn't be so sensitive. I don't know what she means. They passed me back and forth over his open coffin. I was seven. But I don't remember going to the funeral.

Mother is always telling me to comb my hair because I look terrible. Or she says, take off that dress, it makes you look yellow. Father says, leave her alone. Grandmother says Father does not stop Mother from scolding me because he loves her too much. She says the whole trouble is my sister, but I do not understand how that can be because I have no sister who is alive. I have a dead sister who was named Majella. Mother has a picture of Majella and she doesn't let anyone touch it. Grandmother painted it and Mother put it over the fireplace in the parlor. Once I climbed up to touch Majella's face and Mother slapped me so hard I fell off the chair and hit my head on the andiron. I didn't wake up until the next morning and I had a black eye and a big bump on my head. Father said now I was an egghead but he scolded Mother. I heard him when they went into the library and closed the doors.

It takes a long time to climb up to my grandmother's house but I climb up there all the time. That is because I am always afraid. Tell me what you are afraid of, says Grandmother, but I don't know. Sometimes I am afraid to be alone. If I am alone in a room, I get so frightened I start to shake. Sometimes I wake up at night because someone is coming after me. One night I had a terrible dream. I was on fire. I went too near the fireplace and my dress caught fire and I thought, now I will be in trouble, I cannot go to church. Mother, Mother, I called, I am on fire, put me out. But it was night and no one came. So I went upstairs all on fire and stood next to my mother's bed and said, Mother, can't you see that I am burning? But then it was day and the sunlight was in the room and no one was there. I woke up screaming and very hot. Father said I had that dream because I had a fever. But I don't have a fever now and I still have that dream.

When I grow up, I am going to go away from home. A girl named Agnes has to go away from home, I think. My middle name is Louisa and if I went away from home, I could tell everyone my name was Louisa and they would believe me. Of course I am not pretty enough to be a Louisa. Teacher, when you finish reading this, please tear it up. Mother will punish me if she sees I am writing

26

things about her. She does not lock me in my room the way Drusilla's mother does. When I wake up at night, she will not come. That is how she punishes me. I am sorry I wake up thinking I am on fire and calling out, Mother, Mother, I am on fire, put me out. When I sleep at Grandmother's, she puts a big pail of water next to my bed. She tells me not to worry because if I have that dream she will throw the water all over me. Grandmother is not peculiar. She is nice. Mother says I think she is nice because I am as peculiar as she is. Agnes is a good name for a peculiar child. I guess that is what she thought. Even if I am peculiar, I wish I had a different name.

AGNES DEMPSTER
Fourth Grade
North Chittendon School

Well, Margaret, as you can see, the teacher did not throw out the composition, although I did not know that at the time. She must have given it to my mother, and for some reason my mother kept it, and when she died, it was tied into a bundle of papers and photographs and the bundle was marked for me. I wonder why she kept it. Perhaps she was proud of how well I wrote; I was only ten. The other children in the town didn't like to write and were not good at it. But she never said anything about the composition to me and she never changed in her behavior toward me. When I woke at night, she still did not come. And of course she did not change my name. And I wonder what she made of my talk about Isaac Brown's funeral.

Isaac Brown was Bill Brown's brother. Bill managed our farm, and when Isaac died, of course we were expected to attend the funeral. I hardly knew Isaac Brown; he had gone west when I was a year or two old, and when he came back, he helped Bill manage the farm. It was his ambition to develop a new, bigger breed of chicken and I used to play with his children and while we played we were surrounded by chickens, and baskets of feathers to be made into quilts or to be sold. Isaac was a big man but he was mean and one day he punched a cow in the side and it kicked out at him and got him in the stomach and he died; he must have bled to death. Up in the hills, where we lived, there was a superstition that when someone died, you were supposed to pass any children who came to the funeral back and forth over the open coffin. I suppose the idea was that the dead person would get a good look at the child, a good last look, and would

27

be satisfied and wouldn't come back to grab the child later. Who knows? When Isaac died, my mother took me—I was seven—and passed me back and forth over the coffin. I'm sure she thought she was doing the right thing. Everyone else did. Except my grandmother. She said later that she was afraid the women passing me back and forth over the coffin would drop me in there, I was so big. She told me she asked my mother not to take me to that funeral, that at seven, I was too old to be passed over coffins, but when we came home, I was fine, and my mother said, "See, you make a fuss over nothing."

But after that, I started to have nightmares. Isaac Brown never really liked children, and when he saw us near his precious chickens, he would shake a stick at us and make faces as terrible as he could get them, and he could make himself terrible. Even before he died, I was frightened of him. After the funeral, I lay back in my bed and looked up at the ceiling and there was Isaac Brown making faces at me. So I started sleeping on my side. But then I started seeing him looking down at me from all the ceilings in the house. That's when I started going up to my grandmother's. And when I didn't sleep at my grandmother's, I slept in the barn because the cows kept me company. My mother didn't know it, but I didn't sleep in the house much at all.

And that wasn't the end of Isaac Brown. One day, I was playing with some of Bill Brown's children and as usual, there was a big basket of feathers for quilts. I was petting something or other, a toad or a salamander—I always loved anything that didn't bite me—and one of the children took a handful of feathers and dropped it down my back. Then she stood up and screamed at me, "Your back! Your back! Isaac's in back of you! Uncle Isaac's got you!" I didn't know what was scratching at my back and I thought it was Isaac. I started to run and the next thing I knew I was lying on the kitchen table. I'd had a fit. Well, putting the feathers down my back, it's the kind of thing children always do, but I wasn't the same after that. They let something loose with those feathers of theirs. My grandmother said that after that I was always nervous and looking over my shoulder. After a while, I didn't see Isaac Brown in the ceiling, but then I began to see a woman and I didn't know who it was. And I wouldn't eat chicken for years. I still hate the sight of chickens.

My grandmother told me that I would grow out of it, that everyone can grow a shell, and that I wouldn't be in my mother's house forever. Time was passing, she said, and I would forget I had ever been frightened. Well, time passed as it does for humans, leaving the landscape as it always was, that landscape you see when you close your eyes. And it was as if the mists which filled the valleys behind my eyes never rose, but stayed close to the ground, hugging it, hiding everything from view but the few hardy ghosts who could part the fogs and step forward. Were the mists of my childhood worse than anyone else's? I doubt it. But they would not burn off with the sun.

4

According to the common wisdom of North Chittendon, I was a very fortunate child. I was the daughter of a wealthy farmer and the granddaughter of the wealthiest woman in the county. And if that were not enough, I was fortunate to live in one of the most beautiful towns in the state. North Chittendon was only forty minutes from Montpelier and Barre by the branch line of the Central Vermont Railroad and the town was famous for its beauty. It was also, according to everyone, famous for the beauty of the Druitt girls, of whom I was one. My great-great-great grandmother, Cecilia Druitt, was, according to the people of the town, the most beautiful woman in the world, and they used to say that she would have been forgotten soon enough, beautiful as she was, had she not had the uncanny ability to pass her beauty on to her daughters, so that she seemed never to have died. To the people of North Chittendon, the descendants of Cecilia Druitt were forever the Druitt girls, regardless of whom they married. The beauty of Cecilia Druitt was handed down to all the daughters of the family generation to generation. It was handed to me. And so I was a Druitt girl, and so were my mother and my grandmother. My grandmother's married name was Saltonstall; my mother's was Dempster, and of course mine was too, but to the town, we were the Druitt girls.

From the time I was a small child, I was told that artists who vacationed on the shores of Lake Champlain came all the way to North Chittendon to paint the women of the Druitt family. Sculptors, who worked in the marble quarries at Barre, came to North Chittendon to persuade us to pose for their statues. I don't remember anyone coming to paint me, but my grandmother, Eurydice, insisted that I was painted often enough as a small child. There was, according to local legend, a full scale statue of my grandmother in the family plot of the Chestertons, Montpelier's most distinguished family. In the summers, Mrs. Brown, my grandmother's closest friend, a woman who had been widowed after the birth of her fifth child, began taking in boarders who came to sketch the Druitts. It was said that she did a good business looking after the artists and their families, and the people in the town said that she was the next person in line to be congratulated after the birth of a new Druitt girl, because each new Druitt meant more business for her.

Of course, all this talk about the Druitt beauty, which I was supposed to have inherited, seemed like a fairy tale to me. I suppose no mother ever looks like a breathtaking beauty to her own daughter, at least not if she and her daughter are perpetually at each other's throats, as my mother and I were. And the idea that my grandmother was a beauty, well—by the time I knew her, I can be pardoned for refusing to entertain such an idea. Then, too, North Chittendon itself was not overly impressed by beauty. It is startling when one sees something beautiful for the first time; then it becomes something to be taken for granted. And perhaps it is because they live in the midst of such natural beauty that the people of North Chittendon concern themselves less than most with their own attractiveness. They are, for the most part, remarkably lacking in vanity. In fact, great beauty was probably considered a handicap in North Chittendon where those who resembled each other flourished best. They did not stand out. They were inconspicuous. I was undoubtedly right to envy Louise, who was homely, but who fit in so much better with the others than I did.

My grandmother told me she had always known that the Druitt women were as much objects of sympathy as envy. "A man would think twice before marrying a beauty like your daughter," one of the neighbors told her; "taking a wife like that is like waving a red flag in front of all the other men." My grandmother answered that her daughters knew how to behave better than most; she said there had never been a scandal about one of the Druitt girls and there never would be one. The Druitts raised their daughters as strictly as everyone else did. As soon as they were old enough to work in the fields, their mothers sent them out. Grandmother told the other woman that when she had cried because the hot sun would burn her delicate skin and she would look like a tomato when she went to church, her mother had made her father take her into the barn where he had administered a good beating. "You're a farmer's daughter and you'll be a farmer's wife," her father had said.

Everyone knew the Druitt girls worked hard and everyone always said they were uncommonly good with animals. She knew people brought them sick animals, and the girls, before they were even old enough to go to school, nursed them back to health. She herself had brought my grandmother a calf because my grandmother was said to have cured a cow by talking to it. Still, she said, she would be nervous if her son decided to marry a Druitt girl.

And, she said, there was something uncanny in a Druitt family reunion where the grandmothers looked exactly like their granddaughters, the mothers exactly like their daughters. She wouldn't like being a Druitt, she said. You'd see yourself coming and going. There you are and there you go. The woman said she didn't know how my grandmother stood it, hatching creatures who looked like they all came out of the same egg.

My grandmother knew everything that the town said about her. Her friend, Beatrice Brown, saw to that. Bea went to a family picnic, a sleigh-ride, anything, and whatever she heard she told my grandmother. She told my grandmother about two women she heard talking about my mother, Helen, who was my grandmother's youngest daughter. "I feel sorry for her," said one woman. "So do I," said her friend; "but you know what my son says? He says Helen's the worst of Eurydice's girls. She's always talking about how the world is a bigger place than North Chittendon and how she wants to find out about the heel of the sock before she dies in the toe. That's what he said. He walked her home from church one day and she said they lived both in mortal time and in eternal time and she didn't intend to spend all her time on earth in North Chittendon. Just in case there was no eternity, she wasn't going to be cheated. That's what she said."

The two women talked, and as they did, Bea listened. "Eurydice used to say things like that too," the other woman said; "she used to say she was going to leave the farm and live in the city and do great things. We asked her what great things, but she didn't know. Great things. She intended to do them. Well, look at her now. She's up on that mountaintop farm, Cloudy Pastures—did you ever hear of such a name?—and of course they make a fortune up there, but it's up on the edge of the world, and half of the time, when you ride up, she's raking out the mud around the sow or she's hanging up the laundry and trying to keep it from hitting her full in the face, or she's boiling the dirty clothes or she's making soap or she's chasing the cow through the brush.

She didn't get anywhere we didn't get. She got all that money, but they don't use it on themselves. It all goes back into the farm.

"If she stayed inside for a month with some creams from the peddler, she'd be beautiful to look at all over again, but what good would it do her? The laundry doesn't care what she looks like. The pigs don't care. She's a farmer's wife. We all had ideas. Now Helen has ideas. You'll see. One day she'll get an idea about a husband and she'll forget about time and eternity and she'll march into that church blind as the rest of us did." "I don't know," said the other woman; "maybe she won't. Maybe she'll be different. My girl says Helen's moody. They get spoiled, the Druitt girls, what with everyone painting them or carving them." "Oh, I don't think so," said her friend; "they get used to it. It's how they earn money in the summers. Last summer, the three girls sat with Eurydice and all four of them got paid. Eurydice said she'd rather pick berries any day than sit still so long and the girls all agreed with her." "Anyhow," said the first woman, "their looks don't last long. Eurydice's only got a few more years. The Druitts wrinkle up early. Maybe they weren't made for farms." "And were we?" demanded her friend angrily; "and what were *they* made for, pray tell?"

Do you understand that I was told these stories again, word for word, just as I am retelling them now, that my grandmother never forgot a word anyone said to her and years later she could repeat any conversation word for word, just as if she were still hearing it? Do you understand that her voice telling these stories wove a web around me, that each of her stories was like a beam of light illuminating the continent which was still blank and dark for me? She didn't talk much, actually, not until I was born, and then she seemed to realize how empty I was, how I needed to hear a voice, her voice, telling me that life was this way and this way, and she seemed to know that, after years passed, my life would be just as she described hers. Even at nine years old, I thought it was a pity the Druitt women wrinkled up so early. Later, I forgot or thought I forgot I ever heard such a thing. But all my life I've been haunted by a sense of urgency, the conviction that I've started too late, waited too long. Even as a small child, I was determined to rush at life. Perhaps it was something simple; perhaps it was because my grandmother had said that all of us, all the Druitt women, wrinkled up early.

Her stories were disturbing in other ways, too. The things she told me she had said, or my mother had said, or the women of the town had said, were all strange to me. They described their lives and mine in ways I could not recognize. From the beginning, I was choosing between versions of reality. I thought my mother was cold and hard and I did not want to believe I looked like her. My mother herself insisted that we resembled each other not at all.

I used to sit in front of my grandmother's house and she and I would fire at targets she set up on the trees across the meadow; her husband, she told me, had always insisted a woman on a farm had to know how to handle a gun, and so she was intent on teaching me. So we sat or stood in front of the house and fired at the targets she bought by the box. One day I asked her what she was supposed to protect herself from, and she looked at me astonished. "Why, nothing," she said. She looked at the gun, still smoking in her hand. "Well, nothing and everything," she said. She looked at the gun again. "It can't hurt to have a skill," she said at last. But I had stumped her. *What* was the gun supposed to protect her from? And all these years, she had assumed it was protecting her. But she put the troublesome question of the gun's purpose out of her mind, and we went on shooting at targets as she talked. And so, as I learned about my mother's life and my grandmother's I became an excellent shot. And my father was proud of me because I could shoot so well. He would bring all the men on the farm around and on some pretext or other, he would take out targets and set us to competing with each other, and I always won. I kept hoping that one day a man would come up to the farm and he would be a better shot than I was, but no one like that ever came. I didn't like it, being best at anything.

So my grandmother and I shot at our tan paper targets and she told me everything else that Bea Brown had seen and heard at the family picnic. Bea said that the two gossiping women fell silent, and just as they did, Helen, my mother, walked by. She was looking for someone and she was in no hurry. She wore a white, flowered gown and she seemed to float by them. Helen said my grandmother, was always tall and slender, but so were many of the other girls in the town. But Helen, she said, did not look quite real. Her waist, for instance, was impossibly tiny. Her bosom was high and large. Like her sisters, she stepped along lightly, seeming to balance on each toe before resting her foot on the ground. Her ankles were so slender it seemed remarkable that they supported a body even as light and graceful as her own. Her hands were long and thin and white and she frequently raised them to her hair as if to assure herself that it was all in place. What might have been a nervous habit in another girl seemed charming in her. But, said my grandmother, it was Helen's Druitt face and hair which caught everyone's imagination. It seemed a little enough thing, that face, she said, if it was *your* face, but other people could not take their eyes from it.

My mother's face, said my grandmother, was perfectly heart shaped. Her forehead was high, her eyebrows delicately arched. Her eyes were huge and green and almond shaped, surprisingly catlike in her delicate face. Whenever she saw or heard anything interesting, her eyes opened wide, as if she intended to take in the person she looked at through her huge, black pupils. Her nose was straight and turned up very slightly at the tip. Many a man, said my grandmother, had lost his reason, had become deaf to the advice of his beloved mother, at the sight of the Druitt mouth and the Druitt dimple set deeply in the middle of the little round chin. Helen's mouth was bow shaped as if an artist had painted it, as if flesh had not shaped it; her lips were naturally red. All the girls in town had envied the Druitts for generations because the Druitt girls never had to bite their lips to give them color. And when a Druitt looked down, and her long, dusky lashes rested on her pure white cheek, there was not a man in town who remained immune to her charms.

Helen, my mother, had the Druitt hair, thick, black hair, not jet black, but dusky, as if a cloud or mist had tinted it. It was a shade no one had ever seen before, and the artists who visited the town to paint them claimed no one would ever see hair like that again. My mother, who was proud of her hair, had not cut it since her third birthday, and, at sixteen, she wore it in a huge coil on top of her head. The enormous coil of hair set off the delicate shape of her head, her small, sloping shoulders, and the long curve of her neck, which one suitor had compared to a birch bending in the wind. And this beautiful girl was also a beautiful animal whose every movement displayed her appetite for life and reminded everyone who watched her that they, too, had appetites of their own. So the women smiled when she went by, and fell silent, and, after she had passed, they began talking again, and more often than not, she was the subject of their conversation.

"I don't envy anyone in this town," said the first woman, looking after Helen; "we're all the same here. We all end up in west hill. My father, he used to say if we started up a family plot, we should bury the horse in it. The horse was better family to him than the rest of us and lasted longer and cost less."

"Still, I envy the Druitts something," said the second woman. "What?" asked the first. "Their husbands. All the Druitts get good husbands." The first woman looked at her friend and then looked away. "You don't know," she said, "you don't know what goes on up there." "They get good husbands," the second woman insisted. She was angry; her face was flushed.

I watched my grandmother's face when she told me about the Druitt girls, about how beautiful they were, about how beautiful Helen, her daughter, my mother, was. She was utterly unself-conscious as she talked about them, as if they were characters she had read about in a book. Almost always, when she spoke, she might have been reading from a book of fables. She had a sentimental fondness for the characters she had known so long ago. Not until she reached the events which had not yet been neutered by time, did she show any emotion as she spoke of them. And now I see that I was taking down her life on the pages of my own. And later, when I wanted space to write down the story of my own life, her thin, spidery handwriting, covering page after page in faded brown ink, was there before me. In this, at least, I was like everyone else. And I finally realized that my grandmother saw Helen, herself, her own mother, her friend Beatrice, all the women in the town as if she were looking at them through the wrong end of a spyglass. Time had passed. Each year her emotions had been pressed by the years falling on her. She was like a leaf pressed between the covers of a book. The scent disappeared, the flexibility of life slowly drained away, but the outlines remained as clear, the colors as bright.

5

I think my grandmother told me her story as she did because she thought that by blaming herself she would make my mother seem less the author of the misery which blew through our house on the mountain. But that was not the lesson I learned from listening to her. Oh, no. I came to quite another conclusion after hearing the stories of their lives. For one thing, I was impressed by what a patchwork any reality is after all. When she told me about her life, she chain-stitched her own impressions to my mother's and butterfly-stitched Beatrice Brown's memory of the two of them to the rest of it, and finally she had the complete quilt, and it was that quilt that I slept under, so that, at a very early age, I knew that life was made up of miscellaneous fragments that had no business together unless the author chose to attach them one to the other. And I knew that, at any point, at any time, the fabric might give; the pieces might move slowly away from one another, inexorably and without remorse, as continents are said to drift. And I resolved to have something better for my own life, to weave something, something new, a web that would not give. Well, there are people who go out to shear and come back shorn, and I was one of them. Webs should be left to spiders, and the biggest spider of all is the earth itself. I often wonder what would have happened if I had not struggled so in the web. They say that flies do not necessarily suffer waiting for the spider, that something in the spider's web numbs them, and that they die in ecstasy looking at the sun through the crystal-beaded stars of the webs spreading out around them. I wonder if it is true.

My grandmother married Edward Lindsay Saltonstall when she was fifteen years old. Six months later, her father-in-law died, and her new husband inherited four hundred acres of cleared farmland that Edward named Cloudy Pastures. She was soon wealthier than most women in North Chittendon because the Holsteins, on whom her husband had "thrown out" precious money, were becoming known as the best milk cows in that part of the state. Farmers came from all over to breed their cows with one of my grandmother's two bulls. Wherever she went she saw something she had set growing. That, she said later, was how life baited the trap.

She gave birth to her first child, a son, ten months after her wedding day. Within a year and a half, her husband had begun building an addition onto the family farmhouse, and soon the two-story building was one of the grandest farmhouses to be found in Vermont. But my grandmother herself did not change; at least, she did not become uppity, as the people of the town feared she would. She had been raised to be a farmer's wife and now she was a farmer's wife, and when she had children, she had, she thought, all she would ever want. When the men were building a new chicken coop, she would go out and help in whatever way she could. She carried the baby out in a clothes basket and set it down in the grass while she worked along with the men. Then she would go in and cook.

My grandmother said she was not merely caught up in life, she was swept along by it, fascinated by new lives of whatever sort they were; and for the rest of her life, she would tell her daughter, or any woman who would listen to her, that a woman who had just had a baby was out of her mind for six months; she *seemed* to be in possession of her senses, but really she was elsewhere, woven around the baby, weaving herself closer to it or unweaving herself from it, she could never decide which. My grandmother believed she was as happy as a mortal creature could be. She had six children in eight years. Five died.

In the spring, her wild lily beds rioted. They bloomed all summer under the apple tree until falling fruit began to knock them down. Many days began suddenly and ended abruptly with Eurydice's wild flight from her bed, down the stairs, out the front door, down the hill, where she picked lilies in the dark, the grass cool and wet on her bare feet, ran back into the house, set them in a crockery jar and placed them in the center of the table so that she could look at them in the morning. She hadn't a minute all day! In the morning, something or someone would cry. The dog would begin pulling her to the door by her gown. The day could not wait for her. She was always running after it, trying to get aboard before it puffed away down the track. The next night, she would run down to the lily bed again and pick another armful of lilies, resolved again to look carefully at them tomorrow, pick an apple from the branch, put it in her pocket, pick another apple, and, chewing happily on it, would return to her husband's house and bed, hand him the apple from her pocket and jump into bed with him. Usually, she landed on a dog or a cat. It never occurred to her to object to sharing her bed with these furry creatures: a bed, she said, should be like an ark. Hers, said her husband, was not *like* an ark; it *was* an ark.

When they were first married, my grandfather would pick her up, lay her down on the rug, and make love to her there. As time went by, and his back began to hurt, and my grandmother began to complain about the cold and the drafts coming in under the door, my grandfather stopped trying to persuade her to abandon her teeming bed. For weeks, my grandmother brooded. She was worried, afraid that her husband no longer loved her. Then, one day as she was weeding in the vegetable garden, a huge wooden wagon, painted yellow, began swaying up to the curved drive in front of the house. My grandmother stood up slowly, supporting her back with the palm of her hand. As she watched, two men began unloading something long and heavy, but she could not see what it was. It was covered with sheets. She dropped her trowel and her handful of uprooted weeds, the earth smell thick on them, flew to the pump, washed her hands, tilted her head under the bright, cold water, and ran into the house. The men were already halfway up the stairs. She started to call out, *Stop,* to ask them what they were doing, what they had there, but her husband was staring down at her from the top of the stairs. He told her to be quiet. She followed behind the men and stood in the doorway and watched them unwrap the object.

It was a tea-colored fainting couch. She touched it. It was covered with thick velvet; she said it felt like cool skin and fine fur all at once. "It's beautiful!" she said. Her husband smiled at her. "Look," he said; "see this tassel?" He pulled a tassel hanging down from the headrest, and the curved, arched neck of the couch reclined until it was the same height as the rest of the couch. "Can I do it?" she asked. She pushed the headrest back up; she pulled the tassel. She let it down. "What a remarkable thing," she said; "what an intelligent couch." "It's for us," said her husband, "not for the dog and cat and the goat and the raccoon." "Are we going to *use* it?" she asked. "I certainly hope so," said her husband. "Oh, but I don't *want* to use it!" Eurydice gasped; "it's much too beautiful!" "Where would I be," asked her husband, "if I couldn't use beautiful things?"

And he traced the outline of her face with his fingers. "Hmmmp," said my grandmother. "Just for us," said my grandfather; "remember?" She said she would. "And don't go covering it with sheets," he said. "Not even during the day?" Grandmother asked. "Come on, Deetzie," he said. Deetzie was what everyone called her.

After ten years of marriage, my grandfather developed a cough and could not rid himself of it. Eurydice looked around her and realized that if her husband died, she would be in sole charge of four hundred acres, two hundred of them under cultivation, a herd of Holstein cows whose udders were so large they were forever stepping on them and then needing them sewn up—milking them was impossible until the stitches healed—ten goats, innumerable chickens, two vegetable gardens, one flower garden for cuttings to decorate the rooms of the house, a blacksmith shop, a sugaring house, and a farmhouse which boasted ten bedrooms. There were her children, the hired men and their families, her own mother, her sisters, her brothers-in-law who were constantly visiting: they all depended on her. She looked around her and saw that she had not left North Chittendon; she had not even gone to Montpelier, and Montpelier was less than an hour away.

When my grandfather coughed, she began to feel something stir in her throat, something wet, something with a sharp beak. She began to reproach her husband for his carelessness: Why did he insist on going out without his waterproof? Why couldn't he take off wet socks and put on dry ones? Why didn't he take the syrup she made for him from the bark of the slippery elm? She knew he didn't take it. She stood behind the china cabinet and watched as he poured it down the sink.

My grandfather did not know what to do with her. Everything he did annoyed her. If he coughed, she glared. If he did not cough, she told him to go ahead and cough; he had to take deep breaths to get fresh air into his lungs. If he worked all day, she accused him of trying to kill himself. If he told one of their sons to go out with the timbering crew, she asked him what was wrong with him. Was he sick? Was he getting worse? He tried to stay out of her way, but he was lonely and he missed the old ways which seemed to be over and done with and he had no idea why. At night, when she settled into a parlor chair and buried her head in a book, he picked up his farm journal and sat down opposite her. They would begin to talk and he would begin to hope. Then he would cough. My grandmother disappeared behind her book cover. He knew that, behind it, she was glaring at him. "I'll go out and check the barn," he would say, and she would tell him to put on something warm. Even in August she would say, put on something warm. He knew that she could not forgive him for being sick, or if not sick, at least not perfectly healthy, but there was nothing he could do about his cough. He had had it now for four years, and he was still healthy.

He began to criticize little things she did. If she forgot to adjust the damper on the wood stove after she put in a new log, she didn't hear the end of it. When she came into the house with armfuls of lilies, he complained that the house looked like a church funeral. She began to fight back. When she was worried, while she waited for the bread to rise, she rested her hand on her cheek and felt the sharp bone of her cheek against her palm. When her head hurt, she massaged the skin above and below her eyes. She believed she knew the look of her own skull. He never did anything right. The cord of wood for the kitchen stove was cut too short. She was always stoking it. What did they need with another bull? She'd known the cheese factory he'd started with men from the next town would come to nothing. They weren't in the cheese business anyway.

He began to ignore her. But his cough did not leave him. She became uncontrollable. As soon as he came in, the quarreling would begin. If he refused to answer, she talked out loud. She addressed the china cabinet. "You see how stupid it is to cut wood this length?" she asked it. The carved lions' heads didn't answer her. "And now he comes in here to frighten me with that cough. It doesn't frighten me anymore. Believe me," she said to the cabinet, "it doesn't frighten me at all." He would go out and wander over to the chicken coop. He would go out there and cry. Helen had seen him twice. Both times, she fled back to the house, frightened, embarrassed, enraged with her mother.

When Helen was thirteen, she came into the parlor to look for a book she was reading. It was very hot and the house was still. A fat black fly was buzzing against the windowpane. The room looked stunned by the heat, the windows blinded by the hot silver light. Everything was in place. The two red leather wing chairs were drawn up to the fireplace, facing it. Suddenly, she heard a sound. She walked to the hearth and looked over the back of the first chair. It was empty. In the second one, she found her mother staring at the mantel. Eurydice looked up but seemed to be looking through her. "I'm almost forty years old," said my grandmother, "and I've never made a decision." Helen

41

stared at her. "You're thirty-six," Helen said at last. "Thirty-six and I've never made a decision," said my grandmother. Helen, her daughter, my mother, was frightened. She had seen animals like this, dangerously calm, about to become wild. "Don't be silly," she said; "you decided to marry my father." "I married your father when I was fifteen," said Eurydice; "a fifteen-year-old girl is an instrument in the hands of biology." "I don't understand," said Helen; "didn't you love him? You always told him how much you loved him." "A fifteen-year-old girl is too young to love anything *personal*," said her mother. My mother shook her head miserably. "She's only old enough to love being alive. That's all." "I don't understand," said my mother. "No," said my grandmother; "and you won't until it's too late."

As my grandfather's health continued to worsen, my grandmother became increasingly intolerant of him, almost savage. On extremely cold days, when his weakness compelled him to follow the doctor's advice and remain indoors, his wife would complain about how he was always underfoot, how he would never ask her for anything, but would always fetch it himself and replace it the Lord knew where, and she wouldn't find it for weeks, and then it would be discovered moldering behind a picture frame. One morning she came out of the bedroom carrying a half-rotted pear, and started to scream that *she* ran the house; if he wanted something to eat, he should ask her for it, but that if he must take something himself, she would dispose of the remains. The compost heap was outside, not in her bedroom.

My grandfather took refuge in stubborn silence. Helen watched my grandmother with a peculiar horror, for my grandmother had abandoned all attempts to make herself presentable. My grandmother would appear in the kitchen while it was still dark, her long hair uncombed, in tangles, a paisley shawl thrown over her blue flannel nightgown, and begin clattering pots and pans as if her aim were to make as much noise as possible. Her hair fell forward into the frying steak and potatoes; she brushed her hair back with a fat-coated hand. Days passed and still she wore the same costume. If it was cold she padded herself with petticoats which she put on over her nightgown. My mother, who dressed meticulously, was disgusted and ashamed. She tried to speak to her mother more than once.

"I look fine as I am," said my grandmother, a red flannel petticoat showing beneath an old blue taffeta petticoat, both of them over a flowered flannel nightgown, her shoulders covered by a length of heavy, striped cloth which she had once intended to sew into a skirt. Now she used the fabric for a shawl. "I look as good as I need to look," my grandmother said. "Another man would lock you up," my mother said. My grandmother turned and looked at her and my mother burst into tears. "I wish he would lock me up," my grandmother said; "look around. This isn't heaven." Helen stood still, looking at her mother, the tears spilling from her huge green eyes and streaming down her cheeks. "Look around," said Eurydice in a gentler voice; "don't let this happen to you." "Let *what* happen to me?" asked Helen. "This," said her mother helplessly, shrugging, looking around her. "This."

6

I remember that while I was in the hospital, everyone, especially Doctor Train, and you, too, Margaret, was interested in my dreams, probably because, in them, I could remember things I could not remember when I was awake. Or so it seemed then. One of the dreams has followed me all my life: the dream about the clock. By the time I knew my grandmother, she lived in a log cabin in the middle of an upland pasture directly above our farmhouse. She had only the rudest furniture, but she did have a splendid grandfather clock which her mother had left to her sister, and when her sister died, she left it to her. While I sat in the log cabin listening to my grandmother talk about all the lives that had burned so brightly before I was born, I would stare at the clock.

It had a remarkable face. The clockmaker who put it together must have been an ingenious man. As the hands went around, the little sun and the moon and the white fluffy cloud began to move, and eventually the white little cloud would disappear from the clock's face and the gray storm cloud would appear and begin to move across the little sky above the clock's Roman numerals. It would cover the sun and then move off, down the little sky, and the sun would follow it, and a night sky would arrive complete with a moon, and, as the hours of the night passed, the moon would cross the clock face and rain clouds would appear in the night sky, and at six in the morning, the sun would be rising on the face of the clock just as it was rising outside. During the day I loved that clock, but in my dream I found myself in it. And when I was in the clock, I saw the cogs and the wheels turning and interlocking and the wheels were huge; they reached from the ground to the topmost vaults of the sky. And I knew I had to get out of the clock or I would get caught in the wheels.

I saw people who had been caught, and the wheels carried them up to the sky and then dropped them down again, and their faces were all moon colored and their eyes filled with terror. And it always happened that something caught my attention, the way the reddish moon was sailing through one of the wheels, the way a cloud was shredding itself as it became entangled in a wheel's sharp spikes, and I would forget that I had to stay clear of the wheels and then I would feel myself falling toward the wheel and I could see the faces of the others upturned to me. And then I would hear my grandmother's voice saying, "Don't let this happen to you," and I would wake up. But it wasn't until much later that I understood what it was she wanted to warn me about. Of course, as it turned out, the wheels which caught her up were not precisely the same as those which caught me, but they were similar enough. I should have been warned. But I didn't understand her, and the dream did no good. It described what was happening; it could not protect me.

I still dream about the clock. Sometimes I am in the log cabin, looking at it; other times I am wandering through it. I ought to see my mother inside the clock, but I don't. Instead, I see my mother as my grandmother saw her. I never dream about my mother as I knew her. I see my grandmother in the clock. If I see anyone I see her. She told me the story of how she came to live in the log cabin above our house, a story no less complicated, in its way, than the story of how I came to take up residence in the Highbury Asylum for the Insane. And my mother told me the story, too, and it is her version I remember best.

My mother always said that winters made her happy. When she went to the district school, her teacher asked her to write an essay about the winter, and she described winter on the farm as "the good time, the warm time, when everyone had time, when the members of the hive had done their work and buzzed together quietly and sleepily, happy to know each other was there." I would never have described the winter, or any other time, in that way. By the time I was born, the warmth had gone from our house. But my mother had more time before the trouble really began in *her* house, and many of her memories were warm and valuable. Still, when my mother was thirteen and my grandmother was thirty-six, the house became a battleground. My mother dimly sensed that her father was frightened by his failing health, that he would have given anything he had for some sympathy, some comfort, but he would take little or none from his daughter. My grandfather looked to his wife and his wife gave him nothing. And although no one would admit it, each of them knew that Eurydice was afraid of the day her husband would die, of the time when she would be left alone. They saw how she turned on her husband in a fury because he had changed the familiar warm world into a place of skulls and shadows, and her fear turned in the sunlight, in the moonlight, and hatched into hatred, and the hard core of that hatred was her love of her husband and that love was as strong as ever. And so they were caught together: Edward, Eurydice's husband, caught in the trap of his illness; Eurydice, my grandmother, fighting like a cornered thing against the specter of her husband, growing thinner and weaker, month by month; and Helen, my mother, the only child who had survived measles and whooping cough and summer complaint, watching them both, as helpless as if she were watching two children, too reckless or wild to care, moving out into the center of the river where the ice was thin, where the ice would give and no rope could reach them.

One morning in December, Helen was staring out of the window of the parlor across the triangular field which always seemed to point toward the thick pine forest opposite the west wall of the house. She saw the porch dusted by the snowflakes which had blown there with the last gust of wind. The light was queer, somewhere between pink and yellow, and the long shadows of the trees were blue on the high drifts of snow. She stood up on her toes to get a better look at the silent, snow-sunk meadow. The snow had been falling steadily for ten days, and the drifts had blown high against the house. At the same time, snow fell from the roof onto those drifts so that the snow now reached more than halfway up the second pane of all the first floor windows. No wind moved a leaf or a flake now. The snow which had fallen the night before lay cold and silent, glittering in the strange, pale light. Across the meadow, two plum trees rose out of a huge drift and now seemed to be one tree, not two. The sun, small and white, was slowly beginning to mount the sky but its wintry light promised no warmth. A bluejay flew toward the feeder on the house. He pecked once, twice, then flew back into the forest. This was the country she loved. The snow would deepen. The cold would grow solid, palpable, something to be felt with every inch of your skin. The days would glare with their harsh silvery light and the nights would be black and silent, the stars on clear nights brighter than the sun during the days.

From where she stood, the house seemed to float, to be setting sail into the billows and waves of the unending snow. If she stood still enough, she could feel the earth turning beneath her, and the house creaking softly, turning in obedience to the earth. She was absolutely happy. She knew, as she always knew when she was alone looking out at the snow, that the beauty of life lay in its impenetrability, that each winter resembled every other winter because it took so long for the human mind to understand the meaning of the season, to feel the fall of the snow, to learn the lesson of the shrinking sun and the growing stars. She shivered in excitement and hugged her heavy woolen wrapper around her. Her mother was wrong; this was heaven.

Upstairs, her mother was still asleep. Several days before, her father had gone to Boston to consult a specialist in lung disease. They all knew it was hopeless. Nevertheless, Eurydice wanted to know what the man would say. Helen sighed and went into the kitchen. The water was boiling and she began to make the coffee. She liked grinding the coffee beans; she liked the sharp smell. She added some chicory to the coffee beans and turned the handle quickly. The finish had long ago been worn from the handle; the wood was the warm color of raw wood seasoned by the oil of the many hands that had turned it. It had started snowing again, and her attention was caught by the snowflakes, all of which seemed to be tracing figure eights in the air. Then she heard a dreadful crash and her mother's voice, cursing. She ran upstairs and found her mother in the doorway glaring back into her bedroom. In the center of the room was an indescribable pile of bedclothes, mattresses, and heavy pieces of curlicued, gleaming brass. "He said the house is like a pigsty," my grandmother said to her; "you heard him. Well, that's where I'm going. Where is he? He's not back yet, is he?" "He's not home yet," said Helen, backing out into the hall. Her mother had finally taken leave of her senses. "Good," said Eurydice; "I don't want anyone to interfere with me. Get one of the Brown boys." "For what?" asked my mother; "what should I tell him you want?" "I'll tell him," said Eurydice; "don't you ask me what I want him for. I'm still the mother in this house. In this pigsty, rather." Helen did not move. "Go get him!" her mother shouted. Helen ran down the steps and out into the barn.

"It took you long enough," Eurydice said when Helen came back with Bill Brown. "Pick up these things," she told him, "and help me take them out to the pigsty." "The pigsty!" "The pigsty," said my grandmother; "I'm setting up house in the pigsty." "You'll freeze to death!" cried my mother. "I won't freeze to death," said my grandmother; "he thinks I have to take whatever he hands out, but I don't. I'm setting up housekeeping there. I raised that pig and I feel closer to that pig than I do to anyone in this house." "Mother!" exclaimed Helen, "it's freezing outside!" Eurydice ignored her. "Did your father put the wood from the old barn in the shack?" she asked Helen. "It's out there," said Bill Brown. "I won't freeze to death," Eurydice said; "I've got everything I need packed up in the boxes out in the summer kitchen. After we get the bed out there, you and your father can go back and get the boxes out." "Mother!" Helen cried; "stop it! Where will Father sleep? What is he going to say?" "I don't care what he thinks and I don't care where he sleeps," said my grandmother; "I'm tired of doing what people tell me. 'The house looks like a pigsty. Clean it up.' 'A cough is nothing to worry about. Stop worrying.' I want to go see my mother before she dies, but the cow needs watching. No woman must ever think her problems are more important than a cow's. No woman must ever think she is as important as a cow. The cow's fine. My mother's dead," Eurydice said, picking up a comforter and throwing it over her arm. "Mother!" exclaimed Helen; "that happened eight years ago." "The next time I saw my mother, she was lying in a wooden box," said Eurydice. "But he apologized!" said my mother; "he said he was sorry!" "Oh, he said he was sorry," answered Eurydice, picking up another comforter and wrapping it around her shoulders. Helen fled down the stairs after her.

She found her in the little shack which used to house the chickens and the pigs. The night before, its only tenant had been the farm's prize sow. Now, the shack boasted a small wood stove, a cot, a folding chair, and two kerosene lamps which Eurydice was preparing to light. "The brass bed won't fit in here," Helen told her mother. "I know," said Eurydice; "I'm setting it up in the pigsty. Taverns have signs in front of them. I want my bed in front of my house." My mother stared out the crooked little window of the shack. "You've got a huge woodpile under that tarp," she said; "how long are you staying out here?" "How long?" asked my grandmother; "how long? From now on I live here. See those boxes? There are my pots and pans. Those long wooden chests? Full of food." "Oh, good Lord," said my mother; "I can't just leave you here. Please come back." "He said I live in a pigsty," said my grandmother, "and I'm going to live in a pigsty. That's all there is to it."

It developed that they were not snowbound after all. The birds themselves must have carried the news of this new turn of events to the village because one sleigh after another began to arrive at the farm. Even the men who had business with the timber crew in the second mowing managed to pass the pigsty and stare at the brass bed which was slowly acquiring a new quilt of fresh, fluffy snow. Helen refused to come out of the house, even when her closest friend came up from the livery stable with her father. "Is that my friend Emily's rig?" she asked Bill Brown, who was carrying in an armload of wood; "I don't remember her having one like that." "Rented," Bill Brown said; "from Cooper's Livery. I guess she wanted to see our prize pig." "Don't you talk about my mother that way!" Helen flared up at him. "I didn't mean . . ." he said, and he flushed and looked down. Like every other young man on the farm, he was half in love with Helen. "What is my father going to say?" she asked him, avoiding his eyes. "Sometimes," he said, "you just have to give an animal its head. I don't mean your mother's an animal, I just meant . . ." "I know what you meant," Helen sighed.

Sleigh bells tinkled outside. "Oh no," moaned Helen. "I'll get rid of them," Bill Brown said. "Do you think she'll tire herself out?" Helen asked him. "In this weather?" he said; "she's probably tired out already."

But she did not tire. Instead, she seemed to be enjoying herself enormously. By noon, steam was rising up her chimney and the strong smell of beef soup wafted across the snow toward the house and the barn. When Bill came in to tell Helen what her mother was doing, he said it was pretty warm out where Eurydice was. "You know," he said, "it's really very comfortable." Helen sank down in a chair and waited for her father, who had been due back hours earlier. But she was too restless to sit still for long. She put on her boots and her snowshoes, and, wrapped in her father's old bearskin coat, decided to take a walk in the woods. When she got to the far side of the meadow she turned back to look at the house. It was a fine, tall, white house, standing high against the green pines which rose steeply behind it; its shutters gleamed black and its front door glowed red. The sun, which was setting, had struck the windows red gold, so that the house seemed filled with warm, rosy flames. Then she heard raised voices. Evidently, her father was home and he had discovered his wife's new place of residence.

She saw her father trudging back from the pigsty toward the house. He caught sight of her and they began to walk toward one another. "Out for a walk?" he asked Helen. She said she was. "I don't know what to do with her," her father said, "and I don't know if I care. She says she doesn't want me to die but she won't let me live in peace." "I tried to talk to her," Helen said; "she didn't listen." "Maybe," my grandfather said bitterly, "you should have talked to the pig. It has more sense." "What are we going to do?" she asked; "the whole town's been up here looking." "Let them look," he said; "was Bea here? Bea Brown? Your mother still talks to her. Maybe she could handle her." Helen said she would take the sleigh and collect Bea. "Take Bill with you when you go," said her father; "but don't go tonight. If she wants to sleep in a pigsty, let her sleep there. There's no point in ruining Bea's night over it."

The next morning Beatrice Brown, my grandmother's oldest friend, arrived in the family sleigh, got out in front of the shack in front of the pigsty, and knocked at the little door. "Come in," said my grandmother cheerfully, swinging the door wide open. A blast of hot air hit Bea in the face. "It's warm here," Bea said, looking around. She took off her muff and laid it down on the rough table made of planks and bricks. Then she took off her gloves. She shook her head, as if she were barely awake. "Take off your hat and coat," said Eurydice; "visit awhile. I suppose they told you to talk to me." "Well," said Bea, "they told me you moved into the pigsty. I guess you had your reasons."

"Of course I have my reasons," said my grandmother. "That's what I thought," said Bea. Eurydice regarded her narrowly. Then she grinned. "I guess you want to know what they are," she said; "my reasons. It's a long story." "Everything always is," said Bea. "You know," Eurydice said abruptly, "last week I went to see Doctor Baker. I asked him about Ed. I thought maybe he'd tell me something more if I went alone. He said Ed's got a degenerative lung disease and there's nothing they can do about it. First, he thought it was consumption, but when it went along so slowly, he knew it wasn't. He's been sick a long time." "He's been sick almost fifteen years," Bea said sharply, "and you've made them miserable for everyone with your goings on." "He doesn't have fifteen years anymore," my grandmother said. "No," said Bea. They both looked down at their hands. They were seeing Ed as he had looked when Eurydice had married him, tall, powerfully built, with hands like barn doors. He was a handsome man, rugged, and everyone always remembered his brilliant blue eyes. Now he was far too thin, hardly any flesh on him, and he coughed constantly. His large hands were gnarled and their veins were raised and blue. He moved like an old man.

"Eurydice?" Bea asked; "you're frightened, aren't you?"

"Of everything," my grandmother said. "Everything," Bea repeated, staring at her. Eurydice was dressed outlandishly. She wore four or five petticoats over a pair of men's britches. She wore a man's shirt and over it had put on a black waist which she wore unbuttoned. Her hair was wild. As Bea stared at Eurydice, she began to feel the fear that had so transformed her friend. How could she not understand when they had gone to the same school together, sat next to each other day in and day out, shared one another's lunches, slept at one another's houses, bathed in the same huge metal tub from the time they were gawky little geese until just before their marriages? Why, there were times when Bea believed she knew Eurydice's body better than she did her own, they had spent so much time in the warm, soapy water discussing whose nipples were more attractive, hers, which were brownish, or Eurydice's, which were rosy. In the mornings, they would race each other to the two-seater, see which one could finish first, and while they sat, they swatted at each other's breath as it rose in the air, and then they began to pretend that the clouds of breath were bees and puffed the dangerous insects at one another. When Bea got lost in the woods, she got lost with Eurydice, and the two of them lay against each other after saying good-bye to the world and crying for the families which were so soon to be deprived of their company. When her mother was sick, it was Eurydice's mother who sent a wagon full of hampers of food and baskets of yellow spies, her mother's favorite apples, and then Eurydice's mother herself would come down and take Bea back with her, and Bea would live with Eurydice's family until her own mother was better. And when artists came to sketch Eurydice, Bea came along, bringing her friend lemonade, telling her who she saw coming home at twelve o'clock from the direction of the Crocker house.

"You used to be so beautiful," she said to Eurydice. "Don't start that," said my grandmother. "No," said Bea. She fell silent, staring down at the rough, unsanded planks of the floor. She looked up to find Eurydice smiling at her. "I always liked looking at you," Eurydice said. "My mother," said Bea, "always used to say that even a Druitt needs to see an ugly face." "You're not ugly," said Eurydice. A cloud covered the chilly sun and the room darkened. "You can be mad at the world," said Bea, "but you still can't make it do what you want it to." My grandmother didn't say anything. She was staring at the little square of isinglass flickering orange in the door of the wood stove. "If Ed comes out here to get you," said Bea, "you let him take you back in." She waited for Eurydice to answer her, but her friend sat silently, her eyes remote. "What's that next to you?" Bea asked suddenly; "chicken feed? You don't keep chickens here anymore." "I don't know what it's doing here," Eurydice said; "the sacks were outside, so I had Ed bring them in." She picked up a handful of feed and let it drain from her fingers back into an open sack. "Like that," Eurydice whispered; "it goes like that." She started to cry. "Are you going back into the house?" Bea asked. "If Ed comes out for me," she said.

My grandfather came out and took her back in. A month later, he was barely able to get his breath and they sent for Doctor Baker. My grandfather wanted to stay in the kitchen because it was warmest there and he was near everyone; he could see and hear whatever went on. My grandmother objected. She said he made her work harder. She told him that even when he was dying he had to be inconsiderate. "For God's sake!" he shouted hoarsely; "I'm on my deathbed! Can't you let me die in peace?" Two of my grandmother's sisters, there to help her, dragged her away.

"In all my days as a doctor," said Doctor Baker, "I have never seen anything like this. The woman is unnatural." "She can't help herself," said my grandfather. He was interrupted by a rough cough and lay back against the pillows. When they looked at him again, his eyes were wide and staring; he was already pale. Eurydice was inconsolable. Bea came to stay with the family. Whenever my grandmother was awake she wept. She wept through the funeral, and when the lid was fastened onto the coffin, she screamed. Helen refused to speak to her and refused comfort from anyone else in the family. She talked only to Bea. She told Bea that she believed her mother had ruined her father's life and her own out of stubbornness and stupidity. But Bea did not agree. "Out of fear," Bea said, "she ruined her life and his out of fear. You have no right to judge her. People can't help their fears." "I have the right to judge her," said my mother; "if I have any right, I have that one."

7

I am always happy when I think about my grandmother and the stories she told me of her life, especially since I seem to be possessed by the delusion that I was somehow present while all the events of which she told me were taking place. She was a vivid storyteller. Even those who didn't like her for any other reason liked her for that. But my grandmother herself seemed to have ceased existing as an ordinary human being when my grandfather died. Bea Brown used to say that when they buried him the coffin held two people. And it is true that after his death she ceased to exist for the world beyond the farm. She never again went to church on Sunday. She would not tolerate the mention of God in her hearing. She moved through the rooms of her life as if she were a ghost haunting the sites of her previous life.

Eventually, she found living in the house too painful and moved into the log cabin she had built up above, taking the brass bed with her and setting it up in front of the cabin. Still, if she was a ghost, and often an annoying ghost to others, she was a guardian angel to me. She was the only person who did not frighten me, the only thing I went toward without averting my eyes. We belonged together. Because, now that I look back, I am convinced that in some real way, I too was a ghost, a child constructed out of the ebbing and flowing shadows of the lives that had gone before me. But I am getting ahead of myself—probably because it is time to tell you about my mother, and when I begin to think of her, my feet start to drag, my mind begins to wander, and my memory weakens. Well, open warfare between mother and daughter is common enough, but over the years that warfare dies down and eventually the mother and daughter come to an understanding. My mother died before that was possible, but I doubt that we would have come to understand each other no matter how long she had lived. For one thing, most of the reunions I've seen between the generations take place during worried consultations over the feverish body of the daughter's child, when the child's mother and the child's grandmother, both standing helpless next to the cradle, look at one another and see themselves in the other's eyes. But I was never to have children.

The horse does not love the storm which casts heavy, jagged branches down upon the road to trip it up, and that is how I saw my mother—as a storm, an intelligent storm, bent on destroying my life. I came to envy the horse, the cow, the pig, that did not suffer her tending. From my earliest memory, she was a brusque, harsh woman. There was no gentleness in her nature. When an animal was sick she nursed it more efficiently than any machine, and I would feel sorry for the animal so excellently handled, and would take it up myself.

Eventually, I, like my grandmother, was followed about the farm by anything that walked. The farmhands said I could talk to animals. I believed animals understood me and did what I asked them to. They also listened to me when I came into the stables and told them I was frightened and began to cry for a reason I didn't understand; and I would stare up through the ceiling of the barn, through it to the high, cold stars beyond, and tremble with fear. And the only thing that calmed me down was the calm, deep, regular breathing of the animals. Even now, I can see the golden brown fur of my dog's stomach rising and falling; I can see the side of the cow, with its short, rough hairs, rising and falling; I can see the wide green eyes of Stardancer, the cat, watching me until I fell asleep. If only I had a mother or a father like Sam, my grandmother's dog, I would have been happy. I told that to the dog so many times I must have worn out his ear. He was a big shepherd, and when he curled up with me in an out-of-the-way place, he would attack anyone who came near us, even my grandmother, unless I called him off. The only times I felt safe were spent with that dog or with my grandmother, who was, in many ways, like the dog.

I remember riding back up the mountain from my friend Louise's house in town. I got to the farm after dark and the moon was full in the sky and over my head the skies were bright. Perhaps there were fewer lights on in the house than usual, I don't know what it was, but suddenly the night seemed, in spite of the moon, darker than usual. I took the horse into the stable and then began walking back toward the front door of the house.

I don't know why I decided to go in through the front door. No one ever did. Everyone always came in through a shed door or a side door, but there I was, at the front door, when I looked up at the sky, and suddenly I was certain I was dying, that nothing could be done to stop it, and that the angel of death, which I always pictured as a great, golden eagle, was coming straight down for me, plummeting through the air, and was about to sink its talons deep through my hair into my skull and bear me off. I began to shake as if the air had suddenly turned terribly cold and when I tried the door it would not move. It was summer, and the door, which was rarely opened, must have swelled in place and stuck fast. I was sure I had been locked out. I looked up at the sky and the terror returned, this time more strongly. I began to knock wildly at the door, and when no one answered, I pressed my face to the wood of the door, and then began to push my face into the space formed by the door and its frame. I was trying to burrow out of sight; I wanted the house around me like a skin. But the terror kept growing. They were not coming. They were gone and they had left me alone with whatever was flying the night sky. I began to cry. Then I heard my mother's steps. I heard her tug at the door, exclaim, turn around, come back with my father, and then the door flew open, and I, who was holding the knob, flew in with it. "Why on earth did you come in the front door?" asked my mother. My father asked me if the horse had bolted. I said no, he hadn't. "Next time use the shed door," my mother said. The tears were still wet on my cheeks. She didn't see them.

When my mother's father died, she refused to stay with her own mother. She insisted that my grandmother had killed my grandfather and she told Bea Brown that she didn't want to become a woman like her mother. She said she was going to go into town and stay at The Palace, but Bea told her she couldn't do that because The Palace took in anyone; there were men from the quarries staying there, and most of the husbands in town wouldn't let those men in the house. It was no place for her. She persuaded my mother to come stay with her in her boarding-house. My mother kept on insisting that she needed freedom. "Freedom," Bea said, "is for people who have nothing else." "*I* need freedom," my mother insisted; "I don't want this life, mouths everywhere, sucking the life out of you, mouths in the barn, in the earth, in the house, all of them sucking at you. I'm tired of all this weather!"

Bea told my grandmother that when she looked into my

mother's eyes she thought she saw the outline of dark branches against a winter sky and snow wraiths dancing in the air over the frozen mound which was her father's grave. Helen, she said, looked haunted.

And my mother asked Bea if she understood what she meant; did she know what she meant when she said she was tired of all this weather? Bea said she didn't know what my mother meant about being tired of all this weather, but she did tell my mother that she was angry because she wanted to get away from North Chittendon and she was angry at herself because she didn't want to get away at all. My mother couldn't imagine leaving and she couldn't imagine staying, wasn't that true? My mother said it was. Bea said things had once been the same for Eurydice, but when she married, she had been happy in North Chittendon, at least for a while. My mother said she didn't want a fate like her mother's; she said she didn't want the fate North Chittendon was spinning for her. She didn't want to spend her life looking at the hills around her and wondering which one she would be buried under. "Once," said Bea, "your mother wasn't so different from you." "Don't say that!" Helen cried. She said she would do anything to keep her life from turning out like her mother's. Bea told her that she didn't have to worry, that her life would turn out to be *her* life. That was what frightened her; that was the terrible thing.

Oh, whenever my grandmother told me about how my mother came to leave the farm and how she came to live with Bea, I felt sorry for the woman Helen then was. But the woman my grandmother told me about, the woman Bea told me about, was not my mother. She was a person who lived before I existed. It was impossible to listen to my grandmother tell me the story of my mother's life and not to feel sorry for the young woman she described, but had my mother ever been that young woman? I doubted it. And if the young woman of whom my grandmother spoke *was* my mother, then how she changed from the person they described and became the woman I knew was a mystery I could never really penetrate. Or perhaps I did not want to penetrate it at all.

So my mother went down the mountain to stay with Bea. She was determined to go to Montpelier and support herself teaching or sewing, or, as she said at the time, sweeping streets. My grandmother told Bea that she didn't want Helen with her. She didn't want anyone bothering her, and besides, her daughter had good reason to hate her. Eurydice said her daughter could do whatever she wanted to do. She didn't care about any of it. She would care later, but she didn't now. Bea said that my grandmother was not right to wash her hands of her daughter; she said she was ashamed of her. "I don't care if it's not right," my grandmother said; "I'm not like you. I'm not good. I'm not strong." "You're strong, Eurydice," said Bea, "but that's no reason to be cruel." My grandmother said that she couldn't help herself. Bea said that she used that excuse altogether too often.

Of course, my mother, in fleeing the farm, in taking refuge at Bea Brown's, was rushing straight into the trap she was trying to escape. In this she was like almost everyone else on earth, except that most people's paths are not so obviously circular. And perhaps because my mother's path was, I developed the mistaken impression that if I only thought things through enough, avoided making certain obvious mistakes, I could avoid being trapped by life. Because, when I was young, that is what I thought had happened to my mother: that she had been trapped by life on the farm. At that time, even though I was already dreaming that I was lost inside the grandfather clock in the log cabin, I had no inkling of the larger machinery whirring patiently and eternally around me and in me. That knowledge was to come to me only in old age.

On Tuesday mornings, the meat wagon from our farm wound down the twisting mountain road toward North Chittendon, and, out of loyalty to my grandmother's oldest friend, it made its first stop in front of Bea Brown's boardinghouse. It was a large white wagon, and on each of its sides my grandmother had painted a grazing Holstein cow. Above the cow were the black letters spelling out the farm's name: Cloudy Pastures. After Bea chose the cuts she wanted, the meat wagon went off to the far corner of the livery yard, where the townspeople began to arrive even before the driver had time to water the horses.

When my grandmother was first married, she would come down with the meat wagon and visit at Bea's. She brought my mother with her and their children played together. Later, after my grandfather began coughing, my grandmother no longer came into town on the wagon, but Helen, my mother, did. She said she liked to see people, and that was what towns were for, weren't they? In the winter, when the wagon arrived on runners, Helen would warm up in front of Bea's stove, and then tramp off down the street to a friend's house. At three o'clock the wagon would stop at Bea's for her; if she wasn't there, it returned to the farm without her, and everyone assumed she would spend the night, and perhaps the week, at Bea's. So it was not surprising that when she came to Bea's after her father's death, she felt at home even before she crossed the threshold.

She told Bea she felt as if she were melting. Bea, who was ironing, asked her if that felt good. "It does," said Helen; "I've been a frozen pond. It's as if I'm afraid to let people too near me, as if I'd crack open and drown them. What does *that* mean?" "It means," said Bea comfortably, "you can't trust yourself to behave. Now you're beginning to understand your mother." She finished the collar and folded the shirt. "There's the meat wagon," she told Helen. She went out to talk to her son Bill, who had driven it down. Helen sat inside, stubbornly ignoring the wagon. She avoided looking at the window whose view was blocked by the side of the wagon. All she could see through it was the black and white cow her mother had painted and the big, black letters announcing the presence of Cloudy Pastures. "I forgot about the damned wagon," she murmured to herself. She felt as if the farm itself had followed her into town. Finally, she got up and went out.

Bea saw her talking to her son and didn't like it. She didn't want Helen to persuade herself that she loved her son when she was only angry and afraid and ready to grab onto the first person who walked by. Helen asked Bill how her mother was. He said Eurydice stayed in her room most of the time, but now she gave orders and she had stopped crying. Helen asked him if Eurydice asked about her. "She doesn't know whether you're dead or alive," he said bluntly; "she doesn't know whether *she's* dead or alive, and she's too tired to care. My mother thought she might try killing herself, but I told her not to worry; Eurydice's too tired to do anything." "She's too angry to bother," said Helen; "she wants to tell the world what my father did to her by dying." Bill said it did no good to be angry. "Tell that to my mother," said Helen.

Bea heard the cast iron bell fastened to the front door and went to see who it was. While she was gone, she thought, sighing, that her son would ask Helen to go to the church dance and she would accept. Life, she thought in exasperation, walking toward the front door, was so *unarrangeable*.

A very tall and very dusty young man holding a thick, hand-hewn walking stick was standing on her doorstep trying to peer in through the vertical line of little rectangular windows on each side of the front door. "Yes?" said Bea. The young man asked her if this was the Brown house, and when she said she was Mrs. Brown, he introduced himself. His name, he said, was Amon Dempster; perhaps she remembered his father, Cartland Dempster, who had stayed here one summer a long time ago. Probably she didn't remember. "Dempster," Bea repeated. "An artist," he prompted; "a sculptor?" "We've had so many of them staying here over the years," Bea said. He asked her if she had a room; he was awfully tired. He told her he had walked all the way from Burlington. "I wanted to get the city out of my blood," he said. Just then, Helen walked around the corner of the house and started toward them. "Who's that?" he asked without thinking. "Miss Saltonstall," said Bea; "she boards here. I'll show you the room we have available." She looked him over. "Would you mind coming in through the kitchen?" Bea asked him; "you're awfully dusty." "I'd rather," he said; "I know how long it takes to scrub things clean." As they went into the house he looked back at the tall slender girl in the plain blue dress; she was not coming in, after all.

At dinner, Bea's four steady boarders chattered happily with one another. Helen and Amon Dempster sat silently eating, looking from one face to another. They were not yet part of the society around the table. But by supper, Amon, who had taken a bath and a nap, was cheerful and talked easily. Yes, he said, he had walked all the way from Burlington. Why was he so tired of the city? He'd spent his years at the Harvard Law School and apprenticed himself to Caldwell, Cadwallader and Ditch, and he'd had enough of it; the law was a fine profession, he was sure, but all he saw was the wrong side of human nature, children contesting their parents' wills, people who hobbled in swearing they'd been crippled for life by someone's milk wagon, but who straightened up and walked out better than he did when he said he couldn't do anything for them. He was tired of other people's troubles; he guessed that was what it was. "I don't see that you can do much for them anyway," he said; "and if you don't think you can, you have no business being a lawyer. So I left." No, his family wasn't unhappy about his dropping the law; his father was an artist, but the rest of them, all his uncles, were farmers. He had plenty of money and he thought he'd farm. Well, not really farm, he said, but buy a farm and run it.

It was so beautiful here, he said, especially in the upland pastures where the grass was bright green and the snow was still lying on the ground in odd designs and thick, silvery ice was still decorating the cliffs and the rocks.

On his way to town, he came out of a high pasture and found

himself looking at a farm. It wasn't an unusual farm, he didn't suppose, but there was something about it. It was so sunny, and the snow, where it still lay, was blinding. It was so bright there and everything was so well kept up. There was a barn; well, there was a hay barn *and* a cow barn, and then that fine, tall white house with its black shutters. And there were neat corn cribs and a hen yard and the whitewashed coops and their sharp, pleasant smell and just then, a rooster crowed and the other hens began talking to each other, and while he stared past the house, a red fox ran across the pasture and got out under a split-rail fence. The sawed wood was piled up high and in the bright light it looked more beautiful than any wood he'd ever seen or ever hoped to see. He didn't know what it was about the place, but it was peaceful. He wished, he said, his mother was alive to see it. She would say peace lived there. Did anyone know what farm he was talking about? he asked. You came on it suddenly, because the road up to the house was steep and winding and until you turned sharply at the top of the hill, you didn't even know the house was there. He thought it must be the highest farm in the area. He didn't see anything up higher even when he climbed the rocky mountain slope behind the farm. Did anyone know what farm it was? And the strangest thing, right in the middle of the pigsty, was a big brass bed. What a strange sight, but even that seemed to belong where it was.

Bea looked at Helen. The girl had flushed scarlet and seemed lost in contemplation of her peas. "No?" Amon asked cheerfully; "well, I'll find it again. My father," he went on, spearing a piece of lamb, "told me to look for the Druitt girls. Does anyone know who they are? He said they were beautiful enough to be put on the map." He looked up, and, to his astonishment, found Helen glaring at him. "He said he used to draw them," Amon Dempster went on, "and if there were any of them left, I ought to try my hand at it; you know, to see if I had any of the family skill. Well, I don't, but I thought I'd like to see the girls. Do they still live here?" "There are no Druitts in North Chittendon," said Bea. "No?" he asked; "I'm not surprised. My father said they were part of the countryside, the town's best crop, but I said I thought if they were so beautiful, people would have plucked them up and taken them off long ago. Of course," he thought aloud, "if they were married, they wouldn't be named Druitt anymore. Aren't there any left?"

At this, Helen jumped up, overturning her chair, and ran out of the room. Amon looked up in surprise and looked to Bea for an explanation. "Was it something I said?" he asked. "Yes," she said. "What did I say?" he asked, miserable; "all I said was that I saw this peaceful farm and I wanted to find one of the Druitt girls." "You say you studied to be a lawyer?" Bea asked ironically; "you weren't studying very hard, I guess." "She's not—" he stammered; "oh, no! I didn't mean anything!" Bea shook her head. "Whose farm was it?" he asked. Bea surveyed him from under arched eyebrows. "You don't mean—!" he exclaimed. "Her farm," Bea said. "I'll go talk to her," he said. "Before you have a chance to put another foot in it," said Bea, "I better tell you that her father just died." She watched the young man's face. "She's probably out in the barn. She loves animals."

When he came into the barn from the brilliant sunlight outside, he was momentarily blinded. Then his eyes became accustomed to the greenish gold darkness and he began to look for the girl who had fled from the table. He didn't see her. He was about to leave when he caught sight of something blue through the slats of a stall gate. "Miss?" he said; "Miss?" Helen stood up and came to the entrance of the stall. "How dare you?" she hissed; she was shaking with fury. "How dare you make fun of me like that? Who are you to me? You think because my mother disgraced the entire family with that damnable bed you have the right to mock me in front of the whole town? What kind of person are you? What kind of person torments someone he doesn't know? Just to see her suffer?" "I didn't know," he said. "Didn't know?" she said incredulously, her voice rising. "You didn't know it was our farm? 'Peace lives there,'" she mocked him; "you didn't know I was one of the Druitt girls? You just happened to find this rooming house and my mother's oldest friend? Why are you doing this to me? Did your father have something against my father? Is that it?" "I didn't know," he said again; "I was walking for a long time and I came on the farm. I didn't know whose farm it was. I don't know anything about the brass bed. I don't know what disgrace you're talking about."

Helen was holding onto the stall gate with both hands and staring at him. Her eyes were wide and dark green, great, great, deep pools of eyes, like the pools he had seen in the valleys below him when the days were cloudy. "You didn't know?" she whispered. "No," he said; "I didn't know." He saw that she was trembling violently. "Don't you think," he said, "you ought to sit down? You're so upset." "I can't," said Helen. Her eyes didn't move from his face. "I'm afraid to let go." He walked over to her slowly. He held out a hand to her, slowly, as if she were a wild animal who might panic and bolt. "May I?" he asked. She nodded dumbly. He took hold of her elbow. "I'm still afraid I'll fall," she said; "I'm afraid to let go." "Perhaps if I put my arm around your waist," he said; "then if you fell, I could catch you."

"You didn't know?" she asked again. "No, I didn't," he said; "I would never have said a word. I would have died first. Really, I would have." "Perhaps," she said faintly, "you should take hold of me." He slipped his arm around her waist and she fell against him. He realized that he was supporting her entire weight, that she really was incapable of standing. He slid his arm up toward her shoulders and with his other arm swung her up until she rested against his chest. "Now you don't have to stand up," he said, staring into her eyes. She continued to stare back at him. She did not blink. He had never seen anything, not even a cat, keep its eyes open so long without blinking. Then she closed her eyes and let her cheek rest against his shirt. "Do you want to go back in?" he asked her. "Not yet," she said; "if you don't mind." "*I* don't mind!" he said.

"You can't hold me forever," she said after a while. "Where should I put you down?" he asked her. "Come sit with me on the water trough in there," she said, pointing to the stall in which he had found her. "I should have known," he said, when he sat down next to her on the overturned trough; "I should have guessed you were one of the Druitt girls." "Please!" she said; "if you knew how sick I am of the Druitt girls!" He said he didn't know how anyone could be sick of a Druitt girl. "It can happen," she said with a sigh. "Do you want to know," she asked him suddenly, "why the brass bed was in the pigsty?" "Very much," he said. And so she told him. Toward nine o'clock, Bea came out into the barn with a plate of cookies and a pitcher of milk. She said she thought they might be hungry. The two of them were smiling up at her as if they had never known a moment's unhappiness, as if they never expected to know discomfort or misery, confusion or restlessness, ever again.

8

I've always liked thinking about how my mother met my father and came to marry him, and I've always wondered why. At times, I've told myself I like to think of my mother approaching marriage so certain she would be happy, only because I knew she would *not* be happy, and I liked to think about her, there in Bea Brown's house, as a spider likes to think about a fly it sees happily blundering through the air, a fly it knows will soon carelessly career into its web. At other times, I know I liked to think about my mother as she was then because if my mother had once been kind and good she could be kind and good again. The young woman my grandmother described, the young woman Bea described, lived somewhere behind the black shadow that was my mother and someday she might step out and my mother would change back into the person she had once been, and then I would have the mother I wanted; then I would be happy. If that dream never came true, still it was a good dream, and strong. I think I still have it.

Of course, my mother married Amon Dempster, my father. My grandmother was not surprised to hear that one week after her father's death her daughter was already engaged. Life, she said, was like that. Death chewed a hole in the web and life flew about like a winged spider until the hole was mended. My grandmother said that if my mother and father hadn't been staying at Bea Brown's house, there would have been much more and much nastier talk than there was. "Nothing goes on under Bea's roof that shouldn't go on," one woman said to another after church. "Maybe not," said the other, "but the girl's supposed to be in mourning. It isn't right to go courting so fast, just as if she didn't care he was dead. Her father must be turning cartwheels in his grave." "Ladies," said the first woman's husband, "the man was sick for a long time. He must be happy now, knowing his daughter's being taken care of." "Just like a man!" sniffed his wife; "no feelings at all. No sympathy for the dead. No respect for the man who has gone to his rest." "Elvira," said her husband, "sometimes I think I'm listening to a talking turnip." "What did I say?" Elvira asked her companion. "I don't know," said the other woman; "*I* think you were right. Men stick together."

It took my mother some time to muster up the courage necessary to bring her suitor up to the farm. The last time Bill had come down with the meat wagon he told Helen that her mother now spent all her time sitting outside on the brass bed, talking to a pig. My mother was afraid that, at the sight of Eurydice in her five acrid petticoats and black sateen waist left over from going-to-church days, her black, dusky hair rising from her head like a demented cloud, at the sight of her skirt hitched up over her knees, her blouse gaping open across her breasts, Amon would look from mother to daughter, and when he looked again, he would no longer see the girl he thought was so beautiful; he would see the woman on the brass bed and he would turn away afraid that the woman on the bed was the woman she would become. Helen went to see my grandmother alone. She wanted to know if she would sell Amon Dempster the farm.

During the last five years of my grandfather's life, my grandmother had raved on and on about how dreadful it was to live on a mountaintop with no one but a dying man; why couldn't they sell the farm, or leave it, or lease it; if they leased it, they could move into town, and when he got better, they could come back. But her husband had never lived in town. He couldn't imagine waking up in the morning and hearing the noise of strange wagons, the clinking of strange milk cans, looking up and seeing people everywhere. His eyes, he said, bumped into things when he was in town; everything was too close.

My grandmother said she would sell the farm, but she had one condition. She wanted to keep fifty acres for herself; she wanted to build a log cabin in the upland pasture above the house. My mother didn't like the idea: She said it would be like having her living with them. She would always know she was there, looking down at the house. My grandmother told her to worry about her fiancé's finances. She told my mother he might not want the house when he found out how much it cost. "It's the richest farm in this whole part of the state," she said, "and I'm not giving it away." She said that her husband had died making the farm what it was. My mother said that her fiancé's family was wealthy, and he was wealthy in his own right as well. "I'll have better things to do than watch you walking around in the meadow," said my grandmother; "don't worry about me." "What better things?" asked my mother; "shooting at targets?" But it was settled. When my mother married, she moved back into the house she had grown up in and my grandmother moved into the log cabin she had built in the upland pasture.

Helen Saltonstall, my mother, married Amon Dempster, my father, on the first Sunday in October, 1869. She did see Montpelier, after all, on her honeymoon, and she saw Burlington, where my father found the glass irises and daffodils and roses which she later arranged in bouquets for the parlor china cabinets; she went to Quebec and bought peignoirs and worried because she was not as sophisticated as the women she saw there, afraid my father might tire of her. When she asked Amon if he minded, after all, that she was so much less *finished* than the women in the cities, he asked her what women she was talking about, and after that, she saw she had no reason to worry. Bea said she knew that from the first. Amon would never be able to see Helen as she was; she would always be the perfect creature of his imagination. Some men, she knew, were like that. Their imaginations were powerful, and when they loved, their imagination and their love twined together like the roots of two great trees, inseparable, indistinguishable. Men. Some of them were like ducks. They fell in love with the first thing that walked by them. Bea knew how beautiful Helen was, but she also knew that it didn't matter. Some men loved once and their love did not change even if the women did. It was true, she thought, what the town said: The Druitt women always got good husbands.

My mother was married in October because my grandmother insisted that if she waited any longer her fiancé's family would not reach North Chittendon through the storms. When my mother asked her what storms she was expecting, my grandmother said that a hard winter was coming. "Don't you remember?" she asked Helen; "your father said I was his *Farmer's Almanac*." "My father," said Helen, "was too good for this world." "Too good for me, you mean," said my grandmother; "well, you're having your chance. You do better." "I will. Anyway," Helen said slowly, staring at her mother, "I couldn't do worse." My grandmother shook her head. "If your father were alive," she said, "he'd smack you for that." "My father!" cried Helen; "my father was a fool! He put up with you!" Then she stopped, horrified. He had not been a fool. He had loved her mother. He had loved *her,* too, but she was someone who came later. Even in the worst times, it was her mother, the woman who fought and scolded and nagged, whom he loved. He loved the woman who would not let him die in peace. At least, thought Helen, he was never alone with his cough. I thought he was, but he wasn't. She was the voice of his fear and she never left him alone. She hoped she would do better than her mother had; it was the first time that she saw the possibility, far away and fantastic, that she might not.

As I describe these events in my mother's life, I begin to see myself coming closer, and I suppose that is why I linger so over the last of the pleasant scenes. It seems that disaster and I arrived together, and that as I enter upon the stage, the beautiful, happy woman my mother once was is retreating into the wings to change into the costume she wore the entire time I knew her. But perhaps for my father she sometimes changed back. I know that, at her wedding, my grandmother changed back, or at least Bea Brown said she did.

Bea had an attack of nerves before the event. She was afraid that my grandmother would appear at the church in her four petticoats and torn black waist, the little covered buttons ruined, the horsehair showing through their rounded tops. The morning of the wedding, Bea left one of her boarders in charge of the kitchen and went up to get Eurydice.

She did not believe her eyes. There she was, Eurydice Druitt, as she had known her before. Her black hair was shining; she had twisted it into a rope, swept it up and pinned it to the top of her head, where she shaped it into a heavy figure eight which decorated the back of her head and rested luxuriantly on her long, graceful neck. She was wearing a deep maroon dress trimmed in maroon velvet. Old heirloom lace was at her throat and wrists. The skirt ended in a flat, pleated ruffle, and from the way the skirt moved when Eurydice came toward her, Bea knew there was a new petticoat beneath it. There it was again, the breathtaking Druitt face, still heart shaped, the little cleft in the adorable, small chin. The big eyes were green and clear under the magnificent maroon bonnet. Only the skin had changed, darkening and wrinkling with time and so many passing suns. But from a distance she was Eurydice Druitt coming home from a church dance, and when her bonnet shadowed her face, she was Eurydice Saltonstall, looking down at her first-born child. Bea's eyes burned. Bea did not look as she once had. Her pale yellow hair had long ago gone gray; deep lines ran from her nose to her mouth. Her face, which had always been long, was now positively equine. She had lost too many teeth. Her cheeks were sunken. The Druitt women had good teeth. She looked at Eurydice as if she were looking at something unearthly, something that could take her back into the past.

"Well?" asked Eurydice; "will they let me in?" "Where did you get the dress?" Bea asked her; she could barely control her voice. She knew that Eurydice had not come down from the mountain in recent months. "I bought the goods from a peddler," said Eurydice; "I made the dress myself. I copied it from a picture." Eurydice looked like an older and slightly heavier version of her daughter. Perhaps, Bea thought, it would have been better the other way after all, if she had come down looking like the Spirit of Chaos she had been impersonating all these years. Amon would see the resemblance between the two women now.

Eurydice said if she looked human, she wanted to get going; the dress, she said, was tight, and she wanted to get out of it as fast as she could. "It won't hurt you to look human for a while," Bea snapped. "I look like a leaf," said Eurydice, looking down at her hand, "a brown leaf." Bea said nothing. It was bad enough—it had always been bad enough—that her friend was so beautiful, but to complain about not being more beautiful! She glared at her friend. Eurydice, who was watching Bea out of the corner of her eye, saw the poisonous look. She sighed. It felt like old times. Old times were what she wanted to forget.

At the reception, Bea watched Eurydice with Amon's father. He was bending over Eurydice; then he threw back his head and laughed. Eurydice could, Bea thought grimly, marry the father if she set her mind to it. But then Eurydice caught her eye and Bea saw her eyes were green ice. "I am doing this for Helen and for you," said those eyes; "you two think life is worth it. I don't."

A year after my mother married my father, she gave birth to her first child, a boy. Bea told Eurydice that her daughter was living her life all over again. My grandmother didn't think so. "She's not the same as I was," my grandmother said; "she's harder. She stands back. She watches herself and everyone else. She doesn't let herself get taken by surprise." Bea said that Helen seemed just the same as her mother. Eurydice and Helen, Bea said, were not at all different. "She is," Eurydice said shortly; "she's not caught the way I was. Sometimes, when Ed was away, the rooms looked empty. Completely empty, as if there were no furniture in them. I couldn't hear anything. I'd see people's mouths moving and I didn't hear any sounds. The whole world could have folded up and shrunk down to a little seed and blown through a hole in the sky and I wouldn't have cared as long as Ed was there. You used to say my house was like a hive. Well, it was, but not the way you thought. It didn't have a queen. It had a king. Helen's different. Her house is a hive with a queen. If something happens to her husband, she'll survive. If something happens to her, he might not.'' She thought for a moment, drumming her fingers on the table and staring straight ahead of her. ''She's waiting for something,'' she said; ''sometimes, when I see Helen, I think that she's got a twin standing in the shadows, and that twin isn't married to anyone. She isn't anyone's mother. That woman is waiting for something else and won't move forward until it arrives. She stands back and looks at the thin ice we all walk on and won't set foot on it herself. The baby she just had,'' said Eurydice, ''that's not the baby she's been waiting for.''

''I don't understand *what* you're talking about,'' Bea said impatiently; ''she's just like you were. It's her first baby and I'm sure she wants it. It's a nice baby. I hope it lives.''

The baby did not live. It died in its second summer during a deadly epidemic of ''summer complaint.'' My mother cried for two days and then stopped. My grandmother was suspicious. She thought that her daughter had not yet realized that the child was absolutely and finally dead, and that one night, the knowledge would come upon her and she would become wild. But she soon saw that Helen had done her mourning. She had not allowed herself to become too attached to the child. The boy was dead. Eurydice knew that she had been right. The boy had not been the child she wanted. She must have wanted a girl, thought my grandmother. She was waiting for a daughter of her own.

9

When my mother was twenty-one, she gave birth to her second child, my sister. My thoughts about my mother as she must have been in those days are double-edged. For years after the trial, for the first years in Highbury Asylum, I never thought of her. If the doctor asked me a question about her, I answered him, but I believed that what I told him was true: I never thought about my mother. Of course, it is a different story now. When my mother died, I inherited all the family albums and papers. That was all I inherited at that time. After all, no matter what anyone might have willed to me, I could not have done much with it while I was in the asylum. Later, when I was much older, I began to look at the albums, and I saw that my mother and I did indeed look like one another. Often enough, I had to turn over a photograph and read what had been written there before I knew which one of us I was looking at. By then I knew I would never have children, I would never marry. All of family life had spun away from me. I was an empty hive. The bees had decided the queen was dead and the swarm had dispersed into the trees.

At fifty, perhaps even earlier, I began to look at photographs of my mother and pretend I was not seeing her: I was seeing myself. She was not married to the handsome man in the picture. She was not holding the adorable, fat baby with the ashen curls. I was doing those things and I was happy with my husband and child. I was in love with my husband and I loved our farm. And for a long time, I would keep myself happy playing these games. Then I would remember who I was, that my face was hopelessly twisted, that I was alone and that she had taken all I ever wanted away from me. I am almost seventy now, and fifty years after firing the shot, I still blame my mother. Oh, if someone asked me, "Why do you think you fired that shot?" I would not say that my mother made me fire the gun, or that it was my mother's fault, but in a profound way, I still believe she did. And yet I know why I fired the shot, but that more mature knowledge exists simultaneously with the more primitive notion that it was my mother's fault. It will turn out, I suppose, that both explanations are equally true. I, who was so interested in truth, in explanations, in investigating everyone's past so I could learn their motives, learn what drove them forward, in the end always wanted to settle for a simple solution to the complexities I found in life. I could not bear suspense of any kind. My mother claimed I was born in a state of anxiousness, and I believe I was. I can never remember a time, except perhaps a period of six months, the same six months that eventually caused me to fire the shot, when I was not experiencing everything through a barely concealed veneer of panic. The panic boiled up so constantly in its cauldron I might have mistaken it for the source of my being, for my heart itself. Well, here is my mother, as I sometimes imagine myself to be, although when I imagine myself in her place, I am never impatient, I am always kind to my children, and I love my husband. You see, I never believed my mother loved my father.

My father always said that the child and the worst storm of winter came together. My grandmother had refused to go back up to her cabin. She said the baby was coming that day and so was a snowstorm. My mother was evil-tempered all day; she screamed that she wasn't one of my grandmother's cows or pigs or goats and she knew she wasn't having a baby for weeks. As for the flurry of snow at the window, that, she said, was a sun shower. "A what?" my grandmother asked her; "there are no sun showers in Vermont after August tenth." My grandmother went out to look at the sky. My mother complained that there was nothing to see; the sky was all gray, iron gray.

My mother had gone back to doing the laundry and ignored my grandmother. They now communicated by arguing, just as my grandmother had communicated with my grandfather after he fell ill. Helen, Eurydice thought, took after her after all. Helen climbed up unsteadily on a stool and began to drop shirts and petticoats into the boiling water of the huge iron kettle boiling on the stove. Eurydice asked her why she couldn't let someone else do that; Helen's husband, she said, paid good money for a house girl, but there she was, boiling the clothes, doing the heavy work. My father came in and told her he wanted her to stop, but Helen waited until he left the house again, and commenced washing. "No one else does it right," Helen said shortly. "As for me, I don't care whether or not it's done right," said Amon, coming back in; "you wear yourself out with that work."

The snow was falling in large, flat flakes. When they hit the window, they left big cats' paw prints. Soon all the windows looked as if they had been tracked up by wet cats' paws. My grandmother got up and went to the kitchen window. Down the long pasture, curtain after curtain of snow was being hung in the air by the industrious storm. The lavender brown piles of leaves left over from the autumn had gone under. The furrows were filled. The fields were smooth and white. This snow was not going to stop. Eurydice took one look at her daughter's face and knew that she had been right about the baby as well as the storm. They sent Bill for the doctor, but they knew he would not be able to get through to the farm. The roads would be completely blocked within an hour. "If you can't get back, stay at your mother's," my father told him; "Helen will be all right."

It was my grandmother who delivered the baby. She said later that she didn't expect either the mother or the child to live. The baby's head was too large to be delivered normally, and after midnight, Helen began to drift off into sleep and would wake in confusion. My grandmother went to the kitchen hutch and took out a pair of cooking pincers used in making stews; they rescued the chunks of meat which sank to the bottom and began to burn. The next time my mother lost consciousness, my grandmother slid her hand inside her daughter's body and flipped the baby. Then she took the pincers, tied a pad of cloth to each claw, clamped her teeth, and maneuvered the pincers until they grasped the baby's head above each eyebrow. She pulled at the tongs.

Nothing seemed to happen. She applied pressure to her daughter's stomach, then pulled again. The head began to move toward her. The baby's eyes came into the light. Helen's eyes opened. "What are you doing?" she asked her mother. "What am *I* doing?" my grandmother asked indignantly; "what are *you* doing? Push down." My mother pushed down and with a loud pop the baby slid from its mother's body. "A girl," said Eurydice, unimpressed, picking up the baby and sucking at its nostrils, then at its mouth. It began to breathe, its little chest rising and falling rapidly. It did not cry. "Don't do that!" Helen protested; "you do that to calves." But Eury'ice was holding the baby at arm's length and grinning from ear to ear. Another animal, safe at last.

My grandmother said that she knew immediately that this was the child for which my mother had been waiting. Helen looked at the baby and saw the purple marks on her brow and thought even those were beautiful. My grandmother said that my mother fought like a wild animal to stay awake, because she knew that when she slept they would take the child. She angrily rejected any suggestions they made for naming the child, saying that this child was special, that she needed a new name, a name no one had ever had before. Obviously, this new child was special. And, said my grandmother, she was also magical. When her daughter realized that she owed the child's life to her, she actually thanked her. My grandmother said these were the first pleasant words she had heard from her daughter in years.

I have often wondered: What if my grandmother had not come down from her cabin that day? What if she had gone back up, as she so often did, when my mother complained about her presence in the house? What was the special child, the magical child, after all, but the first girl? If she had died, my mother would have gotten pregnant again, and I would have been the first girl. Would I have been the magical one with a new name no one had ever had before? It could so easily have happened that way. If my grandmother had only stayed in her cabin. But she did come down, and when the hands of the clock, which were already pushing my planet into the sky above the Roman numerals, stuck in place, my grandmother, who knew the ways of nature, gave them a push, and there was the magical child, and I became the child of shadows, waiting in the wings.

The magical child was, however, nameless. It made my grandmother uneasy. The roads were not broken to the farm, and no one knew the child had no name, but she was uneasy. A child without a name was not permanent. All her animals had names. "I don't think you want that child to have a name," she told my mother. My mother, who was cooing over the baby, ignored her. "My little wood dove," she chanted, "my little wood dove." "Why not name her that?" my father asked suddenly. "What? Wood dove?" asked my mother. "No," he said; "Majella. It's Latin for wood dove." My mother looked at the child and smiled. "Majella it is," she said. My grandmother objected. She said other children would call her Ella or Madge. No one was going to call her Majella. She reminded my mother that everyone used to call her Hellie and Ellie and Hell. "She won't be in this town forever," my mother said; "Majella is a good name for the big world."

My grandmother watched my mother with the child and saw something strange in them. Her daughter refused to be separated

72

from the child, as if the child were a vital part of her, and now that she had found it, she could not let it go. Helen passed in front of the window opposite her and there was no line of light showing between her body and the child's. My grandmother remembered thinking that my mother had found the part of her that she was missing. Or she saw herself in the child and this time she liked what she saw. She said she was uneasy because she knew a child should be more than a mirror to its mother, but this child *was* more: This child was the reason for her daughter's life. She knew that her daughter was completed by this child, that she felt she had been born to bear this child. When she watched them my grandmother was uneasy, as if there was danger nearby, something she should watch for but could not see, no matter how she tried.

My grandmother thought that when her daughter was up and about she would have to part from the baby. But her daughter lined a huge laundry basket for the infant, and wherever she went, the basket went with her. When Majella was older, but still too young to walk, Helen set her down in a little square cart that my father built for her. The cart was a small, moving playpen and rolled on four rubber wheels. One day, my grandmother came in and my mother was down on the floor pulling the cart after her. "You look like a dog pulling a dogsled," said my grandmother. "We're having fun," Helen said imperturbably. She sat back on her knees and looked at her mother.

"Don't you think she looks like me?" she asked shyly. My grandmother sat down in the carved chair next to the china cabinet. In its curved side glass, she saw her daughter and granddaughter. In the curved glass they were swollen, distorted. Helen had asked her an ordinary question, but she didn't like it, she didn't know why. Helen had never been willing to admit she looked like her. "Well, except for her hair she looks like you," my grandmother said. "Forget about her hair," my mother said impatiently; "what about the rest of her?" "She has your face," said my grandmother; "if her hair was black, she could be you all over again." "I thought so," said Helen triumphantly. "Why is it so important?" Eurydice asked, but either my mother did not hear her or she thought the answer to the question was so obvious that there was no reason to speak. "You do put that child away at night?" my grandmother asked. "She sleeps in a crib at the foot of the bed," her daughter said; "nothing wakes her up." Well, then, thought my grandmother, everything was all right. At least at night, the child slept alone.

73

And I think to myself, Majella slept alone. Alone in the dark. On her back. Facing the ceiling. My grandmother told me Majella always slept on her back. I never could. I am drawing nearer now. Can you feel me? I am coming closer, like bad weather. When I think of the past, that's how I see myself arriving: like a blast of heat, like a drought blue sky bringing no water.

10

It was a very hot day. Outside, there was no shade anywhere. Sunlight penetrated deeper into the forest than it had ever done before. There had been no rain for three weeks and all the men on the farm were occupied carrying pails of water down from the spring at the top of the hill behind the house. Small children came up from town and were given pennies for every pailful of water they brought up to the garden from the creek. The curtains had not been opened for a month; they were drawn tight against the heat. Inside the house the heat weakened only slightly. The little warm breezes which licked the faces of the women were rare. Cooking was no longer done in the winter kitchen. Everything had been moved out into the summer kitchen. The big cast iron range had been picked up and carried out and set down there by eight men.

Outside, the leaves of the great elms were dusty and swollen with heat, their edges curling like paper which had been wet but had dried out in the sun. Day after day, the skies were serenely bright and brilliant. Occasionally the air would grow sultry and the far hills would blur in the haze. "It's going to rain," said Amon, looking at the sky, but in the morning the dampness would be gone, and the haze with it. The mountains were etched against the clear, brilliant sky. Helen came outside and looked across the meadow to the far hills.

"Look at those little clouds," she said; "they won't do any good." "You used to think they were so beautiful," her husband said; "the little grazing clouds. Little sheep over our heads." "What I want to see," said my mother, "is a towering black cloud coming over the mountain."

The hills were still green, but the trees were beginning to pale to the yellows of autumn. In the forest, where the heat held the least sway, the odors were sharper. The pine smell rose into the air with a new vigor. The odor of last year's brown, brittle leaves mixed with a smell of dust foreign to these deep, day-dark acres. The margins of the creek crept inward. Every day a new width of mud showed on each side, and by afternoon the mud had baked into white dust. Everything was ebbing in the bright, malicious sunshine. Helen looked around her and decided to do the wash.

The water had been in the cauldron for two days, and if she didn't do the wash now she would have to empty it out or the cauldron would rust. No one had anything to wear that wasn't permeated by dust. "Wait," her husband said; "it's not work for this weather." She pushed the damp hair back from her forehead. Her clothes stuck to her in the heat. "I might as well do it now," she said; "this weather isn't going anywhere." Amon watched her take Majella by the hand; they disappeared into the dark entrance of the summer kitchen. He shook his head. Helen was pregnant again. When she was pregnant, she washed clothes. It was useless to argue. He had his own work to do. He had to sink a wooden trough into the ground so that he could run water down from the spring at the top of the hill. They couldn't keep bringing the water down by wagon. The horses would all be dead from the heat.

Helen came back out with Majella. She was waiting for the water to boil. She took the little girl with her and sat her down under a tree and began teaching her to play jacks. Majella was five years old. She wanted to know when she could go swimming. "When I put the clothes up to boil," said Helen. "I want to go now," said the child. "Never mind," said Helen; "we're *almost* in the water. Come on," she said, getting up; "the water must be boiling by now." "I want to stay out here," said Majella; "there's Uncle Bill coming down. Right there." She pointed at him. "You come with me," said Helen; "the animals are running loose all over the farm."

Inside, the cauldron was steaming. Helen piled bricks up in front of the stove, climbed up on them and began dropping the clothes in. The steam, the heat, rose up and slapped her in the face. She fought down her dizziness and dropped in the last of the clothes. Then she went outside. "Come with me," she called to Majella. She leaned against the hot, bright wall of the house. Her face was flushed. Her heart was pounding as if it intended to escape from her chest. She could feel her pulse pounding in her ankles, wrists, and throat. Her head was beginning to clear. "Majella?" she called. Where was the child?

Suddenly, she heard a crash and the sound of running water, as if a geyser had broken through the floor of the summer kitchen. She shook her head as if to clear it. "Majella!" she screamed. Her scream mingled with the agonized scream of her daughter. She flew into the kitchen. The cauldron was lying on the floor, its wide mouth gaping at her like a cannon. The clothes were all over. Steam was rising everywhere, from each piece of clothing, from the spilled water. It was hard to see through the mist which rolled toward her like smoke. Then she saw Majella lying on the floor. Her body had been hidden from sight by the cauldron. Her hand rose to her mouth and she crept forward. The child was awash in the boiling water; her drenched little dress clung to her. Huge blisters were already rising on her skin. Her eyes were open and fluttered slightly. "Here I am, Mother," she said in a clear voice. Helen picked her up and almost dropped her; her clothes were as hot as the boiling water. She tried to lift the child up by her arms, but every inch of her was covered by huge blisters. "I'm here," Majella said peevishly. Her eyes fluttered closed. Helen started to scream.

By the time the first of the farmhands reached her, Majella's eyes were open and fixed, and Helen, who was screaming rhythmically, whose eyes were fixed and who did not blink, seemed as far from them as the scalded child. In her hand, Helen clutched the dress from Majella's doll. Evidently, the child had tried to climb up to the cauldron on the bricks, but, unable to reach high enough, had pulled the lip of the cauldron toward her. She had been trying to wash her doll's dress.

11

It is hard for me to believe that I was not there during those dry, hot days. Because when I think of how my sister died, and how my mother grieved, I feel the heat and the grief as if I had been there watching from behind a curtain, invisible but already in need of comfort. I seem to know how it was as if it had happened to me, as if it were happening because of me, as if I myself were the heat, the heat which did not break after the child died, the heat which beat down on the slate roofs of the farmhouse until they glittered and wavered in the tireless sun. The buildings, too, seemed to waver as the sun glared and danced on their white painted surfaces. Time itself had stopped moving. The world could not spin past these dry, hot days. Inside my house, the little body of Majella was sealed in its white, painted coffin. The coffin was packed with ice so that the funeral could be delayed one day, possibly two, at least until Helen could be taken to the services and to the gravesite. But Helen lay in her bed under the roof as silent and immovable as the body of her child. She lay with her face to the wall, and when people came in to her room and called to her, she did not move. When my grandmother or my father forcibly turned her toward them, she stared at them as if she were looking through them to the wallpaper beyond. My grandmother came up and talked to her daughter constantly, although she gave no sign of hearing her. After the first day, my father stopped coming into my mother's room.

The drought outside seemed an extension of my father's state of mind. His imagination could not reach its end: The drought was here and it would always be here. He moved through the brilliant noonlike mornings, beneath the useless afternoon clouds, as if he could not remember a time when things were not caught and held in the drought's hot, dry hand. He could not believe that the drought would one day be over, that he would again have things to which he looked forward, when he would have a wife who walked and talked and cared where he was. The ministers of the neighboring churches announced that on Sunday they would pray for rain. Amon shook his head. God and his crops had withered at once. His child was dead and he no longer had a wife.

On Wednesday, my grandmother came into the barn to find him. The child, she told him, was beginning to smell. They would have to bury her in the morning at the very latest. A shadow fell over them. "Where is she?" asked my mother; "where's Majella?" "She's in the kitchen," my grandmother said, as if she were answering the most casual question in the world. "Let me see her," said my mother. "I don't think so," my father said; "she's all swollen. You won't recognize her." "I want to see her," Helen said. "We have to bury her tomorrow," said my grandmother; "will you be coming?" "We have to bury her?" Helen asked, turning toward my father. "Yes," he said. "She said she was beginning to smell," Helen told him. "She is," he said. "You can look at her," said my grandmother, "if you'll come to the funeral." "I'll come," said my mother.

My mother stood over the little coffin while my father, beginning at its foot, removed the screws from its lid, one by one. When he lifted the lid off, my mother fell forward over the coffin until her face was so close to Majella's that her nose almost touched the nose of the dead girl. "Don't get so close to her," my grandmother said, trying to pull my mother back by the shoulders. "Oh my God and Holy Savior!" gasped Helen. "Come away," Amon pleaded. My mother's hair, which had fallen forward, swept the dead girl's swollen, cold cheeks. She stared into the child's eyes as if she were reading something in them, as if, by sheer will, she could make the child breathe in and out, sit up, climb out over the edge and come with her into her own room. "Close it," she said in a new, hard voice. Amon and Eurydice looked at each other. When my father replaced the lid, Helen continued to stare at the spot beneath which the child's head rested. It was as if she were still looking at her, as if the wood of the coffin had become insubstantial, as if nothing could yet separate them. "So that is what I look like," my mother said.

They steered my mother to the church. They steered her to the family plot in our west pasture. She seemed less human, less aware, than the surrounding trees. The church had been crowded with the family's friends, but at the gravesite only the little family group stood under the brilliant sky. The yellowish grass had been roughly gashed, and the brown earth, which just that morning had been spaded up, was already edging with whitish dust. Oh, how familiar this picture is, thought my grandmother; how many times I've seen this, the little group of people all in black, standing with their heads bent, the two men who would lower the coffin resting on the handles of their shovels. When the service was over they would cover the coffin with dirt. There was only one new thing. The little child, the wood dove, was going under.

After the funeral, Helen, my mother, began to talk. She talked very little, but she did answer questions. She sat in the parlor on the good black horsehair couch and my father would come in there and lay his head on her lap. Absently, she stroked his hair. She was six months pregnant. When Amon went out, Eurydice came to sit with her. "You're going to have another child," she told my mother. "I know that," my mother said. "Maybe you'll have another girl," said my grandmother; "maybe she'll take Majella's place." "No, she won't," my mother cried, jumping up; "nothing will ever take her place! Do you think I want this child! I don't! I want Majella! If I can't have her, I don't want anyone!" "You don't know what you're saying," my grandmother said. "Oh, yes I do," she said in a low voice; "and you know I do."

A hurricane finally drove off the heat. The storm had been growing gradually all day. What had started as a spatter of rain that dotted the dusty roads until they resembled frogskin became a steady, heavy downpour slanting and raging in thick silver lines, first this way, then that. The wind, which had only shrieked in the trees, began to roar and shake the buildings. A black flotilla of clouds rose towering over the mountains and advanced on the house. The little stream grew into a foaming torrent and its muddy brown fingers began to pluck at the edges of the meadow, creeping toward the house. The wind began howling as if it were a living thing someone was tearing apart in the sky above them. By three o'clock in the afternoon the sun was blotted out and the storm's night fell. Trees were beginning to fall in the woods. The apple tree in the front pasture creaked loudly. A loud snap sounded, like the report of a rifle, and it lost one of its largest branches. Green leaves were torn from the trees and slapped against the windows. The dirt paths between the house and the other buildings were foaming brown streams. The men who went out to the barn came in soaked to the skin. Dark clouds rolled over denser, thicker clouds and merged with them. Over the far hills lightning played incessantly. The rain fell like something solid. The water from the creek reached the woodpile at the side of the house. My mother sat at the window and watched the storm. My grandmother watched her.

At ten that night, the storm was still gaining strength. The wind tore a shutter loose from the front of the house and sent it whirling down the front lawn into the meadow and the arms of the apple tree. "Go to bed," Eurydice said at last; "there's nothing you can do about the storm." My mother didn't move. My father said it was hard to go to bed when you didn't know if you would wake up with a roof over your head.

In the morning, the silence woke them. The air was warm and heavy with the smell of fresh wood, crushed leaves, wet earth. The front of the house was a litter of branches that the wind had torn from the trees the night before. Slate shingles had sailed everywhere. The chickens were walking around loose, stretching out their necks, pulling them back. Evidently, the chicken coop had been destroyed by the storm. There would be mice in the basement. They would have come in to get away from the storm. There was a lot to be done. It was over.

In December, my mother gave birth to a girl, easily and fearlessly. When my grandmother held the child out to her my mother shook her head. "You take it," she said. And so I come onto the scene, easily gotten, lightly prized, a lull in the storm, an irrelevant child, not even an anticlimax, not even part of the story.

Don't you think my mother must have seen me as something dreadful, the long, dark, final shadow of my sister, growing within her until finally I unfolded from her and came out into the light? How could she have seen me as anything else? I was there, mocking her loss of Majella by my very looks, because I have seen the pictures, and we did look exactly the same, except for our hair. And as I began to grow, she must have seen me as the child's body possessed by the wrong soul. How could I have been anything but evil to her? How could she have helped hating me? But for a long time, I didn't hate my mother. I hated my sister. She was always there. She was the one who never went away. It was because of her that no one ever saw me for what I was. It is not too much to say that, on the farm, when I appeared, I never appeared alone. My sister was there with me.

12

Perhaps you notice that, as I approach the part of the story that concerns my mother's life after Majella died, and after I was born, I become less and less rational about what happened. I become now as irrational as I was then. There is nothing I can do about it. Almost fifty years after I fired the shot which led me to prison, trial, and the lunatic asylum, I still feel myself caught up in the passions which blew into the air like dust, the ubiquitous dust of that farm. I know there was more to my relationship with my mother than I make out, I know that now, but when I look back, that knowledge rises like the morning mist and disappears, leaving only the glare. After all, my mother sent for me when she was dying, and afterward everyone said she waited to die until she saw me. When it happened, I thought she had stayed alive to punish me by forcing me to watch her die, as if *I* were killing her, but now I know better. To be honest, I know better most of the time. I am almost seventy; still there are times when my resentment of her flares up as suddenly as fire on a dry day. She must have cared for me more than I thought or cared to admit.

Ask yourself: What should I have learned from the events that I have just described? I should have learned that life was hard, that it rarely allowed you to have what you wanted, and that if it did allow you to have it, it did not permit you to hold on to it long. I should have learned that impermanence was at the very heart of things, and that, therefore, there was no such thing as perfection on this earth. These were the things our minister preached to us every Sunday of my early life. How could I not have known them? And then there was the farm itself, disgorging fifty calves in a few days, swallowing up another fifty the following week. I came upon birds dead in the meadow, claw marks visible through their feathers, ugly white slugs beginning to cover them. We had a barn swallow's nest over our side door, and one summer one of them fell down, and I climbed up on a kitchen chair to put him back, and I saw the little bird was swarming with bugs. I was so disgusted I almost dropped him. And then, after I put him back, I saw that the entire nest was swarming with bugs. Well, it was a mud nest after all, mud and straw. I should have known about the impermanence of the world, its blind strength, how it didn't pause for human sorrow; I should have known about the nature of things. I was a farm child. I saw it every day.

And my grandmother was a relentless lecturer on impermanence. I used to go up to her cabin and sit with her on her brass bed; she had set it down under a large plane tree. Some days we talked and fired at targets; other days we just talked. One summer she had one sick piglet after another, and that's how I remember that particular summer, sitting on the bed, my grandmother sometimes talking to the piglet burrowing in the folds of her skirt, sometimes talking to me. She said the pig was no more ignorant than we were and probably he was smarter. Early June. The trees were green again, the leaves still tinged with gold, still delicate, not thickened, not bottle-green as they would be in full summer, when, heavy and flat, they would lie like so many porches in the air. When the clouds blew off down the sky, the sun flooded the scene with gold. The highest pasture was green again. It looked like a pond in the middle of the pines. The grass, said my grandmother, had long ago covered her husband's grave. She said that when she had first visited the gravesite, the earth over the coffin had curved upward; now, of course, it had sunk beneath the level of the meadow. Later, she would go and heap more earth on it. She said she spent more time talking to my grandfather now than she did when he was alive.

She began to think aloud as she always did when I was with her. It never occurred to her to be more careful of what she said to me than she was when she spoke to the pig. Perhaps even to her I was something shadowy. "Well," she said, "when your mother got herself engaged less than two weeks after her father died, I wasn't surprised. She was caught in the wheel. A huge wheel. Everything is attached to it. Like those carnival wheels. You get into one of their seats and the wheel takes you up and you're so interested in how everything looks from so high up, from there, it all looks new to you, you forget you've seen it a hundred times before, you forget you came to see something else, and you go over the top, it's so exciting, and you keep on going round, and then they stop the wheel and open the door to your little basket, the one you've been riding around in, and you're not in it anymore, someone else has taken your place. That's what it means to be young. You're sticky with life. You stick to the wheel. And love is the most wonderful glue there is."

She touched my arm. "While here I am, sailing around in someone else's spring. I'm loose. I'm not alive, not really. When you're alive, you don't understand your life. You don't have the faintest glimmer of understanding. You think only God could understand life. You want Him to change this, change that, make things happen, take an interest in you. As if you mattered to the world. Well, I understand it now. It's a huge machine and all it wants to do is keep on going. I envy this pig. Hunger, shade, farrowing, suckling—all of that, it's enough for him. He doesn't think about love; he never heard of God."

And so I should have learned that life was dangerous, that love was dangerous, that life usually lasted longer than love, that I belonged to the same world as everyone else did and that I could no more escape from its laws than they could. There was even a lesson in the mountains we watched as she talked, dark blue closest to us, lightening through every shade of blue and violet, until the farthest range was indistinguishable from the blue air of the sky. But did I learn? I did not. I hated the world around me and refused to acknowledge it. I needed to believe there could be a different kind of world and that I had only to find it. And my needs were as blind and as undeniable as the pig's. They would not be refused. And so I concluded instead that my mother had never loved my father, nor he her, that my grandmother had never loved my grandfather, and he had not loved her either, that all four of them had settled for some pale simulacrum of love, a cheap imitation. I knew that true love, real love, could not make its way through the mountain passes to North Chittendon. I knew that very young. It was my oldest truth.

Somewhere, I knew, was the one ideal love for whom I was intended, the one perfect love who would catch me up in my own wheel. I knew it would not be the same wheel that had caught my mother or grandmother. It would be a wheel whose high point intersected the arc of heaven; from its top I would see wonders of the human heart no one in North Chittendon even suspected existed. And I believed that even if the people of North Chittendon knew such wonders existed, they would not want them. If they found them, they would not be able to endure losing them. And so they wanted nothing more than the old ways, because they knew those were safe. But I thought I was not like them. Not only could I find the ideal life I saw flickering behind my eyes, but I could survive its loss. Even surviving such a loss was something worthwhile, something heroic. In my innocence, I thought I could.

I now think that only those who hate the real world do what I did. I tried to create an ideal world. What I tried to do was obliterate this life and replace it with another, a more perfect one. And I was sure I could do it. All I had to do was loosen the rope of shadows which tied me to my own past and to North Chittendon. The roads that twist out of the past cease to exist when they cross the border to the future. And I thought I could reach the future untainted by the past, as a balloon might, weighed down by nothing. I did not want a regular, peaceful life like the lives of North Chittendon. I did not want a love like the loves of North Chittendon. I wanted to drift like an unfettered balloon into the future. It did not occur to me that the same sun that lit the past would light the future, that if I took myself into the future, I would be casting the same shadow on the ground before me.

And I think now: was I free at all? Oh, then I thought I was completely free. Now it is natural to wonder if I had any freedom whatever. If I didn't, then I was not responsible for what I did when I got to Montpelier. I was not responsible when I fired that shot. And probably the truth is, as usual, double. I was responsible and I was not. My finger pulled the trigger, but the fingers of the others had closed over mine like invisible net gloves long ago, and were pulling the trigger with me.

I come out into the pasture often, here at Highbury. There are a great many cows in this pasture, and they all cast shadows, but no one worries about whose shadow is whose. They are all the same. I have always loved cows. They are less than human, and therefore happy. I have often wished to be less than human. To be less than human is to be better. To be human is merely to encumber the turning of the wheel. And as I think this, I watch the birds circling in the sky. Sometimes the hawk will begin to circle or glide and a smaller bird will fly directly beneath him. If the hawk is watching something down on the ground, he has no idea that the smaller bird is flying beneath him. If he looks down and sees his shadow, he believes that he alone casts it. His wingspan is huge and so is his shadow on the earth. But if the little bird were to look down, he would see the same enormous shadow and mistake it for his own. He would not know that he was seeing both his own shadow and the shadow of the greater, stronger bird flying above him.

As I look back on my life, I think that it is like the flight of those two birds, one flying beneath the other. The past is the hawk, flying higher; its talons are stronger, its wings wide and majestic. The present is the mouse running from the shadow the hawk casts on the earth, and sometimes it escapes. The future is the small bird flying beneath the hawk, and it mistakes the long shadow on the grass for the shadow it casts. No wonder the future seems such a magnificent thing. But it is only a reflection of what has already happened, the extension of lines already drawn onto a new canvas that takes them up and makes them look new. I believe now that I had almost no freedom at all. I was only free to *believe* that I was free. Nothing challenging that belief could be left standing. I would have destroyed the world to continue believing that I was free, that I could create a perfect world of my own. And I did. I destroyed the world as it truly was.

13

I always believed that it was my birth which had weakened my mother, but my grandmother said that my mother changed after Majella died. She seemed older and more frail. At first Doctor Baker had thought my mother's fainting spells were brought on by her grief at Majella's death, but then he listened to her heart and found that its beat was often weak and irregular. Her heart acted up, he said, and that was what caused her "spells." She clung to my father, and when she was feeling well, she followed him wherever he went. Other days, she would draw the curtains in their room and lie in bed with a cloth pressed to her forehead. She said she was too dizzy to get up, but it was clear enough that she didn't want to get up. One of my earliest memories is of carrying ice up for my mother, and crying if I was not allowed to take it in to her.

When my father was home, he tried to protect me from the shadows he saw reaching out for us, or so I believe now. But he could not admit, even to himself, that the shadows falling over us were cast by his wife, and so there was little he could do. One day I came in from my grandmother's and my skirt and boots were caked with mud. "You're not to go up there anymore!" my mother shouted at me; "I want you down here where I can keep an eye on you. I don't want you playing in the mud like a pig!" "If I can't go up there I'll die!" I cried. "Then die," said my mother. Her voice was cold. I ran out of the room and my father caught me. "Your mother didn't mean that," he said. "Did you, Helen?" he asked her. "If she's going to threaten me with dying all the time," my mother said, rage in her voice. "Can I still go to Grandma's?" I asked my father. He was staring at my mother. "Yes, you can go," my mother said. I never understood why, when I asked one of them a question, the other answered. My mother's voice was hard and metallic, as it usually was when she spoke to me.

It seemed to me that my mother hated me. I was sure that she meant me no good, that she would take back her promise, and that I would not be able to go up to my grandmother's. And I wanted to know why she hated me. I began eavesdropping on my parents' conversations. I heard my mother tell my father that she wanted to make me tougher. She said I was born nervous and I had to get over it, and I wouldn't if everyone coddled me. "I don't see how you're toughening her up by letting her cry alone when she has nightmares," said my father. My mother didn't answer.

My grandmother told me that when I was born I cried constantly. The sound of my high-pitched cry drove my mother to distraction. She would get up, get me from my crib, and thump me down on the bed or couch, and I, frightened, would scream louder. While she changed my clothes, my mother would imitate my odd, chortling cry. One night I woke her and she threw me down so hard that my head bounced against the hard, over stuffed surface of the couch. She was frightened; she knew she could have killed me. But when she had to change my sweater, she pulled me up roughly, yanking me into the air by my arm. In the morning, she went to my grandmother's, told her what happened, and left me there for two weeks. Once, when nothing would pacify me, my mother pinched me and I screamed. Horrified at herself, she put me back in the crib and began to cry. Why couldn't she love me more? She pinched her own arm until it was black and blue. Why couldn't she love me at all? A heaviness stole over her. She was angry because my father had gone out to help with a new toll road, and she had been left alone with me, but now her anger was dissolving into sleep. Perhaps, she thought, she loved the child too much. She told all this to my grandmother, but when she started to say that perhaps she loved the child too much, she began to fall asleep. She said she couldn't think about that, it was a preposterous idea, if she could only fall asleep she would forget about it. And she did fall asleep, almost in the middle of a sentence. My grandmother said that my mother's fear that she loved the child—me—too much continued to haunt her. She thought it was always there, just beyond the limit of my mother's eyesight, just inside the dark border of the forest, the idea that she loved the child too much.

14

They had left me home alone. They had left me alone because I had insisted on staying behind. They were going on a picnic, my mother and father and grandmother. Mrs. Brown and her son Bill and his family were going in two other wagons. The farm was almost deserted. It was a beautiful fall day. Most of the leaves had fallen from the trees. The dark gray elms stood against the sky like exposed nerves. I picked up my cat, Stardancer, and went back into the house. "You'll take care of me, won't you?" I asked the cat and I buried my face in his neck. "They left me all alone," I told the cat. Stardancer, an enormous, tortoiseshell tomcat, lay peacefully in my arms. He began licking my wrist with his rough tongue. "Let's go into the parlor," I said to him.

The longer they were gone, the more frightened I became. It was not that I expected someone to hurt me or that I thought there were dangerous things lurking in the shadows. When I was alone, I felt myself becoming more and more rigid until I felt cold and hard, like a pane of glass, until I felt as if I were a window that was about to shatter. I was most frightened by not knowing what made me afraid. The fear came from nowhere; it made me cold even on the hottest days. It took away my breath until I took little, short breaths like gasps. It came on in seizures, like attacks. Sometimes it began when I saw my father sitting in the library's red leather chair and I would think to myself that I loved him even if he could not see that my mother did not love me at all. At other times I would come into the house, laughing and happy, and my mother would say something ordinary: "Take off your hat," or "Why don't you put your books away and join us?" and the carefully polite tone would let the fear out of its cage. Once it began it would go on for days, and then as inexplicably vanish. Pressing my head into the side of the cow, pressing my head into the side of the cat, curling up on the ground in front of the dog, my head between his front paws, these things would drive off the fear. I thought of the animals as my protectors. It never occurred to me that they might scratch me or hurt me, even accidentally, and they never did.

That day, I took the cat into the parlor and lay down in the middle of the rug holding him. The cat looked into my eyes and began to purr. I didn't know why, but I always felt safer lying on the floor, as if the surface of the earth were a dangerous thing on which to stand, as if I might spin loose from it. The floor had the feel of an animal; lying on the floor, I was close to the skin which kept me from sinking into the crust of the earth. I stared over the cat's pointed ears at the portrait of Majella hanging over the mantel. My grandmother had painted my sister so that, no matter where you were in the room, her eyes seemed to follow you. "See that?" I said to the cat; "she's alive. Don't you think she's alive?" The cat didn't like my tone; he squinted at me and extended his claws. Then he purred and stretched; he rolled over on his back. I buried my face in the dusty, soft white fur of his stomach. He started to bring his back paws forward as if to attack, but relaxed and stretched out again.

"I'm going to stay here until she talks to me," I told the cat. I stared at the portrait. The longer I stared, the more certain I was that the painted eyes could see me. I knew I was working myself into a state, but I kept on staring at the picture of the dead girl. Finally, her hand seemed to move. A wave of panic rose suddenly in me like a tide of heat, and I grabbed the cat and flew out of the room. I pressed my face into the cat's side and burst into tears. I had no idea why I was crying. My cat, who had finally had enough, jumped down, twitching his tail. He squinted angrily at me. "Don't leave me," I pleaded with the cat. "Come back," I asked him. The cat jumped up on the windowsill and watched me.

Perhaps, I thought, there was someone in the house, someone watching me. I went into my parents' room and lay down on the bed. I lay flat on my back and stared up at the ceiling. Nothing appeared there. I got up and sat down in front of my mother's vanity. There I was, three of me. I looked just like the young girl my grandmother had shown me in her photograph albums. My mother. My mother insisted that we did not look alike. She insisted that I looked nothing like Majella. But when my grandmother went through the album, she often had to turn over a picture and read the inscription on the other side before she knew at whom she was looking. "You look so much like your sister, I never know who's who." My father always said he could see no resemblance at all between my mother and my grandmother. There was something wrong with all of them, I thought. They couldn't see what was before their eyes.

I leaned forward to get a better look at myself in the mirror. I saw a beauty mark at the base of my neck. I had never seen it before. Last week, a man in town had died of a disease that began when heavy black beauty marks began appearing all over his body. I unbuttoned my dress and looked at my body in the mirror. There was a beauty mark on my left breast. I had never seen that one before either, nor the one I suddenly discovered on my collarbone. I was going to die. I got up and went into my own room and took off everything I had on. There were uncountable beauty marks. My throat began to tighten until it hurt. I was dying and they would never come home. When they came home, there would be nothing they could do.

I went back into my mother's room and sat down before the mirror. I was so young. I was only thirteen. I didn't want to die. I went into my mother's room and took the bottle of laudanum she kept on her dresser. I filled a glass with water, emptied the contents of the bottle into it, and drank it down. Then I went outside, lay down on the grass, and waited to fall asleep. I patted the grass beneath my hand as if it were fur.

They found me late that night, or Eurydice's dog, Sam, found me. They had searched the farm, they had sent down to Bea's, and no one had seen me. My mother said that I was simply too careless of their feelings to tell them where I had gone, but my grandmother was worried and would not let the matter drop. "Go find Agnes," she told Sam, and the dog trotted off. I had played hide and seek with Sam for years. He thought he was playing the game again. My mother told my grandmother that she was being ridiculous; *she* was going to bed. The dog found me under the lilac bushes and the others found me there, too, still and limp in the deep, wet grass. I had fallen asleep in the middle of a patch of daisies. My grandmother said she screamed when she saw me; she thought I was dead.

They carried me back to the house and sent Bill Brown for the doctor. My mother came downstairs and stood near the wall of the kitchen, twisting her wedding ring around her finger. "She's not dead," my grandmother told her; "no thanks to you." "How could I have known?" asked my mother; "how could I have known what she did?" "How did I know?" my grandmother asked, trying to pour some coffee down my throat. "What was in

the little brown bottle?'' she asked my mother. "Laudanum,"
my mother said. "How can you leave something like that where
she can find it?'' my grandmother asked her; "don't you think at
all?'' "She's upset enough,'' said my father. "I never thought
she would touch it,'' my mother said miserably.

Doctor Baker came and gave me a stimulant. He sat me up
and raised my arms over my head again and again. Finally, my
eyes fluttered open, then shut again. "She's coming back,'' the
doctor said. I opened my eyes. They were all there. I was in the
same place. I considered asking the doctor about my beauty
marks, but I already knew that those dark marks on my skin
were absolutely harmless. It was another kind of darkness I both
desired and feared.

My parents never mentioned the incident again. My grandmother said they wanted to forget it had ever happened, as if
forgetting what I had done would somehow make me better,
stronger, safer. I said they forgot because they didn't care. My
grandmother said they forgot because they were afraid to remember.

15

My grandmother died suddenly when I was almost sixteen. Bill Brown had gone up to her cabin with a load of wood and found her sitting on the brass bed in front of her house, staring out at the blazing autumn leaves. When he called to her, she didn't answer. He went over to her and saw that her eyes were staring into the sun without blinking. Her cheeks were cold. He wrapped her in a blanket and brought her down to our house. My parents sent for Doctor Baker, who said it must have been her heart; sometimes hearts just gave out, it was always the hearts that got the Druitts. But when the women undressed her, they found her stomach hugely swollen. "Well, now I don't know," said Doctor Baker when my parents called him back to look at her again. "Her stomach's been swollen for years," I said; "she said she liked it like that. She said she never was so happy as when she was hatching a baby. She said she never knew how lucky she was to have all those hands grabbing at her skirt. She said she liked her dog, Sam, best because he always dragged her everywhere by the skirt, just like her children did. She said she didn't understand anything until she was old and it was too late." "That's enough, Agnes," snapped my mother. "Let the child talk," my father said. "She's not a child anymore," said my mother; "she doesn't have to babble on."

"Well," said Doctor Baker, "if her stomach was swollen for years, she was sick for years and she knew it." "She didn't care," said my mother. "She did care!" I cried out; "she cared because of me!" "Because of you!" my mother said contemptuously.

Wedged into the crack between the mantel and the wall, my father found my grandmother's last will and testament. "I leave all my earthly possessions to my granddaughter, Agnes Dempster," she wrote; "any and all of my clothes, my books, my plates, silver, and china. Everything in my cabin I leave to her. I leave her my two good leather suitcases in the wooden chest near the front door. I leave her as well my cabin and the fifty acres of land on which it stands. Should she move away from North Chittendon for any length of time, I ask her father, Amon Dempster, to oversee the property for her. My revenues from the sale of the farm held by the Vermont Central Bank of Montpelier are to be held in trust for her until she is twenty-one. I appoint her father the executor of this trust.

"Agnes, do not fight your father over this money. Do you remember that you taught one term of school after the teacher fell ill and you took your entire salary and spent it on face creams that you were going to sell to everyone and make your fortune? I think you sold one bottle and if you want it back, it's behind the third picture from the left on the mantel. When you are twenty-one you will not spend all your money on face creams.

"Helen, I know your feelings remain hard toward me. Still, I ask you to bury me in the plot next to your father's. Helen, I am sorry for everything. If there is anything of mine you want, ask Agnes for it. I am sure she will give it to you." She had signed the document Eurydice Druitt Saltonstall and Beatrice Madelaine Brown had witnessed it. Beneath her signature, Bea had written, "Eurydice Druitt Saltonstall was in her right mind when she wrote this will. February 10, 1896."

"Will this crackpot document hold up legally?" my mother asked. "Oh, I think so," said my father. "She had a witness. None of us is going to try to break the will." "To leave Agnes so much money!" my mother said; "what is she going to do with it?" "Nothing for five years," said my father. "If only Mother could have left her some brains!" my mother said. "Her trouble isn't lack of brains," said my father; "neither is yours."

After my grandmother's funeral, an uneasy peace reigned in the house. One morning my mother woke up, looked out the window, and saw that frost had blasted the garden. Overnight, the flowers and vegetables had blackened and shriveled as if they had been first burned and then drenched. The air was cool and sweet on the cheek, and on the highest mountains a faint dusting of white was already thickening day by day. My grandmother had liked autumn. She had liked every season. My mother came upstairs to look for me. She wanted to know what I intended to do with myself; I couldn't sit around the house for five years waiting to inherit my grandmother's money.

When she reached the doorway to my room she saw me bending over the bed, and on my bed was an open suitcase. I felt her watching me and picked up some folded petticoats and put them in the bottom. "Come in," I said, without looking up. "What are you doing?" asked my mother. "What does it look like?" I asked her. "Don't speak to me that way," she said. I said I would speak to her any way I pleased. "You're not moving out," my mother said; "not until you talk it over with us." "You," I said, straightening up, "have nothing to do with it. I'm leaving tomorrow morning." I went on packing the suitcase. My mother moved forward and grabbed my wrist. "Don't put anything else in that suitcase," she said. "Don't touch me," I said in a low voice; "let go of me." She let go.

"Where do you think you're going to go?" she asked me; "you can't take care of yourself here. How do you think you'll manage somewhere else?" "I can take care of myself," I said. "The way you took care of yourself with Bill Brown's son?" Six months before, I had gone on a hayride with Tom Brown. My father said I was old enough, and moreover, he trusted me. Of course, he was wrong to trust me, and my mother, who did not, was right. I was not to be trusted. I was utterly ignorant of what a friend at school called the sex instinct, and I wanted to learn.

Tom and I were left alone in an old barn. We began sitting closer and closer together until we were pushing against each other. Tom kept fooling with my hair, pulling out one pin after another. Finally, it tumbled down. He said I was beautiful; he began to stroke my leg. An odd tingle began to run up my leg, and further. My nipples stood up against my dress. "Why don't you sit in my lap?" Tom asked. "All right," I said. "You don't weigh anything," he said. His hand was under my skirt. I could see it creeping up as if it were some kind of spider. I felt my face flush hot and red. Through my dress, I felt the heat of his body. The sharp, acrid male smell which rose from his hot skin filled my nostrils. It settled in the back of my throat. His hand moved between my legs and I gasped and lay down on top of him. Suddenly, I felt something hard, something like a stick, pressing into my pelvis. I knew what it was. I was appalled by how strong and how hard it was. I remembered Jenny Saltonstall saying, "They open you up like a clam, all the way, they just open you up, and after that, you bleed like a stuck pig."

I tried to sit up but he pushed me back down. "Let me go!" I cried. "Don't make so much noise," he whispered; "the others will come running." "Let me go," I insisted, beginning to struggle. He let me go. "What's your trouble?" he asked me angrily; "I thought you were having a good time." "I want to go home," I said. "She wants to go home," Tom mimicked cruelly. "I'll walk all the way back," I said. "You don't have to walk," he said; "I'll leave you alone. Next time," he said, "don't start unless you intend to finish. Men don't like girls who do that." I said I was sorry. Now that the danger was over, I felt sorry for him. I also felt a small, sneaky sense of my own power over him. For an instant, I had had that power.

"I want to go home," I said again. "Well, you'll have to wait until the others come back from the woods," he said; "there's only one wagon." "Then I'll wait," I said. "Some girls just don't warm up," said Tom. All the way back, sitting next to each other in the wagon, he and I stared straight ahead, refusing to look at one another. And as we rode, I summoned the sensations up again and again, the tingling in the groin, in the belly, the swelling of the nipples. What if it's true, I wondered, what if I never feel more than this? What if this is as warm as I get?

"You want to move out so that you can take up with every Tom, Dick, and Harry," said my mother. "That's right," I said; "I want to take up with Tom, Dick, and Harry. What difference does it make to you?" "I'm your mother," she said. "You're not my mother!" I cried, slamming the lid of the suitcase shut; "when you take a penny out of a pocket, the pocket isn't the penny's mother. I don't have a mother. If I had a mother, it was Eurydice. Not you!" "I've always taken care of you," my mother said. "Is that what you call it?" I demanded; "is that what you call letting me cry all night? Is that why you killed the cow I raised from a calf? I asked to keep it! Is that why you talk to me as if I were a stranger who just happened to live in this house? I've been to other people's houses! I know how real mothers speak to their children."

My mother turned pale and sat down on my bed. "Don't start in with that!" I cried; "don't start to have a fainting fit. I don't care if you fall on the floor. I don't care if you die. You think because I look like you, you have some power over me. You don't. So what if your shell looks like my shell? That's all you are, an empty shell. You don't have a soul. I hate you! I've always hated you!" "You don't hate me," she said. "I hate you!" I cried out; "you're insignificant. You're nothing at all. When you die, nothing will be left of you. If I ever amount to anything, you'll still be nothing! I'll change my name if I amount to anything! You won't get any credit. You're going to die and the name on your tombstone will be rubbed away. I'd rub it away with my own hands. Insignificant! Insignificant!'' I was horrified. I had thought these things for years. Nothing could have persuaded me that I would ever say them aloud.

"Insignificant," my mother whispered softly. "That's what you are!" I shouted at her. I couldn't stop shouting. "A miserable, insignificant thing. Get out of here! Get out!" I picked up a book and threw it across the room. My mother got up and backed toward the door. She went downstairs and sat on a kitchen chair. "Insignificant!" she whispered again. But I had not scared her off. She came back with my father.

It appeared that Montpelier was far more dangerous than anyone could ever have imagined. There were men there, according to my mother, who did nothing but prey on young girls, secure in the knowledge that the girls were far from their families and that no one would hear of their tragedies. "What tragedies?" I asked. "Don't play innocent with me!" my mother cried; "you know what kind of tragedies I'm talking about." "Tragedy isn't so bad," I said, half to myself, thinking of the life around me, the grim slowing of the wheel, the slow grinding of the grain into dust.

"Tragedy isn't so bad!" said my mother; "Amon, talk to her! She's worse than an innocent! She's a fool!" "Do we have to argue?" my father asked; "she's going away tomorrow." "And," said my mother, who would not be distracted, "your grandmother told me the story of a young girl who went down there to work in a wealthy household, but she never got there at all. She was kidnapped and sold into slavery." "Slavery?" I repeated, biting my lip; "I thought there were no more slaves." "I hope you don't have to find out the hard way," said my mother. "Nothing can be worse than living here," I said. "If you two are going to go on like this, I'm going out," said my father. "So am I," I said. "Don't you dare move," said my mother. My father shook his head, then got up and left.

We heard the side door slam behind him. "You don't know what you're doing," my mother said. "I know," I answered. "You think you're going to leave here and everyone in the world will love you," she said; "they won't. Oh, you're beautiful enough. You won't have any trouble getting a hold of men. But wait until they take you to meet their mothers and sisters. The women will see right through you. That will be the end of it.

They'll see what you're like." "I'll take that chance," I said.
"And when they find out, what are you going to do, try to kill
yourself again?" my mother asked. "Shut up!" I said. "How
many girls try to kill themselves when they're thirteen?" asked
my mother. I picked up my glass of water and threw its contents
full in my mother's face. Little rivulets ran down her face and
dripped onto her clothes. "You see?" she cried; "you see how
well you can take care of yourself?" "If you say another word,"
I told her, "I'm going to take this pitcher and bring it down over
your head." "Go ahead," my mother said; "go ahead. The
constable will be glad to take your suitcases to jail."

"Don't talk to me about jail," I shouted at her; "you killed
your own daughter! You let her spill that boiling water all over
herself. Everyone told you not to do the wash, but you had to
have your way; you had to do it. You killed her. It's not my fault
you couldn't get her back. It's not my fault you didn't want me.
What did you want me to do, get her back for you? It's a good
thing she died before she had to grow up with you!" My mother
grabbed the back of her chair and held on to it. "I can't
breathe," she said. "Don't," I said. "Help me," she said. I
stared at her. She looked green; her forehead was beaded with
sweat. I moved toward her as if I were advancing on a dangerous
animal. I grabbed her roughly around the waist and helped her
into a chair. "Sit there until you feel better," I said; "I have to
finish packing." "I didn't want this," my mother said, looking
up at me; "I didn't want this. Not between us." "There is
nothing between us," I said, and went back to my suitcases.
After a while, she got up and left.

After she left, I remembered how, when I had been much
younger, my mother used to come into my room, slip into bed
with me, and slowly inch closer. But I hadn't wanted my mother
there, and I pretended to toss and turn until finally she had
enough and got up and went out. But I didn't fall asleep, and
after a while, I went into the parlor and fell asleep on the love
seat. When I woke up in the morning, I saw my mother asleep
on the green horsehair couch. I got up quietly and went back to
my own room. Did anyone in the house, I wondered, sleep in
their own beds? My father did. I closed the russet leather lid of
the trunk but did not lock it. There were always things one
thought of at the last minute.

I looked up and saw my mother standing in the doorway.
"I've seen more of you today than I have in the last five years,"
I said. She didn't answer. Instead, she came in and sat down on

the edge of my bed. "Aren't you at all sorry you're going?" she asked me. "No," I said, sitting down in the chair opposite the bed. I ran my fingers along the edge of a cabbage rose curving over the overstuffed arm of the little chair. The armrests were no longer shiny. I had read in this chair, my legs thrown over one arm, my back propped up by the other. I had done my homework and my diary-writing here. I thought of my diaries, and how, at the end of each year, I took one down to the wood stove, and when I was sure that everyone was asleep, I threw it in, the small, rectangular, bloodred book the grain salesman gave us every year. And when the isinglass squares in the door of the wood stove flared orange, I slid the door back, took the poker, pressed the diary down further into the coals, and held it there until the binding itself took fire, and then it was all gone.

"I'll miss this chair," I said. "The chair," said my mother, "didn't raise you from a baby." "Neither did you," I said. "Let's not start all that over again," said my mother; "I tried. I did the best I could." I said that I imagined that was what the condemned said when they felt the noose tightening around their necks. "The noose is around your neck, not mine," said my mother; "when I was a child, I had a friend named Jackie and one day he wanted to go sliding on the ice. He walked straight out onto the river. He didn't look to the right. He didn't look to the left. You know what the currents are like under that ice." "And so he drowned?" I asked, sarcastic. "No, he didn't drown," said my mother; "he was lucky." A cloud blew down the sky and the sun poured into the room. A silence fell between us.

"I suppose," I said, "you'll repaper this room after I'm gone. You never liked that paper much. 'Cabbage roses, cabbage roses. Don't you see enough cabbage roses every time you go out the front door?' That's what you said when I picked it out." "I still don't like the paper," my mother said; "that grayish blue ground. It's like the worst of the winter light. I hate it when those days come. There's no weather, just that gray blue light. And you think that if there's one more day like that you'll start to scream and never stop. Oh yes," she said, "you think you're the only one who feels anything. So did I at your age." The wind blew the frilly white curtain into the room and the room darkened.

"Do you remember," I asked her, "how, when you were giving birth to the baby that came after me, you said, 'Pray, Agnes, pray! The baby's turned wrong. God won't listen to me! Go and pray!'" My mother looked up swiftly and then looked

down at her hands. "Why did you ask me to pray?" "Because,"
she said, "the baby was turned wrong. He was coming feet first.
I thought I was dying." "But," I said, "you thought God
wouldn't listen to you. You thought he would listen to me."
"Yes, yes," said my mother; "I don't like to speak about it. The
child died. I shouldn't have asked you. You were too small.
shouldn't have let you anywhere near me. Is that what you want
to hear?" "No," I said; "what I want to know is, did you know
who you were talking to?" "What?" asked my mother; "what
do you mean? Of course I knew. I wasn't out of my mind with
the pain. I knew who was who. I wasn't crazy. Did you think
was crazy? I've *wanted* to be crazy. Insane. I love the word. Off
in another country, seeing things, a wonderful place where you
can do no wrong. Like heaven." Childlike, my mother wiped her
eyes with the palm of her hand. "Are you crying?" I asked her.
"You always used to ask me that when you were small," my
mother said, sniffling. " 'Are you crying?' You used to like to see
me cry."

It was silent in the room, and the light rippled on my walls as
if the room were a ship and waves from the ocean were reflecting
the sun's light on the walls. It was as if my mother and I were
alone for the first time, as if the dangerous thing between us had
lifted like a treacherous fog. "You knew it was me?" I persisted.
"Of *course* I knew it was you," she said; "who else could it
have been?" I said I didn't know. My mother looked sharply at
me, and then looked away. "About the paper," she said; "it
won't change. It's worn well. It grows on you. If you come
back, it will be here, the way you remember it." "I won't come
back," I said violently. Outside, the wind must have risen. The
curtain blew in and the sun again flooded the room.

"You can't know that," my mother said. "I know," I said.
"You'd die first, is that it?" asked my mother, smiling strangely.
I said I didn't want to talk about it. "At least," said my mother,
"wait until we get the name of a respectable house. There are
places there . . . If you go to the wrong house, it will be a year
before any decent person will let you in. If they ever do." "I'm
not worried," I said.

"Why can't we go into town with you?" my mother asked. "I
want to go alone," I said. I wanted to begin again. I didn't want
my parents' shadow falling over my departure. "Won't you miss
the farm?" she asked. "Yes," I sighed; "I'll miss the farm." In
back of me, through the open window, I could feel the leaves
flaming against the blue sky. The light breeze carried in the smell

of freshly mown hay and the faint but definite odor of mud drying in the sun. "You won't smell that in the city," said my mother; "it's ugly there. Up here, the snow is so beautiful, even when it locks us up in the house, you can't get mad at it. But there, they break the roads right away and the wagons roll through all the time, and the stage, too, and everyone walking back and forth to the mills and the factories, and the snow's black by nightfall. And it's down in the valley, you have to look up to see the mountains." "You're speaking from your own experience, I suppose?" I said. "I've been to Montpelier," she said; "on my honeymoon." "Oh, yes," I said; "the glass flowers."

"We found them in Burlington," my mother said. Burlington! And all these years I had believed they came from Montpelier. "It can't be that ugly or no one would go there," I said, getting up. "Some people," said my mother, "don't have the luxury of choosing between places on the basis of their beauty. They go where they can make money." "Well," I said, "that's what I want to do." I wanted to support myself. I didn't want to take another penny from my parents. "I want you to take one hundred dollars from your father," said my mother, "and put the bills inside your boots." "I don't want it," I said. "If you don't take it now," she said, "we'll come down to Montpelier and give it to you." I looked at the little gold watch pinned to my bosom. "Sixteen more hours," I said, "until I leave." I didn't want to be cruel, but I could not unbend. I was afraid to weaken. I was frozen solid, like ice on a pond. The chill, the coldness between us, kept me safe.

16

Does it seem to you that I exist in flares and flashes in my description of my life? So it seems to me, and so I seemed to live then. But now I am about to tell you how I left North Chittendon. And when I did, I became a continuous being. Suddenly, everything that happened to me became part of everything around me; there were no seams in the web the world wove around me.

And now that I am about to leave North Chittendon in memory, I want to linger, to look at it slowly as I never did before, just as I did fifty years ago, when I first left. North Chittendon! I imagine that now a new family owns the Country Store; there is a new minister in our old pulpit at the Congregational Church, but I am sure nothing has changed in the town. Recently, someone happened to mention that all the branches connecting the small towns to the Central Vermont Railroad had been closed down long ago, and I thought about that for a long time, how now North Chittendon is sealed off from this new century, how it is destined to remain just as it was in 1896 when I first left it.

North Chittendon! I can see it snuggled into one of the deep valleys in the encircling high hills. I can see myself standing in the town square, with the green pasture flung down like a rug over the top of the highest hill and the blue dome of the sky vaulting above it. To the south, Peaked Hill soars into the air, its thick pine forests dying it deep green year in and year out. At its foot, the pastures of the valley divide it from the thick forest which rises up the facing mountain.

A narrow road winds its way up to the top of Peaked Hill, and from the topmost pasture, the water of Lake Champlain can be seen glittering in the far distance. The wind blows hard up here, whipping the clouds into high peaks, tearing the large, cottony clouds into long, thin streaks of white which sail off down the sky and over the town. The wind carries the sounds of the town up to the top of the hill: the soft clink clink of the cow bells, the peal of the church bells, and, on clear days, the sound of the train's deep horn as it pulls into the station.

From up there, the grazing Holsteins are only black and white specks which seem incapable of movement. They remind me, often and oddly enough, of winter. In spring the land turns emerald, and in midsummer, in the high heat, the edges of the pasture brown. The wind blows through the long grasses and the grass seems to rise and fall in waves. As the farmers plow their fields, some of the pastures seem striped; others are rich brown. The familiar patchwork emerges, its margins decorated in autumn by the red and golden flare of the leaves. In November, when the first snows fall, the pasture is no longer green but brown, and it changes again; as the snow fills the furrows, the stripes go under and the hills are white. The pines are darker and more mysterious than ever.

The town rises from the valley against the hills, and from above, its white houses and its three white churches seem tiny, as do the three white steeples climbing into the air as if they would pierce heaven itself and draw grace down upon the town as the big elms bring down the lightning. And then there are the surrounding farms, the trim white houses, the large red barns, the woodpiles growing larger in summer, smaller in winter, and, during any season, the wood smoke rising from each chimney, curling upward, losing itself in the air.

Narrow dirt roads connect the farms to the wider dirt road which links North Chittendon with Montpelier and Barre. The road winds crazily through the farms, between their buildings, from one farmhouse to another. Before the road gains strength and leads out of town, it pauses between two white churches, the Baptist Church, which has a square, four-pointed tower, and the Congregational Church, which is chagrined by its smaller congregation, but boasts a soaring, white tower and a bell whose tones are listened for and anticipated every hour of the day. A little to the side of each church is its cemetery, used by the families who live in town. Farm families usually bury their dead in family plots on their own land.

In winter, when the elms that shade both churches and cemeteries are bare, the two groups of headstones seem lonely, sad, as if they are members of one flock, unaccountably separated. Once a year, twice a year, people from the town will look at the churchyards and say to themselves: They look sad. They look lonely. A pity to divide the dead from each other when their souls were divided enough in life. I see it all again now that, if only in my imagination, I am preparing to leave it. When it held me in its grip, I wanted to see nothing beautiful in it, nothing which would make me regret leaving.

And it is as if I am pausing to say good-bye to the house. It was a beautiful house. It must still be. The double parlors on each side of the front door glowed orange red. The Turkish carpets flamed on the floor. The frilled, thin white curtains fluttered immaculately in the soft breezes of the open windows. The fireplaces in the parlors and in the library behind them were always lit in the winter. The library was painted dark red and its deep shadows and perpetual chill were churchlike and peaceful. My mother's little brown rattan desk was opposite the large, rolltop desk of my father. The whitewashed kitchen behind the library was big and bright; the buttery, whose deep shelves were wide enough to hold one hundred pies, was always full and dark and cool. The dining room furniture was polished until its wood gleamed like glass. Through the two bay windows of the dining room, the meadows unfurled themselves and the mountain ranges seemed the far wall of the house. Upstairs, all the bedrooms were bright with floral patterns, and braided rugs lay warm on the floors. At the top of the stairs, my grandmother had painted a fresco of the farm as it must have looked to someone who came upon it from the high meadow, as my father had.

And I can see the fresco my grandmother had painted in the parlor, an apple tree heavy with fruit, and in the grasses beneath it, the day lilies were blooming orange, and the tiger lilies lifted their sharp wings into the air. The tree seemed to entangle something mysterious in its branches as it stood against a sky which was somehow both an evening sky and a morning sky at once. In the strange light my grandmother had created for it, the tree seemed like a living thing, something half human, balancing between two worlds, drawing the viewer deeper into its darkness, coaxing him out into its light. And on the third branch from the ground, my grandmother had painted a nick in the tree's arm, and above the nick she had painted the initials B. B. and E. D.: Beatrice Brown, Eurydice Druitt. The old apple tree is no longer there, but the fresco might be, the light from the fireplace flickering in its leaves as if the tree were still alive.

Bill Brown once wrote a composition for his teacher about the apple trees. He said that they had been humans whom evil spirits had trapped and turned into trees; trapped in the pastures, on the hills, in the forests, they were forced to watch those they loved, but were not able to move toward them. And so they had learned to grow apples and, when the people they loved were lost, or when their crops failed, they could come to them and eat of their flesh and survive. Bea asked her son about the story. He said it was about his mother; he knew his mother would never leave him and die, but even if she did, she would find a way to get back and take care of him. That was how he got the idea about the apple trees for his story. Oh, now that I am seventy, I can afford to see not only the beauty of the town, but the beauty of the people. If anyone had asked me about North Chittendon when I was sixteen, I would have said that everyone there was homely and insignificant and rough.

Do you see that what I have done is paint the entire background of my life for you as a painter might render the backdrop of a scene before painting in the figures in the foreground? I imagine that was how my grandmother painted the fresco in our living room, the far objects first, the near ones last. So we see things after all. For I did learn to draw in the end in the Highbury Asylum, and it turned out that I did have the family talent for drawing. By that time it did me little good.

Today, I am patient about the passing of time. I see the seasons falling one upon the other, creating the illusion of depth, of perspective. I have tried to call back the seasons, to lay them down one at a time for you, so that when I leave for Montpelier, you will see me in the deepnesses of my sixteen-year-old life. Have I been successful? Can you see the procession, moving from panel to panel, as it does in a medieval painting, approaching the present on its march from the past? Can you tell what is going to happen to me? I like to think you can tell what will become of me, that you can guess even before I tell you, because I believe that everything was destined to happen as it did. I am going to become the most discussed eighteen-year-old in the state and perhaps in the country. The ups and downs of my eighteen-year-old heart are going to be recorded and analyzed in the newspapers and in the houses and in the streets. People will send to the papers asking for photographs of me. And all because I fired that shot. Which is why I am hesitating, looking around. North Chittendon, good-bye. I am leaving North Chittendon to create my own, my ideal, my perfect world. I am about to become the same girl I was then, the sixteen-year-old girl who thought it could be done. And I am going to tell you her story just as she experienced it. I am not going to intrude like the voice of doom, commenting on her choices, her motives, her failings. When I was a young girl, there was no Greek chorus in the wings commenting audibly on my efforts to create a world unlike any world which had ever existed before. I see myself, sixteen, pulling my suitcases onto the porch, my heart beating wildly, fierce with joy because I am going away. And today, if anyone asked me, I would ask for a life precisely like the life of either my mother or my grandmother. I am about to be caught in the wheel. It is about to throw me down on a dark and empty plain.

Montpelier

17

I was taking the morning stage to Montpelier. At five in the morning, I stood in front of the Main Street Post Office where the coach made its second stop. It also stopped in front of Bea Brown's boardinghouse, but I didn't want to see her. I was an hour early. I sat down on one of the suitcases, spread out the skirt of my good green wool plaid dress, and waited. The sky was soft and silvery. It was slowly taking up the pink tinges of the rising sun. The upper reaches of the sky had lightened, but the valley was still sleeping in the pale blue predawn light. And then the sun tilted over the jagged mountain, the highest one in the range surrounding North Chittendon, and the streets flowed with silvery light, and the long black shadows of the trees ran and fluttered in the breeze, and the long rectangular shadows of the houses stretched out as if to pull everything back into darkness, but the sun continued to rise and the shadows drew in their claws.

I sat forward on the suitcase, straining to catch a glimpse of the stage. When I saw the faint, rosy cloud of leaf-dust in the distance, I jumped to my feet and picked up both suitcases. As the stage approached, I put one down and waved violently. The stage was a marvelous contraption, gleaming of bright red enamel, its trim painted black, and inside, smelling of dust and old leather and the excitement of hundreds of voyages undertaken for urgent reasons. "Destination?" asked the driver. "Montpelier," I said proudly. "Two-fifty," he said, unimpressed. I went inside and settled down into a corner seat. "It's so comfortable," I said aloud. "Its springs have been dead and gone a long time now," said a cracked voice from the depths of the coach; "wait until it gets going." I peered into the darkness and saw a little old woman sitting opposite me. She was so old she appeared ageless and sexless. She reminded me of the dried apple dolls Grandmother made me each Christmas. She was dressed in a black outfit which caught and reflected what little light there was; her cap, too, was made of the same black material. I doubted that she had any hair left underneath it. That dress, I thought, must be as old as she is. She looked like a drowned woman floating under black ice. I shook myself. It was all morbidity. I was leaving.

The stage started up suddenly, jerking me back against my seat. I grabbed ahold of the worn leather strap fastened to the coach wall. "No springs," said the old woman; "I told you." But I didn't pay any attention to her. We were driving straight into a cold wintry sun that sat in the middle of the horizon like a great, round door, and when we emerged on the other side, I would remember nothing of my previous life. Nothing from the past would have the power to touch me. I leaned out the window as if I wanted to talk to the sun. And then the road bent slightly to the left and a giant elm that had lost all its leaves was outlined against the sun like a skeleton, like something barring the door. I closed my eyes. I was not going to dwell on such sights. When I opened my eyes, the flaming hills were rushing by as if the world were on fire, as if the world of which North Chittendon had been a part was consuming itself and was no more. The world was bending to my will at last. I laughed in pure ecstasy. The old woman lifted her hooded eyes, looked at me, and went back to sleep.

Much later, she opened her eyes and told me that it was going to snow. "How do you know?" I asked her indulgently. I had patience with the whole world today, even old women who told the weather by consulting their bones. "Because it's snowing on the high mountain," said the old woman; "look over there." I could see nothing. "At my age," said the old woman, "you're either blind or you can see everything coming from miles away. Nothing close, but things as far away as the future." "Are you sure it's snowing?" I asked her. I didn't want anything to interfere with my arrival in Montpelier. "I see it up there," the old woman said. "But it's too early to snow," I cried. I was outraged. How could the weather do this to me? The old woman shook her head. She looked at me as if to say, undoubtedly, that I had lived someplace all my life and this wasn't the first time I had seen weather pull a surprise out of a hat, but at the first frustration I forgot everything I had ever known. "Too early to snow!" the old woman said; "well, that's what it is to be young. Only wishes are real." The snow had come down the mountain and now met us on the road, sailing toward us in straight lines. I was becoming more and more agitated. The old woman watched me curiously. I didn't want her there. I wanted to be alone in the coach.

"Do you think we'll get there?" I asked her. "Oh, we'll get there," she said. "Today?" I asked. "I expect," said the old woman; "it's too early for the worst snow of the winter. We have all day. I expect we'll get there." "I wanted to get there before dark," I said, throwing myself back in my seat. I was appalled at my tone, how sullen I sounded. "I don't know where to stay," I said, "and I was going to ask some of the shopkeepers." "Well, if that's all you're worried about," said the old lady, "my daughter runs a rooming house. On Chapin Street. I think it's pretty run-down and old-fashioned, you know, but it's cheap. Some of the things that go on there, well, what can you expect if she rents to men and women, but she says she has to live just like anyone else. It's respectable, though. I say my daughter keeps the place respectable by those great iron spectacles she wears. I wouldn't stay there myself. But the people there say it's fine. If you want to know her name, it's Iris Trowbridge. Some of her boarders call her Mrs. Trough-bridge behind her back. That's because her house backs right up to the stables. It can get pretty fragrant in the summer." "I like stables," I said. "Oh, well, then you should be pretty well set up at Iris's," the old woman said. She went back to sleep.

In the face of the hard, driving snow, the stage slowed. The animals had trouble keeping their footing. The driver, for all his years on the road, had difficulty keeping to it. I stopped staring out the window; it had been hours since I had last seen the faint flare of orange leaves through the falling snow. When I got out of the buggy that had taken me into town, Bill Brown had handed me an enormously heavy bearskin cape that had belonged first to my grandmother, then to my mother. "She wanted you to have it," he said. "Take it back," I told him. "I won't," he said; "leave it in the road if you don't want it." Instead, I had draped it over my second suitcase. When I got into the stage, I folded it and laid it down on the seat next to me. Now I was glad to have it on.

Suddenly, I heard voices. A rider had come toward us and was talking to the coachman. The old lady took her cane and began banging on the door in the partition in back of her. Outside, the voices went on. Inside, the banging continued. The driver climbed down from his perch and came around to the side.

"What is it?" he shouted. "What did he say?" the old woman asked him. "He says there's a bad storm over Montpelier and the roads are blocked in the city. Don't worry none. A sleigh from the stable will take you where you're going if the stage can't get in." "I hope we don't have to pay twice," said the old woman. "You don't," he said, turning around and clomping back to the front of the stage. "That must be some storm," the old woman said. "We'll never get there," I cried in despair. "You get everywhere if you wait long enough," the old woman said.

Oh, how I hated her! The patience of a tortoise and as wrinkled! "Imagine," I heard her mumbling, "someone being in such a hurry to get bitten by bugs at Iris's." I pressed my face to the window. I knew that any minute the driver would stop, come out, and tell us that we had to turn around and return to North Chittendon. "Please," I prayed, "let me get to Montpelier. Don't let the snow stop the stage. Let me get there and I'll never ask for anything else again." I screwed my eyes tight, concentrated, and repeated the prayer. I believed what I was saying; I believed that if I got to Montpelier, I would never want to ask God for anything again.

The stage did not turn back. The animals plodded slowly along, and the stage, slipping this way and that, followed after them. The old lady began banging on the partition once more. This time, the driver slid back the small door in the wall which separated him from his passengers. "What now?" he called. The old woman wanted to know what the road was like. "As long as it doesn't rain and freeze up, we'll make it," he said; "nothing to worry about." It was better, I thought, that it was happening this way, that I had to suffer and worry so before arriving in Montpelier. I had a theory about suffering. If you suffered now, you didn't suffer later. I was glad to be suffering now. It was a good omen.

"It's going to rain," said the old woman. "I don't care what it does!" I burst out; "no matter what it does, I'm going to get there if I have to *walk* the rest of the way!" "The insanity of the young," said the old woman. I looked at her. "Insanity?" I echoed. "All the young are mad," she said. So she didn't mean anything by it. I put the remark out of my head as I had put by the glimpse I had, or thought I had, of a woman's figure gliding behind a tree across the road from the post office just as the stage pulled up in front of it. The woman had moved like my mother, but it was dark; probably all I had seen was a shadow. Why would my mother get up in the middle of the night, come secretly into town, and hide behind a tree to watch me leave? It was impossible. I hadn't seen her.

The coach stopped and the partition slid back. "We're waiting here for the sled from Montpelier," said the driver. The old lady nodded, as if half asleep. I asked the driver if I could come out and watch for the sleigh. "Stay in there where it's warm," he said; "you'll catch your death out here." He banged the partition closed.

Finally, the sleigh drew up next to the coach and the driver helped us out. "A bit early for trouble, ain't it?" said the driver as soon as he saw we were settled. "It is," I said emphatically. "Just how much trouble is trouble?" asked the old lady. "Well," said the driver, "it snowed and then it rained and now it's freezing up. You can't ask for more trouble in October." "It's downright freakish, that's what it is," said the old woman. The driver asked us where we were going and the old woman said she was going to the Montpelier Inn, right down the street from the courthouse, but the young lady was going to Iris Trowbridge's place. "A newcomer, eh?" asked the driver, smiling at me. I beamed. "How far are we?" I asked. "We're getting there," he said; "we're coming to the fringes. Too bad you can't see it clear, though. There's nothing like looking down on that gold dome from up in the hills." "It is clearing, though," I said, looking toward the horizon, where a thin band of bright light shone under the dense black clouds. "It'll be dark before you can see anything," he said. "What's your horse's name?" I asked. "Trouble," he said; "just the horse for this weather. You can't trust her near another horse or a stranger, but she's the most surefooted thing short of a mountain goat. It's a good thing, too. The streets are like glass." The black horse with the high, arched neck stepped slowly and steadily down the road. When we rounded a turn, houses came into view, and in back of the most distant houses, I saw the sky flaming red. I started to say what a beautiful sunset it was for such a stormy day, but then I realized that the red flare was climbing the eastern sky. "Fire," said the driver, following my gaze; "and a bad day for it. It's taken three houses and it's after the ones on both sides of the ones that are gone. See the volunteer firemen there?" He pointed. "They're trying to stop it before it gets the block."

As we drew closer, I heard a low, strange wail; it grew louder, died down and out, then swelled again. "The siren," the driver said. He reined in his horse. A crowd of sightseers had gathered on the street across from the burning houses. Every now and then a gust of wind blew hot air and burning cinders toward them and they would leap backward, covering their eyes with their hands and crying out in fright. "Damn fools," said the driver; "can't think of anything better to do with their time than watch a house burn to the ground." "It looks like the Huggins house is going up," said the old woman. "Looks like it," the driver agreed. Just then, one of the front windows shattered and the sharp splinters of glass from the pane seemed to leap outward. "The heat does that," the driver said. "No, no," said the old woman; "look!"

At first they didn't know what it was they were to look at. Flames were leaping from every orifice of the house. They roared up the chimney and clawed at the sky. Long arms of flame leaped from the windows on one side of the house. From the other, funnels of smoke poured with flames licking behind them, lighting the dark smoke garishly. I watched it and thought that this was what hell was—a fire that could not be stopped. Then the old woman grabbed my arm. "Look!" she said; "not at the chimney! At the window that just burst out." As I looked, the dark figure of a man seemed to separate itself from the darkness and smoke. "There's someone in there," I whispered. I leaned forward, holding on to the seat in front of me. The man in the fire was climbing out through the window. I saw his shoulder come clear of the building and then he seemed to reach back in as if to pick something up. He swung his legs over the windowsill and for an instant his torso seemed to disappear into the darkness inside. Then he straightened up, and, carrying something, slid out through the window onto the lawn. A wild cheer went up from the people standing on the other side of the street. The young man was carrying a girl in his arms. Some people ran up to him and took the girl away from him. Others gathered around him, offering him water, trying to wipe the soot from his face.

"It looks to me like he saved one of the Huggins girls," the driver said. "That's what I call a brave man," said the old woman. "Or stupid," said the driver. "I never had any trouble laying my hands on a stupid man," said the old woman, "but a brave man was always hard to get hold of." The man in question was laughing and shaking his head and trying to free himself from the crowd of people, all of whom wanted to shake his hand. "I wonder who he is," said the old woman; "I've never seen him before." I sat still. I was hypnotized by what I saw. The man was young. He was tall and slender and wore a plaid flannel shirt and dark brown pants. I could not see his face clearly.

Suddenly, the firemen began shouting and pushing people away from the burning house. "It's going to fall," said the driver. I watched as the roof of the house seemed to rest on the four walls of fire. Then the front wall fell forward into the street and the roof seemed to stand still in the air as if it were floating there, and it gave up and fell to the ground with a crash.

He could have saved me, I thought. I could feel myself being carried out of the building in the stranger's arms. I couldn't see his face. I didn't know if he was light or dark. It disturbed and excited me, knowing that I might meet him and talk to him and never know that he was the man who had rescued the Huggins girl. I didn't know who she was, but I was jealous of her. I told myself she was probably hateful and ugly. It would be worth it, I thought, to be trapped in a burning building if one could be rescued like that.

The sleigh started up again. Gradually, we stopped seeing smoke and then ceased to smell it. The sleigh paused in front of the Montpelier Inn and the old woman got out and the driver got down and helped her onto the porch. "Where to?" he asked me, coming back; "Iris Trowbridge's?" "Is it a good place?" I asked. "As good as any other," he said. We drove off under the unreal trees, the great elms whose branches met overhead, whose huge leaves were burdened with snow. Every now and then the wind blew and rustled the branches and the snow was shaken down from the leaves. Green and red and gold began to appear in the winter fastness around us. The trees seemed to be stepping through the snow back into their own season. I hardly noticed. As if I had stared too long at the sun, the image of the young man stepping out of the burning house onto the white lawn burned in my eyes.

"Daydreaming, miss?" asked the driver, as he pulled up in front of a rambling white frame house. "Trowbridge residence," he said, pointing to the sign which swung from an L-shaped support. "I'll take the suitcases in and come back for you," he said, but I was in no mood to wait an instant longer than necessary. I scrambled out behind him and we entered Mrs. Trowbridge's together. "Good luck, miss," he said, tipping his cap and going back out. Good luck, I thought. I had already had it. I had never had such a glorious, such an exciting day, and it was not yet over.

18

I found myself alone in an empty room. I felt strange, exhilarated, as if I had been struggling for years in a web and had just now managed to pull free. Everything looked remarkable; everything had significance. The objects in the room were hieroglyphs whose meaning I did not yet understand. A single candle burned on the desk. It had almost burned down. Its flame would sink, then spring up suddenly, casting wild shadows over the wall and the floor. Outside, the rain clouds were gone, and the white, bony moon was full. The room's white walls reflected the eerie violet light brilliant on the snow, and when the wind blew, the shadows of the leaves flickered within. I unfastened my cape and laid it across my suitcases. The house appeared to be deserted. As my eyes grew accustomed to the half-light, I saw a wide room with two small windows, and at its end, a passageway led into the depths of the house. Across the room, facing the front windows, was a large railway stove with a metal footrest in front of it. I walked over to the stove and put my hand near its potbelly. The stove was not very hot. There was no fire showing in the isinglass square, no glow lighting it from inside, so I knew the fire was dying out, but I didn't dare disturb the wood basket next to the stove. After all, this wasn't my house. I liked the look of the stove. It looked like a cast iron person whose head had been cut off. I lingered near it as if making friends with it and then turned back into the room.

In one corner was a fixed, small desk with a slanted top. A small inkbottle, some extremely rusty pens, an ink-stained blotter covered its surface. An old register, a large rectangular book with a marbled cover, rested on top of the desk. I opened it. "Courtesy of G. Winthrop Thrall. Insurance for All Purposes. 1861." I closed the book, touching it gently. It was October 17, 1896 and I was nearly sixteen. On an impulse, I opened the book again. I had opened to August 1st, and across the top of the page, someone had written, "fair—wind Easterly. Took five cents off Jim Gowan. Took his receipts for toll road." Suddenly, I felt all the lives around me, the lives which had passed before I was born, the lives that were still continuing on, the lives whose coming I would intersect and interrupt. I could feel them beating against me like a wave. Blood flush after blood flush rose from my stomach and burned in my cheeks. I wiped the perspiration from my forehead. If I had not known better, I would have thought myself ill. As it was, I did not believe such excitement was possible.

I began to wander through the room from object to object. Between the front windows was a small mahogany table, over which hung a matching mirror. A triangle was chipped from one of its corners and a crack extended diagonally across its surface. It was fly specked; even in the violet light, I could see that. Behind the stove hung quarter-sheet advertisements of auction sales, a lithograph of Penny Sidwell in *East Lynne* at Town Hall on the second of April, 1860, and a hand-drawn flier proclaiming the arrival of the Kickapoo Indians. They were to give an entertainment next month in Morrill's Hall.

There were three other doors to the room in addition to the one through which I had entered. One led to a passageway at the end of which were the side steps, one led to a small washroom, where two cracked and dingy bowls were surmounted by tarnished faucets, and above them hung worn brushes and virtually tooth-less combs. Beyond these hung a roller-towel, stained and crimped by wet hands. It was frayed and gray. The third door bore a sign which stopped me: Barroom. I could hear my heart pounding. Suppose it was true? Suppose this was not a respect-able house? Suppose there were people here who did things to you? The wind roared outside. I could see it circling the house, coming down, lowering its claws. A wind like that, I thought, could take off the roof.

"Hello," said the room. I jumped and turned around. A young girl about my age was standing near the little, slanting desk, staring at me. She looked amused. "Oh, don't worry about *that*," she said; "there hasn't been a barroom there for fifty years. Mrs. Trowbridge doesn't like spirits or tobacco. She says enough of either and men start spitting things up, and she has enough to do without mopping floors all day long." I stood there and stared at her; my tongue felt glued to the top of my mouth. "Can't you talk?" she asked me; "I know. You're shy. Aren't you shy?'' Dumbly, I nodded. "No one needs to be shy with *me*," said the girl; "I'm Polly Southcote. I board here and work in the furniture factory and sometimes I help out around here. I earn a lot of money." She said it proudly. "I have to. I have a big family in Boston and they're always starving. My father had a relative there and he thought he'd get work, but he didn't. Well, anyway, I know what you're here for. You're here for a rich husband." She made the last statement in a flat, almost bored voice. "A rich husband?" I asked; "what makes you think that?" "Well," said Polly; "you're very pretty, aren't you? I suppose you've heard that before? When a pretty girl comes here from the country, that's what she comes for. A rich husband. Oh, don't worry," she went on, "you came to the right place. There are plenty of rich men here. This is the state capital, after all. Senators, lawyers, they're all over, more of them than leaves on a lawn. Businessmen, bankers, they're all here."

"Have you found one?" I asked her. "Me?" said Polly; "well, look at me. I don't have any illusions about my charms. Oh, I have a good enough figure and men start after me on the street, but when they see my face, they turn around and look the other way. Look at me, dunnish hair, not too thick. It wouldn't shine even if you varnished it. A long face like a horse and teeth like a horse's too. A long, straight nose that looks like it's trying to slide down to meet my chin. A forehead so high you could skate on it. And two little beady eyes with dark blue circles under them whether I sleep enough or not. You're smiling," she said, smiling at me, "but it's true." "You're exaggerating, you know you are," I said, laughing. "Go ahead and laugh," said Polly; "it's a face to laugh at all right." "I'm laughing at that ridiculous picture you painted of yourself," I said. "But you wouldn't call me beautiful?" Polly asked, suddenly serious. "No," I said reluctantly. "Good," said Polly; "I hate women who lie and flatter." "But I wouldn't call you ugly, either," I said; "you look just fine." "To you," sighed Polly; "but you're not a man."

Suddenly, I felt the quiet moving in from the four corners of the room. I didn't want her to leave. "I bet you've already found someone you like," I said. "Maybe," said Polly. "You have!" I said. "Well, if I've found him, that doesn't mean I have him," Polly answered; "it just means I know where he is." "Where is he?" I asked. She looked at me as if she were trying to guess my motives. "He works for the Highbury Asylum for the Insane," she said. "Oh," I said. I tried to repress a shudder but I didn't succeed. My mother had always said an asylum was the worst place on earth, worse than a hospital, worse than prison. "Well," Polly went on, "he's not insane, but he tells a lot of funny stories about what happens there. He says there's a new supervisor and he made all the attendants wear uniforms so you could tell the workers apart from the patients. He has to live out there six days a week. Are you going to be staying here? If you're going to be staying here, you'll meet him. He comes by for me. He's not rich, but I suppose you've already guessed that. What would a rich man want me for?"

I looked around the room. It was shabby, just as the old woman in the coach had said it was, but I had an odd notion that I belonged here, that if I had been meant to live somewhere else, I would have met someone else and she would have told me of another house. "I've seen cleaner places," I said. "Oh, don't worry about that," Polly said; "Iris, I mean Mrs. Trowbridge, gets cleaning fits and it's all you can do to get out of the house without sliding on a wet floor and sliding right on out the door. That's when she starts coming into your room with pots and mops and pails of water and you think you're going to mildew before she gets done. There's plenty of privacy here and the people are nice. You'll meet them at meals. They're mostly old. The food's good too, and it's cheap here. If you take two meals a day, you pay seven-fifty a week. There's no point in paying for breakfast when you can carry out rolls in your pockets and we all have coffee pots to warm up things on the wood stoves in the halls. You can borrow mine until you get one of your own. No, I wouldn't take breakfast." She looked appraisingly at me. "You country girls always have big pockets," she said. "I think I'll take breakfast," I said; "just to see whether I like it or not." I blushed. It wasn't a question of hunger but curiosity. I wanted to know as much about the house and the people in it as I could.

I was uncomfortably aware of the one hundred dollars in my boots, fifty dollars under each of my heels. I wouldn't touch that money. I was saving it for an emergency. Still, I was uncomfortable to be standing on it, knowing it was there. "I have enough money for the first two weeks," I said; "then I have to find a job." "Just enough for two weeks?" Polly said; "that's cutting it close. Well, Iris, she'll trust you for it once she gets to know you. This place has lots of advantages. Elegance isn't one of them, but you're not used to elegance are you?" She watched me through narrowed eyes. "Well, maybe you are, but you won't find it here and you won't need it," she said; "those elegant places, well, you can't move without a chorus of voices saying, 'And when will you be back, Polly?' or, 'Why don't you introduce your young man to us, Polly?' or, 'Polly, surely you're not going to take that young man into your room?'" "You can take men into your rooms here?" I asked. "As long as you leave the door open," Polly said, "and if a suitor gets stuck here because of the weather, Iris lets him sleep in the kitchen." I must not have seemed impressed enough because Polly peered narrowly at me. "You're awfully white for a farm girl," she said; "well, even if you don't have a man you want to take to your room, and even if you don't know what to do with him when you get there, it's better to have the chance if you want it, isn't it?" "Yes," I said, "I suppose." "I guess you don't know much about life yet," said Polly; "I guess you'll learn."

"This house," I said, "is it—?" I broke off, embarrassed. "Is it what?" asked Polly. "Disreputable," I said, flushing hotly; "do girls get bad reputations from staying here? I know you wouldn't," I said hastily, "but would I?" "Oh, my," said Polly, "you *are* an innocent. You're working out, aren't you? You're not staying with relatives or with family friends. Any girl who works out isn't thought much of around here. If you're really worried about your reputation, you ought to get a job as a house girl with an old Montpelier family and they'll chaperone you and everyone will assume you're good and proper. You'll never know you left home." "That's not what I want," I said; "I just didn't want—" "Look," said Polly, "things can be pretty free and easy here, but you won't turn into a scarlet woman because you're staying here. Iris doesn't like trouble. She doesn't like gossip. If a tenant complains about the goings-on in the house, she throws *him* out and she hints to everyone that *he* wasn't behaving. She doesn't care what anyone does as long as they don't bother her. 'See no evil, hear no evil, speak no evil,' that's her motto. If you don't wake her up at night, she doesn't care what you do or whose room you're in. And she comes from an old Montpelier family herself. Everyone thinks very well of her. No one believes anything wrong goes on in her house. So if you're going to board out, this is the best place. Of course, if you meet your rich man, you'll have to convince his family that you're not a fallen woman, but you'll be able to do that. Everyone does it. Even the girls who live in *really* disreputable houses."

"How can I stay here?" I asked her; "what do I have to do?" "Oh," said Polly; "where are my brains? There's only one room left, on the second floor in the back, down the hall from mine. It's got a trouble, though. It's cheek and jowl to the stable in the back. You have to take in pretty strong smells." "That's fine," I said. "Well, then," said Polly, "I'll take one suitcase and you take the other. Don't worry, Iris will be grateful I got you settled in. I'll tell her in the morning. She'll know you're here." "You're sure?" I asked, picking up a suitcase. I was suddenly exhausted. The suitcase seemed enormous. I followed Polly up the narrow flight of stairs to the second floor. Every step squeaked. "You don't have to keep secrets here," she said; "no one comes out of his room to see who's doing the squeaking. Not even in the middle of the night." At the end of a long hall, the girl threw open a wooden door and backed in, holding the suitcase and the cape. "Well," she said, looking around her; "do you like it?"

The room was long and narrow and the ceiling was high. The wallpaper was deep chocolate brown and covered with a diamond-shaped pattern, and in the center of each diamond was a pink rose. The paper must have been pretty once, but the roof had evidently leaked many times, and the paper had bubbled away from the wall, dried again, and here and there it had crumbled altogether, flaking away from the wall, exposing the pattern of the wallpaper beneath it. That paper, I saw, had been striped and bluish gray. The bed, pushed against the wall opposite the window, was narrow and its mattress looked thin. Its frame was painted white, but rust showed through the paint. A single bulb hung from the ceiling and someone had adorned it with a preposterously frilly white shade. The last tenant, I thought. I wondered what she was like. Small splinters of moonlight showed beneath the frame of the window where it met the wall. The room would be cold. In the middle of the wall opposite the door was a small wood stove. "I thought the stoves were in the hall," I said. "They are, but the heat doesn't get as far as this room," Polly said; "this room has its own stove." The floor had been painted gray, but the gray paint was wearing thin and green paint was showing through beneath. "Iris tried to scrape these floors," Polly said, "but you know that old buttermilk paint. Nothing gets it off." I nodded. I had already forgotten the cracks between the windows and the walls, the bubbling, decaying wallpaper, the last tenant, clinging to the bulb as a ruffled shade. "I love it," I said; "it's just what I was looking for." The bells in a far steeple began chiming the hour. It was ten o'clock. "You must be tired," Polly said. I didn't answer her. I was staring, mesmerized, at the walls, the bed, the stove. It was all mine. "I'll help you unpack tomorrow," she said; "I'll stop by Iris's room. If her light is on, I'll tell her she has a new boarder."

I took off my boots and lay down on the bed fully clothed. I heard a horse stamp and neigh and I felt the tremor through the walls of my room. There was a faint smell of hay in my room, even in that weather, even with the windows closed. I had not eaten all day, but I was not hungry. Whenever I was excited, or very happy, or very upset, I stopped eating. I had once gone without eating for three days and would not have known what I was doing had not everyone constantly asked me when I was going to eat something. I always said I would eat later and they assumed I did. Then they went on a picnic and I had taken my mother's laudanum. All that was over. I was finally free of the country. The people in North Chittendon were all ghosts. Only I was alive. I was alive in a new, unknown world and I did not want to close my eyes on it. I wanted to keep staring at the room, but the first time I shut my eyes, I was sound asleep.

19

At first, I thought I was dreaming. I thought I was back home. There was an occasional rattle of carriage wheels, the thud and stamp of horses' hooves on plank floors, the scraping of shovels, frequent oaths, and sharp slaps accompanying the men's commands to the animals. Whack! Evidently, a horse had refused to move. Stamp! Snort! I opened my eyes slowly. I was not in my own barn. I was in a boardinghouse in Montpelier. I jumped out of bed, grabbed my boots, poked in them until I felt the packet of fifty dollars in each, repeated "South Central Savings," the bank I had promised to deposit the money in, and laced up the boots as quickly as I could. I looked down and saw that I had missed passing the lace through one eye. "Damn!" I said, throwing myself back down on the bed, beginning again. "Take a drink out of the horse trough if you can't wait for the bottle," I heard a man's voice saying. Where was he? I looked around the room. He was in the stable behind the house. I thought I heard pigs and chickens, but was that possible? The sun was up, and through the thin, grayish curtains, I could see the light gilding the metal gutters of the building in the rear of the boardinghouse. Then came a raucous squealing and grunting of pigs, the rapping of a flat stick on flesh, the cackling of fowls, and the whirring and cooing of pigeons. I stayed at the window, held by the sounds, the old melody, but then feet began to clatter up and down the passages and stairways. I heard voices demanding various articles—water, towels, soap, blacking—and then came the rattling of latches and keys in rickety locks. The people in the house were waking up.

My face, reflected in the room's pitted mirror, was clean. I hadn't thought to ask for a basin and water. My hair was still in place and I patted a few loose strands back where they belonged. I began slapping myself all over, trying to rid myself of the dust

I had accumulated on the trip. From a room not far from mine, I heard terrific, regular snores. Someone else was still in his room. I began to smell the odor of steak and fried potatoes and coffee cutting through the smell of hay and manure. I took a deep breath, swallowed, and went out into the hall. It was empty. I crept down the stairs, following the sound of voices. I might have been entering a cage of lions, I was so frightened. And then I was standing in the entrance to a huge dining room. Inside was an enormous rectangular wooden table and perhaps twelve people were sitting at it. As I looked at them, their faces seemed to flatten and blur. I could not move.

"Well, well," said Polly, seizing my elbow and steering me forward, "our newest boarder. I've saved a place for you." "But," I whispered, "I thought you didn't eat breakfast." "I don't," she said; "I'll watch you. I'm keeping you company. Sit here," she said, pointing to a chair. I slid into the seat. I tried to look around the table. I could see that everyone's smile was friendly, but I was afraid to look directly at anyone, as if, should I look at them too hard, they might vanish.

"You know," said Polly, "you didn't tell me your name." "Agnes Dempster," I told her. When I looked up again, an old man at the end of the table was smiling at me. I smiled back. "Are you playing with that bread or eating it?" Polly whispered to me. I picked up the thick slice of bread and slipped it to her. She began chewing happily. "Eat your potatoes," she whispered to me, her mouth full; "I'm not used to a big breakfast." I put a forkful of fried potatoes in my mouth, and found, to my surprise, that I could swallow it. I smiled at Polly and looking around the table, I saw that there were other young people staying there. I became conscious of one of them staring at me from across the table and looked up again. He's a handsome man, I thought. His eyes, I decided, looking down at my plate, were his best feature. They were large and greenish brown. They reminded me of the color of the creek bed when the sun shone on it. He had fine features, I thought, but he looked like every other handsome man I had ever seen. I imagined that he was tall, although it would be hard to tell until he stood up. He had broad shoulders, but then so did all the men at the table.

"Who's that?" I asked Polly. "That's Frank Holt," she whispered; "all the girls in town are mad for him." "Really? Why?" I asked, but I wasn't interested in him. I was staring at the man next to him. He was absorbed in eating, and his blond, straight hair fell forward over his forehead. He kept pushing it

ack, but it fell in his eyes again and again. "Bad as swatting
ies," he said, smiling at me, brushing his hair back once more.
Why don't you just leave it?" I asked. "But, miss," he said,
lushing deeply, "it isn't tidy." "It isn't untidy, either," I said.
Ve smiled at each other. Then we noticed that all conversation
ad stopped and that everyone was listening to us. We resumed
ating hastily. He had, I thought, beautiful skin. I had never
oticed a man's skin before. It was as if he had swallowed
unlight and little suns pulsed everywhere in his blood. His eyes
vere bright blue, and when he smiled, the little crinkles around
is eyes made him appear older than he was. He saw me
vatching him. "It's hard to eat when everything's so new," he
aid. I was grateful to him. At home, everyone would have said,
Look at her. She can barely swallow. She's going to make
erself sick."

"Well, good-bye, everyone," he said, getting up; "I've got to
et there early today. I'm three flowers behind." "Who's he?" I
sked. "Charlie Mondell," Polly said; "the girls are mad for
im, too." "Who aren't they mad for?" I asked. "Practically no
ne," said Polly; "are you going to finish that steak?" I cut the
est of the steak in half and slid my plate over to her. "We're
riends, aren't we?" I whispered. Surprised, she looked at me.
"How old are you?" she asked. "Sixteen," I said. "Oh well,
ixteen," she said; "that's why you have to ask. Look who's
taring at you." I looked up. Frank Holt was staring at me as if
e could not believe what he was seeing. "If anyone stared at
ne that way," said Polly, "it would give me the willies." "I'm
sed to it," I said; "besides, it's not *me* he's staring at." I
esitated. "It's this," I said, tapping the skin on the inside of
ny wrist; "this shell. He's staring at me because it's beautiful.
Ie's not staring at *me*."

"What are you talking about?" Polly asked me; "if you're
eautiful, you're beautiful. Don't try to tell me that it doesn't
nake a difference. You walk around for years knowing that
ou're beautiful and the whole world loves to look at you more
han anything else because you're beautiful and all that gets to be
part of you. Oh, no," she said bitterly, "I don't believe beauty
s only skin deep. It sinks in. Because people treat you different-
y. And pretty soon, you see yourself the way they see you.
You're beautiful, all right." "That's not true!" I said. "It is!"
aid Polly. I didn't answer her. "Why isn't it?" she asked at last.
"Because," I said, "I don't *feel* beautiful. Because no one I
ared about ever looked at me as if I were beautiful. They

125

certainly didn't treat me as if I were special.'' Polly chewe
silently. "Well," she said finally, "someone is looking at you
if you were beautiful now. Don't look. Frank's still staring.
you ask me, you could catch him or Charlie or both.'' "Don't
silly," I said. "Really," said Polly; "you could." "Both?"
asked, grinning. "Both," said Polly; "what do you think
them?"

"Well, this one, Frank," I whispered, "he's good-lookin
enough, but he seems, oh, I don't know—ordinary. He's n
deep, is he? The other one? Charlie Mondell? He seems awful
nice. I wish I knew him." "Don't worry," she said; "you will."

"Well, Polly," said a loud female voice; "you've got a frien
at last." I looked up and saw a tall, large-boned woman wit
brown hair and olive skin looking down at the two of us.
suppose," she continued, "this means putting up with months
whispering at the table all over again. I've spoken to her about
I don't know how many times," she said to me, "but she wi
whisper. So you're the new girl. I'm Iris Trowbridge. Don
stand up. Whenever anyone here stands up, they knock some
thing over. The mice sit under the floorboards with their tongue
out, just waiting. I'll see you at dinner," she told me; "if yo
want to find me before that, I'll be in the office. The room yo
came into last night." I watched her leave. She didn't walk ou
she swept out. "She looks foreign," I whispered. "There's
rumor she's a gypsy," Polly said. "But I met her mother!"
said. "Maybe her father was a gypsy," said Polly.

"What do they do?" I asked Polly. "Who?" she aske
"Frank Holt and Charlie Mondell." "Oh, them," Polly sai
"they're stonecutters. They work in the quarries at Barre. The
make a lot of money at it, especially Frank. Look," she sai
abruptly, "don't worry about them. Go and ask Mrs. Trowbridg
what she knows about a job. You've only been here one nigh
You can't go boy crazy until you have a job." "Boy crazy!"
said, pushing back my plate; "I'm not boy crazy! I've neve
even met a boy I've liked!" "That kind always falls hardes
once they become sixteen," said Polly; "well, I've got to mov
off or I won't get to work before the whistle. I hate to be late.''
She left me alone with four old men and one old lady.

When I left the Trowbridge house, I stood still, blinking in th
brilliant sunshine. There was no trace anywhere of yesterday'
storm; overnight, the snow and ice had melted, drawn back in b
the earth. The leaves were still blazing. It would not be hard t
persuade myself, I thought, that the events of yesterday ha

never occurred. Yet I was here. I could see the gold dome of the courthouse gleaming far down the street. The steeple bells were chiming the hours. The train whistle was deep and spoke with an ominous voice. I wandered down the street past the Century Hotel, its three layers of terraces fancifully decorated and painted white so that the building looked like an enormous wedding cake. I was walking on sidewalks, not edges of pastures, not dirt roads. It would, I thought, take me the rest of my life to get used to sidewalks. They were marvels! No matter how long I lived, I would still be astonished by sidewalks.

I kept walking and found myself going over a bridge. On the other side were block-long, gray wood buildings; they marched up the street, and when the street turned the corner, they turned with it. Factories. Factories and rooming houses. I crinkled the piece of paper on which I had written the name Mrs. Trowbridge had given me: Mrs. Ellwood James, 11 Chapin Street. "If you can sew from a pattern," Mrs. Trowbridge had said, "that's the best place for you. The work's easy and the company's good." I asked her what Mrs. James would pay me. "She pays by the piece," Mrs. Trowbridge said; "the faster you are, the more you get." But I wasn't ready to go inside. I wandered from street to street and finally found myself in the center of the town common. I sank down on a bench and looked around me.

"Tell your fortune?" asked an old woman, coming up to me. She seemed to have risen out of the ground. I hadn't seen her coming toward me. "How much?" I asked. "Five cents," she said; "for you." I nodded and the old woman took my hand. I started to pull it back; I didn't like strangers touching me. My mother always said that I didn't like to be touched at all; perhaps she was right. "You have an unusual lifeline," the old woman said; "you have already died and been born again. See here and here? It's broken in three places. You'll die and be born again three times." "Just three?" I asked. "Don't joke about your lifeline," she said sternly; "it's the writing on the wall. It's fate. It's the past and the future." "All that in my hand," I said slowly. I was put off by the old woman. Fortune-tellers were frauds. Everyone knew that. "Tell me something else," I said; "something you see in my hand." "You know how to shoot a gun," she said. I nodded. "Am I right?" the old woman asked. "Yes, yes," I said. If she was a fortune-teller, why didn't she dress like one? She was wearing an ordinary dark purple dress. "But you didn't bring your gun with you," she said. I am crazy, I thought, to be talking to this crazy old woman. "And you have rich feet," she said, smiling. "What does that mean?" I asked startled. "I read it in your hand," she said; "I don't know what it means." "Here's your five cents," I said, getting up. "You'll be famous," the old woman called after me. I thought of all the times the fortune-teller who had come to North Chittendon had told me the same thing. They must all say that, I thought.

I was utterly disoriented. I felt as if I had stepped out of normal time. It had been autumn when I left North Chittendon but during the trip we had entered another season, another year, for one day and one night, a year that was still spinning somewhere, going on with its round of seasons, its winter storms; I had only visited that world for a few hours, and now was in the world I had always known once more. But for a short time, while the snow had hidden the material objects of the world, I had seen the ideal world I always knew existed somewhere behind the surface of this one. When I was a child, the wallpaper on which my grandmother had painted the fresco of the farm had separated; it had been damp for months and finally the seams of the wallpaper parted company. Suddenly, there were rips in the painted sky. I felt as if I had arrived in Montpelier by walking through one of those rents.

Autumn was still flaring here, and the odor of wet leaves blew everywhere. The birds were brown and dust colored, suited for long flights, and they swept high over the dry fields. The robins were late leaving, faded and rusty, their new feathers showing smoothly mottled through their old coats, their wings and tails uneven and ragged from discarded feathers. They were flying high in small flocks, perching and chasing and calling to one another in the tops of the tallest trees. Flocks of cherry birds flew here and there, now alighting in the trees, now flying high in the air, changing directions suddenly, filling the air with their curious screaming twitter. From the bridge, I saw the lily pads were no longer smooth, but had been gnawed ragged by fish and turtles, while here and there on the banks, a red cardinal flower still bloomed, and in the trees around the square, a red tanager still flew. High above the immense trees which shadowed the river a magnificent golden eagle soared in slow circles. Every thing was feeding on everything else. The seasons would devour one another. Something would devour the years. There had to be something that would last. I thought of the design my grandmother had stitched into all the petit point covers for my mother's chairs and piano stools; she had never seemed to tire of it. A snake devouring its tail. She had seen it, she said, on the

128

back of a Chinese robe someone wore down at Bea Brown's. If I was thinking about North Chittendon, I told myself, it was time I looked for employment.

An hour later, I was back at Mrs. Trowbridge's, excitedly telling her that I was employed; I would be starting work in the morning. "That's nice, dear," she said, without looking up; "dinner will be ready soon." I bit my lip and went up to my room, closed my door, and leaned against it. I was crying. I had thought that Mrs. Trowbridge would be so excited for me. But why should she be? She didn't know me; she probably wouldn't recognize me if she met me on the street. I threw myself down on the bed and sobbed bitterly. Nothing had happened. I had come to a place where no one cared for me; no one cared what would happen to me or knew what already had. I had never felt so lonely. But I knew this was the price I would have to pay for freedom. I told myself I should not be so upset. But I could not stop crying. I dug my fists into the mattress as if I expected the room to tilt and throw me to the floor. What had I expected?

I lay with my head turned to one side, so that one eye was buried in the pillow, the other staring at the white sheet. I had no life now unless I created it myself. A tundra: That was what the sheet looked like. I let my fingers creep along the little ridges and wrinkles of the sheet as if they were the hills and valleys of a new world whose contours I wanted to memorize. I missed everything, but I didn't want to go back. I closed my eyes. Next door, the stamp and clomp of the horses, the odor of the stables, expanded to fill the vast, empty spaces I had suddenly discovered in my room. I fell asleep.

A knock at the door woke me. "A letter for you," Polly said, coming in. "Why are you back here?" I asked her; "aren't you supposed to be working?" "I'm home for dinner," she said. "Home," I repeated. "Don't you want your letter?" she asked. "Who would be writing me a letter?" I asked; "no one knows where I am." I tore it open. It was a letter from my father, telling me to dress warmly, to make inquiries about the house in which I had chosen to live, and to do the same for any employer I found. He also exhorted me to put my money in the bank at the first opportunity. "They must miss you," Polly said; "they must have sent this on the next stage." "He may," I said; "my father. He may miss me. Not my mother. She wouldn't miss me. She never knew I was there. I wish they'd forget about me altogether. My father probably sent this to the stage coach office and asked them to find me for him. I wish he'd leave me alone. I wish he'd forget about me. My mother forgot about me long ago." "You know how to get back at your mother?" Polly asked me; "forget about her. That's the only way." "I can't," I said; "she's stitched to me. Like my shadow." "If you want to walk around with two shadows," she said, "you'll spend a lot of time tripping yourself up." "Don't worry," I said; "I won't trip. People in Montpelier don't cast shadows." Polly turned to look at me. "People here are the same as people everywhere else," she said. "I'm not," I said; "I changed the minute I got here."

We went down to dinner together. I looked around the table. The two young men I had seen in the morning were not there. I felt a sharp stab of disappointment and was surprised and angry at myself. From one minute to the next, I had no idea of how I was going to feel. "If you're looking for Frank and Charlie," Polly whispered, "they don't come back from Barre until supper. They take dinner pails to work." I glared at her. But she knew. I was disappointed that they weren't there.

After dinner, the sun was too brilliant; it hurt my eyes to look at it. I had worn myself out, and if I did not sleep, I would have a headache. I went back up to my room and lay down on the bed. I traced the ridges of the sheet with my fingers. Already they seemed less alien. Someone was yelling at a horse, asking it to move off his foot. I grinned into my pillow.

In the dream, I was in Grandmother's kitchen, but the table was not the one in my grandmother's kitchen; it was the one in my mother's. I was hungry and I was circling the table, waiting for my grandmother to put down the heavy, white platter she was preparing. Then I saw there was something on the table and I went closer to it. It was something brown. I did not want to see it after all. I looked out the window, but I could see nothing. Someone had painted over the windowpanes. I thought that they were painted because someone had died. I came back to the table. It was foolish to be afraid of something lying motionless on a table. I held on to the edge of the table and bent over it. I knew what it was. It was a doll's head lying upside down on the table. I turned the doll's head so that its eyes stared up at me. It had such beautiful hair! It was warm brown hair, the color of old honey. I picked up the doll's head and pressed it to my chest.

"Don't you see," said my mother, "the doll has no body." "The doll has no body," repeated my father. "I can make it a body," I said; "I can sew the head onto a body." "It has no body," my grandmother said sadly.

The doll's head was made of porcelain. It had beautiful blue glass eyes which opened and shut when you tilted the doll's head forward and back. I looked into the hollow neck of the doll to see what held the eyes in place, but it was dark inside the doll's skull. I put the doll's head back on the table. I spread out its hair. Then I saw the crumbs from the tabletop had caught in the long brown hair. I tried to comb out the crumbs with my fingers but they would not come out. "Leave the doll alone," said my mother; "it has no body."

But I was afraid rats would come and chew on the crumbs and chew the doll's hair. I picked up the doll's head and pressed it to my dress. "But the doll has no body," my mother said again. But it does, I thought; it does. They just don't see it.

I woke up, shivering, not knowing where I was. I got up and went over to the mirror. I pulled up the little stool that stood near the foot of the bed and sat on it, looking into the mirror. "It's me, it's me," I kept telling myself. I heard footsteps running up and down the steps. Someone was shouting, "Just a minute, I'll get it and be right back." "Has anyone seen my umbrella?" one of the old women called. "Aren't the cars back from Barre yet?" Mrs. Trowbridge was asking in exasperation. "I belong here," I told myself, still looking in the mirror; "I do. It's me after all. Get up and go downstairs," I told myself, as if I were my own grandmother, "forget the dream." I wasn't certain, but I thought I had dreamed it before, perhaps many times before. But when I came out into the corridor and felt the excitement sweeping through the halls of the house, I smoothed my skirt, flew into the washroom, splashed water on my face, and plunged into the grimy towel, coming out in time to reach my seat in the dining room before Polly walked in and sat down next to me.

20

For the first time, I felt as if time were passing and as if I had
suddenly stepped into its quickly flowing current, and the current
was sweeping my past further and further down the river. It had
not been much of a past, I thought; it had been an emptiness, a
prison, and its song had been the low sad song of mourning. I
was like an animal that had been pent up all its life. I wanted to
run, and nothing on earth could have convinced me that the
bright green fields I saw beyond my stall bars would ever come
to an end. I wanted to run right off the edge of the earth, and I
knew, because I was young, that I could always get back, that
there was no place where things came to an end, no gray place
where I would float, lost and terribly free, beyond the sound of
any other voice.

I wanted to *burn* up. And so I found myself rubbing and
pulling against the marvelous, storybook fabric of Montpelier.
And at the same time I burrowed into that fabric. I was
fascinated by everyone around me. I watched people alone, with
their friends, in couples, and I knew that they were all happier
than I was. No one else seemed as alone as I was. I was
consumed with envy of the young men and women who drifted
together through the streets. For several days, I followed a young
couple past Mrs. James's house, and, when I finally turned back,
I was late to work. The two of them were utterly oblivious to the
rest of the world. The second day that I followed them, the girl
turned around, looked at me, and smiled. They didn't say a word
to one another. When they passed the last of the buildings on
their way to the Barre cars, they walked with their arms around
each other. They would bump into one another and laugh softly.
I wanted someone who would love me the way that girl was
loved. I wanted to love someone the way she loved the young
man with whom she walked.

I told myself it was preposterous to make myself unhappy because I had not yet fallen in love. After all, I had company. My days of solitary confinement were over. For the first time, I felt as if I were living with people. If anyone had come up to me and said, "Someone told me you weren't raised by people; you were raised by eagles," I would have told them that what they had heard was true. That was exactly how I felt, as if I had been brought up by alien beings, inhuman things.

But now, when I woke up in the morning, I couldn't wait for the day to begin. I was still taking breakfast at Mrs. Trowbridge's, not because I was hungry, but because I loved sitting at the table with the others. Frank and Charlie were always at each other; Charlie told me they had grown up together. Polly was well aware of my interest in the two of them. When they talked to each other, she would stop in the middle of a sentence so that I could listen to what they were saying. "It's useless to talk to you when they're around," she grumbled at me, and we began to talk after supper, because by then everyone was in his own room. When we were alone, she said, she knew she had my full attention.

One morning when I came in, Polly looked up at me and raised her eyebrows, looking over at Frank and Charlie. Something interesting was going on. I slid into my seat. "Good morning," Frank said. He barely looked at me, but a wave of heat washed over me. Whenever I felt his eyes on me, I was overcome by a nervousness, a restlessness I did not understand. I would have to order myself to sit still, to stop fidgeting, to stop rolling the crumbs back and forth across the tablecloth. I looked at Charlie, who nodded at me. The two of them seemed angry.

"What do you think of her?" Frank asked Charlie. "Who?" asked Charlie. "The new girl at the quarries," Frank said. "Don't tell me you're interested in the new one, too," said Charlie; "I thought you were interested in that one with the same name. Jane Holt." "I'm not interested in Jane Holt," Frank said. "The new girl," Charlie said; "she's young." "Too young for me, you mean?" Frank asked in a tight voice. "Just young," Charlie said. They glared and chewed. "What business is it of yours?" Frank asked suddenly; "I know what you're thinking about. You better keep quiet or I'll shut you up." "You'll shut me up?" Charlie said; "you couldn't even shut me up when we were kids and I was smaller." They sat there, glowering at one another. "What now?" asked Charlie; "are you going to get a commission to do a woman's head? You could. They just give me the flowers and letters." "She's not worth carving," said Frank; "but it's an idea." "Not one you haven't had before," Charlie said; "that's how you got into such a mess the last time. You always get into trouble when you take a professional interest in them." "Shut up, will you?" said Frank. "Anyway," said Charlie, "her brother works in the quarries."

Polly looked over at me. We were pretending to eat. "Anyway," said Frank, "she seemed more interested in you than in me. She brought you some water. She didn't even look at me." "She did seem more interested in me, didn't she?" asked Charlie. He put down his knife and fork. "Just sneak up on her in your respecting way and she'll have three kids before you get to take her on a hayride," Frank snapped. "That's enough," Charlie said, flushing. "Things are always so simple for you," Frank said bitterly; "always right or wrong." "They're even simpler for you," said Charlie; "they're always wrong." "Good day, everyone," Frank said, pushing his chair back fast. Charlie reached out and caught it before it hit the floor. "I'll catch up with you," he said. "Don't bother," said Frank. "Well," Polly said to me, "get up, get up. We're late."

And then we were out on the street. The streets flowed with rivers of women dressed in their plain black dresses, all on their way to work. Polly and I started out together. Occasionally, Frank and Charlie walked a little way with us, usually teasing Polly about her fiancé, or asking me how I stood such a numbskull for a friend. They were comfortable with Polly, but I was still strange to them. They asked her what the foreman said when she painted five chairs all over with roses and painted the sixth with pansies. Didn't she think the housewife who ended up with the set would notice? Oh well, she should hear the foreman if they made a mistake carving a name on a tombstone. It was a good thing for her she wasn't a marble cutter. Polly said she could spell even if she couldn't carve, which was more than they could say. And so we would walk along laughing, and when they turned off for the Barre cars, I would look after them as if they were walking away from me forever. "Come *on*," Polly would say, pulling me after her; "the whole street can see you staring at them." Oh, I was in love with the mornings.

I could not wait for the day to begin, and at night, when I got into bed and blew out the candle, I cried because it was over. Polly said I was the most emotional creature she had ever seen in her life and I said I wasn't so emotional, was I? and she said, yes, I was. "Much more emotional than other people?" I asked her. "Of course," she said. "Of course?" I echoed, surprised. I thought all people spent their time laughing or crying or lying in their rooms with cool cloths on their heads because they had headaches or were in despair. "Most people," said Polly, "are just like potatoes. They're nice and solid and nourishing and they all look a lot like each other. They don't mind living in the ground if they have to. They have a good, thick skin. That's all there is to them." "A potato," I said, "has a lot of eyes." "Well, if a person were a potato," said Polly, "it would have lots of eyes and they'd all be closed. You only close your eyes when you need to sleep. You have to see everything." "Everyone's like that!" I said. "They're not," Polly said flatly; "you know the way you cross-examine me about everyone and everything in the house? Other people don't pay attention to every little thing. They certainly don't waste time thinking about them." "But," I said, taken aback, "surely you believe that everything is worth looking at? Everything is worth understanding?" "No," said Polly; "I don't. Oh, I'm curious, more than is good for me. I'm a dreadful gossip. My mother always said so. I want to know everything, but I don't know what it means. Who knows what it means? Who cares what it means? If you wait long enough, you find out what it means, so why should I knock my head against a stone wall?" "But," I said slowly, "just figuring things out is fun." "Oh, please," said Polly; "how many people do you know who like to figure things out? Most people can't think for more than a minute at a time." "I can," I said. "Well, that's what I said," Polly answered, pushing back her hair; "you're not like other people." "Is it bad to be different?" I asked. "What kind of a question is that?" Polly said, pulling the pins out of her hair. It began tumbling down her shoulders. "I've got to wash this," she said; "do you want to help me?"

"*Is* it bad to be different?" I asked her. "Pour some more water over my head," she said. I did. With her hair wet, she looked like a sharp-faced little animal. A rat. Rats, I thought, were more appealing than I had realized. "It depends," Polly said, "on what you want. If you want to live just like everyone else, it's not good to be different. It's harder for other people if you're different." "Why?" I asked. "Why?" she repeated, staring up at me; "because if you're always upset about something, or excited about something, and someone loves you, you're a lot more trouble than someone who's like a potato. And besides, not everyone wants to know about everything. A lot of people think it's better not to know too much. 'A person mustn't notice everything.' That's what my teacher used to say when I tattled on someone in the class."

I had slumped down on a high, three-legged stool in back of the metal washtub. She had to be wrong! I wasn't less suited for life than anyone else. "More water," Polly called out. Then she twisted around to look at me. "You see?" she said; "you see? We have a simple talk and you're sitting there all miserable. And you have to ask me if you're not the same as everybody else?" "What I'm worried about," I said after a while, "is that I'll never find anyone who can love me. Especially since I'm so hard to get on with." "I didn't say that," sighed Polly. She stood up in the tub and I took down the sheet from the shelf over the stove so that she could wrap herself in it. "Go out and see if the hall's clear," she said; "I forgot my nightgown." "It's clear," I said. "You'll find someone," she whispered to me as we scurried down the hall; "everyone does." "Even the people in the Highbury Lunatic Asylum?" I asked her. "They have no trouble," she said; "if they don't find someone, they make someone up." "What I want," I said, watching Polly get into her nightgown, "is to find someone who doesn't think I'm different. I want to find someone who's just like me." Polly looked at the comb she was beginning to tug through her hair; it was practically toothless. "Wouldn't that be pretty boring?" she asked me. "Well, not exactly like me," I said, flushing. "Maybe," said Polly thoughtfully, "the best place for you to look would be the Highbury Asylum."

When Polly started across the little, arched bridge which led over the river to the factory, I began to walk down Chapin Street. It took me forever to get to work. I was perpetually stopping to look up at the hills rising over the buildings of the town, and then I would look at the buildings in front of me as if I wanted to swallow them. I passed one brick building every day, and every day, I took as long as I could before coming up to it. It was the most beautiful house I had ever seen. A long time ago, someone had painted the house white, and after that the owners had let the seasons remove the paint slowly, so that now the building was rose colored and glowed in all lights, even the slate gray light before a storm. Some day, I thought, I would live in a house like that. I would stop and look at my boot against the sidewalk and marvel at the existence of the street, of my foot resting on the cement, and at its presence in the city. And then I would go into Mrs. James's and on up to the second floor where seventeen of us spent the day making men's shirts or women's dresses. On the third floor, in the attic rooms, three girls did fancywork for trousseaus and baby clothes. I knew I could do that sort of work best, and I knew I would be paid more for doing fancywork, but I liked the second floor better. The girls' chatter never ended, everyone teased everyone else, and we traded pieces of things with one another. I was dreadful at sewing in pockets, but very good at sewing in linings, and the girl on the other side of me was delighted to sew in my pockets if I would do her linings. And in the beginning, I made a great deal of money. I sewed very quickly and well. But every now and then, Mrs. James would come into the rooms, look around, and then she would say, "Are you rich, Agnes? If you're rich, you can afford to daydream," and I would feel myself turning scarlet. After a while, the girl sitting next to me would nudge me the instant she caught sight of Mrs. James and so I escaped her disapproval.

And so the days went by. After a heavy snowfall, I would get up before breakfast and go out to watch the enormous snow rollers press down the snow on the streets. I thought it was the most wonderful sight. Polly asked me if there hadn't been snow rollers in North Chittendon and I said, no, there hadn't; at least I didn't think there were any there and I certainly hadn't seen them. I loved watching the teams pull the six-foot-high rollers. When I told Polly that I thought it was a marvelous contraption, she sighed and dragged me after her, muttering that next I'd be telling her the snowflakes which fell on Montpelier were especially beautiful just because they fell here. Of course I thought they were.

Then, one morning at breakfast, Polly asked me if I wanted to go to the fair. "What fair?" I said; "I thought they only had fairs in the summer?" "What fair?" Charlie asked her, looking up. "Is there going to be a fair?" Frank asked, putting down his knife and fork. "Yes, there's going to be a fair," Polly said to them, putting down her fork. By now, we both shared a plate. Mine. "Why are you two sophisticated things so interested?" she asked them. "When Eddie and I went to the fair last summer, you laughed at us. You said you guessed you'd just pass up an opportunity to see the biggest squash in the county." "Oh, well," Frank muttered. It was curious, the way his eyes darkened when he was annoyed. "Well," said Charlie, "the truth is, it's a little grim in the quarries." "You've been looking gloomy lately," I said, without thinking. "Have I?" he asked.

He looked at me as if seeing me for the first time. "I guess I have," he said finally; "I knew when I came here I'd be carving tombstones and I knew I wouldn't like it. Some days I like it less than others." I asked him why. "Because," he said, "there was an epidemic before you came here and I'm working on a huge stone. Ten names, ten sets of dates. A whole family wiped out at once." "I thought that you got used to it," I said; "like doctors." "He's used to it," Charlie said, glancing at Frank; "I'm not." "Neither am I," said Frank without looking up. "How many more names have you got to go?" I asked Charlie. "Seven," he said. "That's a lot," I said. "It is," he said.

"Well," I said to Polly, "what kind of fair is it?" "Oh," she said, her mouth full of potatoes, "naturally, the Kickapoo Indians are coming." Charlie and Frank groaned together. "What's wrong with the Kickapoo Indians?" I asked. "Wait, wait, let me finish," Polly said; "they have sleigh races and sleigh rides, a magic show, a beauty contest and a fortune-teller and a play of some kind and a square dance." "A square dance in all this snow?" asked Frank. "They're setting up a wooden platform and then a tent," Polly said; "I think it's a good idea to have a fair in the middle of the winter when everyone starts to feel so locked up." "I don't feel locked up," I said. I felt the three of them staring at me. "What's wrong with the Kickapoo Indians?" I asked again. "Tell her," Charlie said to Polly. He was smiling at me.

"The Kickapoo Indians come to every fair," she said; "they do the same thing every year. They gallop into a tent and gallop around the tent a couple of times waving tomahawks, and they shout and shed feathers." "Shed feathers?" I repeated. "They're the rattiest Indians you ever saw," Polly said. "They fall off their horses," Frank said, looking up from his plate; "I don't know if they're really Indians. No one does." "Well," said Polly, "they're going to have that thing you like so much. You know, you hit the platform with a mallet and the one who hits the hardest gets a prize." "It sounds wonderful," I said. "It does?" Charlie asked. Now he was grinning at me. "Yes," I said, embarrassed; "it does." "Then do you want to go with me?" he asked.

I dropped my fork in my lap. I felt Polly picking it up and I saw her hand putting it down on the table. "Oh yes," I said; "I would." "We can all go together," Polly said; "Eddie's getting off from the asylum." "Good," said Frank; "I could use a fair." From beneath my eyelids, I studied him. He was brooding about something. Everything he said always seemed to mean something more, as if he only said half of what he thought and didn't care whether or not you guessed the rest. From the way Charlie glared at him, I could see that he didn't want Frank coming along. "Well," said Polly quickly, "Frank can dance with me. Eddie won't dance. I love to dance. My brothers taught me." "Frank loves to dance, too," said Charlie; "you can bet his brothers didn't teach *him*." Frank chewed on, silent.

"Well," said Polly later that night, "I'm not surprised." "You're not?" I asked; "I'm amazed." "He's been watching you from the beginning. I told you. Besides, you said you were looking for someone like you. He's like you. More or less." I wanted to know how he was like me. "Oh, he takes things hard," Polly said; "and he likes animals. He's nice." "I'm not nice," I said. "You're not as bad as you think you are," Polly said. "I have a terrible temper," I said. "So does he," she said. "I'm moody," I said; "you told me that yourself." "All right," Polly said; "I never said you were identical twins." "But he is nice, isn't he?" I asked her. "Yes," she said; "are you going to ask me how nice he is? Don't ask me how nice he is. I don't know. I'm not going to the fair with him." She crossed her arms over her breasts and studied me. "I'll be glad when this fair is over with," she said; "you're not going to be in your right mind until it's over."

On Friday, the day of the fair, I had a dreadful time keeping my mind on my work. Mrs. James caught me staring into space twice even though the girl sitting next to me had nudged me in time. Once when Mrs. James came through, I was very lucky because she didn't look down at my work. I was in the middle of sewing in a pocket so that it hung outside of the pants, not inside, and as soon as Mrs. James left, I gave my neighbor the pants and she ripped out the pocket and stitched it back in for me. I was not doing a very neat job with her lining, but she said nothing about it.

Suddenly, all I wanted to do was leave and go back to my room. I looked down at my dress and decided that what I was wearing was more attractive than the dress I intended to wear that night, but the dress I was wearing needed cleaning. And I wanted to change the way I wore my hair. I was tired of wearing it as I did, in a crown of braids on top of my head. A person, I thought, ought to look different if she were going to a fair. So I pretended to have a headache. Mrs. James paid us by the piece, but she didn't approve of our leaving early. She had her own idea of how much work we ought to get done in a day. "Don't try this too often," the girl next to me said; "she never believes you're sick, not even if you're covered with splotches." But Mrs. James let me go. As usual, I had to turn my pockets inside out in front of her; she was always sure we were going to steal some of the material we worked on. One of the other girls said that plenty of material was stolen, and it was stupid of Mrs. James to look in our pockets because no one put anything in them. She had a whole quilt she was cutting out from pieces she had taken from the James house. She said she would show me how to do it. With hair like mine, she said, it shouldn't be hard. I said I didn't need any quilts. She said I could make something else. "A person *never* has enough quilts," she said, looking at me oddly. If I would only keep my mouth shut more often, I thought, I would fit in better everywhere. But then I was out on the street, and I forgot about everyone else.

At four o'clock I was in front of my mirror. I had taken all the pins out of my hair and unbraided it and let it all down. I shook my head at my image in the glass and felt the hair sweep against my thighs. I looked like a great cone of hair. Some of the girls wore part of their hair up in a braid and part of it in loops over their ears. I thought I would try it. I braided too much of my hair and the two loops looked like very long rats' tails. So I started again. The next time the braids were fine but the loops were so thick they began invading my cheeks and threatening to cover my eyes. I took it all down and began again. Outside, the sun was beginning to set. The metal trim on the livery stable was gleaming like molten brass. I looked in the mirror again; it was hopeless. Whatever I did was worse than what I had done before. My arms were tired from reaching up over my head and my shoulders hurt from twisting around to catch the strands of hair as I wove them into braids. I had washed my hair the night before, and now every single thread of it wanted to float off in a different direction from the others. I started over.

The sun was no longer lighting up the stable and in the window the light was dimming. Five o'clock! I only had an hour left. I decided to ignore my hair and clean my other dress. I took down my little bottle of ammonia and water and began wiping the skirt down with the cloth I kept wrapped around the bottle. But the skirt was so full and my arm so tired that I seemed to be getting nowhere. Finally, after cleaning the lower half of the skirt, I picked up the bottle and sprinkled it heavily over the top half of the skirt. When I tried to wipe it down, I saw that the fluid was sinking into the skirt where I had so recklessly spilled it and that the drops were quickly blending into one another. The skirt looked wet. What was I going to do now? My skirt was wet and my hair was loose like a wild thing. I thanked heaven that Charlie's room was on the third floor, because if I flew down the hall to Polly's room, I wouldn't run into him looking like this.

And just then, the door opened. "Oh, good heavens!" Polly exclaimed; "what happened to you?" I took one look at her and started to cry. She looked from me to my skirt and then at my little bottle of cleaning fluid. "Oh, I see," she said. "All right," she told me, "stop that bawling. We only have half an hour. You can't go like that." "But I don't know what to do with my hair!" I wailed; "and my skirt is wet!" I started crying again. "Stop that crying," she said; "you know what you'll look like with swollen red eyes? Worse than anything you're worrying about now." I sniffled. "Blow your nose and let's get going," Polly said; "just braid your hair and we'll dry the dress."

I protested that I always braided my hair. "Well," Polly said, "braid it differently. Wear it in one big braid on the side. A lot of the girls do that when they walk out. Charlie likes hair that way." "How do you know?" I asked her. "His sister wears it that way. She visited him this summer and he said he liked her hair in a braid like that." Before I had a chance to say anything else, Polly was whacking away at my head with a brush Bill Brown had given me years ago. He used it to curry the horses' manes and it was the only brush that would get through my hair. He got tired of having me come out to the stables to have my hair brushed, and gave me the instrument to use on myself. "Your hair is thick," Polly grimaced, yanking the brush through it and pulling my head backward. "Sorry," she said, attacking my scalp again. "Comb," she said finally, and I gave her my big metal comb, the one the farm blacksmith had made for me. "My grandfather used to have a comb like this for horses," Polly said. "It is a horse comb," I said. She raised her eyebrows and drew out a hank of hair, backing slowly away from me. She was almost at the stove before the hair dropped through the comb. "I've never seen such long hair," she said; "I wish I had hair like yours. Mine hardly covers my head. My mother always said she ought to have my head sodded." "I hate my hair," I said; "it's so much trouble." "It's beautiful," Polly said; "don't complain. You always complain about the wrong things." She finished the braid, secured it with a band of rubber, and asked where my ribbon box was.

Then she was ready to attack my skirt. By now, my head was pounding from the many assaults on it. "We'll dry it over the stove," she said. "Here, watch me. Put this sheet under the skirt and rest the skirt on top of the stove for a few seconds, then take it off and move it. Don't keep it there or it's going to burn. I've got to go downstairs and tell Eddie we'll be a few minutes late. I'll be right back." I stood at the stove, watching the little mist rise up from the black surface of the skirt. I moved it so it would not burn. And then I began to think about the fair, about how, this year, there was supposed to be some marvelous new exhibit from France, and how we were not taking supper downstairs but would make a supper of what we found at the fair, and the next thing I knew, I smelled burning wool. "Oh, no!" I gasped, looking down. There was an ugly, scorched patch right in the middle of the skirt.

The door opened. Polly flew into the room, sniffed, and ran over to the stove. "Oh, I knew it," she said in disgust; "weren't you raised to do anything right? I never heard of such a helpless thing coming from a farm. Well, you can't wear *this,*" she said, holding the skirt up and regarding it grimly; "you'll have to wear your everyday skirt. Put it on. Hurry up. Everyone's waiting. Your hair looks wonderful," she babbled, hurrying me into my other skirt, buttoning the row of little buttons on my bodice. "You've got your shoes on," she said; "that's something." I tried to look at myself in the mirror, but Polly was dragging me after her. "I shouldn't have worn my hair this way," I told her as we went down the hall; "I'm not used to myself like this." "Just forget about your hair," she said. "Let me look in a mirror," I pleaded. "Look at your reflection in the window," she said. She was out of patience, and merciless. "I can't get used to it," I said; "are you sure he likes hair in a braid like this?" "Yes, I am," said Polly; "he told me so."

When we got downstairs, Frank, Charlie, and Eddie were waiting for us. Once we were outside, Polly and Eddie began to get ahead of us and I found myself walking down the street between Charlie and Frank. "You look different," Frank said; "I guess it's your hair." He peered at me. I blushed. I don't know why. "I like it," he said, "but Charlie won't." "Why don't you keep quiet?" Charlie asked him; "I like her hair fine." "You don't like your sister's hair when she wears it like that," Frank said. I flushed and bit my lip. I jammed my fists into my cloak pockets; my hands seemed to want to move of their own accord, to unfasten the band of india rubber and to unbraid the hair. I had no command of myself whatsoever. I couldn't believe I was there. It made me feel happy and protected, walking between them, but Charlie seemed angry at Frank. He didn't want him there. Perhaps, I thought, he wants to be alone with me. I smiled into the darkness. Then I told myself Charlie was angry at Frank for something that had happened at work; he couldn't be jealous. Not over me.

"It's not that I don't like my sister's hair," said Charlie; "I don't like my sister." I took a deep breath. "Do I look like your sister?" I asked him. "Certainly not," he said; "speaking of sisters, Frank, what does yours look like lately? Frank loves his sister," Charlie said to me; "he was brokenhearted when his sister got married. I thought he was going to try and stop the ceremony," Frank glared at him and began walking faster. "Catch up with Polly," Charlie said.

"Does he really love his sister?" I asked Charlie. "Who knows?" he said; "who knows if he loves anybody?" "Everyone loves something," I said. "Oh, yes?" he said, smiling at me; "has that been your experience?" I said it was. "You've been lucky," he said. "Don't you?" I persisted; "you must love something." "Oh, me," he said; "I love too many things." What did he mean? Did he love too many girls? I hoped not, but if he did, I had no chance with him, not with my braid hanging over my left shoulder, not with my moods. "Anything that comes up and nuzzles me, anything that hasn't eaten all day, anything like that," he said; "I'll take it home with me. My family used to say I was born to be a priest." "Oh," I said, enormously relieved. Girls did not come up to him and nuzzle him. He had not been talking about girls. "Well," I said, "carving the stones is like being a priest." "How's that?" he asked, stopping in his tracks. "Doing the carving," I said; "for the family, it must be like the last blessing." "Do you think so?" he asked, looking down at me. He was very tall. The moon was bright and it lit his blue eyes and his eyelashes shadowed his cheeks. Suddenly, he looked young, and, inside of his strength, fragile. And suddenly I wanted him to hold my hand. "I do," I said; "I do think so." I saw his hands were deep in his pockets and sighed.

All my life, for as long as I could remember, I only grew attached to men who somehow seemed in need of my protection. There was one little boy in the third grade who was thin and pale and barely spoke to anyone, and for one winter, I got up an hour early, fussing over my dress and hair, hoping he would talk to me. I insisted I be taken to school early because I wanted to start the fire in the stove for the teacher, but really I wanted to see him. His name was Lloyd. For one year, I had a mission. I was determined to make Lloyd talk, to look at me. I was going to be the one to cheer him up. And then the school term ended and I forgot about him. And one summer, Grandmother said I disgraced myself by following Bill Brown around like a love-sick pup. I had gotten it through my head that he was unhappy because of his wife, whom I frequently heard scolding him, and I used to wander after him, looking at him with pity. I thought he knew what I was thinking: that I believed he was perfect and that he should forget about what his wife had to say and go back to being happy, as he had been when I first knew him. My grandmother used to say that I fell for any sick cat, any lame dog, and now I fell for any sick male. She said when I got to be old enough, I was going to have to watch out or else I would bring home some hopeless man just because he was helpless in the world and he would hang like a millstone around my neck for the rest of my life.

I thought about this as I walked along with Charlie Mondell. I told myself he was no sick cat, but I could see that he was not perfectly happy. And what I said seemed to matter to him and often appeared to make him happier. There was nothing wrong with that, I thought, looking over at him. His hands were still in his pockets. I wanted to be of use to someone. I wanted to be the person someone else could not live without. I wanted to be the sole source of their happiness. But Charlie had said he loved too many things; they all made him happy. But they couldn't make him *very* happy.

When I looked down the road, Polly and the other two were out of sight. "It's not much further," Charlie said. "I don't mind," I said; "I love walking." "You're very energetic," he said. I knew without looking that he was grinning at me. "You're not really happy here?" I asked him; "in Montpelier?" "No," he said; "I should have stayed on farming or gone further from home. I'd be happier doing marble work on buildings, but I'd have to go to New York City for that." "New York City!" I whispered. "I guess I wasn't ready to go to the city yet," he said. "Will you go?" I asked. "Oh, one of these days." He looked down at me. "How old are you?" he asked me. "Sixteen," I said; "why?" "Well," he said, "sometimes you seem older and sometimes you don't." We had stopped walking. "Would you be offended if I held your hand?" he asked. I yanked my hand out of my pocket so fast I nearly tore the lining. "There's supposed to be a new exhibit from France," he told me in a soft, new voice. "I hope so," I said. "I can't wait to see it," he said. I said I couldn't either, but for all our impatience, we were walking more and more slowly. Other couples were beginning to pass us. Some turned back and looked at us. I squeezed Charlie's hand. "You're really very nice," he said. "Didn't you think I was?" "Well, beautiful girls," he said, "they're usually concerned about themselves and their looks and how many beaux they can keep dancing on a string. I guess I think they're not really people." "Maybe," I said, "you're tired of all those beautiful girls you see standing around in the quarries. The ones you carve out of marble. All beautiful girls aren't made of stone." I was devoutly grateful for the darkness. I had flushed beet red. What was I going to say next? If Polly were here, I thought, she would be stuffing a sock into my mouth. "They're not all dead either, are they?" he said, and he bent down slowly and kissed me lightly on the lips. "I'm sorry," he said. "Don't apologize," I said. He started to laugh. He took my hand and swung it in his. "Polly said you were nice, but you're better than that." "What do you mean?" I asked. "I don't know," he said.

Others were in front of us, and we were soon part of a crowd waiting to file in through the fair gates. We began wandering through the fair, stopping at various booths, looking quickly at the exhibits of fancywork, getting on line for fried dough, then going on, munching away at the sugar-powdered bread. We were looking for the French exhibit. By now, we had heard a great deal about it. It was something called The Automaton, a machine which looked exactly like a person. "I see the sign for it!" Charlie cried; "come on." He began leading me through the crowd over to a tent within a tent. We stood on line and waited for the attendant to let us in. We went inside, and there it was, the most incredible thing I had ever seen. It was a machine which looked just like a man, and it was dressed in ordinary street clothes, but its hands and feet were painted white and its eyes were wide and unblinking. At a signal from the attendant, the machine began to move.

It was standing behind a small table upon which rested a bottle of wine and a small glass, and its arm began jerking down through space, as the minute hand moves on a clock face, in tiny, disconnected, stiff motions, until it reached the bottle. It took forever for the automaton to pick up the bottle, but when it did, it began to pour the wine into the glass. "How does it work?" I whispered to Charlie, who shook his head at me, staring amazed at the mechanical thing. The thing was raising the glass to its lips. "Is it going to drink it?" I asked; "how can it drink it? Is it hollow inside?" The thing slowly drank the wine, and then, as if the effort were enormous, it began to move its lips, which, like its arm, seemed to move in response to clockwork wheels and cogs somewhere behind its mask of a face. Finally, it was smiling. I was astounded by the machine, by how perfectly it worked, by how well it imitated life.

And then it began to frighten me. I thought of myself, that afternoon, doing and redoing my hair. The automaton no longer looked so innocent. All around me, the people in the crowd were gasping in astonishment. I kept moving closer and closer until I was right in front of the machine. I could feel Charlie's eyes on the back of my head, but I could not stop staring at it. The thing was both dead and alive at once. So it was true that it was possible to be dead and alive at the same time! And then I saw that it was not a machine at all. It was not a clockwork imitation of a living thing, but it was a man who was pretending to be a machine. "It's alive," I whispered to Charlie; "it's not a machine." "It isn't," he said, bending forward. "It *is* a man," he said. Then he looked down at me. "Come on," he said; "come away from here. It's frightening you." "No, it's not," I said. "It is. Come on," he said. He took my hand and led me away from the automaton. I looked around me. The world seemed drained of color. The faces of the people were dimensionless. I was cold. I was afraid to move. I thought that if I lifted my hand to my eyes, it would move as the arm of the automaton had moved, jerkily, mechanically.

"It's scary, isn't it?" Polly said, materializing at my elbow. At the sound of her voice, something in me relaxed. Color returned to the world around me. "Oh," she said to me, "everyone's fooled. Everyone I talked to said he thought he was a machine." "He," I said. "Yes, he," Polly said, looking at me sharply; "it makes you think, doesn't it?" She linked her arm through mine. "It makes you wonder about these men. Are they real or aren't they?" "I'm real," said Eddie, taking her other arm. "So am I," said Charlie. Frank glared at all of us and said nothing. "*He* wasn't impressed," Polly said, looking at Frank; "he said he knew it wasn't a machine right away." "He ought to know," said Charlie. "I want to go over to the square dance," Polly said. "I can't dance," I said. "I'll teach you," Charlie said; "let's go."

But when we got to the dance, he couldn't teach me. I would go stiff, and halfway through a series of steps, *allemand left, allemand right, swing your partner, swing your corner,* I would turn the wrong way, and instead of facing Charlie, I would end up staring at another girl in the square with us. "Just keep trying," Charlie said, but the more I tried, the stiffer I became, until I was sure I resembled the mechanical thing we had just seen. "I think," I said miserably, "you had better dance with someone else." "Just relax," said Charlie; "it's not hard. Half the fun is in making mistakes." "Then I'm having too much fun," I said, trying to smile. I could feel the press of tears behind my eyes. When the dancing started up again, I knew I was going to cry. I was furious at myself; I seemed to be two people, one of them bent on embarrassing the other. I heard the fiddler plucking at his strings. Then I saw him tightening them. I knew my eyes were starting to shine.

"All right," Frank said, coming up behind me, "it's time to trade partners." "What?" Charlie asked. "Time to trade partners," Frank repeated, putting his hand on my shoulder. "Come on, Charlie," he said, "you always said I could teach anything to dance. You take Polly." Charlie didn't say anything. He looked at me. I couldn't bear it, dancing so badly while he tried to convince me that I was doing as well as everyone else. I didn't care whether or not Frank knew I danced badly. And his hand burned on my shoulder. The weight of it felt inevitable. I could no more imagine moving away from him than I could imagine flying to the top of the tent. "All right," I said.

As Frank led me off, I saw Polly's expression. Her eyes had narrowed and her head tilted slightly to the side. When I turned to look back at Charlie, I couldn't see his face. He had turned his back on the dancers and was talking to Polly and Eddie. The dancers were forming a huge circle, and as we approached it, my feet began to drag. "Don't worry," said Frank, "we're not going there. We're going into the corner so you can practice. Then you won't be so worried about people looking at you." "Oh," I said, relieved; "thank you."

Frank did not dance with me as Charlie had. It didn't occur to him to explain or to demonstrate anything. Instead, he just seized me and pushed me through the paces of the dance. And I felt lighter than air, as if I were a marionette and someone had just seized control of me. "See how easy it is?" he said, after he had swung me and pulled me and yanked me twice through the steps. "No," I said, "it's not easy. I'm just going to the right place because you pull me there." "What difference does it make how you get there?" Frank asked. He twirled me under his arm, pushed me away from him with one hand and pulled me back with the other. "You're dancing," he said flatly. "I'm not dancing," I said, starting to smile; "I'm spinning." "Do you like it?" he asked. "Oh, yes," I said, "but I wish I could learn." "You want to learn?" he said, grinning at me; "then learn." And he began twirling me under his arm, then holding me by both hands and spinning me around in a circle with him, pulling me toward him until my face was buried in his shirt, pushing me back. "Learning?" he asked me. "No," I gasped. "You're moving under your own steam," he said. And I realized that I was.

I no longer cared about the steps. I wanted to move quickly, to feel my body moving wildly. When Frank began to spin me around, I spun on. When he pushed me away from him, I leaned back against the air behind me as if I trusted it to hold me, pulling myself further from him, and when he pulled me back toward him, we rushed together. I started to laugh. "This is fun," I said. "Good," he said. "I suppose," I said, "it's more fun for me than for you. You're a good dancer." "I'm having fun," Frank said. And just then the fiddling stopped. My cheeks were hot, I was out of breath, and as we walked back to the others, I smoothed down my hair and tugged at my skirt, which had twisted slightly while we danced. "She can dance," Frank said to Charlie. "So I see," Charlie said; "Agnes, tuck in your blouse." "Is it loose?" I asked, twisting around, pushing my blouse down under my skirt with both hands. "It's not loose," said Frank. "It was," said Charlie. "It's nothing to argue about," said Eddie. "I can't dance," I said to Charlie, avoiding his eyes; "he pushed me this way and that." Charlie nodded as if to say he had known that all along, but he didn't look at me. He glowered at Frank. "I think I'll see Agnes home," Charlie said. "Unless you want to stay later," he said, looking at me; "you could come home later with Frank." "Come home with Frank!" I exclaimed; "I came with you."

We went outside. The night was bright and the clouds that drifted across the spangled sky were silvery blue. "It's cold out here," I said, "after dancing. It was hot in the tent, too." He didn't answer me. His silence frightened me. I began to feel the old fear that in the silence, in the emptiness, something terrible waited, waited like a ghost ready to spring from the cold darkness in which it lived. I could not tolerate fear or suspense. To me they were the same, and soon the fear itself would become a further source of fear. I was afraid that, in an attempt to free myself from its hold over me, I would do something wild, something dreadful. I would start to scream or throw things, or turn on the person next to me and try to scratch out his eyes. I had never done anything of the sort, but that, I thought, was only because I had been lucky.

I looked at Charlie's profile, closed, remote, and I stopped in my tracks. "You and Frank don't get on well, do you?" I asked. "No," he said shortly. "Why not?" I asked. "Why are you so interested in Frank?" he asked. "I'm not interested in Frank. I'm interested in you and why you're so mad at me because I danced with him." "I'm not mad," he said. "You are," I said. He looked down at me. "Maybe I am," he said; "come on. Let's walk. It's too cold to stand still out here." The bright blue light reflected by the drifts of snow cast an eerie spell over us. "We look," I said, "like we had already died and gone to some strange blue place. Don't I look strange to you?" "No," he said. I had never done that before, said what I really thought to someone else. I had always been too afraid of what other people would think. I was afraid that they would think I was crazy. Charlie didn't seem to think so; perhaps he simply didn't notice. But the fear, whatever it was, was ebbing, and I could once again take deep breaths and release them. I no longer had to remind myself to breathe in and out.

We walked along in silence, the snow crunching beneath our feet. If I don't think about it, I told myself, I can do it. I'm going to count to three, and when I get to three, I'm going to do it. I counted to three. My hands refused to come out of their pockets. I counted to three again. My hands were still in there. Suddenly, as if of its own accord, my hand slid out of my pocket and into the pocket of Charlie's coat. He looked down, surprised, and stopped walking. "Well," he said. He was smiling. "I'll take my hand away if you don't want it there," I said. How could I have done such a thing? "Don't move," he said. I felt his fingers wrapping around mine. He bent down and kissed me on the cheek. "You're beginning to like that," Charlie said. He was grinning at me. "I am," I said. "Come on," he said; "you're going to freeze."

We were coming to the little arched bridge that crossed back into Montpelier's business section. "Why are you and Frank always at each other?'' I asked again. "I didn't want him dancing with you,'' Charlie said. "Why should you be worried about me?'' I asked. Oh, I was disgusted by myself. By now, I knew he was jealous, but I wanted him to tell me he cared for me. "Because,'' Charlie said, "friends can share a lot of things, but not girls. At least I can't.'' "But,'' I persisted, "you've been snapping at Frank for a long time now, before you even knew I was sitting there at Iris's table.'' He kicked some of the snow into the air with the toe of his shoe. "Look,'' he said, "have you ever had a puppy outside, and when it was outside, it was running loose, and everyone said what a great dog it was? Then you bring the dog in the house and it eats up the rug and chews up the bottom step and gnaws a hole in the wall. That's what Frank's like sometimes. Just wild. You can't say he's doing anything on purpose. You can't say he broke the bottom step because he knew someone would fall on it and break her neck. It just happens. But if you know he knocks things down and you let him in the house and someone gets hurt, you blame yourself.'' We had stopped walking again. "Do you understand what I mean?'' he asked me; "I don't mean to spread mud over him, but Frank's that way. There are animals who don't understand they're making you unhappy. He's like that. My sister took up with him for a while and she was never so miserable in her life.'' "Why?'' I asked, starting to walk again, tugging him after me. "She thought if he was spending so much time with her, he had to be serious about her. But it never occurred to him to think about things that way.'' "Oh,'' I said. "Oh, well,'' he said, "someday a woman will come along and sink her claws into him and he'll settle down. Some woman who bats him over the head with a rolling pin. That's what he needs. A witch with a broom. That's what he understands.'' "I guess he doesn't want a witch with a broom,'' I said, laughing. "Well, maybe she can't push forward through the crowd around him,'' Charlie said, smiling, "but that's what he needs.''

We were three houses away from our own. "You're sure,'' Charlie asked me, "that you don't want to be one of that crowd?'' "I'm sure,'' I said. "Well, then,'' he said, "do you like walking in the cold? If we want to see each other without a crowd around, we'll have to walk out after supper.'' "I love to walk,'' I said. "When it gets to be spring,'' he said, "it will be much nicer. We can go on picnics.'' I reached up and traced the outline of his eyebrows, feeling the ridge of bone beneath them. "Your bones are lovely,'' I said. I wanted him to kiss me again.

I wanted him to come to my room. "I'll look for you tomorrow night after supper," he said, and we went in and went to our different floors.

I stayed up waiting for Polly. I had to tell her about everything, as if I thought life was so ephemeral that one's own memory was not sufficient to preserve it, as if I believed that if something pleasant had occurred, it could not have happened to me. So I needed confirmation, a witness. Polly came in and flopped on my bed without taking off her cloak. "You really don't think, do you?" she asked; "how could you dance with Frank? Can't you see Charlie's jealous of him?" I said that I hadn't seen it before, but I saw it now. "I suppose that's the end of you and Charlie," Polly said; "he drops a girl like a hot potato if she so much as looks at Frank." I told her what happened after we left the fair. "Well," she said, "good for you. I didn't think you could do it. You must be learning more than sewing from those other girls at work." I asked her if she liked Charlie. "Charlie's too good for this world," she said. "What about Frank?" I asked. "The world's too good for Frank," she said; "forget about Frank. You may be pulling the wool over Charlie's eyes, but I can see what you're up to." "I'm not up to anything," I protested. "You're after Frank," she said. "I'm not!" "Time will tell," said Polly.

I told Polly that I had wanted Charlie to come to my room but he hadn't. "Well, that's what I wanted to ask you," I said slowly; "what things do men like?" Polly stood up and bent over me. "Don't ask for trouble," she said in a low voice; "don't start that. You're too young. Charlie knows you're too young. You're not ready yet." "How do you know I'm not ready yet?" I asked indignantly. "Because you have to ask," she said.

I lay down on my bed and stared up at the ceiling. What did I want her to tell me? I had grown up on a farm; I knew how animals coupled. But humans, I thought, were different. When a woman met the man who was right for her, not only their bodies joined, their souls rose over them, floated above them like a canopy, and joined together as cleanly and seamlessly as two clouds stirred together by the wind from the deep places between their souls. But while their souls mated above them, their bodies were busy, touching one another in special ways, intricate ways, delicate ways, about which I knew nothing. Men and women are not animals who feed upon each other during a season of blood, driven into one another's arms by the same machinery which drives one season after another through the sky. Perhaps, I thought, Polly did not want to tell me anything because she didn't know enough herself. My friend in North Chittendon had said that the sex instinct drove men and women together. I knew better. Men and women came together to free their souls, to cancel the flesh which separated them, to join their spirits together. When men and women joined bodily, they rid themselves of their bodies. Through their bodies, they became free of them. When they coupled the world of the spirit would become visible to them. Perhaps, I thought sleepily, Polly didn't understand that. I had always known it.

All that winter, Charlie and I went out after supper and walked. We walked out of the city and into the fields. If the roads had already been broken, we followed them for miles. When the weather began to turn warm, I began to fear that we would somehow be separated by the changing seasons. As the snow began to melt and to run in rivulets, I held tighter to Charlie. We now walked with our arms around one another's waists. I could not believe how easily it had happened, how I had become so like the women I had envied when I first came to Montpelier. And then, one day, Polly said that she guessed I would be marrying Charlie, wouldn't I? I stared at her. "What for?" I asked; "so I can feed more people to west hill?" "What?" asked Polly. "Nothing," I said. "What was that about west hill?" she asked me. "Nothing," I said again. "What's west hill?" she asked. "The cemeteries in North Chittendon are on west hill," I said; my voice was sullen. "Don't tell me," Polly said, "that you think you're going to escape all that?" "All what?" I asked. "Births and deaths, all of that," she said; "don't tell me you think you're too good for it or that you're so special life won't bother you with little things like births and deaths." "I don't think anything," I said. "Oh, yes you do," she said; "you think you're too good for this life. You think there's some other way to live." "No, I don't," I said. "Don't you want to get married?" she asked me. "No," I said; "not yet." "When?" she asked me; "when do you want to?" "I don't know," I said; "there's something else I want to find first." "And what is that?" Polly asked; "a world where there's no west hill?" "Never mind," I said; "you wouldn't understand." "And why wouldn't I understand?" she snapped at me; "what am I, some kind of mindless rabbit? Just because I want to get married and have children?" "Then go ahead and have them and leave me alone!" I cried, running out of the room.

And after that, everything changed. It was as if Polly had cast a magic spell. Before, I had seen Charlie as part of me. When we separated, I imagined something intangible stretching invisibly between us, connecting us wherever we were. But now I was aware of the spaces between us. I was floating free. More and more, I observed myself from a distance, as if I had split into two parts, and the one who watched, the one who floated, tiny and detached, in a corner of the room just beneath the ceiling, had no connection with either me or Charlie. I scolded myself; I constantly rehearsed Charlie's virtues. I told myself he would make an ideal husband and I believed that to be true. But when I told myself I loved him, I did not believe it.

More and more when we were together I found myself watching myself go through the motions of talking to him, hugging him, listening to him. I saw myself pick up my arm to lay it across his chest; I saw my hand move to his cheek, and I did not know why I was doing these things. And the fear began to return, the old, inexplicable fear that things were not right in the world, that something dangerous was hiding just out of sight. And, as I drew away from Charlie, I became more and more aware of Frank. I watched him out of the corner of my eye. He was unhappy; I saw that. He was restless and didn't know why. I saw that he wanted something but had no idea of what it was. There was something he wanted and he couldn't find it. But he would, even if he had to devour the ground and the sky themselves. I was sure of that. And in the meantime, he was lost. I could feel it, the emptiness in him, the crying out for something he didn't know he missed. And I wanted to move closer to him. Charlie must have sensed a change in me, because, whenever possible, he arranged it so that the two of us did not eat with the others. He teased Iris, bargained with her, annoyed her, until she would pack up our dinners in tin pails and we would take them outside and eat our dinners on a rail in a snowy field. I loved being outside at night, and would not have thought much of these winter picnics, but Polly did. She asked me why Charlie wanted to keep me away from everyone else, and I said I didn't think that was it at all. Then, she said, I was a lot thicker than she had taken me for.

"Well," I said at last—even if I could not be honest with myself, I could often be honest with Polly—"when I'm with him, I think there's something wrong. I love to hold his hand and I love it when he kisses me but I don't want him to do any more. It's too—" "Too what?" she asked. "Ordinary," I said. "Did you tell him that?" Polly asked me. "Of course not," I said. I didn't tell Charlie that often, when I was with him, I thought about Frank and wondered what he was doing and what it would be like if *he* were in the meadow with me, not Charlie.

"Maybe," said Polly, "you'll feel differently when you've been with him more." She didn't sound convinced. "I don't think so," I said; "it would all be so *settled*." Polly sighed. "Sometimes," I went on, "I try to get closer. I do. You know, I put my hand inside his shirt and I feel like someone else is doing it. I want to make funny faces. Like this," I said, wrinkling my nose. "Do you think it will get better?" I asked her; "I *want* to love him. I do love him." "Not enough," she said. "You can't be sure!" I cried. Now that I had admitted the truth, I wanted to take it back, to undo it. "Well," Polly said; "I don't have to be sure. You do. I feel sorry for Charlie," she said slowly; "and you, too." "Why me?" I asked. "Because you want things you can't get," she said; "not from anyone. And you two seemed good together, that's all." "It may turn out that way yet," I said. "Not if you keep looking over your shoulder at Frank," she said. "I'm not!" I said angrily.

Winter wore on and the snows melted, the muddy roads dried and the fields turned green in the sun, and Charlie and I began to wander out into them for our suppers. I knew that the other girls with whom I worked envied me and thought I was perfectly happy and I knew how useless it would be to explain how uneasy I felt, how I felt divided in two, never wholly in one place, always watching myself with Charlie as if he and I were two people with whom part of me, another self, had nothing to do. And oddly enough, this growing uneasiness somehow affected my work for the better. Now, when I went to work, I sewed furiously, as if my life depended on quickly finishing what I had begun. I came early and stayed late. I did all of my own work and many of my neighbor's seams. I concentrated on every stitch and every tangle in the thread. I never made a mistake. I knew I had reached the height of success at 11 Chapin Street when Mrs. James no longer looked through my pockets at the end of the day. Of course by that time the other girls had taught me how to sew pieces of cloth inside my skirt, or how to fold them into tiny squares and pin them under the heavy coils of my hair. I no longer left work with the same barely controlled impatience which had pushed me home through the streets three months before. I wanted to see Charlie, and if I knew he was not going to be there, I felt bewildered and lost. But I was not eager to find him, either.

One afternoon in July, he and I were lying on a blanket on top of Bald Hill. We were both lying on our backs, our heads on our clasped hands. The sun was warm and our eyes were closed. I felt, rather than saw, Charlie's shadow fall over me and he kissed me. I opened my eyes, pulled his head down toward me and kissed him back. He smiled at me and I smiled back because I was happy. I was completely there. The tiny version of me which sometimes escaped and watched me from a point somewhere above me was nowhere in sight. Charlie began touching my lips, my nose, my cheeks, the line of my hair against my forehead. "You're drawing me," I said. He said he was. "You're lovely," he said. "I know you think so," I said, pushing myself up on one elbow and pushing him down flat on the blanket; "you're lovely yourself." And I began tracing the lines of his face.

He had a beautiful face. His cheekbones were so high. The bones of his face were all so sharp and clean. He had fine, strong looks. "You have such wonderful skin," I said; "even in the dead of winter, it had such lovely color." I picked up his arm and turned it this way and that. Its gold hairs lit up in the sunlight. I ran my fingers down the long, strong bone of his arm. "Men aren't supposed to be lovely," he said. "Well, you are," I said. I bent over him, kissed him, and lay back down on the blanket. Then I felt his hand unbuttoning my blouse. I waited patiently to see what would happen next. His hand slid under my chemise. He cupped my left breast and when I didn't move, he began tracing circles around its nipple. I felt it grow hard under his finger. "Well," he said. "Will the other one do the same thing?" I asked him. He turned to me and lay partly across me and cupped both of my breasts in his hands. "Do you like that?" he asked. "Yes," I said, "I do." My body felt warm, lit, as if I were a candle to which he had taken a match.

He looked around and then began to take off my blouse. "No," I said, suddenly afraid, "someone might come." Instead, he slid his hand under my skirt. My clothes felt too hot and too tight. I was breathing in short little gasps. Under my skirt, I had on nothing but my petticoat. First one hand, then the other, slid up the inside of my thighs. I felt my body begin arching in a way it never had before; I felt my pelvis lifting off the ground. Now he was lying on top of me so that his chest was rubbing and pressing against my breasts until they caught fire. My body was arching and bucking uncontrollably beneath him. I was frightened and ashamed. I was afraid he would disapprove of me. I remembered the animals on the farm and how they had behaved when one mounted the other. Now I was like one of those animals.

But Charlie didn't seem to disapprove of me. His finger was sliding inside me, and for an instant the shock of feeling something penetrate my body, which all my life had been sealed tight as an egg, chilled me and made me draw back. But then I felt the hardness of him, his body pressing against mine and withdrawing, then pressing harder, and something warm and wet swelled in my pelvis and its heat spread throughout my body which began following his as if it had a mind of its own, as if it wanted to press itself upon the hardness of him and never come loose. And then I felt something strange, something deep inside me drawing in and letting go, something tidal constricting my insides, then releasing them, again and again, and I was aware of the extraordinary, intense heat, which I knew came from inside me. And suddenly, Charlie let me go and fell back against the blanket. "I'm sorry," he whispered; "I'm afraid I got your skirt wet." "Don't worry about it," I said, looking down; "it's not wet." I looked at him. "But your pants are," I said; "we can wash them out with a little water and they'll dry in the sun." "I don't have anything else to wear in the meantime," he said. "Don't worry," I said; "when you want to get up, I'll stand guard. Anyway, maybe it won't be noticeable." I felt relaxed, rubbery, as if I didn't have a bone in my body. I remembered the hayride in North Chittendon and how the Brown boy had said that some girls never warmed up. Well, I wasn't one of them. I stretched, giddy with relief.

"I'm surprised," Charlie said finally; "I didn't know you felt that way about me." I didn't say anything. "Sometimes," he went on, "I think I'm not what you're looking for, that I'm too easy for you. You want someone harder, someone who'll cause you more trouble. You want some kind of a challenge." "Why do you say that now?" I cried. For the first time in months, I felt completely happy. "Maybe it's you," I said; "maybe you're the one who doesn't want things coming too easily. Maybe you don't want happiness." He looked at me and shook his head. "You know better than that," he said. "I don't understand," I said again, "why you're saying this *now*." "Now?" he said; "I don't know why. But you think about it. You think I'm happy all of the time and you don't really like it." "I know you're not happy all of the time," I said impatiently. "Compared to you, I am," he said; "isn't that what you think?" "No," I said, "you have your moods." "Like yours?" he asked. "No," I said; "not like mine. I have too many moods. I don't think it's a good thing to be so moody." "But you think there's something wrong with me because I don't have so many moods," he said; "you think that if I really saw the world the way it was, I'd have just as many moods. Don't you?"

I was shocked into silence. It was true that at times I thought of Charlie as an adorable, simple creature, but then, I told myself, I thought of all men that way. They were well-intentioned creatures of abnormal physical strength and they were easily taken in by women. When I was a child and busy pursuing Lloyd, the shy boy from my class, he never noticed anything odd in my mysterious appearances wherever he happened to be; he always mistook our collisions for coincidence. Men, I thought, were incapable of understanding how women schemed and plotted to entrap them, to bind them, to bend them to their will. I did not expect one of them to understand me more thoroughly than I understood myself. "I don't know what you mean," I told Charlie.

"You," he said; "I've seen how your moods come on. Someone shows you a new baby and you start to cry. Polly tells you she's thinking about getting married and you start crying. When I ask you about it, you say you're crying because you're happy." "I do cry when I'm happy," I said. "That's not the only reason you cry," he said; "you cried when you saw the new baby because you thought about what it would be like if it died. As soon as you see anything you care about, you start to cry because you're afraid it will die." "Because I know it will die," I said softly. "Well, I'm not like that," Charlie said. "No," I agreed, "you're not." "So you think I don't care much about things," he said. "No," I cried, "I don't believe that!" "You do," he said; "you can't believe that happiness and seeing the world with your eyes open can go together." I didn't answer him.

I was thinking about how often the thing I looked at seemed to turn immediately into its opposite, how just before, in the meadow, I had traced the lines of his face until the image of his skull had begun to emerge from beneath the rosy flesh I was admiring. And I thought the surface of the world itself was like a mirror. The surface was bright and shiny and reflected wonderful pictures, but when you scratched through the mirror, you came down to the dark black backing behind it. Underneath everything was that blackness. If you followed a human life long enough, it ended in blackness. It ended in the earth. Life began when energy grabbed hold of some dust and would not let it go. And when it did let go, dust was all there was. Women married and gave life to dust. It was worse to be a woman than a man. Men did not have to watch their creations crumble in the wind. "You think I'm morbid," I said sadly. "I don't care if you're morbid," he said, "but you care because I'm not." "It isn't true!" I cried; "it's just not true!" "I think it is," he said. "Even if it is, and I don't think it's true," I said, desperate, "I could change." "That's what I've been hoping," he said. He sounded so unhappy, so desolate that I wanted to get up and put my arms around him. "You look unhappy enough now," I said. "And you like me better this way, don't you?" he said.

Finally, we went down the hill toward the town. "Two more days until my sister gets here," he reminded me. "I know," I said; "I've been dreading it. She won't like me." "Why not?" he asked, surprised. "Don't sisters always dislike their brothers' girls?" I asked. "Not that I know of," he said, regarding me quizzically. "All right! All right!" I exclaimed; "I know that I always expect the worst and I know that you don't. That doesn't mean I care for you any less." "We'll see," he said.

And at supper, Polly kept looking from me to Charlie, and her eyes would rest on him in puzzlement before returning to me, but when she came in to my room that night, I told her nothing about what had happened on Bald Hill. I would tell her, I decided, eventually, after Charlie had forgotten what he had said to me.

When I came into the dining room that night, I saw that Frank wasn't there, but I didn't dare ask anyone where he was. When Polly came in, she told me Frank had gone back home to visit his family and wouldn't be back for a while. "If you ask me," she said, "he just wants to get away from Charlie's sister. I don't know what went on there, but all you have to do is mention Madge's name and he starts to look like a thunder cloud." "A whole week," I said. "Well, it's a long way to Quebec," said Polly; "he can afford a vacation anyhow. I guess there's someone back home waiting for him. Anyhow, that's what Charlie always says." We chatted on idly. I said I couldn't imagine going home voluntarily; I had to force myself to write letters and they were insultingly short when I did write them. Then Polly said she wished she had a real home to go to. She asked me if I would embroider some things for her trousseau because she loved my fancywork, but she couldn't pay me much, and I told her not to worry about it. I didn't want any money. I had already finished six handkerchiefs with raised strawberries in a design of white on white. I knew that after a few weeks of wear, the different shades of white would all blend together, and no one would notice the differing shades of the same color, but I wanted her to have the same handkerchiefs the girls on the third floor made for the legislators' wealthy wives. Ever since Polly had decided to get married, I had been making her a quilt. Every day, I came home from work with a new piece of cloth stitched into my skirt. I worked on the quilt while she watched me and I took her advice about which colors looked best next to each other; after all, the quilt was to be for her. It was my own design: a sun in the center, and from it radiated stylized rays, wave upon wave of them as the quilt grew.

21

Finally, Charlie decided to take me to the Barre quarries. I had been after him for months. I wanted to see what he did all day. He said we might as well go before his sister arrived, because once she came, it would be impossible. She was, he said, a magnet for accidents and the quarries weren't the safest place in the world and he didn't want to have to explain how his sister happened to fall into one of the yawning chasms that cut through them. We went next door to the livery stable and woke up the owner, who was sleeping on the porch. It was Sunday and the whole city was quiet. Charlie persuaded the man to rent us two horses, but first he had to convince him he wasn't attempting to work on the Sabbath. I sighed. I had come a long way from North Chittendon, but some things, it appeared, did not change.

The day was flawless, and the mountains receded into the distance as far as the eye could see. "I can count thirteen," I said; "thirteen ranges." "Fifteen," said Charlie; "you have to keep looking." "I can see fifteen," I said finally; "I can see more!" We rode on. I was completely, utterly happy. "How many ranges are there?" I asked him. "No one really knows," he said; "some of the men think they can see twenty-one of them. Frank does. Maybe he can. He's got good eyes."

We could see great gashes in the hills above us, as if an enormous bird had come down and raked its claws deep through the earth. Scarred earth. "What's that?" I asked Charlie; "are those the quarries?" He said they were, and that when we got closer, we would have to get down and lead our horses. If they made a misstep and went down, we would go with them. I was a good rider and wanted to take the risk and ride them all the way into the quarries but Charlie wouldn't hear of it. "I'm not gambling with you," he said. But I was disappointed. I asked

Charlie when we would have to start walking the horses. "Oh, you'll know," he said.

The landscape was beginning to appear strange to me. I looked at the hills and the trees and the grass on both sides of the road and everything looked as if it were covered by a thin white curtain. I blinked my eyes hard. I must have ridden too long looking into the sun. I rubbed my eyes to clear them, but the whiteness covered everything. Had I burned my eyes? I started to rub them, but Charlie leaned over and grabbed my arm. "Leave your eyes alone," he said; "it's the dust. It covers everything for miles around. Watch. The horses' hooves will start sending it up in clouds." I looked down; the hooves seemed to be disappearing into a little mist which rose up everywhere around us. The land around us was becoming discontinuous. A hill would begin to swell and then drop off suddenly, as if cut through by a knife. I began to look for a hill, any hill, which had not been subjected to such surgery, but I could not find one. "How do they do it?" I asked Charlie; "how do they cut through the ground like that?" "Dynamite," he said; "they blast it out." He signaled me to stop. In the distance, I could see the long gray sheds which I knew housed the stonecutters during the week. I was fascinated by the landscape. I recognized it; it was not alien to me. As if I had been here before, I looked around me at the sudden, deep gaps in the earth, the chasms whose jagged walls yawned so dangerously. Even the dust and the smell of the dust were familiar, as if I had breathed this air many times before. "Come on," Charlie said.

We got off our horses and led them down the road, which, as it approached the sheds, became narrower and skirted deep gorges. We were going around in back of the stone sheds and as soon as we passed them, I stopped, stunned by what I saw. For as far as the eye could see, tombstones rose from the ground, cutting their outlines into the clear blue sky. There was an uncanny air of activity about the stones, as if they had just been carving themselves into existence before we had interrupted them. Some of them were turned at an angle to the others; others rested on their backs, displaying their legends to the sky. Coats were thrown over the shoulders of some stones. Tools of various sorts rested on many of the stones, especially on those which had only been partially carved.

I looked back at the stone sheds. They were dead and quiet, but expectant, as if they were waiting for something, as if, I thought, the dead who belonged to these stones were waiting in there until their stones were finished. "This," said Charlie, "is where I work. It's not pretty, is it?" I looked around me. "It is," I said; "it's beautiful. It's very strange." Charlie looked at me, troubled. "Beautiful," he said; "what's so beautiful about tombstones?" "It's the purest graveyard I've ever seen," I said. "You mean because there are no dead bodies here," he said, "just stones?" "No," I said; "it's as if this is where death gets manufactured. It's death's factory. It's the most beautiful factory there is, where things are both dead and alive at once." I looked ahead of me, my eyes wide. I didn't want to blink. I didn't want the scene to fade. I wanted to memorize it. I felt as if I had somehow come to one of the sources of things, and that while I was there, I could learn something very important.

"Death's factory," said Charlie; "that's ghastly." For an instant I had forgotten he was there. But he was there, and he was angry. "We don't cause the deaths," he said; "we just carve the stones. Someone has to do it." "I know," I said. "It's not beautiful here!" he said angrily, kicking a pebble into the chasm. "No," I said slowly, "I suppose it's not. It's peaceful, though." "It's peaceful today because no one's working," he said; "come on. I'll show you where I work."

We picked our way through the monuments that tended to crowd the margins of the little path we followed. "All the way up on top," he said; "I like to get as far away from everyone else as I can." A small distance behind the last row of monuments I saw two stones, one with a coat thrown over its back. "That's where I work," Charlie said. "Why do you go so far back," I asked, "behind the others?" "There's less dust, for one thing. See that pail?" He pointed to what looked like our old well bucket. "We don't bother with flasks. We fill that up with water and put a wooden lid on it to keep the dust out. I must drink four or five of them a day, the dust's so bad in your throat. It's everywhere. In the winter, the sheds sound like they're coughing. The dust makes our eyes burn and dry out. Someone's always got a new way to take care of your eyes, but nothing works. Frank won't try anything anymore. He wants to see the stone and do a good job and if he has to see it through dust, he will. I don't bother about it anymore, either. It's here and so are we." I looked down at the stone on which he was working. Lucy Pendergast. "Who was Lucy Pendergast?" I asked him. "If I don't already know, I never try to find out," he said; his voice was tight. "Let's go back," I said; "it's Sunday. Why should you spend another day here?" He had bent down to look at the stone and was running his finger over the grooves which formed the *P*.

"Well," he said, straightening up and looking at me, "*you* haven't been here before. I have a surprise for you." He took me behind the stones on which he was working and showed me a little, cylindrical column of marble. "I've been carving this for you," he said. "I only just started this last flower," he said, pointing at it, "so you could try your hand at it yourself. When it's finished, you can use it for a doorstop." "It's beautiful," I said, kneeling down and touching it. "Well," he said, "Frank does better with flowers than I do, but it's not bad." "Let me try carving it," I said. He said I could try, but I had to be careful. He showed me how to hold the little chisel and how I had to strike it with the hammer. "Now don't change the angle," he said, "or you'll shear off the stone instead of shaping it." He covered my hand with his and maneuvered the chisel into position. "Ready?" he asked. I said I was.

I hit the chisel with the mallet and the raised portion of stone sheared off. "Oh no!" I cried, looking at the smooth place which I should have helped make into a flower. "I thought it would happen," he said; "I expected it. I'll carve a medallion to cover that space and then keep going with the garland on the other side." "It's not ruined?" I asked. I looked about me. The many stones glowed rose as if they were living things. I would have liked to make one of my own. "It's not ruined," Charlie said; "see?" and he began chipping away at the stone. "Well," he said, "it will take too long to show you, but here and here . . ." he sketched imaginary lines with the chisel, "there'll be a medallion, and the roses will arch up on either side. If you hadn't broken off the stone, I probably would have done it myself anyway. This way the design will be more interesting." I wiped my hands on my skirt. Dust streaked its folds. "You see?" Charlie said; "some of the men wear dusters and hats, but I can't bother. The dust gets in anyway." "You're never dusty at Iris's," I said. "No, because by then I've been to the stables and gotten a good dunking. Frank, too. Look here," he said, walking down the field to the next stone; "look at this." A stone, covered by a dust-colored cloth, stood by itself as if in defiance of all the others. "Guess who's working out here all by himself?" Charlie asked me, yanking the cloth from the stone so that it sailed through the air in a thick cloud of dust.

On the unfinished stone, a mother bent over the child she held in her arms. The expression on her stone face was warmer than anything in life; the child in her arms was plump and healthy and stared up at its mother as if it were seeing the face of heaven itself. I knew that I was looking at a relief carved upon rose-colored marble. But I could not see it as it really was. As I looked at it, the mother and child took on the hues of flesh and blood; they were only temporarily inanimate. At any second, they would begin to breathe. I had simply come upon them after they drew in one breath and before they took another. I didn't realize that I had moved toward the stone, or that I had touched it until, feeling its cool surface, I drew back, frightened. They were not alive, after all. How could he do that? I asked myself. How could he create life out of stone? *That* was what I wanted to do! And then I thought of the little stone column Charlie was carving for me, and how I had sheared the flower from its garland and my heart broke. "It's beautiful," I said, still staring at the stone. "It is," said Charlie; "he has a talent." "He could do better than this!" I exclaimed; "he could carve *fine* statues!" "Yes," said Charlie; "he could."

I looked at him, confused. Why had he shown me this stone? He knew, evidently, how I would see it. "I don't have a talent," he said; "I'm only very good at what I do. I'm only one of the best. He's different." "Yes," I said. "This is what he loves," Charlie said; "the stones. He loves the people he carves himself. He can't love anything else. The stone people don't change." "You're being unfair!" I cried; "you don't know that's true! I wish I had a talent like his, but would it mean I couldn't love anything but my stones if I did? He must have loved someone *once* to be able to carve things that way. You can see that by looking at it." "You can see it," he said; "I can't." "I can see that you're jealous of him," I said; "that's plain enough." "Of his carving?" he asked. "Of course of his carving!" I said; "what else have we been talking about?"

Charlie rested his arm on the back of Frank's stone. I wanted to knock his hand from the stone, as if he had no right to touch it. "I hate this place," he said, looking around. "Everyone who works here dies faster. The dust kills you. They say people are made of dust, but enough is enough. Once the coughing starts, you know you've fallen into one of these slashes in the earth and you know you're not getting out. But Frank thinks the place is beautiful. Just the way you do." "You can't expect everyone to see things the way you see them," I said. He regarded me speculatively. "If you and Frank fight so much," I asked, "why do you stay so close together?" "We grew up together," he said; "he's like my brother." "You don't like your brother much, do you?" I asked. "Brothers and sisters don't usually like each other much," he said, "at least not while they're young." "Then I don't see why they bother with each other until they're older," I said. "If you had a brother or sister, you'd understand," he said. "I had a sister," I said; "once."

I was staring at Frank's carving. I stooped down before the stone and peered closely at it. I could see the chisel marks, but I knew I was looking at life imprisoned in marble. "Well," I said, getting up, "let's look around some more." Charlie said we would have to leave soon because we would have to have the light when we led the horses down the trail. I was in no hurry. I never wanted to leave.

As we wove down the hill between the stones, as we approached the stone sheds where the marble cutters worked all winter, I turned back and looked at the stones glowing in the gold and rose light. "I hate to go back," I said; "from here, it looks like a little city. See how the outline of the stones against the sky looks like the houses in a town?" "It's safe to ride now," Charlie said, and he helped me onto my horse. He seemed sad. "What's wrong?" I asked. "Oh, nothing," he said; "I wish you hadn't liked it so much." "Why shouldn't I?" I asked; "it's where you work." He shook his head. "Can I come back again sometime?" I asked. "Of course," he said; "I'm always there." And so we rode back, talking more happily the further from the quarries we were. Everything I saw was lovely. Everything made me laugh. I giggled easily when Charlie said something about my eyes or my hair. I was still under the spell of the quarry stones.

And when we came down the road, down into Montpelier, it seemed to me that we were descending into another town of such stones. But then the people began to move around us; carriages rolled by us and the world of the quarries rose in the air like dust, and, although its odor lingered in my nostrils, it was gone.

We went slowly down the main street, letting the reins dangle and the horses walk at their own speed. We had to pass in front of Mrs. Trowbridge's house to get to the livery stable behind it, and as we came toward the house, the door flew open and Polly ran down the street toward us. "Hurry up!" she called; "someone's waiting for you!" "For him?" I asked. I assumed that Charlie's sister had arrived early. "No, for you," she said; "get rid of that horse and get back to the house." "Why?" I said; "what happened?" "Someone's here to take you home," she said; "your mother's dying. She sent someone for you. He's waiting for you in the kitchen." "I don't want to go home," I said, shaking my head. The world had gone cold. "I *can't* go home!" "Just get rid of the horse," Polly told me. "Charlie, take her to the stable. I'll meet you there."

At the stable, I got down reluctantly. Suppose I went home and never came back? If I went home, I would turn back into the person I had been before I left. I couldn't go home. I couldn't take the chance. Why did my mother want me there? I was just getting free of her. "She's terrified," I heard Polly say to Charlie. "Do you want me to go with you?" Charlie asked. "No!" I burst out. "Why not?" Polly asked. I looked at them hopelessly. I was afraid that if either of them came with me, they would never come back. Or, in some way, they would come back changed. I didn't want them exposed to it, whatever it was, the contagion, the blight which fell on everyone who came near Cloudy Pastures.

"Listen here," said Polly, grabbing me by the shoulders; "you're coming back. If you're not back in two weeks, we'll come to get you." "Don't come," I said. My voice was hollow and dark. "We will," she said; "we'll come. Won't we, Charlie?" He nodded. "We'll come on the cars," she said; "it isn't far. Nothing's going to happen to you." She took my hand and we walked back to the house. "Agnes," she said, "walk a little faster. Look how you're worrying Charlie." "I have to pack," I said at last; "I can't go home without any clothes." "I packed a suitcase for you," said Polly; "it's in the parlor." I glared at her. "You won't forgive yourself if you get there too late," she said. "Oh, yes I will," I said. "Well, if you're going to go, you might as well get there on time," she said. "She won't die," I said; "she can't die; that's her trouble." Polly and Charlie looked at each other. "I'll write to you," Charlie said. "I'm not going to be there long enough to get a letter," I said. Charlie said he would write to me anyway.

Bill Brown was sitting on one of the little button-tufted chairs in the parlor. I had never seen him look more uncomfortable, more thoroughly out of place. I had forgotten how big he was. When he stood up, I expected to see his head go through the ceiling and his arms through the walls. "Well, Agnes," he said awkwardly; "your friend, has she told you?" "What's the matter with Mother?" I asked abruptly. "Heart," he said; "it's giving out. The doc says her lungs are all filled up with water. She don't barely breathe. She asks for you so much she gets

166

tired, so your father, he said to take the buggy and go and get you. We better go on.'' ''Don't you want something to eat? Aren't you thirsty?'' I asked, desperate to delay. ''Oh, no, your friend here brought me some lemonade and cookies.'' Polly avoided my eyes. I heard horses stamping in front of the house. I looked out the parlor window and there it was, our black buggy, and the circular emblem with the letters *CP* at its center. Cloudy Pastures. I should, I thought, have gone further away from home. ''Well,'' I said, standing up; ''good-bye.'' Polly came over to me and kissed me. ''Don't touch the quilt,'' I told her; ''you'll ruin it. I'll be back.'' I went over to Charlie and kissed him. He flushed. I touched his hair. ''I'll be back,'' I said again, more to myself than to him.

''I see you made yourself some friends,'' Bill Brown said as we left the house; ''do you want to sit up front with me or inside?'' ''Up front with you,'' I said. Suddenly, I was afraid of being alone. If my mother was dying, I thought, she could be anywhere, even in the air above us. I was, I realized, becoming hysterical. My mother was right where she always was, in our house in North Chittendon. Even if she died, I would know where she was. She would be in the family plot, right next to Majella. Really, I thought, I never wanted to be alone. Never. I twisted around in my seat so that I could watch the Trowbridge house out of sight. But then I turned back, facing the road before us. I did not want to see Montpelier recede in the distance, and until we could no longer see it, I pretended to be asleep.

''How's my father?'' I asked Bill. ''He'll be better when you get there,'' he said. ''I hope they don't expect me to stay,'' I said; ''I'm not going to.'' ''I guess they don't,'' he said. ''What's wrong with my father?'' I asked Bill suddenly. ''Nothing much,'' he said; ''he runs fevers.'' ''Why?'' I asked. ''The doctor doesn't know. Your father says it's because he's getting old.'' ''You're just as old,'' I said; ''are you running fevers?'' ''No, Agnes,'' he said grimly; ''I'm not. You ought to show him some attention. You treated your animals better.'' The horses galloped on. ''My animals,'' I said, ''never hurt me.'' ''No?'' he said; ''what about that dog? The one that almost took out your eye? Your memory works just the way you want it to work.'' ''I can't,'' I said; ''I can't show them attention. I would if I could.'' ''Try,'' he said. I pretended to fall asleep again.

I felt rather than saw our entrance into North Chittendon. I knew when we passed Harding's Livery, the post office, the schoolhouse with its dark windows and locked door, Bea Brown's house, Louise's house. Not until I began to feel the horses straining up the steep ascent to our house did I open my eyes. And then we came around the sharp bend in the road, and there it was, the tall white house, as if I had never left. I knew I was walking inside with my head down, like a convict, as if I were being arrested and was ashamed because I had been caught. At the last moment, I looked up at the sky. The moon was there. So it was the same world after all. I hesitated so long in front of the door that Bill Brown thought I was having trouble opening it, and pushed it forward for me. We had come into the kitchen, and I saw at once that nothing was as I had left it.

My parents' bed was set up in front of the kitchen stove and the room was filled with a strange, rasping rhythmical noise. As I approached the bed, I realized that I was listening to my mother breathe. Just then, someone touched my arm. I jumped, startled. It was Bea Brown. "What's causing that?" I whispered. "She can't get her breath," Bea whispered; "come into the parlor. It's a terrible job for her to breathe in and out. She's in the kitchen because she's always cold and your father found out that drinking ice water makes it easier for her to breathe, so she chews on ice and that makes her colder. It's a terrible thing to watch." "And to hear," I said. "At least you're here," Bea said; "now she won't waste her strength asking for you." "Bea," I said, "don't expect a warm family reunion. I know she's sick but everything else is the same." "She's not sick," said Bea; "she's dying." We went back into the kitchen. "Don't say anything to disturb her," Bea whispered to me.

My father was not there. When I asked Bea where he was she said he went out to get some ice, or at least that's where he said he was going, but she thought he went out and cried where my mother couldn't hear him.

Bill Brown pulled up a kitchen chair and set it down next to my mother's bed and I sat down on it. "Hello, Mother," I said, bending over her. She was propped up by pillows, a pack of ice sat on her chest, and on the little table drawn up to the other side of her bed, crushed ice filled a tall glass. Her eyes were closed. She looked so fragile and blue. She looked younger than I did. I could see the violet veins in her eyelids and the blue vein throbbing at the side of her temples. It was like watching myself struggle to breathe. Why had I never seen the resemblance before? We looked just like one another.

Her eyes opened. "Agnes," she said. And she smiled. And when she smiled, her face lit up. The illness which had descended on her seemed to draw in its claws. Her breathing improved. "Are you happy?" she asked me. I saw that talking cost her a great deal. "There," she said; "are you happy there?" I said I was. She motioned to me to bend over her. "Here," she said, talking slowly, a few words at a time between each difficult breath, "here you can feel the wind sucking you out through the walls." She stopped talking and picked up the glass of ice and sucked on it. "Have you?" she asked. "Have I what?" I asked her. "Felt it," she said. I said I had. "I feel it now," I said without thinking. She nodded and pressed the ice against her chest.

Bea bent over me. "Tell her you love her," she whispered in my ear. I looked at my mother beneath two blankets in the middle of July, sucking on bits of ice, looking up at me and smiling. I wanted to tell her I loved her but the words froze in my throat. "Tell her," Bea whispered to me. I motioned her away. "Mother," I said; "try harder. Try to get better." Her hand fluttered against the blanket. "Try," I said again. She motioned me closer. "I've had enough," she said with difficulty; "enough." I bent over her. "Do you want to die?" I asked her. She didn't answer. "Don't you care?" She shook her head. No, she didn't care. "Has it been so hard?" I asked. I was talking to a stranger. I didn't know her. Her lips shaped something. "What?" I asked. "The wind," she said; "the wind." My father had come in through the buttery and stood at the foot of her bed. I looked up at him. He looked much older than he had only months before. I was surprised at his resemblance to Charlie, or Charlie's to him. Their coloring was similar. So were their faces. Even the way they moved. I looked around the room, my eyes automatically seeking my grandmother, Eurydice, and suddenly I remembered that she was dead. And as soon as I looked for her and did not find her, the fear caught hold of me until I could barely sit still on the chair next to the bed.

I got up and wandered to the window and stood staring out. On the stove, a covered pot was coming to a boil, the steam lifting and dropping its lid. My father would need someone to cook for him now. "You'll need someone to do the cooking," I said aloud, and then, horrified, I broke off. I hadn't intended to say anything. My mother's loud breathing, the silence waiting beneath it, had worked on my nerves. "What's the matter with you?" Bea asked, grabbing me by the arm; "if you can't behave, go up to your room." I walked over to my father. "I'm going upstairs," I said; "I'm tired. I'll be down in a little while." He nodded at me as if he didn't know who I was, as if he hoped to remember soon. I went into my room. My mother had kept her word. Everything there was as I had left it. Still, the room looked smaller, darker than I remembered it. Its air was thick with old sorrows, fears, recriminations. "Cabbage roses," I said aloud, sighing. I sank down in the chintz-covered chair and stared out at the sky through the window opposite me. And I fell asleep.

In the dream, my old cat, Stardancer, was outside walking in front of the window and he was much bigger than he had ever been in life. He was bigger than the house itself. And, as he went by, I could see that someone had done something to his fur, but at first I could not see what it was they had done. But as he continued to pass and repass in front of the window, I saw that someone had sewn hooks and eyes into his skin so that all along his silhouette hooks and eyes were sewn into his flesh as if they were necessary to keep his fur suit attached to him. I could see how the stitches must have hurt him and I called him over to the window and he came, pressing his side against the windowpane. But when I tried to remove the hooks and eyes, I could not find the threads by which they were attached and I could do nothing for him. "Wait for me," I told the cat; "I'll find a scissors and I'll be right back," but the cat howled and lay down along the side of the house. He began to cry and his cries made me more and more uneasy and I tried to get up and look for the scissors. And then I woke up. The sound of my mother's breathing filled my room. I sat up and looked slowly around. She must be worse. I ran my hands up and down the skin of my arms as if I expected to find the hooks and eyes there. I had not had a dream like that since leaving North Chittendon.

I came downstairs and saw the doctor bending over my mother. "She's worse," my father said to me. I wanted to go over to him, to touch him, but I was incapable of it. "She's not trying," I said. "She can't," my father said; "her heart's going. They can't do anything for her." I looked up and saw Bea staring at me from the other side of the room. I knew she wanted me to tell my mother I loved her, but I could not. "Say good-bye to her," my father said. I could do that. I went over to the bed. "Mother," I said, bending low over her. Her eyes flicked open and shut and open again. "Good-bye," I said. She was trying to say something. I bent closer to her. My cheek was almost against hers. "Good," she said; "good." "Good what?" I asked. "Fortune," she whispered. "Good fortune?" I asked her. She nodded and her mouth struggled into a smile. I wanted to touch her. I wanted to cry, but instead a lump constricted my throat until it hurt to swallow, until the air I breathed in was painful. "I'll sit here," I said at last. She shook her head. "No," she said; "sleep." And she closed her eyes. But I was beyond sleep.

I put on my mother's old shawl and went out into the meadow. One of the dogs followed me. I didn't know this one. It was one of the many collies on the farm. "What do you suppose," I said aloud, "they're doing in Montpelier now? If she has to die, I wish she would die soon. It would be better for her and better for me, don't you think so?" The dog wagged his tail. I sighed and looked up at the sky, which had drawn back from me. Its vaults were higher and further away than ever before. I lay down on the grass. The dog licked my face. He did not think I was a monster because I wanted my mother to die now, not later. Would I keep on breathing if it took so much effort? No, I wouldn't. I was, I thought, looking for something to live for and had not yet found it. My mother must have found what she wanted. Even now she fought to breathe. But I hadn't found what I wanted; Charlie was not who I wanted. I told myself I shouldn't be thinking about him now, not when I was here and he was so far away. The dog licked my face. I turned over and buried my face in the grass.

When I came back into the house, the first thing I heard was muffled sobbing and I knew that my mother had died. Bill Brown had his arm around his mother, and my father was sitting next to the bed, holding my mother's hand. "Come away from there," I told him. He didn't move. I became aware of the silence through which I moved; it was thick and viscous. I could barely move in it. I had to get out of the house. I had to go back to Montpelier. "I'm going up to bed," I said aloud. I knew everyone in the room was appalled at my behavior, but I could not speak to them and I could not stay where I was.

In the morning, I said I would stay in North Chittendon until my mother's funeral was over and then I was going back. My father looked surprised but did not object. The funeral, he said, would take place the next day. He said he didn't know what to do about a stone because my mother had said she didn't want one of her own. She had insisted the weather would remove her name soon enough and she said that Majella's stone would serve them both well. But, said my father, he thought she ought to have her own stone.

The next morning, Bea woke me and told me to get dressed because we were going into town for church services. I was numb. When I dressed myself, I barely felt my own hands on my body. Sounds seemed to come to me through a deep, unlit water and beneath that water, I slowly moved. "Here," Bea said, handing me the black dress I had worn home the day before; "I cleaned it for you." I put it on. "Don't you feel anything?" she asked me. She was not reproachful, only curious. Bea was always a practical one. Yesterday, my mother was alive and, had Bea been able, she would have forced me to behave as she believed a daughter should. Today, my mother was dead and I was alive, and so Bea was concerned with me. My grandmother always said that Bea could not hold a resentment in her hand for ten minutes at a time. We sat in the kitchen for several hours, supposedly praying for the dead, and then went into town. It was a very hot day and few people came to the service. The coffin was open and Bea had arranged orange day lilies in a crescent around my mother's head. She was bloodless and the bones of her face had risen up against the fabric of her skin. Already her skeleton was breaking through into the light. I watched it all coldly.

And then I thought it was raining, and looked up in surprise, because we were in church, and even if it were raining, I should not be getting wet. I put my hand to my face and felt my cheeks; they were drenched and slippery. I looked down at the bodice of my dress and saw that drops of water had fallen onto it. When I touched the black poplin fabric, it was damp. Carefully, slowly, I raised my hand to my hair. My hair was dry. I didn't understand it. I looked out the window. The sun was shining. There wasn't a cloud anywhere. And with a shock I realized that I was crying and that I couldn't stop. It was as if my body and I had parted company and my body had decided to mourn my mother's death even if I had not. I observed Bea putting her arm around me with a detached curiosity and listened to the pet names she whispered to me. But I continued to cry. I cried all the way back to the farm and then all the way to the burial plot in our west hill. I stood still, crying, while the coffin, now closed, was carried from the wagon to the hole in the earth already prepared for it. I watched the men lower the coffin into the ground and watched them draw their earth-stained ropes up again. When my father threw in the first handful of dirt, I heard the pebbles dance on the coffin lid. They sounded like hailstones. And I don't know why, but that sound made me laugh.

I stopped crying and started to laugh. I saw Bea watching me in consternation and I ran partway down the meadow, kicked off my shoes and began running down the road toward the farm. Partway there, I stopped, took off my hat, and began waving it in the air by its ribbons. I felt as if I were on fire with energy and I laughed for the sheer joy of it. I was still laughing when I came in sight of the farm buildings, and I ran from one to another, wreaking havoc. I opened the door to the pigpen and chased out the pigs. I opened the door to the chicken coop and would have gone into the barn and turned the horses loose had not Bill Brown, who had followed me down, grabbed me and pinned my arms behind my back. "All right," he said; "that's enough." That, I thought, was the funniest thing I had ever heard. I screamed with laughter. "You're upset," he said; "you're not yourself." "Then who am I?" I asked, convulsed at my own joke. I laughed until my sides hurt and my muscles ached and I could barely get my breath. "Anyone who laughs like that will be crying before long," said Bill Brown, and suddenly I stopped laughing and twisted around to look at him. "If I let you go, will you tear up the place?" he asked me. "No," I said, "I don't want to tear anything up. I just want to leave."

"I'm sure that can be arranged," Bea said, coming up behind us. "The whole town's going to be talking about this, Agnes, the way you ran around laughing without your shoes on or your hat." "Would it have been better if I'd had on my shoes and my hat?" I asked, starting to laugh again. Bill Brown looked at his mother and shrugged. "This, too, will be forgotten," he said. "I'm grateful for one thing," said Bea; "I'm grateful that God saw fit to take your grandmother before your mother." "What does my grandmother have to do with this?" I asked, giggling. Bea, I thought, was becoming cloudy with age. "She didn't take well to funerals either," Bea said. "Agnes, I talked to your father and he thinks you ought to go back to Montpelier. He wants you to stay, but he thinks you'll be happier there. And your mother made him promise not to try to keep you here. So Bill will take you back." "Now?" I said. "If you want to go now." I said I did. This time, when I watched Bill put the suitcase into the back of the buggy, I again felt as if I were escaping from a dangerous place, but this time I was afraid that perhaps there was no fate for me at all, as if the doors of the houses everywhere were, one by one, locking against me. I no longer felt as if I had a place to which I could return.

22

When I came into the office of the Trowbridge house, it was dark and empty, as it had been the first night I arrived, but this time, there were noises coming from the dining room. I put my suitcase down in front of the little desk and rested my hands on it. I heard the sound of the train whistle as the train pulled into Montpelier Junction. Nothing had happened. Everything was where it had been when I left. "Thank God," I said aloud. I pushed open the swinging door and went into the dining room. Polly and a young girl I had never seen before were sitting at the table, talking and laughing. Polly jumped up when she saw me. "You're back," she said again and again; "you're back." "I'm back," I said, embracing her stiffly, looking over her shoulder at the other girl. "Who's she?" the girl asked Polly. "Oh, I'm sorry," Polly said; "Agnes Dempster, this is Charlie's married sister, Madge Piersall." We said hello to one another and I sat down. "Just call me Madge," said the other girl. I was about to answer her when the door opened and Frank walked in.

He was wearing some kind of uniform, navy blue with bright blue buttons. There were gold epaulets on his shoulders. My throat constricted. My heart beat so hard I was sure the other could hear it. "Are we at war?" I whispered. "War?" Polly asked, astonished. "War?" echoed Charlie's sister, looking at me from beneath raised eyebrows; "are we at war?" "You mean," Frank said, his eyes on me, "because of the uniform? Is that why you're asking?" "Yes," I said. "Well, it practically takes a war to get me into it," he said, "but it's only my band uniform. I played with the band when I was home. We were marching for the patriots of Quebec." "Oh," I said. I wondered why he was still wearing it. "He's still wearing the uniform," said Charlie's sister, "because he knows how dashing he looks, don't you, Frank?" "Right," said Frank. I saw how the air crackled between them. "Aren't you back early?" I asked Frank; "I thought you were staying away longer." "Well," said Frank, "Madge was coming down here to see Charlie so we came down on the train together." "But weren't *you* supposed to come earlier?" I asked Madge. "Oh, I had more things to do than I thought," Madge said. She was talking to me, but she looked at Frank. "And I had to finish a stone," said Frank, "so I decided to come on back." "Well," I said, "the ride must have been less boring for the two of you if you could talk to each other." "It was," Madge said solemnly. I felt Polly's eyes on me.

"Where's Charlie?" I asked them. "He's gone to Rutland," said Polly; "he'll be back any time. He has to cut a new name on a stone. They thought it would be cheaper to bring him there than to send the stone here." "He won't like that," I said. "No, he won't," Polly said, looking around the room. "So you're my brother's girl," Madge said slowly. "Her mother just died," Polly cut in hurriedly. "That's funny," said Madge, "my brother doesn't usually go for the pretty ones. That's more Frank's way." "Madge," Frank said. "Well," Madge said, "even Frank seems to have given up on the pretty ones. He thinks the nice plain ones make the best wives. They make the least trouble. They know who comes first, don't they, Frank?" "Keep on talking, Madge," he said. "Well, you'll keep your promise, won't you?" she asked him; "you'll invite me to your wedding, if you have a wedding, if anyone in her right mind will marry you." "I'm not worried," Frank said evenly. "You're right not to worry," Madge said; "the girl you've got designs on ought to worry." "Are you going to make a scene?" Frank asked her. "I don't know," Madge said. Her voice shook. "Well, just in case you are," said Frank, "I'm going out. I'll be back later." He got up and the door swung shut behind him.

In the ensuing silence, I inspected Madge. She did not resemble Charlie in the least. Her face was almost square and her hair was a dusky blond which she parted in the middle and then wore pinned to the back of her head. She had cut her hair so that one large curl covered each side of her forehead. Her lips were round and full and her cheeks were the cheeks of a child, plump, as if she had candy hidden in them. Her eyes were large and dark. She would be pretty, I thought, were it not for her nose. It was wide and doughy. I admired her blouse. It was made of a light, white striped cotton and its bodice was shirred and its sleeves short and puffed. The neck was low and a narrow double ruffle decorated the neckline. She wore a little gold chain around her neck. The long maroon skirt she wore matched the color of the flowers in her blouse and she had sewn the skirt's panels so that the grain ran at right angles to one another. She looked, I thought, like something that had stepped out of a magazine. Then I saw that she was watching me as intently as I had been watching her.

"Polly said your mother just died," she said. She was utterly unsympathetic. I said she had. "That's why you're wearing black?" she asked. I nodded, but that wasn't why. I gave very little thought to my clothes. It was easier to keep up a black dress than a white one. It was full summer, and I had only one dress which was brightly colored, and even that was not white; it had a beige ground. "I hate to wear black," Madge said; "it's so dull and uninspired and it makes me look yellow." She looked at me critically. "I suppose you like it because it sets you off," she said; "it doesn't set me off at all." I didn't know what to say to her. I wished Charlie were there.

And, magically, he came into the room. When he saw me, he walked straight over to me, put his arms under my shoulders, lifted me into the air and hugged me to him. As I felt his warmth against my body, I realized how cold I was. I nuzzled against him as if I wanted to burrow through his shirt and on into his chest. "I see you've met my sister," he whispered into my ear; "don't mind her." I sighed and my arms crept upward and around his waist. I forgot the others in the room with us. "She died?" he asked me. "She said she'd had enough," I whispered back. He nodded. His chin pressed against the top of my head. "You don't have to live forever to know how that is," he whispered. I tried to look up to him but I did not want to move my head from his chest. I became aware of a button pressing into my eyelid and moved my head slightly.

"Well, I'm back," I heard Frank say. Charlie let me go and we turned around to look at him. "Well, he's back," said Madge; "stop the world. The conquering hero is back. Hail him." "Ignore her," Charlie said to Frank. "Out doing heroic deeds?" Madge asked Frank. "What is she talking about?" I asked from the safety of Charlie's encircling arm. "Didn't you tell her?" Madge asked Frank; "didn't you tell her how you rescued that poor girl from the burning building? *I* know you wouldn't have gone through fire for a man or even a boy, not even for a poor, innocent baby, but a pretty girl in a burning building, naturally you were heroic. I guess the Huggins family is still grateful to you. I guess the Huggins girl is still on fire about it, isn't she?" Madge asked. "Madge," said Charlie, "shut up. If you don't shut up, I'm taking you to the Inn and you can explain why you had to pay so much for board when you get back home." "All I did was congratulate him," Madge said; "I never did congratulate Frank properly. It was in all the Quebec papers. They said he stepped out right through a wall of flame." "Madge," said Charlie; "I'm not telling you again. Cut it."

The world had stopped. People were moving in flickering light. When they spoke, their voices crackled. I pulled away from Charlie and turned to Frank. "I saw the fire," I said in a hoarse voice. No one said anything. "I saw it from the sleigh. I saw you carry the girl out through the window." "Lucky girl," said Madge. Out of the corner of my eye, I saw Charlie go over to his sister and jerk her to her feet. Then he dragged her out of the room. I could hear them arguing in the office, but I couldn't hear what they were saying. I heard the blood in my ears, roaring. "I saw you," I said to Frank; "on the way to Montpelier. On my first night here." Frank looked quickly at me and then looked away. He was embarrassed.

"It was nothing big," he said; "I didn't think. I heard someone crying and I went in. If I'd thought it over, I wouldn't have done it. The papers made too much of it." The walls of the room spun away from us and out into space. The ceiling floated weightlessly above us. The wind ripped through the room in which we stood. There was no one in the world but the two of us. "I saw your stone," I said; "the mother and child." He waited to see what I would say next. I couldn't take my eyes from his face. His eyes were slightly slanted, almost oriental. His nose was long and straight and his mouth was sharply defined and beautifully shaped. For the first time, I saw how his lips always seemed to be slightly pursed, how his cheeks always appeared to be sucked in as if he were considering something inadequate or displeasing in the world. He had a distinguished look, a superior, even arrogant air about him. He looked like an artist, I thought, or something created by an artist. His moustache was precisely cut to fit the curve of his mouth, and above his thin, arching eyebrows his dark hair was combed back from his high forehead in precise waves. I could not remember seeing it tousled or falling into his eyes, as Charlie's always did. I knew I was staring shamelessly.

"I saw your stone," I said again; "I've never seen anything so beautiful." "It's for the Huggins family," he said. He was watching me, puzzled. "Three of their children died in the fire," he said; "I didn't save them all." "No one could have expected you to," I said. He watched me quietly. My eyes refused to move from his face. I saw that, even when he was angry and upset—and now he was both—his face was still pale. Even in the height of summer, he was pale. "I think," Frank said, unbuttoning his coat, "I ought to go help Charlie out." The voices from the office were louder and louder. Frank put his coat across the back of the chair. I was surprised by the width of his shoulders, by the narrowness of his waist. He looked at me with curiosity and annoyance. He didn't like being stared at, but he didn't know why I was staring at him. "She's very rude," I said weakly. I should have recognized him, I thought. I should have realized he was the man in the fire. "Madge?" he said; "I guess she has her reasons." He went out into the office and I heard his voice join theirs. For a while, their voices grew louder. I moved toward the chair and touched his coat gently. I rested my hand on the coat's shoulder as if someone were inside it. Then I heard someone crying, and Charlie, exasperated, saying, "I told you so, Madge. Goddamn, it always ends this way!" And then it was quiet.

Polly came back into the dining room. "Well, that's over," she said, sinking down into a chair; "that sister of his is a little beast, isn't she?" I said she was certainly rude enough. "Rude!" exclaimed Polly; "my, aren't we being charitable today!" I said I thought Madge had beautiful clothes. "Oh, when are you going to grow up?" Polly burst out; "can't you see she's been up nights for weeks making clothes to impress us with when she got here? Well, not us. She wants to impress Frank. You can bet she doesn't dress herself up like the prize hen in the roost just for her husband." In the morning, I thought, I would go to the dry goods store and buy several lengths of new fabrics, and I would look at the fashion books and see which designs I wanted to copy. Mrs. James didn't expect me back for days. "Oh, I see," Polly said; "Frank's caught ahold of you at last." "Frank?" I asked, as if I didn't know who he was. Polly shook her head. "He's only rescued one girl," said Polly; "the others are more like Madge. Do you know what I mean?" she asked. I said I did. But I didn't care what she meant. I could see him in front of me, his body turned away from me, the fire behind him. I could see him pull free of the smoke and come toward me, the flames close behind him. That night, I had been upset because I couldn't see his face, because I might never know who he was. I knew who he was now.

And when he came back in, Charlie seemed to know that something had changed. "My sister's stuck in my bed," he said. "I tied the door shut," he said without a smile. "Tied it shut?" I echoed. "I don't want her going into Frank's room and raising the roof," he said. He seemed to be avoiding my eyes. I know I wasn't looking directly at him. "They weren't supposed to be here at the same time," he said apologetically. He looked over at Frank's jacket. "He's a good musician, too," he said. He asked me about my trip home, and I told him it had been terrible and I was glad to be back. He regarded me sadly, as if, were he not in control of himself, he would have something less pleasant to say. He looked at me as if he no longer believed a word I said. "I think," Polly said, watching us, "that we all ought to go to bed. Everyone has to work in the morning." I would, I decided, go back to work in the morning, but first I would buy fabric and take it with me to Mrs. James's. Charlie, when he kissed me goodnight, kissed me formally on the top of the head, as if I were someone else's wife.

23

The next morning, I woke early. The room was still dark, and behind me, the livery stable was quiet. I breathed in the pungent odors of the horses and the hay. I felt as if I had awakened in a different world. I turned over on my back and thought over the events of the night before. I looked up at the ceiling fearfully, as if I expected my mother's face to materialize there. When it didn't, I felt both relief and disappointment. I looked at the dark blue square of the window. Lately, all my emotions seemed double-edged.

I got up, washed my face, and sat down in front of the mirror. I began brushing my hair, but when it came time to braid it up, I rebelled. It was time to wear my hair differently. I brushed all the hair into a tail which I held straight up over my head. I slid my hand up and down the rope of hair, studying the different ways my hair fell into a cap-shaped wave around my face. Finally, I had what I wanted. But I could not pin it up yet. First I had to braid the rest of it. I pinned the braids in a coil on top of the waved cap of hair. I looked just like the most sophisticated girls at Mrs. James's. I took a handful of steel hairpins and thrust them into my hair. I would not look sophisticated if it all came tumbling down in the middle of breakfast or when I was walking on the street. Then I surveyed my clothes. I had nothing respectable to wear. I would need four or five new dresses. I took out my beige lawn dress and laid it across the bed. Then I looked at my watch. It was only five o'clock.

I lay down on my bed. I was looking at the door, wondering when I would begin to hear footsteps, and I saw the handle turn. Then the door opened and Madge was in the doorway. Without thinking, I asked her how she had gotten out. "My fruit knife," she said, reaching into her pocket and showing it to me. "It's preposterous of him to lock up his own sister. Don't you think so?'' I sat up. I didn't want to lie on my bed while a madwoman armed with a fruit knife was loose in my room.

"Don't worry," Madge said, watching me, "I'm not crazy. Not anymore, anyway." She sat down in the chair opposite the bed and looked me over. "You are beautiful," she said. I waited. "You've heard that before?" she asked. "Many times," I said. "Who is Frank going about with now?" she asked bluntly. I said I didn't know. "You must," she said; "you're always with Charlie and Charlie's always with him." I said that they hadn't been together very much lately. "You're getting in the way, are you?" she asked; "good for you. You *must* know," she insisted, her tone threatening. "I really don't know what Frank does or who he sees," I said; "I didn't even know he was the man in the fire until you said something about it. Why do you want to know?' "To get even," she said. "For what?" "Do I have to tell you?" she asked. "Yes," I said; "I think you do."

But just then my door opened again. Charlie strode in and hauled his sister out of the chair. "All right, Madge, that about does it," he said; "I'm putting you on the train." "You. don't have to worry," she said, smiling strangely; "she didn't tell me anything. She said she didn't know." "She doesn't know," he said. "Why won't you let me make him miserable?" Madge asked him; "he deserves it. You know he does." "He's miserable enough already," Charlie said; "he doesn't need your help." "He's not miserable," Madge said; "he doesn't know what misery is." "He doesn't know what happiness is, either," Charlie said, "but you don't let that trouble you." "You didn't know how mean my brother was, did you?" Madge said to me. "Charlie is not mean," I said. "If you don't walk through the door," Charlie told her, "I'll push you through it. If you don't pack up and get on the train quietly, I'll tie you up like a heifer and put you in the baggage compartment." "Madge," I said, "go with him." "We'll see you at breakfast," Charlie said. He steered his sister out of the room, glaring at her.

I lay back down. Frank was evidently busier than a butterfly in spring. But from the beginning, Charlie had insisted Frank was not happy, and now that I was thinking about Frank, I did not believe he was happy either. Of course, if he constantly discovered women like Madge it was no wonder that he wasn't happy. I thought about the night of the fire and how I had seen Frank lean back into the flames and then lean forward, carrying something in his arms. That night, although I could not see his face, although I had no way of knowing whether he was twenty years old or seventy, I was sure that the fabric of this life had ripped neatly to reveal the perfect world for which I was always looking, and that he was the perfect man for whom I had been looking, the man who could step through the doorway from this world to the other one, the man who could walk through the fire and come out unscathed. It was as if the man for whom I was fated had appeared to me in a vision. And now I thought the same thing. When I closed my eyes, I saw Frank's face in front of me and I wanted to reach out and touch him anywhere: on his eyelid, his nose, the inside of his wrist, the arch of his foot.

There had to be another person who fit you perfectly so that the two of you together formed one whole. I thought about Madge and wondered if she had ever believed that she and Frank were created for one another, and I decided that she could never have let herself believe such an outlandish thing. She was vindictive, vulgar; she wanted to hurt him. I couldn't imagine hurting him. Just thinking about it made my eyes fill with tears. I would fight the world to keep it from hurting him. A man who could carve as he did! A man like that was capable of enormous love. I wanted that love. If necessary, I thought, I would *teach* him to love me.

I drifted in and out of sleep, but whenever I woke up, I was obsessed by the same problem. Even though Frank and I lived in the same house, we rarely saw each other except at breakfast and supper, and then we were surrounded by at least ten other people, one of whom was Frank's best friend and the man everyone thought I would eventually marry. What would I do about Charlie? In spite of everything, he and Frank were really very loyal to one another. I remembered, uneasily, how Charlie had once knocked down another stoneworker because the man had said something about Frank's mother. When I asked him why he was defending Frank, he said he wasn't defending Frank; he was defending Frank's mother. Poor Charlie, I thought. In the end, I knew he would decide that however things worked out, they had worked out for the best. It wouldn't take him long to find someone else. But how was I to get Frank alone? Running into him at work was hardly practical since he worked in the quarries, and no matter how I tried, I could think of no excuse for arriving there out of the blue. Of course, I thought, if Charlie's sister died, I could take the message to him and then I would see Frank, but Charlie's sister looked healthier than I did and it was unlikely that I would receive any important news first since I spent the day sewing at Mrs. James's. I decided to go down to breakfast late because Frank usually came in after Charlie and I had already begun eating; perhaps I would bump into him on the stairs.

But I didn't. When I walked into the dining room in my bright summer dress, with my hair done up differently, everyone in the room stopped to look at me. They were all half-finished with breakfast. But Frank was not there and neither was Charlie. "You're late," Polly said; "I saved you half." She pushed the plate over to me. "Where are they?" I asked her. "Oh, you missed it," she said; "Charlie dragged Madge off by main force. She said she was coming in here to eat some breakfast. Frank said her husband would be anxious to get her back, and she started shouting at him, she said he better not mention her husband, he'd never be as good as a hair on her husband's head, and Charlie, he asked Frank to help him get Madge to the station. I must say she went quietly once she heard Frank was going along too." "Someone should take their breakfasts out to them," I said; "they didn't have anything to eat. I could do it myself." "To Barre?" Polly said; "don't be ridiculous. They won't starve to death. You wouldn't want to go out there just to see Frank?" "Of course not," I said. "Can't you let Frank be?" she asked me softly. "I don't go near him," I said.

Frank's room was on the second floor near the front of the house. Next to his room were the linen closets. If I knew when Frank was coming in or going out, I could go to the closets for an extra towel and run into him in the hall. Everyone would think that was why I was there: to get another sheet or towel. "What are you thinking about?" Polly asked me. "About Charlie's sister. She's completely crazy," I said. "Not completely," said Polly; "before she got married, she used to go around with Frank. I don't know why she's still so mad at him unless—" She flushed. "Unless what?" I asked. "Unless nothing," she said. "You don't think I can interest him, do you?" I asked. "I don't see why you'd want to," she said. "He's very talented," I said. "So is the man who does the bird imitations at the county fair," she said. "He's not happy," I said. "If you want to make people happy, you should talk to Eddie," she said; "they need new people at the asylum." "I can't think of anything more worthwhile than making someone happy, especially if you're the only one who can," I said. Especially, I added mentally, if the person you're making happy is like no one else on earth. "I can see there's going to be no talking to you," said Polly. She put down her fork and inspected me. "Nothing," she said slowly and with emphasis, "is going to make Frank happy. Nothing. If God created another world just for him, he wouldn't be happy in it." "I don't know why you're so against him," I said. "Let's go to work," Polly said.

As we walked along, I told her about my plans to sew four or five new dresses and she sighed and shook her head. "It would be simpler to go to the general store and buy a bear trap and set it out in front of Frank's door," she said. "The dresses," I said, "are for me, not for him." "Oh, please," Polly said. I waited until she crossed the bridge to the factory, and then turned back into town, but when I got to the Emporium and was standing before the bolts of cloth, I didn't know what to do. I didn't know what kind of dresses Frank liked. I had no idea what patterns or colors would both suit me and please him. I picked up bolt after bolt, holding them up against me and looking at myself in the mirror, imagining myself as Frank would see me, imagining him watching me as I moved from the mirror to the counter and back again. "This is a pretty pattern," said the salesman; "all the lawyers' wives seem to like it." I looked down at the light blue watered silk. I had never liked blue, but I thought Frank did. I had heard him telling an old woman at the house that her blue dress suited her wonderfully. In the end, I took all the salesman's suggestions and bought enough material for six dresses. And then a display of hats caught my eye and I stopped.

When I finally left, I was carrying three packages of yard goods and a red and white striped hatbox. "Can you manage, miss?" the salesman asked me, and I said I could, and I backed out of the door and promptly collided with someone. "I'm sorry," I said without looking up, trying to keep ahold of my packages. "Why don't you just hand some of them to me," the man said, and I looked up, and there was Frank grinning down at me. "You're supposed to be at work!" I exclaimed. "So are you," he said. "Well," I said, blushing, "I have to take these packages back to the house and then I'm going to work." "Are you going to let me carry them or not?" Frank asked. He was laughing at me. I felt my cheeks burning. "Here," I said, handing him one package, and as I gave it to him, the two beneath it slipped out of my hands and fell to the ground. "You give me all the packages and you carry the hatbox," he said.

"I didn't see you at breakfast," I said stupidly. My hand, where he had touched it, tingled as if needles were pricking it. My breasts felt swollen against the cloth of my chemise. Little beads of sweat covered my forehead. Silently, I thanked God for clothing, which covered everything. At that instant, I would have liked to cover my face as well. I was sure everything I thought was reflected there for Frank to see. "Well," said Frank, "Charlie and I went to see his sister off." "Was she," I asked, "calmer?" "No, I wouldn't say she was any calmer," said Frank. "Did you really grow up with Charlie?" I asked him. I wanted to listen to his voice forever. He spoke with a slightly unfamiliar accent; it was like Charlie's, but different. I had never noticed it before. "With Charlie and his sister. We all went to the same school." "She came in to see me this morning," I said. Frank stopped walking. "Did she?" he asked. "She wanted to know what girl you walked out with," I said. I didn't dare look at him. "I told her I didn't know." "When I was three, I asked Madge to marry me," Frank said; "I should have stopped right there. She still thinks she owns me." I nodded. "I'm sorry she bothered you," Frank said; "you're too young to understand girls like Madge." "I'm not so young!" I protested, insulted. Now he was smiling at me. "I'd like to see your carving again," I said boldly. "Well," he said, "ask Charlie to bring you down on the cars. Bring a cloth to cover your mouth. That dust is punishing." "I remember the dust," I said; "if you wait for me, I'll walk along to the cars with you." "Oh, no," said Frank; "don't bother. I've got another stop to make. I'll tell Charlie I saw you." I wanted to throw the hatbox down on the ground, to stamp my foot, to burst into tears, to kick him in the knee, but I smiled pleasantly and thanked him for his help.

When I got into my room, I hurled everything on the floor, flung myself on the bed and burst into tears of rage. He didn't even see me! He thought of me as a little sister, or worse, as Charlie's girl. What could I do? I thought of waiting outside his room some night with a sad tale, but if I concocted a sad enough story, Frank would go get Charlie. And then it occurred to me that if I went to work, one of the girls there might know something about Frank, and the next thing I knew, I was running down Chapin Street as if someone were chasing me.

I went up the stairs slowly, and paused at the window on the landing and looked down the street. Perhaps I might catch a glimpse of Frank. But the street was empty. I went on up to the work floor. On the second floor of the house, Mrs. James had knocked down all the walls so that the second story was one enormous room bisected by the wide stairs leading up to it. At one end of the room were the ten-foot-long cutting tables. Two of the girls, who had worked there for some time, were cutters, and they often cut out fifteen dresses at once. Every time I saw them cut through so many widths of material at once, my blood went cold. If they should make a mistake, they would work for weeks to repay Mrs. James for the damage they had done.

I stood in the doorway, watching the sixteen other girls, their heads bent over yards of dark cloth. Everyone's hair was tightly bound up; it was too much trouble to keep track of one's hair and all the threads of the fabric at the same time. Each girl sat next to a long bench which was narrow at one end and equipped with tall wooden pegs which held our large cones of sewing threads and our scissors. In front of the pegs a little trough was hollowed out for our pins and needles. The lower half of the bench broadened out into a small cutting bench which we could use as a pressing board or a cutting board of our own. The light, which came from the windows of the side walls, was never good, and many of the girls wore spectacles which slid lower and lower on their noses as the day went on. Some of the girls wore clip-on spectacles which held on to the bridge of their nose because, they said, these did not give them headaches. They were forever taking them off and massaging their noses. The spectacles left bright red marks which took some time to go away. They told me that I would have to get glasses sooner or later. Everyone did. It was doing such close work in such dim light.

Toward noon, as the light brightened, the girls began to look up and begin talking, but dinner pails did not appear until three, when the light began to fade. Few of us wanted to eat more than we wanted light to work by. In winter, we ate earlier because it grew darker earlier; in summer, the girls who brought their pails often did not open them until supper and they were not unhappy to do so because they not only got more work done, but had one less meal to pay for. None of them had much money. When I came in, the light was brilliant and so the girls were silent. I sat down next to my bench and waited for Mrs. James. Someone had picked up and finished the dress I had been working on the week before. Mrs. James came over with a bolt of black silk and handed me the pattern for a skirt and a shirtwaist with leg-of-mutton sleeves. There were intricacies to the collar which she wanted to explain to me. I was surprised at how impatiently I listened. I had my own plans for the afternoon, and the collar was the least important part of them.

"Did you hear a word she said?" asked Florence, the girl who sat next to me. I shook my head. "We heard your mother was sick," she said. "She died," I told her. "Oh, well, no wonder," said Florence; "when you get up to the collar, I'll show you. It's really hard. We spent the last two days ripping them out and doing them over. I could do them in my sleep now." I got up and spread out the heavy fabric and pinned the stiff paper pattern to it. "What *are* you doing?" Florence asked me, covering my hand with hers. "Look," she said, "you didn't lay out the fabric right. The two good sides should be on top of each other." I looked down at my bench and shook my head. "I'll do it," Florence said; "you work on my lining. Here," she said, a few minutes later, dropping the cut-out pieces in my lap and taking back the waist on which she was working.

"I guess your mind isn't back yet," she said. "I've been thinking about how I should go to church more," I said, without looking up from the cloth; "what church do you go to?" "The Congregational," she said; "what church did you go to at home?" "The Congregational," I said. I heard tin pails beginning to click open. I let my work fall into my lap and looked up. "We had quite a rumpus at my house last night," I said. I waited until I saw the girls near us prick up their ears. "My friend's sister was staying at the house and she had the worst quarrel with Frank Holt you ever saw. I never saw anyone carry on like that. Her brother had to tie her up in her room." "Who's her brother?" asked Florence. "Charlie Mondell," I said. "Your Charlie?" she asked me. "Yes, my Charlie," I said with a sigh. Evidently, she didn't know Frank.

"I know Frank Holt," one of the girls said; "he goes to the church I go to." "What church do you go to?" I asked. I was sure she wouldn't answer me; I was sure she and everyone else would see I was too interested. "Oh, the Methodist," the girl said; "do you know Frank?" "He lives in the same house I do," I said; "he's a good friend of the man I go about with." "You wouldn't think Frank Holt would be beating down the church doors," the girl went on, "but there he is, every Sunday. Sometimes he comes with a girl, but usually he doesn't. He's not bad looking." "He looks foreign," said the girl next to her, without looking up. "I like the looks of Charlie Mondell better," she said; "he came to church with Frank last week. Who was he sitting with?" she asked the girl next to her. "Charlie? He was sitting with Carrie Holcomb. He used to go around with her, remember?" "Carrie Holcomb?" asked the first girl; "the same one who used to work here? I didn't know she ever went around with Charlie Mondell." "Well, I haven't seen him with her for a long time, not since last winter. That's about when he took up with Agnes.''

"Gossip, gossip," said Mrs. James, passing through the room; "gossip takes the food out of hungry mouths." "That woman," said Florence, as Mrs. James swept past us; "she's always on her way to her favorite entertainment. An execution."

"Florence," I said, "who's this Carrie Holcomb?" Florence regarded me over her sandwich. "She's just someone Charlie used to go around with." "How much did he go around with her?" "Quite a lot," she said, getting up and brushing the crumbs from her skirt. "Quite a lot," I repeated; "and now he's going around with her again." "He sat with her at church, that's all. That one over there," she said, indicating a girl on the other side of the room; "she's a troublemaker." "Who's a trouble-maker?" the girl asked; "I see Frank at church every week, that's all. Last week, he was there with Charlie." "You didn't have to tell her," said Florence; "not about Carrie." "There's nothing to tell about Carrie," said the other girl; "I ought to know. After she saw Charlie, she spent the afternoon crying on her bed."

"Who does Frank go to church with?" I asked. "Don't ask her anything else," Florence whispered to me. "Jane Holt," said the other girl; "sometimes I see them walking."

"Who's Jane Holt?" I asked. "Don't ask her anything!" Florence hissed at me. "No one special," said the other girl; "she's not even as pretty as I am. She's sure not as pretty as you are. But she's rich. She comes from one of the old Montpelier families. Her grandfather was a senator. Her father owns the big dry goods store. The Emporium." I thought of my packages waiting for me at the boardinghouse. I had been shopping in her father's store. "What's she like?" I asked. "Why are you so interested?" the girl asked me. "I told you not to ask her anything," Florence whispered; "she'll make something out of anything you say and tomorrow she'll be retailing it all over Montpelier." "I like Frank," I said; "he's my friend, too." "He doesn't have lady *friends*," the other girl said sarcastically. "Why do you always sound as if you know what you're talking about," asked Florence, "when we all know your head is as empty as a watering can." "Don't start fighting, girls," said Mrs. James, sweeping back through the room. "Don't pay any attention to her," Florence whispered to me. "Carrie Holcomb," I said. "Forget about it," said Florence; "she wanted to bother you." "She didn't bother me," I said.

188

In the weeks that followed, as the light, which was still brilliant, grew thinner, as the nights fell earlier and grew colder, I went out walking with Charlie after supper. I went obediently and out of duty and because I did not dare return to the loneliness in which I had lived before I met him. But a new light washed the world clean for me, and there were times when I thought I was somehow seeing the world through Frank's eyes, not my own. Wherever I was, I imagined what he would say if he were there. I saw his face as he looked out over the fields steeping in the inky light. All day, as I sewed at Mrs. James's, I was really at the Barre quarries watching Frank work on his carving of the mother and child. When he was thirsty, I took the pail down to the pump, filled it, and brought it back up to him. In that other life, into which I was moving more and more, Charlie did not exist at all. I wondered how Charlie put up with me as I now was, one foot in the world in which we walked, one foot in another. And in that second world, I was always with Frank. Regardless of where Charlie and I went, I was walking through the Barre quarries with Frank. When Charlie said something to me and I looked at him blankly, he patiently repeated what he had said. I knew he thought I was still upset, that I had yet to recover from my mother's death. And as he talked, I thought how ludicrous life sometimes was.

I had been in love with Frank for six weeks, praying that he would fall ill so that I could nurse him, coming down to breakfast late hoping to meet him on the stairs, chewing my potatoes forever because when he sat across from me I was barely able to swallow, staying up until all hours of the night, sewing by the light of the kerosene lamp in my room so that I could wear my new dresses to breakfast, getting up early so that I could arrange and rearrange my hair because a new hairstyle might catch his eye, and all this time Frank did not have the slightest idea that I cared whether he lived or died. As far as he was concerned, I was in love with Charlie, and Charlie, whom I did not love, commented enthusiastically, even passionately, on each new swirl of my hair, on each new pattern I stitched into the dresses I wore to breakfast and supper. My silences made him solicitous of me. But I didn't want to be made happy; I wanted to make Frank happy.

On the first Sunday in October, Charlie decided to hire two horses and ride out into the country for a picnic. The leaves were radiant in the light, and the cool, sweet air touched the skin, exhilarating and chilly. The sky had taken on the faint green cast of an autumn day. We rode until we passed an overgrown meadow which must once have been part of an apple orchard. In the center, one of the trees, enormously old, had already lost all of its leaves, and its small, wrinkled apples hung from its branches like little gold balls. Blackbirds swooped down into the tree, cawing loudly. They flew in wide, eccentric circles and I realized that the birds were drunk. They had been eating from the apples hanging on the tree, and the apples had fermented right on the branches, and I thought how much like one of those birds I was, flying through the air in a strange new light, mesmerized by a perfectly ordinary tree which had, suddenly, become something wonderful beyond the limits of this world. But the part of my mind which saw this had no influence over the rest of me, which reeled in the sky with stupefaction and delight.

We spread out a blanket I had brought back with me from home and I began to unpack the hamper from Mrs. Trowbridge's house. The air was filled with the tolling of church bells. I looked at the sun. It was almost one o'clock. "Why are the bells ringing?" I asked Charlie; "services are over." "Someone must have died. They toll the bell once for a death, and then it tolls once for every year of the person's life," he said. He tilted his head to one side, listening. "It's the Baptist Church," he said; "I can tell the bells apart." "I've been thinking of going to church more often," I said. "I didn't think you had much religious feeling," he said. "Why should you think that?" I asked; "because I let you touch me?" I heard my voice; it was angry. "No," he said; "of course not." "Then why shouldn't I have religious feeling?" I asked him; "I do. I just haven't been going to church." Charlie looked at me oddly. "That's really what I meant," he said; "some people are religious in a daily way. It's part of their routine, that's all. They don't have to go to church." "I suppose," I said, "that someone who goes to church is better than I am. Whether or not they appreciate the world God created for them. It doesn't matter whether or not they see the beauty in things or love other creatures in the world." "I don't know why you're going on about this," Charlie said, frowning; "I'm not full of religious feeling myself. I go to church because I've always gone to church." "What value is there in that?" I asked; "what value is there in going out of habit?" "Do you really want to know, or do you want to argue with me?" Charlie asked me. "I really want to know," I said. "The value is in doing the usual things. In going back to what you know. It makes you feel safe." "Like a child with a toy," I said. "Something like that," Charlie said, staring down at the grass. His voice was strained.

"Surely," I persisted, "there's more to it than that. There must be people there you see who you care about. Or is that part of going back to the usual things?" "It is," said Charlie. "Who is Carrie Holcomb?" I asked him; "is she one of the usual people?" "What's going on here, Agnes?" he asked me, his cheeks flushing. "I just happened to hear that you went to church with Carrie Holcomb every week," I said. "Well, I don't," Charlie said; "drop it." "You did that week I went home to North Chittendon," I said. "Either you're asking people about me," said Charlie, "or the girls you work with are talking." "But it's true, isn't it?" I said. "If she's there, I sit with her," said Charlie. "If you're getting tired of me," I said, "you ought to tell me." Charlie regarded me suspiciously. "What are you up to, Agnes?" he said. "What am *I* up to?" I asked him; "apparently, you and Carrie Holcomb were all over the city together before I came here." "I don't understand what that has to do with you," he said. "It has something to do with me if you're still seeing her." "I'm not still seeing her!" he burst out; "we go to the same church!"

"I can't trust you anymore," I said sadly. "Look, Agnes," he said, "I used to care for Carrie Holcomb. I don't anymore. I didn't ask you for a list of all the men you took to before I met you." "There weren't any men before I met you," I said. "What are you up to?" he asked me again. "Did you make love to her?" His face darkened. "I don't see that you have a right to ask that question. She's nothing to you. Her life is none of your affair." "You did make love to her!" I cried; "if you hadn't, you'd tell me straight out." "No, I wouldn't!" he said; "a man doesn't talk about one woman to another. It's not right. You shouldn't ask me." We sat in silence, staring out over the hills. "I think," I said at last, "that it would be better for all of us if we didn't see so much of each other." "All of us?" he echoed. "You and me and Carrie," I said. "Carrie has nothing to do with us!" he shouted. "I don't see it that way," I said. I looked straight ahead. I could feel him studying me.

"You're not worried about Carrie Holcomb," he said slowly; "you know I don't care about her or anyone else. You're just looking for an excuse." "An excuse for what?" I asked. "An excuse to bring this to an end," he said; "well, you don't need an excuse. If you want to call things quits, that's up to you." "I'm not the one who started going around with someone else!"

I cried. "Go ahead," he said, "talk yourself into it. Tell yourself it's my fault." "It is!" "My sister told me you were after Frank," he said. "Your sister," I repeated, hoping he would not notice the goose bumps that had suddenly appeared on my skin, "was not exactly reasonable while she was here." "When it comes to Frank," Charlie said, "she has a sixth sense." "What does Frank have to do with this?" I asked, turning on him; "you're just trying to get the subject away from Carrie Holcomb." "I don't want to talk about this anymore," Charlie said. "Why?" I asked; "because it's true?" He looked at me and then up at the sky. "Let's go home," he said. "Why?" I asked; "it's still early." "There are some things I want to do," he said. "What things?" I asked.

"Look, Agnes," he said, "if you're doing this because of Frank, think again. You don't belong with him. You'll never understand him and he'll never understand you. You met my sister. She's a perfectly calm person when she's not around Frank. You saw what she was like here. He did that. He didn't do it on purpose, either. She knows that. That's why she's so bitter. She says she dug the pit she fell into all by herself."

"Maybe he didn't love her," I said. "He didn't love her and he doesn't love her now," said Charlie, "and he doesn't love you now and he won't love you later because he can't love anyone." "I don't believe that," I said. "I was right," Charlie said; "it is Frank you want after all." "No," I said; "I just don't believe he can't love anything. I told you before. He hasn't met the right person." Charlie looked up into the hills above us. "They say mountain lions love each other," he said, "but I wouldn't want one of them falling for me." I said nothing. The gold dome of the courthouse was coming into view. "I've been wanting to move closer to the cars anyway," Charlie said. He saw the panic which contorted my face. "Don't worry," he said bitterly; "you can always come talk to me when you have trouble." "Don't move away," I whispered. "I'm not going to stay there and watch you and Frank, if that's what you have in mind," he said. "You won't have to," I told him; "Frank's not interested in me." "Not yet," he said in the same bitter voice; "but you haven't started in yet, have you? And I haven't told him you're not my girl anymore. That's what you want me to tell him, isn't it?" I turned scarlet, but I did not contradict him, and we rode into town without exchanging a word.

That night when Polly came into my room I told her nothing about the argument I had with Charlie on Bald Hill. She asked me how Charlie was, and I said he was fine, and she wanted to know if we would like to go on a picnic with them the next weekend. I said I wasn't sure. Well, then, she asked me, what about walking out together tomorrow night after supper? I said I'd been working long hours at Mrs. James's and Charlie was pretty worn out, too.

I felt as if a world, a very good world, were coming to an end. I was almost seventeen and I had spent the happiest days of my life in Montpelier, in this room, and with Charlie Mondell. On the one hand, I was not in a hurry to sever his life from mine; on the other, I saw the story of our lives together as a page to which I wanted to touch a match. And when I did, I would watch it flare into light as it never had in life, and then it would settle as gently as tissue-thin bits of ash. I might never be as happy again. I had never been as happy before. Still, Charlie was not who I wanted. I said nothing to Polly because I knew that in the morning Charlie would tell everyone at the table that he was planning on moving away and she would know why immediately.

But the next morning Charlie said nothing about leaving Iris Trowbridge's. He joked with Polly and Frank, but when he turned to me, he was strained and his eyes were stunned. Confused, Polly examined all of us and then asked if we wouldn't like to walk through town with Eddie and her when he came for her that night. Charlie said he thought we all ought to go and asked Frank what time he would like to meet. Frank seemed slightly surprised to find himself included in our plans, but fell to considering and said that eight o'clock would be just about right. And so, for four weeks, the five of us were inseparable. I saw what the trouble was. Charlie, who was always such a realist, was unable to act on, or perhaps to believe, his own conclusions. I saw how things were, and my heart twisted. But I could not really feel sorry for him because I could not believe that he would really be unhappy to lose me. In the face of all the evidence. I denied the strength of his attachment to me. And my own view of things was, of course, distorted.

When the five of us walked, I watched Frank out of the corner of my eye. If Charlie bent down to pick up a rock and I found myself next to Frank, I felt as if I were filled with heat and light and I would not have been surprised if, had I held my hand up to the sky, it glowed in the dark. Everyone joked about how clumsy I had become, when before I was surefooted as a goat, but I was not clumsy at all. I was forever watching Frank out of the corner of my eye and hence I failed to see the rocks and hollows that appeared in the road in front of me. I watched his profile, aloof and lonely, and it seemed to me that wherever Frank was, the currents were fast and dangerous and he would soon be swept back by them. And so I would talk to him, or try to. I wanted him to hold on to me as a drowning man holds on to a rope thrown to him. I wanted him to know that, no matter how dark and empty the world was, I was in it and I would not leave.

"Look at the moon," I said to Frank; "it looks like someone's been carving it." "Chewing on it is more likely," he said. All of us seemed to wander down the road, but we wandered purposefully. Except Frank. He always seemed adrift. I was always afraid that, if he went into the woods, he would not come back again. On some nights, I thought the danger of the woods drew him in; on others, I thought he wandered from the road and into the darkness looking for something like oblivion, anonymity. And one night, I knew that he found himself an intolerable burden, and that in the woods he lost himself. I thought this was a very important and very remarkable thing to know, but I could not tell Polly because I knew what she would say. She would say that Frank was right and that he *was* intolerably burdensome. But that was not what I meant.

Charlie would understand what I meant, but I knew better than to speak to him about Frank. I knew I was cruel in letting the walks go on as if nothing had changed. I knew it would be up to me to put an end to them. But I did not know how. I told myself that I had no opportunity to change our routine, but the truth was that I was afraid of change. I was afraid that, if Charlie decided to remove, Frank, who would have no idea he was the source of the upheaval, would decide to go along with his friend and then they would both be gone. So I waited, and so the five of us drifted, first under the falling leaves, and later, under the bare branches of the trees and the first powdery snow.

Then, Florence asked me to come home with her one night after work. She and her sister lived in a large loft in one of the factory rooming houses and I was to teach her sister some new stitches and her sister was to teach me how to embroider grapes so that they looked as if they were carved, not embroidered, on the fabric. We made a supper out of crackers and dried beef and I was walking home when I heard someone call me. "You're out late," Frank said, catching up with me. "Not very," I said. He asked me if I thought it would snow again tomorrow. "Oh, no," I said; "it won't." He said that I sounded awfully sure, and I stopped and turned to him and said that as far as I knew, I had never been wrong about the weather. "That's a useful talent," Frank said; "there aren't many running in my family, although they say my mother's side has a talent for fits." "Fits," I said; "they said I had a fit when I was a child. Someone put chicken feathers down my back and told me a dead man was trying to get me." "Children are beasts," said Frank. "Don't you like them?" I asked. "They're all right," he said. "Does your sister have any children?" I asked. "How did you know I had a sister?" he asked. I said that Charlie had told me. "She's got three," Frank said; "she'll never get off the farm now." "Does she want to?" I asked him. "*I* wanted her to," he said in a tone I had come to know. "You must miss her," I said. "I do," he said.

I asked him how he came to be a stone carver. "My father was a stone carver," he said; "he taught me. I started out whittling things from wood. Then I just went on to stone. He didn't want me coming to the quarries. He had to leave soon enough because of his lungs. That's how he got into farming in Canada. Now he can't do much but wheeze, but he's got my two brothers there to help him. He does all right." He looked at me, surprised. "You didn't ask me about my father, did you?" he said. "No, I asked you how you came to be a stonecutter," I said. "Oh," said Frank.

"If I were your father," I said suddenly, "I wouldn't be happy about your being here either. You're so much better than this place. I never saw anything as beautiful as that stone you were carving. You could be a real sculptor and your statues could be in museums and parks and the whole world would come to look at them! You could be famous!" "Famous?" said Frank, smiling down at me. "Yes," I said; "you could." "It takes a lot to be famous," said Frank. "But you have a lot," I said. "It takes more than talent, Agnes," Frank said, turning serious; "it takes character." "You have character," I said. "I'm not so sure," he said slowly. "Of course you have character!" I exclaimed. "All of it bad," he said, smiling. "Don't belittle yourself!" I cried. He stopped walking and looked at me, surprised. "How can you believe that?" he said; "you hardly know me. You can't have heard much good about me." "What I've heard doesn't matter," I said; "I know what you're like. I saw the stone." "Oh," he said slowly; "you're taken in by the stone." "Taken in!" I exclaimed. We were passing the town common and the tower bell was beginning to strike the hour.

"Look, Agnes," he said, "come sit down here for a minute. People have a mistaken idea about artists. They think that the artist creates with the best part of himself and he carries that part of himself wherever he goes. Do you understand?" "Of course I understand," I said; "and it's true." "It's not true," Frank said; "some of us can only find that part of ourselves when we're working. The talent doesn't really belong to us any more than a bird belongs to a tree. The bird belongs to the nest of its mother. A talent can come to roost in some very bad people. When I carve, I've got a kind of fever. When I stop carving, I'm like anyone else. It's easy to be romantic about artists, but we're just the same as everyone else." "What nonsense," I said. "Why is it nonsense?" he asked me. He seemed amused.

"Because you could always turn that talent to something else," I said; "you could try carving your life the way you carve stone." "No," he said; "that's nonsense. That's not possible." "But you could try," I insisted. "Why try when you know you're going to fail? Life isn't perfectable. Nothing in life is." "There has to be something!" I whispered. "Why?" Frank asked, looking intently at me; "because you want to believe in perfect things?" "I *know* there are perfect things," I said. "You know more than I do," he said. "Your stone is perfect," I said, flushing to the roots of my hair. "It's not perfect," he said. "Then it's close enough!" I cried, exasperated. "Perfect things last forever," Frank said; "nothing on earth lasts that long." "Mountains," I said, "mountains do." "Nothing man-made lasts that long," Frank said patiently. "Oh, you're wrong!" I cried; "there is a perfect world somewhere behind this one, and when something perfect comes into being in this world, it lasts forever. Somehow or other it does." "Somehow or other?" Frank repeated. "Yes!" I said; "everything isn't destroyed! Unique things aren't destroyed!" "You know that for a fact?" Frank asked me, half-joking, half-serious. "I do," I said. "What does Charlie make of these ideas?" he asked. "Charlie?" I said; "I've never talked to him about this." "Why not?" Frank asked. "It never came up," I said. "It never came up," he repeated, looking at me thoughtfully.

We got up and began walking toward Mrs. Trowbridge's. "What perfect thing do you want to do?" he asked me. "Marry, have children, go about multiplying," I said; "that's what I'm supposed to do, isn't it?" "So they say." "But it's not what I want to do," I said; "at least it's not what I want to do first. *I* want to be famous," I said, shocked at myself. "As what?"

asked Frank. "Not as someone's mother!" I burst out; "children don't last. Not much longer than you do. I want to be famous because I do something that lasts." I stopped and looked at him. "You must think I'm horrible," I said. "Why should I think that?" he asked. "A woman's supposed to want to get married and have children," I said. "Well," he said, "you said you did. Sooner or later." "I don't want to have them at all!" I burst out. "Did you tell that to Charlie?" Frank asked me. "I never thought of it before," I said miserably; "I never realized I'd turned out like this. So different from everyone else. It's terrible to be so different." "It's not terrible and you're not freakish," he said; "just don't marry a man who wants a dozen children." I was crying. "All men want children," I said. Frank took a handkerchief out of his pocket and handed it to me. "No, they don't," he said; "I know I don't. Some men are as different as you are." I cried on.

"Well," said Frank, "you have to be famous at something. What do you want to be famous for?" "As a painter," I said. "Can you paint?" he asked. "I don't know," I said; "I don't think so, but painting runs in the family. All the women in my family were known for their painting. My grandmother painted frescoes and portraits. I've never tried." "Because you're afraid," said Frank. "Of what?" I asked him; "I'm not afraid of failing at it. I'm used to failing at things." "Failing at something isn't hard," said Frank; "it's succeeding that causes the trouble. All of a sudden you have the thing you wanted and it turns out not to be as good as you thought it would be. I go home and my father looks at me and says, 'I could never have been so good if I'd had three pairs of lungs,' and then I feel as if I've stolen something from him." "He must be proud of you," I said. "He'd be happier if he was the one doing the carvings he likes so much," Frank said, his voice tight. "You can't help it," I said; "you didn't ask to be born with more ability." "The irony of it is that he has the persistence to get somewhere. I don't." "You could have it," I said. Once again, he stopped walking and looked down at me. "Do you think so?" he asked me. I said I did. "You know, Agnes," he said, "if you'd like, I could teach you something about drawing and if you liked it, you could go on to painting." "When?" I asked; "when?" "Soon," he said; "I have something to do after suppers for a while, but I'll be back by nine o'clock." "Do I need special paper?" I asked him. "Just get some brown wrapping paper and some charcoal," he said.

When we came up to the Trowbridge house, I knew Charlie was watching us from one of the windows. It was as if I could see him right through the walls. I saw him move through the parlor and out through the front door and then he was standing in front of us. "Have a nice walk?" asked Charlie. "I ran into Frank on the way home from Florence's," I said. Charlie scanned the night sky. "Did Agnes tell you I'm thinking of removing?" he asked Frank; "there's an empty room in the Hinckley house. I've been thinking about it." Frank looked at Charlie and then at me. "No," he said slowly; "no, she didn't say anything about it." "I'm surprised," Charlie said; "we talked about it a long time ago. I asked if there might be a room for you," he told Frank, "but Mrs. Hinckley said she only had one." "I'm happy where I am," said Frank; "I see you all day anyhow." He went inside. "Charlie," I said, "I want to talk to you." "Go to bed, Agnes," he said.

24

That Saturday, Charlie packed up his things and he and Frank carried out the wooden, slatted crates he had borrowed from the market and put them into a small wagon he had rented from the livery. Polly had gone to the asylum to spend the day with Eddie, and I drifted behind them as they carried the boxes out of the house and then went back in for more. I looked into the boxes as they went out and was surprised at how many books Charlie had. Really, I had not been very curious about him. After they started downstairs with the last of the boxes, I stood in Charlie's empty room and found myself touching the wall as if I wanted to pat it or soothe it. Without the books on the shelves, without the paintings on velvet which Charlie's mother and sister so often sent him, the room seemed immense, and as I stood there, it seemed to be growing larger still, until I felt like a small, black dot in the middle of an immense plain of snow.

And then I realized I was lonely. I looked down and saw that I was again dressed in black. I sighed and walked over to the window of Charlie's room. He and Frank were talking and Charlie was holding the horse's reins loosely in his hands. Then they looked back at the house, and the wagon began moving. I wondered what life would be like without him. Why was a room without things in it so cold? I hugged myself closer. I told myself he hadn't really known anything about me, but he had loved me anyway, and so, I reasoned, he really was something of a fool. Or if he was not a fool, he was shallow because he had fallen in love with my face and body. And, I thought, my eyes following the street down which the wagon had disappeared, he had not had my body. The pure, hot contempt I now felt for him warmed me. And then I was crying. I wanted him to come back, not because I loved him, not because I cared for him, but because I was used to him. I hated to part from anything. I went back to my room. I lay down on my bed and felt the blood thudding above my eyes. I wanted to sleep. There was nothing in the world I wanted to look at.

A knock at the door woke me. I sat up in confusion. The room had darkened, and from my window I could see the full, swollen moon. "Come in," I said, expecting to see Polly. My voice was curiously flat. I had not sounded like that since leaving the farm. The door didn't open. "Come in," I said again. I could feel the hand on the door knob, hesitating. "Are you decent?" asked a voice. It was Frank. "Yes," I said. He came in, carrying an awkward, badly tied bundle. "I have something for you," he said; "there's an artist over at Mrs. Hinckley's and he gave me all this paper and some charcoal. The paper doesn't suit him but it should be just fine for you. When he gets his new pastels sent down from Toronto, you can have his old ones" I was speechless. Frank filled my room. He pressed against my lungs, taking away my breath. He was a wall behind which I was sealed. His mouth was at my throat and I could not speak. "You said you wanted to learn drawing," he reminded me. "Yes," I said; "I did." Idiocy had me in its grip. I could neither talk nor move. "How about tomorrow night?" Frank asked. "Tomorrow," I repeated. "Nine o'clock," Frank said; "or is that too late?" "Too late?" I echoed. "No," I said, hearing my voice coming from far away, "that's just fine." "What do you want to draw?" he asked me. "Flowers," I said. "They're good to start with," Frank said; "try it before I get here." I nodded. He smiled slightly and left.

I crept up on my bed until I was sitting on my pillow with my back against the headboard. Who was he, with his hooded eyes and superior look, to come into my room and make me fight for sight and breath? I looked down at my hand, as if to be sure it was there. I knew how the mouse felt when the hawk seized it. It was an enormous thing to be picked up and devoured, to be forced to exist inside the vessels of another body, with one's heart pumping someone else's blood. The room was emptying itself of Frank and returning to me. I was taking myself back. And suddenly, I had a presentiment of what was to come, of the enormous fire which would roar through the house of my body, of the flames that would leap from my eyes and my mouth. I knew I would hear myself saying things I dared not think. I knew the fire would climb the precious, necessary internal walls I had built up as carefully as any drone in a hive. I knew what force the wind would have when the fire burned it and sent it roaring into space, and I didn't know how I would stand against it. But I also knew that I no longer wanted to live in these clean rooms, tindery, dried out by time, these walls like fallen leaves which had dried and crinkled and thinned under the hot, enormously distant sun. I wanted the fire. I was almost seventeen and nothing had happened to me. I had been born expecting something to happen. I had lived all these years knowing that I was set apart from others, but not knowing why. Now I would find out what I had been born for.

And suddenly I didn't want to know. As if it were in my room, I saw the cogs and wheels of my grandmother's enormous clock spinning against the opposite wall. And I saw myself on the wheel, and as it turned, my dress caught in the cogs of a smaller wheel and I saw myself being pulled apart. And then I looked up higher and saw myself rising on the great wheel which turned the moon and the planets in the little sky above the clock face and I was taking my place among the stars. It was glorious there, floating between the planets, watching them turn slowly, seeing, at last, the dark side of the moon. And the music which sifted through everything was like rain entering the hot, dry earth.

And I knew that the great wheel which rose so easily was not what I wanted. I wanted to be torn this way and that. I wanted to suffer terribly and rejoice terribly before I began my climb up the sky. And as I thought that, I saw myself as if from above, in my small, narrow room, in my black dress, cowering at the head of my bed like a trapped animal, and I was flooded with shame. I had no right to such desires. I was too small, too insignificant. I was like my mother. And then the familiar rin in me rebelled and I felt myself turn on life once more. I was not going to be like the porcupine, walking stupidly down the road waiting for someone to club it to death.

I got out my little bottle of ammonia and water and moistened my washcloth and swabbed my dress with it, cleaning it. I looked in the mirror and saw for the thousandth time that I was beautiful. I saw the long shadows my eyelashes cast on my cheek. I saw how gracefully the shadows outlined my cheeks beneath their bones and I shook my head. Oh, it was easy enough to see how a man made his mark in the world, but how did one woman set herself apart from the others? All women married and had children. There was nothing extraordinary in that, no accomplishment one could take pride in personally. At the end of one's life, what did one say: I, animal six trillion and two, have spawned three more of my kind and nourished animal six trillion and thirty-four for all of my years, and if one said that, then God would be pleased. *He* would be pleased, but I would not. Life should do more than spin on like an idiotic top someone had set in motion but could no longer stop. I *never* wanted to go to my rest. There had to be something of oneself that outlasted death. If I was the only monument my poor mother had, then she was damned. She had lived for nothing. I did not want to be a monument to anyone, not even to my grandmother, whom I adored. I looked into the mirror. It was ridiculous, wanting what I wanted. I wanted to transcend my own nature. I was like a cow wishing for wings. I felt my breasts and imagined them heavy with milk. The idea revolted me. I saw the baby as if it were in the room, lying on the bed, and I hated it. I wanted myself for myself. I was not ready to become the caretaker of another living thing which would, like me, eventually turn futile. I wanted Frank. I wanted the fire. I wanted myself. But I was afraid. And so I took my shawl down from the hook and went outside.

I intended to walk until I was too tired to think, until my body grew weary of toying with my mind, and then I would return to my room and sleep. But instead I found myself wandering in the direction of the Hinckley house, and I saw one of the girls from Mrs. James's, and I stopped her and she gave me directions. I turned down Crown Street and stood in front of the Hinckley house as if I wanted to apologize to it for being there. Then I went in. A small, steel-haired woman was sitting inside a railed-in enclosure. I went up to the counter. "We have no more rooms," she said, looking me over as if she didn't like what she saw. "I know," I said; "I came to see Charlie Mondell." "What's your name?" she asked in a cold voice. "Agnes Dempster," I said. "I'll see if he wants to see any Agnes Dempster," she said, getting up.

"Well, Agnes," said Charlie, coming up to me. "It's all right, Mrs. Hinckley," he said. "Well, that's a relief," she said; "we've had one scene too many here lately." "What does she mean?" I asked him as I climbed up the stairs after him. "Someone here's been having trouble with a hysterical girl," he said; "he moved here to get away from her and she keeps coming by and when he won't see her, she throws stones at his window or she gets a ladder and tries to climb in. I guess she hid in the washroom one night and came out after everyone was asleep and the whole house was raised up when he tried to get her out. Mrs. Hinckley's not as bad as she seems," he said, hesitating at his door. "Come in," he said, finally looking at me. The room was large and plain. Against the wall facing the street, Charlie had stacked his crates. Some of the paintings on velvet were already hung on the walls. "It doesn't look like home yet," said Charlie, "but it will." "Can I sit down?" I asked him. I sat down in the big Morris chair near the bed, and as if its touch loosened something in me, I started to cry.

"What are you doing here, Agnes?" Charlie asked, ignoring my tears. I looked at him, surprised. In the past, my tears upset him, and when he looked at me, his features would become all blurry and soft, as if the sight of me crying was a catastrophe he could not bear to witness. Now, his expression did not alter. I felt a new thrill of respect for him. Perhaps it was not so easy for a woman to manage him after all. "What are you doing here?" he asked again. "I missed you," I said. "That's not a good reason for coming," he said. "It isn't?" I asked. "Don't play the fool with me," he said; "you know why I moved away." "Because you thought I cared for Frank," I said. "Because you don't care for me," he said. "I do," I said. "Not enough," he said; "let's not start that all up again. I don't like to suffer, not if I don't have to." "No," I said; "I guess you don't."

I was thinking about the picnic on Bald Hill and how he had lain on top of me and how my body had arched to meet his and part of me wanted him back. But as I looked down at the arm of my chair, I saw that man and that girl and that hill existing in someone else's past, not in mine. Those two would marry and have children who resembled them and they would all lie down under the pasture together, peaceably, like animals who were buried, appropriately enough, beneath the land on which they had once fed. I looked up at Charlie. "You see," Charlie said, looking at me, "how little you think of me?"

"It's not you," I said; "it's me. I want to get out of the pen life puts you in. I want something more than the kind of life I saw when I was a child." "Oh, you'll get it," Charlie said. There was something hard in his voice. "Do you think so?" I asked, as if he had the power to give it to me. "I think so," he said; "you'll have a good teacher in Frank. To find another world all you have to do is hate this one enough." He got up suddenly and went over to the window and stood with his back to me, staring out into the street. "I don't think that's fair," I said. "You don't think that's fair?" he asked, turning on me; "why should you? You don't even know what I'm talking about." "I don't hate this world," I said; "I love it. I love everything in it."

"Except people," said Charlie; "except for people's lives. You think there's something hateful in a happy life." "No, I don't!" I cried; "I want happiness!" "Is that what you think?" he asked me. I said it was.

"Ask Frank about the farm," he said at last. "Why? I know all about farms. I grew up on one." "You don't know farms the way Frank does," Charlie said; "ask him." "All right!" I said, infuriated; "I will." "Ask him soon," said Charlie. "I'll ask him when I want to ask him," I said. "Well, of course I can't tell you what to do," Charlie said. "No," I said, "you can't." "You haven't asked me about Carrie Holcomb," he said. "Carrie Holcomb?" I echoed. "The girl you were so jealous of. The one who made you decide we shouldn't see each other anymore." I looked down at my hands, and when I looked up, he was regarding me coldly. "Carrie Holcomb's getting married next month," he said; "not to me." "Oh," I said; "I'm sorry." "You should be," he said, holding out a hand to help me up. "Will I see you again?" I asked him. My throat was swelling shut. "You'll see me again. Frank and I are always around together." "You must hate me," I whispered. "Just ask Frank about the farm," he said.

He didn't offer to walk me home, and I made my way through the bluish gray streets myself. For the first time since coming to Montpelier, I was afraid to go back to Mrs. Trowbridge's, to enter my room, to lie down on my bed, because I knew that as soon as I fell asleep, my shadowy self, who I had avoided for so long, would step out of the darkness in the corner of the room and would lean over me until I had breathed her in like a mist that was hovering over the ground. When I looked at Iris's house from the other side of the street, I seemed to see it through a memory of the old cemetery in North Chittendon. It had been raining then, and the rain suddenly stopped, but thick mists still shrouded the cemetery next to the Congregational Church, and as I watched, the mists seemed to be chewing on the stones, grazing on them, while in back of the cemetery, the mists were beginning to rise slowly as if reluctant to leave. I told myself to forget about the cemetery, and I walked quickly through the front yard, into the house and into the office. There were no sounds downstairs.

When I got to my room, I opened the door and stood there with my eyes closed. When I opened them, the bulky, badly wrapped package was there waiting for me. For a minute, I had hoped it would not be there, that I had only imagined its existence. I circled it as if it were something dangerous, as if it were momentous, as if, should I pick it up, it would become the cornerstone of the rest of my life. I thought of Charlie in his room on Crown Street and I could see the light burning in his kerosene lamp and I knew that was the light of safety. I took a deep breath and picked up the package.

Polly came in without knocking. "What's that?" she asked. "A package of drawing paper," I said; "Frank's going to teach me. To draw. I don't want to hear anything more about Frank. No one has a good word for him." "Do you know what a fool you are?" Polly asked me. "I'm sure that you think so," I said, "but I don't want the same things you do." "You mean you wouldn't marry someone like Eddie if your life depended on it," she said angrily. I put the package down on the patchwork quilt which covered my bed. "I don't understand," I said, "why everyone thinks I disapprove of them just because I don't disapprove of Frank." "You will," Polly predicted. "Look, Polly," I said, "if everyone keeps on attacking Frank all the time, I won't want to have anything to do with anybody but him. I don't like it. I care about him and I'm not ashamed to say so. He doesn't care about me. He's only going to teach me how to draw. So it's a waste of time, all this fussing about Frank." "Would you marry someone like Eddie?" Polly asked me.

Hadn't she heard a word I'd said? "No," I said; "not because there's anything wrong with him, or that he's not good enough. I want someone like me, someone who's looking for something you just can't point at, something you can't even see, but you know it's there." I looked at her. "You must think I'm crazy," I said. "Yes, I do," she said; "if you think you can find something like that with Frank." "Do you think I can find anything extraordinary at all?" "I doubt it," she said; "when you get a little older, you'll doubt it too." I said I didn't think I would; I said I thought I would die looking for something better than what I had already seen. Polly twisted the little silver ring Eddie had given her. "Didn't you ever want to find something better, more wonderful than anything you'd ever seen before?" "No," Polly said; "no. This world seems full of wonderful things. I just—" She looked at me helplessly. "I just don't see how to deserve them. The things that are already here." "Oh," I said, "I don't feel as if I deserve *anything*. But I want something miraculous all the same." "As long as it doesn't already exist?" Polly asked, smiling faintly. I smiled back at her. "As long as it doesn't already exist," I agreed. "Then it would be all yours when you found it," Polly said. "Exactly," I said.

Polly sat down on the bed and picked at the strings tying my package. "I want more company in the world than that," she said; "I wouldn't want to find a world and be the only person in it, even if it was miraculous." "I don't want to be the *only* person in it," I said. "Two is a very small number," said Polly. "No, it's not," I said; "two is the perfect number." "Well," Polly said, "there were two of them in the Garden of Eden and that didn't work out so well in the end." I didn't answer. If I found my Garden of Eden, no God in the universe would have the power to throw me out. "I better get to bed," Polly said; "you probably want to sit up and think about Frank." "Forget about Frank," I said sharply. "I guess I'll have to," she said; "if you won't." "I won't," I said. "If your mother was alive," Polly said, "I'd write to her." "Well, she's not," I said.

After Polly left, I undressed and sat on the bed, the package in my lap. I could not bear to unwrap it. I saw Frank giving it to me; I saw the way his mouth tightened as he tried to hide his delight in giving it to me. I held it as if I were holding Frank. The tower clock struck eleven. I was late getting to bed. Finally, I threw back the quilt, put the package on the pillow, and crept into bed. I lay still, watching the moonlight waver on the walls and then turned over on my side, hugged the package to me with one arm, and fell asleep. In the morning, when I woke, I was curled into a little ball around it. I lay in bed, stroking it as if it were an animal. The rising, gilded edges of a good dream which I had already forgotten still hung in the room, and the peace around me was alive. It was the air I breathed. And then I began to think about Frank, about how sly and secret had been his smile as he handed me the gift, and I saw again the little, round bone in his wrist and how sweetly it showed against the skin. He would be in the dining room and we would both be thinking about the paper he had given me, and how, that night, he would come to my room and teach me to draw. I put on my blue watered silk, looked in the mirror and decided I was too pale, took it off and hurriedly threw it across the bed, and put on my dark red plaid dress.

When I sat down at the dining room table, I was so afraid of staring at Frank that I hardly dared look at him, and when I did look up, I saw him staring at me, puzzled. I was relieved when he got up to go, because now that he was gone, I could think about him in peace. Polly ate her half of my breakfast slowly;

she, too, seemed abstracted. "That's new," she said; "teaching someone to draw." I asked her about Eddie and whether or not she still intended to marry some time during the winter, and she said she guessed not. She still had to work at the factory and the roads between Montpelier and the asylum often weren't broken for days at a time. It wasn't a problem for the Highbury people, she said, because most of them didn't leave the grounds of the asylum much anyway, but if she had to get in to work everyday, it would be bad for her. She didn't want to get fired. I thought about the quilt I was making for her and how I would have a chance to make it bigger. I was glad she was not going to marry and leave me alone just now. "When do you think you'll do it?" I asked. "Do it?" she said; "you make it sound like a crime. I don't know." "Aren't you in a hurry?" "Oh well," she said, looking sideways at me, "not really. Not anymore." "You're not tired of him?" I asked. "Tired of him?" she said; "I'd like a chance to get tired of him."

Outside, we joined the tide of girls flowing toward the factories. "Why weren't you happy with Charlie?" she asked urgently; "I can't understand it." "It was all my fault," I said; "I keep looking for a man who's, well—remarkable. Exceptional. As soon as I see one thing wrong with someone, I can't look at him again. I'm horrible when I'm disappointed in someone." "What faults did you find in Charlie?" she asked me. "I don't know," I said miserably; "Charlie said he wasn't unhappy enough for me and that he didn't make me unhappy enough." Polly stopped walking. "Did he hit you?" she asked; "did he go around with other girls?" "No," I said; "he was just what you said he was, too good for this world. Maybe he was right and that's what I didn't like about him." She shook her head and we began walking again. We were almost at the bridge. "I'll see you tonight," I told her and headed for Mrs. James's.

As I walked down the street, I thought that today would be unbearable. When I woke up, I knew it would be unbearable and it was. It was now seven-thirty in the morning and Frank would not come to my room until nine tonight, and before he came, I would have to sit across the table from him and converse with him and everyone else as if nothing unusual had happened. I climbed up to the second story of Mrs. James's house sighing every step of the way. It seemed unusually dark inside, and then I remembered that I had been walking into the sun before I came in. I hung my cloak on a peg and sat down next to Florence.

"Don't we look cheerful today," she said; "and you haven't

even seen what we've got to do. Everything is navy blue or black. Our eyes are going to fall out. If you do the lining, I'll cut out your suits." I stitched away at the lining, but I was really elsewhere. I was in my room, and Frank was leaning over me, showing me how to draw a flower. And I could see that he wanted to leave because he had been there for a long time. The idea that he would come to my room and then leave again stunned me; I stopped with my needle halfway through the rough blue cloth. I had to think of a way to keep him there. I would like to seal him in my room forever. "I hear Charlie Mondell is a thing of the past," Florence said, handing me the cut-out suit. She nodded in the direction of the girl who had told us about Carrie Holcomb. "That one," said Florence; "she knows everything about Charlie." "Carrie Holcomb's getting married," I said, "and not to Charlie." "Oh," said Florence, impressed. She had a weapon to use against the other girl when we opened our dinner pails. "She says you're going after Frank Holt," Florence said. "I'm not going after anyone," I said; "we're all friends. He and I live in the same house, that's all." "Frank Holt looks like he belongs on the stage," she said. "He deserves better than that!" I exclaimed without thinking.

I pretended to be absorbed in my work, but I could feel Florence's eyes on me. And then I forgot her altogether. I had to find a way to bind Frank to me, and then, once the two of us were together, far from the rest of the world, he would have to leave the quarries and go to a wonderful place where his customers wanted statues for their houses and their gardens, and eventually, they would stand in museums, and even their shadows would be precise and heavy and beautiful in the dust-flecked light. And of course he would take me with him. "Good Lord, give me that!" Florence cried, snatching the pants from my lap and throwing the pair of pants she was working on into mine. "Good morning, Mrs. James!" she sang out, smiling brilliantly up at her as she passed by. Mrs. James turned around to look at Florence, but Florence was industriously bent over the pair of pants on which I should have been working.

"Where has your mind gone?" Florence asked me as soon as Mrs. James was out of the room; "you're sewing these so that all the stitches will show on the right side of the cloth. It's a good thing I saw you before she did." She shook the pants out on her lap and pointed to the seam. "You know," Florence said, "that is really very bad work. If you keep that up, she'll get rid of you. You'd think this was your first day here." "I'll be careful," I said. "I won't be sitting next to you forever," said Florence; "what happens if I get sick? You've got to take care of yourself." "I'll be careful," I said again.

My mind returned to Frank, the way he had carried in the package as if it were a baby, the way he had set it down as if it might break, even though there was only paper and charcoal inside. "You know," Florence said, "I've heard a lot about Frank Holt." And suddenly I was telling her all about him, all about the package, about how, that night, he was going to teach me to draw. "Oh," said Florence when I caught my breath, "so that's what's the matter with you. I've heard that he doesn't have the best reputation in the world." "People don't know him," I said, angry. "Whether they do or whether they don't," she said, "I wouldn't let him catch you so fast." I shook my head. I couldn't wait to be caught.

"Here she comes again," Florence said, without raising her head. I picked up a needle and pretended to thread it. "I'll be glad to get married and get out of here," Florence said; "at least then I'll be working for myself." "You are now," I said; "you're working for money, that's all." "It's different," Florence said; "here you're working *just* for money. The work isn't anything." "I don't see why washing dishes is anything," I said, picking up the fabric and inspecting my work; the seam was straight and the stitches tight and regular. "That's an improvement," said Florence.

The day ticked by slowly and finally I was out on the street, running toward the Trowbridge house. I filled my pitcher and Polly's with water and went upstairs and began bathing myself with a wet towel. Then I took out the high, circular box of lavender powder which once belonged to my mother and began dusting myself all over. I began to imagine Frank was dusting me with the puff, and my body, as I watched it in the mirror, looked more rounded, more flushed, more smooth than I had realized it was. I smoothed a little powder on my cheeks and I saw myself paler, older, with huge dark eyes which seemed to belong to an older, more mysterious version of me. I smoothed a little more powder on my face; I was transformed by it. Now, I thought, I would not look like a young child. Now I would look like a grown woman. I unstoppered the bottle of lavender water and poured some over my shoulders and breasts. Finally, pleased with the results, I put on my petticoats, my camisole, and then my red plaid dress. I looked at myself in the mirror once more. Frank, I thought, must be taking his bath in the livery stable. I liked thinking of him dressing as I dressed, as if, somehow, the two of us were really in the same place. Now, I thought, he would be stepping out of the tub; now he would be toweling himself off. When I started down the steps, he would be near the door of the livery stable, crossing the yard toward the back door of the Trowbridge house, and when I entered the dining room, he would just be coming in.

The dining room door was open and I walked in. Polly looked up at me and dropped her fork. "What's wrong?" I whispered to her as I slid into my seat. "What happened to you?" she asked me; "are you sick?" "I'm not sick," I said; "why do you think I'm sick?" "Your skin," she said, staring at me; "it's dead white! You look like you've been eating arsenic!" "I powdered my face," I said; "doesn't it look all right?" "You look like a plaster wall," Polly said; "go wash it off." "I think it looks sophisticated," I said. "Have it your way," she said; "when Frank gets here, he's going to take one look at you and tell you to forget all about drawing until you feel better." I got up and fled into the washroom. "You look *a lot* better," Polly said, picking up an ear of corn, "but you still smell like a lilac bush." I started to jump up again, but Polly grabbed my arm. "Sit still," she said; "the lilac water will wear off."

I chewed absently, watching the door.

Every time I heard someone approaching it, I went rigid with expectation. How was I going to stand it, having to watch Frank while everyone at the table watched me? "Eat," said Polly. Iris was bringing out the apple pies but Frank was still not there. "He's missed supper before," Polly whispered to me; "he must have gone home with Charlie." "With Charlie!" I said. If Frank had told him that tonight he was going to help me learn to draw, Charlie might have tried to keep Frank with him. I said as much to Polly. "Charlie isn't like that," she said. "Maybe he just forgot," I said; "Frank, I mean." "What did he tell you?" she asked me; "that he'd see you here or that he'd come to your room at nine o'clock?" I said he told me he'd come to my room at nine o'clock. "Is it nine o'clock?" Polly asked me, and when I said it wasn't, she told me I was worrying about nothing.

But I was sure he was not going to come. I went into my room and sat in the chair next to the wood stove and stared at the empty chair next to my bed. I heard footsteps coming toward my door and jumped up and opened the door before anyone had a chance to knock. "Oh, it's you," I said when I saw Polly. "Well, don't act as if you hate me just because I'm not Frank," she said. "Quiet!" I hissed; "he might hear you." "He's nowhere about," she said; "I took some extra biscuits from the table. I thought you might want them for tonight." She fished them out of her pocket and I took them gratefully. "Do you want me to sit with you and wait?" she asked. "No," I said; "no." I wanted to be alone when Frank came. "I guess you want me to leave," she said. I nodded, embarrassed. "Why don't you start drawing something before he comes?" she said, pausing in the doorway; "that way it won't be so obvious." I wanted to ask her what wouldn't be so obvious, but I didn't want to keep her there. I sat down and began sketching on the outside of the package. I looked at what I had drawn from every possible angle, I even turned it upside down, but no matter how I looked at it, it still looked hopeless. Then someone knocked at the door and I jumped.

"I'm not late, am I?" asked Frank, coming into the room. He bent over my chair and looked at the flower I was drawing on the wrapping paper. I seemed to have drawn a sunflower on a rose's stem. "Well," said Frank, "I see we have our work cut out for us." He took the package away from me, unwrapped it, put the pile of paper on the bed, and handed me a single sheet. "Now," he said, giving me a piece of charcoal, "you have no idea about perspective and you can't draw from memory. I'll be right back." And he disappeared.

I felt my eyes burning. After waiting so long for him to come, he walked in and then walked out. I wanted to pick up the neat pile of paper lying on the bed and fling it into the air. And then Frank walked back in carrying an iris. "What's that made of?" I asked. It looked like a dried flower, but it was too shiny and white for that. "It's made of marble," he said, smiling; "I carved it. Here," he said, holding it toward me; "get a good grip on it. It's heavy." I settled the marble iris in my lap and looked from it to the picture I had drawn. "It's no use," I said; "I can't draw. This," I said, looking at the flower, "is perfect." "It's not bad," he said; "give it to me and I'll put it on the candlestand and you can sketch it." I gave it up reluctantly. "Do you think," I asked, "I could keep it in my room for a while? The iris?" Frank frowned slightly. "I could sketch it when I'm home," I said. "If you want to keep it for a while, keep it," Frank said. I said I would take good care of it. "Let's get started," he said.

"Don't hold the charcoal so tightly," he said, bending over me; "don't hold it so close to the tip." His hand closed over mine. "Like this," he said. I felt his hand, felt him bending over me, felt his breath behind my ear, and forgot I was supposed to be drawing. "Don't get discouraged," said Frank; "you're not doing so badly. Look at the petals closest to you. See how some of them look long and thin and their bottom edges look straight? You have to get used to seeing things the way they look, not the way they feel, or the way they looked when you had them up close. You have to draw it the way it looks from where you are, even if it doesn't seem right. Try it." I started again. This time the flower I drew bore a faint resemblance to the iris. "That's better," said Frank, bending over me; "you're still not seeing right, though. Here and here," he said, touching my lines with the point of a pencil. "Look." He took the charcoal from me and redrew one of my curved lines so that it was straight and then bent at a right angle to itself. Then he elongated a vertical line and suddenly I was looking down at an iris. "That's wonderful," I said.

"You're better at it than you think," he said; "start again." I drew another iris. It looked like a nightmare cousin to the marble flower on the candlestand. "Again," Frank said, fattening the leaves on my drawing, shadowing the petal which hung over like a tongue. I tried once more and showed him what I had done. "You're getting there," he said; "again." I was on my fourth sheet of paper. I looked up at Frank. His eyes were wider than I had ever seen them. His lips were parted in a slight smile and every now and then he nodded as if what he saw delighted him. "Once more," I said; "I'll wear out your patience." "I don't have any patience to wear out," he said; "ask anyone." I said he was one of the most patient people I'd ever met. He smiled at me. I had never seen him smile like that before. He smiled as if he were happy with the world. I forced myself to look away from him and back down at the paper. "How is this?" I asked when I finished. "Very good," he said; "you'll be good at it after all."

There was a knock at the door and Polly came in. "Oh, you're busy," she said; "I'll come back later." "That's all right," Frank said; "I've got to get on to bed. I'm going to be at the quarries until the middle of the night tomorrow." He smiled at Polly, who was watching him open-mouthed.

"Who was that?" Polly asked when he walked out. "Stop it, Polly," I said. "What did you do to him?" she asked; "does Frank have a twin? Was that his twin?" "Stop," I said. "The person who walked out of here was *nice,*" Polly said. "I told you he was nice." "You ought to get a job as a lion tamer,"

Polly said. "Polly," I said, "he's a nice person." "I think I'll just wait and see what happens. I wouldn't have believed it if I hadn't seen it with my own eyes. He said he was going to teach you to draw and that's what he's doing. And he was smiling like any other human being I've ever seen. What did you do to him?" "I tried drawing that iris," I said, pointing to the carved flower. "I can think of a lot of girls who ought to have thought of drawing that iris," Polly said. She shook her head and said she would see me in the morning.

I put out the lights and got right into bed, but I couldn't stay still. I had to get up and look at the drawings I had made, and when I looked at them I again felt Frank bending over me. The third time I got up, I decided to leave the lamp unlit because I had few matches left, and to study the sketches in the morning. And just as I was falling asleep, I began to think of what Frank had said when he left my room, and I realized that he hadn't said when he would come back to teach me again. I felt myself stiffening with fear; I heard the mocking voices of the girls at Mrs. James's saying that Frank had no women friends, and I, who had gone to bed so happy, ended up crying myself to sleep.

When I woke up, I wasn't sure where I was. I looked at the dark brown wall with its dried pink roses and saw, with relief, that I was not in North Chittendon. Then I listened for feet on the stairs, and when I heard none, looked at my watch. I was late for breakfast.

When I came in, Frank smiled happily at me. "I saved you the softer half of the steak," Polly said; "it's only fair. It's your meal." I nodded and began chewing. "Eat fast," said Polly; "I don't want to be late." I chewed and watched Frank from beneath my lashes. "My," Polly said, "you look calm, even if you are red around the eyes." "Calm?" I asked. If, by waving a wand, I could have sent all of the people at the table to kingdom come so that Frank and I could have been there alone, I would have done them in without thinking twice, that is how jealous of his attention I was. I looked with particular hatred at the old woman who sat next to Frank. She often told him endless stories about her life as a girl in Rutland, long, involved stories about her mother and sisters, all of whose names began with *M*.

I tried to get his attention. "I have a flower in my room," I said to Frank. He nodded at me and smiled. "It's wonderful to have a spring flower blooming like this," I babbled, "in the wrong season." He smiled at me and nodded his head. I could feel Polly turning to me, about to ask me what flower? what flower? but I reached under the table and slapped her hand. She didn't know I was talking about the marble iris. She raised her eyebrows and lowered her eyes. "Well," Frank said, getting up, "I've got to move along. Keep working," he said, looking at me, and the door swung shut behind him.

I sat still, furious with disappointment. "He didn't say when he'd come back," I whispered to Polly, my mouth full of potatoes which I could no longer swallow. "Chew slowly and swallow those down," she said; "I don't know why you can't swallow whenever you're upset. There are people like that in Highbury." She stabbed another potato and ate it up. "What do you want him to do?" she asked me; "you don't expect him to announce when he's coming in front of the whole zoo here, do you?" I said I didn't, but I thought he could have found a way to let *me* know without letting *them* know. "So now you're angry?" Polly said. I said yes, I was. "Well, I certainly never thought I'd be defending Frank," she said, "but you have to show a little sense. You have to act as if you trust him even if you don't. He said he'd teach you to draw starting last night and he showed up when he said he would. I guess he knows he didn't finish teaching you to draw. You have to act like you know he's coming back. You have to believe it, too, or you'll drive yourself crazy." "I'll believe it when I see it," I said. "You still have that marble flower in custody," Polly said; "he'll be back for that." "He might come for it when I'm not home," I said. Polly looked at me, disgusted. "Well," she said, "this is how being too beautiful gets you into trouble. You think you should get whatever you want right away. If Frank comes around, he'll come around in his own time. If he sees every little thing he does upsets you, he'll find big things to do to you. Men are like that. They have too much energy for their own good and the best of them use up most of their energy controlling themselves. I tell you, Agnes, you'd better grow up. If you want Frank, find a way to make him suffer. Then he'll never go away."

Never go away! Make him suffer! All I wanted to do was make Frank happy and I was sure I was the only person who could. "He has to be afraid you'll throw him over," Polly said, "or he'll pull away. You'll see." "But if I make him happy, why should he want to pull away?" "Because he's afraid," she said. "Of being happy?" I asked. "Of being so close to anyone else. He *won't* get too close." "He has to get married someday," I said; "he'll have to get close to someone then." "Do you think so?" Polly asked me; "I don't. I think he'll marry someone he doesn't have to get close to." My hands on the table felt leaden. I didn't want to work. I wanted to go back to bed. The tablecloth was grayer and more stained than it had been an instant before. "It's not that I think I should have everything whenever I want it," I said; "I don't believe I'll ever have anything I want." "That's why you get so frantic," Polly said; "you think every chance is the last one." "Oh, how do you know!" I cried. "How do I know?" she asked, and looked significantly at Frank's empty chair. "Will you come on?" she hissed at me; "straighten your skirt. Wipe your mouth. Good Lord!"

And then we were out on the street, going to work as if nothing had happened, as if Frank had never come to my room. "What would you do if Eddie died?" I asked Polly suddenly. "Well, I couldn't marry him, then," Polly said. "But how would you feel?" I insisted. "I'd feel like it was the end of the world," she said, "for about six months. And then I'd start to feel better and I'd start to look around again." "Would you marry again?" I asked her; "if you were already married?" "Of course," she said; "I'd have to find someone I cared about as much. That would take a long time, but I'd do it. Life doesn't stop."

It doesn't start, either, I thought, walking along next to her, until you find the one man in the world for whom you were made. I believed in second chances for some people, but how could there be a second chance for me when I believed there was only one person who was perfect for me and that I had found him? If he left me, or if he died, the door to the world would swing closed against me. And the key to the door would be buried with him.

"I don't believe there's only one perfect person for you," Polly said; "I know you do, but it's all silly, romantic nonsense. Suppose you were in China? Don't you think you'd meet your perfect person there and he'd be all you ever thought about? It's all accidents and more accidents. It's an accident you came to Iris's house and not someone else's. That's what life is. Accidents." "I think," I said, "that there's some kind of destiny in back of our lives, and it pulls us through the cloth and you only see the threads when you pull hard on the seams of the fabric." "I think that's nonsense," said Polly; "I think that's just ridiculous. You hold your own life together. There's nothing attached to you. Marionettes move around by strings. People move themselves around. Destiny is all the accidents that happen to them. You're not a quilt! If you pull too hard on the place

215

where the fabric is sewn together, what happens to a quilt? You rip the fabric, that's all. There's no such thing as destiny, and if there was, I wouldn't want to rely on it.''

I looked away from her, and suddenly, on the other side of the street, I saw Frank coming toward us. He was deep in conversation with a man I had never seen before and was talking with great animation, and, as he spoke, his hands moved forcefully through the air. I turned around to look back at him, and could see that he was still talking, still gesturing. There was such energy there! Usually, he affected a languid, almost bored air. ''Isn't that destiny?'' I asked Polly; ''coming across Frank when we were talking about him?'' ''First of all,'' she said, ''we weren't talking about him. Maybe you were, but I wasn't. Second of all, we've talked about him a lot of times and he hasn't appeared in front of us. It's an accident.'' ''You and your accidents,'' I said, annoyed. I started to step into the street, but Polly yanked me back. A heavy wagon rumbled by. ''They say love is blind,'' she said, ''but I don't think they mean you actually stop seeing everything in front of you. Didn't you see that wagon?'' I said I hadn't. I had been thinking about Frank and how he had looked talking to the man on the street. I wanted him to talk to me that way. I wondered who the other man was. I wished him off the face of the earth. And through it all, I heard Polly telling me to look upstreet and downstreet before crossing. ''I'll be careful,'' I said. She snorted.

That night, Frank came to supper, smiled at us, excused himself early, and we did not see him again. The next morning, he smiled at me and left for work without mentioning my drawing lessons. Polly watched me curiously. After five days, I told Polly that Frank had forgotten all about me and that she might as well relax. After a week went by, I picked up the marble iris, went down the hall with it to Frank's room and stood in front of the door without daring to open it. I didn't want him to think I disliked having the flower in my room. But after ten days, my resolve broke. I had not been sleeping at night, and at meals I could not eat. My clothes were loose and my cheeks looked sunken, and Polly, who was the recipient of my un-touched plates, said she hoped this fuss over drawing lessons came to an end before she swelled out of her clothes altogether. On the eleventh night, I went into my room, stood in front of the marble iris, and burst into tears. ''You're going back to your own room,'' I told it; ''he doesn't care about you, either.'' I picked it up and went down the hall. My cheeks were hot and my heart was pounding in anger and exhaustion. "If the door isn't locked," I told the iris, "I'm going to put you inside. Otherwise, I'm leaving you out in the hall." I thought about the poor iris, standing in the hall where anyone could break it or steal it and almost began crying again. Polly was right. I was on the edge of hysteria.

I pushed Frank's door open. He was leaning over a small table in front of his window. "Oh, hello," he said, standing up; "I was just coming to your room." Then he saw the iris in my hands. "Don't you want to draw anymore?" he asked. Pure, liquid hatred bubbled behind my eyes. He saw none of it. If I loosened my hands, if I let the iris slip through them, it would shatter on the floor. "I'll hold that for you," he said, taking the iris from me. "I would have come by sooner," he said, "but I have a new commission and we've been settling the details. They want me to carve four walls of a mausoleum, but they want so many things on it, it would have to be bigger than a courthouse. Now we're down to a weeping willow, an urn with a cloth draped over it, and a sheep. After I get those things in, I can use my imagination." "A weeping willow?" I said. "A lot of people want weeping willows," he said; "I'm going to carve one weeping in a rainstorm so it looks as if the whole landscape is crying." "Doesn't the man who wants the mausoleum want the sun shining?" I asked. All the carvings I had ever seen were cheerful, as if, in the world to come, no one could imagine such a thing as rain. Everything in the next world, I thought, should be self-sufficient, should contain whatever was needed within itself. "The sun will be shining on the other panels," Frank said; "when someone's miserable, he can sit in front of the weeping willow, and when he's happier, he can sit in front of the lamb playing in the sun."

We went into my room and I sat down and Frank handed me the paper and charcoal as if teaching me were something he did every day. I started sketching, but my hand shook. Frank put his hand over mine. "Stop," he said; "you're nervous." "No," I said, "I'll be all right." I didn't want him to leave. "Well," he said, looking down at the paper, "maybe you're tired of that iris. Try drawing me. Some people are better at portraits." He sat down on my bed and turned toward me.

I looked at his face, so finely molded, at the high, pure line of his eyebrows, at the cheeks with their high cheekbones, at the flesh which seemed so tightly, aristocratically drawn over them, at the finely carved mouth which as always seemed pursed as if in disapproval of existence, and I despaired of drawing him. To my horror, I saw fat tears splashing onto the paper. "What's wrong?" Frank asked, paling. "Nothing," I said, rubbing my eyes with my hand; "I'm just tired." "I should have thought," Frank said; "Charlie told me how hard you work." "I don't work that hard," I said. I thought of how badly I had done my work that week and began crying again. "I'm sorry," I said; "this is what happens when I don't get enough sleep." "Do you want me to come back some other time?" Frank asked. "No," I said; "don't go away."

He sat there quietly, watching me cry. I could not stop. I was crying with rage and frustration and relief. I was crying about everything for which I had not cried before, my mother's death, my grandmother's, all the bitter disappointments of days spent inhaling and exhaling empty air. I cried because I was sure Frank would get up and walk out of my room thinking he was well rid of me, a human version of the weeping willow he was preparing to carve in stone, and then I felt his hands on my shoulders. He was standing in back of me. "It's all right," he said; "everything will be all right." "How do you know?" I asked him. I seemed to speak easily through my tears, as if they were not really mine, but fell as water did from a waterfall, while I stood somewhere behind the curtain of water. "It always turns out all right," he said. I kept on crying. I took deep breaths, and when I breathed out, I found I had no breath left. I could not breathe through my nose. "Look at you," Frank said gently. He took out his handkerchief and gave it to me. I looked at him questioningly. "Go ahead," he said; "blow your nose." I blew my nose and went on crying. "Should I tell you a funny story?" asked Frank. I tried to smile. "I better not," he said.

He came over to me, picked up the piece of paper before me, and sat back down on the bed. He drew something rapidly, then held it up to me. It was a sketch of my face. "That's how miserable you look," he said. "I look terrible," I said, looking at it and crying. I covered my eyes with my hand; I thought if I couldn't see him, I might stop crying. I looked up, startled. He was standing over me. "You're still crying," he said. I nodded. He bent down and kissed me on the cheek. Then he kissed me on the lips. I heard myself take a long, shuddery breath and I knew I had stopped crying. "I think," Frank said, "you had better lie down on the bed." He stretched his hand out to me and I took it. He pulled me to my feet and steered me to the bed. "Lie down," he said. So this is how it will happen, I thought, stretching out on the quilt, feeling the soft mass of the pillow against the hard, throbbing bones of my skull.

But Frank was sitting in the chair I had vacated. He was watching me. "Better?" he asked. "Yes," I said, "I think so." I lay there watching Frank and listening to my breathing return to normal. "Do you really think it is possible?" he asked me; "do you think I could move on and do statuary?" "I know you could," I said. "Why are you so sure?" he asked. "I knew it the instant I saw that carving at the quarries," I said; "when I was a child, sculptors used to come to North Chittendon and we saw a lot of their carving, or pictures of their statues, and nothing any of them did was half as good as yours, and almost all of them were famous." "North Chittendon?" said Frank; "why did sculptors come to North Chittendon?" "To sketch the Druitt girls," I said, horrified by my own words. I had never intended to tell anyone about my family or the town in which we lived or what had happened to any of us and why.

"The Druitt girls," he said; "that sounds familiar." "One of them was the model for the bronze statue near the courthouse," I said. "Now I remember," Frank said. He stared at me as if he were seeing me for the first time. "You look like the statue," he said. "She was my grandmother," I said. "The statue?" he asked, smiling. "No," I said, "the woman who sat for it. Or stood for it." "Well, she brought good luck to that sculptor," he said; "I guess you know what you're talking about. Some, anyway." "I know your carving is better than anyone's I've ever seen," I said. "Better than the statue near the courthouse?" "There's no comparison!" I cried. "I'd like to try it," he said softly; "if I didn't make it, I could always come back here." "You won't have to come back here," I said. "How can you be so certain?" he asked. "I'm not certain about much," I said, "but I'm certain about this." He seemed to be turning things over. "Well," he said, getting up, "you better get some rest. I'll come back tomorrow night." "When?" I asked shamelessly. "Right after supper, if you're not too tired." "I won't be," I said. "If you're really not tired," said Frank, "we could go for a walk first."

25

The next day dawned leaden and the sky was the silver gray color of frozen ice. The feel of snow was in the air. All day, I looked at the sky, hating it, as if by sheer will, I could prevent it from snowing, as if my will were strong enough to keep the snow tight within the seamless clouds over our heads. When I finished up at Mrs. James's, I ran down the street and watched the sky. I felt the peculiar moist chill of the air on my cheek and knew it would soon be snowing. "Don't snow," I pleaded with the sky as I ran up the stairs and into my room. "Don't snow," I whispered, looking out the window.

At supper, the old woman sitting next to Frank began to harangue him about how it was certainly going to snow tonight and it would be a bad snowfall too, because when it snowed a lot, her hip hurt, her knee hurt, and she couldn't bend her fingers. The snow became everyone's topic. One of the elderly gentlemen said it would never snow because the sky wasn't dark enough; someone else said it was too early in the year for a heavy snow, but almost everyone else said they wouldn't be surprised by anything the weather dreamed up. What did I think? someone asked me. "About snow?" I asked. I guessed it wasn't going to snow. I was enraged with everyone at the table. It was certain to snow if they kept on talking about it. I looked over at Frank and saw him nodding pleasantly while the old woman lectured him about the dangers of walking in snow, slipping on ice, and how her husband had once almost choked to death when he had taken a deep breath and breathed in some hailstones which went down the wrong way. Frank looked at me and smiled. Undoubtedly, he had long ago given up the idea of walking. I pushed back my plate. "Ready?" Frank asked me. Astonished, I said I was.

Outside, the first snow had begun falling. The sparse flakes fell toward the ground, then blew upward with the next gust of wind. "Don't breathe in," I said; "you might choke." "I won't breathe at all, how's that?" he said. We walked along in silence. "Where are we going?" I asked after awhile. We had already passed the factories and the last rickety buildings that marked the outskirts of the city. "The woods," said Frank; "there's something there I want to show you." "What?" I asked; "a snake or a bear?" "Don't worry about that," Frank said; "I always take a pistol when I go into the woods." He patted his coat pocket. "It's an old habit from the farm." "Is it loaded?" I asked him. "Not yet," he said.

"Well, then," I asked, "what good is it? By the time you got it loaded, the bear would have eaten you." He took the pistol out of his pocket, fumbled for two cartridges, and loaded it. "Feel better?" he asked me. "I'm not sure," I said; "now that you've loaded it, I expect something to happen." "A bear or a snake?" he asked me. I started to laugh. I felt silly, giddy, childlike. It was as if the whole world had emerged from the fog through which I was accustomed to seeing it. I felt light, as if the wind itself could pick me up. I laughed happily. It was all so new. Frank looked at me and smiled. He never laughs, I thought. I wonder why.

I stopped and looked back at the lights of the town. The snow, falling lightly, was whitening everything. "Come on," said Frank; "we've still got a way to go." We walked for more than a mile and then Frank stopped, looked across the field at a clump of trees in its center and said we were there. We left the road and began cutting across the ridged, snowy field. The ground beneath our feet was frozen and lumpy. The snow was beginning to stick to my cloak. I began brushing it off, but as quickly as I did so, it settled again. We were in front of the dense clump of trees. "Are we here?" I asked Frank. "We are," he said. "Where are we?" I asked. "Just follow me," he said. We picked our way between the trees into the center of the grove. "Here we are," Frank said.

"All I see are tree stumps," I said, going closer to them, intending to sit down. "Look closer," Frank said. I stooped down to look at one of them. "Wait," said Frank. He kneeled down and brushed the snow carefully from the stump. I sank down next to him. "It's carved!" I exclaimed. "They all are," he said; "this is where the stonecutters used to bring their children in the summers when they weren't working in the quarries. A lot of the children started out carving right here, right on these stumps. My father used to bring me here. I did my first carving here," he said, looking down at the stump. "If there were a moon, you could see it," he said; "a bear's head." "Put my hands on it," I said. Frank placed my hands on the stump. "I can feel its teeth!" I said. "All I ever thought about were bears," he said; "bears and more bears." "I don't think I ever thought about bears, except when I was coming home at night," I said.

I stood up and looked around me. The snow was heavier, the flakes larger. He began brushing himself off. "It's no use," I said; "I already tried. We might as well give up and stand here. We'll be the two statues of the field." "No," said Frank; "let's go back." "We could sit here," I said. Frank sat down on one of the larger stumps and I sat down next to him.

"Why didn't you stay on the farm?" I asked him. "Oh, you don't want to get me started on that," he said. "Yes, I do," I said. "You know all about it," he said; "you grew up on a farm." "We owned the farm," I said; "another family did most of the work." "You know," Frank said; "you know how it was, how beautiful it was. It's true there's nothing as beautiful as the sun coming up over a field. I miss the farm, but I could go on for hours about how horrible it was, how brutal it was. I got up at five o'clock every morning. When I was four, my cousin and I fed the calves. If it was thirty below, that was too bad. She laughs about it now but I remember it well enough. I went out sick to feed the animals because the animals had to be fed and my uncle told me a farmer never got sick. The important thing was the animals. Then when I got older, it was cleaning out the barn and milking the cows and getting the manure out, and that was something after the snow started, dragging out the carts of manure. They'd start steaming before you were out the door. It was always thirty below on that farm. Even in the summer." He looked at me and smiled tightly. "I don't like to talk about it," he said; "it's haunting an old place."

"In this light," I said, irrelevantly, "my hand looks blue." Frank looked over at me and shook his head. "When I was a child," he said, "I don't think I was three, I used to walk in front of the reapers and pull up the black-eyed susans because the cows didn't like them, and when I had a big armload, I'd throw them over the stone fence. Well, then they'd bale the hay, and the flowers I threw out of the pasture dried in the sun and the wind blew the seeds back in, and the next year, we'd have an even better crop. Summer people love that flower. It's just a damn weed to me. The way they multiplied, the way they grew back and took over. Those damn flowers! Do you know what I'm talking about?'' "I think so," I said. "And when the cows were ready to calve, one after another, all night long and all the next day and the next night, I was out there delivering calves with a good case of measles because you had to take care of them. That's all I ever heard from my mother or father. You have to take care of them. They weren't *my* animals. I was the only animal on the farm that didn't matter. If you walked on two legs, you didn't make any difference. I got sick of it.'' He kicked his heels back against the stump we sat on. "You probably think I left to get away from the work," he said; "everyone does." "No," I said; "I don't." "And then, after getting up at five morning after morning, there'd be a drought and everything turned brown and you might as well have spent your time sleeping all day. It wasn't hard to think the land was after you and wanted to punish you for something. Anyway, I got away as fast as I could.''

I was staring through the trunks of the trees across the white field, and I saw how the smooth, white curve of the snow as it lay on the ground was like the curve of a woman's body, and I saw how the farm was like the body of a woman which lay down under the sun and under the freezing snow and perpetually and relentlessly produced uncountable swarms of living things, all born with mouths open and cries rising from them into the air, beaks open and cheeping, long-boned muzzles opening like the jaws of alligators, as if they would swallow the world whole, hooved things or webbed things or claw-footed, all demanding attention, all wobbling to their feet, bent on perpetuating themselves, the chickens laying their eggs God knew where, the cows, swollen with their first calves, going all the way back to their beginnings, making nests for themselves in the woods, having forgotten those strange animals, men, who unlike them had only been walking the earth for a short time, the dogs running loose and chasing the horses in the pasture through the low, grazing mists, the spindly colt trembling to its feet and crushing the skull of the kitten hidden by its mother in the stall straw, the empty fields calling out for crops like barren women who sang in voices as inescapable as the air and who would not be comforted, filling themselves with weeds and bushes and small trees with long roots which had to be pulled up or the forest would take back the farmland, while the women of the farm nursed the sick animals and fed them and fed their family

223

and the men who came to help with the harvest and none of the women ministered to the men any more than they ministered to any other living thing, unless, of course, the man was dying. They ministered to the many creatures of the female earth and the earth was a pitiless female, and man was only one poor animal among many, a necessary son, not loved, but necessary, not special, not unique, and when the wind rose and tossed the leaves in the graying sky, that was the woman's voice, not the man's, and so was the lightning and the thunder, and the drought was her anger and her terrible silence. I had always known how it was.

"It's no life, being on a farm," Frank said aloud. Then, as if he had been reading my thoughts, he added, "everything's gelded so it won't run or chase the young females in the pastures. Everything has to get as fat as it can. They keep the bull penned up and then drive him from one cow to another until he's half dead because they want the calves born when they can feed on the grass and it's easier if they're all born at once. I hated it. My mother didn't have time for us. My sister had some time, but not much. There's no end to it. It's insatiable, the land. Life. It takes. It doesn't give back." "Everything alive is insatiable," I said; "even you. You must want something or you wouldn't still be here. You wouldn't go on living." "Wanting something is one thing," he said; "getting it is another. Anyway, sometimes I don't think I've gone on living."

"Not all women want to populate the earth," I said abruptly. "I never knew one who didn't," he said, turning to me. "I don't," I said. "You don't want children?" he asked me; "you said that before but I didn't believe you." "No," I said; "I don't. At least not yet. A baby's just a stupid lump of flesh. It's all mouth. It can't give you anything. It just takes. It lies around starting to look like you, and you look at it and it's getting ready to replace you. At least animals get up and start taking care of themselves. No, I don't want children. I'm enough trouble for me." "Well, I don't really want them," he said; "but if you don't, you're the only woman I've ever heard of who doesn't." "Well," I said, "my mother had three children, and all she wound up with was me and I wasn't worth much to her." "Why not?" he asked. "We didn't get along," I said; "we fought about everything." "Your teeth are chattering," he said; "we ought to get back." He looked at me. "I never *heard* of a woman who didn't want to have children before." "That's the

224

third time you've said that," I told him. "Well," he said, shrugging.

"Let's come back here when the snow melts and we can see the carving," I said. "We will," said Frank. For an instant, he put his arm around my shoulders and then stiffened, as if remembering something, and took his arm away. "Agnes," he said, "I want this to be different." "Different?" I said. "I like you," he said; "you're not like everyone else." I felt my heart swell. I wanted to reach out and touch his cheek. "I'm not so different," I said softly. "Yes you are," he said.

As we walked in the silence, as I saw the round moon trying to smoke its way out through the silver clouds, I saw how it was. I thought about all I had ever heard about Frank and knew it was all true, that he only loved marble women, that he had no use for flesh and blood. But I saw something more. I saw that he was in rebellion against the earth and its ways just as I was. I knew that when he walked he felt the hungry mouths beneath his boots. He knew how thin the sky was and how implacably the clockwork moved behind it and how the moon and the sun moved through the sky for their own reasons, turning their indifferent faces from us. We were the same. We wanted a world which was not yet here. I looked up at Frank's face, gaunt in the moonlight. He did not have my will. If the world seemed like a woman who gave nothing, I would be his world but I would be everything to him. If he wanted to leave Montpelier, I would make him leave and I would go with him. I would take care of Frank. There was nothing else I wanted to do and I knew I was the only person who could care for him. No one else would ever understand him. "What are you thinking?" Frank asked me. "Nothing," I said.

We began taking longer and longer walks. On some nights, Frank did not come back to the house until nine, and I would curl up in my chair near the window and watch the street, waiting to catch a glimpse of him. Often enough, he woke me up when he opened the door. The snow fell constantly all through October and there were times when I heard myself talking as the snow fell; I feared the snow would bury the words beneath its drifts. There were times I felt as if Frank and I were walking at the bottom of a vast shaft which time had sunk through the air and as we walked the snow, like time made visible, was covering us, and by the time spring came and melted the snow we would have gone under. "I'm always surprised by how light the snow is when it's falling," I said, "and how heavy it is when you have to shovel it." "Everything mounts up," Frank said.

As if my mind were stitched to my feet, I began to talk as I walked along. I told Frank about my sister. I told him about the composition I had written saying that I hated my name and I told him about the child in the woods. I told him about my grandmother and her brass bed. "She never put the bed back inside the house?" Frank asked me. "No," I said; "she never did." "Didn't the neighbors come up and talk to her? Didn't the minister?" "Probably," I said; "I wasn't born when it happened. I only heard about it." "Didn't you think it was strange?" he asked me. "No," I said; "well, yes. I did. But at least she didn't always put up with what life handed her." "Rebellion is a waste of time," Frank said. "It is if it doesn't get you anywhere," I said. "Where did it get your grandmother?" he asked me. "Off by herself, where she wanted to be!" I said violently.

I thought of her, lying under our west hill and I saw her lying beneath the ground as if beneath a quilt. Sound asleep. She was not dead. "If my grandmother made a mistake," I said, "it was stopping. She should have gone on rebelling until she got something she really wanted." "Most people get what they really want," said Frank; "they don't think so, but they do. They *like* to think life cheated them. They *like* to think they don't have what they want because they don't want to admit it, but a little bit of life makes a person happy. People's eyes are bigger than their stomachs. They want more than they can swallow. They don't really want to be happy because then they have something they can lose. They want to be content, and the less they have, the easier it is." "My grandmother wanted to be happy, and my mother did, and so do I!" I said angrily. "People who are happy," Frank said, "fit in with everyone else. They're part of the herd." "I don't want to be part of the herd!" I burst out; "you're not part of it! You're different!" "No, I'm not," he said sadly. "You are!" I insisted; "you have to be!"

We walked on. I told Frank about how my mother forbade me to go to Louise's house when she saw I was happier there than I was at home. I asked him why they had been so mean. "Because they were too busy or they didn't know any better," he said; "there's never any more to it than that." I insisted that there had to be more to it than that. "If there is," said Frank, "I don't want to know about it. There's no point in going over these things." We had come to the end of the cleared road. "If we walk any further," Frank said, "we'll be in snow up to our necks. Let's turn around."

"No," I said; "I'm going to lie down in it," and I flung

myself down in the snow and found myself staring up at the thick cold stars. "They look like salt on a blue cloth," I said. "Get up," said Frank; "you'll freeze." "I'm perfectly warm," I said; "nothing gets through this fur cape. The snow's comfortable." "All right," Frank said and stretched out beside me. "I feel like an idiot," he said. "Why?" I asked; "didn't you ever lie down in the snow before?" "I told you," he said; "snow was something to move from here to there. Falling trouble. That's all it ever was to me." We lay on our backs looking up at the sky. A small flock of clouds was grazing its way past the moon. "Well, do you like it?" I asked. "It's nice," Frank said. "If it didn't melt, you could carve it," I said. "But it does melt," Frank said. I was angry. I didn't want to think about the snow melting.

"Did they ever find out anything about the baby in the woods?" Frank asked; "the one your father found?" "No. We knew they wouldn't. Or my mother and grandmother knew they wouldn't. They said that a woman who left her baby to freeze in the snow and didn't even leave a bit of cloth on it wasn't going to let herself get caught. We never knew who it was." "Some women don't show when they're pregnant," Frank said. I didn't like to think about the baby in the woods. When I was a child and unhappy and pulled the covers over my head, I remembered the baby in the woods and was sure that they had found me in the woods and had brought me back to my mother's house, dead, and somehow she had done something to me so that I seemed to be alive again. It was a waking dream, one that I had had repeatedly.

"I don't see how a woman could leave a baby in the woods," Frank said. "Why not?" I asked; "you said that you didn't want children." "Yes, but once they're here, that's different. It's murder." "Maybe," I said, "she had something worth murdering for." "Murder," said Frank, as if hearing the word for the first time. I was thinking about my mother and her silences, of her bitter outbursts when I wanted to visit a friend, of her headaches which kept her in a dark room as if she were a tulip bulb in storage for the winter, of how politely she spoke to me when she was not angry, as if I were not her daughter, as if she could not see me, as if she did not know who I was and did not believe I existed. "There are lots of ways of committing murder," I said.

"I'm getting cold," Frank said, pulling me up. I began thwacking the back of his coat and the snow puffed into the air. Then Frank started brushing off my cape and I saw his face coming toward mine like a planet out of the heavens and I felt

227

his lips on mine. I clung to him as if I expected to be pulled away from him; I kissed him back so hard I could feel his upper lip push back and I felt his teeth under my lips. I was hot, as if I were standing under an enormously powerful dark sun. I wanted him to take off my cape, drop it in the snow, and press me against him. I drew back to look at his face and Frank held me away from him. "I'm sorry," he said. The sky pressed down on the top of my head; I was being pressed into the earth, taking root at last. As we walked back, I thought: I will get what I want. All I have to do is wait.

Time was like a sheet of paper that had divided itself in half, one part bright with light, the other dark. I had no use for the days, no use for the distant white sun which did its best to warm the earth, which, even in the depths of December, turned the sky a brilliant blue. The days were long, sterile, snow-covered meadows which I had to cross to reach the nights. The days were boxes in which I was sealed with sixteen other girls, all of us stitching mindlessly like seventeen unimportant Fates sewing on unimportant cloth with irrelevant threads. If only I were sewing for Frank, I thought, looking down at the cloth, I would not mind it. I would not mind if my fingers dried and split and bled. Instead, I thought bitterly, I sewed on, with my skin whole and I sewed for strangers. I hated them, whoever they were.

When I came home from work and lay down on my bed, and Polly came into my room, I only shook my head and listened to her tell me what the factory girls were up to or when she and Eddie planned to get married. They were going to get married when they could move into a little house on the grounds of the asylum. I said I would miss her if she left, but I wasn't sure I would. Like everyone else, she was becoming more and more irrelevant simply because she was not Frank. She said she was going to go on working in the factories after she married, at least until she started having babies. She said she wanted to have a baby once a year for four years and then she'd have eight hard years, and after that, her life would be her own again. "Why have them at all?" I asked her. "It's not exactly as if you have a choice about it," Polly said, looking at me oddly. "You told me about the girls at the factory who got rid of theirs," I said. "You don't get married if you want to get rid of babies," Polly said impatiently. "Why not?" I asked. She didn't answer me. "I never should have told you anything about that," she said at last. "Why not?" I said, looking at my watch; it was almost supper time. Frank would be coming back. "I'm not pregnant," I said.

"The girl I told you about," Polly said, "she told me it was easier to have a baby than to get rid of it." She jumped up nervously and went over to the stove. "It's stuffed with wood," I said lazily. "You're not pregnant, are you?" I asked. "I thought I was," she said. "What was it like?" I asked. "Terrifying," she said. "Why?" I asked. "Why? They would have fired Eddie. They would have fired me. We would have had to leave. It would have been so hard." "Why?" I asked. "Because it wasn't what we planned on," she said; "let's talk about something else."

"Would Eddie have left you," I asked, "if you were having a baby?" "Left me?" Polly cried; "he would have married me right away. He wanted to marry me this summer when it happened. But then I would have worried about it, why he was marrying me, because he wanted to or because he thought he had to." I said all men weren't like Eddie; I thought about the woman who had left the child in the woods. Polly sighed and looked at me critically. "Some men wouldn't throw a rope to a drowning man, either." "It's more than that," I said. "No," she said; "it isn't."

She looked out the window. It was quiet downstairs. "The cars must be late getting back from Barre," she said; "I'm not surprised, not with all this snow." She turned back into the room. "Have any of the girls at work ever said anything about a Jane Holt?" Polly asked. "I've heard that name somewhere," I said. "They say Frank sees her," Polly said; "it's odd, their both having the same last name." I sat up suddenly and stared at her. "When someone starts talking about babies," Polly said, "it's about time she knows all about the man she goes around with." "Wait," I said; "the girls mentioned her. They said her father owned the Emporium. But that was months ago! He's been with me ever since." "From what I hear," said Polly, "he's been with both of you."

I leaned back against the headboard and thought. Of course. That was why he came home at nine o'clock; that was why we left so late. But, I thought, there must have been weeks when he did not see her at all, because there had been weeks when we had gone out immediately after supper. Polly watched me working it out. "What are you going to do?" she asked me. "I have no choice," I said; "I hope he chooses me. There's no world without him." "You have to stop thinking that way!" she said; "he's not worth it." "Don't say that!" I said; "he's worth everything in the world and more." "I shouldn't have told you," she said. "You keep saying that!" I said; "but you say everything you want to say." "I'm trying to do the right thing," she said. "It's not up to you," I said; "*I'll* decide what's the right thing!" She said it was time to go down for supper, but I said I wasn't hungry and I wasn't going down. I sat on the bed and thought. I heard the clatter of dishes and the scrape of chairs pulling up to the table and I thought of Frank, sitting there, and I thought I could pick his voice out from the others, but still I did not move.

Jane Holt! Who was she? One of those pale, good Montpelier girls who were obedient to their mothers and fathers, who went docilely into other people's households as hired girls to earn money for their finery, and at the appointed time came out and married one of the proper young men of the town. They were all the same, those girls. You could order them, by number, from a catalog of proper, lifeless girls just as you could order beets from *Burpee's Seeds*. I would tolerate Jane Holt's existence if I had to, but I didn't like it. There had to be something I could do. And then I remembered. I'd seen her. Florence had pointed her out one afternoon when we stopped into the Emporium after work. She was a thin, nicely dressed girl. She was not pretty. Frank would not choose her simply because she had come along first.

I sat down in front of the mirror and began pulling the long hairpins out of my hair. But I had seen her. I knew her. She was so *good*. She would wait patiently, sure Frank would choose her in the end. If I knew about Jane Holt, then Jane Holt must know about me. If someone pointed me out to her, she would tell herself she had nothing to fear because I was only another girl who roomed in the same house as Frank did; she would never believe that he would take an interest in me, a common girl, working out. I boarded out and sewed in a tailoring establishment; *her* father owned the Emporium. I conjured her up once more. There she was, limp and pale in front of the spools of ribbon in the Emporium. She couldn't be more than eighteen, I thought, but her skirts already seemed dragged down by grimy little hands. Jane Holt would ruin Frank's life. Even if he wanted to see more of her, I had to stop him. She didn't deserve him. She didn't understand him. He would be better off dead than married to her. *I* was the one he had been born for.

My hair was loose. I told myself I had better hurry, because when Frank finished eating, he was sure to come up here and see why I hadn't come down to dinner. I began taking off my clothes, folding each article neatly, as if I were packing things I never intended to wear again. I picked up the neat pile of clothing and placed it on the chair near the stove. Then I put on my nightgown and sat down before the glass, brushing my hair. I pulled half of it forward so that it fell over one breast and my stomach. I brushed the rest of it over my shoulder. Then I picked up my shawl, threw it over my shoulders, looked out into the hall, and seeing no one there, ran its full length, and pushed at Frank's door.

It was open. I closed the door behind me. The marble iris stood peacefully on a low shelf. A few charcoal sketches were tacked to the walls. The room was neat. There was nothing out of place. It seemed empty, as if no one lived there. My own room always looked as if it were occupied by someone who had finished shedding one of the many skins she sloughed off every day. My clothes lay around like so many forgotten selves. Every day I resolved to be neater, and every day I produced chaos. Something in me had no sympathy for order. I looked around Frank's room and sighed. Order lived here. Order was important to him. The feather comforter was neatly smoothed out on the bed and the pillow was precisely in its center. I went up to the bed, took a deep breath, and turned the covering back. Then I sat down on the edge. I was moving mechanically, in stages. I told myself to pick up my legs and put them on the bed and I lay one leg down on the bed and then the other. I looked down at my body, sitting on Frank's bed, my back propped up by his headboard. It was cold in the room. I pulled the covers up over my lap. I was wearing one of the rough white cotton nightgowns that my grandmother used to make by the dozen. It was long-sleeved and fell loose from the shoulders. Only one button fastened its front, which was slit from the neck to the belly. One button, my grandmother used to say, made things easier when you were nursing babies. I felt for the button and opened it. Then I waited. I didn't think about anything. I didn't know what to expect. I had come to the place where the tracks ran out, where no one had gone before me. Had time passed? I didn't know. I waited.

The door opened and Frank came in. I didn't smile. I didn't blink. I couldn't move. "My God," said Frank. He shut the door quickly behind him. His brows furrowed; his lips were pressed together. He looked as if he were about to cry. "No," he said, "this isn't right. Get up." He might have been talking to a stick. I sat there, looking straight at him. "You don't know what you're doing," he said; "get up." I shook my head. "Damn!" he said, kicking the foot of the bed. "What is it you want?" Frank asked me. "I love you," I said.

And then I waited for the world to come to an end. I wondered, calmly, how it would happen. Would he pick me up and drop me down on the hall rug? Would he start packing his bag and walk out the door and go to Mrs. Hinckley's and ask Charlie to let him stay there? Would he take me back to my room and leave me there alone? If he did, I would never eat again. I would never get out of bed again. "You don't love me," said Frank. "Don't tell me how I feel!" I said, flushing; "I love you. I love you more than anything in the world. Why shouldn't I? You're worth loving. You're the only person I've ever met who was worth loving." Frank sat down in the chair and studied me.

"Do you love me?" I asked him. "I'm not in bed with you, am I?" he asked. "What does that mean?" I asked. "If I didn't care about you," he said, "I'd be in that bed." "Is that the only way you can think of saying you love me? By not getting into this bed?" I asked him. "I can't say it at all," he said. "But you do love me?" I asked. "A little," he said. "How much?" I asked. "How much? Oh, one petal of that iris." "But not the whole flower?" I asked him. "Not the whole flower." "One day you might," I said. "I might." "Do you love anyone else more than me?" I asked. "No," he said, "I don't." I patted the place next to me. "Not here," he said; "you're the one who likes the snow so much. Go back to your room and get dressed. Everyone's talking as it is. We don't have to make it easier for them."

I jumped out of bed and flew down to my room. He might love me! He might! I was dressed and back in his room before he had put on his coat and hat. He came up to me and put his hands on my shoulders. "Idiot," he said. His voice was gentle. He let his hands slide down over my breasts and they rested there. He nodded slowly, as he always did when something pleased him. "You can always change your mind," he said; "in fact, I wish you would." "I can't," I said, and as soon as I said it, I knew it was true.

I knew where we were going without asking. We were going to the thick grove of woods with the carved tree stumps in its center. The snow had been falling heavily all day and the roller had not yet pressed down the surface of the road. By the time we stood in the middle of the trees, I was exhausted. "We're not going to get undressed out here?" I asked Frank, uncertainly. "Just lie down," Frank said. He sounded both stern and harassed.

I lay down in the snow. Frank stood over me, indecisively, as if, even now, he might turn back.

I stretched my arms up toward him and he sank down next to me. He lay there, rigid. I turned on my side and began stroking his forehead, running my finger along the line of his eyebrows, along his lips, down the long line of his nose. "I've been thinking of growing a beard," he said. "Have you?" I said. I began kissing the lids of his eyes, his cheeks. I nuzzled between his head and shoulder and kissed his throat. I didn't want to kiss him; I wanted to bite him. I wanted to swallow him whole. I felt Frank fumbling with his clothes and then he lowered himself onto me and pushed me deeper into the snow. "Wait," I said. I wanted to see him without his clothing. I wanted to see what was pressing against me. I wanted to see the long, hot maleness of him before he entered me.

"Should I stop?" Frank asked me. "Oh, no, don't stop," I said. Frank pushed himself up by his arms; the lower half of his body separated from mine and then I felt something warm and hard pressing against the sealed chamber of my body. I looked up and saw Frank staring down at me, expressionless. "What's wrong?" I said; "are you stuck?" "No, I'm not stuck," he said; "Agnes, let's stop." I reached down and took his organ in my hand and began caressing it. My fingers traced its little ridges and folds; they burrowed in the fig-shaped testicles until I felt them flatten and harden under my hand. I ran my hand along the little line of fur that rose from his groin to his navel, and, just as I had forgotten what was pressing against my body, I felt the hot flesh entering mine. I felt Frank begin to move slowly inside me and I felt the doors to my body open. I was home in my own skin. He had been separated from me for so long, and now he was back. I felt my body arching to meet his in a way that was familiar but new in its violence. A warm flush was spreading through my groin, up into my stomach, down into my thighs. And then Frank began pushing in deeper and I wanted to cry out against the pain, but my body rose to meet his and I heard a wolfish voice, crying, and realized that it was my voice crying out in pure pleasure and triumph. And Frank began to thrust harder against me, and I felt something tear, and something warm began to leak out between my legs, and then I heard Frank groan and another stream of something warm and wet flooded me like balm against the pain. Frank lifted himself away from me and lay down beside me. I touched myself; I felt swollen and bruised and warm. I held up my hand in the moonlight. "It's bloody," I said; "will I stop bleeding?" So this was how it happened; this was how bodies took possession of one another, how all the secret places of your body were opened for the new being who, mysteriously, was able to find the key.

Frank dug in his coat pocket and pulled out a huge kerchief. "Here," he said; "use this. It'll stop the blood." I put the cloth between my legs, but the bleeding didn't stop. I felt the cloth grow heavier as the blood drenched it. "Don't worry," Frank said, his voice remote; "you won't bleed to death." "I know I won't bleed to death," I said, "but I don't want to bleed anymore. I'll never get this skirt clean." I reached up behind my head and scooped some snow into a ball. "What are you doing?" Frank asked me. "I'm going to put this snow between my legs," I said; "the cold will stop the bleeding." "I thought," Frank said slowly, "you'd be hysterical. I never thought you'd be so practical." The snow between my legs felt wonderful. The throbbing was lessening. The bleeding was slowing. "How long are you going to be able to keep it there?" Frank asked. "Not too long," I admitted. "You're not hysterical at all," he marveled. "No," I said, stretching out carefully in the snow. I reached down and removed the ball of snow, which was beginning to melt. "But I'm hysterically happy," I said; "I hope you're happy with this body. Now it belongs to you." I felt a cold, hard silence next to me. "What I mean is," I said quickly, "I don't feel alone anymore." I scooped up some snow and packed it between my legs and rolled over toward Frank. "I could do this day and night," I said; "the only thing wrong is the time. There should be bright light here so that I could study every inch of you. I want to *memorize* you."

Without thinking, I buried my face in his stomach and began kissing the hairs running down his belly, and when I came to his organ, I didn't stop. "God!" he gasped. I began to take little bites of his flesh. "I've always wanted to eat a person," I said, raising my head. I went back to biting him. "God," Frank said again, rolling toward me, and once more he was inside me, and this time it did not hurt; it was only sore. I saw Frank smiling at me. "You really did like it?" he asked. "Of course I liked it," I said; "you are the most wonderful thing!" Am I?" he asked. "You are! You know you are!" I said, and I began tickling him between the ribs. "That's enough," Frank said; "are you ready to get up?" "No, I want to stay here and freeze to death," I said; "life will never get any better." I felt sleepy, dreamy, perfectly safe.

"Agnes," he said, "get up." I got up, waiting for the blood-gush warm between my legs, but I had stopped bleeding. "I've ruined your handkerchief," I said sadly. "I'll burn it when I get home," he said; "you'd better hide that skirt." "I think I can wash it out," I said. "Are you sorry?" I asked him abruptly. "No," he said, "I'm not. I don't want you to be, either." "I could never be sorry," I said. "I feel," I said, gesturing helplessly, "as if my heart were warm and white and were sailing around like a swan on a dark lake." He squeezed my hand. "We came back here sooner than we thought," I said. Frank put his arm around my shoulders and drew me to him and we walked together, matching our strides, as if we were joined at the hip.

"You really are happy with me, aren't you?" he said. "Oh, yes," I said, holding him tighter, "I am." "What do you want from me?" he asked. "I want you to want me," I said. "That's all?" I nodded. "This is the damndest thing," said Frank, looking from the ground to the sky and back, as if he wanted to be sure that it was the well-worn, familiar world after all.

26

When I wakened, I was floating somewhere in a seamless, bright light which had no discernible source. I looked toward my windows but did not see them, and then I realized that the sheet was over my eyes. When I pushed the sheet back, I saw that someone had drawn the white curtains, and the sun, which shone brilliantly outside, was lighting the room with a warm, pearly radiance, and I knew that Frank had come in, covered me with the sheet, and pulled the curtains. I held the sheet before my face and looked at the light shining through it. I knew that the whole world had changed utterly. I knew that the peculiar radiance filling the room now filled me as well. I got up and dressed slowly, smiling at the walls, at my pitcher and basin, at my skirt, circling in the air in front of the stove. I went over to the skirt and looked at it. When it dried, there would be no trace of blood. It was too bad. I ought to have kept something from the night before. I heard a scratching at the door, and, as I was about to open it, Frank stuck his head in and said he would see me downstairs. When the door closed, I stood in the middle of the room and laughed. I had never been so happy.

I began lacing up my boots, and as I bent forward, I became aware of the new soreness inside me. So this is what it feels like to live in one's body, I thought, to move into it, soul and all, to know that your body was really your own and that it was your own soul looking out through your own eyes. I was sorry that I had not suffered more for what I loved, so that the Fates themselves would see how much I was prepared to endure now that I had found what I wanted. Outside, a wood dove burbled on my sill. I was not surprised to hear it there, in the middle of the winter. I went down the steps, slowly, enjoying the way each step bore my weight. The world and I fit together so well! There was nothing too small to delight in. I wondered how long this could last and I saw no reason for it ever to end.

When I came into the dining room, everyone looked up and smiled as they always did, and I beamed back. I had never realized how lovely they were, how kind, how unfailingly polite. The sunlight struck the silver-plated candlesticks on the sideboard and sent stilettos of light flashing through the room. I sank down into my chair and grinned at Polly. "What's that foolish grinning about?" she asked me. "I got a good night's sleep, that's all," I said. "Hmmm," said Polly. Then she looked at my plate. "Well," she said, "you won't start eating until Frank comes in, so I'll start on some potatoes." She began chewing. I smiled at her. I loved her. She was loyal and intelligent and she never gave up on anything. I wished, for the hundredth time, that I was more like her. From the corner of my eye, I could see the rusty crack in the ceiling paint which betrayed the existence of a leak Iris had not yet repaired; I saw how the green paper and its weeping willows bubbled away from the walls, and yet everything was beautiful to me. I was, I saw, possessed by a kind of double consciousness: I saw the flaws around me but they did not matter. My eyes were changing the essential nature of things. The bubbling wallpaper, which had so annoyed me in the past, such incontrovertible evidence of Iris's tightfistedness, was now adorable, an expression of her personality; her house was like no other. I loved the crack in the roof over our heads because it was *our* roof. This must be, I thought, how a new colt feels when it stumbles over its feet trying to reach all parts of the world at once. I was in love with the world, every stick and stone in it.

I was starving. Under Polly's stunned gaze, I gobbled down my half of the potatoes. I felt a sudden stab of sorrow for the blood I had lost the night before, not because I had lost it, but because I had not been able to see what I was losing. I thought about lying in the pure white snow, under the rock-salt stars, and I again lamented the absence of light. I remembered the feel of Frank's body against mine. I remembered his flesh, hot and hard under my hand. The uneasiness which had afflicted me when I had gone to Bald Hill with Charlie was gone. In its place was a complete acceptance and a ravenousness for more. I was like a starving person who had suddenly found the only food I could eat. Blood, even the idea of blood, had always revolted me, dizzied me. Not now. I knew that girls sometimes took off all their clothes when they were with men, but I had never been able to imagine how they stood it. Now I was eager for a chance to take off all my clothes and watch Frank remove his. I had no shame. I could even imagine what it must be like to have a baby. Of course Frank did not want a baby and neither did I. I thought of it, growing inside, a deformed little dwarf pulling down its mask to form its face, and its face was my face, and I thought of it ready to enter the light, a small, terrible replica, its tiny fist woven out of the reproaches and hatreds and disapprovals it would have for me simply because I was its mother. And then I leaned sideways to borrow Polly's fork and I again became conscious of the soreness at my center, and I thought the baby need not look like me; the baby might look like him. And if it did, there would be two of him, and as he got older, the baby would look like Frank, and I would see what he had looked like before I had ever met him, and when Frank and I died, the baby would live on, and it would have other boys who would look like Frank, and Frank would never die. But I still did not want to have a baby.

I saw Frank come in and studied him without appearing to lift my eyes. That was one of the few talents I had perfected in North Chittendon. I watched him sit down, pick up his knife and fork, and saw how he looked at me and smiled. Finally, I looked up. "There's a show tonight," Frank said across the table; "do you want to go?" I was so startled I started to hiccup, but I nodded my head violently. "Drink some water," said Frank. Polly reached over and slapped me on the back, harder, I thought, than necessary. "What kind of show is it?" Polly asked him. "Some play or other," he said; "it's called *Only One Life*. Some of the cutters have been to see it and they say it's pretty good." "It must be wonderful to work normal hours," Polly said gloomily. "Why don't you come with us if Eddie can't get off?" Frank asked. I glared at him but he didn't notice. "I'll get three tickets," Frank said, getting up. "I'll see you tonight," he said to me, and he was gone.

"Are you finished?" Polly asked me, but I didn't answer. I was speechless with rage. Didn't she have the sense to know she wasn't wanted? After all this time spent waiting to be alone with Frank, how could she spoil everything by coming along? I pushed back my plate angrily. Polly and I left the house without speaking; when we were out on the street, I walked faster and faster, trying to leave her behind. Finally, I felt her grab the back of my skirt. "Agnes, stop," she said; "you're running down the street." I slowed down but refused to look at her.

"I know why you're angry," she said; "you don't think I

should come with you tonight. I wouldn't be coming if I'd had time to say I wasn't coming, but he was too quick for me. You better not let Frank know how you are. You'll scare him off." "What are you talking about now?" I demanded. "Frank likes having people around," she said. "Who doesn't?" I asked. "You don't," she said; "you like to study people and when you're finished, they could fall down dead in front of you and you wouldn't care." I stopped and stood still. Two girls stepped off the sidewalk and into the street, passing us. "After the show, I want to go for a walk with him," I said. "After the show, I'll have a headache," she said; "all right?" "Fine," I said. "Do your best," she said; "exercise your moral character, as the reverend says." "Damn the reverend!" I said. "Be careful about that too," Polly said; "Frank takes religion seriously. When he takes it at all. Charlie told me Frank's mother and sister are pious creatures." "Pious," I said. "Just keep your mouth shut and you won't have to worry about anything," she said.

By the time I reached Mrs. James's, my anger had faded and was replaced by a senseless contentment which I knew had nothing to do with my surroundings. I looked at the sixteen other girls, all sewing diligently in the bad light, all looking furtively at the doorway so that when they laid down their work and gossiped, they would not be caught by Mrs. James. It was early in the morning, but the airless room was already acrid. Florence always said that when she walked through the room she could come back and tell me who wasn't tending to her clothes. But if I sewed all afternoon, I could stop at the Emporium and buy Frank a sticky bun and in the morning, I could give it to him to take to the quarries. And tomorrow afternoon, I could go by some of the shops on my way home and buy him something for Christmas. Christmas was only three weeks off. My birthday was next week. I decided not to tell Frank about it. I would only be seventeen. I didn't want to remind him of how young I was.

I looked up and saw two girls watching me from the far side of the room. I leaned over and said something to Florence. "They're friends of that Jane Holt," she said; "I heard you've been keeping company with Frank." I sewed silently. "Which one of you do you think he'll pick?" she asked me. "I wouldn't know," I said. Florence inspected me. "You think he's already chosen you, don't you?" "No," I said, "I don't think anything." "Who's he taking to the show?" she asked. "Me," I said. "Oh," said Florence; "well. I guess Jane won't like that. I wish I were going. They have such exciting theatricals at the

239

Barre Opera House." "The Barre Opera House!" I exclaimed; "I didn't know it was in Barre." "You'll have to take the cars," Florence said, stitching away. "Is it an opera?" I said; "I've never been to an opera. I might not understand a word of it." "It's not an opera; it's a play," Florence said. "I'm relieved to hear it," I said. "You're sewing your skirt to that pair of pants," Florence told me.

After dinner, Frank and Polly and I started out for the Barre cars. I didn't want to cling to Frank, so I drifted loosely, as if he and Polly were together and I were tagging along. But Polly began to either walk ahead or inexplicably lag behind, and finally Frank took my arm. "It's a beautiful night," Polly said, catching up with us and linking her arm through mine; "you'd never believe it was below zero out." "No," I said, looking at Frank. Couples were drifting down the side streets and back onto the main street toward the cars. I saw that some of the girls had dressed their hair with brooches and bits of ribbon and I was sorry I hadn't thought of decorating my own more elaborately. Its style, I thought with a sigh, was elaborate enough. I had so much hair and it was so heavy and pliable that I wore it in the most intricate ways.

We were among the last on the cars, and the crowd pressed me against Frank. When the jostling car didn't throw me against Frank, Polly did, and when I turned to look at her, she opened her eyes wide, as if she didn't know who I was. When we got off in Barre, I stood and looked around me, amazed. The women were so elegantly dressed. There were men in frock coats and bowler hats. Surely we had come more than just a few miles. "Come on," said Frank. We could see a brilliantly lit building, its three verandahs strung with colored paper lanterns, and a little band was playing on the bottom level. "They set tables up on the porches for refreshments," Polly said. "At intermission," Frank said. I said I thought I would be too excited to eat, but Frank said he wouldn't be, and Polly said she probably wouldn't be too excited, either; she was never too excited to eat. Frank took out our tickets and told us we were going to sit in the twelfth row. "That's good and bad," he said; "it's good because you can see and hear everything, but if the costumes are falling apart and they're just half sewn, you can see that, too. And when they have an old battle-ax playing a young girl, you get a pretty good look at her wrinkles." "I'd rather sit up close," I said; "I don't want to miss anything." "Remember the time all of us came out last year?" Polly asked Frank, "and that actress kept spitting through all her lines and you said the only reason I was dry was because I was wearing a hat?" "We were sitting too close that time," Frank said.

We climbed over the people who were already seated and I leaned forward and watched the heavy velvet curtain for signs of life. Frank and Polly were considerably calmer. Polly inspected the audience as if that were the real show. "I see four girls from the factory," she said, collapsing back against her cushioned seat; "and I thought I saw Charlie." "He's coming tomorrow night," Frank said. "Oh," I said. Polly looked at me. "Well," I said, "I guess all of Montpelier can't fit in here at once." Then I saw the curtain twitch and I fell silent. *Only One Life* was about to begin. Frank unfastened my cape and draped it over the back of my chair while I stared straight ahead, motionless.

The curtain rose heavily into the air. A young girl was sitting in a rowboat in the middle of a painted river, pretending to row to the other side. Then she rowed back to the middle of the river, and, thinking she was alone, jumped out to swim. A spotlight shone on a man who was watching from behind a painted tree on the riverbank. Just then, a large bird began to dive at the girl who had gotten back in the boat and she waved her arms, trying to frighten it off. Evidently, the man on the bank mistook her intention and thought that she was having difficulty with her boat, because he began removing his shoes and shirt and dove into the water. Meanwhile, the girl had successfully frightened off the bird, but the young man found himself caught in the deadly currents of the painted river. The girl saw that he was in danger of drowning and began to row toward him. After great difficulty, she brought the boat close enough so that the young man could climb into it. Then she rowed to shore and helped the young man, who was exhausted from swimming, down the path to her father's residence. She and her father appeared to live in a large mud hut shot through with twigs. "That's a house in the country," Frank whispered, leaning forward, "according to a city painter." Polly laughed. I wanted him to be quiet. I wanted to see what would happen next.

When the curtain came down, I refused to leave my seat. I was afraid when it rose again we would not be there, and I would miss some of the story. Frank went out and came back with glasses of lemonade and two little bags of biscuits. "Did you ever hear such silly dialogue?" Frank asked Polly. She shook her head. I stared at both of them. The dialogue was wonderful, the people were real; on the stage, lives sped before me like stars falling through the sky.

When the curtain went up again, a messenger came with an urgent message from the young man's father asking him to return home at once. In pathetic tones, the young man explained to the girl that he would have to leave for a short time, but he would return, and when he did, he would take the girl away with him and they would live together eternally. But as soon as he left, a moneylender appeared on the scene and threatened the girl's father. If her father did not pay his debts immediately, he said, he would evict father and daughter. Lightning flashed overhead. Just as it appeared that all was certainly lost, a new young man walked out of the woods and toward the girl and her father. He said he was a friend of the first young man and that, if she would promise to marry *him,* he would lend her the money she needed. After much hesitation, the girl decided to marry the second young man in order to save her father's honor, but unknown to her, the man who performed the ceremony was not a minister at all. The curtain fell as the young girl and the man to whom she thought she was married stood in front of her house while the young girl's true love walked out of the woods and gazed upon the two of them in horror.

The curtain rose on a funeral scene. Evidently, the false husband had gone rowing with the young girl's father and both had been drowned. After the funeral, the young girl decided to go to the city to find work and her employer was her first love's fiancée. "This story is too complicated for me," Polly whispered; "how do they dream those things up?" "Shh," I said. "So many things can't go wrong in one person's life," she whispered. I slapped her hand. The girl's true love was happy to find her once more but unhappy to discover her working for his fiancée. However, his fiancée seemed to spend a great deal of time with the minister. At last, I began to suspect that the minister and the man's fiancée would get together, and that the girl, after all her suffering and sacrifice, would be reunited with the man she had rescued from the river. After all, they were fated to be together. And so it happened. When the final curtain came down, tears were running down my cheeks.

"I guess you liked it," Frank said, grinning. "I did," I said; "it was wonderful." "What about you, Polly?" he asked. "Oh," she said, "I'm still trying to work out the twists and turns of things: I never saw such a complicated story." "They're all the same," Frank said. "Well," Polly said, "I don't think they should try to show someone drowning on a dry stage." "It looked real to me," I said. "*All* of it?" Polly asked. "All of it!" I said; "it was terribly realistic." "Her life must be more exciting than ours," Frank said to Polly.

My eyes were burning. I didn't want to listen to their dissections of a wonderful story. "Did you see the way the girl rowed?" Frank asked; "she kept pointing the oars up in the air. I thought she was signaling to the bird." "Oh, for heaven's sake!" I exclaimed. "Don't tease her," said Polly; "she's never been to a play before." "*Only One Life,*" said Frank; "I felt as if I spent three lifetimes there watching it." "That's enough," Polly warned him. I felt his eyes on me. "When we get back," he whispered in my ear, "do you want to go for a walk?" "Yes," I said; "if we don't have to talk about the play." "We're only teasing," he said gently; "sometimes I forget you're younger than I am." "Only four years younger!" I exclaimed.

We joined the steady flow of couples returning to the Barre cars. Every now and then I heard someone call Frank's name, but by the time I turned to look, whoever it was had vanished. On the car, I sat next to Polly, and Frank stood over us. The two of them talked to each other over the top of my head. Frank said something to me and I nodded. Polly poked me in the ribs and I nodded at her and smiled. I wanted to think about the play. I could see the young girl standing with her false husband while the man she really loved walked slowly out of the woods toward them. How terrible it must be to marry the wrong man! I thought about the heroine's life, how conveniently it had shaped itself to her purposes, drowning her false husband and spendthrift father, causing her arch rival to fall in love with someone else and freeing the field for her, and I thought, I have never had luck, I will have to make my own luck.

I looked up at Frank and smiled. I knew I was beautiful. I knew other men on the cars were watching me, and that Frank knew they were, but I knew how people grew accustomed to beauty and that, finally, it had little influence over them. I had to find another way to bind him to me. Passion could not be enough. Probably one got used to that just as one got used to beauty. And as the scenes of the play kept passing before me, I saw with surprise that I knew what Frank's expression had been at every point. I saw him raise his eyebrows as the thick rope, painted the same blue as the stage, yanked the boat this way and that as the girl pretended to row. I saw him cast his eyes up to heaven as the imposter came upon the stage dressed as a minister, and I remembered how he hissed at him along with almost everyone else in the audience. I must have watched him as closely as I watched the play. I must have seen it through him, as I was now seeing the cars, the people, and the landscape outside. I saw everything through him.

When we got off the cars, Polly announced that she had a headache and wanted to go home, and Frank said that was too bad; it had been awfully stuffy in the opera house. Evidently, he didn't suspect that Polly and I had manufactured the headache together. "Do you still want to go for a walk?" he asked me; "it's late. It's almost twelve." I said I still wanted to go. "You'll be awfully wrung out in the morning," he said. I said I would just sew more slowly. "Where do you want to go?" he asked; "it's a long way out to last night's field." "Last night's field," I said; "I want to go back to last night's field." "All right, then," Frank said, taking my hand.

The wind sent the surface snow whirling into snow devils. "You're not saying anything," Frank said. "Neither are you." He hugged me to him, and we walked, matching strides. "I could walk," I said, "over the horizon and on through the morning and into tomorrow night." He laughed. "You'd be pretty tired," he said. "But it would be worth doing," I said; "to see how far we could get." "Sometime we'll try it," he said. "When we don't have to go to work in the morning," I said, and then I was staring at him, wondering what it would be like if forty-five years had suddenly passed and we were walking down this road in our sixties, safely past passions, past everything but an enormous, snow-covered love for one another. Frank asked me what I was thinking about. "I was thinking about what it would be like to be old," I said. "How old?" he asked; "twenty?" "No, old. Sixty or seventy. I wonder what it's like to be that old. I never thought I'd live to be very old. I always thought I'd die young. I still think I will. But I don't want to, not now. Now I want to live forever." "I never thought about it," Frank said; "however long I live is long enough for me." "That's because you haven't found what you want yet," I said; "wait until you start on your statues. You'll be afraid every day is your last." "Is that how it seems to you?" Frank asked. "Mostly it does, I guess," I said.

We cut across the field and came to the clearing. "Does Charlie know about this place?" I asked. "No," Frank said, "I never told him about it." "Then it's our place," I said, relieved; "don't bring him here. Don't bring anyone else here. Have you ever brought anyone else here?'' "No," he said; "what's so special about this place?" In the moonlight, his face looked intense, strange. "It's yours," I said; "you came here when you were a child, before I even knew you existed." "Before you were even born," he said. He sat down in the snow and held his arms out to me. "I'm getting better at this," he said; "come on."

And when it was over, and when we were fastening our clothes, I started to cry. "Why are you crying?" Frank asked. "Because I'm happy," I said; "I always cry when I'm happy. At least I do when I'm this happy. My *bones* are happy." "Your bones?" he said, smiling. "They're singing," I said; "can't you hear them?" "You're crazy," he said. "No, listen," I said, and I put my cupped palm over his ear. "Don't you hear them?" "I hear them; they're roaring," he said; "they're not singing." "That's how happy bones sing," I said, brushing his hair back from his face. "What a high, smooth forehead," I said, stroking it. I kept smoothing back his hair and felt his cheek turn lazily under my hand. "Do you still have the gun?" I asked him. "In my pocket," he said; "it's a habit. We never went out at night without one. It was wild out there in Canada." "Are you a good shot?" I asked. "Not bad," he said; "can you shoot?" "Oh, yes," I said; "my father and the farm's manager taught me when I was tiny. Then I practiced with my grandmother. I can hit anything, at least when I have a little practice. They would never have left a woman alone on the farm unless she could use a gun. My grandmother shot a mountain cat a year before she died and everyone around said they hadn't seen one of them in years."

"My grandmother's idea of hunting," said Frank, "was to go along with my grandfather and then set herself down on a log in a clearing, and she'd sit with her rifle and wait there. If something happened to walk in front of her, there was some chance she'd get it." "Did she ever get anything?" I asked. "Well, one year, she was the only one to get a moose. My father said it wasn't fair, because the moose obviously thought she was another tree and he pitied the moose its last moments, shot by something it knew all its life and thought it could trust. My father had a vivid imagination." "I don't like hunting," I said. "I do," said Frank; "it's a challenge." "Trying to think like an animal?" I asked; "is that it?" "I do that all the time," said Frank. "So do I," I said, "but that's why I can't hunt them. I couldn't be the thing closing in on them." "The way I always figured it," Frank said, "was that someone had to shoot them, and it might as well be me. They started me out young enough. I had a dog that got caught in a trap. They made me shoot him." "Your own dog?" "*Because* it was my own dog. They said I should have known better and kept him tied up when I wasn't around." "I would never have shot my own dog," I said. "You would have if you'd lived with my family," he said. "No," I said, "I wouldn't have." "What would you have done?" he asked. "I would have died with the dog," I said. "It's easy to say," Frank said, sitting up; "anyhow, I never had another dog after that."

"Just how well can you shoot?" he asked, staring through the tree trunks which outlined themselves sharply against the silvery sky. "Well, after ten or so practice shots, I don't have to sight the target. I can close my eyes and point the gun and hit whatever it is. That's how they taught me. I had to see the sights in my mind's eye, not just at the end of the gun." "I can't shoot nearly that well," said Frank. "It's a useless talent," I said; "I have to find a useful talent. If I could carve, that would be something." "It's no profession for a woman," said Frank. "I might be able to write," I said; "my teacher always said I could. Of course, she was only from North Chittendon, so her opinion wasn't worth much." "You could write better plays than that thing we saw tonight," Frank said. "Oh, I don't think so!" I exclaimed; "that was wonderful!" "You don't know if you can do it unless you try," he said. "I want to do *something*!" I said. "I know," said Frank; "it's one of the things I like about you." I stared at the trees, dark against the sky. "If I had a choice, I'd rather paint," I said.

"You won't do anything if you freeze," he said; "let's get up." "I won't freeze," I said; "I'm healthy as a horse." "Even horses get cold," he said. "You know," I said, while we were walking back, "I've been trying to think what I remembered first. First in my whole life." "Mostly what I remember," he said, "is coming into the kitchen and seeing my mother standing in front of the kitchen window looking out. She usually had a wooden spoon in one hand and a bowl of something on the table. Half the time she was crying. No one ever knew what she was crying about." "Maybe she wasn't happy," I said. "Well, it's obvious she wasn't happy," he said irritably, "but we didn't know why." "Maybe she didn't love your father," I said; "if you're in love with your husband, you'd be happy." "My parents loved each other, and they still love each other, and they're still unhappy," Frank said. His voice was hard. "If I

246

loved someone and he loved me," I said, "I don't think I could be unhappy." "That's a nice thought," he said.

"When you dream," I asked him, "what do you dream about?" "I never dream," he said. "You must. Everyone dreams." "Well," said Frank, "if I dream, I don't remember when I wake up. I have enough trouble keeping my eyes on everything in this world." "Don't you think," I asked him abruptly, "there's more to this world than you can see? I look around and I can't believe that we see everything there is." "We see everything there is," said Frank; "when they turn the earth over with a shovel, we see the rest of it." "That's horrible!" I said. "A lot of the world is horrible," Frank said; "most of it is." I burrowed into Frank's shoulder. The world could not be horrible with him in it.

As we came to the Common, the clock struck four. "You're going to be sewing very slowly tomorrow," Frank said. "Are you going to be here for Christmas?" I asked him. "I suppose," he said; "I'm in no hurry to go home." "You don't want to see Madge?" I asked, trying to laugh. Frank stopped walking. "What did Charlie tell you about Madge?" he asked. I said he hadn't told me anything. "I might as well tell you before someone else does," he said; "someone will. Charlie will. I know him." I said I hadn't seen Charlie for weeks. "Madge had a baby and got rid of it," he said; "she said it was mine and that she knew I didn't want a kid. She blamed it all on me." "Who did Charlie blame?" I asked. I was surprised by my voice, calm, neutral, as if we were discussing the week's laundry. A baby! His baby! No wonder she had been so angry! No wonder she had wanted to make him miserable! "He didn't blame anyone," Frank said; "he was just disgusted with both of us. He said she ought to have known better and I ought to have known better and he ought to have known better than to leave us alone."

"Were you ever sorry," I asked, "that she got rid of the baby?" "Well, I never wanted to marry Madge," Frank said; "I guess if she'd left a baby on my doorstep, my mother would have taken care of it. Every now and then she starts in crying and when we ask her what's wrong, she says she'd be fine if she could only have another baby. No, I wasn't sorry. I wouldn't have known what to do with a baby. They would never have stood for it back home, letting me run around loose while its mother walked around unmarried. They would have come for me in the middle of the night, and if I hadn't married Madge, they would have hung me from a tree. That's how it is there." "Did you love her once?'' ''I never loved Madge,'' he said; ''I *told* her I'd never marry her.'' ''I guess,'' I said, ''you don't want to get married. Some men don't.'' ''I didn't say that,'' Frank replied.

When I got back to my room, it was almost five in the morning. Outside, the sky was already lightening. A baby, I thought. So that was what was wrong with Madge. She'd gotten pregnant. I rubbed my hand over my stomach. I wondered if the same thing could happen to me. No, I decided, it couldn't. Then I sat back against the headboard and thought. It could. But I had found a new world, and it was worth the risk. It was worth whatever I had to pay to keep it. My lids were closing. Polly had told me stories about the factory girls who got pregnant even though they took so many precautions against it. There were remedies they used, syrups made of pennyroyal. There was a doctor in Clarendon Falls who came to their rooms if the syrup didn't work. It was always possible to undo things, I thought, but it was not always possible to do them. My hand was still resting on my stomach, and I thought of Madge, and a hot flush of envy rose from my stomach and burned in my chest and my cheeks. That ridiculous woman, that loud, vulgar person, had walked around with Frank's baby inside her. Still, I told myself, she was far away, and Frank did not intend to go home for Christmas. Most of the people in the boardinghouse would go home, and he and I would have the house to ourselves.

In the dream I was at the bottom of a hill and I was looking up toward a knot of people who were standing in front of a bright, white building. I knew they were waiting for me, and I tried to make my way toward them, but my legs would not hold me. Each time I took a step, I sank to the earth and then struggled upright again. As soon as I saw I was standing, I looked down at my feet and then at the ground under them so that I would not make a misstep, but each time I would feel my legs numb beneath me, as if they had been bandaged for a long time and the tight bandages had just been taken off. Suddenly, I noticed the white picket fence on the other side of the sidewalk and I crawled up to it and pulled myself upright.

I began hitching myself along, pulling myself from one picket to another. The group at the top of the hill had turned toward me but did not move closer. I tried to see who they were but they were too far away. There was one man and three women. The women were beautifully dressed and their colorful dresses blew in the wind. I saw the wind blow my skirt out in front of me and I saw that my skirt was black. I kept struggling to reach the four people at the top of the hill, and suddenly I could walk, and I walked quickly up to them. But when I approached them, they turned their backs to me and I still could not see who they were.

I opened my eyes, sure I had dreamed this many, many times before. "I hate that dream," I said out loud. I thought of the dream of the doll's head on the kitchen table. It was a horrible dream, but I liked it better than the dream about the people on the hill. I didn't understand why I dreamed about the people who turned away from me. I always found the people around me unutterably strange, but in the dream, all the people who seemed strange were familiar, very familiar, and it was my fault that I could not recognize them. "What an awful dream," I whispered to myself, as if all the people in the world wore masks and when they took them off they were all the same; they only seemed to be different. I wondered if everyone in the world had dreams which so mocked their ambitions.

The house was shaking itself out of sleep. The familiar cries from the livery stable next door came through the walls. From downstairs came angry voices quarreling over a towel, and then Mrs. Trowbridge's powerful voice shouting, "Get out of here, all of you!" Someone was invading her kitchen. I got up slowly and cracked the thin layer of ice that had formed in the washbowl and splashed the water over my face and throat. My eyelids felt thick and swollen. I went to the dresser to find my watch and saw a letter stuck into the mirror's frame. I knew the handwriting. It was from my father.

"Dear Agnes," he wrote; "how are you keeping? It has been four weeks since getting word of you. If I don't hear soon, I shall send Bill Brown to Montpelier and instruct him to bring you home for Christmas. No working girl is too busy to come home for Christmas. As you can imagine, we are all pretty dragged out here since your dear mother left us. There is little in the world to comfort me and I should like to see you. You know, Agnes, there are not so many of us left. I have directed a letter to business acquaintances in Montpelier and they hear that you are well enough although they have not themselves seen you. Please reply by return post or I shall send Bill Brown. Your affectionate father, Amon Dempster. P.S. This is the fourth I have directed to you since your return to the city. I assume that the others have miscarried and that you did not receive them."

I stared down at the brief letter, furious. I had received the three previous letters from my father, and had read them next to the wood stove, dropping them into its leaping flames as soon as I finished them. I did not want to be reminded of North Chittendon. I did not want Bill Brown coming to get me as if I were still a child in the schoolyard for whom the walk home was too hard. I sat down on the bed and began scribbling in pencil: "Dear Father, I cannot imagine what happened to your other letters. Of course, you know the city is full of thieves and they steal our mail in hope of finding money. Please do not enclose money in letters to me. Everyone says you must send money orders if you do not want your letter stolen. I cannot come home this Christmas because I promised my friend, Polly Southcote, that I would help her care for the house in the owner's absence. Mrs. Trowbridge will be visiting her relatives for Christmas, and I will find this exercise in responsibility a salutary one. Don't you agree that it will be? I should find it too painful to come home right now. The memories are too vivid. I am sure they will dim with time and then I shall be eager to come home. Perhaps I will come home for Easter. Please do not send Bill Brown for me. He had no love for Montpelier last time and it is unkind to require him to make such a strenuous journey. I hope you are keeping well, and you may be sure I think of you and pray for you often. Your loving daughter, Agnes."

There, I thought, hastily folding the sheet of paper and placing it in the envelope. Now no one will bother me. Probably, I thought, nothing would work out as I planned it. Frank would go home with a friend for Christmas dinner and I would be left here alone. Polly would go home with Eddie, or stay out at the asylum with him, and I would stay in my room, my head under the pillow, attempting to sleep through Christmas. Still, it was worth the chance; I was going to mail the letter to my father on the way to work. Frank and Polly were still eating when I left. I had to stop at the Post Office.

27

The sky was ominously gray and low. It seemed to have collapsed on top of the horizon where its mists were blunting the mountain peaks. There was a strong wind blowing from the north. It caught in my skirts and pushed me down the street as if it wanted to clear the street for someone more important. It tugged at the coils of my hair as if it wanted to see them floating on its strong gray tides. Snow, I thought, snow. Not the peaceable snow which fell gently and thickly, but the driving snow that, coming down in thick, chalky lines, erased all outlines of the visible world, snow so thick that it ate the hand you held out in front of your face. The kind of snow that the strong, hard wind would ship into drifts that curled at their tops like cresting waves and inside whose curves rested thick blue shadows. This was world-building, world-obliterating snow, and I thought how wonderful it would be to be shut in the house with Frank. I looked up at the sky. It was blackish gray. If he went to Barre, he might not get back for days. I started to run down the street toward the cars, but then I realized how it would look if I ran up and insisted that he return to the house because otherwise he would be trapped by the snow. Everyone would be certain I was mad.

I turned around and walked slowly back to Mrs. James's. For every three steps I took, the wind blew me back one. Dark clouds were climbing the north mountains and thickening the sky. I grabbed the door handle, pulled the door open against the force of the wind, and ran up the stairs. I was the only one there. Mrs. James came in and came over to me. "Oh, Agnes," she said, "the girls upstairs are behind on the fancywork. I want this tablecloth finished up. Would you work on it?" She held it out to me. It was to be embroidered with the same raised strawberries I had stitched so painstakingly onto Polly's handkerchiefs.

"You can work on it down here on the second floor with the other girls," she said, "but then you'll get paid the usual rate. Everyone on this floor gets the same salary. You'd get paid more upstairs." "I'd rather stay down here," I said. "You country girls are all the same," she said. "You mean we're all stupid, don't you?" I said. "Agnes," she said, "don't be so sensitive." "But that is what you meant," I said; "I'm not stupid. I like to be with my friends." "Well," she said angrily, "stay with your friends. Here." She dropped the white silk cloth in my lap.

Florence arrived, hung up her shawl, and came over, blowing on her hands. "It's getting cold," she said; "do you think it's going to snow?" "I know it is," I said; "what happens when there's a blizzard? How do the men get back from Barre?" "Sometimes they stay there," Florence said; "sometimes the boardinghouses send out sleighs or the livery stable does. Last winter, the men were stuck there for five days." "Five days!" I said. The other girls were beginning to come in and take up their places. "It's snowing," said the last one in; "do you think it will stick?"

When I looked at the window, a curtain of snow was weaving and reweaving itself out of different white threads. As the morning wore on, the sky darkened and I moved my chair to the other side of Florence's so that I would be closer to the window. The heavy snowflakes hit the glass, melted, and then snaked down the panes. "You know," I said to Florence, "I'm going down to look outside. I don't think we'll be able to get home if we wait until five or six." Outside, a white sea seemed to have flooded all of Montpelier. It swept across the streets, burying the curbs, and curled against the walls of the houses. The bushes wore thick caps of snow. In another hour, the drifts would be too deep to walk through. The men might be stuck at Barre and I had no intention of staying at Mrs. James's. I went back in and found Mrs. James standing over my empty chair. "Florence said you wanted some fresh air," she said. "Yes," I said; "I have a headache." I volunteered to take the white silk tablecloth home with me and said I would work on it at home when I felt better, but I knew perfectly well she would not let it leave her house. "Finish it tomorrow," Mrs. James said, glaring at me. "Try and get out as soon as you can," I whispered to Florence.

I was the only person on the street, if that was where I was. The ground beneath my feet swirled and changed shape as easily as the air through which I moved. The buildings were only specters glimpsed through the thick white veils the air had

ecome. I drew my scarf over my mouth to keep from breathing
 the snow. The air was alive, breeding one creature after
 ιother. At that instant, I wouldn't have been surprised to see
 rank materialize out of the snow and dance in the air in front of
 ιe, such a creature of my imagination did he seem. When I
 ιame in, Iris stuck her head out the kitchen door and said she
 as glad someone had made it home, and she hoped I had
 mething to read because she was the only other person in the
 ɔuse and she had plenty of baking to do; she didn't think she'd
 e going downstreet for a while.

Before I went into my room, I went into Frank's. How could I
 ιave thought it was cold and impersonal? It was orderly and
 recise, as Frank was. The same drawings were on the wall, but
 new one was on the wall near his bed, and as I went closer, I
 ιw it was one of my drawings of an iris. I sat down on the bed
 ιd touched its quilt as if it were a living, breathing thing. I got
 p and sat down in the chintz-covered chair near the window.
 itting in Frank's room, I did not miss him. I saw that I was
 ιaring the back of my chair with an unironed shirt. That, I
 ecided, was what I would do. I would take it to Polly's room
 ιd iron it. I had watched her heat the irons on the hall stove and
 ring them into her room often enough; I shouldn't have any
 ouble.

The stove in the hall was hot. I warmed up the irons. I went
 ιack into Polly's room and stretched out the shirt on the board
 ʰhich fit on her dresser top. At last I was ready. It took me
 venty minutes to iron the collar to my satisfaction, and by the
 me it was done, I was already tired. I thought that next I ought
 ɔ do the cuffs, because I could finish them without moving the
 ɔllar about. But then I had to decide whether to iron the front or
 ιe back of the shirt. I decided to do the back. The shirt began
 ɔoking better and better, but I saw to my horror that the collar
 vas wrinkling and that somehow, I had pressed a crease into it. I
 tarted to iron the front of the shirt, but the collar somehow crept
 eneath one of the irons and was creased again. Meanwhile, the
 rms hung down, wrinkled like grotesque, long, fallen leaves. I
 ιt down in the chair and started to cry. I had pictured Frank
 ɔming home, finding his shirt, beautifully ironed, resting on his
 illow, and I would have come in and buttoned it for him and it
 vould have been my love for him which had made me capable of
 ɔning a shirt. I had never ironed anything before in my life. I
 ɔned the sleeves, but the whole shirt was a pattern of knife-
 harp creases. Life was impossible. It was better not to attempt

anything than to try and fail. I looked out the window at th thickly falling snow and began crying again. The irons wer cooling. I folded the shirt and glared at the window. If th weather were better, I would go down to the Emporium and bu another shirt. How Jane Holt would laugh if she could see m here with this ruin of a shirt! *She* would know how to iron. *Sh* was properly brought up.

I looked at the shirt. Even the Emporium couldn't save m Frank's shirts were handmade. I remembered that when he tol me about his sister he said she sewed wonderfully well and mad all of his shirts. I lay down on Polly's bed next to the shirt an looked at it as if it were a map of the rest of my life, a map o which there were no smooth places.

The sound of a slamming door woke me. "Well," said Polly leaning over me, "you're breathing. What's this?" She picke up the shirt by one arm and dangled it in front of me. "It's little big for you, isn't it?" she asked. "It's Frank's shirt," admitted miserably; "I tried to iron it." "Well, you succeeded, Polly said, starting to laugh, "but it looks like it fought back The next time you tell me you come from a rich farm," she sai "I'll believe you." "What am I going to do about the shirt?" asked. "What will you give me if I iron it for you?" she aske "Anything!" I swore; "anything you want! We'll go to th Emporium and you can pick out whatever you can carry." "I te you what," said Polly; "you go down and fill the water pitche and I'll iron the shirt for nothing. After all, I eat half yo breakfast every day." "It's past help, isn't it?" I asked he "Oh, you are a fool," she said; "it's only a shirt. You didn burn down a city." "Did I burn it?" I asked her, horrified. "N you didn't burn it, but you didn't sprinkle it, either, and yo didn't get the irons hot enough and you didn't iron its parts in th right order, but otherwise you did a fine job. Go heat up th irons and I'll finish it before supper." "You won't have time," said. "Oh, please," said Polly; "watch." But I was afraid watch. "Tell me when you're finished," I said. "I'm finished, she said a few minutes later. And there it was, the red plaid shir creaseless, good as new. "Don't tell him you did it," I begge "I won't, but maybe you better," Polly said, "unless you wa to end up ironing all his shirts." "I don't want to do that," said. "I didn't think so," she said.

"Well," said Iris, as we sat around the table that nigh "should we send a sleigh out to Barre?" "Oh, Iris," Polly sai "it's a waste of time. Nothing can get through there. The haven't even broken out Main Street yet. Besides, Frank and Charlie will get back. You'll see." "I miss Charlie," Iris said. "I guess he's happier where he is," said Polly. "Don't talk about him as if he died," I said without looking at either of them. "You really think Frank will get back tonight?" Iris asked. Polly nodded and mashed her stew potatoes into a reddish mound. "Why do you think he'll get back?" I asked her. "Snowshoes," she said, her mouth full; "wherever he is, Frank behaves as if he's in the middle of the wilderness. He keeps snowshoes here and in the stone huts at Barre. So does Charlie. One winter, they were the only two who came home the morning after the first bad snowfall." I asked Polly if walking on such deep snow wasn't dangerous. "Frank says it's dangerous only if you don't have snowshoes," she said; "he ought to know. Charlie told me he once lived out in the woods for six weeks in the middle of the winter." "Why does he do things like that?" I asked. "He thinks you have to take care of yourself," she said; "in case the world should happen to come to an end a few feet away from where you're standing." She looked at me. "You're going to drown in your stew," she said; "when did you get to bed last night?" "Late," I said; "I'm going up." "Stop in my room and get your shirt," she said.

I picked up the shirt and walked down the hall to Frank's room. I thought of him walking through the thick snow which was obliterating all landmarks and I thought of all the stories I had heard about hunters who lost their bearings in the woods and wandered in circles until they died. I put the shirt on Frank's dresser, closed the door, and lay down on his bed. He would wake me up if he came in. If he didn't come in, I never wanted to wake up.

I woke slowly and swam up from the bottom of a dark sea. A hand was on my shoulder; then it moved to my face. "Frank?" I whispered. "Shhh," he whispered, "I just got back." "On snowshoes?" I asked. "On snowshoes." "It's no night for walking," I said. "No," he said, "but I could light a candle and we could pretend we were outside." I sat up and started to undress. "I ironed your shirt," I told him as he took off his trousers and folded them over the back of the chair. "I know. I saw," he said.

Frank was running his hands along my breasts. I sat still, transfixed by the sight of his body. I felt the strong, tough ridges of his shoulder blades. I ran my hands over his knees. "You have the most beautiful body," I said; "I've never seen it *all* like this.'' With my index finger, I circled his navel. His organ swelled and straightened and stood away from his belly. "Aren't you tired?'' I asked him. "I am, but he isn't,'' Frank said looking down. He kissed my left breast, then my right and then he began to enter me. "Are you still sore?'' he asked, stopping. "Hardly at all,'' I said proudly; "you know, you don't even have to touch me. All I have to do is look at you and even if I am sore, I forget about it.'' Frank groaned and pushed into me and I felt the heat welling up inside me and my body moving uncontrollably. I put my arm over my mouth and bit down on it to keep from crying out. The warm, wet fluid was inside of me and Frank's body was motionless on top of mine.

He was exhausted. He must have fallen asleep. I tried to roll him to one side without waking him, but his eyes opened. "It was worth coming home to find you,'' he said, turning on his side and watching me. I was doing my best not to shiver. I was half-frozen. "You're cold,'' Frank said, getting up. I picked up the towel from the bedside table and draped it on Frank's organ which was still erect. "That comes in handy for many things,'' I said. He looked down and smiled. "You know,'' I said, "if this goes on long enough, I'm going to become a perfect idiot. I'm idiotic with happiness.'' "But cold all the same,'' said Frank taking the towel and throwing it at me.

He came back with two blankets and covered me carefully, then crawled in next to me. "Do you have all your clothes?'' he asked me; "it's best not to let everyone know what we're doing.'' "I have everything,'' I said; "I can get up in the middle of the night and go back to my room.'' "No,'' he said; "just get dressed and go down first. It's all right as long as we don't go down together.'' "Everyone will know eventually,'' I said. "Let's keep the old things guessing,'' he said. "When will the others get back?'' I asked him, but he didn't answer. His breathing was deep and regular. He was sound asleep and I watched his face, watched how the candlelight cast fringed shadows on his cheek until the candle finally sputtered and went out.

In the morning when I woke up, I felt as if I were floating in a yolk of light. I watched Frank get up. I wrapped my arms around him so that he could not get dressed, and, in inexplicable bliss, watched him put on the freshly ironed shirt. "I love you,'' I said without thinking. He turned toward me, troubled. "If you don't love me,'' I said, "don't worry.'' "Two petals,'' he said. "You love me two petals of the iris?'' I asked. He nodded. "That's a

256

improvement," I said. Frank looked out the window. "It's still snowing," he said. "You must love me," he said finally; "you ironed that shirt." "And that convinces you?" I asked him. "It does," he said, "especially since I know you can't iron anything, not even a handkerchief." I picked up his pillow and threw it at him. It was a while before we went down to breakfast.

28

That morning everything and everyone was snowed in. I stopped on the landing downstairs and saw that the city was gone and in its place was a polar sea adrift with bulky icebergs, all unaccountably sending up corkscrews of bluish white smoke. I scanned the landscape for something black, a branch, a twig; there was nothing. The trees were covered with snow, and the branches, the heavy boughs, the small twigs, all were outlined in heavy, fluffy snow. Every now and then, the wind rose, shook a branch, and it snapped into the air releasing its white powder as plants sometimes released their seeds into the air in the spring. Little powdery explosions were taking place everywhere, as if the snow were fighting for its right to remain, to keep its hold on the world. I leaned forward, trying to see the branch after it was free of its snow, but I always looked too late. No, there were no black branches. The snow was still falling and it was going to continue falling.

I looked at the world beyond the window and thought how much and how senselessly I loved it. I thought about the person I had been before I came back from North Chittendon and found Frank, and it was like trying to remember a stranger or an old story. I remembered the girl who believed that part of herself sat, legs crossed, high up in a corner of the ceiling, watching everything she did, disapproving. I remembered the perpetual state of panic and terror in which she spent her days, and how on some days it was difficult to do anything, even to get out of bed, even to pick up a knife and cut a piece of meat, and I felt sorry for her. But I no longer knew her.

I was not the same person who had gone to Bald Hill with Charlie and lain beneath him while I floated over myself, reproachful and frightened, turning cold. Now time, my old enemy, was precious to me. I could never wait for the days to begin because somewhere in them Frank moved. And I was driven by a new hunger, a constant hunger for his body. I had never seen anything so remarkable. He was the man in the fire. He had walked home on top of the snow. There was nothing he could not do.

I thought of the marble frieze in Barre and hoped someone had covered it against the snow. Of course, it would have to stand outside eventually, but I didn't want to think that his carving, his life, was susceptible to the ravages of time. Headstones gave up their letters. The wind diminished the carvings. Little boys threw small stones at the bigger ones. Picnickers sat on the stones and they fell over; they broke apart. He had to leave Montpelier and Barre and find a place where he could carve things which would stand inside, safe from the weather. The weather was time made visible. There were places where he could be safe from it. Eventually, I thought, the Barre stones would be monuments to forgetfulness, to the bliss of pain ceasing. It was a sad and futile job, carving headstones. No wonder Charlie had not liked it. Puff! Puff! Puff! Another regiment of twigs was fighting something unseen in the sky. Such small smoking muskets, such lovely rifles.

That was what had changed in the world. There was no more *as if* to things. It was not as if I were watching a fairyland outside; it was a fairyland. I did not adore Frank as if he were a god; he was a god. It was not as if I worshiped him; I did worship him. The world was as it was. The hollow had become solid. I looked down at my hand and loved it, not because it was my hand, but because Frank loved it and touched it. If I could have everything I wished for now, I would wish never to be separated from him. He was the light in the sky. He was the sky. Puff! Puff! Puff! I wished the snow well. It was keeping the men home.

Everyone at the table was talking about the snow. As I slid into my seat next to Polly, it seemed to me that Iris looked at me strangely. Well, perhaps she knew. There was nothing I could do about it; if she threw me out, I would move to another house. "How much?" the old lady who sat next to Frank asked; "three feet?" "Five feet," Frank said, "and ten-foot drifts in the open fields." "Ten feet," said the old woman; "when it melts, we'll be flooded." "You worry too much," said the elderly man on her other side. "When we're all sitting up in the attic waiting for the rowboats to come, then tell me I worry too much," she said. "We haven't had a flood in forty years," the old man said. "Are we going to have a flood?'' the old woman asked, turning back to Frank. "If it warmed up tomorrow and stayed warm, we could have a flood," he said; "but it won't." "Don't ever be sure about the weather," said the old woman; "the weather's killed more people than old age." Frank smiled at me.

"Let's go out," I said suddenly; "it's so beautiful out there." "Go out!" said the old woman; "the drifts are over your head!" "Only into the yard," I said; "I love snow." "The Beautiful," said the old man; "that's what we used to call it. The Beautiful. 'I'm going out to shovel the Beautiful,' I used to tell that to my wife a thousand times a winter." "If you're going into the yard," Iris said, bending over me to take my plate, "be careful of the back steps. You won't be able to see them." "You couldn't fall down out there if you wanted to," Polly said; "you can fall in, not down." "Come with us," Frank asked her. "No," she said; "I've got a lot of work to do for Iris. If the factory stays closed, I'm going to be short of money." One by one the people at the table got up and drifted off.

Finally, Frank and I were alone. A little round vase sat in the middle of the table. In the spring Iris filled it with flowers, but she never removed it. It sat on the table all year long.

"A crystal ball," I said; "should I tell your future?" "No," said Frank, "I don't want to know." "How about your past?" I asked him. "I don't want to know about that, either," he said. He was uncomfortable. "Well, then," I said, pushing the vase away from me, "I won't tell your fortune. I'll look into the vase and tell you what the weather is. In your mind." "Fog and more fog," said Frank. "I don't see fog," I said; "I see wide plains full of snow and there are no mountains anywhere. No matter which way you turn your head, you can see the sky meeting the earth. The sun is going down and the land is purple and red. When you turn around, you can see for hundreds of miles. You can see so far you can see tomorrow's weather starting toward you. You can see the future coming closer."

"That's not bad," Frank said; "I used to want to go out West. It's like that there, all flat, no mountains in the way of the horizon. Everything stands clear of everything else. You can tell where one thing leaves off and the other begins. I loved it there." "Do you want to go out West?" I asked. "I did," said Frank; "now I'm thinking about cities. I could study with someone in a city." "Study?" I asked. "With a sculptor," he said; "someone better than I am." "There is no one better," I said. "Yes," he said; "there are a lot who are." "If there's someone who can

260

teach you, then you ought to go," I said. "If I thought there was any point to it," he said; "my family would never understand. You can't eat a statue. A stone crop, it wouldn't mean anything to them." "You're not like them," I said; "*I'm* not like my family." "We're all like each other, more than we want to be anyway," he said. I brushed some crumbs to the side and leaned forward. "What about your father?" I asked him; "you said he used to be a stonecutter until his lungs gave out. He should understand."

"Well, he doesn't," said Frank; "and it was more than his lungs. He's got rheumatism in his hands. They're all twisted and deformed. They look like the roots of an old tree. It looks like something was busy carving him. But he still carves. Wood, not stone. He holds the chisel in his twisted hand and it works as well as anyone else's good hand, probably better. The walls are covered with things he's carved. He's got a talent." "Then why don't you see any point to it?" I asked; "the things you make are so beautiful." "There's no point in it for *me*," said Frank; "everything has a point for my father. He loves the world and everything in it. I don't." He looked at me. "Give me the vase," he said. "I see time passing in it," he said, "and I see myself, carving. And there's only one way to keep things above the ground and that's to carve them in stone, and while I'm carving one thing, other things which I care for more are going under and I'll never be able to get them back. And I won't even know I care about them until they're gone. And I don't see the point of carving some of them while others vanish. I don't see the point of caring for things that vanish. Sometimes, I don't think I love anything." He looked at me, miserable. "Do *you* understand?" he asked. "That you have to fight to keep what you can because otherwise it will be taken away?" I asked; "yes. I understand that." "Whether you fight or not," said Frank, "everything is taken away." "But if you fight," I said, "you keep things longer." "And is that worth it?" he asked me; "fighting just to keep something longer? If you have to lose it anyway?" "It's worth it," I said. "Why?" he asked. He was staring into the upended vase.

"Because some of the things are so splendid," I said; "they're so splendid, they're just like fire. They burn you up. I want to be burned up like that, not just crated up and packed away in the earth." "What things?" he asked; "what things are so splendid?" "You are," I said; "I don't care what you think of yourself. I see you the way you should see yourself." I thought for a moment. "I have complete faith in you," I said at last; "there's nothing you can't do." "With you around?" he asked, smiling strangely. "With or without me," I said. He looked at me hard and I felt myself flushing under his gaze. "Maybe you're right," he said at last; "maybe there is a point." "Of course there's a point," I said; "otherwise we might as well lie down and die right now." "Most of us could," Frank said, "and it wouldn't make any difference in the world." "It would make a difference to my world," I said, "if you lay down and died." "I know," he said, watching me; "and I don't understand it. Get your cape and let's go out."

We went out the back door and fell into the drift. "You're the damndest thing," Frank said, pulling me upright. "You said that before," I said; "what does it mean?" "I don't know," he said; "I guess when I'm with you, I'm happy." We played aimlessly in the snow, throwing snowballs at each other, falling into drifts, and only when the snow soaked through our clothes did we start back up the stairs to the kitchen. Puff! Puff! Puff! The trees were firing at the sky. Everything fought for what it wanted.

When the roads to Barre were cleared, Frank went back to work. I began buying sticky buns and fancily wrapped candies at the Emporium. If they were small and well-wrapped enough, I hid them in his boots. The sticky buns, wrapped in two wax papers, went into his coat pocket. Christmas was coming closer and I still had no present for him. I asked Florence where to look because I could find nothing at Holt's Emporium. It was bad enough buying other things from Jane Holt's family, but I didn't want to buy his Christmas present at their store. Florence said she knew of some shops off Main Street and she would go with me after work. We came in one morning at seven-thirty so that we could leave at four and drifted off down Main Street.

"Well," said Florence, "I feel like a lady of leisure, being out here without the whole mob bobbing around." "It's nice," I said. She said we were going to a Mrs. Goodknight's. She ran a shop right out of her house and everyone said she had the nicest and the most unusual things, but they were a little dear. "The person I want this for," I said, "well, nothing is too good for him." "Are you still seeing Frank?" Florence asked me; "the rumor mill says you're always with him." "We live in the same house," I said. "I don't know why you're so closemouthed all of a sudden," Florence said; "I won't tell anyone what you say. Anyway, people see you walking out with him at night. No one here has anything better to do than wear out their elbows leaning on their windowsills and watching everyone else go by. Who is the present for?" "My father." "Oh," she said, "is it?" "Yes," I said, "it is. Look, Florence," I said, turning on her, "why don't you tell me something? Do the girls still say he's seeing Jane Holt?" "If you're worried about that," Florence said, "you should ask him." "I'm asking you," I said. "They say he doesn't. But Miss Gap Tooth says Jane thinks Frank is going to marry her anyway." I brushed some imaginary hairs away from my face. "Why does she think that?" I said; "if they know Frank doesn't see her anymore?" "He's been around Jane a long time," Florence said; "at least a year before you got here. I guess they think so much time goes by and you're engaged. They say Jane thinks he'll come back to her when he gets finished with you." "To someone he doesn't see?" I asked. "I didn't say he was engaged or that I thought he was engaged," Florence said; "you asked me what the girls were saying." "Let's forget it," I said. "This way," she said, and we turned down Bell Street. "Where does Jane Holt live?" I asked. "On Willow Drive, the big white house in the center of the circle there. I thought you were going to forget about her."

I thought about Jane Holt, pale, plain, like every other girl in Montpelier, and I felt sorry for her. Frank would never talk to her about wanting to go to the city. He would never talk to her about his father's hands, or his mother, standing in the kitchen crying. She would never know him. Even if I died tomorrow and she somehow got him to marry her, she would never live with him, not really. He would be a shape, an outline, something opaque between her and the light. He would look at her and wonder why he had ever thought there was any purpose in daily life. She would look at him, sure he was happy, locked out of the world he and I moved in together. And now he spent so much time with me, he would have to see her in the middle of the night, or in the middle of the day when he was supposed to be at work, if he saw her at all. Still, I wished there were no such person as Jane Holt. She could give him the contents of the Emporium for Christmas, while I, who stopped at her father's store every day to buy Frank buns or candy, was fast using up all my extra money. I would have to be more careful or the money my father had given me to put in the bank against an emergency would be gone. Well, buying things for Frank constituted an emergency. There was nothing more urgent than making him happy.

We rang the bell at Mrs. Goodknight's and waited. A tall, thin woman, horse faced and sallow, let us in. "Are you factory girls?" she asked us, stopping in the hall. I said no, we worked for Mrs. James. "The things here are very dear," she said. I said I knew that, but if I could find something worthwhile, I would be glad to pay her price. She opened the small-paned glass door and we walked into a parlor filled to overflowing with objects; inkwells, pens, powder boxes, silver shaving kits, comb and brush sets, picture frames. Silverware and silver services gleamed darkly from all the shelves.

I saw a heavy rectangular object, covered in red and white velvet, and in the center of its cover, a brass replica of the liberty bell with an embroidered version of the stars and stripes set in its cutout center. "What is it?" I asked Florence. She put it down on the edge of the table. "I think it opens," she said; "try the latch." I opened the latch and the decorated panel fell forward. "It's a photograph album," I said, turning the thick cardboard pages. Each page had slots for two photographs and the pages themselves were covered with a thick, shiny paper painted to look like red leather. The slots cut out for the photographic portraits were arched. It was a magnificent album. And then I turned the last page. Now I saw why, when viewed from the side, the album had such a strange, triangular shape. Under the last page was a little writing desk. A little ink bottle and two pens were fastened to its floor by gold brackets. The last page of the album had no cutout slots for photographs and formed the writing surface.

"It's a cunning thing," I said to Florence. "It's very nice," she said; "it must cost quite a bit." I pulled on Florence's sleeve and she bent toward me. "Do you really like it?" I whispered. "I think it's the most beautiful thing I've ever seen," she said. "How much do you ask for it?" I said, finally looking at Mrs. Goodknight. "Ten dollars," she said coldly. "Ten dollars!" said Florence; "Agnes, that's too much!" "Your friend is right," said Mrs. Goodknight; "it's too much for a working girl. I have other albums." She bent down and took out a plain album covered in rust velvet. "That one's three dollars," she said. "I want the other one," I said. Florence put her hand on mine but I shook it off.

I could barely wait to pay for it and take it home. "Do you think he'll like it?" I asked Florence. "Anyone would," she said.

I went back to my room and took out the handkerchiefs I had embroidered with Frank's initials. I sat down in the chair and began sewing them together until they formed a large square. Then I laid the album down in its center and wrapped it in the white cloth. I imagined Frank unwrapping it; I saw myself telling him how to cut the threads which bound the handkerchiefs together, and I saw his surprise when he realized the wrapping was itself a present. Life was doubly magical. I lived it twice now, once in anticipation, once in actuality. I felt the pleasant weight of the album on my lap and I imagined it filling with portraits of the statues Frank would carve. Then I thought about the little writing desk hidden beneath its pages and wondered if I might someday have the audacity to try writing something myself. One of the girls at work said she had a sister who lived in New York City and worked for *The Ladies Home Companion*. I sighed and went to the oak cupboard and put the package on the bottom shelf beneath a blanket and several pairs of boots. I had done very little drawing. It was foolish to think about writing. Only Frank held my attention.

The house was already emptying as one person after another set off to join their families. Polly said she would be gone for most of Christmas day herself, because Eddie could not get off from the asylum. Iris was going to visit her sister in West Townshend and would be gone for six days. The old woman and the old man were taking the train to Burlington where they would be met by their families. Polly and Frank and I would be left alone in the house, and on Christmas, Frank and I would be completely alone. I had to talk to Polly as soon as she came in; I didn't know how to boil water but I was determined to cook Frank a splendid dinner. If I could get Polly to mix everything up for me, I would try not to burn it.

The night before Christmas, I woke up in the middle of the night, crept out from beneath Frank's arm, put on his coat, and ran down the hall back to my own room. I took the package from the bottom shelf of the cupboard and scurried back down the hall. I put it on Frank's dresser and crept carefully into bed. I didn't want to wake him. I lay on my back, my head turned toward him, and watched him breathe. Eventually I was thirsty, but I didn't dare move; I didn't want to wake him. My eyes traced the blue veins on the inside of his wrist which lay, defenseless, on the blanket, the thicker blue veins on the side of his neck, and I must have fallen asleep, because when I next looked at Frank, he was sitting up in bed watching me.

"I see a package on the dresser," Frank said. "Yes," I said, "you do." "Is it for me?" he asked. "It is," I said. As he went to get it, I stopped breathing. Suppose he didn't like it? Suppose he saw how expensive it was and thought I was trying to buy his affection? He unwrapped the album slowly. "What is it?" he asked. "Oh, I see." He unfastened the latch, and just as I had done, began to turn the pages until he came to the little writing desk. "It's beautiful," he said, "too beautiful for me." "No, it's not," I said. He opened his bottom drawer. "This is for you," he said. He had carved a small, wooden replica of the marble frieze I had seen at the quarry. "Oh," I said, "I don't deserve it." "Don't deserve it?" he echoed, puzzled. "Well, a person should do something important to deserve having something important like this," I said, hugging the carving to me, my eyes filling. "You're a fool," Frank said, sitting down on the bed and pulling me onto his lap; "you deserve a lot more than that."

He began stroking my hair and I began to sob. "You're crying because you're happy?" he asked. I nodded, my head against his chest. "Do you want to get married?" he asked me. "To who?" I asked. "To me," he said. "Do you want to get married?" I asked. "I asked you, didn't I?" he said. "Yes," I said, "I do. When?" "Not for a while," he said; "not until I save some money." "When you save some money, will we go to New York?" He stroked my hair. "Yes," he said, "we will." I thought about Jane Holt and the rumors I'd heard about their engagement. "I hope you don't ask a lot of girls to marry you," I said. "I've never done it before," Frank said; "there's a first time for everything, I guess." "You sound surprised at yourself," I said. "Well," he said, running his finger down my nose, "everyone gets married sooner or later." "And I happened along at the right time?" I asked, burrowing into him. "Who knows?" Frank said; "stop talking."

We sat still, looking at the album as if we were afraid to look away from it. "Are we hungry?" he asked me, "or are we going to sit here all morning looking at each other?" "We're hungry," I said. "Well, look here," Frank said, "Polly told me your secret. I know you can't cook, so I'll make breakfast. I'm a good cook. When my mother was sick I used to cook for the whole farm, sometimes for thirty people at once." "I can learn to cook," I said. "You don't have to cook," he said; "you don't have to do anything. Except maybe stand around naked this afternoon and let me sketch you." "Wait," I said, and I picked up the cloth I had wrapped the album in. "See?" I said, pulling a thread, and the handkerchiefs separated and fell, one after another, into my lap. "Eight of them," I said, "with your initials." "*F. H.*," he said, running his fingers over the embroidery. Originally, I had intended to embroider each with an *H*, but since there was a Jane Holt somewhere in the world, I decided on the double letters. "I'm the one who doesn't deserve you," he said. "Let's not argue about it," I said.

I sat in the kitchen, leaning at the table, my cheek propped up by my hand, watching Frank cook. I had never been so happy. I wondered if I would ever be so happy again, and I thought, no, I would not; it was not possible to be this happy more than once. Every so often, Frank looked up at me and smiled; he looked softer, younger. "Is this what it's like to be happy?" he asked me. I said it was. "Then I guess there's a point to things," he said. He sat down opposite me. "Go on, eat," he said; "I won't poison you." "I ought to be the one to do the cooking," I said. "Oh, please," he said. I started to laugh. "You sounded just like Polly," I said. "I can think of worse people to sound like," he said, and I nodded. I was thinking about Easter and that I would almost certainly have to go home then.

"Frank," I said, "if we're going to get married, do you want to come home with me? You could meet my father. You could see the famous brass bed." "North Chittendon?" he asked; "you want to go back there? You want to take this disreputable fool back to meet your father?" "I want to go if I can go with you," I said. "All right," he said, "let's go. When?" I said I had promised to go home for Easter. "Easter it is," said Frank. "What do you want to do today?" he asked me. "Go back up and get back into bed, go for a walk, have you draw me, go for a walk again." "Fine," he said.

It was strange and wonderful, being alone in the house, as if we were already married and had shrunk the whole, unsafe world to this small place of peace and safety. I told Frank that before he began sketching me I wanted to write my father and say we were coming. "He'll never believe it," I said; "I think one of the last things I said to him was that I'd never get married." Frank said that he didn't believe any of this himself. "Use some of the paper in here," Frank said, taking a sheet from the album and handing it to me. "But it's for you!" I said. "I don't write letters much," he said; "there's plenty left." "You don't write letters?" I asked, looking up at him. Did that mean that he didn't want the album? "Now of course I'll have a reason to write letters," Frank said, seeing my face; "it's a wonderful thing." I sat back, relieved.

"Would we stay one day or two?" I asked him. "We could stay two," he said, "if you want to. I've got enough money to take time off." I would have, too, I thought, after I went to the bank on Monday. As I wrote my father, telling him when we would probably come, I thought about Louise, and whether or not I wanted to see her. Of course, there was no one in the world I wanted to see but Frank. Still, I knew that Frank liked my interest in people; he had said more than once that he envied my ability to make friends. I didn't tell him that although I made friends easily, I often had no use for them. They were irrelevant as the trees that defined the nature of the landscape or the season but did not draw your attention. I said that I didn't make many friends and he said I did. There was Charlie and Polly at the boardinghouse and he had seen me around the city with the girls at work. I said he had just as many friends; Polly and Charlie were his friends, too. "But they don't really talk to me," he said, "not the way they talk to you." I said I didn't know what he meant. "Well, the old woman told you how she had to take care of her brothers and sisters and got so frantic she tied them all to the parlor chairs and left them there for a whole afternoon," he said. I sighed. When the old woman talked to me at the table, I barely listened. "I'm sure she'll tell you all about her life if you talk to her," I said.

"I've tried," Frank said, "longer than you have. All she ever wants to talk about is the weather." "Ask her questions," I said. "What questions?" "*Anything*," I said; "ask her if she had sisters or brothers. Ask her if she was ever snowed in, and if she was, how she got out." "It's none of my business," said Frank. "It's not an improper question!" I said; "she can't *not* have been snowed in. Whatever she says, you'll have something to talk about." Frank stared at a spot above my head. "You know," I said at last, "I don't think you want friends or you'd ask them questions without thinking about it." "You're wrong," he said; "you don't know how much I want to be ordinary." "I thought you said you *were* ordinary," I said. "Oh, I mean ordinary in ordinary ways," he said, flushing.

Frank got up and stood with his back to me. "Everyone has a right to their privacy," he said; "it's not right to pester people with questions." "People don't want to be private about everything," I said; "that's loneliness." Frank sat down and looked at me. "Do *you* really want to hear the answers to all those questions? How many sisters she had? What they did when they were snowed in? You *know* what they did. They were bored.

They read and they ate." "I know what they did and I also want to hear the answers to the questions," I said. "Why?" "Because it's important to hear the sound of another human voice."

But now I was pulled up short. I really didn't believe what I was saying. I believed there was only one person I needed or would ever need, and that person was Frank. Yet here I was, I, who had spent my childhood talking to animals, here I was telling him how important it was to hear the sound of a human voice. And still, I knew that what I was saying was true. Where was this wisdom coming from? It was as if Frank was my child and I was like a cat who had just had kittens; suddenly, I knew what to do. I knew what to say. I looked over at Frank. I loved him so. I could kill for him, easily and without thought. I could even *think*, if it did him any good. "That's what people are for," I said; "they make you feel better because they're around."

"You make it sound like cows in the barn," Frank said contemptuously. I took a deep breath. "Everyone underestimates the poor cows in the barn," I said. "They talk to each other in their own way. I envy the cows in the barn." I thought about the barn at home, and about Dierdre, my cow, and the warm, full feel of her side, rising and falling against my body. "When I wake up at night and see you in bed, I know how the cows feel out in the field," I said; "they must feel invulnerable. They can swallow a bumblebee and it doesn't hurt them. Probably cows are a great deal happier than people." "Cows!" said Frank. "I wouldn't mind being a cow," I said; "if I could get rid of my mind. That's what you should ask the old woman," I said, losing patience at last; "ask her how she'd like to be a cow." "At least," said Frank, "an answer to that question might be interesting."

But the truth was that the circle of my interest was constantly narrowing. When I first came to Montpelier, everyone fascinated me. It was as if their lives contained the answer to the riddle I sensed at the heart of my own. I loved to hear about how the old woman had dropped three rats she found dead in her barn into her husband's stew and then denied knowing anything about it even though she refused to touch her own plate when the stew was served. Frank would come upon me lost in a discussion of clothes which were starched so stiff they cracked like glass when they blew in the wind, and he would drift off with a faintly irritated look. And I was afraid that he would think I was young and silly. So I told Frank that the people around me interested me as characters in a book might, and he said that all he ever saw me reading were romances, and he couldn't imagine how such uninteresting people could ever get to be characters in any sort of book. Frank said it was a good thing he was a sculptor and not a writer, because a model could have the mind of a beet, but if she were pretty enough, that was all you needed. I said I thought spending the day with a beet could be pretty tiresome, but Frank said it wasn't. You didn't think about the beet. You thought about what you were carving. *Your* beet was always interesting.

Now, I was drawing away from the people around me. It was as if I had a disorder of the eyes. I seemed to see everything but Frank out of the corners and Frank was the only one I could see whole. He was the only one I wanted to see. More and more, I had become irritated by the friendly presence of the old people at the table. When they paused to talk to Frank before we left for work, they used up two minutes of the precious ten we had, and I would be in an agony until they finished talking to him. And I knew that I did not want him to have friends; I wanted him to have no other friend but me. I wanted the city to empty out and leave us alone forever. A miracle had joined me to Frank, as if the clockwork gears inside both of us had meshed and now worked perfectly, while before, we both kept poor time, or no time at all, struck the wrong hours, or stood about, dead and empty, like stopped pendulum clocks.

I watched Frank over the top of the letter I was writing to my father. I was beginning to fear other people. If they would only leave us alone, we would twine together so tightly that nothing could separate us. It was as if my mind were a lens, and all the light there was focused on Frank. And I wanted him to look at me in the same way, to burn me with his attention, but I knew he did not love me that way, not yet. He would be happy to see Polly when she came home and I would not. Really, in spite of what he thought, he was the social one. I wanted no one but him. When Polly came in, she would not be my friend; she would be someone who took Frank's attention from me. I felt Frank's eyes on me and began writing again. "Dear Father," I wrote, "I will be coming home the day before Easter. I will be bringing someone home with me and we will have a surprise for you. I shall not be able to stay past Easter Sunday because I am expected back at work. Christmas away from home has been very dreary. Your devoted daughter, Agnes." "Well, that's settled," I said, folding and sealing the letter.

"If you're finished," Frank said, "I'll draw you," and he got up and went out into the hall and put more wood in the stove.

"You should be warm enough now," he said. "Are you going to keep the door open?" I wailed. "There's no one here," he said. "I know," I said, "but the door . . . If we leave it open, some-one's sure to come by." "We could go to your room," he said; "you have your own stove." "Leave the door open," I said, defeated; I liked his room better than mine. When I was in it, I felt as if he had swallowed me and I breathed from somewhere deep within him.

I took off my clothes and stood in the middle of the room with my hands over my eyes. The house was absolutely silent. "Are you drawing yet?" I asked. "No," he said. I peered at him through two fingers. "I never saw a body like yours before," he said; "it has no flaws. You don't even have a scar." "Then draw me," I said, "and get it over with. I don't know how the models do it." "I never saw a model who looked like you before," he said. "Are you drawing yet?" I asked again. But he had stolen up behind me and grabbed me around the waist and carried me to the bed. "Those are good breasts," he said after he lay me down; "and the curve of your stomach and the inside of your thighs. It won't be easy to carve that." His fingers were sketching the outlines of my body in the air. "I'm supposed to learn drawing, too," I said, and I began unbuttoning his shirt and his trousers. "Wait a minute," he said, and he got up and shut the door. "You don't have to shut it," I reminded him; "no one's here." "Just in case," he said, kissing my breast. "Are your bones singing?" he asked me. "No," I said, "but they will be."

When I woke up, the room was darkening. I got up and lit the kerosene lamp. The bright yellow light filled the room like sunshine. Frank was sound asleep when I took out the wooden carving he had given me and sat down in the chair near the lamp and began drawing it. "That's not bad," Frank said, looking over my shoulder; "look at it harder. You don't see everything full face, even if you think you do. The mother's forehead," he said, pointing, "stops in a straight line. There."

"It's a wonderful birthday present," I said. "A what?" Frank asked; "a what?" "A wonderful birthday present," I said flushing; "my birthday just went by. I forgot about it." "When was it?" he asked, watching me. "December seventeenth," I said; "I was seventeen." "Why didn't you tell me?" "I didn't think it was important," I said; "I was thinking about what to get you." "Or maybe you thought I wouldn't get you anything," Frank said, looking at me angrily; "Charlie used to tell me he thought I was cheap." I sat still, stunned, hugging my carving. What had I done now? "I didn't want to remind you," I said; "you're so much older and smarter than I am." "Didn't you think I would get you a present?" he asked, intent on an answer. "I never thought about it," I said; "if I'd thought, yes, I would have expected a present. But I didn't think about it." "Did Charlie tell you not to expect anything?" he asked. "I haven't spoken to Charlie in weeks! In months!" I protested. He shook his head.

He might as well be on the moon, I thought; he's not in the same room with me. "I don't want anything," I said. My pride was rising with my blood. "I don't want anything but you and if I have to ask you to stop scolding me just because I didn't tell you when my birthday was, I'm not going to do it. I don't even know when *your* birthday is." "November eleventh," he said. "Well," I asked, "what do you want for your birthday?" He came and sat down on the arm of my chair, but he was staring into the slice of blue distance the window allowed us. He bent down and began nuzzling my shoulder. "I'm sorry," he said. I didn't answer. "I am," he said; "sometimes I forget. I think you'll be like other people." "Other girls," I said. "Other girls," he agreed. "And I'm not?" I asked. "No, you're not," he said.

"Why am I so different?" I asked, suddenly, for the first time annoyed at being set so apart. "I can't explain it," he said; "you know how bad I am at people." "At people," I said. He talked about them as if they, like mathematics, were a subject to be mastered. I was uneasy. I was not completely unlike the rest of the human race even though I had often enough felt as if I had nothing in common with it. Other girls fell in love as I had. I knew that. I wanted to know what Frank disliked in the other girls he had known. Perhaps, I thought, I should talk to Charlie once more after all.

"Hungry?" Frank asked me. I said I was. "We're having beef stew," he said; "there's plenty for Polly if she gets back home tonight." I crossed my fingers behind my back and prayed that she would stay late at the asylum. "I'm going to try sketching you tonight," Frank said, "whether or not Polly comes home. I keep on trying and then something comes up." "Then we'll have to go to my room," I said. "And you'll have to uncover your eyes," he said; "otherwise, it's not the pose I had in mind." "What's wrong with it?" I asked, teasing; "you could make it a statue of justice. Justice is blind." "And a good thing for me it

272

is," said Frank; "no, I think I'll leave the subject of justice alone."

I sat at the table, watching Frank stir the contents of the large metal pot with a wooden ladle. I got up and went to the kitchen hutch and started to take down the plates. "Set out three plates," said Frank; "just in case." "You know," I said as I was laying down the last plate, "I wish I could go out to the quarries with you and watch you. Just for a day," I added hastily. Frank paused in his stirring. "You could," he said. "Charlie'll have a fit and the foreman will have a fit and everyone in the stone shed will be jealous and they'll all waste their time looking at you, but they're not going to get rid of me. You could come." "Tomorrow?" I asked. "If you can get off," he said; "why not?" "What will you tell people when they want to know why I'm there?" "I'll tell them you're interested in learning to carve." "No one will believe that!" I protested. "They're not going to believe anything I say, so what difference does it make? Anyway, it will be pretty clear. You'll be there because I want you there."

"Everyone will gossip," I said. "I may not know people, Agnes," said Frank, "but I know gossip. They'll gossip whether or not you come to the quarries. By morning, everyone who wants to know who spent the night in this house will know we were here alone." "Suppose we don't want them to know?" I asked. I felt a queer panic, as if the others were a pack closing in on us where we stood in our bright spot of light. "Then you lie and say things were some other way," said Frank; "gossips don't care what's true. They take whatever they can get. If we say we weren't alone and say Polly was here, or that the old man was here, they'll be busy for a month straightening things out. A lie is as good as the truth to a gossip. I know. My sisters live on gossip. All women do." "I hate gossip," I said. "I know," said Frank; "but that's not natural in a woman, is it?" I watched him, worried. "I hate gossip, too," he said.

Polly blew in the door, followed by the wind and a few furiously swarming snowflakes. "Here," she said, putting a bottle down on the table; "made by the poor patients at Highbury. Blackberry wine. It's good. Drink some. Don't worry about it. I had some last night and I'm still here. It was nice out there. They had the patients cooking all week and decorating the rooms. They should have sold tickets. Some of the performances were pretty good, too. One of the women danced on top of three tables. As soon as we got her off one she was up on another. She can dance, though."

After I drank my second glass of blackberry wine, I was no longer angry at Polly for coming home. Everything was beginning to amuse me and I giggled at everything they said. "She's drunk," Polly said, laughing at me. "I never had anything to drink before," I said, giggling. "Good Lord, take the bottle away from her!" Polly said, and Frank slid it down toward her, where she took firm charge of it. "I feel like the party from the asylum is just going on here," she said happily. "Very nice," I said. "I meant it well," she said, laughing. "She's coming with me to the quarries tomorrow," Frank told her. "You are?" Polly said; "don't you have to work?" "I can miss a day," I said. "You're getting reckless, aren't you?" she asked. "It's just one day," I said. "And Eve said it was just one apple," said Polly.

"Should we tell her?" I asked Frank. "What?" he said. "What you asked me," I said. "Why not?" he said; "she'll find out soon enough anyhow." "He asked me to marry him!" I exclaimed. "He did?" Polly said, looking at Frank. "I did," he said. "And you, of course, said yes," Polly said, looking at me. "I did," I answered her. "When are you getting married?" she asked Frank. "Not for a while," he said; "I have to save enough money to set up house. Not for a year at least." "I suppose you're going to meet her family?" Polly asked, her eyes on him. "We're going to North Chittendon for Easter," I said. "Good Lord," said Polly. "We've been talking about going to New York for a while now," Frank said. "You know," said Polly, "I think life is simpler at the asylum." "Don't try to change her mind," Frank said, the smile fading from his face. "Nothing could change my mind!" I cried. "And there we have it," said Polly, filling her little wine glass. "Stop in my room tonight," she said to me; "if you can find a minute." I felt Frank glare at her.

When Frank fell asleep, I slid out of bed and went down the hall to her room. "You're really getting married?" she asked me, and when I said I was, she said I better stop taking days off from work or we'd never have enough money to get married. "It's dangerous to keep a man like Frank on a hook too long," she said. I told her that I had a great deal of money, but I couldn't have it until I was twenty-one, and Polly asked me if I'd told Frank anything about that. I said I hadn't because I was afraid he wouldn't like it if he knew I was really rich, or was going to be rich, when he didn't have any money of his own. "He might not like it," Polly said; "who knows? He's got the queerest kind of pride. But it shouldn't make any difference. At least this way you know he's not after your money. By the way, what do you want for your birthday? Frank gave me some money to buy you something because you're going to the quarries with him tomorrow and he won't have time to go himself. So what do you want?'' ''A beaded bag,'' I said; ''if you have enough money.'' ''I have enough money,'' she said, ''and I know just the one to get you. The one with the spiderweb pattern.''

29

The next day the house was still deserted, and Polly packed a dinner pail for Frank and for me. "I hope you both don't wind up without work by the end of the day," she said to me, handing Frank the pail. "Try not to get killed," she told me. Fortunately, we did not have to walk past Mrs. James's and did not run into any of the girls with whom I worked, but when we got to the line for the Barre cars, there was Charlie. "I've kept a place," he called to Frank, and he watched me, expecting me to turn around and go back toward town. "She's coming to the quarry today," Frank said; "she wants to see what it's like." "She already knows what it's like," he said. I said that I'd never seen the quarries in winter. "There's nothing to see in the winter," said Charlie; "just men working in the stone shed." "I want to see Frank working," I said.

"She's going to be the only woman in the stone sheds," Charlie said. "I can look out for her," said Frank. "I don't think it's such a good idea," Charlie said. "Forget about it," Frank said; "it's only one day." "What happened to your job?" Charlie asked me. "It's waiting for me," I said. The car was beginning to take on passengers. "You stand between me and Frank," Charlie said, yanking me in after him. "No point in starting a riot on the car," he said, avoiding my eyes.

The car jolted and started forward. "How have you been, Agnes?" Charlie asked. "She's been fine," Frank answered. "Fine," I said. "How are things back home?" he asked. "Oh, I don't know," I said; "I haven't been back since my mother died. But I'm going home for Easter." "We're going for Easter," Frank said. "I see," said Charlie. "No, you don't," Frank said; "we're getting married." "In March?" asked Charlie. "No, not for at least a year," said Frank. "A lot can happen in a year," said Charlie. "What?" asked Frank. "You're the one with the

276

imagination," Charlie said. "Do you two fight all the time, or only when I'm around?" I asked. "They fight all the time, miss," said a voice behind me. "That's what I thought," I said. "Don't speak to people you don't know," Frank whispered to me. "Now's a fine time to worry about it," Charlie said.

We got off the cars and began the long walk up the quarry hill road. Charlie said he'd see us later and caught up with someone ahead of us. It was a beautiful, blue December day, crisp and cold, without wind, and the snow glittered everywhere. I wanted to put my arm through Frank's, but now that we had turned off for the quarry, I was the only woman on the road and was the center of everyone's attention. "We go around to the far end of the stone shed," said Frank; "I work in the back." "As far away from everyone else as you can get?" I asked; "that's what Charlie told me." "I don't like having people looking over my shoulder," he said.

I looked around for the little city of stones outlined against the sky, but it was gone. Everything, I realized, must have moved inside. In the spring, the little city would rebuild itself. Frank opened the small door in the back and we went in. The noise was deafening. I looked around, confused. "Coughing," said Frank; "that's the sound of men coughing." "You have to get out of here," I said. "Everyone who works here coughs," Frank said; "come this way."

"Hello, everyone," said Charlie, taking up his place at the station next to Frank's. "Well, Agnes," he said, "what are you going to do here all day? Besides ruin your lungs?" "I'm going to watch Frank," I said. "Watch Frank," he repeated, raising his eyebrows; "a worthy ambition." "Shut up, Charlie," Frank said. I walked over to Charlie's station and looked at his stone. It was an obelisk twisted round with ivy. "What do you think?" Charlie asked me. "I think it's lovely," I said; "it's very simple." "It's going to get a lot simpler if I don't do a better job on the ivy," he said. "What happens if you don't get it right?" I asked. "Then Frank comes to the rescue," he said. "It looks all right to me," I said; "aren't ivy leaves more pointed than that?" "Yes," Charlie said with a sigh; "they are more pointed than that."

I went back to Frank's station and looked at his stone. It was a high, arched stone surmounted by two weeping willows, and on the front of the stone a house stood out in relief. It looked exactly like Iris's house. "Did the house die?" I asked Frank. "Gordon Woodruff died, and his family said that they couldn't bury the house with him, so putting it on his stone would be the next best thing. His name goes here," he said, pointing to the space above the house, "his dates here," and he pointed to the space beneath the yard. "How long will it take?" I asked. "Two more weeks, three more weeks. Stonecutting takes a lot of patience. It's the only thing I've got patience for."

"You can say that again," said Charlie, looking over at him. "You're not so long on patience," I said to Charlie. "You hear that Frank?" Charlie asked; "she's defending you." "Do you two chip at each other all day?" I asked. "It makes the time go by," Charlie said. One of the men came over to Frank and said he had an extra dust coat if I wanted it and Frank thanked him. I put it on and sat down behind his stone.

The dust was beginning to rise in the air and the sun was climbing the thin blue sky and the dust motes were fat and gold and lazy. I watched Frank through them and I watched the men working over their stones in the golden haze and I thought I had never seen anything so utterly safe. This was a country without women. This was the male hive, a magical place where men's dreams could be born and grow without the help of mothers and daughters. This was what Eden was like before women entered the garden and I was privileged, I was allowed into this pure place. I watched Frank work. I watched him bend over the stone and study its surface. I watched him begin to chisel out the first letter in Mr. Woodruff's name, and as I watched him and the others, I saw that another kind of birth was taking place here, and that these men were midwives to dreams born of their own minds, and that these dreams, incarnated in stone, could not fail. This was a corner of eternity. These men were its priests and Frank was the best of them all. I watched his muscles move under his shirt and I longed for him. Even death stood aside for him. His stones blocked death's path; they stalled oblivion. All the men here were remarkable, carving stone pages for a great book, all of whose texts said the same thing, that there was no end, that the ending was only life beginning again.

"Are you bored yet?" Frank asked me. "I could stay here forever," I said. "Look at the stone behind you," Frank said; "I bought it for myself. I want to sculpt you if I ever do the drawings of you first." I turned around and looked at the smooth, black stone. "This must have cost a fortune!" I said. "I won it," Frank said. "Won it!" I exclaimed. "On a bet," said Charlie. Evidently he was listening to every word we said.

I sat back and watched the men work in the motes of gold

light. The chisels clinked and chipped. Someone would call out for help in moving a stone. Someone else would stand up, look down at his work, and curse. There were no such things as women in the world. I was a premonition of a creature that had not yet come to exist. No wonder, I thought, the men who worked here loved it so in spite of the dust, in spite of the air which burned in their lungs and brought blood to their lips. It was a primeval place; it was one of creation's workshops.

"Is it better or worse than you thought?" Frank asked, sitting down next to me. "Better," I said; "it's unearthly." "You see things in such an odd way," Frank said, shaking his head; "I can't imagine anything more earthy. If we were honest, we'd carve worms on these stones and put an end to the nonsense." I stared at him, horrified. "These stones," said Frank, "they're fancy covers for rot." "Stop!" I cried. "Why do you have to spoil everyone's dreams?" Charlie asked him. "Leave him alone," I said automatically; "he was talking to me." "You spoil some ideals or they spoil you," said Frank; "it's always better to look facts in the face." "Assuming you know what they are," said Charlie; "you must have your own Book of Revelation, you're so positive about everything." "Are you hungry?" Frank asked me. "She'll have a better appetite in front of a weeping willow than she'd have in front of carved worms," Charlie said. "Let's take our dinner outside," I said. "Don't worry, I'll be quiet," Charlie said.

I opened the dinner pail. Polly had packed thick slices of roast beef, four pieces of apple pie, thick slices of sage cheese, two doughnuts, and four walnuts. Two jars of milky sweetened coffee stood up in one end of the pail. "She must have emptied out the kitchen," I said. "Don't worry," Frank said, "I'll finish whatever you don't eat." Charlie had taken his dinner and joined a group of men at the far end of the sheds. "It *is* peaceful here," I said. "So is a cemetery," he said. "No," I said; "you *must* see how beautiful it is." "I don't," he said. "You will," I said. "Optimist," he said, biting into a doughnut. A terrific commotion began at the far end of the shed and I looked up, frightened. "Don't worry," said Frank; "it's the Italians. They get into fights every day. But they're the best cutters here. Do you want to go look?" I said I did.

We wandered over to the source of the noise, and when the men saw me, they stopped shouting and began babbling happily at me. I couldn't understand a word they said. "They want you to look at their stones," Frank told me. I went from one to another. Evidently, they specialized in madonnas. I stopped in front of a frieze depicting a monk who sat on the ground behind a lion and a tiger, while above his head, birds flew in an arc like a halo. "Is that Saint Francis?" I asked. *"Il Santo, si,"* said an Italian man happily and then they were all offering me part of their dinners. Frank smiled and shook his head, and we went back.

"What do you think?" he said. "Of their carving?" I said; "They're not nearly as good as you are." "Love is blind," said Charlie, who had returned to his stone and was sadly contemplating the ivy crawling gracelessly up the obelisk. "Not entirely blind," said Frank; "she can see what's wrong with that ivy." "She should have brought a book," Charlie said; "she's going to be bored to death. I'm bored and I'm working."

But I wasn't bored. I was afraid that, when the day was over, night would roll into place like a stone and I would never come back here again. "I wish I could come every day," I said; "I would if I could." "You'd get bored faster than you think," said Frank. "No, I wouldn't," I said; "if I could, I'd come here and draw. I could do it if I knew you were right here all the time." "Don't encourage her," Charlie said. I glared at him. Frank was looking at me oddly. "Why should I be so important to you?" he asked in a low voice; "I'm not so special." "If you took a piece out of the mountain over there," I said, "it would only be a piece of rock, but if every time you looked at the mountain, you noticed the piece was gone, it would be the most important part of the whole mountain range. When you're here, everything's here." "I don't know what you mean," Frank said. "I do," said Charlie, "and she has a lot of growing up to do." "Lay off, will you?" said Frank.

By the time the men were ready to leave, I was drunk with happiness. I walked down the quarry road looking over my shoulder at the stone sheds until Frank grasped my wrist firmly and steered me after him. I saw the deep chasms in the earth and felt as if I could walk over the columns of empty air to the solid ground beyond. "She's in a daze," I heard Frank say. "It doesn't take much to make some people happy," Charlie said. His voice came from far away. The cars swayed back and forth, returning to Montpelier. If there were other people in the cars, I didn't know it. I closed my eyes and I was moving through a space filled with a golden dust, and at the end of it there was a door, and I knew it would open if only I kept knocking at it. The important thing was to keep on knocking. "Wake up," said

Frank; "we're home." "She's tired," Charlie said. I said I didn't know why I should be so tired; I hadn't done anything but watch. Charlie hesitated on the corner of Crown Street as if there were something he wanted to say and then turned the corner and waved. "Jealous," said Frank, dismissing him from his mind.

After supper, I went upstairs and lay down on Frank's bed. He wanted to go out for a walk, but I was too tired. In the dream, I was out in the snowy fields with Frank and the snow was perfect for molding and Frank had carved a snow statue of me and was working on new statues of cows and lambs and horses. I lay down in the snow and watched him and then I asked him to make us a house, a big house with three bedrooms on the second floor and two on the first floor, and I wanted a porch that curved around the house and a gazebo in the far corner of the meadow. And Frank started building the house, and I could see that by morning he would be finished and then we would move in. And as he worked, I slept. I woke just as the sun was coming up, and the rosy sky reflected its warm blood onto the statues which were coming alive and were just about to move. I lay in the snow with my arms stretched out toward them, waiting for them to come to me, and then I saw that the sun was rising and it was large and hot and I saw the animals running with water; their ears were melting, their flanks were sinking, and when I finally turned to the house, I knew what I would see. Already the second story was collapsing into the first, as if a fire had raged through the bottom story, and while I watched, the pillars supporting the roof collapsed and the porch fell into what was left of the drift and I saw that the meadow itself was thirsty and hot and was drinking in the snow as it melted, and I picked up some snow and held it in my hands, hoping to save it, but my hands were hot, I had not realized how hot they were, and the snow melted and ran through them and out into the ground. And the snow which had stuck to my skirt melted and my skirt was wet and I looked around the world and saw that it was washed clean but also washed empty, and I began to cry. And the sky was boastfully empty of clouds and seemed to be saying that the drifts of snow would never come again.

I woke in an empty desolation, and I was confused, because I seemed to be sleeping in snow. And then I saw that I was in Frank's room and I had turned on my side and the whiteness into which I stared was only his pillow. I turned on my back and looked at the ceiling, a relief map of cracked, split paint. I wanted to have good dreams, not dreams like these. And then I thought that perhaps my dreams were unpleasant because my life was not, and I remembered that I had had some good dreams once, when I was still in North Chittenden. I would, I thought, getting out of bed, rely on my life and not on my dreams. I could always wake up out of a bad dream.

It was astonishing how quickly time passed now that I wanted it to slow down. Frank was still not back. Probably he had gone to find Charlie. I sat in the chair near the window and looked out, but the blue snow shone in the silvery light, enigmatic as ever. I took my nightgown out of Frank's bottom drawer where I now kept it and crawled into bed. My body felt heavy and drugged.

And I was having more and more trouble concentrating on my work. The day at the quarries had spoiled me. Here I was, stitching on lifeless cloth which wore out and stained and was thrown away or cut down or used for rags, while there, the men were creating beautiful invulnerable things. And I could not imagine introducing Frank to my father. I could not begin to imagine what my father would make of him. Bill Brown would not like him. He had never liked anyone I cared for. When I bent over my sewing, I felt the old, pure panic return as I thought of Frank walking in the door to that house as if he were walking into the mouth of a bottomless well. And I would shake myself and tell myself it was all nonsense and finish what I was doing. And then I would find myself slowing down, seeing Frank entering the kitchen, and there was my mother, coming out of the shadows toward him, and I wanted to pull him back or make her go back, but I could not decide what to do first and so they would come closer and closer to each other. "You look like you're dreaming with your eyes open," Florence said to me. "I am," I said, shuddering. She asked me what the trouble was, and I told her I had to go home over Easter but didn't really want to. She said I would when I got on the train. I said I hoped I would but I doubted it. A hundred times a day, I was tempted to throw down my work, tell Mrs. James I had a headache, and run off to the cars. And now I really had headaches. I would rip out a seam and begin again and from the way the light fell in the window, I knew it was not yet twelve o'clock and I could not imagine remaining where I was for another six hours. Then I would take out the beaded bag Frank had given me for my birthday, and every time I looked at it, I smiled because he had been just as interested in seeing what it looked like as I had been. On each side was a spiderweb, outlined in black, shiny beads. I loved it. It was always cool, even when the room was stifling, and when my head began to ache, I would look at it, and if looking were not enough, I would press it to my forehead.

My life began at night when I left Mrs. James's. At night, Frank and I wandered the streets of Montpelier and I thought that ghosts must walk as we walked, and I looked around us as if I expected to see someone suddenly make himself visible to us. We talked without thinking. We said whatever came into our heads.

I asked Frank what it had been like, coming here from Quebec, going so far away from home, and he said he didn't feel as if he'd gone anywhere at all, not with Charlie snapping at his heels every inch of the way. "You wouldn't want Charlie to go back?" I asked him. "I never did before," he said; "now sometimes I wish he weren't here." I said that there were times when I wished everyone in the world would go away but him and he smiled. "Are you used to women loving you so much?" I asked, my voice shaky. "I guess I am," he said; "I never made any sense of it. But I take it for granted. That's what Charlie says." "Is that why you love me?" I asked; "because I love you so much?" "Well, that helps," Frank said; "but that's not the reason. I don't know the reason." "How much do you love me?" I asked; "the whole iris?" "Not the whole iris," he said. "Then why do you want to marry me?" "Because I love you as much as I'm ever going to love anyone," he said. "Are you disappointed?" he asked after a while. I said I wasn't. And it was true. I knew he would come to love me as I loved him.

"Do you think I'm beautiful?" I asked him after a while. "I don't think there's a person on earth who wouldn't think you're beautiful," he said. "Is *that* why you love me?" I asked. "No," he said; "I never much liked beautiful women. Madge was right about that. 'Spare me a beautiful woman.' That's what my father used to say, and I guess he was right." "Why?" I asked. "Oh, I don't know. They're so taken with themselves. They expect so much. They think they just have to stand here." "I told you I'd learn to cook," I said unhappily. He was beginning to see it, that I was of no use. "I didn't mean you," Frank said; "you're different." But when I asked how I was different, he couldn't answer me. "Don't you get used to my being beautiful?" I asked him. "I don't think about it much," he said, "but then sometimes, when you're doing something, reaching up for your cloak or looking over your shoulder, it's brand-new. What's gotten into you, anyway? Why are you cross-examining me?"

"I'm just nervous about going home," I said; "it's only a week away."

Frank sneezed. "Oh, you're getting sick!" I cried; "we won't be able to go!" "Don't pin your hopes on that," he said; "I never get sick. Anyway, the best medicine is going on with things, so sick or not, we're going. Maybe you're ashamed of me. Maybe that's why you're so worried." "Ashamed of you!" I cried; "I'm afraid they'll make you see me the way I really am." "I see you the way you really are," he said; "you'd be fine if you only stopped talking." I relaxed and then tightened my grip around his waist. "You always hold on to me as if I'm about to blow away," he said, smiling down at me. "You might," I said. "It would take some wind to blow me off. You're smaller," he said; "you'd go first." "True," I said. "Do you want to go to the Barre Opera House?" he asked; "they're having another theatrical. This one's called *Kyra's Fate*." I asked him if he thought he could live through it. "If I can't, can I sleep on your shoulder?" he asked. "You shouldn't have asked that," I said; "now if you don't sleep on my shoulder, I'm going to be disappointed."

I took my hand out of Frank's pocket and began burrowing up the sleeve of his coat toward his shoulder. "You're warm in there," I said. "I guess you want to go home," he said, and we went back. "You get into bed first this time," I said, and when he lay down, I began circling the bed, as if I were going to leap in without warning. "Come on," said Frank, "you're making me nervous." "Close your eyes," I said. He closed his eyes and I climbed up on the stool at the foot of the bed. "Keep them closed," I ordered him. "I'm getting cold," Frank complained, and then I jumped over the low footboard and fell flat on top of him, and the bed, always creaky and wobbly, fell with a crash to the floor. We heard feet running down the hall toward our door. "Get behind the cupboard," Frank said. "No, it's all right, Iris," I heard him say; "the rope springs gave. I'll fix them tomorrow. Tell everyone to go back to bed." He closed the door and latched it. "Come out," he said; "I guess you won't complain if we have to sleep on the floor." "I guess not," I said, looking at the wreckage around me. "You know why I love you?" Frank asked me; "because you're the only woman who ever thought of destroying something as big as a bed. Sometimes," he said, reaching out for me, "you remind me of a puppy." "A puppy!" I said, biting his ear in outrage. "Well, what did I say?" he asked; "puppies chew your head." "I'll do more than chew your head," I said. "You know," he said, "I'm glad the bed fell down." "Why?" "Because," he said, "now it can't fall down again."

30

It was the day before Easter, and we were at Montpelier Junction waiting for the train. I kept leaning forward, looking for the train. "Stop that," Frank said, pulling me backward, "you're going to fall under it when it comes. You're worse than a child." I said I thought I saw it. "You don't, that's a cloud. You'll feel it before you see it," he said; "it makes the ground shake."

"I wonder what the roads will be like at home," I said; "you never know about March. Sometimes the mud's terrible. When I went into town, I never knew if I'd get back." "Stop worrying," Frank said. I looked around me as I always did when I was leaving, as if I wanted to memorize the scene so that, if I never see it again, it would not be lost. "It looks like December all over again," I sighed, "before it started snowing." The drifts were granulated and shrinking under my eyes. The world looked shopworn, worn out by months of bearing up under the heavy snow. "Spring's coming," said Frank; "just try to stop it." "It's always foggy," I said; "I hate fog. It blots things out. It's not pretty." "It's pretty when it's rising over a lake," he said. "No, it's not," I said. "I'm not getting into an argument about fog," said Frank. "It's always foggy in the morning on the farm," I said. "Will you stop worrying?" Frank said; "look for the train." It came and we got on, and as soon as we were settled, I opened the dinner pail Iris had packed for us and began feeding Frank. "Open up," I said, popping a piece of roast beef into his mouth. "You're going to choke me," he said. "Well, then," I said, "you feed me." I was sulky. "You know what?" said Frank; "I'll be happy when this is over."

As the train began slowing down for North Chittendon, I flattened myself against the window. There were the familiar hills, the familiar curve of the river, a leaden silver thread gleaming dully under the winter sun. And then I saw the two spires of the churches, the headstones of their twin graveyards, and in the distance, I could see Bea Brown's house. "Tuttle's Hardware," I said aloud. "You're glad to be home," Frank said, smiling at me. "I guess I am," I said, surprised.

Bill Brown was waiting at the station with the buggy. "I guess you're the surprise," he said to Frank. "That is Frank Holt," I said; "Frank, this is Bill Brown." "Well, get in, whoever you are," said Bill. He was getting crankier as he got older. "Don't you want to ask him anything?" I whispered to Bill; "don't you want to know what he does all week?" "He'll be telling your father soon enough. No point in going through it twice," Bill said. I shook my head. Frank smiled into the air.

When we turned the hairpin corner and the house sprang into view, I began babbling. "There's the garden," I said, pointing to a plot enclosed in chicken wire east of the barn. "And there, on the southern side of the house, the field's full of pear and apple and peach trees. And the path goes down to a grape arbor, and the back of the barn's all grown over with a grapevine, and in the summer, you should see the west side of the house: it's all candy-tuft and bachelor's buttons, pansies, foxglove, trumpet-vines, heliotrope, striped grass, sweet william, sweet peas, hollyhocks, geraniums, morning glories, oh, it's wonderful!" Out of the corner of my eye, I saw the stand of lilac branches bleak against the sky and I remembered lying down beneath them, intending to fall asleep there and never wake up again. I looked away. "No sunflowers?" Frank asked. He was grinning at me. "They grow all around the barn." "Oh," he said, "good. I thought there might be something missing."

The carriage stopped and I found myself in front of the door and I felt Frank behind me and Bill behind him. My father opened the door. "Well, Agnes," he said slowly. "I'm glad to see you," I said, without moving toward him. I was afraid of what he might do, what he might have become. My mother was gone. He was alone. He might turn on me and tell me I had no right to bring a man into the house when my mother had just died. He might think I had no right to anything if he had nothing himself. "So you're Agnes's surprise?" he said, moving around me, stretching his hand out to Frank. "He's Frank Holt, Father," I said; "he's a stone carver." "Well," said my father, looking at both of us oddly, as if he were suddenly looking at a sky with two suns, not one, "you must be tired. You probably want to show Frank all over the place." "I want to take him up to my cabin," I said suddenly. "Well, we've been taking care of it for you," my father said. "My grandmother left me her cabin when she died," I said to Frank; "let's go up there. Can we take the horses?" "They could use the exercise," my father said. "It's foggy, though. You know the trail. You go first."

We rode up the twisting path to my grandmother's cabin. There it stood as if she were still in it, as if she might come to the door if only I called loudly enough. And there was the brass bed, gleaming in the dull light. "That's the bed?" asked Frank. "That's it," I said, dismounting. We tied up our horses and went in. A thick dampness filled the air. An odor like decaying leaves pressed against the walls of the room. "My father said they heat up the place every few weeks to keep out the damp," I said; I guess it can't be done." There were spiderwebs everywhere, but otherwise everything was in perfect order. The familiar, pale dust from burned wood covered all the surfaces.

"What's this?" Frank asked, picking up a picture on the mantel. "Oh, that," I said, coming up to him, "that's an old portrait of my grandmother. One of the sculptors did it when he was here in the summer." "You look exactly like her," Frank said. I didn't answer. My throat was tightening. If I looked just like her, why wasn't she here? If I looked just like her, why couldn't I peel off an outer layer and give her back her own body and have her come back to me? I dug my fingers into my arm as if I wanted to tear the flesh from it. "What's wrong?" Frank asked. "Nothing," I said. How I hated these portraits, the photographs, the resemblances! They did no good. But I knew I could not explain what I meant to Frank because I did not know what I meant myself.

"Look at this," Frank said, pointing to the bottom corner of the little portrait. "F. S. Chappell," I read aloud. "He's one of the most famous sculptors in America. And in Europe," Frank said. He looked at the portrait in awe. "He came here?" he asked; "F. S. Chappell?" He stayed here part of one summer," I told him; "well, not right here. He boarded in town." "Good Lord," said Frank. "Was he so remarkable?" I asked. "At twenty-five, he was filling orders for the president of the country," Frank said; "and the British Museum bought three of his statues." "Oh," I said. Frank put the picture down and looked from it to me. "I can see what he was doing in North Chittendon," he said. "Now you have me," I said; "you can start working yourself." I wanted to get as far from that portrait as possible. "Your grandmother left you the cabin?" Frank asked. "Yes," I said. "What about the portrait?" "It's mine," I said. "Could I borrow it?'' he asked; ''just for a while? F. S. Chappell in my own room. It would be my own fault if I didn't live up to it, wouldn't it?'' ''You don't have to live up to anyone,'' I said. ''Can I borrow it?'' he asked again. ''You can have it,'' I said; ''you know that.'' I felt defeated. I didn't know why. ''I like it up here,'' Frank said; ''it feels so far away from everything. It's an enormous farm. That's not just an ordinary farmhouse your family has.'' ''No,'' I said; ''it's a wealthy farm. My family has money.'' ''You can tell that by looking around,'' Frank said. ''We should come back up here someday,'' I said; ''this is the only part of the farm that feels like home to me.'' ''It's a hard place to leave,'' he said, ''a farm like this.'' ''No one in my family ever managed,'' I said; ''let's go down.''

We went into the main house, but it was empty. ''The cows,'' I said; ''they must be loose.'' ''Or the horses,'' said Frank; ''he'll be back.'' We wandered from room to room. ''The kitchen's the worst place,'' I said; ''my sister was scalded here, I was born here, and my mother died here. My room's not bad. Nothing ever happened there.'' I went into the room next to mine; someone had cleaned it and stacked wood next to its stove. ''It looks like you're staying here,'' I said; ''I'll get some linens for the bed.'' ''It's already made up,'' Frank said, and he pulled me toward him. ''The house isn't so bad, is it?'' I asked, pulling away. ''It's a fine house,'' he said, ''an impressive one.'' ''I feel like a child in here,'' I said. ''Everyone does when they go home,'' he said.

At supper, my father and Frank chatted about the farm and Frank told him about the quarries and what kind of work he was doing and what kind of work he wanted to do. My father was older and thinner. He couldn't last much longer, I thought. He was wearing out. Already his skin had the look of fallen leaf-flesh. I watched the two of them through blinding tears. I loved them both. ''Well,'' said my father, stopping to consider Frank's plans for New York, ''I don't see why you couldn't do that. The city's full of people and they all come from somewhere.'' ''Agnes and I are going after we get married,'' he said. ''Married?'' said my father, putting down his fork. ''In about a year,'' I said hurriedly; ''Frank wants to put away some money first.'' ''Do you want to wait a year?'' my father asked Frank. ''I don't have much choice,'' Frank said.

''Well, he might, mightn't he, Agnes?'' asked my father. Frank watched us, puzzled. I was afraid to look at either of them. ''He doesn't know,'' I said. ''Know what?'' asked Frank.

"My grandmother left me quite a bit of money," I said; "it's in trust until I'm twenty-one." "I'm the trustee," said my father; "I might be able to free it up." "She wouldn't have wanted that," I said; "she wanted me to wait until I was twenty-one." "I don't want it," Frank said, his voice angry. "Well," said my father, "it's worth thinking about. You could get on with your ideas." I was afraid to look at my father. He ate on, oblivious to the storms he was stirring into the air around him. Frank had stopped eating altogether. "We're going to go out for a walk," I said. "Well, come back early," said my father; "I've only seen you twice in the last year." "I'll come back early," I said.

Outside, the stars were bright tips of ice showing through the indigo surface of the sky. "The ground's still frozen up here," I said; "you don't have to worry about the mud." Frank walked quickly. I had trouble keeping up with him. When we were safely into the border of trees, he turned on me. "Why didn't you tell me about the money?" "What money?" I asked. "*Your* money," he said; "you didn't tell me you had money of your own." "I didn't think it made any difference," I said. "How couldn't it make a difference?" he asked me; "you've been playing a game with me. You're no poor working girl. You don't need a husband."

I stood there, struck dumb. I didn't know where to begin. "I never said I was poor," I answered at last. "You didn't have to," Frank said; "you knew how it looked." "But I want to support myself!" I said; "I don't want to take any money from my family! That's why I left! I never decided about my grandmother's money. I don't have to take it. I've never counted on it," I said, and as I said it, I knew it was true. "And as for a husband," I said, "I wasn't looking for a husband so that he could earn money for me. I was looking for something different. I didn't want a provider," I said, starting to cry; "I wanted someone to love."

"Why didn't you trust me?" Frank asked, his voice softer. "I did trust *you*!" I cried; "I was afraid you wouldn't want me if you found out about the money! I'm always afraid you won't want me!" "Why?" asked Frank, his eyes on mine. "I don't know," I said; "it seems like such a miracle that you want me at all. I don't know why it happened or how it happened and I'm always afraid it will just go away." "Just go away?" he echoed. "Everything always has!" I cried. "I don't understand you," he said; "you sent Charlie off. He told me himself. If I walked away, half of Montpelier would be knocking on your door." "I

290

don't want half of Montpelier!" I cried. I turned away from him and looked into the woods. I couldn't see anything beyond the trees in front of me. "I did trust you," I said; "I didn't trust myself. I didn't believe you'd still want me. I know how important it is to you to do things your own way. I know you don't want help from anyone, especially not a woman." "Agnes," he said, "that's how I was brought up. The man's supposed to take care of the woman, not the other way around." "Well, I'm sorry," I cried; "I didn't ask my grandmother to die and leave me her money. If you don't want me to, I won't take it." "I don't know what to think about the money," he said. I started to sob.

"Agnes," he said, "stop shaking." He pulled me to him and wrapped his arms around me. "I still want you," he said; "stop shaking." I took a deep, shuddering breath and collapsed against him. "What do you want me to do about the money?" I finally asked. "Nothing," he said; "leave it there until you're twenty-one and then make up your mind. Nothing's changed." "Nothing?" I asked. "Nothing," he said. "My father just brought it up to make trouble," I burst out. "No, he didn't," said Frank; "he was only trying to be helpful." A shooting star sailed across the sky. "I should teach you where the stars are," said Frank; "there's Orion." He pointed at it. "There's the Big Dipper. There's the North Star. It's good to know." "In case of emergency?" I asked. "In case," he said. "Tomorrow let's shoot at targets," I said; "my father likes it, too." "On Easter Sunday?" asked Frank. "No one will know what we're doing up here," I said. "Oh, well," said Frank, "I guess it's all right."

We went back. I put off going to bed. I didn't like sleeping alone, but then Frank began talking to my father and I saw they would be up late into the night. It had been years since I'd talked to my father, much less listened to him. When had it started, the silence between us? When he killed my pet cow? I was nine or ten when he'd done that. It must have begun before that. I could not remember a time when I felt free to tell him what I thought. I must have been born resenting him. Poor Dierdre the cow. Mother said she was too expensive to feed when she didn't give milk. I felt the old resentment, and as if I were a small child again, I sat up in bed as if I intended to get up and burst into the parlor and start shouting. I lay down again. I was angry. I was angry because I was sleeping alone.

In the morning, a stony light filled the room. I got up and went to the window. The sky was the color of an iced-over pond on a cloudy day. The snow glared dully; spring was always late coming to this farm. I got dressed and went into the barn and looked for the old wooden trunk near the rear entrance. There it was. Under a length of coiled rope were the targets my father had bought from Tuttle's Hardware. There were hundreds of them; he must have expected our target practices to go on forever. But when I remembered practicing, I remembered my grandmother, not my father. I picked up ten of the targets and took them back into the house. Their edges were yellowing. "What's that, Agnes?" my father asked, coming over. "Oh," he said, "I'm glad you're keeping up your shooting." "I haven't been," I said, "that's the trouble. Can I borrow a pistol of yours? Frank has one of his own."

"I've kept your grandmother's for you," he said. He went over to the gun cabinet, took a key from the ring, and unlocked it. "Here," he said, "it's small, but its balance is good. It works like a clock. It won't jam. Of course, you have to keep it clean." "I'm not taking it back with me," I said; "I don't need a gun. I just want to practice." Frank came down. I handed him a napkin. "Sit down," I said. "Do you need help with the cooking?" he asked. "My father's cooking," I said; "he learned while my mother was sick." "A man should know how to cook," said my father. "Frank's a very good cook," I said. "Bread must be easy after marble," my father said.

I sat down at the table and inhaled the odor of fresh butter. It had been some time since I had smelled it. Iris got her butter from a dairy and she liked it fancy; she said there was no point in working herself to death running the best boardinghouse in the city and then smelling it up with country butter. The rich, thick, rancid smell filled the kitchen. It was a sour smell, but good. I had missed it. Frank was buttering his bread thickly; evidently, he liked fresh butter too. "It's good to be home," I said at last. "You know you can always come back here," my father said. "You can, too," he said to Frank. We smiled at him. "I got the targets," I said; "they were just where I last saw them." "Agnes is a good shot," my father said. "That's what she tells me, but I don't believe her," Frank said. "Well, let's go out and see," said my father. I watched how slowly he got up, how stiffly he moved. "You should have had more children," I said suddenly as we walked out into the yard. "More children?" said my father; "three were enough." "But you only wound up with one," I said.

"I had a good life," my father said; "in spite of everything."

"I'll go set up the targets," I said, walking across the narrow end of the field. I fastened three targets to three trees and came back. Then the three of us stood behind a line of sticks and began firing. "You know," I said, "I don't think any of us hit anything." A cool wind was beginning to shake the black branches. "That's what happens when you don't practice," said my father; "your young man was right. You can't hit the broad side of a barn." "Well, I haven't had a chance to practice yet!" I said indignantly.

"Look at that," my father said to Frank; "I bet you didn't know that about Agnes. You can't go up against that one and expect her to lie back and let you beat her. She'll race anything. She used to race the dog across the river and she cried when he beat her. She liked it better when the dog got older and she won. But she wasn't happy then, either. She didn't want the dog to get old. Isn't she after you about sculpting?" my father asked him; "doesn't she want you to teach her?" "No," said Frank; "she wants me to teach her to draw. Mostly, she just wants to watch me." "I don't try to race Frank," I said angrily. "Why not?" my father asked; "you used to race me. I always let you win, but that's something else." "I never race him," I said, "because it would be like racing against myself." "Still," said my father, "we're going to be out here all morning until you start hitting that target, Agnes. I know you well enough for that." "You can go in," I said; "Frank wants me to learn to use the gun again." "If you took more time sighting down the barrel, you'd do better," my father said. I said I knew that; I just wanted to shoot a few times for the fun of it.

Then we settled down to firing at the targets. I was surprised at how it came back, how the world narrowed down to those black concentric circles which would spin everything away from me unless I stopped them and began to fire. "She's hitting the target now," said Frank. "What did I tell you?" said my father; "as soon as we settled down, she remembered how to use the gun." "Let's go look at the targets," Frank said. We walked down the field. "You hit it every time," Frank said. "She usually does," said my father. "You hit it five times," I said to Frank. "But I missed twice," he said. "Now you know what her special talent is," my father said, winking at Frank. So that was what they had been talking about after I went to bed—what I was going to do with my life. "Let's do it again," I said; "ten shots apiece." "You should give me a handicap, Agnes," said my father; "these old eyes can barely pick out the trees." "No handicaps," I said. "If your sight's that bad, you ought to go in and get a rifle." "A rifle!" snorted my father; "I should be able to hit a target with a pistol even if my eyes are bad." "That's what I thought," I said.

We went on shooting until we were all hitting the targets most of the time, and then my father told me to shoot without sighting along the barrel of the gun. He said he wanted to see if I could still do it. I said I didn't think I could. I looked hard at the target and raised the gun, stared at the target, closed my eyes, and fired. I opened my eyes, repositioned the gun, stared at the target, and fired again. "Ten," Frank said finally; "let's take a look." "I don't believe it," Frank said; "you hit the target every time. Your pattern's wider, but you hit every time." "It's a skill that runs in the family," said my father; "in the women, anyway. I couldn't do it. But her grandmother could shoot a fly at eighty paces and she didn't sight the target either." "Could you teach me?" Frank asked. I said I would try. My father said he would go in and start dinner, and the two of us stood on the edge of the field, firing at the trees. "I can't do it," Frank said at last; "I *have* to look through the sights." "You have to pretend you're looking through them and then not look," I said. Frank fired at the target. "I can't do it," he said; "I have to look." "Well, it is an utterly useless talent," I said. "No talent is ever useless," he said. "This one is," I said. "No," said Frank; "if you can do this, there must be other things you can do that are useful." "For instance?" I asked. "That's what I'm trying to figure out," he said.

We walked back to the house, our hands clasped, our free hands still holding the pistols. "You know," Frank said, "today is Easter Sunday. I almost forgot." I said I hoped no angels were flying over the pasture. I stopped and listened. The deep tones of the Congregational Church bell were faint in the air. "Your father said he asked about your friend Louise, but she was working away from home." "It's just as well," I said; "we would have sat around smiling at each other without saying anything. I guess there isn't much to say after all this time." "You wouldn't have believed it when you were younger, would you," Frank asked me, "if someone had told you you'd have nothing to say to Louise?" I shook my head. "I never thought I'd want to hear the end of Charlie," he said.

But I was thinking about Easter and how we had spent it firing into the edge of the darkness, as if something dangerous were waiting for us; that was what it would have looked like to someone watching from above. But there was no one up above watching us, and there was no danger. It was being home, the house still standing, unchanged, most of the family gone, that made me see things so strangely. When we got inside, I could not wait to return the pistol to my father, and until he locked the cabinet, I was on edge.

31

When we returned to Montpelier, something small but definite shifted in my view of things. I saw Frank differently, but I could not say how. I clung to him more than I ever had before. I got through the days at Mrs. James's by telling myself that I was working for the day when Frank and I could leave for New York. But I no longer had any patience with Polly when she hinted that Frank was only an ordinary human being after all, and if she criticized him for anything, I flared up at her. Some balance was off, and the clock was ticking wildly.

And I blamed everything on the visit to North Chittendon. Again and again, I saw Frank standing on the edge of the field, firing at the target, and my father standing next to him, firing too. I had attacks of the old fear and I began to tell Frank about them. I called them the "nameless dreads," because that was how they felt to me. And when I was alone, I blamed Frank for having come home with me, for talking to my father, for wanting the picture of my grandmother, for acting like anyone else's future husband. And then I would turn on myself and ask what it was I wanted of him; he had behaved precisely as I had expected him to. Yet when he was there he had seemed ordinary.

And then I would draw up my knees and hug them with my arms and tell myself that it was not Frank I was angry at. I was angry at myself, coming home like any love-sick girl with a boy she had found to marry, and I would scold myself and tell myself that I was angry at Frank for asking me to marry him, for coming home with me, for not shooting as well as I did.

But when I wore myself out, I would admit the truth: I was afraid of Frank. He was pulling me into ordinary life. Then it wasn't Frank's fault, after all. I would be angry at anyone I loved. And I saw with horror how little things about him were beginning to obsess me; how, when we made love, he would draw in his breath in little hisses, as if he were in pain, and I would tell myself that I would get used to it, that in a few weeks, or in a month, it would be a dear sound because it was his. I saw how little he understood of what people told him. I saw that my own moods went unnoticed by him unless I told him of their existence, and there were times I thought that even bursting into tears would not be enough to get his attention. And at the same time, I clung tighter and tighter, as if something were trying to take him from me, as if something outside of myself were the danger when I knew there was no danger but me. And because I was afraid of myself, I clung to him harder, as if *he* could drive off whatever fears I had about him. I saw that I was sewing myself into a sack, but I didn't know what else to do. I only felt safe when I was with him, yet he was the source of the danger. It would all pass, I told myself repeatedly, as soon as North Chittendon wore off. I had only to get through so many weeks, so many months, and everything would be as it was.

But the nameless dreads did not stop. After two weeks, I began coming home from Mrs. James's early; there, my head hurt and my stomach hurt, but when I had gone two blocks, I would feel better. I was using up the money I had in the bank. I drew half of it out and hid it behind a loose board in my wall. I told myself that I had to stay at work, that I could not earn a living working only three days a week, but it did no good. I would walk back to the Trowbridge house, go into my room and go to sleep. On some days, I would sit down in front of the mirror and comb my hair, trying out one style after another until I heard the front door slam and felt the tremor of the slamming door go through my room and my rigid body.

"What's wrong with me?" I asked Frank one night. We were walking under a chewed skull of a moon. "Why can't I calm down?" "Are you worrying about something?" he asked me. "That's just it," I said; "there's nothing bothering me." "Maybe that's what's the matter," he said; "you need something to worry about." I looked at him sharply. Charlie would say something like that, not Frank. "Why did you say that?" I asked him. "That's what my father used to tell my mother," he said comfortably, "when she complained she was worrying about nothing." "Did she stop?" I asked; "worrying about nothing?" "I guess she did," said Frank; "she wasn't one of the world's gayest people. Usually she had plenty to worry about." "She wasn't crazy?" I asked. "Crazy!" he exclaimed; "my mother!" "Well," I said, "it feels crazy to be worried about nothing."

"She used to worry about the skulls in the walls," he said, "but I don't blame her. It was my father's fault." I asked him what on earth he was talking about now—skulls in the walls. I was going to have nightmares for weeks. It was just like Frank, to try cheering me up with skulls.

"When we bought the farm in Three Forks," Frank said, "before that it was empty for years. My dad said it was full of lice, and squirrels were running in and out everywhere, and the whole place was full of cats. He smoked out the lice and set up a stove for my mother in the parlor and we all moved in and then he began knocking down the walls because the old plaster was shot, and the walls were full of cats' skeletons. They must have gone in between the lathing strips somehow and then they couldn't get out. They found all kinds of things in the walls. A book, a baby's shoe, an old umbrella. Some of it must have fallen in while the house was going up, but my mother thought someone put in the little shoe on purpose. And corncobs. Hundreds and hundreds of corncobs. They were supposed to line the walls and keep the house warm, but they didn't. They did feed a lot of mice, though. You can't imagine how dusty that house was while he was knocking down the walls. We slapped each other all the way to school and we were still dusty when we got there. Well, you can imagine it. You've been to the quarries. Sometimes I think I'm meant to live in a cloud of dust for the rest of my life." I squeezed his hand. "Don't worry," I said. The clenched fist in my chest had relaxed and let go. For a while, I was free.

"Do you want to come home with me?" Frank asked; "it's beautiful there. You'd like it." The coldness was back. "Yes," I said, "I'd like to go." Then I thought I'd try telling the truth. "I'm afraid of meeting your family," I said; "I'm afraid they won't like me." "They'll like you, and even if they don't, it won't make any difference." "What if your sister doesn't like me?" I asked. "My sister?" he said, surprised. "Charlie told me you were her favorite." "My sister will like anyone I like," he said; "she's got three kids. Did I tell you that? They don't look like her and they don't look like her husband. You know how old she was when she met her husband? Twelve. My parents made her wait until she was fifteen. She said she didn't understand why at the time, but she does now." "When do you want to go?" I asked. I had never heard Frank say so much at once. I should remember to ask about his sister more often. "When do you?'' he asked. "In the summer," I said; "it's so beautiful here in the spring."

"Do you feel better?" Frank asked. I said I did. Frank said we should start back. I asked him if he knew anything about bees, and he said they'd had hives on the farm, but he didn't know anything about them except that they stung and made honey. I said I had a book about them; I'd brought it back from my house. "That's a funny thing to get interested in," he said; "Iris doesn't want any bees around, I can tell you. She doesn't like anything that flies, not even butterflies." "Oh, I don't want any bees," I said; "I've just been thinking about them. They're strange."

Recently I had had trouble sleeping, but that night I fell asleep immediately. It seemed to me I was still awake when I heard a voice calling me and I struggled to wake up, but I couldn't. "Your bees are swarming," a voice said; "wake up. They're swarming." "They're not my bees," I said, closing my eyes. "Wake up. They're swarming," the voice said again, and in the dream, I got up and went out. I was standing in front of my grandmother's cabin and it was snowing even though the apple tree was heavy with blossoms. "They're not swarming," I said; "they only swarm in summer," and I turned to go back, but the voice again said my bees were swarming. I walked over to the hive, which was near the house, at the edge of the woods. The hive was misted over by a golden mass of small bodies flying like comets and their little wings flashed like metal as the bees flew and looped and buzzed in triumph because they were free of the hive. Inside the hive, a new queen was tended to by the drones, but the bees who had escaped did not know about her. They were flying with their own queen and they flew until their queen had no breath left. I watched the bees flying so furiously and getting nowhere and finally I saw them beginning to settle near a cracked, lightning-struck elm.

I walked over to the tree, slowly. The buzzing of the bees filled everything; it had risen from the earth to the sky and fell back down upon me. I saw that the queen had settled on a low branch of the elm and while I watched, the drones, tired of flight, began to join her, tens of them, hundreds of them, thousands, until they formed a dark cloud around her, until they hung from the branch like a tear-shaped clot of blood, a clot that would not fall, live blood hanging from the tree, living blood, murmuring to itself, its sound filling the air. Now I was supposed to do something. If I did not give them a new hive, the dark, moving clot of bees would hang there telling its story to the air and then they would fly into the woods and find a home in the dark. And somehow I knew that I was the hive, and that when the bees entered me they would not sting. I knew that they expected me to come closer and that they would enter me through my mouth and my eyes and my nose and they would not hurt me. And I did not want to go near them, and my feet would not move. Now the bees began swarming again, and they swarmed around me; they hung from my arm and my arm fell to my side under their weight. They were crawling all over me; some of them were stinging each other to death, and the dead bees fell at my feet.

And then I saw a bee circling my head and I could not move. I knew she was the queen bee and there was nothing I could do to escape her. I opened my mouth and she entered. And then the other bees were around me and I saw the mountains and the trees through a veil of small, hurtling dark shapes. And then the horizon cleared and I knew they had entered me and I was their hive, but I felt no different, perhaps a bit more content. But I did not want anyone to know that I had taken in the dark clot of bees and that they moved inside me, the queen ruling over them all. She was laying her eggs; the drones were feeding her. She was eating the royal jelly. She was all that mattered.

And then I was walking through the fields and I came to the hive, which was outside of me, and I didn't know how it got there. I thought the bees were still within my body, and I saw that on the ground, in front of the entrance to the hive, were little creeping, hopping things, and when I looked closer, I knew they were the used-up bees, the tired workers. Their wings were tattered or utterly broken. They had not grown old. They had worn themselves out for their queen and the fur along their throats had been worn down by their passage through uncount- able rough flowers. I picked up one bee and placed it on the sill of the hive. The bee did not try to enter. There was no place for it, weak, worn, in the hive. It crawled about outside the murmuring door and fell to the earth. It did not mind; it died with the others, peacefully and without rebellion. It had done its job.

I bent over and loosened the lid of the hive. My bare fingers sought for and found the queen bee. I knew that she would not sting me. I held her between my fingers. Then I sat down and watched the hive. It took little time. The world of the hive unraveled. The drones interrupted their rhythmic flights over the fields and began to fly about erratically. The bees massed darkly on the threshold as if crying aloud to the heavens and the hum of the colony changed; it was no longer steady and contented. It was the sound of agitation, the cold knowledge that the world was coming to an end. I went back to the hive and replaced the queen. The bees buzzed loudly and the flights over the field resumed immediately. I watched the drones flock around the queen, tending to her, inspecting her, feeding her, crawling nearer to her. Their ecstasy was unimaginable.

They had their queen and they resumed their life of work and contentment. Death was nothing to them. I did not understand why the queen refused to defend herself against a person's hand when it plucked her from the hive. I wanted to pick up the queen again and feel her furry body against my bare hand, but this time I did not dare touch her; the bees knew me now and they were waiting for me.

And then I heard a voice saying, "Your bees are swarming," and I turned back to the forest, and from every tree, a dark mass, shaped like a tear, was hanging from a branch, and I said, "Oh, no, there are too many; they will have to go to someone else," and at the sound of my voice, the bees began flying toward me and the sky went dark.

"Wake up! Wake up!" Frank was saying. He was shaking me by the shoulder. "Wake up!" he said urgently; "you're screaming." "It's the bees," I said and burst out crying. I held on to him while my eyes searched the room. There were no bees anywhere. "The bees?" Frank asked. "In the dream," I said; "they were coming at me." "It was only a dream," Frank said, smoothing my hair; "it was only a dream."

But I didn't seem to wake from that dream. While we ate breakfast, I heard the bees. While I sewed at Mrs. James's, I saw the bees, hanging like a clot of living, stinging blood from a far branch. And I didn't want to talk to Frank about the bees; I wanted to talk to Polly. I decided to leave early and find her at the factory. She wasn't there. The foreman told me she had gone back early to the Trowbridge house and I ran down the road back to Iris's.

I burst in on Polly. She was in the kitchen, ironing. "I had the most terrible dream last night," I said, falling onto a chair, trying to catch my breath. I told her about the voice calling me and how I had swallowed the bees and how I had picked up the queen and ruined the hive. "What does it mean?" I asked her. "I didn't know you knew so much about bees," she said. "I've been reading about them," I said; "we had honeybees on the farm." She kept on ironing. "What does it mean?" I asked again. "Well," she said, "I have a book of dreams, and it says that when you dream about blood, you're going to get your little friend." "Little friend?" I said. "You're going to start bleeding," Polly said; "that's what it means to dream about blood. No, wait," she said, resting the iron on the board. "It can also mean you're going to have a baby." I fell back against the chair. "It says that in the book?" I asked her. "That's what it says about blood. I don't know about bees." "But the dream was about bees!" I said. "You said the bees looked like a clot of blood." "That's what they looked like, but the dream was all about *bees*." "Well, don't start to cry about it," Polly said; "you aren't, are you?" "Aren't what?" "Worried," she said; "you've been bleeding every month, haven't you?" "I don't keep track," I said; "I just expect it to work out." "What?" Polly asked, staring at me; "you don't keep track at all?" "Not at all," I said. "But you *have* to," she said urgently. She picked up the iron and attacked the shirt's sleeve. "That's what the dream is for, then," she said; "it's warning you to keep track." "I won't get pregnant," I said; "I can't." "That's what they all say before they get into trouble," Polly answered. "I *won't* get pregnant," I said; "I refuse to get pregnant." "Oh, Lord," said Polly. "Besides," I said, "I know I'm all right this time. My breasts are all sore and my back hurts." Polly went on ironing.

"I don't think the dream had anything to do with babies," I said. "Then what did it have to do with?" "Hives. All those bees have to die for the queen. It's horrible." "Not for them," she said; "no one understands bees. Maybe the queen bee is the mind and the rest of them are the body." "I don't think so," I said. "No one knows," she said. "Once we had a hive with two queens and one of them killed the other," I said. "That's what the crazy people are like," Polly said; "two minds in one body." "It wasn't a dream about crazy people," I said annoyed. "I didn't say it was," she said, flipping the shirt over. "It was awful," I said. I could still feel it, the bees inside me, buzzing, moving under my skin. "Don't go near any bees, that's all," Polly said; "maybe it's an omen. A friend of mine got stung by a bee and swelled up and died. Her tongue turned black and choked her. You wouldn't like hives anyway. There aren't enough men in them." "Wherever there's a man, there's a hive," I said. "What does that mean?" she said, looking up. I shook my head.

"That dream is about getting into trouble," she said to me; "you have to be more careful. You can get pregnant just like everyone else." "I can't," I whispered. "Did a doctor tell you you can't?" Polly asked. "No, but I know I can't," I said. "You mean you want to think you can't. That's nonsense, and nonsense is fine as long as you don't believe it. You can get pregnant, and if you don't watch out, you will." "Let's not talk about it," I said. "Do you know how to be careful?" she asked me, and when I said I didn't really, she began explaining it to me. "I don't like the sound of it," I said. "Just think about the bees," she said. "I don't want to think at all," I said. "Spoken like a true bee," said Polly. And later that night, I began bleeding.

And for the first time in my life, I was relieved to feel the blood leaving my body. I walked through the streets of Montpelier and saw the lilacs swelling thick with sap and the forsythia drifting in the wind and the tulips, which had escaped the winter's long teeth of ice and the tunneling spring moles, waving in the breeze, and I felt my own spring descend on me. The critical eye which had stared so at Frank had closed and I was happy. But while I walked, I kept my eye on the swelling world. I saw how the vines, gray and dead against the black shingles, were sprouting green and would soon be waving with leaves. I thought about how hard it would be to cut the vines down now that their little roots were growing tight against the walls, and how, during the winter, it would have been easy to rip their sheaths from the wall, but the householder never thought of it; in winter, the vines looked dead and so they were protected. The mind of the hive, I thought, ticked in all natural things. What was the mind of the hive, what was the queen bee, if not the biological command to survive, to propagate? And I looked down at my stomach, flat under its black skirt, and was thankful that I had escaped the universal command to blossom and ripen into something beyond oneself. I had something beyond myself: I had Frank. And so April passed, and then May. I came to walk alone during the day instead of staying in and gossiping with the girls. The mechanical rhythm of my feet on the stones, of my heart beating harder as I climbed uphill, soothed something in me that needed quieting. More and more, I wanted to be alone, to think, although when I returned to Mrs. James's, I could not say what I had been thinking about. Florence asked me what I thought about when I walked and I told her I thought about emptiness. She said she couldn't imagine that was a very interesting subject, and I said she'd be surprised.

. Mrs. James stopped me after work one day and told me she'd be happier with my sewing if there were more of it. She said I should make up my mind about the job; if I didn't want it, there were plenty of people who did. The next day, I went out to the quarries with Frank. I brought a book, but I never opened it. I stared at him, working under an apple tree, and I watched the slow stem of a lily begin emerging from the stone. The sound of the chisel against the stone made me drowsy, and while I watched Frank work, I was utterly happy. I decided to come back the next day, but Frank asked me what Mrs. James would say and I decided I had better go to work. My head began to pound as soon as I got there. I got up and went to look for Mrs. James.

She was in the front yard transplanting day lilies. I said that my father was coming to Montpelier and wanted to take me with him to visit relatives for a week, but naturally I would not go if she would dismiss me because of my absence. "Well," she said, digging at the soft, brown earth, "a vacation may be what you need. Why don't you think of doing embroidery when you come back?" "It takes so much concentration," I said absently. "What else do you have to think about?" she asked, standing up. I stood there, silent. "Well?" she asked. "I thought I would leave early today if I might," I said; "to pack." "Go ahead," she said; "but when you come back, you better settle in to work or you'll have to look elsewhere." "I'll settle in," I said.

I walked back into town and over the bridge to the factory. It was only three o'clock. It would be two hours before Polly finished. I sat down on the little stone bench across from the long gray building and waited for the time to pass. The sky darkened. The whistle blew. I didn't know where the time had gone or what I had been thinking about. "Hello," I said, looking up and seeing Polly standing over me. "Now what?" she asked me; "is someone sick?" "Nothing's wrong," I said; "I left work early, so I thought I'd come and meet you." "You're leaving work early all the time," she said. "I'm taking a week off." "You're going to be out of money," she said. I nodded. I would have to take out my last fifty dollars at the end of the week. I would write my father and tell him that I had been ill and unable to work. I knew he would send me whatever I asked for.

"It's tiresome," I said, "the same thing, day after day."

"That's life," Polly said; "repetition." "Not my life!" I exclaimed, surprised at the violence of my feeling. "What else can you do?" she asked me; "waiting on tables is hard work." "But it would be different," I said. "You're looking for trouble," she said. I said I wasn't, that all I wanted to do was go with Frank when he went to work. "That would be fine if you were a rich woman," she said, "but even then, you'd get bored. You have to do something yourself. You can't watch someone else all the time." I said I thought I could. She said she didn't think Frank would like being watched day in and day out, it would drive him crazy, but I said he seemed to like it.

"I looked up bees in my book," she said; "if you dream about bees, it means a storm is coming or trouble is brewing." "Dreams don't mean anything," I said. "Well, you were the one who wanted to know what the dream meant," she said; "queen bees, hives. I don't dream about things like that. I dream that I've finished washing the kitchen floor, and when I wake up, there it is, all filthy. Or I dream that I'm already dressed, and when I wake up, I'm late." "I wonder if it meant anything," I said; "all those bees and that strange queen." "Bees are strange altogether," said Polly.

All the next week, I went to the quarries with Frank. Frank, Charlie, and some of the other men moved his stone further away from all the others, and we were alone under the twisted apple trees. I remembered Bill Brown's telling me how he had once thought of apple trees as women who were turned into trees by an evil magician, but the trees fed their children anyway by learning to grow apples. Would I ever look at nature that way, as something so kind, so fundamentally good? I doubted it. I watched Frank's marble lilies begin to float up from the layer of marble in which they had been submerged and I floated in the warm sunshine. Every now and then, an apple would fall near me with a curious, dull thud, and if I were hungry, I would pick one up and eat it. "Don't eat too many or you'll get sick," Frank said; "they may be falling but they're still pretty green." I picked up an apple and fed it to him while he worked.

"Do you mind having me here so much?" I asked him. "It's good having you here," he said; "but if you lose your job, I'm going to have myself to blame for not chasing you back. I don't have enough money for both of us. If I did . . ." "If you did?" I said. "If I did, I'd tell you to forget about the work and stay out here forever." "Maybe I should," I said. "I wish you could," he said. His eyes were green, gold-flecked. "But you don't want to use my money," I said, pulling up some grass and dropping it on my skirt. "No, I don't," he said; "it's wrong for a man to sponge on a woman." "I don't see it that way," I said. "No," he said, "but you don't want to use your grandmother's money either." "What would you think if I changed my mind?" I asked him; "would you want to get married?" "Agnes, I'd like to have my share saved up," he said, laying down his chisel and turning to me. I felt myself go hot with anger. "What would happen if I wanted to get married right away?" I demanded. "I suppose we could," he said slowly; "do you?" "No," I said. "You just wanted to see what I'd say, is that it?" he asked; "you thought I'd changed my mind?" "No," I said; "it's not you. I don't seem to know what I want lately. All I want is to come out here with you." "Well, you're here," he said, "and you can stay as long as you want."

When the week ended, I didn't go back to Mrs. James's. My father sent me a check for seventy-five dollars and instructed me to write him if I needed more. Then one day in the middle of June I feel asleep under the apple tree and when I woke up, I heard Charlie and Frank talking in low voices behind me. "What does she do out here all day?" Charlie was asking. "She reads and she draws. Sometimes I draw her," Frank said. "Doesn't she work anymore?" Charlie asked. "No, she just comes out here." "Is she going back to work?" asked Charlie. "I guess," said Frank. "Listen, Frank," Charlie said; "you're not thinking. Suppose something goes wrong between you two? What's she supposed to do then? She doesn't have a job. She doesn't have friends anymore. She's always out here with you." "We're happy," he said. "Everyone's happy," said Charlie, "and Polly says she doesn't sleep much anymore. How's that?" "That's over with," Frank said; "she had a bad time after I went home with her." "Why? Did her father try to shoot you?" Charlie asked. "We got on fine," Frank said. "I don't like it," Charlie said. "You don't have to like it," Frank said; "we like it." "So she's what you want?" asked Charlie. "She's what I want," Frank said.

And then I dreamed about the bees again. This time I was carrying the queen bee in my hand and the other bees followed me, humming miserably, and I wanted to give them back their queen, but I could not make myself open my hand. And I woke up, terrified. The room and everything in it was thin, unreal. I bit my arm and was grateful for the stab of pain, for the resistance of the bone beneath the skin. I looked at the calendar on the wall opposite the bed; it was the end of June. I tried to remember when I had last bled and I could not. Frank lay next to me, sound asleep, turned on his side, facing me, his arm flung straight out over the pillow, his cheek resting on his elbow. The dark hairs of his arm gleamed in the early morning light. In April. I had been sick in April and May. But June! I had spent June out at the quarries and I would remember if I had taken a supply of rags with me. I would remember if I had looked for washrooms or wells or pitchers of water. But if I had not bled in June, I was three weeks late. I looked at Frank, sleeping. He was so sweet when he slept, so helpless, so innocent. I always felt uneasy watching him sleep, as if his soul floated in the air about him and if I touched it, I would harm him somehow. I watched him now and thought about one of the fairy tales my grandmother had read me. It was about a young girl who met the prince of her dreams and he married her and they were to live happily ever after if only she did not try to look at him during the night, and naturally, she could not resist the temptation, and lit a candle and the hot wax dripped and woke her prince who at once turned into a panther and left her. And that was how I felt, watching Frank as he slept, as if looking at him so closely might burn him, change him, take him from me. I tried to remember how the story ended. Did she get him back? And if she did, how did she do it? But I couldn't remember whether it ended well or badly.

And then I saw the calendar on the wall staring at me like a square eye and I went cold with fear. I felt my stomach. It was as flat as ever. I had to talk to Polly. I had listened to the girls at work; it was not unusual to skip. There were girls who had skipped six months at a time and nothing had happened. I slid out of bed and covered myself with a huge paisley shawl. I had to see Polly. But I already knew. I was not going to bleed at all. I stood at the foot of the bed, looking at Frank. His body was sweet and long and every night he was hot and warm against me. When we lay together, I felt as if we were creating the world. When we came together, we were one whole thing, and when we separated, we were the two halves of the earth. And now I saw that I had indeed been the earth and that Frank had been its gardener; he had tilled the earth and I was bearing fruit, and it was the fruit of his body and therefore precious, but I knew that it was impossible. "I can't keep this baby," I whispered to myself and I went down the hall to Polly's room.

I rapped softly on the door and went in. Polly was standing in the middle of the floor, her hair brush raised above her head. Her rough linen nightgown had yellowed from endless washings and ironings. In the early light, with her blond hair loose about her bondy shoulders, she looked like a fragile, precocious child. "You were right about the dream," I said, sitting down on her bed. "It was warning me. What am I going to do now?" She lowered her arm, looked at the brush, and put it down on the dresser. "You better tell me what you're talking about," she said.

"I haven't seen my period for seven weeks," I said. "Oh, no!" Polly said; "are you sure? You said you didn't keep track." "I'm sure," I said. "You told me you knew about a doctor who'd get rid of it." "I can't tell you about that doctor," she said; "he'll only go near the same person once. He's afraid if he comes back a second time, he'll find the police waiting for him. If I get ahold of him for you, I wouldn't be able to get him for myself later." "But there's nothing wrong with you," I said. "Not yet," said Polly, "but I never believed I'd never get in trouble just because I didn't want to get in trouble." "I heard the girls talking," I said urgently; "they said there were things you could drink." "There are," Polly said; "I can get you the syrups. That's not hard. There's one made of pennyroyal. A lot of the girls use it. And taking a bath in very hot water after you drink it. Sometimes it brings it off."

"Would you get me the syrups?" I asked. "But how do you know you're in trouble?" Polly asked; "are you sick in the mornings?" I said I wasn't. I was sleepy all the time. Otherwise I felt fine. But I knew. "You knew you couldn't get pregnant the last time I talked to you about it," Polly said. "I was wrong," I said. "Are you going to tell Frank?" she asked me. "Not unless I have to," I said. "What does that mean?" she asked. "If the syrups and the bath don't work, I'll tell him. The men must know about doctors." "Yes," said Polly, "they must."

"Frank's baby," I said softly. Polly looked up, startled. "Look, Agnes," she said; "you're going to marry him. You don't have to get rid of it. You could marry him now and have the baby." "He doesn't want it," I said. "But he doesn't even know you're in trouble!" "He doesn't want children at all," I said. "Never?" Polly asked. "I don't think so," I said; "I don't think he'll ever want them." "What about you?" she asked; "do you want them?" "No," I said. "Are you sure?" "If I had the baby," I said, "I'd have to choose between the baby and Frank. He'd leave me if I had the baby. I'd die if I lost him! I would!" "You're going to have a baby some time," Polly said; "are you going to spend your life worrying about Frank leaving?" "No," I said; "I'm not going to have a baby now or ever!"

"Sit down," Polly said, patting the bed; "stop jumping up and running around." I sat down again. "Why do you want to marry him if you don't want to have children?" "I want to marry *him*," I said; "only two people sign the marriage certificate. The man and wife. I don't want to marry him *and* some strange children I don't even know! I don't want anyone *but* him!" "You're upset," said Polly; "you're not thinking clearly." "But don't you understand?" I asked her; "I'm perfectly happy with him now. I want to go to New York with him and help him with his work. I want to be with him all the time. I want to be his *wife*. That's all." "He'll want more than that when he gets older," she said; "all men do." "No, he won't," I said. "Then there's something wrong with him," Polly said; "and Frank always takes the easy way. It's easier to have a house and a family than not to have it. It's easier being like everyone else." "You don't know what you're talking about!" I cried; "just because Eddie wants to fill up a house with a collection of dwarfs who look like him doesn't mean it's the only way to live!"

Polly got up, picked up her brush, and, with her back to me, began brushing her hair. "If you're not going to tell Frank," she said, "you better get dressed and cheer up. You look like you just came from a funeral." "How long will it take you to get the syrups?" I asked her. "I can get them tomorrow and if you can come home for lunch, I'll give you the hot bath. Iris is off somewhere or other for the next few days. But if it doesn't work, then I think you should tell him." "Then I'll have to tell him," I said; "you won't help me." "Don't keep turning on me just because you're miserable," she said; "you wouldn't act any differently in my place."

We went downstairs and I smiled at everyone and listened to the old man tell me how to graft branches onto apple trees. When Frank caught my eye, I smiled at him and raised my eyebrows. I got up and got our dinner pail and we left for Barre. I was like the sky, clear and bright, and then I would remember that I was "in trouble," that awful phrase I had heard since childhood, and I would go cold and numb. But I told myself that tomorrow everything would be better; I would drink the syrups Polly got from the girls at the factory and I would sit in the hot water and I would get rid of it. There was no need for Frank to know; there was no need to frighten him. I watched him going

309

about his work and my heart ached. I knew that if I told him, and if I said I wanted him to marry me, he would do it and we would never go to New York. We would stay here and I would take care of the baby and I would become just like my mother and he would begin to cough and become like his father and both of us would be lost. I could not do that to him, I had to rid myself of the child.

The next morning, I told Frank that I wanted to stop at Mrs. James's to pick up some things I had left behind and I had some shopping to do downstreet, but would come with him tomorrow. He said he'd miss me and kissed me good-bye. I watched him walking down the street and thought that I never saw him walk away without fearing that I was seeing him for the last time. I would drink anything to keep him happy, anything, rat poison, lye, arsenic, anything that would let us remain together as we were now.

Polly came home early and gave me two little brown bottles. "Drink the pennyroyal first," she said. She watched me swallow it down. "You have to pour this into a glass of water first," she said, taking back the second bottle. She filled a glass and gave it to me. I poured a purplish liquid into the water; it spread through it like ink. I drank it down. "Ugh," I said; "it burns." "The girls said it can't hurt you," she told me; "I hope they're telling the truth. Now you're supposed to wait a half hour and then you're supposed to get in the tub. I'll start up the pots." She took the huge pots from the cupboards, filled them with water, and set them on the stove. "It's hot in here," I said after a while. "It's going to be a lot hotter when you get in the water," she said. "All right," she said, "take off your clothes and get in. I'll fasten the doors." I put my clothes on a chair and got into the portable metal tub. "This is very hot," Polly said; "tell me if you can't stand it." She picked up one of the pots and emptied it into the tub. "I can stand it," I said; "make it hotter." She picked up another pot and poured the water in. Steam rose in the air. "That's awfully hot," Polly said, worried; "do you want me to put in some cold water?" "No," I said, "put some more hot water in." She had filled three pots, and carried the last over to me. "I don't know about this," she said; "it's too much." "Pour it in," I said.

I sat in the steaming tub and waited for Polly to pour in pot after pot of water. When I heard her coming toward me, I would take a deep breath, as if I were filling the inside of my body with cool air against the onslaught of the heat. "Isn't that too hot?"

Polly asked again and again, and each time I said it wasn't. The kitchen drifted in steam. I was lost in a little ocean of fog. My knees appeared and disappeared in the mists rising from the tub. I couldn't see the walls but I knew that the windows and mirrors were sheeted in fog. "I want to see what that water's like before I put any more in," Polly said. I saw her drift down through the steam; she stuck in her elbow. Her hair was clinging to her face in wet wisps. "Ouch!" she cried; "that water's almost boiling! What's the matter with you, Agnes? I told you to tell me if it got too hot." "It's not too hot," I said. "Yes, it is too hot," she said indignantly.

"Put more in," I said. "Oh, no," she said; "if you want someone to kill you, get someone else." "It won't hurt me," I said. "Look at you!" she exclaimed; "you look like a boiled lobster!" "Well," I said, "the heat makes my blood pound. I feel like my head's about to open up." "Maybe you better get out of there," she said uneasily. "You said I had to stay in at least an hour," I said. "You've been in there an hour. Come out." "A half hour more," I said. "I'm watching the clock," she said. "I wonder what it is," I said; "the baby. Whether it's a boy or girl." "Right now it's not much of anything," she said; "just blood. Don't start thinking about it that way, as if it were a person. Think of it like the mumps. Otherwise it's going to be harder. You know, when it's gone." "It won't be hard," I said. Polly sighed. "Miss Know-It-All," she said, pulling a stool up next to the tub. "You know, Agnes, sometimes I think you'd be a lot easier to understand if we just assumed you meant the opposite of whatever you said." "I tell the truth," I said. "That's a perfect example of what I mean," she said. "I do tell the truth," I said sleepily; "when I know what it is." "You usually don't," she said shortly. I didn't answer. I was drifting somewhere over my body. "I'm thirsty," I said. "I'll get you some water." I gulped down the contents of the glass and then gagged. "What did you put in it?" I asked. She *was* trying to kill me. "Salt. They told me to make sure you drank salt water or you'd be pretty sick from the heat. I wish Frank could see this." "I'm doing this for Frank," I said; "I'd do anything for Frank." "I hope you don't have to," she said. "Don't you think you should ask him what he wants first?" she asked me. "Let's not start that again," I said; "it's my baby and my body. So far."

I leaned my head against the smooth wooden rim of the metal tub and I drifted pleasantly. "Being cooked isn't so bad," I said; "I wonder where that expression came from: 'Your goose is cooked.'" "I think you better come out of there," Polly said; "you're not right." "If it works," I said, pushing myself up, "how long does it take before I start bleeding?" "Usually not more than a day, but one of the girls said she went three days before she saw any blood." "Three days!" I exclaimed. "*If* it works," she said. She put her hand in the water. "I don't know how you stand it," she said. "I would stand worse for Frank," I said. "Ten more minutes," she said. "What are you going to do in ten minutes?" I asked her; "you can't drag the tub out with me still in it." But I had underestimated her. When the ten minutes were up, she came up to the tub carrying two sap buckets, submerged them, filled them with water, and poured them down the sink. "Enough is enough," she said. She went from the tub to the sink and back again. My belly was dry in the air; the water was sinking around me. "I guess I'll come out," I said. I started to stand, but the room spun around me. "Here," Polly said, grabbing me under one elbow, "hold on to me." I climbed out and my legs began folding under me. Polly pushed me onto the stool and put her arm around my waist. "That water was too hot," she said. I said I would be all right. "Try standing up again," she said. This time my legs held. I put on my robe. "Do you feel any different?" she asked. "Not yet," I said. "I'm coming up with you," she said; "I'll bring a book." "What book?" I asked, wavering up the steps. I put my feet down carefully. If I fell backward, I would fall on her. *The Report of the State Commission on The State Lunatic Asylum in Massachusetts*. Eddie gave it to me." "Not for your birthday, I hope," I said, going into my room. It looked unfamiliar, as if it belonged to someone else. I was hardly ever in it anymore. I lay down gratefully on the bed. "No cramps," I said; "should I have them?" "Not yet," she said; "go to sleep. You look sleepy."

I must have fallen asleep because a terrible wave of nausea woke me and I jumped out of bed and ran over to the basin of my washstand. Something scalding pushed its way out of my stomach and up through my throat. "It's the syrups," Polly said. I tried to straighten up, but another wave of nausea swept over me and I vomited again. Finally, I was retching uncontrollably, my stomach in spasms and nothing coming up. "If you don't stop soon, I'm going to have to get the doctor," Polly said. I shook my head, leaning over the basin. "You're not even bringing up water," she said. I shook my head again. I was holding tightly to the stand with both hands. My shoulder and neck muscles hurt, my chest muscles felt as if they had been tightened around my skeleton, and my back was stiff and sore: I didn't want her to call the doctor. Eventually my body would have to wear itself out.

And then my teeth started chattering. "Oh, Lord," Polly said. She took down my bearskin cape and wrapped it around me. "If you're not better soon," she said, "I *am* going to get the doctor." "I'm not throwing up anymore," I said. She asked me if I could go back to bed and I said I could. By now, my whole body was shaking. Polly took the winter blankets out of the cupboard and covered me with them. "No cramps?" she asked me. "No cramps," I said. "Do you want anything?" "I want Frank," I said. "I better clean this place up first," she said; "he won't be home for hours, so you might as well go to sleep." I was trembling less violently but my teeth still clicked together. "If the doctor came," Polly said in a low voice, "I wouldn't even know what to tell him you took." "I'm getting better," I said; "you won't need to call him." I clamped my jaws together to stop my teeth from chattering. "Still cold?" Polly asked. "I'm getting warmer." I looked over at her, sitting on the chair, her knees drawn up to her chin, the state commission's report open on the chair's arm. "Don't go away," I said. "I'm not going anywhere," she said.

When I awakened again, the room was dark and Frank was standing over me. "Polly said you were sick," he said. I said it was nothing; it would pass over. I was much better already. "You don't look too kicky," he said. I said I would be kicking soon enough. "Do you want me to stay with you?" he asked, and I said I did. He sat on the stool at the head of the bed and stroked my forehead and my hair. He got up and went to the washstand and dipped his handkerchief into the water pitcher and wiped my face. "You're a better nurse than Polly," I said. "I've had more practice," he said. "More practice?" "In the barn," he said; "sitting up with the animals. None of them had your looks." "You must be tired," I said after a while. "Not really," he said; "it's good to be taking care of something again." I reached up and touched his cheek. How I loved him! And then I thought about the trick my body was playing on us and I went cold. "Don't worry," he said, watching my face; "you'll be fine." "I don't want to sleep here alone," I said. "Wait until everyone goes to bed and I'll carry you to my room," he said. "I love you so," I said and started to cry. He looked at me, troubled. "I don't know why it is," I said, "but I can't say that

313

without starting to cry. I'm sorry." "I love you, too," he said His voice was soft and hesitant. I turned on my side and looked at him. I wiggled over to the edge of the bed and worked my head into his lap and wrapped an arm around him. "Poor thing," he said, holding me tighter, "poor thing."

I heard Frank moving around the room and opened my eyes. He was buttoning his shirt and smiled at me in the glass. "You look better," he said. "I want to come with you," I said "You'd be better off in bed," he said. I got up and went over to him, hugging him from behind as if I wanted to press myself into his bones. The warmth of his body! The hardness of it! I began to pull him back toward me and then pushed him forward until he and I were rocking together. "All right," he said, "I guess you're strong enough. I was worried. You never get sick." "I only lasted a day," I said. "It seemed longer," he said.

I went into the washroom and put a clean rag between my legs so that, if I began to bleed, I would see the evidence at once Then I went into the dining room and sat down. The food looked lumpish and the smell made my stomach turn. I poked at my food and Polly watched me slyly. "Eat all of it," she said. "I'm not hungry." "Has the sun come up yet?" she asked me. I looked at her blankly. "Oh, no," I said, "it hasn't."

And after three days passed, I saw that it was not going to come up. When I was at the quarries, I perpetually drifted into the woods, slipped the piece of rag from between my legs looked at its sad whiteness, and replaced it. I went off so often Frank began to notice and I said the heat made me restless. I said I was looking for a place where I could practice my shooting, but I didn't have a pistol yet; I'd left my own at home. Frank said I could use his, but not in the woods up there, because the men walked through them all the time and he didn't want me to shoot anyone. "Do you think it will be hard? Getting used to New York?" I asked him. If I thought hard enough, if I imagined another life strongly enough, it would begin to exist; it would suck the power out of this life, which had so suddenly taken a wrong turn.

"For the first week, maybe," said Frank; "once you learn how to get to work, once you have a place to sleep, and once you know where two or three stores are, you're pretty well acquainted with the place." "But it must be hard to belong there," I said; "everyone's so important." "I guess," said Frank, working away, "you stay with the unimportant people while you're unimportant and wait until you get important

314

enough to worry about the others." "I wish we were there now!" I burst out. "Aren't you happy here?" "Of course I'm happy here!" I said. "A year isn't so long to wait," he said, going back to work; "actually, it's only ten months. We used up two." I touched the tip of the rag through my skirt and felt it move against my skin. Under my skirt, it was as dry as ever.

I would have to tell him. Polly would not tell me the name of the doctor she knew. I could, I thought, ask Charlie. Out of the corner of my eye, I could see him working. As usual, his straight blond hair was falling into his eyes; as usual, he was tossing his head to lift the hair from his forehead. By three o'clock, he would have given up and he would tie his handkerchief around his forehead. I could not ask Charlie. He would only tell Frank. I tried to think how I would tell him. I felt foolish, silly, as if I had done something thoughtless which could easily be undone, the sort of thing someone might do and then think about and shake his head over, smiling at his own ineptitude.

32

That night we walked out into the fields. It had rained the night before and the smells of summer were pungent in the air. Swallows swooped above us, cutting the vivid blue sky with their sharp wings. Something flew in front of us, trembling through the air. "A bat," I said aloud. "I don't think so," said Frank; "it's a big moth." I had thought up nine hundred ways of telling him but I could remember none of them. "I think I'm in trouble," I said. I felt ridiculous, as if I were one of the actors at the Barre Opera House, as if, suddenly, I was living on the wooden stage in the middle of the third act of *Kyra's Fate* and I was dragging Frank into this preposterous drama with me.

Frank stopped dead. "What did you say?" he asked me. "I said I think I'm in trouble." "Why?" he asked. I told him about the skipped period, the syrups, the hot bath. "None of it worked?" he asked. "No," I said, "it didn't. They say frail girls do better with the syrups. I'm too healthy." "Let's walk," he said. "What do you want me to do?" I asked him. "What do you want to do?" he asked, bending down and picking up a rock. He threw it across the dark field. "I want to do whatever you want to do," I said. "Oh, God," said Frank. "Well, it is your baby," I said. "I know it's my baby," he said; "I'll take the responsibility." "I mean it's *your* baby; you might want it." "It's also your baby," he said. I said we weren't getting anywhere. "You didn't harm the baby with the syrups, did you?" he asked. "Polly said the syrups didn't do anything to you if they didn't work; she asked the girls." "So the baby's healthy," he said. "Well, it's certainly holding on," I said. And suddenly, I saw it, in its moon blue darkness, curled up around itself, its fist in its mouth, stretching out and curling back up again, awash in the tides of my blood. It knew all about us already; somehow it did. Even if I sent it to the other side of the world, when it saw us, it would recognize us.

"Do you want to have it?" Frank asked. He was watching me intently. "Do you?" I asked. "I want you to have what you want," he said. "I want you," I said. "You want me," he repeated slowly, nodding his head. My throat was swelling. It was my fault. I should have learned how to be careful; I should have believed this could happen to me. If I had known more, if I had known there were times when I should have slept alone, it might not have happened. But I would never have paid attention to rules. I would never have let calendars keep me away from Frank. I hadn't believed the laws of nature applied to us. I still didn't. "I'm sorry," I said, and I started to cry. "It's not your fault," Frank said. "It's got to be someone's fault!" "It's not anyone's fault," he said; "it's nothing personal. It's what bodies do. They make more bodies." I listened to his voice; it was harder, bitter. I remembered how he had described the farm and how he had felt there. I would have the baby, and he would resent me because I was heavy and sick and swollen; when he wanted to talk, I would have to nurse the baby or change it. When he wanted me to come to the studio, I would have to stay at home with a croupy infant. There would be no peace, no freedom. I was the one who had made him think about leaving the quarries and going to New York and now I was to be the one to take his ambitions from him. I couldn't do it. "Tell me what you think!" I cried; "I don't know what I think. You tell me first." "I don't know what I think, either," he said.

"You have to know!" I cried; "you've been through this before!" "What's that supposed to mean?" he asked. I looked at his face in the moonlight; he looked cold and far away. "Madge," I said; "you got Madge pregnant and you didn't want that baby." "I told you," he said; "she got rid of it without telling me. Madge doesn't have anything to do with this." "Yes, she does!" I said; "if you didn't want that baby, why should you want this one?" Frank kicked a stone into the air. "What are you doing, Agnes?" he asked me. "Doing?" I said; "I'm trying to be honest." "Trying to be honest about Madge?" he asked; "you know that subject's trouble." "Do you want a baby?" I asked. "If you mean would I go out and order one from the store, I wouldn't," Frank said, "but this is different. It's here. Or it could be here." "Do you want a baby or don't you want a baby? Yes or no?" I demanded. "For God's sake, lower your voice," Frank said. "Why won't you answer me?" I said, bursting into tears. I moved away from him and we walked down the path as if there were already someone standing between us.

"What are you thinking?" I asked, my voice rising. "No matter what I say," Frank answered, "you're not going to like it. If I say I want you to have the baby, you won't like it. If I say I don't want you to have it, you won't like it." "Don't worry about what I'll like!" I said; "tell me what you want! Tell me the truth!" "I don't know," he said; "all women are the same. If you don't have the baby, you'll never forgive me. If you have it, you won't forgive me. Or yourself. It doesn't matter. You won't forgive one of us. Well, you talked to Madge. I told her from the start I didn't love her. She said she wanted to lose her virginity and she picked me. That's what she told me. And then she got rid of the baby and went crazy." "I won't go crazy." "There is no good answer," Frank said; "that's the trouble. Whatever we do, we're going to regret it." "I'd only regret not having you," I said. Frank came closer and took my hand. It lay inert in his.

"What if we had it to do all over again?" I asked him; "what if there wasn't any baby and I asked you if you wanted to have one and we could make up our minds now? What would you say then?" "Then I'd say no," Frank said; "I'd say I didn't want a baby right now. But we don't have it to do all over again. There's no point in thinking that way." "Yes, there is," I said urgently, seizing both his hands; "we have it all to do all over again. If I give the baby back, we can start over." "Give it back?" Frank repeated. "If I get rid of it," I said. My voice sounded hollow. I felt hollow, like a dried gourd, a few loose seeds shaking uselessly inside me. He didn't want the child. "If I get rid of the baby," I said, "we'll still get married?" "Yes," he said. "We won't start over altogether?" I asked; "we'll only go back to the time before I got in trouble?" "That's right," said Frank. "I wish it never happened," I said. "It was part of everything else," Frank said. "No, it wasn't," I said; "we decided about everything else." "We decided about this, too," he said; "we knew it could happen." "I didn't!" I cried; "I never thought about it!" "Never?" Frank asked me, angry; "where did you think babies came from? Goddamn, Agnes! Be honest!" I started to cry. "That's right," he said, turning on me, "cry! That's what women do when they're wrong. They cry. I thought we were both in that bed together, but I was wrong. I was in there all by myself." I dug my fists into my eyes. "Ouch!" I cried. "What's the matter now?" he asked me, exasperated. "I think I got something in my eye." "Blink it a lot," he said. "It's still there," I said. "You really a nuisance," Frank said. I started crying again. "Keep on crying. You'll wash it out." "It's not out," I said. "Good Lord," Frank sighed, "come on."

We crossed the field and came to the brook. In the moonlight it glittered silver black. "Kneel down on that rock," Frank said. "Now lean forward—slowly—and put your head in the water and keep your eyes open. It'll wash out. You'll see." I picked my head up, dripping. "Is it out?" Frank asked. "Yes," I said. He held his arms out to me and I buried my face in his shirt. "If you want the baby, let's have it," he said. "I don't want it," I said, "because you don't." "And I don't want it because you don't," he said; "we're going in circles." "I don't want it," I said; "I don't." "Are you sure?" "Yes," I said; "I am. But I don't know what to do now. Polly knows about a doctor, but she won't tell me who he is. She says he'll only come near each girl once. She said the men at the quarries knew about doctors." "You want me to find one?" "Yes," I said. "They say it's painful. And dangerous," Frank said. "So is having a baby," I said. "If you're sure," said Frank, "I'll find out tomorrow." "Do I have to stay home?" I asked; "if you're going to try and find out?" "No, you can come. Everyone will know why I'm asking anyway."

"Polly says if we're going to do it, I should do it as soon as I can," I said. "Polly, Polly," he said; "does she get to vote about this?" "She's my friend," I said; "I was frightened." "So you talked to her first," he said. "I didn't want to tell you at all," I said. "Why?" "Because I knew how it would be," I said; "I knew you'd be unhappy." "Why shouldn't I be unhappy?" he said; "this is something to be unhappy about." "I don't want you ever to be unhappy," I said. "You can't prevent it," he said; "you shouldn't try." His voice was soft; he put his arm around me. "I will try," I said; "that's what I want to do with my life. I want to make yours perfect." "Perfect?" Frank said, smiling for the first time that night; "me? By now, you ought to know it can't be done." "Well, I don't," I said comfortably, and we walked back to the house, our arms around each other.

The next night, we walked along the car tracks toward Barre. "I got the name," Frank said; "Grimsby. He comes to your room and takes care of it there. I guess it's pretty bloody. It takes a while to get back to yourself." "When can he come?" I asked. "He's in Barre," Frank said; "he can come almost any night.

He won't come during the day. He wants to come this weekend because it's a holiday and there probably won't be many people around the house on Monday." "Two nights from now?" I asked him. "That's fine," Frank said. I looked at him. We were two criminals, plotting. We were planning an attack on me. I didn't want to be attacked the next night. I wanted one night's grace. "We'll have to pay him!" I said suddenly. "I'll take care of it," Frank said; "don't argue with me. I'll take care of it." "Let's not talk about it anymore," I said; "not until it's over. I don't want you to be there, either. I don't want you to see it." "I can't be there," Frank said; "that's one of the doctor's conditions. I guess some of the men have gone crazy and knocked him around. He won't stay if the man stays." "I'll ask Polly to stay," I said. "I already asked her," he said; "she said she would. She said Iris wouldn't be back for at least ten days, so we're in luck. No one should find out." "You go over to Charlie's and stay with him," I said. "Why?" he asked; "do you want to be sure where I am?" "Something like that," I said. "Why?" he asked. I said I didn't know.

33

"No, no," Polly said, coming into my room; "put your hair up. It's supposed to be awfully bloody. We'll have enough trouble cleaning you up." "I have to pin up my hair?" I asked. I started to lift it but it fell through my hands and I sat there helplessly, the hair falling over one eye. "Do you really want to do this?" Polly said, coming over. She picked up my brush, pulled my hair back, and expeditiously braided it. "There," she said, "that's done." She looked me over. "Are you sure you want to wear that nightgown?" "What's wrong with it?" I asked her. "It's white. Wear something dark. It won't stain." "I have a blue one," I said faintly. "It's in my second drawer." "I'll get it," she said; "stick up your arms." She pulled off the white gown, folded it, laid it on the bed, and helped me on with the dark blue-flowered gown. "You look like you're ready for the slaughter," she said, standing back, looking at me. "I am, aren't I? That's what's going to happen, isn't it?" I asked. "You can still change your mind," she said. "Frank doesn't want children," I said. "I don't know," she said; "most men go along with their women when it comes to children." "Frank isn't most men," I said; "he has a future." "Everyone has a future," Polly said. "Not like Frank's," I said. "So you're doing this for him?" she said. "No," I said, "I'm doing it for myself too. When is he coming? Grimsby?" Polly looked at her watch. "About another hour," she said; "maybe he'll come early." "I wish it were over," I said.

Someone knocked at the door and both of us jumped. "I'll get it," Polly said. A short, plump man with dark hair walked in behind her. He had a doctor's satchel and set it down on the dresser. "Who's the patient?" he asked. "I am," I said. I was not in the room, I told myself; I was not there. If he touches me, I thought, my heart will stop. He began laying out his instruments on the table scarf. One was long and tubelike. Another looked like a triangular knife at the end of a long stick. I looked at his face. His skin hung loosely from his skull. His lips were thin and bitten and the top of his head gleamed yellow under his oily hair. I didn't like him.

"Who's got the money?" he asked. "It's here," Polly said, holding out an envelope; "you can have it when you're finished." "Now or I don't do it at all," he said. She hesitated, then handed him the envelope. "Where's the man responsible?" he asked; he was washing his hands in the basin. "He's at a friend's house," I said. "Keep him away from here," he said. "You don't have to worry," Polly said. "Lie down," he said to me; "on your back." I did as I was told. "Spread your legs," he said. "Give me that tube," he told Polly. I felt something cold slip between my legs. It pushed into me until I thought it would rip me open inside. "You're in trouble all right," he said. "Hold it," he said to Polly. I turned my head and watched him take the long, narrow knife from the dresser.

"Look, girls," he said, "we've had a lot of trouble with the law lately. You're going to have to use the knife yourself. I'll put it in position, but you'll have to turn it and push it in." "Just a minute!" Polly hissed; "we're not giving you all that money to do this ourselves. You promised to do it!" He threw the envelope down on the bed next to me. "It's yours," he said; "I'll just pack up." "No," I said, "you have to do it." "Little lady," he said nastily, "I don't have to do anything I don't want to do." "Well, you better do this," said Polly, "or I'll get the police." "That's ugly talk," Grimsby said, walking toward her. "Get away from her," I said; "put the knife in place. I'll use it." "You don't have to do that!" Polly cried; "that's not what we're paying him for." "Let's get it over with," I said. "See how sensible your friend is?" Grimsby told Polly; "and she's the one who has to use the knife."

"Now," he said, bending over me. He stank of sweat and smoke; my stomach turned. "Take deep breaths," he said. "I'm slipping the knife down the tube. I'll tell you when it's at the entrance to the cervix. You'll feel it. You'll have to push it in. Work it back and forth. Like this." He held his wrist near my head and twisted it back and forth. "Like that," he said; "work it in slowly." "Will it hurt?" I asked. "It's a knife, isn't it?" he asked. He went back to the foot of the bed and bent down between my legs. I saw his hand holding the knife and then it disappeared into the tube. When I felt the sharp, stabbing pain, screamed. "You can't scream," he said; "you'll have to keep quiet." "Can't you give her something?" Polly asked. "If I give her something, she won't use the knife right," he said; "she can drink a whole bottle of whiskey afterwards." "You promised to bring some powders!" she said. "I've got them," he said; "you can give them to her later." "All right," he said to me, "are you ready?" I fought down the nausea and the chills and said I was. "Start working the knife," he said.

I had to bend forward to reach the handle. I began twisting it as he had told me to. The pain was unimaginable. It was both sharp and dull at once and it flooded my whole body. "Keep going," he said; "you haven't even begun." I pressed harder and felt the knife puncturing something inside me; hot blood began to drip between my legs. Terrible cramps were spreading through my back and traveling around my sides into my stomach and groin. "I can't," I said; "I can't push it any more." "It's not too much further," he said; "keep working on it. You can't stop now or it will all be wasted." I was crying, one wrist in my mouth so I could bit down on it, and my other hand working the knife in deeper and deeper. "I can't do it," I said; I was drowning in my own sweat. Sweat was pouring down my forehead and dripping into my eyes. The pillow was drenched.

"Finish it!" I heard Polly say to him. "Don't threaten me," he said; "she has to do it herself." "You're going to regret this," Polly told him. "I doubt that," he said.

I stared at the ceiling and let my mind float loose and then I was watching the girl lying on the bed, the one with the knife in her hand. "That's it," said Doctor Grimsby; "twist it around once more." I did what I was told. "Finished," he said; "I'll take out the knife." My arm dropped over the edge of the bed. Wave after wave of pain crashed over my body. I was drenched in my own perspiration, my own odors. I heard Polly demanding the powders and I knew he was giving them to her.

"She'll bleed for a while and then she'll have cramps. She'll be all right in the morning." "And if she's not," said Polly's voice—it was coming from the middle distance—"then we don't call you, do we?" "Don't call me," he said; "I never saw you before." "Get out of here," Polly said, "or I'll shout the house down." "You're all the same," the doctor said; "you can't wait to get me here and then you can't wait to get rid of me." "Just get out," Polly said. She slammed the door after him and burst into tears.

"I'm sorry," she said, coming over to me, wiping her eyes;

"you're the one who should be crying." I wanted to say something, to thank her, but the pain was so thick, so urgent, I was afraid to open my lips. Scream after scream had massed its feathery wings right behind my teeth. "I'll put this powder in water," she said; "do you have cramps yet?" I shook my head. "Maybe we better wait for them," she said. I could feel the blood pouring out, drenching the bed. I pointed toward my stomach and Polly picked up the sheet. "Oh, God," she said, "you're bleeding to death!" She ran over to the washstand and picked up some of the cloths we had cut out of old gowns; then she began packing them between my thighs. "It should stop the bleeding," she said; "I'll press them against you. Does it hurt?" I shook my head no. Of course it hurt. I could feel the blood drenching the cloth, and the cloth, drenching with blood, pressing against my thighs. "It's not stopping," she said. She pressed more cloths between my legs. "I think it's slowing down," she said at last. "Can you stay here alone for a minute? I'll go and get some more rags." I nodded and heard her run off down the hall. The bloody rags were heavy. Suppose I died? For an instant, I saw myself from up above, as an eagle must see its prey, and I knew it made no difference, because no one single thing made a difference; it was only the whole machine spinning on that counted. Nothing was important in itself.

And when Polly came back, the cramps had begun and I was writhing on the bed. "You have to lie still," she told me; "you're starting up the bleeding." I looked up at her, hopeless. "Try to lie still," she said. She was holding the packed cloths between my legs. "Do you want me to get Frank?" she asked. I shook my head. I never wanted to see Frank again. He had found this doctor. He had done this to me. "Don't blame Frank," Polly said softly. I turned my head and looked at the floor. "I could never go through this," she said, starting to cry. I reached for her hand and squeezed it. "It's not worth it," she sobbed; "it's not."

I shook my head. I saw it all now. The world was an ashen place. There was nothing so shiny as the sun, and the sun would not tolerate competition. It burned up all that rivaled it. The sun was the cannibal's eye. It was hungry for everything, and it tired of everything quickly, and when it tired of things, it burned them. Then it began again. Love could not last in this world. Evil could last because it was a principle of life; it could not last in individuals. Neither could love. Nothing lasted in individuals. Promises and lies. They kept the young going. The older ones knew better; they were cynical. They were only curious. Curiosity was the passion that lasted. Curiosity survived. I looked at the floor and felt nothing. If the window had opened and my arm had blown off in a cloud of ash, I would not have been surprised.

I looked at the basin on the washstand. Something was moving under the lid of the basin. I stared at it. It was a dark shape, fluttering. It was a large moth. It was going to start flying. But it didn't fly. It moved forward and I saw the sharp nose of a mouse underneath the two dark deerlike ears. I screamed.

Polly stood up and ran to the head of the bed. "What is it?" she asked. "A mouse," I sobbed; "a mouse. Over there. By the basin." Then I clamped my mouth shut again. The cramps continued, but they were not as strong. "Am I still bleeding?" I asked. I couldn't tell. The rags were so full of blood that a steady stream trickled from them, down my thighs and onto the bed. "I don't think so," Polly said. "You really are something, going through all of that and then screaming about a mouse." I tried to smile at her. I wanted to turn on my side, but when I started to turn, Polly pushed me back down on my back. "Don't move," she said; "the bleeding." I decided that it was safe to talk, but when I did, my voice was hoarse. "I'm stuck to the sheet," I said. Polly lifted the sheet and said that I was. The blood was drying and my nightgown was glued to the sheet and to my skin. "I'll clean you up later," she promised; "try to sleep." "I didn't know blood was so sticky," I said; "human blood, I mean." "Go to sleep," she said. "I can't sleep on my back," I said; "maybe if I drank that powder." "I don't know," she said; "anything we got from him . . ." "I don't care what it is," I said; "give it to me."

My sleep was dark and sludgy and filled with heat, as if the sun had chosen to set right in my room. At times I thought I heard voices, but I wasn't sure. I might be dreaming. I thought I heard Polly telling Frank to come back in the morning because I didn't want to see him yet, but I wasn't sure. I was back in North Chittendon and the bells were ringing madly and I went into the Congregational Church but no one was there, so I started up the stairs and no one was on the second floor either. I found the ladder that led up to the tower and climbed up to the platform, and there, circling in the air above me, was Mr. Chatham, the sexton, hanging from the bell rope. "You have to come down from there," I told him; "that's no way to ring the bells." And then I was out in the snow with my father and we were walking across the fields on snowshoes, and my father said that we had to keep going because if we didn't get there it would be terrible, and I said I was tired and wanted to go back, but he said I'd get lost if I went back by myself and I had to come with him, and we finally came to a field and he said we were almost there; he could tell by the tracks.

And we came into a field hidden by the trees, and there were almost fifty deer crowded in, their bones showing through their hides, their eyes big. They wanted to run from us but they were too weak. They were starving. They had wandered into this field to eat the grass before the heavy snows fell and the snow trapped them and they did not know how to get out, so they stood, huddling together, starving, waiting to die. My father picked up his rifle and began shooting. "Aren't you going to shoot?" he asked; "it's a mercy. You can't let them live like this. They'll starve to death." But I could not shoot them. They were happy dying together. Why couldn't he see it? It was better to starve to death, together, in peace, as they were doing, than to run about the world filled with food, alone in the endless wood. But they were falling, one after another, one on top of another, and finally there was only one left, and when I saw that one look around, stunned, when I saw her profile, its eye turning toward me, I raised my rifle and shot her and when I saw her start to fall, I turned back and walked through the woods. I followed my own tracks. I didn't care if I lost myself in the woods but I knew I would not be lost. We had not done the right thing when we shot the deer. The deer knew how to die. And I was wandering through the fields looking for other deer who had come together to die, but I couldn't keep going. It was so hot.

When I opened my eyes, Polly was sponging my face and neck. "You have a fever," she said. I told her I'd be all right if only I could have something to drink. She left and came back with the warm pitcher. "Drink as much as you want," she said, lifting my head with one hand and holding the glass with the other. I drank down one glass, then another, but when I asked for a third, Polly said no, I would begin vomiting. I lay back and closed my eyes. "I feel like I'm on fire," I whispered. "I'll give you some more water soon," she promised me. Then I started shivering and the bed began shaking beneath me. "I'll get more blankets," Polly said. "Don't let them get bloody," I said through chattering teeth. "Don't worry," she said. I fell back to sleep.

When I woke again, I was swimming in a milky light. Polly was asleep in the armchair next to the bed. I felt stiff and sore and hot; I tried to turn sideways in the bed, but I was stuck to the sheet. I lay still. Where was Frank? I had only dreamed about him. He hadn't come to see me. My eyes were burning, and my lips. The palms of my hands burned, the soles of my feet and the backs of my knees. I wanted water but I didn't want to wake Polly. She opened her eyes and looked at me. "What time is it?" I asked. She looked at her watch. "It's five in the morning," she said; "Friday morning. You've been sleeping since Wednesday night." I took a deep breath and ran my hands along my body. I was still alive. "Where's Frank?" I asked. "I don't know," she said; "he came by Wednesday night, but I sent him away. Does anything hurt?" "It still aches," I said; "there. Where the knife went in." "I think you'll be all right," she said; "you're not so hot. For a while you felt like the stove." I turned my head from side to side on the pillow. "Do you want to try getting up?" I said I did. Polly said she'd have to get a pail of water, there was so much blood. She didn't want to pull the rags away; she'd have to soak them off. I asked her what we were going to do with all the bloody things. "We'll burn them," she said; "you're cold anyway. Now's a good time for a fire." "Let's do it tomorrow," I said; "I'm tired." But Polly said I had to do it now because almost everyone was out on excursions to Lake Champlain and tomorrow everyone would be pretty curious about why she was taking pails of water in and out of my room.

Polly brought in the water and a new supply of rags. She gave me one and told me to start cleaning my sides and my stomach. "You'd better start washing off your face, too," she said. "My face?" I said. It felt stiff and caked, but I hadn't thought about it; I thought it was the fever. "You must have reached down and then touched your face," Polly said. I asked her for the mirror. She picked it up and gave it to me. It lay on my stomach, a warm, dark wooden oval with a long, shaped handle worn smooth by years of use. I was in no hurry to look into it. Finally I picked it up. Caked stripes of dried blood covered me from forehead to chin. "I look like an Indian," I said, and I picked up the cloth.

The blood took longer to wash off than I expected. It was like removing paint. First, the top, dried layer came off in chipped pieces, and then the blood underneath, still moist, came off a little at a time. "Sandpaper would be faster," I said; "I'm using up this cloth and I'm not even finished with my face." "I'll help you, we'll get done," Polly said.

It took us a long time. We began washing the blood from my

sides and Polly began peeling the sheet away from me. I asked for a rag and worked on my right side. "All right," she said at last, "if you can roll toward me, I'll push all the sheet under you, and then you can roll to the other side and we'll get the sheet out. It's ruined." I rolled over and the soreness in my stomach throbbed and spread. When the sheet was gone, I sank back with relief. My forehead was beaded with sweat. But we weren't finished. The stiff rags were still between my legs and the mattress, which I had only glimpsed, was a red map of blood. "Talk to me while I do this," Polly said, beginning to wash my inner thighs; "I'm nervous about touching these rags." "What are we going to do about the mattress?" I asked; "it's ruined, too." "Well, if you can sit up in the chair," she said, "I'll cut out some of it and put in something to fill the hole and then we'll turn it over. But we'll have to get rid of it and get another. It's going to smell." "We could put naphtha flakes in it," I said; "that would cover the smell." "That's a good idea," said Polly. She was biting her lower lip. Then she took a wet rag, squeezed it so the water ran down between my legs, and began swabbing me again. "They're coming loose," she said; "maybe we should leave them there until I clean your back." "Let's do it now and forget about it," I said. She began pulling gently at the rags, but they stuck. "More water," she said wearily. Finally, she began to tug more energetically at them, and one after another, they let go. I had gotten used to all the packing between my thighs; now I felt hollow. "Am I bleeding?" I asked her. "No, you stopped. I think you're better." I turned on my side and she washed my back. "This is very good of you," I said. "You'd do the same for me," she said. "I hope this never happens to you," I said. "It's bad luck, that's all," she said. "Is that what you call it?" I asked her bitterly.

"Here," she said, "let's put on a new nightgown." I slipped the new one over my head. My hair in its long greasy braid fell heavily over my left shoulder. I tugged at it. It was still attached to my head. I reached up and felt my scalp. It was still covered with hair. "I thought maybe it had all fallen out," I said; "I thought maybe I was bald." "Well, you're not and we have to wash it," Polly said. "At the asylum they sometimes wash people's hair when it's still all braided like that. It might be easier on you." "If it's easier on you," I said, "go ahead." Polly helped me pull myself onto a chair so that it supported the upper half of my body and my head dangled over a large basin. I pushed against the cushions so my full weight would not rest on the chair; it was painful to sit up. "Oh, I don't know," she said, pouring warm water over me, "I think it would be easier to unbraid it." "Go ahead," I said. She washed my hair. "It feels wonderful," I said; "I can't remember anyone ever washing my hair before." I felt her strong fingers massaging my scalp. "This hair is going to take weeks to dry," she said. "If I can sit up a little," I said, "we can hang it over the headboard and let it dry like that. That's what I usually do with it. It's so heavy when it's wet." When we were finished, Polly stood back and looked at me. "You're human again," she said. I said I was starting to feel human. Every now and then my wound throbbed and I squirmed, changing position.

"Where's Frank?" I asked finally. "I don't know," she said; "he's been gone since Wednesday night. Didn't you send him to Charlie's?" I said I did, but I didn't know if he'd gone there. "He'll be here soon enough," she said, sinking down into a chair. "You've been here all along," I said; "aren't you going to be short of money?" "It's not so bad," she said; "Iris is paying me to look after the house." "I want to pay you something," I said; "I wouldn't be all right if you hadn't stayed." "I don't want any money," she said.

I watched her struggling to stay awake and watched her fall asleep. She looked worse than I did. I slid down in my bed, my hair fanning out over the headboard like a thick black fringe. Later that night, Eddie came in and Polly asked him to pick me up and hold me while she turned my mattress over and then she covered it with a clean sheet. "You're not cold?" she asked me; "if you're not cold, I'll open the window and we can get some fresh air in here." She opened it and the cool night breeze blew in like a promise of better things.

"Where's Frank?" I asked her. Again she said she didn't know, but she imagined he was pretty upset too and was probably off drunk somewhere. "He doesn't care," I said; "he's probably gone off with that Jane Holt." "Don't be silly," Polly said angrily; "he hasn't seen her for months. He's upset about you." "He's angry because of what I did," I said. "Stop looking for trouble," Polly said; "when he gets here, you'll find out what he thinks. I don't see how he could be mad at you." "If he wasn't mad at me, he'd be here." Polly sighed. "You don't want to stay alone tonight, do you?" she asked. I shook my head. "Well," she said, "I sleep like a stone. If you could move over to one side, I could lie down there with you." I pushed myself up with both hands and slid over to the edge of the bed. "Come on," I said. The minute she got into bed, she was sound asleep. I watched her sleep, her chest rising and falling, and eventually the rhythm of her breathing began to put me to sleep. I had never slept with anyone but Frank before. I was pleasant, the warmth of another body.

In the morning, Polly was still asleep when I woke. I reached up above my head and felt my hair. It was almost dry. I heard the doorknob turning, and Frank opened the door slowly and tiptoed in. He saw Polly sleeping next to me and smiled. He put his finger to his lips, pointed to the chair, tiptoed over, and sat down. I felt as if the sun had suddenly walked into my room, as if the long night was really ending, and as I looked at him, the red rays of the rising sun were horizontal in the room. And then I thought that if he went away now and never came back, there would be a different kind of dawn for me, a different world would begin because it would have to begin and I knew I would walk into that world and make my own way. Perhaps it would be best. I looked away from him. But when I looked back, he was staring at the pile of blood-stained rags in the corner of the room and his face contorted in pain, and the old love for him welled up in me like new blood. I wished Polly were not here; I wished she were on the moon. As if I had never seen him before, I saw how tense his body was, as if it were ready for something. I saw how he held his head, slightly stiffly, and how the very air around him seemed charged. I wanted Frank in bed with me. I smiled at him and pointed to my hair, hanging like a curtain over the back of the bed. He shook his head. He pointed to the water glass on the washstand, and when I nodded, he got up and filled the glass and tiptoed over to me. Polly was beginning to stir. Her eyes opened as I was finishing the last of the water. "Oh," she said when she saw him; "you're here. Can you stay?" He said he would. "Wonderful," she said; "the changing of the guard." She got out of bed, looked down at me for a minute, and then went over to Frank and squeezed his shoulder. "I'll see you both later," she said.

"Are you hungry?" Frank asked me. I realized that I hadn't eaten anything since Tuesday, and now it was Saturday morning, but I wasn't hungry. "I'll go down in a few minutes and get you something," Frank said; "you have to try and eat." I didn't say anything. "Is Polly going to burn those rags?" he said. I said she was burning some of them now. "The fire's burning down," he said, and he picked up half of the rags on the floor, opened the stove door, and stuffed them in, pressing them down with the

330

long iron hook which hung from the side of the stove. "It smells terrible," I said. The rags had taken fire. "It's windy," Frank said; "the smell will clear out fast." I nodded and looked at him. I was afraid to close my eyes lest he vanish while I was not looking.

"Are you ready to get up?" he asked; "you're still fastened to that bed by your hair. I'll fix it for you." He got the brush and came over to the bed. He lifted my hair from the headboard and I bent forward and it dropped about my shoulders and fell over the sides of the bed. He tried brushing it but tangles stopped the brush. "I don't understand," he said; "I used to do this for my sister." "You're not used to so much hair. You better give it to me," I said, taking the brush, and I began attacking my hair energetically. But the activity made my wound ache. Faint cramps spread through my stomach. Frank saw my grimace and took back the brush. "You have to be more ruthless with that hair," I said; "you better get the metal comb if you really want to get through it." "This looks like a horse's comb," he said. "It is," I said. He worked patiently on my hair. "One side is done," he said. "I'll do the other side," I said. "No," he said; "let me finish."

When it was done, he sat back and looked at me. "You look better than ever," he said. I didn't answer. I felt hollowed out, empty, neutered. "I thought you were going to die," he said. I looked away from him and looked down at my hand lying on the blanket. "I feel as if I did," I said; "I feel like someone else." "You're fine," he said; "you are." "I don't feel the same," I said; "I feel like this happened because I did something wrong." "You didn't do anything wrong." "Or there was something I didn't do," I said vaguely; "I don't know. I can't explain it." "You look the same," he said; "in a few days, you'll be the same." I felt an inexplicable anger surging in me, rising into my throat, and I looked at the sheet, my eyes stinging. "I feel different," I said. "About me?" Frank asked. "Not about you," I said, annoyed; "there are other things in the world besides you." He nodded his head and avoided my eyes. "I guess it will be a while before we get back to where we were," he said; "I guess it must have been pretty terrible."

"Where were you?" I asked abruptly. I didn't want to be comforted, not yet. He moved restlessly in the chair. "I went over to Charlie's Tuesday night and Polly sent me away when I came back here. After that, I just stayed out at the quarries. There's a lot to do out there. I have two commissions." "It must be nice to have a real job to do," I said. "It is," Frank said; he was watching me, his eyes narrowed. "What kind of things do you have to do?" I asked. "Two stones," he said; "as usual. One's a plain stone with a lamb on its crest, but the other's better. It's a full scale angel. If you want to model for me, this is the time to do it." "I don't feel like an angel," I said. "No," said Frank. "Look," he said, "Charlie wants to see you. Do you want him to come?" "No," I said; "I don't want to see anyone." "What about me?" he asked; "do you want to see me?" "I feel as if I ought to be locked away from the rest of the human race," I said. "Don't say that," he told me. "That's how I feel," I said. He was running his fingers up and down the arm of the chair, tracing the grain of the wood.

"Are you going to stay with me?" I asked him; "you don't have to." "I know I don't have to," he said; "I want to." "Maybe you better get something to read," I said; "I keep falling asleep." "I'll be right back," he said, getting up. He came back in with his sketch pad and pastels. "You're going to draw?" I asked him, incredulous. "Yes, what's wrong with it?" "You're going to draw *me*?" "You," he said; "as usual." "Don't draw me," I said; "I look like a monster. Draw anything else." "You look fine," he said. "I'll put the sheet over my face," I said. "All right," said Frank; "I won't draw you. I'll work on new designs for the stones."

He took out a piece of paper and I watched him angrily. I had no control over my moods. One minute I was overjoyed to see him, just as he had looked when I saw him last, sketching as if nothing had changed or would ever change, and the next instant, I was inexplicably furious that he sat there drawing as if nothing had happened, as if I were not different, as if nothing had been lost, as if we would wake up tomorrow, ask each other what had happened to the last four days, and go on as we had before. I pretended to sleep and watched him through flickering lids. He was so much stronger than I was, so much safer. He had a purpose in life and I did not. I was useless. It was no wonder this terrible thing had happened to me. I had made a mistake. I hadn't attached myself strongly enough to the world. I was attached only to Frank. If he had been attached only to me, he would not have the strength to put up with me now. He was attached to me and he was attached to the world. Everything had to have more than one purpose; everything had to have more than one thing it could do.

Frank went down and came back with some biscuits and a

glass of milk. "Come on," he said; "eat." I picked up the biscuit and took a bite of it. It felt like wet paper; I couldn't bring myself to swallow it. Frank came over to the bed, picked me up, and held me in his arms. "Swallow," he said; "swallow or I'll drop you on the floor." I swallowed. "Take another bite," he said. I finished the biscuit. "If I put you down, will you drink the milk?" he asked me. "Don't put me down," I said. He carried me to the chair, sat down, and settled me in his lap. "Are you all right?" he asked me. I said I was. My head was resting against his chest and I felt his heart beating against my eye and cheek. It wasn't his fault that I didn't know what I wanted from life. I wanted to go back to where we were before it all happened, and at that moment, I knew I could.

"Look at your hair," Frank said; "it's trailing down on the floor." "I should put it up," I said. "I'll braid it for you if you want," Frank said; "I'm good at it. I used to braid my sister's." "All right," I said. I felt the brush against my scalp and the pull of my hair dragging my head back and letting it go and the world shuddered and came to rest. I reached up and covered Frank's hand with mine. "I wish we were at the quarries," I said.

If I could only get out of this room and get back there, everything would be all right. I felt like a sponge full of unshed tears. The sun on the hills would dry me out. I would pose for the statue of the angel and I would watch the pure, clean, motherless bodies of stone growing slowly around me, and the dust would settle on me and rub itself into my skin until I was part of that marble world. I would be washed clean by the brilliant blue light, by the warm, golden sun. The dust would heal me.

34

I was not prepared. I was not prepared for the weakness, for the shifting weather of my moods. I looked out at the sheeplike summer clouds, altering their shape and hue all day long, growing fat and dark and predicting rain, then shrinking and stretching out into white streaming banners, and I thought that the inside of my mind must look like that sky. Frank came to my room in the morning and coaxed me to eat. I would choke down part of what he brought me and promise to finish the rest, and after he was gone, I would creep down the stairs and throw out what I had not finished. At night, he would sit in my room sketching. Two weeks had passed and I was still unable to force myself out of my room. "Don't you want to go for a walk?" Frank would ask me and I would always say the same thing: "Maybe tomorrow." And I could see that he was becoming more and more restless, and finally he would get up and say he was going out for a while. He couldn't sit still so long; he'd be back.

I had trouble staying awake. I seemed to exist in a dream, and so I never knew when Frank came back in, but one night I woke up and found myself being carried down the hall into his room and he lay me down in his bed. "Don't worry," he said, pulling the covers up under my chin; "I'm not going to touch you." And I turned on my side and twined myself around him. I slid an arm under his shoulder and hugged him with the other. I put my leg over his hip and did not relax until I was as close to him as it was possible to get. And then I cried for the happiness of being so close, for the nights I had spent alone and feverish, tossing on my own bed, for the confusion within me which I could not understand but which blighted my days. I cried because the nameless dreads came from nowhere and for no reason; it was as if rain began to fall on a perfect, blue day and there was no cloud, not anywhere in the sky. I cried because when he left for

Barre I was tormented by dreadful headaches, and when he came back I could not remember how I had spent the day, yet it was gone. And when he asked me to come with him the next day, I would sink into a sleepiness from which I could not escape.

Then Frank came home one night and said that enough was enough. I was getting weak from staying in bed. If I kept it up, I wouldn't be able to walk at all. He was getting me up and taking me out if he had to carry me. I got out of bed and the room whirled around me. By the time I finished dressing myself, I was exhausted; I was too tired to brush my hair. "Forget your hair," Frank said; "put on a hat." He picked up my white cloth hat and fastened it to my hair with a hatpin. Then he picked me up and carried me down the stairs and out into the yard. "Now you're going to walk," he said. I walked at his side as if I were drunk, bumping into him, drifting crazily off. I complained that walking made my head hurt and he said that was because blood was returning to my brain. He said I was like someone who had been in a cast and now that the cast was off, I was numb. That was all that was wrong with me. "Tomorrow night," Frank said, "we're going further. We're going all the way to the clearing with the carved stumps." "I can't!" I wailed. "That's what you think," he said.

The next night, the same night began again. Frank insisted that I get dressed and come out, and I threw myself down on his bed and refused to move. Frank pulled me upright and threw my clothes at me. I lost my temper and threw them back at him and was about to attack him with both fists when he grabbed me and pinned me down. "I don't know what you're mad at, and I don't care," he said; "but you're going out." I dressed slowly, glaring at him. I went down the steps behind him and found them solid beneath me. We started to walk out toward the fields, and my legs, which were cramped and sore, did not buckle under me. "Walk faster," Frank said. I said I couldn't and that I certainly couldn't walk as far as the clearing. "We'll see," he said. I would tell myself that I would walk to the next clump of trees and no further, but then we would pass it and we were still walking. Finally, we came to the field with the grove at its center, and in the center of the grove, the carved tree stumps. "I don't want to go in there," I said. "Well, I do," he said. He seized my wrist and dragged me in after him. "Lie down," he said when we came to our old place. "No," I said; "I don't want to lie down." "Why not?" Frank asked; "do you think I'm going to force you here when I don't bother you in bed?" "I just don't want to," I said.

"What do you want?" he asked me. "Nothing. I just want to be left alone," I said; "I'll get back to the way I was. You have to leave me alone." "I've been leaving you alone and you've been getting worse every day," he said. "I can't get any worse than I was after that doctor came!" I said. "You have to put that behind you!" he said. "How can I put it behind me?" I asked him; "when it could happen again? I can't put it behind me without putting you behind me!" Frank was tracing designs in the earth with a stick. "You could always enter a convent," he said. "I don't think that's funny," I said. "No one ever said I had a sense of humor," he answered.

We sat there in silence. The moonlight filtered down like a luminous dust, silvering the leaves. "What do you want me to do?" I burst out; "tell me what I should do! Do you want us to go on the way we were? It could happen again! You don't want children and I'd have to get rid of it all over again." "You don't want children either," Frank said, his voice remote, his face turned away from me. "You don't care about me!" I heard myself saying; "you don't love anyone but yourself! You love dead women! It's no wonder you like carving them in stone so much! They're what you want!" And then it was quiet. I waited for Frank to say something, but he sat where he was, expressionless, his hand holding the stick, tracing circles in the earth. My eyes burned but I didn't cry. "Aren't you going to say anything?" I asked finally. "What about?" he asked; "you said everything." "I didn't mean it!" I cried; "I don't know what I mean lately! I don't know what I think or whether I think at all. I can't sleep and my head hurts and I can't get out of bed and I don't know what to do all day. I didn't mean it." "You meant it," Frank said.

"I'm sorry," I said, crying softly. "There's nothing to be sorry about," he said. "You *have* to forgive me!" I cried; "I'm not in my right mind!" "You're in your right mind all right," Frank said. "Let's go home," I said; "all I want to do is get in bed with you and go to sleep." "No, Agnes," he said. And then I started to sob. Frank said he thought it would be better if we slept in our own rooms for a while, and I cried harder. I said that we could sleep together the way we used to, I was just frightened, I would get over it, I hadn't meant a word I said, I just wanted to go home and I wanted us to get back into bed. "You really think I *am* a monster, don't you?" Frank asked; "you hink I don't care whether or not you get in trouble again." I said I didn't think he was a monster; I knew he didn't want to get me in trouble; he hadn't gotten me in trouble in the first place, my body had, and I kept on crying and pleading with him; I wanted him to come back with me, to get into bed with me, I wanted him to promise he would forget what I had said. But he sat on the stump, tracing patterns in the earth. I seized him by the shoulders and shook him. "Promise!" I insisted; "promise!"

"Promise!" he shouted, standing up; "you promised me you wouldn't want children! You promised me you wouldn't have them!" My hands fell to my sides. "I don't want children," I said, crying; "I kept my promise. I never promised not to get in trouble. I didn't believe I could get in trouble. But I didn't have it! I got rid of it! What more should I have done?" "Meant what you said," Frank answered. "I did mean what I said!" I insisted; "if you just had patience! I'll be just the same. I promise I will!" "Don't make any more promises," he said. "But I haven't broken any!" I cried; "I haven't changed. I still have the same feelings for you." "Do you?" he asked. I said I did. I kept on crying.

"Please!" I begged him; "please let's go back to your room!" "I don't know," he said. I could see he was wavering. "You have to let me come back," I insisted; "I'll die otherwise." "What do you mean, Agnes?" he asked. "I don't know what I mean," I said, "just let me come back." He didn't say anything and I sank down on a log and sobbed. If he did not take me back with him, I would kill myself. I would wait until he was asleep and I would steal his pistol and I would shoot myself. "I know what I did wrong," I cried; "I shouldn't have tried to look into the future. If I get in trouble again, I'll get in trouble again. It was worth it. It would be worth it again. Please take me back!"

What had I done? Why had I said such things? If he didn't take me back, I would lie on the floor in the hall outside of his room. I would follow him to work. He would *have* to take me back! "I don't know why you want to come back with me," he said. "Because I love you!" I cried; "I love you! I always have! I don't want to be alive if I can't have you!" "Don't say that, Agnes," he said, looking up at me; "no one should be that important to anyone else." "You're that important to me!" "All right," he said; "let's go back." "Say you forgive me," I pleaded. "Let's just go back," he said.

We walked back to the boardinghouse and every step I took

set loose a new flood of tears; they were unstoppable. I cried all the way up the stairs and while I was undressing and after I got into bed. "You're here," Frank said; "you can stop now." But I kept crying because I could not stop and I held tightly to him because I was terrified of driving him away by my tears, by the words I had spoken before which he would think of as he fell asleep. I was sure that I had driven him away from me, and tomorrow, when I woke up, he would be gone, and the more frightened I became, the more I clung to him. He lay next to me stiff as wood. Finally, when I had given up and turned on my side, Frank turned to me and put his arm around me. "Go to sleep," he said; "for God's sake, stop crying."

When I woke, the morning light was slowly transfusing the room. My arm was under Frank's shoulders and my other arm was wrapped around his waist. I looked around cautiously, as if there was something I was afraid to see, and then I remembered what had happened the night before. I stretched my legs slowly; they were sore and cramped but I had no intention of remaining in bed. I had to make Frank forget what I had said; I had to make him forget that I had turned on him as if I hated him. It was my fault. Anything that happened now would be my fault. It had always been that way. It was nothing new. I watched him, asleep on his back, and was afraid of what he would say when he opened his eyes. The fear rose in me and I forgot to breathe. My nose was still stuffed from crying all night.

I slid out of bed and began to dress silently in front of the window. I held on to the edge of the dresser when I put on my shoes because I didn't want to wake Frank with the chair's creaking springs. As I was bending over to lace my second shoe, I saw Frank wake up and turn to look at my side of the bed. He saw I wasn't there and sank back on the pillow, staring up at the ceiling. His cheeks sucked in and his eyebrows arched as if he were angry. He turned and saw me, holding on to the dresser. "You're up," he said without expression. "Yes," I said; "I'm going with you." "Oh," he said; "are you?" "You said I had to get out more," I said. He didn't answer. "I'll go down and tell Iris to pack a dinner pail," I said. When I looked at him, I felt as if I were looking at a house closed down, boarded up, the owner gone indefinitely.

Breakfast was a gloomy affair. I was afraid to speak to Frank and he did not seem anxious to speak to me. Polly watched us both, toying with her potatoes. "Well, well," she said, "into every life a little rain must fall." Frank looked at her as if he wondered who she was. "I see you got her up and around," Polly said to him. "Oh, she's loosened up, all right," Frank said, his face closed. There was no point in trying to talk to Frank now. I might say the wrong thing and he would forbid me to come with him to the quarries. I tried to imagine it, standing in the front room, listening to Frank telling me to stay behind, and I knew I would begin to scream uncontrollably, throw things, attack him, and finally I would be carried off, sobbing. My body was a shell which could barely contain its energy and the energy was fury, a pure, fiery fury which seemed to have come from nowhere but possessed me now as a fire possesses a burning house. I felt Frank's eyes on me and pretended to swallow a piece of steak; when he wasn't looking, I took it out of my mouth and hid it under a potato. I did not want to do anything for which he might reproach me.

We walked to the cars in silence. When Charlie said good morning, I was pathetically grateful to him. And I thought, this is how things go wrong. One mistake and there is no going back. And, as if I were many years older, I watched myself living with Frank in silence; I saw myself trying to make him talk, trying to make him as he had been when I first knew him; I saw myself enraged at his indifference, and I knew that it was possible. It was; the road I was on now could be the road to hatred, not love. It's not possible, I told myself. It's not. I conjured up an image of Frank at work on one of his stones. I *was* on the right road; there was no one else in the world like him. There was no one else I could love.

I asked Charlie if he had been back home lately, and he said he didn't think he'd be taking a vacation that summer; he was happy enough as he was. "I heard you were sick," he said. I told him that I had had a bad attack of influenza. "That's odd," he said; "Frank said it was appendicitis." "Well, at first the doctor was confused," I said. I looked sideways at Frank. He was staring out the car window. He would not look at me. "How is your ivy going?" I asked Charlie. "Better," he said; "you should see the points on those leaves. The customer is always satisfied, though. No matter how bad my ivy is, you don't have to water it." "Don't run yourself down," I said. Frank looked over at the two of us as if he had never seen us before and hoped never to see us again. Charlie told me about the false alarm they had on Crown Street when one of the girls started a fire in her stove and forgot to open the damper. She ran through the house screaming fire, fire, and smoke poured out all the downstairs windows, and when the firemen found out what it was, Mrs. Hinckley told the girl that if she ever did that again, she'd have to find another place to live. "Someone worse than I am," I said; "I didn't think anyone was." "This one used to live in a mud shack somewhere or other," Charlie said; "I don't think she knows what to make of washrooms." "They're places you go to get water to put out fires in your stove," I said, and we started to laugh. Frank looked at me and glanced away. The reproach was clear enough: Charlie could make me happy and he could not. "Well, good-bye," Charlie said when the cars began slowing down for the quarries; "I guess you two have things to talk about. I'll see you up on the hill."

"It's obvious enough to Charlie that we're not talking," I said as Frank and I began walking up the hill. He walked along silently, absorbed in the horizon. "We've lived together for a long time and we never had a fight before," I said. No answer. "How long has it been?" I asked; "almost a year? We've never argued. I think that's remarkable. It is, really." Frank kicked a stone into the air. "Aren't you going to talk to me at all?" I asked. He shrugged. "If I loved you just a little," I said, "then I'd only get a little upset with you. But I don't love you a little. I adore you. I worship you. That's why I got so mad." He still said nothing. "When my mother and father fought," I said, "it was over with in a few minutes. They'd fight about whether or not the apples had to come in before the storm or whether or not they should try drying them on the roof. That's all they had to fight about. You shouldn't blame me so much. I wouldn't have said such awful things if I didn't care about you so much."

"It might be easier living with you," Frank said, "if you didn't care about me so much. Did you ever think about that?" "How can you say that?" I asked, stopping, seizing him by the arm; "would you really want me to care for you less? Just so things would be easier?" He took a deep breath and pursed his lips as if he were blowing smoke rings. "Sometimes I think that's just what I want," he said. "But if you couldn't have one without the other," I said, frantic, "if you couldn't be loved the way I love you without the fights, you'd want the fights, wouldn't you? You wouldn't want to spend all your life arguing about apples and whether the cow should be penned up because she might be ready to calve?" "It might be better than hearing someone tell you that you only loved dead women," he said; "a fight with you isn't like a fight with everyone else. That wasn't just an ordinary fight." "You have to forget I said that!" I

340

insisted; "I didn't mean it! I'll never say it again!" "Oh, I'd say once is enough," said Frank; "I thought you meant I wanted to kill *you*, I liked dead things so much." He kept his head turned away from me; I could not see his expression.

And then the fury again welled up inside me. "You are killing me!" I hissed; "you know you're the only thing in the world I care about and you're punishing me for getting angry at you. Don't you think I've been miserable enough? Don't you think I've been sick enough? Do you have to make it worse? No wonder you're so insulted by what I said last night! Some of it must be true! Otherwise, why would you want to torture me like this? Because I love you? Because I'm stupid enough to love you?" I stopped suddenly, the rage, like a candle flame, snuffed out. I did not understand this fury. It seemed born of the fever and it broke out against my will as if a part of me were determined to annihilate everything around me. I was afraid of it; it made me turn on others when I most wanted to soothe them or draw them closer to me. Then I saw that Frank had finally turned to me.

"Am I killing you?" he asked me. "Yes!" I said; "you are! I wait for you to say something and I forget to breathe. When I was bleeding, and everything hurt so, I thought I was doing it for you and it was all right. But it's not all right now. Not if you won't talk to me! Not if you can't forgive me for losing my temper once! It was your fault, anyhow. You made me get up and get out of the house. You made me walk to the field. I wasn't ready to go. I would have jumped on anyone. You don't have to take it so personally. If Polly had been there, I would have jumped on her. You just can't see anyone but yourself." "You mean I'm selfish?" Frank asked. "Yes," I said; "you are. Selfish and conceited. And you don't understand anything. If Charlie had been there, I would never had said such horrible things to him. I don't care that much about him. But you don't understand that, do you?" Frank glanced at me. "I understand that," he said. "No, you don't." "I do," he said, "and I'm not angry. Let's forget about it." "Do you mean it?" I asked him. He nodded. "Well," I said, "you're still all the way over there on your side of the road." He shrugged slightly. I knew he could not bring himself to move closer. I walked toward him and bumped into him, hard. He smiled tightly and awkwardly; stiffly, he put his arm around my waist. "It's not the first time someone told me I'm selfish," he said at last. "You're not so bad, really," I said. "Even if it takes a while," I said, "it's worth it, getting back to where we were. You think so, don't you?'' "I guess,'' he said. "Do you love me?'' I asked him. "Yes,'' he said. "How much?'' "Let's not start that again,'' he said.

We had gotten to Frank's station and I sat down under the apple tree and settled the sketch pad on my lap. It was going to be a hot day. The last two weeks had been damp and little gnats thickened the air like a living dust. I reminded myself that Frank had just said he loved me and that he wanted to get back to where we were, but I was not reassured. I felt as if something ominous was happening even as I sat there watching him. It was as if the ground under us was no longer solid and we both stood on ice and it was cracking under our feet and the current was carrying us in opposite directions. And the more frightened I became, the angrier I grew. I stood up suddenly and the sketch pad fell into the grass. "I'm going to look at Charlie's stone,'' I said.

Charlie was sitting on a log staring at his ivy-covered obelisk and when he saw me he looked up and smiled. "Sit down,'' he said, moving over. I hesitated, looked back at Frank, and decided to sit down. "Well, what do you think?'' Charlie said, throwing down the little twig on which he had been chewing. "The ivy's certainly a lot more pointy than it was,'' I said. "Look, Agnes,'' he said; "I want you to tell me the truth. If you walked up to this stone and someone asked you what kind of leaves were growing on it, what would you say?'' "I'd say they were ivy leaves.'' "Thank God,'' Charlie said. "Very pointy ivy leaves,'' I added, irrepressibly. I had always teased Charlie. I rarely teased Frank. "Oh, that's all right,'' Charlie said, "as long as people know it's ivy. The carving doesn't have to be good but it's got to be recognizable.'' I smiled at the obelisk. It certainly showed signs of industry. "The weather will round off the leaves,'' I said. "Well,'' he said, "I wouldn't be one to mourn if one of my stones was split to pieces by lightning.'' "Do you think you'll keep at it forever?'' I asked him. "No,'' he said; "I'll go back to farming. As soon as I have enough money to buy a good farm and hire some help. If Frank hadn't come down here, I'd probably be back home carving a stone here and a stone there and doing odd jobs and working for my father. I don't mind it. We have a good time there.'' I nodded. Charlie was lucky. He belonged at home and he belonged here on the hill.

"What are you going to do?'' he asked; "after Frank finishes carving a statue of you?'' "Oh, I don't know,'' I said; "go with

Frank when he goes to New York." "Do you really think he'll go?" Charlie asked. "Why not? He said he wanted to." Charlie shook his head and looked over at Frank. "Some people don't like to be too good at anything," he said. "Frank's not like that," I said. "If you're good at something, people expect a lot more of you," Charlie said; "do you think he likes it? Having a lot expected of him?" "I never thought about it," I said; "he took good care of me when I was sick. And later on, too." Charlie nodded, bent down, picked up the little twig and began chewing on it again.

"What are you thinking about?" I asked. "You," he said; "are you coming out here every day?" "So far," I said. "It's no good, Agnes," he said; "you have to find something for yourself. You can't expect him to fill up the whole day and the whole night. Even if he wanted to, he couldn't do it."

"Even if he wanted to?" I repeated. "He's not the kind to give that much to anyone. Or want that much from anyone. Believe me. I know," Charlie said. "I think you're wrong," I said. "Well," said Charlie, "he'd respect you more if he knew you had a life of your own. He wouldn't take you for granted. Anyway, if you really want to go to New York, you ought to save some money." "I don't know if Mrs. James will take me back," I said. "You could ask," he said; "she's not the only person in the city who hires girls. Mrs. Hinckley needs someone to wait on tables." "I'm still wobbly," I said, starting to laugh, picturing myself under a tower of dishes, all of them slipping from me and skittering across the table at Mrs. Hinckley's boarders. Charlie laughed too. "You know," he said, "you hardly laugh when you're with Frank." "Oh, but I *beam* with happiness when I'm with him," I said. I heard the irony in my voice, the bitterness. It astounded me. "You see?" said Charlie; "he's not the only one you have to worry about. You'll bore yourself to death." "Believe me," I said, "I'm not bored when I'm with him." "You're only human," Charlie said; "things will bother you. If he's the only one there, lightning's going to strike him the same way it strikes the only tree in a field." "I'd never hurt him," I said. "I guess that's why he wasn't talking to you this morning," Charlie said. "Maybe you're right," I said; "it wouldn't hurt me to talk to Mrs. James." "Or someone else," he said. I looked over at Frank and saw that he had stopped working on his stone and was sitting under the tree. "I better go back," I said.

I asked Frank if he was hungry; he said he wasn't. "It's finished," he said, pointing at the stone. The little lamb was curled on top of the arched stone, its small snout poking aggressively into the air. Its front paws were folded back beneath its body and its back paws disappeared beneath its round rear haunches. The lamb had an embryonic air, as if it had not yet been born and was looking into this world through the curtain of another. From a distance, the lamb looked like a seal. Its small ears were flat against its head. Its nostrils were wide as if it were smelling the world for the first time, and its mouth looked inexpressibly weary and wise. That lamb, I thought, did not belong on top of a tombstone. It deserved better. I said there was something about it, I didn't know what, but the lamb looked like every animal there was. When I looked at it, I thought about a pony I'd had, my grandmother's dog, Sam, and my cat, Stardancer. "That's what I wanted it to look like," Frank said; "all animals. But you can tell it's a lamb?" "Yes, you can tell. It's too bad it has to go to a graveyard. It's a waste." "I don't want to talk about New York right now," Frank said.

"What do you want to talk about?" I asked him. "I saw you talking to Charlie," he said; "he's always saying you ought to get a job. I think you should, too. It's getting pretty far into the summer. A lot of girls have gone home for the season. Everyone floods in with the fall. This is the best time to look for a job." "Why are you so eager for me to get a job?" I asked; "you never mentioned it before." "A lot of things never got mentioned before," he said. "All right," I said; "if you want me to get a job, I'll get a job." "It's not as if I'm asking you to do something strange," Frank said; "every woman works unless . . ." "Unless what?" I asked. "Unless she's staying home." "With children," I added. "With children," he said; "it's not healthy to stay home in an empty house." "All right," I said, choking down my outrage; "I'll talk to Mrs. James." I opened up the lunch pail, took out a doughnut and began chewing on it as if I hated it and wanted to destroy it as quickly as possible. I did not understand myself at all. One minute, I was sitting in the sun, watching Frank, convinced I was watching one of the world's ideal creatures moving inexplicably through this tattered world, and the next minute I wanted to shout at him, to slap him, to walk away from him and never see him again.

I took out another sugared doughnut and began devouring it. Halfway through eating it, I stopped. Either I did not eat at all or I ate as if I never expected to see food again. I was like the weather that came before the worst of the hurricanes; one minute, the day was sunny and the wind blew sultry, and the next moment, the sky went dark and the wind blew cold. I looked at Frank, sitting next to me, and I felt nothing whatever for him, but I knew that in five minutes, I would be awash in adoration, and if he moved away from me, I would want to die. I was not fit to live with. This moodiness, this uneasiness, was left over from the fever. If I stayed out here with Frank, I would turn him against me.

"I've been thinking of going home for a while," I said; "just for two weeks. It would be good for me. When I come back I'll be the same as ever." "I think it's a good idea," Frank said, his lips tightening. He had been quick to agree. "Will you miss me?" I asked. "Of course I'll miss you," he said. He looked at me suspiciously, as if he wondered what I was driving at now. "I'll miss you, too," I said. "Will you?" he asked me. He was staring up at the leaves flickering overhead. "Of course I will!" I cried. I got up and bent over him. His face was a mask of confusion and pain. "Let's go out to the field tonight," I said; "the way we used to." "Are you sure?" he asked me. I was sure. I had to stop worrying, I had to forget about everything but Frank. If I didn't, I thought, he would forget me. I kneeled down next to him and began stroking his forehead. "That feels good," he said after a while. I was thinking about the coming night, half dreading it, half anticipating it. I would never have believed that I would want to make love to Frank so that I could be sure he would continue loving me. I kept stroking his hair and felt his body relax against mine. "When you come back," he said, "if you're not too tired, would you pose for that angel?" "I'll pose for the angel," I said. "My black angel," he said, looking from me to the black stone. "I'll write you," he said. "You don't have to," I said; "I won't be gone that long." "I want to write," he said.

35

No one knew I was coming home, so I left my bags at the train station and started walking. I went past the two churches, their graveyards, the general store, the livery stable, Bea Brown's house. Then the houses thinned out, the roads were bumpier and full of ruts, and soon I was walking uphill, past the valley farms, up toward Cloudy Pastures. After a while, the sun grew hotter and I unbuttoned my black waist and walked on in my black skirt and white blouse. I heard the sharp report of a rifle in the woods and wondered what someone was after now. It wasn't a good time for hunting anything. I stopped before I turned the corner and came into view of the house. They would not be there. My mother and my grandmother were gone. I was the last of the Druitt women. When I turned the corner, I had to remember I was the last of them. My father was the only family I had. I was going to take long walks through the woods and practice firing at targets until I was as good a marksman as I had ever been. I was going to stay here until I wore out whatever the fury was which I had swallowed down whole and which now buzzed inside me like so many bees. When I returned to Montpelier, I would be no trouble to anyone.

I was in no hurry to see the house, far less to enter it. I turned off the road and cut through the woods until I found the little trail I had cleared as a child; it went straight to my grandmother's cabin. It was overgrown with goldenrod and milkweed and small trees the size of ferns were beginning to grow up in it, but it was still a path. The cool of the forest made me aware of how hot I had been and I sat down on a boulder and looked around me. Up above, the aspen leaves were quivering in the golden light. There was a crackling of twigs, a snap, a shower of leaves falling toward me, and I heard the squirrels pass overhead. Bluejays cawed in the boughs. The sound of the creek, running over its interminable brown and gold and gray stones, was faintly behind everything. It was August, high summer, but there was something definite and curiously insubstantial in the air, like silent mourning bells announcing the end of the season. In the fields near me, the cattle were untroubled, their jaws grinding the last of the grass, their large, fat tongues drinking the clear brook water. But there was something in the air, a sad note the weather played upon the instrument of the bone-stretched skin. And I found myself angry at it. Autumn's long fingers were stealing into the woods, rubbing the leaves between her fingers as if she were a prospective buyer testing out cloth. She would want whatever she found. How long was it until the first killing frost? It was the middle of August. Sometimes the frost came before the end of the month. The nights were already cooler. The little summer insects buzzed around my face. They were like the flowers. Death would come for them when they were at their best, and they would enter death without having suspected its existence or knowing that it was waiting for them. It was not the same for humans. Death came for humans before their dreams hatched; death was the fox who came early and broke the eggs open. One morning the flowers blazed with color. The next morning they lay burned and blasted, blackened by the first frost, their seeds promising their resurrection. Oh, I envied them, those things with their feet in the ground, those things with their wings buzzing them through the air until the cold brought them to earth.

I looked around me. In October, the leaves would be off the trees; the fallen leaves would be beaten flat by heavy rains and the first fall of snow. The bony ledges of the earth would begin to show, the earth's skeleton shedding its unnecessary flesh. The earth. It had only one body and that body was immortal. It did not have to die itself and trust that it would be reincarnated in its descendants. It would reincarnate itself endlessly and it laughed at all the creatures on its surface who could not do the same. Soon the mornings would be cauldrons of mists, slowly rising and clearing as the mornings ticked by. If the spirits moved in those mists—and so many people here believed they did—what would they want to say to us? See how indefinite are our shapes, see how tenuous our hold on this world grows? See how we fight to return, now that we have shed our skins, now that we are only water? What are you doing to bring us back? they ask and ask again, and the sun rises, heating the land, driving them upward into the branches. And it is no wonder we dread the feel of the mists. They are insistent. They want everything from us.

A cowbell sounded close at hand. A cow must have wandered into the woods. One of the men would be after her. I got up and began climbing up the path toward the cabin. I wasn't ready to see my father. I was afraid he would look at me and instantly know what had happened. And yet, I looked exactly the same. I looked better. I had so little to do I spent all my time fussing over my hair and mending my clothes. I wondered what it must have been like for my parents, living here, sending me to school with the others, coming into town and seeing us throwing snowballs at one another in the schoolyard, or hearing the school bell ringing dully in the middle of the day, proclaiming fire or illness, working steadily away as the seasons changed one into the other, smoothly, not jolting mechanically from summer to autumn to winter as they seemed to do for me. To them, the seasons were not separate rooms, equipped with doors, which could close, locking you in one season, leaving you banging on the door begging for admission to what came next as they were for me. It occurred to me that I did not know what happiness was, and that it might be madness to forge a new kind of happiness which I could claim as my own when I did not yet know what the ordinary, common sort of happiness was. The exotic flowers we crossbred on the farm never lasted as long as the wild ones which grew naturally. And it was impossible to create something out of nothing. Whatever I created had to grow from what was already here. How could I create something worthwhile out of materials I thought unworthy to work with? Because I did. I thought of the earth as unsatisfactory, a poor mother to its children, a huge, round, immortal creature which held out the promise of happiness and permanence and beauty only to snatch it away.

Even under the trees, even in the thick pine shade, the heat was beginning to make me dizzy. I remembered leaving school and walking downstreet to Louise's house. She had the chicken pox and was kept at home, but I was allowed to visit because I had already been sick with it. I had to pass the Common and the children playing there turned on me and began throwing snowballs at me. They were not angry at me. They did not want to hurt me. It was just something to do. I suppose they expected me to stop and join the fight. But I was frightened and I began to run, and of course they ran after me, and by the time I ran up the steps to Louise's porch, I was blubbering and I got quite a scolding from Louise's mother. "A great, gawky thing like you," she said, dusting the snow off my coat, wiping my eyes, "not to fight back. To run! I'm ashamed of you, Agnes." She raved on, picking up some snow, molding it and throwing it at a boy lingering near the house. "No wonder they chased you!" she exclaimed. I wondered what she would say now if she knew what I had done. Of course now there was no one chasing me. There was only the threat of this season, preparing to dissolve into something else. I pushed aside some heavy pine boughs and came out into the clearing in front of my grandmother's cabin. The key to the front door was tied onto a little ribbon pinned into my pocket. I took it with me wherever I went. When I was upset, I put my hand in my pocket and rubbed it between my fingers. I believed it brought me luck.

The heavy chocolate brown wooden door had been recently repainted. I took out my key but the door swung away from me into the depths of the room. So he wasn't taking care of it! If my father left the door open like this, anything was possible. I walked into the room, stepping carefully. Perhaps someone else was in there, a tramp or an animal. When I crossed the room, I stopped in front of the fireplace and listened. Across from me, the door opened and I heard someone gasp. I looked up, frightened, ready to seize the poker from the fireplace and attack. It was my father. "Helen?" he said. "Then it's true," he said; "you can come back." I was furious. It had happened again. I wanted to pick up the poker and beat him over the head until he lay senseless on the floor. He had mistaken me for my mother.

"No, Father," I said; "it's me. Agnes. I came back." "Agnes?" he said. "Agnes," I repeated, "your daughter." "Agnes," he said again; "I thought it was your mother." "I know," I said; "you must have been thinking about her." "I'm always thinking about her," he said. "I'm sorry I startled you," I said. He shook his head inconsolably. "For a minute, I thought she was back," he said. "The dead don't come back," I said. I looked nervously around the cabin. I didn't believe that the dead didn't return. I wanted them back, but I wanted my grandmother, not my mother. "Sometimes," said my father, "when I'm falling asleep and looking out the window, I think I see one of them. They both look just the same. My dead don't come back the way they were when I last saw them. They come back the way they were when I first saw them." "In dreams?" I asked. "In dreams," he said, "of course." "Maybe they really do

349

come back," I said. "No, they don't, Agnes," he said; "I only see them when I'm falling asleep. It's dreaming, just dreaming with my eyes open. It used to happen when your mother was alive. I'd look up and see her coming toward me and when I looked again it would be a weed waving in the air."

"What are you doing up here?" I asked him. "I come up twice a week to look after the place," he said; "you know that." "I didn't see your horse outside," I said. "It is good for me, climbing up here," he said. I nodded and looked around. Nothing had changed in here; nothing ever would. The cabin was a mausoleum after all. "I should be asking you what you're doing here," said my father; "is your young man with you?" "No, I came alone," I said; "I was afraid I'd tire him out, I was sick so much, and when I started getting better, I was so cranky I wasn't fit to live with. So I thought I'd come home because you're used to my wicked ways." "You were never wicked," he said. Without warning, my eyes filled. "Did you have enough money?" he asked me; "I sent you almost two hundred dollars, but I was afraid it wasn't enough." "I still have some left," I said, "in my shoe. When I go back, I'm getting a job again and I'll pay you back." "You don't have to do that," he said. I said I did. I had to wash off all traces of the ink I had smeared all over the picture of my life.

He asked me if I was hungry, and I said no, I was thirsty, and we went outside to the well and he cranked up the bucket and held it in both hands while I drank from it. "Feel better?" he asked me. And I did. As we walked down to our house, I said I'd be happy to try cooking if he'd try eating what I cooked, and he said he'd be happy to have someone cooking in there again, and if he didn't like the results, he'd just saddle up and go into town and order breakfast at Mrs. Brown's. "She still takes in boarders?" I asked. "Oh, yes," he said; "no one's told her she's getting old. She went out last winter to get some wood and she fell and broke her hip and she would have been lying there for days but Bill came by with the meat wagon and took her back in. The doctor told her she was a damn fool and Bill's trying to get her to close up and come up here to live with him but she won't hear of it. If anyone tells her she's old, she'll just crumble like a cake of dust. But by now her hearing's so bad, I don't think there's anyone who can tell her the bad news, so I guess she'll just keep on going." "I should go and see her," I said.

"What about Frank?" he asked. "He's a little fed up with me, I think," I said. "What about you?" asked my father; "are you a little fed up with him?" "A little," I said. "When you first argue," said my father, "it's the end of the world. But you get used to it. The same sun comes up the next morning." "I hope so," I said. "You know it does," said my father. "He said he would write to me," I said after a while. "Watch out for this branch," my father said; "it's going to snap back." I held the branch and followed behind him. "I guess he'll write, then," my father said; "you know, Agnes, I always believed you could get anything if you really wanted it. The trouble is, you have to want something to get it." "I guess I want Frank," I said. "If you do, you'll get him," my father said. "Are you always so sure about everything?" I asked him. "Well, I'm not sure if you want him," said my father. "Why?" I asked; "I just told you I did." "You're here, aren't you?" he said. I followed him down the path, glaring at his back.

"Did I tell you your friend Louise died?" he asked me. The air roared in my ears; the gnats flew into my eyes. "No," I said, "you didn't." "She froze to death. Right after she moved to Sharon. She went out visiting and came home in the middle of a storm and lost her way and in the morning when they went out to look for her, they found her holding on to the fence in front of the house. She must have been feeling her way along, trying to find the house. She was expecting, too. Can you imagine it? A country girl doing something so foolish?" "Why didn't they look for her right away?" I asked. "They thought she'd have the sense to stay with whoever she was visiting, but she didn't. Her mother moved away. She's gone out to Ohio to live with her mother. Her husband's gone West, too. It's a tragedy." "Poor Louise," I said. I could see her there standing in front of me, crying, because the others were telling her she was ugly; I could see her unbuttoning her blouse when the other girls decided to undress, and I wished I were back with her, back in that time I had thought was so dreadful. I should never have left Louise. She was a town child. She never understood snow. "She wasn't a country girl," I said aloud; "she always lived in town." "That's true," my father said; "I never understood why people cared so for town." "It has its advantages," I said. But now, when I thought about Montpelier, it seemed dangerous; so much more could go wrong there. But that was what I wanted, I told myself, a place where the best and the worst could happen and life stretched out its wares in front of you and you were willing to pay for what you took. That was my trouble, I thought. I wanted everything but I didn't want to pay the price. Nothing ever happened here. Boredom was too high a price to pay for peace.

"You know, there was real excitement here last week," my father said; "up at Mrs. Butcher's farm. A tramp broke into her house. There's been a lot of that lately, so there's nothing new in that. But when he went into the kitchen, he found Mrs. Butcher lying on the floor in a pool of blood and she was bleeding from the wrist. So the tramp tied a towel around her hand and hitched up *her* horses to *her* wagon and drove her into town and brought her to the doctor. And the doctor said it was a good thing that he brought her in when he did, or she surely would have died. And then he asked the tramp how he knew Mrs. Butcher, and the tramp said he didn't know her at all; he'd broken into her house looking for some food or money. So the doctor called the sheriff and they locked him up. Well, now it's all anyone talks about. Half the world thinks the man behaved like a Christian because he saved the woman's life when he could have run off and let her die, and the other half of the people think he ought to be tried for breaking and entering, and they think *he* stabbed Mrs. Butcher. But she told the papers she'd cut herself cutting onions and the tramp never hurt her at all. It's all *The Argus* writes about. They may have to let him go yet if she won't press charges and now they say she won't. Of course her family is at her to do it. They say she was lucky, but what if she'd turned around and seen him and he was in an ugly mood? What do you think?'' "He must have been simple," I said, "to admit the truth. He should have made up some kind of story. Everyone thought he was a hero until he told them he wasn't. People need heroes." "Just what is the trouble between you and Frank?" asked my father. "Nothing," I said; "I might as well try cooking tonight." "No," said my father, "tonight I'm taking you to the Inn. I never took your mother there enough."

The first week passed sweetly enough. The honeysuckle had climbed the back wall to the house and its fragrance filled my old room. In the mornings, two hummingbirds trembled up and down on the warm currents of air. I peeled potatoes in the kitchen and watched them shrink into small white balls beneath my inexperienced hands, but when I cracked the eggs, they landed in the bowl, not on the table, and I no longer burned the toast or set fire to the butter melting in the heavy pans. And when I was finished with breakfast and had set the peeled potatoes in a bowl of water, I would take down an old net scarf of my mother's or grandmother's, and walk up to the cabin, where I ate my lunch. From there, I could see the whole farm: the tilled patchwork of the hills, the black and white cows ambling here and there, in and out of the shady patches, the birds swooping down into the apple trees, the ducks sharply white on the sparkling brook, the chickens milling around in the yard, every now and then flying up into the air in a madness of wings. And sometimes I would see my father, small and toylike from my vantage point, leaving the house and starting out on the path up to the cabin and I would lean back against a tree and wait for him. When he came up and found me, we would sit there, looking out over the farm. If he said anything, I listened. I had little to say myself. He was a good man, after all, and I was glad to be back.

One day I was up above the cabin and I saw the mailman stop at the house and knock at the door, and a few minutes later, my father came out, something white in his hand, and started along the path up the hill. I knew the letter was for me and I didn't want it. The last week had been enchanted. Time had stopped. But the letter, heavy in my father's hand, was pulling on the great wheel, starting it up again. A bee buzzed near my ear, and I brushed it away. I remembered the wasp's nest, built above the shed door, and reminded myself to tell Bill Brown about it. It wasn't a safe place for a wasp's nest to be. There were two swallows nesting above our front door. I wanted to stay until the nestlings left. I didn't want to see the letter.

"Something for you," my father called from below, waving the envelope. I got up and walked down the path toward him. "It's from Montpelier," he said; "I brought up some apple cider, too." I took the bottle from him and sat down. "Don't you want the letter?" he asked. "Of course I want it," I said. "Well, open it," he said. "I thought I'd drink some cider first," I said; "I'm thirsty." "Well, I'm bursting to know what's in it," he said. I sighed and tore open the letter. "Dear Agnes," Frank wrote, "I hope this letter finds you well. I know that when you left you were subject to sudden changes of heart and I guess I know the reason for that. I guess you know that I was unhappy to hear some of the things you said about me. I know that I am not the best, but Agnes, I am not completely heartless, and I guess you know that, too. I hope you will remember that it was some of your fault that we were fighting. You say you know it was, but there have been times when you looked at me as if you did not know anything of the kind. I hope you will answer this letter so I can get it by Monday or Tuesday and not have to worry another week about how you are. I know you will try to do what is best for us and I will try to do the same. I gave some thought to coming down there to see you but I know you would not want me to. I seem to find my room larger than it was. When you come back, we will start on the angel. I have resumed going to church, but will break off when you return. I am not in danger of becoming too saintly, as you well know. Well, that is all for now. Frank Holt.''

"He wants to know when I'm coming back," I told my father; "I'll probably be going in a week. Maybe two. I feel much stronger." "You look much better," he said; "of course, I'll miss you." "I'll miss you, too," I said, and I meant it. "You know," I said, suddenly, "whatever I want to do, I always stop in the middle and get frightened. I'm so afraid of making mistakes. Sometimes I think I do things fast, without even thinking about them, so I won't have to worry about making a mistake. Well, then, whatever happens, it isn't my fault because I didn't really decide. Do you know what I mean?" "You have to make mistakes," said my father; "you're only human." "You didn't make a mistake about my mother?" I asked him. "About your mother?" he said, astounded; "no. Not about your mother." "What did you make a mistake about?" "I never should have tried to keep sheep," he said, grinning at me; "I guess I don't have much to regret, do I?" "No," I said; "you know what? I think I'll stay up here and take a nap in the cabin." "Go ahead," he said; "I've got to get on back down anyway." We were sitting on the boards of the brass bed.

I went into the cabin. It was cool and musty and the curtains were drawn so that the cabin glowed with a snowy light. I went into the small bedroom and lay down on my grandmother's bed. I envied my father. He thought there were times he could see them, the ones who were gone. What had he called it? Dreaming with his eyes open? I wanted to see them, too. Perhaps if I slept here, I would see her moving through the room. I turned on my side and clutched the pillow as if it were a living thing. No, I wouldn't be surprised to see her walking through the room. And the sun must have tired me more than I realized, because the bed was floating beneath me and I knew that in seconds I would be asleep. And in the dream, I was waking up in the same room and across the room from me there were no windows. Instead, there were three doors, and I looked for the door through which I had entered the room, but it was gone. I knew that I had to find the right door if I wanted to leave the cabin. I got up and stood in front of the doors and I thought for a long time before going closer to them. All the doors were the same black, painted wood, varnished to a high shine. They all had shiny brass knobs whose surfaces were unscratched. I could see my image in each of them, distorted and swollen. Finally, I decided to try the middle door.

I opened it and behind it was a wall of dirt shot through with the deep roots of trees. Oh, I thought, this door goes out into the deep earth. I closed the door and considered the other two. I'll try the one on the left, I thought, but when I opened it, I saw the same thing: a wall of earth webbed through with thick tree roots. I smelled the strong odor of wood rot and dampness. I closed the door and tried the third. It, too, had nothing behind it but earth. So I am buried in this cabin, I thought, and I went back to the bed and sat down. And then it seemed to me that I heard sounds behind the doors. I got up and pressed my ear to the one in the center. On the other side were low voices, murmuring.

I opened the first door and the earth was gone. Instead, a steep, wooden flight of stairs led down into the ground beneath me. But I don't want to go down there, I said, and opened the door on the left, and it too opened on a flight of steps, as did the third. I decided to go down the center stairs, and as I went down, I felt my shoulders ache and then stab with pain. When I reached up to touch my right shoulder, I felt something solid and feathery, and as I kept going down, I saw that I was growing wings. I stopped and looked about me. The way down was narrow. I was not sure I wanted to see the bottom. Then a voice said, "You have to come down if you want to see me," and I didn't know who it was, but whoever it was frightened me, and I ran back up the stairs, and as I ran, my wings grew smaller and smaller until they were gone altogether.

I woke up on my back, staring at the ceiling. The white light was bright in the room. "I'll have to leave," I thought.

But I was still in no hurry to go, and on the tenth day of my visit, I heard my father ringing the big brass bell which hung from the arch of the barn door. He and my mother always rang that bell when we had visitors, but I could not imagine why he was ringing it now. Perhaps he needed help. I jumped off the brass bed and ran down the path toward the house. No one was in the yard. I jerked open the side door and went into the house. My father and Charlie were standing in the middle of the kitchen. "You have a visitor," my father said. I stood still, dumbfounded. "Frank told me where you were," he said apologetically. "Why?" I asked. "I told him I wanted to talk to you and I guess he wanted to know when you were coming back," he said. "I guess you've met my father," I said. "If you don't mind," my father said, "I have to get back to the fields." "Go ahead," I said.

"Let's go outside," I said; "there's a nice rock ledge I always sit on." "So this is where you live," Charlie said; "it's pretty grand." "Yes, I know," I said; "what are you doing here? Really?" "I was wondering how you were. After your appendicitis." "Influenza," I said. "You and Frank should really get that straight," he said. I felt as if he had dragged all of Montpelier up to Cloudy Pastures with him. I would not have been surprised to see my room at Iris's floating like a square balloon above his head. "Did Frank ask you to come?" "No," he said; "I wanted to." "He didn't mind?" "I guess not," said Charlie; "he told me how to get here." I sat there, stubbornly silent. "I know you've been having trouble," Charlie said; "that's why I thought I'd talk to you." "What am I?" I asked, smiling bitterly; "another Madge?" "Maybe worse," he said. "Maybe worse!" I exclaimed. "Well, my sister's got a lot wrong with her, but she always knew what she wanted." I didn't say anything. "She wanted Frank," Charlie said; "you did, too. Once." "I still do." "Not the way you used to," he said. I said that wasn't true, and he said if it wasn't, why had I left Montpelier? I said that lately I'd been having trouble controlling my moods and when I was blue I turned on Frank, so I came home to calm down. "And are you calmer?" Charlie asked me. I said I thought I was. Probably I would be going back to Montpelier soon.

"Madge just had a baby," he said; "a girl." He seemed to expect me to say something. "Good for her," I said at last. "She says she doesn't even think about Frank anymore," he said. "I know what you're getting at," I said. "Frank said you wanted to start over. As if nothing had happened. I guess that's what Madge did, except she didn't start over with Frank." "Just how did she start over?" I asked. "She lost a baby," he said; "now she has a baby." "I don't want children," I said. "Well, if you're going to live with a man, you're probably going to have them, so you have to decide whose babies you want." "I can live with someone and not have children," I said. "Can you?" he said. "Anyone can," I said; "if they really want to." "They may not live very long," he said; "not having children. From what I hear, it's dangerous not having them. You ought to know

356

that by now." "Then don't have any," I said impatiently; "let's talk about something else." "About Frank," Charlie said; "if he thinks you don't want him...Well, he won't wait around." "Has he stopped waiting around?" I asked. "Not yet," Charlie said. "If I had a baby, what do you think he'd do?" I asked. "Well," said Charlie, "if it looked like him, you'd probably never get him out of the house." "He told me he doesn't want any," I said. "That's what he thinks," Charlie said; "that's not what counts. What counts is what you think." I shook my head. "Maybe you're too young to know what you think," Charlie said; "how old are you now?" "I'll be eighteen in December," I said. "Why don't you just wait four years and you'll know what you think and you won't make any mistakes." "And what am I supposed to do in the meantime?" I asked him. "You won't have trouble keeping busy," he said.

"You know," I said, "I don't really know what we're talking about but I'm glad you came." "Are you?" he asked. "I wish I'd fallen in love with you," I said. "So do I," he said sadly. "I'd try again," I said, "if I thought it would do any good. But Frank...well, from the minute I saw him, I knew that was the person I'd been looking for. I was born for him. I don't suppose that makes much sense, does it?" "Not when you're here and he's there," he said; "he sent you this photograph of him." Charlie took the little picture out of his billfold. "A photographer came to the quarries," he said.

I took the photograph. There he was, his eyes hooded, his cheeks drawn in, his mustache precisely clipped, his eyes far away and slightly stunned. "Was he looking into the sun?" I asked. "I don't think so," Charlie said; "it was pretty cloudy." I touched the photograph and my heart pounded. It was Frank in that picture, locked up and shrunken, waiting patiently behind that little window. I had to go back. I took Charlie up to my grandmother's cabin. At the house, I served supper and he ate with us and then I took the buggy and drove him to the train station. "You're an odd-looking Cupid," I told him, as we stood at the train station. "I wasn't trying to play Cupid," he said. The train was pulling in. "I'll see you on Monday," I shouted over the noise of the train; "that's when I'll be coming back. Don't tell Frank. I'll surprise him."

At home, I lay on my bed looking at the cabbage roses on the wallpaper, trying to see where the pattern ended and joined the next identical cabbage rose. I had never been able to do it before and I could not do it now. But if I traced them long enough with my eyes, I would fall asleep. I would love this house, I thought, if I hadn't lived in it. I would love the world, I thought dreamily, if I didn't have to live in it.

In the morning, the smell of frying steak filled the house. I must have slept late and my father was doing the cooking. I found my blue watered silk dress hanging in the closet and didn't turn away from it to the familiar black dress I had been wearing. When I went downstairs and sat down at the table, I saw that a large package, clumsily wrapped in newspaper, had been set down at my place. "From you?" I asked my father. "From Charlie," he said; "he asked me to give it to you today. He said after what you'd been talking about, you'd take it the wrong way if he'd given it to you yesterday. He seems pretty concerned about you." "He always was," I said. "Well, I guess it's something to make you forget you were so sick," he said; "he told me you didn't snap back too well." "Everyone's talking about me lately," I sighed. I picked up the package. "Don't drop it," my father said; "it's heavy as can be." It was. I put it down and got up to get a knife to cut through the twine which tied it. "It's probably a stone," I said. "Oh, he didn't seem the kind of young man to play tricks," my father said. "No, that's not what I meant," I said; "he's a stonecutter, too." My father moved the pan from the fire and came over to watch. "I don't know. I was a farmer and I didn't give your mother a plow for a present. I gave her glass flowers. Save the twine," he said, and, as I unwound it, I gave him the end of the string. He began wrapping it around his hand. I had forgotten how it was on the farm. Nothing went to waste.

"Well," I said, folding the paper away from the object, "I wonder what it is." And then all the paper was off and a miniature obelisk covered with ivy was sitting in the middle of our kitchen table. My father looked at me, astonished. "What is it, Agnes?" he asked; "it looks like a tiny tombstone." "That's what it is. It's a copy of one he was making." "It's very nice," said my father, regarding it nervously, "but why did he want to go and give you a thing like that?" I didn't answer. I touched the obelisk. "Stone is always cool," I said. "It's one pretty strange present," said my father. "He knows I like tombstones," I said; "they're so pretty. I once told him I wished I could have one of my own without dying first. I guess now I've got it." "What's that growing on it?" my father asked; "ivy?" "It's supposed to be," I said, smiling. "Well, you can tell what he meant," my father said. He went back to the stove, and I sat down at the table, looking from him to the obelisk. It seemed to attract and focus all the sun's rays. It was the brightest object in the room. "You know," I said, "I think I'm going back Monday. I've been here two weeks." "He said you'd probably be going back then," my father said. "What else did he tell you?" I asked. "Nothing else," said my father; "don't go getting jumpy again."

My father went out and I was left alone with the obelisk. These stone things had a song of their own; if you tilted your head just the right way, you could hear it. I looked around the room to be sure it was empty, and through the windows to be certain no one was coming. I picked up the stone and held it against my stomach. That was what the stone was for: a monument to the child I had let go. Charlie was right. Someday, I would have a child and then I would want the one I had given away. That was how I would get it back. Then it would never have died. I took out the little square card with Frank's photograph on it. He was sealed in it, as if he floated under transparent ice. It was time for all of us to come alive again. I went upstairs, changed into my old black dress, and went up to my grandmother's cabin to say good-bye. I looked longingly at the bed, but it was a double bed. It would never fit in a boardinghouse. And, I thought, running my hand along its cool curves and curlicues, it belonged here.

36

The early morning train to Montpelier ran ahead of schedule, and I reached Montpelier Junction before ten o'clock. The passenger wagons were not going into town for another half hour, so I hired a carriage and went in myself. The obelisk was in my suitcase along with the few dresses I had taken with me and an album of photographs I had found at my grandmother's. When I came into Iris's house, the silence was as absolute as it had been the night I first arrived. I looked around indecisively. I assumed that Iris had kept my room for me, but I had left without speaking to her and I wasn't sure. I would go up, I decided, and see whether the room was as I had left it.

Just then, Iris came into the little room. "Oh," she said, "you're back. Your room took a lot of work. We had to get rid of the mattress and it took days to get the smell out of things." I said I had some pretty bad bleeding last month and we couldn't get it to stop. "That's what Polly said, too," she answered, watching me curiously; "she said she was pretty worried, but she didn't send for the doctor. That's not like Polly. She's so sensible." "Well, we thought it would stop any minute," I said. "I guess it did eventually," she said. "Yes," I said. "You didn't come out of your room for a long time," she said; "I wondered how you were going to pay your board but I guess that wasn't a problem." "No," I said, "my father sent me the money." "What are you going to do now?" "Look for a job again," I said. I didn't know why she was asking me so many questions. "Did you keep the room for me?" I asked. "Of course," she said; "Polly paid the two weeks' rent." "I'd better pay her back," I said. "Yes," she said, "a girl like Polly doesn't have money like that to give away." "No," I said. I went upstairs feeling as if I'd been thoroughly scolded.

The room was just as I had left it. The wallpaper cracked and bubbled in all the same places. Even the bed looked the same. I put down my suitcase and sat on the edge of the bed. There was a new mattress. It didn't sink in as the old one had. I looked on the shelf and saw my bottle of ammonia and water. I took down the rag and cleaned off my dress. Then I went down, washed my face, and set off for Mrs. James's.

I thought I would ring the bell when I got there. I was afraid that if I walked in, Mrs. James would assume I thought I could come back as if nothing had happened and she would throw me out in a rage. But she was working in her garden, digging up bulbs. "Are you putting those away for the winter?" I asked her. She sat back on her heels and looked at me. "No," she said, "I'm burning them. They have a disease." At that instant, I felt as if I could see Florence and the others through the walls and I wanted to be back inside with them. I looked at the pile of diseased bulbs and repressed a shudder.

"Well," she said, "what do you want?" "I want to go back to work," I said hurriedly, afraid she would cut me off; "I was sick a long time, but now I'm better. I went home to North Chittendon, but now I want to come back and work here. I know you said you were giving me my last chance that other time, but I'll work hard now." "I don't need girls to make clothes," she said; "I have all the girls I need for that." She stood up. She was a short woman who always seemed taller than everyone around her. "I still need someone to do fancywork," she said; "I have a lot of orders for christening gowns and trousseaus. It's that time of year," she said. "I can do the fancywork," I said. "Not on the second floor. You'll have to work on the third floor with the other girls doing the same thing. It causes too much trouble to mix the girls together. You'll earn more on the third floor. We've been through that already." "All right," I said, "I'll do the fancywork and I'll stay on the third floor." "Of course you can eat your dinner with anyone you want to," she said; "just don't discuss wages with the girls on the second floor. They can't do the fancywork, but they're jealous of the fancy wages." "When do you want me to start?" I asked her. "You can start right now," she said; "if you really want to work." "I really want to work," I said, and followed her up the stairs.

As we passed the second floor landing, some of the girls looked up and I tried to catch Florence's eye, but she was bent over her work. The third floor was the attic floor and the walls of the room sloped crazily and the two circular windows on each side admitted even less light than the windows on the floor below. Two girls were firmly installed in front of each window. "Find a place in the center," Mrs. James told me; "Lilian, give her the tablecloth and the napkins and show her the transfer. Mrs. Hopsbaum wants day lilies all over everything. It would be easier to pick them. Well," she said to me, "you're going to have your hands full. They're a common flower, but they're not so easy to embroider." I said I would do my best and she nodded and went back down.

Lilian was a large-boned, unpleasant-looking girl whose nose seemed permanently red. Thick brown freckles covered her face, thickening over the bridge of her nose, and whenever she said something, her face flushed meatily. When she bent over me to show me where to begin tracing the design onto the cloth, I found myself pulling away from the sharp, tangy odor of her dress. She smiled nastily as if she knew how uncomfortable she was making me. "Well," she said at last, straightening up, "do you understand?" I said I did. "You better," she said; "when you work on this stuff, you can't make a mistake and rip it out without ruining the fabric and she takes the money right out of your pay. You can end up owing her money after a week's work. I know." I nodded and bent over the embroidery hoop. "Who taught you to embroider?" she asked me; "the schoolteacher?" "My mother," I said, "and my grandmother." "In the winter?" she asked sarcastically; "when you weren't in the fields?" "I was never in the fields," I said. "Oh, a great lady," said Lilian; "we heard all about how you came to work whenever you wanted to. You better not do that here. It just makes more work for the rest of us. There are only six of us up here and she always takes in enough work for eight." I said I had no intention of missing work. My eyes were burning. Either I would throw down my work and try to gouge out her eyes or I would start to cry. "Leave her alone," said one of the girls near the window.

I took a deep breath and drew the orange thread through the yellow linen. "Aren't you going to take off your jacket?" the girl near the window called to me; "don't let Lilian worry you. She's not in charge of us." I took off my black jacket, hung it over the back of the chair and picked up the hoop. "It's hot in here," I said to no one in particular. "Complaining already?" Lilian asked me. "Leave her alone," the other girl said again. "It's all right," I said; "I can take care of myself." I put down the hoop and went over to Lilian. "She's right," I said, "leave me alone or one night I'll lay for you, and when I get through with your eyes, you'll never see anything again." Then I went back and sat down, astonished at myself. I hadn't done anything like that since I was a child, and then I'd only fought to protect Louise.

I picked up the hoop and looked at it. It was true; I had never fought to protect myself. I looked up and saw Lilian staring at me, her eyes wide and fixed. "Don't worry," I said; "I never bother anyone who doesn't bother me." "I wouldn't threaten me," she said. "It wasn't a threat," I said; "it was a promise."

"You've got your nerve," she said; "I guess that's what Frank Holt likes about you." I stitched away, silent. "You've been away, haven't you?" she asked me; "well, you know what they say. When the cat's away." "What are you talking about?" I asked her. "He came to church with Jane Holt," she said; "I guess that's still going on." "Jane Holt," I said; "it's been a while since I heard that name." "I guess you'll be hearing it quite a lot now," she said; "from what I hear, they're going to get married." "He'll never marry Jane Holt," I said. "How do you know?" Lilian asked. "I know," I said, stabbing my needle through the cloth. "Well, you're certainly prettier," said Lilian, "but men don't always want the prettiest ones." "I guess you'd know," I said. "You don't have to be so nasty," she said; "I was only warning you fair and square. If you don't do your share of the work, the rest of us have to do it." "Oh, I see," I said; "now you're only trying to make friends. By telling me about Jane Holt." "Well, you must know about that already," Lilian said, "everybody does." Her face had flushed so that her freckles seemed to have disappeared. "I'm not worried about Jane Holt," I said; "he bumped into her at church. That's all." "I don't think she's worried about you, either," said Lilian. "Oh, shut up, both of you," said a girl sitting in back of us.

I sewed steadily and only when the girls began opening their dinner pails did I realize that I was hungry. But I had come straight here and had nothing to eat. "I'll be right back," I said, getting up and going downstairs. Florence was standing up and stretching. "Oh, you're back," she said; "it's hot in here. Are you stopping to eat?" I said I was stopping, but not to eat, and she took a doughnut out of her pail and handed it to me. "Let's get out," she said; "it's an inferno in here." I said it was worse upstairs. "I'm not surprised to see you, but I'm surprised she took you back," Florence said when we were out on the street. "Who else can embroider day lilies so fast?" I asked her. "Day lilies?" "Orange day lilies on mustard yellow linen," I said, wrinkling my nose; "someone thinks it's beautiful." "I've got some cloth for you," Florence said; "I sneaked it out when you

were gone. Did you ever finish that quilt you were doing?"
"No," I said, "but I'll finish it now." "Are you better?" she
asked me. I said I was. She was so good to me, so kind. And
yet, most of the time I barely knew she existed. "Good," she
said softly. Did she know? Did everyone know?

"I've been hearing about Frank Holt again," she said. "I
know," I said; "this creature upstairs says he's been seeing Jane
Holt." "Well, he sat at church with her anyway," Florence said.
"She'll never marry him," I said. "How do you know?"
Florence asked. "Because I will," I said. "Who's the creature
upstairs?" Florence asked; "Lilian? I'd watch out for her."
"I'm not worried about Lilian," I said. "She's big and she's got
a bad temper." "I'm smaller but I've got a bigger temper," I
said. "You?" said Florence; "you don't have any temper at all."
"Oh, if my mother were alive, she'd tell you another story," I
said. "The girls say you're going around with Charlie Mondell
again," she said. "I'm not," I said; "he's Frank's friend. He's
mine, too. I'm going to marry Frank. Before next summer. Don't
tell the others. We're going to New York." "New York!" gasped
Florence. "He's very talented. He needs to get out of here."
"Poor Jane Holt," said Florence; "I didn't think there was any
truth to that story about her getting back with Frank." "Let's go
in," I said; "it's impossible to cool off today. I might as well get
some work done."

I worked on my day lilies the rest of the afternoon, but Frank's
face floated between me and the cloth. If these stitches were
stitches in his heart, I thought, what a tapestry I could create to
cover the floor, the ceiling, the walls, all our days, all our visions
of each other, of the world around us, and whoever came into the
room would be stunned by its beauty and would never want to
leave.

"You're dreaming," Lilian said. I looked over at her; there
she sat, red and raw boned, laboring over a white rose on a black
scarf. "I'm getting a lot more done than you are," I said. "My
friend told me men always go for the bitches," she said, "and I
guess it's true." I dropped the hoop into my lap and scrutinized
her, wondering what to do to her. "Watch out for her, Lilian,"
one of the other girls said; "look at the expression on her face."
I liked that better. I'd rather have them afraid of me than feeling
sorry for me, trying to protect me. "What could she do to me?"
Lilian asked loudly, but there was a quaver in her voice. "Do
you want to find out?" I asked her. She didn't answer. "Don't
worry," I said; "there's always a man who's looking for some-

thing no one else wants so he'll never have to worry when the mailman comes." The blood rose in Lilian's cheeks; even her wrists and the backs of her hands were red, but she didn't say anything. I went back to my sewing. Every now and then, I slipped the little photograph of Frank out of my pocket and studied it—it would not be long now—and glared defiantly at Lilian who was trying to see what I was looking at. "Get on with that rose before the beetles get it," I said. I was going to keep this up forever. It was wonderful, attacking the world.

At five-thirty, I put down my work, folded it neatly, put it away, and ran down the steps and all the way back to Iris's. I splashed water on my face, yanked open the door to my room, and put on my blue silk dress. I sat down in front of the mirror and waited for the sound of footsteps. I could feel Frank coming closer. I could see him, standing over the others on the cars. I could see the cars pulling into the station. Then I heard footsteps running down the hall and I forgot to breathe. I stared into the mirror, watching the door. Polly burst into the room. "You're back!" she babbled happily; "you look wonderful! You look better than ever!" I got up stiffly and went over to her. She threw her arms around me and I hugged her back. "Where's Frank?" I asked her. "Frank?" she said; "he's at work. He'll be home any minute." "What's this I hear about Jane Holt?" "Jane Holt!" she exclaimed indignantly; "aren't you even going to say hello to me?" "Hello," I said, hugging and kissing her; "what's this about Jane Holt?"

Polly flung herself down on my bed. "Oh, it's nothing," she said; "he's been feeling sorry for himself since you went home. She waits for things like that. She sits around like a spider waiting for him to get upset so she can comfort him. I guess that's what's been going on." She looked me over. "You've changed," she said; "something's different." "I found my temper, that's all," I said; "and I went back to work today." "Good!" Polly said. "And I spent all my time frightening this red thing called Lilian," I told her. "Good Lord," said Polly; "I know that Lilian. Something's gotten into you all right." "My grandmother's ghost," I said. "Oh," said Polly. "So to speak," I said. "What are you going to do about Frank?" she asked me. "Get him back," I said; "let's go down. I want to lurk at the door and surprise him." "You're not entirely changed," Polly said with a sigh.

Downstairs, I hid behind the parlor curtain and watched the street. And I realized I didn't expect to see him. It was almost as if I had ceased to believe in his existence, as if I now believed he was a creature of my imagination, and because he was, he could not come walking down Main Street toward the house. The world I had been trying to accept since returning from North Chittendon had no place in it for him. And then I saw him, walking quickly toward the house, a sketch pad under his arm, scowling, covered with dust, and I realized that he would go to the livery stable to wash off before he came into the house and that I ought to be hiding at the back door. I ran through the house and took up my post near the entrance to the kitchen. Iris saw me, raised her eyebrows, and said nothing.

When I saw him coming toward the door, the blood pounded in my cheeks and my body flushed, the heat rising up from the soles of my feet to the top of my head. I saw him reaching for the doorknob and I opened the door and blocked his way. "Agnes," he said. His eyes were blank. "I didn't know you were coming back," he said. "Come into the parlor," I said. He followed me in and set the sketch pad down on the little slanted desk. "Why didn't you tell me you were coming back?" he asked. His voice was odd, formal. "I wanted to surprise you," I said. Oh, it had begun again, the old hunger for him, the desire to feel the bones of his arm encircling me, caging me up, protecting me from the rest of the world until his arms became the only world there was, the space I fought to live in, the only place I had ever belonged. No wonder I had been tigerish with Lilian. The other half of my body was back. I was no longer turning, bisected, like the half-moon, bleeding jaggedly into the night sky. I thought about North Chittendon and how I had contemplated staying there and I told myself I must have been mad. But Frank did not move toward me.

"Did you miss me?" I asked, my voice so cold that I did not recognize it. "Of course I missed you," he said. "Aren't you going to kiss me?" I asked him. He bent down and kissed me on the cheek. "Not in front of everyone," he said. I said I didn't care about everyone. "I do," he said. I felt limp, like a puppet whose strings had been cut. "After supper," he said; "we could walk out to the field." He spoke without enthusiasm. "All right," I said. "First I have to stop over at Charlie's," he said; "then we'll go." "I'll come with you," I said. "No," he said, "I'll go alone. It won't take me long."

And suddenly I could not stand it, not touching him, but close enough to see the little violet veins in his eyelids, the little white creases at the corner of his mouth where the sun did not penetrate, and I threw my arms around his neck and clung to him, pressing myself against him, my head burrowing into his chest like an animal desperate for its old home, breathing in his musty smell which always reminded me of herbs in the garden, holding on to him as a vine must hold on to its sheltering wall. And then I felt his stiff body relax, and his head burrowed into my shoulder and I knew he had given in; he had taken me back. "Oh, I love you. I do," I whispered, my head against his shoulder, and his head, buried in the curve of my neck, nodded. We let go of one another and stood still, looking at each other. His eyes were shiny. "I'm sorry," I said. "Don't apologize," he said, "it's over." We went into the dining room and Polly looked up, startled. Then she smiled the wide smile which lifted her ears toward her hair. So it was true; everything would be all right. I saw myself kissing Frank in the parlor's cracked mirror and I felt as if I were waiting for a coronation, not for my dinner.

When Frank came back after supper, we started out for the fields. I was shameless. I ran around him like a puppy, tickling him from behind, running around in front, throwing my arms around him and kissing him until his face was wet. And as we walked, he began to smile. In the bluish light, he seemed far away, not yet a creature of flesh and blood. There was something challenging in that remoteness. And with every step, my desire for him increased. If it had been a sleeping animal since the night of Doctor Grimsby's visit, it was awake now and it stretched its animal claws through my human hands. I could not stop touching him.

I unbuttoned his shirt and ran my hand over his nipples and around his stomach as we walked, and all the time I kept on chattering: about North Chittenden, about how it was cooler there than it would be here for weeks, and when I began to tell him about my friend Louise, and how she had died, my hand was slipping beneath the belt of his trousers and when my hand finally closed around his organ, I stopped in sheer ecstasy. Then I slid my hand further down and began stroking his testicles; I felt them wrinkle and flatten under my hand. I worked my hand further under his belt and began pinching the smooth skin between his thighs. I heard Frank breathing in little hissing gasps. "Agnes," he said, "you'd better stop. We'll never get to the field."

But I could not stop. I opened his belt. I unbuttoned his pants. I cupped his organ in both my hands. I licked his chest; I bit at his nipples. "Come into the woods," he said, pulling me after

367

him. "The ground's wet," he said. "We don't have to lie down," I said, feeling for him. I didn't want him to ask questions; I didn't want him to ask me if I was sure. He picked me up and held me against the tree behind me and I pushed his pants downward and saw his flesh gleaming in the moonlight. I tried to bend sideways to reach the back of his knees. "Keep still," he whispered; "I don't want to drop you." And then I felt him enter me, and I felt my insides swell with warmth, and when I felt the warm, wet liquid spurting inside me, I felt healed. Deep inside, a high, wailing voice stopped crying and fell back into a deep sleep. Frank lowered me to the ground. We were panting. "Do you want a handkerchief?" he asked me. I said I had one in my pocket. I dried myself with it and then looked around for a stream to wash it out in. "Do you still want to go to the field?" Frank asked me. "Yes," I said; "I do." "Then wait until you get there and we'll wash things out then." I nodded and we started off.

It had only rained lightly the day before and the ground in the clearing was damp. I said I didn't mind it and lay down, reaching for Frank. He lay down beside me. "I feel like *years* have passed since I was last here," I said. He lay quietly, looking up at the cloudy sky. "But I'm back now," I said, turning over and kissing him on the mouth. "I guess you are back," he said, turning toward me and I felt, with relief, his hand tugging my skirt upward and I arched my back so that he could push my skirt out of his way entirely and then our bodies locked together again. "I didn't know if you'd come back," he said later. "Not come back?" I asked; "and leave you here alone? You must have been out of your mind." I traced the line of his eyebrow, then the line of his cheekbone and ran my finger down his chin and under it, along his neck.

"I got my job back," I said; "Mrs. James took me back embroidering. I'm on a different floor and I don't like it as much but I get paid more." "Good," Frank said. "The only bad thing is," I said, "I won't be able to come out to the quarries with you." "That's just as well," said Frank, "your lungs fill up with dust just like everyone else's." "If you go out on weekends, I can come with you." He nodded. "Are you still going out on the weekends, or are you going to church instead?" I asked. "I've been going to church," Frank said, "but I guess I'm not fit to be there." "I'll go to church with you," I said, "if you'd rather go to church." "No," he said, "I wouldn't." "Good," I said.

"You know," I said, rolling toward him and propping myself up on one elbow, "I feel so fortunate to be back. I can't imagine what made me leave. You are so wonderful," I said, lying back down and stretching my arm across his chest; "there's no one in the world like you. I could never love anyone else like this. I'd follow you everywhere if I could. I'd never leave you alone even for a second. And you have no faults! I wish you had some so I could show you how little they mattered to me! Oh, I know what the iron feels like when the magnet pulls it. You don't know what it's like to be in love with you! It's like being crazy. I forget how to talk. You could tell me to do anything except to stop loving you. It's like a flood. There's no limit to anything when you're nearby. It's wonderful," I said, sinking down on him. I could feel his heart pounding beneath me.

"I don't think I could love anyone like that," Frank said at last. A cold chill raised bumps on my skin. "Don't say that," I said; "you will." "I don't think so," he said. I pushed myself back up and looked at him. "Don't worry," he said; "I don't think I want to love anyone like that. I'm not sure I want anyone to love me that much." "Why not?" I asked quietly. I had gone cold with fear. "What do you think you want? Do you want to marry someone you'll love a little better than your favorite pipe? That's what most people's loves are like." "I *am* most people," Frank said. "No, you're not," I insisted; "you know you're not. We talked about this before." "I have a talent for stonework," he said, "not for love." "Stop it!" I cried; "you love me. You know you do!"

"What about you?" Frank asked, sitting up. "Why should you be willing to marry me when you know I don't love you the way you love me? Isn't that as bad as marrying a woman who doesn't love you much more than she loves her knives and forks?" "No, it's not as bad," I said, starting to cry, "because I know there's no one else in the world I'll ever love. If I can't have you, I won't have anyone. I *can't* love anyone else. And," I said, choking down a sob, "I know I can make you love me as much as I love you." In the darkness, Frank made an impatient gesture. "Even if I can't," I said, "it doesn't matter. I love you so much that you wouldn't have to love me at all."

"What does that mean?" Frank asked me. "It means that no matter what happens, I'll always love you as much as I love you now, and if things go wrong, I'll still love you as much, and after a while, you'll see, you'll see that there's nothing else in the world you can trust as much or rely on as much; there's no one who cares for you as much and who doesn't change from day to day, and you'll change, just because I love you, and either you'll start to love me the same way or you won't. It won't matter, because the way I love you will *never* change. It can't." "Everything changes," Frank said. "Not this!" I cried. "All right," Frank said; "we'll see. I'm afraid you'll be disappointed. When you see I can't love you the same way, you'll . . ." He hesitated. "I'll what?" I asked. "You'll turn on me," he said. "I'll never turn on you again," I said. "I wish I could love you the same way," he said; "I wish I could love anything the same way." "You will," I said, bending over and kissing him on the lips. He started to turn his head away, gave in and turned back to me, but this time, when his arms closed around me, I felt fear, cold and hard as metal.

When we got back to the boardinghouse, Frank seemed to assume that we would both sleep in his room. I was, I told myself, worrying about nothing. I should have waited until I was back longer, until he was used to having me back. It did not do to jump on people when they weren't expecting you. My intensity had frightened him. That was all it was. But after we got into bed, and after Frank had fallen asleep, I lay awake, listening to him breathe. He couldn't have meant what he said; he couldn't believe he wanted someone to love him less than I did. Finally, I got up, took my watch over to the window and tilted it toward the moonlight. It was three-thirty in the morning. I had to sleep. I had to work in the morning. But I could not sleep and the darkness was beginning to frighten me. I was afraid to look at the window, as if I expected to see a face there. I scolded myself, telling myself that I was too old for this childish nonsense, but it did no good.

Finally, I gave up. I turned over and shook Frank's shoulder. "Wake up," I said; "I want to talk to you." "What time is it?" he asked, not opening his eyes. "Almost four in the morning," I said. "What's the matter?" he asked. "You didn't mean it, did you?" I asked; "you didn't mean you didn't want me to love you so much?" "Oh, Agnes," he sighed, "go to sleep." "Say you didn't mean it," I insisted. "I don't know what I meant," he said. "Tell me you love me as much as you used to," I said. "I love you as much as I used to," he said; "now can we go to sleep?" "I'm serious," I said; "it's important to me. I have to know." "I have to sleep," Frank said, "but you don't seem interested in that." "Tell me you want me to love you," I repeated. "I want you to love me, all right? Go to sleep." "Say you don't want me to love you less," I said. "Agnes," he said, "I'll say anything you want if I can get some sleep." "All right," I said; "you go to sleep and I'll lie here staring at the ceiling." Frank propped himself up on his elbow.

"Look, Agnes," he said, "I didn't mean to say anything to upset you. I love you. You love me. You knocked me off, coming back suddenly like that. That's all." "Are you sure?" "I'm sure," he said. "You're not just saying that so you can get back to sleep?" "No, I'm not," he said; "if you want to stay up all night and talk about it, let me know and I'll get up." "Don't be silly," I said; "I know you have to get some sleep." "So do you," he said; "lie down and I'll put my arm around you." I lay down and turned on my side and Frank put his arm around me. "Go right to sleep," I told him; "you have to get up early." I could feel him shaking his head.

And so we settled into a life that was the very image of the life we had lived together before I returned to North Chittendon, and if anyone had asked me what had changed, what made me watch Frank out of the corner of my eye as if he might be up to something dangerous, what made me open my eyes slowly every morning, as if I suspected the day of treachery and the ground of shifting beneath my feet, I would have been unable to say. Often enough, I found myself thinking about Charlie and wishing that I had been able to fall in love with him; then I would turn on myself and ask myself why Charlie should seem preferable to Frank in any way. I remembered how, when I spent time with Charlie, I always felt as if I were divided into two creatures, hopelessly strange to one another, and I could not understand why I regretted the course my life had taken. And then there were days when I woke up convinced that Frank did not love me at all and that he had not yet realized it, but he would eventually and then he would turn away from me and I would not be able to make him turn back.

And I went over it constantly. What made me so sure anything, much less everything, had changed? In the mornings, we ate our breakfasts together and joked with Polly. In the evenings, we drifted outside after supper and wandered through the fields beyond the city. As the nights grew colder, we stayed in our rooms, sketching and reading, and sometimes I worked on Polly's sunburst quilt. She was definitely to be married a week before Christmas, and I wanted the quilt ready by then. While Frank worked, I watched his face. It hadn't changed. Yet when he looked at me, I believed he didn't really see me. When we lay together at night, there was something purposeless in our pleasure.

We began to go to my room because I had the stove and the house was cold. Sometimes we would sleep there until morning because we did not want to give up the heat. One morning in October, Frank woke up first and I saw him standing in front of the little obelisk on my dresser. "Where did this come from?" he asked. "It's been right there since I came back from North Chittendon," I said. I was wondering how cold the floor would be and if I wanted to put a towel down on it before I stood up. "Charlie made it, didn't he?" Frank said. "Who else would have made it?" I asked; "you must have seen him working on it. Anyway," I said, pulling on a thick black woolen stocking, "I told you he gave it to me when he came down to our house." "No, you didn't," Frank said. "You just don't remember," I said, standing up. I had on nothing but my black stockings; once they were on, I felt warm. I sat down on the bench in front of the mirror and began brushing my hair. "Put something on, for God's sake," Frank said. "Why?" I asked; "no one's going to walk in here." "Suppose Polly came in?" he asked. "Polly knocks first," I said, brushing my hair back, away from my face. "Doesn't that hair drive you crazy?" he asked me; "some mornings when I wake up, it's lying over your face like a shroud." "I don't want to cut it," I said; "I've always had it. I wouldn't know myself in the mirror without it." "Oh, it's beautiful," he said, "but it's not very practical."

"Practical for what?" I asked. "Well, at night you're always turning over on it or lying on it or getting it in your mouth and after you wash it you have to sit around for hours waiting for it to dry." "I have nothing else to do," I said; "here. Take the brush." Frank took the brush and worked on the hair which fell beneath my shoulders. "I help you brush your hair and Polly helps you wash it," he said; "don't you think it's a lot of trouble?" "No," I said; "I could do it myself if I had to. But I don't." I wondered suddenly about Jane Holt's hair. It must be thin and short, I thought. "You like this hair well enough," I said, starting to pin it up, "when you want to sketch me for an angel or a statue of Niobe. Angels don't look right with close-cropped hair." "I think," said Frank with an abstracted air, "I'm going to try cherubs for a while. They have little ringlets." "Go borrow someone's baby," I said, standing up and pulling my skirt on over my head. "Why don't you get dressed from the inside out, like other people?" Frank asked. "Is that how other people get dressed?'' I asked; "I didn't know. I put the warm things on first. Everyone does who comes from a farm.'' "I guess,'' said Frank.

He was standing in front of the obelisk again. "He'll never get anywhere doing work like this,'' Frank said. "He gets far enough,'' I said. "If I hadn't come along,'' he asked me, "would you have married him?'' "No,'' I said; "I didn't love him.'' "You thought you did once,'' he said. "I was wrong,'' I said, lacing up my shoe. "What made you decide you wanted me?'' he asked. "Oh,'' I said lightly, picking up Polly's quilt and looking at it—it was almost done, but I needed some scraps of red—"I didn't decide. It was decided before I was even born. Somewhere up in the stars we were a little constellation and then everything got rearranged and we fell down here and wandered around until we met each other here.'' "Sometimes,'' said Frank, "I think you believe that nonsense.'' "I do,'' I said, folding up the quilt. "You didn't look at me and think I'd make a good husband or a good father, nothing like that?'' "Nothing like that,'' I said cheerfully. "I could fix the ivy leaves on this thing,'' Frank said, turning back to the obelisk. "You leave that alone!'' I said.

In November, some men were waiting for Frank when I came home from work and Polly took me into the parlor and said she thought they had come all the way from New York and wanted Frank to come with them. She saw the expression on my face and asked me what was wrong and I said my head hurt. It had begun hurting as soon as she told me about the men from New York. They had nothing to do with us. *I* was the one who would persuade Frank to go to New York; they could only interfere. Frank came home and the men went up to him, and from the kitchen, I watched him talking to them. They smiled a great deal; they offered him cigars and little, flat packages wrapped in gold foil. Their vests sported heavy gold watch chains and their shoes shone and reflected the lights in the room. There were four of them and they were all plump and jolly in their manner; it was clear enough that they were rich. I hated them. I was afraid they might take Frank from me. He might not want to take me. He might want to go to New York first and find a place to live and ask me to wait and come down later. I never wanted to be separated from him again. Frank came into the kitchen and told me that he had to go with the men to the Montpelier Inn to talk about business and he'd be back late but he would stop by and see if I was awake. "If I'm not awake,'' I said, "wake me up.''

He went into the parlor while I watched from my post behind the kitchen door.

I went into Polly's room after dinner. "I can't bear it," I said, throwing myself into her chair; "I wish I were dead." "What's wrong with you now?" she asked. She held up a darning egg with a blue sock drawn over it. "Oh, give that to me," I said; "you're hopeless at darning." "Did anything in particular happen," she asked me, "or have you just gotten tired of this vale of tears?" "He's going to go to New York with them and leave me here," I said; "I'd rather die." "You'd always rather die," she said; "you'd rather die than think about spending a day by yourself. You're worse than you were before you went home." "You don't understand," I said. "You're right," she said; "I don't." "Here," I said, throwing the darning egg into her lap, "it's all done." "Don't throw things with needles in them," she said; "anyway, you two wanted to go to New York." "That was before," I said; "things are different now." "I don't see how," said Polly; "he's always with you." "I don't know how either," I said, "but they are. He complains. My hair is too long. I get dressed from the outside in. He doesn't think I should steal cloth from Mrs. James even though everyone else does. He gets these queer attacks of righteousness. He doesn't think he wants to carve any more angels. He thinks he wants to carve cherubs." "So what?" asked Polly; "he can't go on sculpting you forever. It's ridiculous to be jealous of a cherub." "Who cares about the cherub?" I flared up; "he can go around carving snakes and goldenrod. He's tired of me. That's what it means." "I don't see it," Polly said, considering another sock. "Give me *all* the socks," I said, exasperated; "I can't talk and watch you make a mess of them." She threw the things over to me. "Don't throw things with needles," I mocked in a high, childish voice. "Well, I shouldn't have," she said.

I worked away on the socks. "Don't you have any black thread?" I asked, and she threw the spool over. "He wants someone easier," I said; "he wants someone who won't love him so much." "Did he say that?" Polly asked. "Yes," I said; "at least he said he thought he didn't want someone who loved him so much." "When?" she asked. "Right after I came back." "Does he keep saying it?" she asked. "No," I said, "he doesn't." "He was just put out because you went home," she said. "You always see everything in the most cheerful light," I said; "why is that? Is it laziness or stupidity?" "It's neither, Agnes," she said, "and I'm not going to fight with you, so you

might as well pull in your claws. It's experience, that's all."
"It's your experience that things always work out for the best?"
I asked, astounded. "If you wait long enough," she said, "they
do." "If you wait long enough, they dress you up nicely and
give you a shiny box of your own if that's your idea of a happy
ending," I said. "That is *not* my idea of a happy ending," she
said.

I got up and walked over to the window. There was no one on
the street. "I don't know if I can keep it up," I said suddenly.
"Keep what up?" Polly asked. "Work," I said; "I'm not there
ten minutes and I start to get the blues and the next thing I know,
I'm falling asleep over my work and my fingers feel like they're
made out of lead. The only good part of the day is fighting with
Lilian. By the time I go down to find Florence, I'm dizzy. My
head hurts and I'm sick to my stomach. All I want to do is come
home and go to sleep. I could stay in here for weeks and not
come out if I didn't have to eat." Polly sat up and looked at me.
"That's not good, Agnes," she said; "there are people like that
in Highbury." "Love-sick," I said softly. "They don't call it
that," she said. "I don't know what to do," I said, starting to
cry. "Don't do anything," she said, getting off the bed and
standing behind my chair; "just keep going. Everything will
work out one way or another. That's the whole secret—just
going on. One foot in front of the other. *You* expect to jump right
off the earth and pull down whatever you want, right out of the
sky, and then when you can't do it, you turn all blue and cloudy.
Try not to think about Frank. Do things by yourself." "Like
what?" I asked; "I already walk all over the place by myself
when he comes home late." "Stay in the room and try drawing," she said; "that's what you said you wanted to do."

"I can't," I said. "Why not?" she asked. "I'm too tired. I
look at the paper and start to fall asleep." "Force yourself,"
Polly said. "I can't," I said. "Can you see him?" I asked her.
"No," she said, "he wouldn't be coming in the back way
anyhow." "Oh, I wish I were dead!" I cried; "I can't stand
worrying anymore!" "I wonder what Frank would say when he
tripped over the body," she said. "Is he coming?" I said,
jumping up. "No, he's not coming," she said impatiently; "but
I'm going to bed. Cheer up. Read something." I picked up her
copy of *The Other Woman*; or, *A Young Girl Fallen*. "The other
books are more cheerful," Polly said, "but I suppose that's no
recommendation." I said it wasn't and went back to my room.

I heard the men shouting in the livery stable. I heard the

animals whinny and stamp. I heard the voices dying out in the house and the footsteps, one by one, going down the hall and not returning, doors slamming and not opening again, and I lay down on the bed. If he went to New York with them, if he left without coming back here, I would follow him there. He would not go without me. He woke me out of a confused dream in which I had taken a chisel to a cherub's head and was methodically chipping off its curls while people raved behind me and trains were late or had already left.

"What did they want?" I asked, sitting bolt upright. He sat down next to me and smiled. "They want me to do some work for them," he said; "one of them saw one of my angels this summer, and they want me to do as many as ten statues for them. Angels, lambs, weeping willows, anything I want. They have a lot of money. I didn't know people had that much money." "Are you going to do it?" "Why not?" he asked; "it won't change anything. I'll stay on at the quarries and work there. It's a year's work, maybe more." "You look pleased with yourself," I said. "I am," he said; "aren't you pleased with me? You're the one who thought I was better than the others." "You don't have to go to New York?" "No, but I could go after I finish," he said; "we'd have enough money." "We would?" I asked. "Plenty," he said. "Agnes, I know it's late. Let's go for a walk and celebrate." I got up and put my bearskin cape on over my nightgown and slid my feet into a pair of boots and we clumped down the stairs. It was impossible to wake anyone in the house. Everyone worked so hard during the day.

"I don't believe it," Frank said as we walked along, "to come all the way out here. Just to find me!" "I'm not surprised," I said; "I said so from the start." "You were just biased," he said, putting his arm around me. "I still am," I said.

"Are we going all the way out to the field?" I asked him. In the darkness owls were hooting back and forth. The moon was only a china chip in the high, domed sky. "Do you want to?" he asked me and I said I did. "Well, how will they arrange it?" I asked him when we got there. "Will you ship the things down when you're finished, or will they come for them?" "I'll ship them down," he said; "there's no reason for me to go." "But the people who commissioned the stones might want to meet you," I said. Frank sighed. "Well, *I* would," I said, "if I paid a lot for a statue and someone special did it." "That's the only trouble," Frank said. "What is?" I asked. "I do the sculpting and I ship the stones down, but they carve their own names on the stones," he said. "They carve the names on the stones?" I asked. "No," he said, "they sign their names to the stones. The way a painter signs a painting." "What?" I asked; "they sign your stones?" "Those were their terms." "And you agreed to them?" I asked; "you agreed to let them steal your work?" "They're not exactly stealing anything," Frank said; "they're paying me a heavy price. I'll get to work with better stones and designs than before. It's a great opportunity." "For them!" I cried.

"I shouldn't have told you," he said. "Write them and tell them you'll be glad to do the work, but you want to put your own name on it," I said. "I'm not doing any such thing," said Frank. "Even these *stumps* are signed with the children's right names!" I exclaimed. "It's not the same thing," he said; "maybe later, I'll go down to New York and find where they put the statuary and let people know I did it." "How stupid can you be?" I demanded; "they'll never let you near that statuary once they put their names on it. You'll never see any of it again! I bet if you go down there and try to find out where your statues went, they'd have you arrested." "Don't be silly," he said. "They would!" I shouted. "Agnes," he said, "what do you want me to do? It's a good opportunity. It's not perfect. But I'll get experience and we'll have the money to go to New York." "You can't start compromising!" I insisted.

"I don't think of it as a compromise," he said; "I'll still do the carving. That's the most important thing. I'm not as ambitious as you are. I'm not as confident as you are." "I'm not confident about myself," I said; "I'm confident about *you*." "Look, Agnes," he said, "let's drop it. I'm going to do it. If I'm so good, I can be good in New York one year later." "I won't let you do it!" I said without thinking. "How are you going to stop me?" he asked. "All I meant was that you shouldn't do it," I said. "Well," he said, "I don't agree with you. I thought you'd be happy about it." "I'm not," I said icily. "You could ask them to change the terms." "They won't. That was the whole point of coming so far. They want someone who'll let them claim the work as their own." "You could try," I insisted. "No," he said, "I couldn't." I sat silently, rage tightening my body.

"You know, Agnes," Frank said at last, "maybe it would be better if I moved into another boardinghouse and we didn't see each other so much. I get on your nerves. You know I do. I'm always disappointing you. I'm perfectly happy about this new arrangement with the New York sculptors, but you're not. Maybe if we lived in different places for a while, we'd get along better." "Don't you love me anymore?" I asked. I didn't recognize my own voice. "I love you," he said; "I just think it might be better if we didn't live in the same house." "Why?" I asked; "would it be easier for you to see Jane Holt?" "Who told you about Jane?" he asked. "I've known about her from the beginning," I said; "is that why you want to move, to be near her?" "Jane has nothing to do with this," he said; "I hardly ever see her." "That's not what the girls say," I told him. "The girls," he said contemptuously; "it always surprised me that you didn't listen to everything the girls said." "Well," I said, "they knew about Jane." Frank stood up and looked out through the trees toward the field. "I told you," he said; "Jane has nothing to do with this."

"Do you love Jane?" I asked him. He didn't answer. "Are you going to marry her?" "I'm not talking to you about Jane," he said; "she's just a girl I know from church. That's enough." "You wouldn't move out, would you?" I asked; "not really?" Frank shook his head and stared toward the field. "All this nonsense about your wanting me to love you less," I said uncontrollably; "that's all it is. You don't *want* anyone to love you." "You're starting again," Frank said; "you said you wouldn't do this again." "*You* said we'd never be separated again!" "Just for a while," he said. "Is that what you told Jane?" "I'll ask around at the quarries for a place to stay," Frank said.

And then I thought about the quarries; the sheds filled with stone after stone, the heavy marble dust sifting slowly down through the golden wintry light. I saw myself sitting in back of Frank while he bent over his stone; I saw the powdery light paint gold swatches over his red plaid shirt and I started to cry. "Don't cry," said Frank; "it's the best thing." "No, it isn't," I said; "if you move out, I'll kill myself." "Don't threaten me, Agnes," he said; "it won't do any good." "I'm not threatening you," I said; "if you leave, I'll kill myself. That's all." "You're hysterical," he said without sympathy. "Well, I guess you're used to girls threatening to kill themselves for you!" I cried; "but I will! I know how!" "You'd shoot yourself?" he asked me; "you don't have a gun." "I'll steal yours some night when you're sleeping and I'll shoot myself."

"Not me?" he asked, as if he were genuinely curious. "Shoot you!" I sobbed; "I'd never shoot you! I love you!" "I can't live

378

this way," Frank said; "if every time we have an argument you threaten to kill yourself, it's impossible." "I won't threaten," I said; "if you'll stay. I'll never say that again." I sensed his wavering and I began sobbing uncontrollably. I knew that no matter what he said he could not bear tears. "But it might be much better," he said in a lost voice; "we're together too much. We might have less trouble if we weren't always in each other's hair." "I'd rather die," I sobbed. "Then forget about it," Frank said bitterly; "I'll stay." I locked my arms around his waist and cried on. "You can't keep me that way forever," he said; "if we're not happy, we can't keep on like this." "We'll be happy," I said. The little piece of moon, like a chip of eggshell, shone in the sky over us.

After that, it seemed as if Frank was always working. At home, in our rooms, he sketched and resketched the figures he intended to carve. He stayed later and later at the quarries, working by kerosene lamp. I barely arrived at Mrs. James's on time because every morning I was afflicted by wrenching nausea or a pounding headache and then I had to fight to finish out the day. Now, when I stopped at the Emporium, I looked at the patent medicine display first. Every day, I arrived at work with a new nerve powder or a new headache cure, but none of them worked. A week before my birthday came, Frank gave me a beautiful plum-colored hat decorated with ostrich plumes. "Did you pick it out yourself?" I asked, trying it on. "No," he said, "Mr. Holt knew who you were and I asked him to pick out something suitable."

I put the hat down on the bed and looked at him bewildered. "Mr. Holt?" I said; "Jane Holt's father?" Frank nodded. "Doesn't he know who I am? I mean, doesn't he know about us?" "I don't know," said Frank; "he was glad to help." I put the hat back on. Even Frank was not cold-blooded enough to buy a hat for one girlfriend from the father of another if he was up to something. Perhaps, I thought, this was his way of telling Jane I was the only one he cared for.

That week, when it was not snowing, I arrived at work in the hat. Probably it was the hat which set Lilian off. "You look like you came out of one of the theatricals," she said when I first came in wearing it. "Thank you," I said, sitting down. "Where did you get it?" she asked. She sounded as if she suspected me of trapping it in the woods. "A present," I said, taking out the pins and laying the hat down in front of me. "It's from the Emporium," she said; "I know. I saw it there." "Good for you," I said. I reached into the depths of my pocket. Some dry lint and three different brands of headache powders. I would take all of them at noon. "I saw your friend Frank Holt a few nights ago," she said. I nodded. I would give myself three minutes before I began embroidering the velvet mantle scarf which was to be my lot for the next two or three days. "He's with Jane Holt again," Lilian said. "He's been working late," I said, taking off my cape and letting it fall over the chair in back of me. "I guess he can't work without company," she said. "What do you mean?" I asked. "Well, maybe that's what you call work," she said, "walking all around the Commons."

She went on talking, but I no longer heard her. My head was throbbing and I was afraid that if I moved suddenly I would begin vomiting. "I'm sorry," I said, "I have a touch of the flu." "The flu nothing," Lilian said; "you don't like hearing about Jane." Jane! She spoke of her so familiarly, as if she were real. "How do you know her?" I asked. "We went to the same school," Lilian said; "but she only works for families her parents approve of. She's working for the Ludlums on Cherry Street. I wouldn't mind working for the Ludlums. You should see Mr. Ludlum." "What's she like?" I asked, finally picking up the heavy purple velvet on which I was embroidering white pansies. "Like everyone else," Lilian said; "boring." "Is she pretty?" I asked. "Like everyone else in town," Lilian said; "not very pretty. When she fixes up her hair and puts on a good dress, she's not the ugliest thing you've ever seen." "Frank says she's very religious," I said, as if we were in the habit of discussing her. "I guess she's religious enough," said Lilian; "you know the type. When she has time off, she's in the parlor embroidering a sampler, and the legend says, 'Be Not Weary in Well Doing.' " I nodded. I knew the type. She was the type to congratulate Frank on his New York commissions; she was not the type to threaten to kill herself if he told her he would not be seeing her for a while. I had to find Frank. I looked at my watch, but it was only ten o'clock.

When I was walking home, I saw Charlie in front of me and ran down the street until I caught up with him. "Hello," he said. "Hello," I said; "where's Frank?" "Frank?" he asked surprised. "Frank," I said, "your friend." "Didn't he tell you he was working late?" Charlie asked, his face flushing. "I guess he forgot," I said, trying not to begin crying right then and there. I had never been so disappointed. "He's pretty puffed up about these new commissions," Charlie said. "I don't know why," I said, "not if he can't put his own name to them." "Still," said Charlie, "it's a compliment, being asked. They didn't ask me." "If they'd asked you, would you have done it?" "Probably," said Charlie; "but it's a different story, my carving is. I'm not proud of it. Anyone could claim to have done it. In fact, I wish someone would."

"Does he work alone out there?" I asked, abruptly changing the subject. "I guess he does," Charlie answered slowly. "Is it safe?" I asked him; "out there in the middle of nowhere?" "You know Frank," Charlie said; "he always has his gun." "It must be lonely out there," I said. "He's got all those women standing around on pedestals," Charlie said. "Maybe I should go out and keep him company." "No, Agnes," Charlie said, "I wouldn't do that. It isn't safe groping around there at night." I said I guessed it wasn't. We were in front of Mrs. Trowbridge's house. I said good-bye and turned in, then stood on the front step watching Charlie go out of sight.

I went upstairs, hung my hat on a wall peg, and lay down on the bed. My eyes would not focus properly. Every now and then the objects of my room slid apart as if they were really composed of two layers, as if the world were preparing to double itself. It was the suspense that was making me sick. I had not felt right since Frank had mentioned wanting to move and I felt worse now. It occurred to me that he had begun working later and later almost immediately after our quarrel over the statuary and I began to rethink the matter of the hat. Perhaps he and Mr. Holt were on very good terms and Mr. Holt believed whatever Frank told him. Once I had believed whatever he told me. Probably Frank had told him that I was an old friend or a cousin or Charlie's sister. He could lie easily. I had seen him do it. I got up and went down for supper. Polly would be getting married in less than two weeks. Her family had refused to attend a wedding held in a lunatic asylum, and Iris had offered her the use of the boardinghouse, even though Polly said it was only trading one asylum for another. I asked her why she didn't want to be married at home, and she said that the house in Massachusetts had never been built back up after the chimney fire two years ago and it wasn't fit place for a wedding. So her family and Eddie's were coming to Montpelier. I was to be her maid of honor and I was going to wear a dark rose brocade dress I had almost finished. Her wedding quilt was packed neatly in a white carton. I didn't want anything to spoil her wedding. I would find out what Frank was doing, and if there was anything to be done, I would do it later.

I sat down quickly, almost overturning my chair. "What's wrong with you now?" Polly said; "can't you see?" "Headache," I said; "the powders don't help." "I know they don't," Polly said; "they make you worse. Where's Frank?" "He's supposed to be working late," I said; "try to stop that biscuit platter when it goes by. I don't think I can eat anything else." "What do you mean supposed to be?" Polly asked. "I think he's working, all right," I said; "on Jane Holt." I told her about the quarrel we had over the New York sculptors. "Oh, Agnes," she said, "you are an idiot! Why couldn't you have let him be happy?" "Because," I said angrily, "it's not fair. They shouldn't be stealing his work. He's a fool to let them do it." "I suppose you told him that," Polly said. I said I also told him I'd kill myself if he moved out.

"You didn't!" Polly said, putting down her fork; "don't you know that's the surest way to get rid of someone! You are a fool!" "I mean it," I said softly. "Then you're even more of a fool," she said; "you don't think Frank would kill himself if both you and Jane ran off with his best friend, do you? He'd go right on with his work, and next week he'd have someone else waiting for him." "No, he wouldn't," I said. Polly bent over to me and whispered into my ear. "You stop thinking that way!" she said; "you keep that up and you won't have to visit me in Highbury after I get married. I'll have to come and visit you there in the locked ward." "I'm not killing myself yet," I said. "I told you to stop that and I meant it," Polly said, flushing. "Thinking of killing yourself over a man who asks you to marry him and then goes around with someone else! If that's what he's doing, you'll be well rid of him." "I don't think so," I said. "Eat," said Polly; "I'm disgusted with you." When we finished eating, I told her I was going out for a walk. "Where?" she asked suspiciously; "Cherry Street? Where Jane Holt works?" "No," I said, "just a walk."

But I went to the livery stable and asked Mr. Emmett if I could hire a horse for four or five hours. And then I rode past the courthouse, the two churches, their bells tolling eight as I passed, the train whistle sounding like a desolate beast behind the hills, and galloped along toward the quarries. I tied the horse up at the foot of the hill and climbed up to the stone sheds. I was wearing my black dress and moved among the trees like a living shadow. The quarries were silent and deserted; the moon was hidden behind the candlelit clouds. I knew the paths. If I had been less familiar with them, I would have been frightened. When I came to Frank's stone shed, I walked along its side toward the back. The brilliant yellow stain of kerosene light spilled itself out on the snow. I moved quietly and slowly, pressing myself against the outer wall of the building. I heard someone laugh and I bent forward cautiously. Frank was standing in back of a half-carved angel which had stepped thigh-deep from the pink marble he worked on, and leaning against the angel's feet was a small, slender blond girl who I knew immediately was Jane Holt. I watched her take a banana from a paper bag, peel it, and offer it to Frank. He shook his head and bent over the stone. So it was all true. I had always known it.

When I was back on the main road I dropped the reins and let the horse find his own pace. I knew we were reaching town when I heard a church bell tolling, and then I realized that someone important must have died, because it was tolling without a stop. Cherry Street. That was, I thought, the last street before the fields on the edge of town. I rode over to Cherry Street and looked at the houses. There were only three of them. I remembered someone saying that the Ludlum house was painted blue and had black shutters and I saw it was the house on the corner. I reined in the horse, turned around, and went back to the livery stable. I paid Mr. Emmett and went back into Iris's and up into Frank's room.

There was the red and white plush album, sitting as it always had, in the middle of the dresser. I turned it over, opened it, and took out three sheets of paper, three envelopes, and dipped the quill pen into the little ink bottle. Then I sat down and began to write. If Frank came in and found me at this, he would be furious and we would begin to fight. I *wanted* to fight, and this time, I wouldn't make any mistakes. I would say whatever I needed to say to get him back.

"Dear Jane Holt," I wrote, "the girls say you are receiving the attentions of a very bad fellow named Frank Holt. Possibly he calls upon you because he thinks it is nice you have the same last name. But you ought to know that he is already spoken for. He has been engaged to another girl for over a year and a half. He has gotten two girls in trouble, one here and one in Canada too. He boasts that he will get many another girl into trouble before he is done. I guess he will take you out to the quarries and get you in trouble there as he has done this to all of us before. He will not rest until he has undone you altogether. The girls say you are a good girl so I am writing to warn you. I guess you already know that what I am saying is true." I looked at it and was pleased with it, and signed it, "More sinned against than sinning."

Then I made another copy addressed to Mrs. Holt and a third for Mr. Holt. Mrs. Holt's would go to the house on Willow Drive, Mr. Holt's to the Emporium. I addressed the three envelopes, folded the letters, and slipped the sheets inside. There was no point in sealing them; I wanted everyone in the world to read them. Then I went back to my room, slid the three envelopes between the pages of my grandmother's photograph album, and got into bed. When Frank slipped into bed next to me, I pretended to be asleep. I would think of a way to start an argument soon enough, I thought, falling asleep. In the morning I mailed the letters, and then I settled down and waited. For the first time in weeks, my head was not aching.

The next evening, Frank came into the dining room, saw me, and asked me to come into the parlor with him. "What's wrong?" I asked; "aren't you hungry?" "I'm hungry," he said; "have you been writing letters?" I said I'd written to my father a few weeks ago and I supposed I should have written again. "That's not what I meant," he said; "have you been writing to Jane Holt?" I said I didn't even know Jane Holt. "Well, someone's been writing to her about me," he said, watching my face; "someone called 'More sinned against than sinning.'" "Can you find out who it is?" I asked. "I want to know you're not doing it," he said. "Why?" I asked; "is Jane Holt so important to you?" "No," he said, "but you are." "I'm not doing it," I said cheerfully. "Good," said Frank. "But if someone's writing her about you," I said, "they must have a reason. Do you see her?" "I don't want to talk about it," Frank said. "I don't want you to see anyone else but me," I said to him; "we're engaged." "I can't promise you that, Agnes," he said. "But you have to promise me," I said; "we're engaged." "Maybe not anymore," he said in a low voice. "You'll always be engaged to me," I said, staring at him. "*Did* you write those letters?" he asked. "No," I said.

"Look, Agnes," he said, "I told you I'd go on living here, but I'm not going to promise I won't see anyone else. And don't threaten to kill yourself. It won't do any good." "It might," I said; "I don't have to take the world on its own terms. Maybe you do but I don't." "Do what you want," he said; "you will anyway." "Don't you love me anymore?" I asked. "Not the way I used to," he said; "no." "You just stopped?" I asked. My voice was calm. Someone else was speaking, using my voice. "I've just fallen out of love with you," he said; "I don't know why." "*When* did you fall out of love with me?" I asked; "when I had the abortion?" "No," he said, "not then." "Then when?" I demanded; "you must remember when it happened. It's the least you could do!" "Well," he said, his cheeks sucking in—he must have been biting them—"when you went home to North Chittendon." "But I went home because I was so upset!" I cried; "I didn't want to trouble you!" "You went home because you didn't want to see me," Frank said; "be honest for once." "Be honest!" I exclaimed; "I'm always honest!" "You didn't want to get away from me when you went home?" he asked. "No," I said. "If telling yourself lies cheers you up, keep doing it," Frank said to me.

"So you took up with Jane Holt because *I* didn't love *you* anymore?" I asked, incredulous. "Something like that," Frank said, regarding me coldly. "And you tell me *I* lie to myself?" "You do," he said; "you don't begin to be honest." "I *never* lie!" I insisted. "We all lie," he said, "especially about ourselves. If we want to live with ourselves." He was looking at me with something suspiciously like pity. "You started to see Jane Holt while I was home?" I asked. "Yes," he said impatiently, "I did. But it's nothing serious." "You haven't decided which one of us you want?" I asked sarcastically. "Not really," Frank said, uneasily. "*How* will you make up your mind?" I asked. Frank raised his eyebrows. He pressed his hand to the window-pane; when he took his hand away, the prints of his five fingers and his palm had melted the ice crystals on the pane. "I thought I'd let some time go by," he said. "And what am I supposed to do while time is going by?" I asked. "If you don't want to wait, you don't have to," he said. "That's not fair," I said; "you know I'll wait. You know I'll do whatever you want." He shrugged slightly.

"You can't mean what you're saying!" I burst out; "you promised me everything would be the same. We are getting married." "No," he said, "we're not. At least, right now we're not. I'll stay with you but I don't want to get married. Maybe I will later. Maybe I won't. Maybe *you* won't want to get married."

For an instant the words he said made no sense. They were strange words, syllables in an animal babble. And then for an instant I saw us from above and we were two puppets, two mechanical machines, and behind us the wheels turned and lifted our arms and legs and put words in our mouths which spilled out and ruined us, and all the while the wheels turned in response to something great and dark and ugly which floated overhead and decided our real futures which had always been waiting for us. And I stared at him, wondering why. All those nights together, all the joking, all the days at the quarries, it had all really happened. How could it all be undone? What could have poisoned past happiness and turned its course away from our future? Or did the past keep changing so that happy things unhappened and unhappened, as wool unravels, and finally the present is only an illusion, something imaginary, built on empty space?

"You'll never marry Jane Holt," I said. "I don't want to marry anyone," Frank said; "I'm not meant to be married." "You'll never marry Jane Holt," I said again; "if you marry, you'll marry me." He turned on his heel and went into the dining room.

I went back in and sat down next to Polly. I would not look at Frank. "What now?" she whispered to me. "I'll tell you later," I said. "Tell me now," she said. "He doesn't want to get married anymore," I said. "Then let him go," she said; "you can do better." "There is no one better," I whispered back.

37

Polly's wedding was two days off. I had prepared Mrs. James and she did not expect me back until after the wedding. Iris sent Frank to Charlie's and I slept in Polly's room with her so that we would have two extra rooms for the members of her family. Iris borrowed beds from friends and turned the attic into an impromptu dormitory. I helped Iris letter place cards and worked away in a corner on the special bridal cloth Iris had asked me to make for Polly; it was to be her present to her. Its borders were three inches wide, and each border represented Montpelier in a different season. Iris had insisted on having the cloth done in white on white. I thought it looked ugly and said so, but Iris said white on white was all the fashion, and Polly ought to have fashionable things. The napkins I had made her, I thought sadly, were also white on white. At least the sunburst quilt had all the colors of the rainbow. When I was not working on the wedding preparations, I thought about Frank, about how he no longer considered himself engaged to me, about how he was waiting for something to happen which would make it easier for him to decide which of the two of us he wanted, and while I thought, I cried. As soon as the wedding was over, I was going to go to Barre and buy a gun. Florence had moved to Barre to be closer to her father and I would tell anyone who asked that I was going to visit her, and then I would buy a pistol on my way to her house. I was tired of fighting for breath. I was tired of pretending that any stories in which I figured could ever end happily. If Frank wanted to be rid of me, he would be. But first I wanted to see Polly safely married.

The afternoon before the wedding, both Frank and Charlie arrived virtually invisible behind huge bunches of gladiolas, and we took the flowers away and began setting them up in vases throughout the parlor and dining room. "This is good of you, boys," said Iris. "Here," she said, pressing something into Charlie's hand, "go buy as many more as you can. I should have thought of it myself." Frank was attentive to me, even courtly. I paid little attention to him. I did not trust myself. I was afraid that I would stop the wedding in the middle and begin shouting that I too was supposed to be married, and there was no justice in the world and men could not be trusted and we should all go home. So I avoided him, and the more I stayed away, the more closely he followed me.

"Are you still upset?" he asked me. "Yes," I said, turning away and going into the kitchen. "You're taking it too hard," he said; "I didn't say it was for forever. I just don't want to get married now." "Well, you're not," I said, "so you don't have anything to worry about." Just that morning, I had mailed three more letters to the Holts. "I'll be right back after the wedding," he whispered to me. "You better tell that to Jane," I said, picking up the tablecloth and sitting down next to Iris, who was peeling carrots. "I'll see you later," Frank said. I nodded. One week, I thought. If he didn't change his mind within one week after the wedding, I was going to shoot myself. If I didn't shoot myself first, I would go talk to Jane Holt, and *then* I would shoot myself. Yes, that was it; talk to Jane Holt and then shoot myself. He wasn't going to marry her, not after I spoke to her. But what if she were deaf to reason? She might listen to me and go right on planning to marry him. Then I would have to use the gun. I would not stand by and watch the two of them destroy my life.

The next morning, Polly's family and Eddie's relatives arrived for an eleven o'clock wedding breakfast. The boarders had been served their own meal an hour earlier than usual, and in spite of their grumbling, had agreed to stay away from the downstairs rooms. We went through the rooms, adding water to the vases full of white gladiolas. We watered the pots of white geraniums which bordered an improvised set of steps, boards on bricks, covered with sheets. The wedding platform was made of slats which rested on top of neatly stacked bricks.

All of the eggs were cracked into their bowls. The butter sat in the middle of the huge frying pans. The toast, buttered and sugared and sprinkled with cinnamon, was cut into large triangles and laid out on platters. Pitchers were set out for milk and the large coffee pot was bubbling on the stove. A large tea kettle was already whistling and boxes of exotic tea from the Emporium were set out on one of the long tables near the cups and saucers. Trays of little sandwiches, their crusts removed, were everywhere. When Frank and Charlie came in, each carried two large bottles that they held by the neck like dead geese. "Champagne," they said, and Iris said she guessed we had better wash some more cups. And then it was time for me to go up and get dressed so that I could help Polly. The ceremony was to begin at one o'clock.

I went up to my room and began unfastening my black skirt. The rose brocade dress lay on the bed. I was curiously unwilling to get into it. I touched it gingerly. The material was thick and rich. I had made it well. I took off my black waist and laid it down on top of the skirt. First, I thought, I would brush my hair. Then the door opened and Frank walked in. "Is that what you're wearing?" he asked, looking at the dress on the bed. He wore a black rented suit and a boiled white shirt. His black tie was rich and knotted so that it resembled a scarf. "It's very pretty," he said. I said that he looked handsome himself. "If you give me the brush," he said, "I'll help you with your hair." I handed the brush to him. He worked away steadily and gently; often enough, when Polly helped me, she lost her temper and almost pulled my head from my neck. "Do you sleep with her?" I asked him. He stopped brushing my hair, then began again. "No," he said. "But you might later," I said. "I might later," he said, handing me the brush.

His hand rested on my shoulder. "What went wrong?" he asked me. His voice was thick with confusion; his head was tilted as if he were hoping to hear an answer from the air itself. "I don't know," I said; "do you?" In the mirror, I saw him shake his head. "Right now," he said, "it doesn't seem as if anything did happen." In the mirror, I watched his face. "If we could only stop time," he said. "Where would you stop it?" I asked him. "Here," he said. "Here?" I asked; "right now?" "Right now," he said. He was right. Right now, I was absolutely happy. He was once more the handsome, remarkable man I had first seen, the one who had saved me.

Then I looked down at my watch and saw it was almost twelve-thirty. "I have to get finished," I said; "I have to help Polly. She'll be here in a minute otherwise." "Do you think she'll be happy?" Frank asked me. "Of course she'll be happy," I said; "she can't imagine being unahppy. Besides, he loves her." "She loves him, too," Frank said. "I guess," I said, "she must. She's stuck to him long enough." "It's more than that, Agnes," he said. I took a deep breath and looked at my dress, lying on the bed. "I know," I said; "it's just a different kind of love." "That doesn't mean it isn't as good," Frank said. "I never said it wasn't, did I?" I asked. "Maybe we could go out walking after the wedding," he said. "Yes," I said, pinning the last braid in place; "I want to talk to you."

I went into Polly's room and she was sitting on her bed, crying. "What's wrong?" I asked. Polly never cried. "I'm going to miss it so much," she said, wiping her eyes, and then starting to cry again. "Miss what?" I asked. "All of it," she said; "the walls, the floor, the dresser. You." "Me?" I echoed; "you're going to miss me?" She nodded and continued crying. "Stop crying," I said; "you'll be all red and puffy for the ceremony." "It won't be the same there," she said, crying. "It will be better," I said. "Even if it's better," she said, "it still won't be the same. I hate change. I always want something better, but I never want anything to change." "Neither do I," I said; "neither does anyone. But you can't carry everything on your back like a snail. First you'd have to drag this boarding-house onto the grounds of the asylum and then you'd have to go back and get your family in Boston and soon there'd be no room for you. Things have to change." Polly blew her nose. "You always sound so sensible," she said, "when you're talking about someone else."

"Come on," I said, "get dressed." She was wearing a deep purple traveling dress with a high collar. The pleated collar stood out slightly from her neck. Her skirt was full, and black grosgrain bands divided it into panels. I had given her my hat; it matched her dress. "Well," I said, when she was dressed and sitting primly on her bed, "you look very lovely." "I look better," she said. "No," I said, "you look beautiful." And she did. It may have been her expectant air, it may have been the wide, round shadow of the hat which darkened half of her face, making her mysterious, even exotic, but she looked changed. "Stand up straight during the ceremony," I said. "Why?" she asked; "do I usually slump?" "You don't slump but you don't want to slouch down at your own wedding," I said. She looked at her watch. "Ten minutes," she said.

"You don't have any doubts?" I asked. "Well," she said, "if I were God, I wouldn't have cut the world from this pattern, but as long as this is how things are, I don't have any doubts. I've found the man I wanted. We're happy together. We want the same things." "What things?" I asked. "Children," she said, looking away from me, "a place of our own. We like helping people. We like to work hard. We like each other." "You're supposed to love each other," I said. "We were lucky," she said; "we liked each other first." "Do you still," I asked, "like him?" "He's my best friend," she said, standing up. I inspected her for dust, for threads, and when I found nothing, I took her hairbrush and brushed her off just in case.

I stood in back of Polly and Eddie while the minister performed the marriage ceremony. It was, I told myself, something I had to live through, and when it was over, I could see to my own life. And then Polly and Eddie were hugging and kissing one another, and Polly kissed me and Charlie kissed me on one cheek and Frank kissed me on the other. We drifted through the rooms, eating the dainty sandwiches, drinking the champagne, and then we sat down and watched Polly open her presents. Frank and Charlie had pooled their funds and bought her a large silver serving tray and she stared at herself in it as if she saw herself transfigured by what had just occurred. She unwrapped Iris's tablecloth and held it up for us to look at and I marveled at it as if I had not made it, as if I had never seen it before in my life. Then she opened the box with my quilt in it; she had not seen it since I had begun it almost eight months before, and when she shook it out and the multicolored sunburst fell over her lap and onto the floor, she began crying and saying she would miss me, and I told her to fold up the quilt and open the other box, and she took out the white linen napkins with the white strawberries I had embroidered on them and began crying again, and finally she went on to the other presents, and I thought, this is a good way for things to end. If this were a play at the Barre Opera House, it would end here. And then we talked for a while and Polly and Eddie left, waving as the carriage drove them away. They were going to New York for five days and when she came back, Polly said, she would tell us what it was like so that we would hurry up and want to get there. And then I turned around and looked for Frank.

He was standing on the top step in front of the door, looking after the carriage, and he turned toward me. "Let's go for a walk," he said. "Do you want company?" Charlie asked. "No," said Frank. We started walking in the direction of the fields. It had been raining all week and the cleared paths were slick where the rain had frozen on top of the snow. The drifts of ice glinted beneath the pale sun like glass. The rain was stopping. It was little more than a mist now. "Your shoes are getting wet," Frank said. I said I knew. "You'll catch your death of cold," he said. I said I wished I would. "Maybe we should go back," he suggested. "I don't mind wet feet," I said. We walked along slowly; the snow beneath our feet was slippery. We slid every which way, clutching at each other. It was warm for December, and I opened the top button of my cape. "It's colder than it looks," said Frank. Finally, we stopped opposite the clearing to which we usually came. "You don't want to go in there," Frank said, "not with that dress on." "I really don't care," I said. "I'd carry you," he said, "but the snow's so deep under the crust of ice, I'd fall in with you." "We can sit over there," I said, pointing to a fallen tree just to the side of the road. "This is better," Frank said; "if you fall, that frozen snow can scratch you up pretty badly." I nodded. More than anything else, I wanted to see the stumps again. But I had decided to agree with everything he said. I wanted him back.

"Well," he said, looking at me almost shyly, "did you decide anything?" "I didn't think it was up to me to decide," I said; "you're the one who's paying attention to someone else." A thin, cold wind blew down from the mountains, lifted a veil of snow, and blew it over us, glittering. I brushed the snow from my eyes. "I wonder where that came from," Frank said; "no clouds at all up there." "They're climbing Bald Hill," I said; "they'll be here soon." "Anyway," he said, "there aren't any now." And then all my good resolutions evaporated. I had to know what was going to happen to me. I could feel each nerve in my body. They were like snakes, alive, writhing, barely contained by my skin, all of them sinking their forked tongues into the base of my brain. I said I wanted to know what his intentions were. He asked me what I meant.

"Do you want to marry me or don't you?" I asked. "No," he said, "not right now." "When do you expect to make up your mind?" I asked him; "if it's made up, I think you should tell me so." He was silent a long time. One of the clouds over Bald Hill tore loose and floated down the sky toward us. I watched it with dread. Lately, everything seemed portentous, an omen, as if the world wanted to warn me and then mocked me when I wouldn't be warned. "I guess it's made up," he said at last; "it's too hard with you. I can't do it. I know you think you can do everything," he said, looking quickly at me, "but I couldn't live that way." "What do you mean?" I asked him. "You always say you don't mind it, that I don't love you as much as you love me," he said. "But *I* mind it. I can't live with you, knowing how you feel. You think you're better at loving things than I am. Well, maybe you are. Charlie thinks you are." "You talked this over with Charlie?" "Well, Agnes," he said, "I had to talk to someone. I didn't get too far. He says it's all my fault." "Why?" "Well, when I said it was just bad luck, he said it was more than that. He said I didn't like life and that was why everything I touched turned bad. So I asked him if that was a crime, not liking life, and he said maybe it was." "What did you say?" I asked. Perhaps this was the way, I thought; perhaps I could convince him that I could teach him to like life.

"He said he thought you were the same way. He said you always talked about how wonderful I was, and how I was from some other world, not this one." "I *do* like life!" I cried, outraged; "you know I do! I may not love every single stick and stone in it, but I adore the things in it that I do care for. I adore you." "Charlie said I shouldn't forget that you didn't want to have children," Frank said. "You don't either," I said. "I'm not sure about that," Frank said; "but someday you're going to want them, and it will all be too hard. I can't do it. Not with you." "I really don't know what you're talking about!" I said; "why should things be harder with me than with anyone else?"

"Because you expect so much. You expect so much from me. You expect so much from yourself. You'll never be happy if you think I don't love you as much as you love me. You'll keep trying to make me love you as much as you love me. I don't want that. I have to feel I'm as good as you are. I don't want to be the person who can't give enough. I want to be important to someone." "You are important to me," I said, dully; "you're the only one in the world who is important." "Why?" he asked, "because you saw me before you were born? It's not because of what I'm really like. You don't really care about me. You care about this perfect person you think I'll become. I don't *are* about perfection. I have enough trouble getting from day to day without breaking the law." "I don't know how you can say that," I said, watching two blackbirds flying across the field; "you must be out of your mind." "If I'm going to get married," he said, "I'll be happiest with someone who can stand me the way I am," he said. "I love you the way you are!" I exclaimed. "No, you don't," he said; "if I said I wanted to marry you and I wanted you to stay home taking care of the children and cooking my dinner, and that I wanted to be just like everyone else in the world, you wouldn't want it that way." "No," I said, "because you're not like everyone else in the world." "I told you from the beginning," he said, "I'm talented at stone carving. Nothing else. When it comes to anything else, I'm no different than anyone else. If I'm anything, I'm worse." "That's not true," I said dully. "It is. Charlie told you. Polly told you. Agnes, I'm trying to be honest with you. I don't feel things the way you do. I'd cheat you if I married you." "You could never cheat me," I said. "I'm cheating you now," he said; "I'm somewhere between you and Jane. That's not how you want it." "No," I said.

"Look, Agnes," he told me, "sooner or later, I'll want to get married. Just because it's the easiest way out. That's the way I am. It will be easier to have a wife than to keep renting rooms in a boardinghouse. And I'll want to have children because it's easier to have them than not to have them, and I don't hate children or marriage, either. I just don't want to be swallowed up by anything. But you, you're—" He broke off. "I'm what?" I asked. "Insatiable," he said, slowly; "insatiable. I can't live with someone like that. I'd always feel like a criminal, the one who wasn't giving enough. I'd feel like you were an animal in a cage that I was starving to death. You wouldn't *want* me to live that way." "But," I said, "you wouldn't mind coming home to the same woman all the time or having children? If they didn't make any trouble? If they made you happy?" "No," he said, "if I made them happy." I was groping in a fog, hoping for inspiration. I wanted him back, but I didn't know what to say. I was terrified. Insatiable! Suppose he was right.

"Don't you want to go to New York?" I asked. "Not really," he said; "I never did. You wanted me to go. If the work I do is good enough, people will find me. If they don't find me, they won't find me. So what?" "So what?" I said; "they *won't* find you. Maybe once you're dead, someone will come out here and say, 'Oh, he was a genius but a primitive one. If only he'd been taught. But it's rude work. Let's mention him in the fine print in case anyone's interested in local artists.' That's what they'll say." "That would be good enough for me," Frank said; "it would. But it wouldn't be good enough for you. That's the trouble. I don't care about it. I'm not ambitious. I don't see the point." "Why don't you?" I asked, my voice shaking; "why? Are you lazy? *Everyone* wants more."

"Lazy?" Frank asked; "you know I'm not. But I'm realistic. I'm going to die sooner or later, and no matter how many statues I carve, no one's going to remember me after I'm gone. I don't care if people remember me. I don't think I want them to. It's a rough tunnel, going through life, and you should go through it as smoothly as you can and when you get out, leave the ground as lear as you can for the next person." "Is that your philoso-hy?" I asked, genuinely surprised. "If I have one, that's it," e said; "the world's not much good. You can't fight it and win, o you take what you can. I'm not ashamed to wave a white flag nd take whatever I can get. I guess I think that's what happiness s." "Like having a soft cushion behind your head on a train ide?" I asked scornfully. "Exactly," he said, his cheeks indrawn.

"It's giving in," I said; "it's surrendering. It's not happiness." "Surrendering," said Frank; "it *is* surrendering. But what else can ou do?" "You can fight back!" I cried, desperate. I knew this vas my last chance. I had to make him see it. "Don't you emember what it was like in the fields? Can you imagine what it elt like to me after we made love? It was as if every single cell n my body sprouted wings and started flying about inside wildly. felt as if I could fly! I wasn't in this world! And you! I know ou wanted more. You don't really want to ramble through the ears like a cow rambling through the fields. You don't really vant to have them carve 'He was just like everyone else,' on our tombstone!" "They could carve much worse things," rank said. "No," I said; "I don't believe it. I've watched you vork. I've seen the way you *shine* when you work on your tones. You know you could do it! You could live a better life! You don't have to compromise!" "Agnes," Frank said, putting is hand on my shoulder, "for a while I believed that. I don't nymore." "Why not?" I demanded. "I'm not strong enough," e said softly; "I saw that after the abortion. I saw what you'd o through for me. I could never do the same kind of thing for ou." "You wouldn't have to," I said; "you're not a woman." 'You know what I mean," he said; "I couldn't sacrifice myself he way you did. And to go to New York and try to do important vork there, I couldn't. I don't have it in me." "You have the alent," I said, jumping up. "But not the character," he said; "I now I don't have the character. Can't you see that?" "I could ave the character for both of us!" I said. "We're right back vhere we started," he said; "I don't want it that way. Would ou be happy if you saw I was going to spend my life doing the ame kind of work I'm doing now?" "No," I insisted, "and ou wouldn't either."

"Well, then," Frank said, standing up, "I guess I have made decision." "You're going to marry Jane," I said. "Jane is a ice, simple girl," he said. "And she's happy all the time, just ike a cow in the field?" I sneered. "Not all the time," he said, 'but enough. She knows there's plenty wrong with me and it doesn't seem to bother her. She doesn't care." "That's because she doesn't care about you," I said. He didn't answer. "Are you going to marry her?" I asked. "I might," he said. "You mustn't," I said suddenly; "you'll be lost. You have to remember what it was like! You have to want something better!" "Agnes," he said, "I don't. What's here is too good for me." "Why do you keep saying things like that?" I cried. "Because they're true." I stared into space. "Do you want me to keep calling on you?" he asked. "No," I said, "but I can't help myself." He held out his arm to help me up. "You'll see it," I said; "you'll see I'm right. I know you will." He shook his head and we went back to the house.

I found Iris in the middle of the parlor, sweeping. "Look at your shoes," she said; "they're soaking wet. Put on some dry socks." "No," I said, "it's all right." "You'll catch your death," she said. "I hope I will," I answered. I went upstairs, undressed, and got into bed. On Sunday morning, I heard the bells ringing but I did not stir and when Frank came in I told him I was unwell and sent him away. The world had pulled away from the sun and was spinning loose, one cheek after another turning into the darkness.

38

No one in F. R. Edwards' Hardware Store seemed surprised that I wanted to buy a revolver. I told the man who waited on me that my father wanted a revolver and I had promised to bring one home for him, and in the meantime I wouldn't mind having it by me because I got home from work so late and the streets were all deserted. The clerk took out three revolvers and laid them on the counter and I picked them up and sighted along their barrels, but none of them was what I wanted. He brought out three more. One was small and compact and fit nicely in my hand. "That's a good choice," the clerk said, picking it up himself; "it's an Ivers-Johnson double action center fire. It's a thirty-two caliber. You can always get cartridges for it. It's real handy if you know how to use it." "My father's a good shot," I said; "I'm not bad, either."

I picked up the revolver after he put it down. It felt like my grandmother's pistol; it was growing warm in my hand. I knew I had already chosen it. "Well," I said, "if I'm going to take it, I better get some ammunition." "How much do you want?" "Oh, about seventy cartridges," I said. "I can give you a special price of fifty or one hundred," he said. "Fifty," I said; "would you wrap up the cartridges in one package and the gun in the other? I have to visit a friend and I want to put the things in my pockets." He said he would. I paid him, and put the gun, wrapped in brown paper, into one pocket, the package of bullets into the other. "They're heavy," I said, "the bullets. If I jumped into the water with these things in my pockets, I'd drown." "That's a new way to use a gun on yourself," he said, smiling. "A person has to have imagination," I said. "Don't let children get near that," he said as I started out. "Children?" I said; "don't worry about it." He nodded and smiled.

It was four o'clock. Florence would not be back at her house until after six. I went into a tea shop and ordered a pot of tea and a little cake in fluted white paper. I could walk from here to the quarries; I should go see him one last time. There had to be something I could do, something I had not yet thought of. I paid the waitress and left without touching anything on my plate.

Outside, the wind was rising and it whipped the little hairs which I could not pull back in front of my eyes until I seemed to be looking at the world through a black bramble or wire net. The cold made my cheeks burn, and my hands, sunk in my pockets, were frozen within their gloves. The trails up toward the stone sheds were slippery and I picked my way along slowly. By the time I got to Frank's shed, I was tired of slipping on the ice and went in the closet door. I would have to walk the length of the shed to reach him. Charlie saw me first and stood up, his brow furrowing. Then Frank saw me. He stopped working and stared at me. "I came to Barre," I said; "I was going to visit Florence but I had some time to kill, so I thought I'd come here." The sheds were as beautiful as I remembered them. I stared at Frank's angel. There I was, standing in pink marble, my body complete, half of my face having risen up from the deep marble waters, the other half submerged.

"Is that one of the ones you're giving away?" I asked Frank. "It's one of the ones I'm selling," he said. "To the men from New York?" "That's right," he said; "did you come here to talk about that?" "No," I said; "I don't know why I came." Frank nodded. "Well, sit down," he said; "I have to get some work done." "For a minute," I said. Perhaps the place would work its own magic. Perhaps he would see I was as much his creation as he was mine.

"I didn't know you were so friendly with Florence," Frank said. "Well, now that Polly's gone," I said. He nodded again. I stared at his shirt. I saw the muscles of his shoulders working beneath the soft plaid flannel. Perhaps when he turned to me, he would say, "Let's go to New York. We're back to where we were." But he kept on working and then he asked me if I was eating supper with Florence and I said I was. "We'll walk back into town with you, then," he said. I sat back and watched the men around me work. The little marble houses, the marble people, the men moving in the pollenlike dust, creating everything. And he was going to shut me out of this, and he had no idea how terrible it would be for me to be shut out, and I saw how ridiculous it was; how the quarries meant more to me than they did to him; *he* was the sculptor. I was only an irrelevant visitor, a thick column of dust, a ghost.

"Four-thirty, I've had enough," Frank said, putting down his chisel; "let's go." He asked me again about Florence, but I said I'd changed my mind; I was going back to Mrs. Trowbridge's after all. We sat next to each other on the cars going back to Montpelier. "What are you thinking about?" he asked me. "Oh," I said, "I was hoping you'd change your mind." "No," he said, "I don't think so. If you were just easier..." "If I was?" I asked. "Well, then I'd just as soon marry you as marry anyone," he said, "but you're not easy. Let's not start it all up again." "I could learn to be," I said. "People don't change," he said. "They do," I said; my voice was flat and gray. At Mrs. Trowbridge's, I went into supper with Frank, and then, in the middle of the meal, I began to think about the stones glowing in the dusty light, and I looked over at Frank, and suddenly he was the jailor with the key who was locking me out of that world and I wanted to get away from him. I told Frank I was going out for a short while and would be back later. He looked at me suspiciously but said nothing.

I went to Mr. Emmett's livery and asked him if he minded my practicing shooting in his yard and he said, yes, he certainly did and it was a bad idea to shoot anywhere within the city limits. I asked him where I could go and he said to go up to the top of Bald Hill. I took a horse and rode up. No one was there. From the top of Bald Hill I could see the whole city. I could see Iris's house. I could see Cherry Street where Jane Holt worked. I could see the Emporium, the two churches, the dull gold dome of the courthouse. I loaded the pistol and thought that nothing had gone right for me since I had come here. If only I had gone somewhere else. I looked down at the buildings outlined in the distance and thought of the tombstones outlined in the golden light. One was a miniature of the other. I shook my head and tried to concentrate on what I was doing. It wouldn't have mattered where I had gone. Somehow everything would have turned out the same way. Frank would have been waiting for me wherever I had gone, like fate.

I picked out a branch and began firing at it. With each shot, the branch got smaller. With each shot, the branch trembled and a piece of it flew into the air like a small bird flushed from its nest. The gun was easy to handle; it did not kick when it fired. Its balance was good. I resumed firing.

"What in hell are you doing?" Frank's voice demanded

behind me. I turned around, startled. "Targets," I said. "Up here?" he said; "are you crazy? You can't go around shooting this close to the city." "Mr. Emmett said I could," I answered. "I know," he said; "I saw you going over there and I asked him where you'd gone. Mr. Emmett doesn't know everything. Where did you get that gun?" "I bought it," I said; "you come home so late now. I walk around alone. It makes me feel safer." "You're not planning on using it on yourself, are you?" he asked. "Would you care?" I asked him. "I don't want to talk about it," he said. "Would you?" I persisted. "Of course I'd care," he said; "I wouldn't lie down and die, though, if that's what you're hoping." "I didn't think so," I said distantly. "Look," Frank said, "just put the gun away and let's go for a walk." We started back to Iris's. "It doesn't do any good to talk to you," I said. "What do you mean?" he asked. "I tell you things and you don't understand them," I said helplessly; "perhaps I ought to write you a letter." "Write me a letter," he said, "but put the gun away before you get yourself arrested." I snapped open the cylinder, emptied out the cartridges, and put the gun in one pocket, the bullets in another. "Happy now?" I asked. "Yes," he said; "you look exhausted." "I am exhausted," I said. I could barely pick up my feet. "You go to sleep," he said; "I'll go for a walk." He's going to see Jane, I thought, but the fog was thickening around me. I went up to his room and sat down on his bed.

As soon as I lay down, the exhaustion vanished and was replaced by an unnatural, excited wakefulness. I got up and got out a sheet of writing paper. It was useless, writing to Jane Holt. I would have to go and talk to her if I wanted to make an impression on her. I began to write Frank a letter. "Dearest Frank," I wrote and as I began to write, I felt sorry for us all, for Jane, for Frank, for me. We were all caught. We were all doomed. I was not the only one caught in the trap. "Don't blame love-sick girls for they were made thus by loving," I wrote. "Jane is not to blame if she loves you. She could not do otherwise. A beautiful girl is worth something, too, but a very good, willing, self-sacrificing girl is worth much more. If I were one of those luke-warm, indifferent, loveless beauties, and I asked you to take me, you could become a sacrifice to marriage, and I would never ask you to sacrifice yourself for me on marriage's altar. Jane would not, either, if she knew what she was asking. It is the one who loves almost to distraction who is the best, and I am that one.

"She is the premium wife whose fervid, glowing, devoted whole-souled love spills forth daily, whose love knows no limit, who is spellbound, magnetized, and entranced, turned to stone, beside herself when her love appears, whose love, torrentlike, sweeps all before it, making all possible allowances for imperfections in the loved one and magnifying to the greatest degree all his desirable and lovable traits of character and she who does this reaches heaven on this earth, and she enters it in hand with her beloved, as I would surely enter it with you.

"If you listen for it, you will hear the voice of the little soul who went before us calling to us, asking us to come toward him together. Once we are joined together, all the difficulties we have seen will show themselves for what they are: mere mirages, clouds which appear in the morning and burn off under the noon sun. I ask you to enter that world with me because I am sure it is there and I know that I cannot enter it without you and you cannot enter it without me. There is nothing on this earth that can oppose a love so pure and strong. Everything else is delusion.

"Turn away from the miserable world and come with me. Others will see how happy we are and envy us, as they already have. You have already lived with me in this world. The angels who guard the door to the garden are lowering their crossed swords. If you come back now, we will never have to leave again. I have not wanted to love you, I have not wanted to forsake the world for you, but I have had no choice, and when I look about me, I have no regrets. You shall not either. Come to me. It is for us that the cherubs sing. Forgive me if I sound like a pagan who has made a man my god, but I am a pagan and you are my god. Do not turn away from me. Your ever-faithful Agnes."

And when I finished the letter, I pushed the paper back, and began to cry. I would talk to Jane Holt before I gave it to him. Then, if the letter failed, the world would fail. I folded up the letter and put in my photograph album. Then I crawled into Frank's bed, hugging the album to me.

I saw the light widening in the window, but I could not make myself get up. Frank had not come back. I wanted to go see Jane and I was so hungry that I thought about nothing but hunger for hours on end, but I could not make myself get up and go down to the dining room. When the house was quiet, I stole down to the washroom and then went back upstairs. And I stayed there. After two days in Frank's room, I was oblivious to hunger and thirst. If Iris had not brought me biscuits and milk, I would have eaten nothing. Frank had asked me what was wrong, and when I said I was sick, he said he would ask Iris to bring me something to eat. But when he came in, I usually did not answer him and he would leave. On the morning of the third day, I got up, dressed, and went downstairs for breakfast. Soon, I would go to Jane Holt. I would talk to her and tell her all about Frank and she would turn away from him. But I could not decide when I would go; I could not decide anything. I was like a pendulum which ticktocked between terror and confusion, confusion and anger, anger and sorrow. And then I would be overcome with a hilarity which made everything I saw comic, two-dimensional, utterly without significance. So this, I thought, is what it means to be lost. This will pass, I told myself, crossing my fingers; everything passes. At night, I was beginning to pray. It was always the same prayer: Make this stop. Make him take me back.

And then I tried to plan. I would go talk to Jane Holt. If she didn't agree to give Frank up, I would give him my letter. If he didn't agree to come to New York with me, I would shoot myself. It was such a simple plan. Of course, Mrs. James would never give me back my job, but now that I had a new plan, such a simple new plan, I didn't need a job. Still, I didn't want to talk to Jane Holt. Talking to her would be such a brazen provocation of the Fates. Jane Holt, I thought, poor and thin as she was, was my fate. I wondered what Polly would say if she heard what I was thinking. I was making no sense, even to myself.

The door opened. Perhaps Frank had come back; perhaps he had changed his mind. But it was only Iris. "Oh, Agnes," she said, "Polly stopped by yesterday but she said she couldn't get you up. She asked me to give you this. She said you'd know what to do with it." She gave me a little package wrapped in brown paper and I undid a corner of it; inside was a nightgown I had embroidered for Polly last winter. "She tore it and doesn't know how to fix it," Iris said. I would fix it and fancy it up. I would talk to Jane Holt tomorrow. I was glad to have an excuse to put it off another day. I spent the rest of the day embroidering pansies all over the front of Polly's nightgown and when Frank came home, I pretended to be asleep. When he left to take a walk, I got up and started to write another letter. The other one, I decided, was too passionate. It would only drive him away.

"Dear Frank," I wrote, "the future is a wonderful place and everything in it is always wonderful because all horizons are imaginary, all the people are unreal, but tinted with the hues of the imagination, and hence shine more brightly than creatures of this world. How pleasant it must be to see one's imaginary wife moving pleasantly through one's imaginary rooms, stooping over one's baby, which is perfect and never cries and never sickens simply because it does not exist in the real world but in the world of imagination. All it has to do is grow older and grow more and more like you, which it does, for in the future all things grow according to our dreams.

"And in the future, whose creatures obey the rules of the heart, there are no differences of opinion between husband and wife because the wife is not real, but a creature of the imagination, and she moves as the heart does and is forever in tune with it. Is it any wonder that you turn from such marvelous pictures of domestic life to creatures of this world and turn away, horrified by what you see? But is there anyone or anything in this world who would not pale when compared with the creatures of your imagination? The reveries of a bachelor are wonderful precisely because they are reveries; the dream of reality can be more marvelous than reveries, but the reality cannot flower without love, which, like the sun, forces the flower to bloom, however hostile the climate. We have not entered that future land which we glimpse in our imagination, because we have not accepted the limits of the ordinary."

I stopped and looked at what I had written. I did not believe a word of it. I believed that the real world was worthless, a pale imitation of the true world which our imagination had created between us. Even if our imaginations had created it, I believed the world of our imaginations was the only reality there was. Still, I thought, bitterly, Frank would find truth in what I had written.

I went back to my room, sat down on the bed, and began to write. "The child I gave back," I wrote, starting to cry, "is waiting for us to recreate him and bring him back," and I went on in that vein, no longer conscious of what I was writing, every now and then getting up for a new sheet of paper and when I had finished, I saw I had written twenty-six pages. He would *never* read such a long letter. I sighed and took the letter into his room and put it under a board in his floor where he kept his extra money and the cartridges for his gun. I would leave it there and when he found it, it would take him by surprise; perhaps it would change his mind. Then I climbed into Frank's bed and tried to sleep. I knew when Frank slipped into bed beside me, but I did not move. I kept my eyes closed until I fell asleep.

At five o'clock in the morning, I went back to my room and sat down in front of the mirror. My hair was in place. That seemed important. I put on my plain black dress and put my mackintosh on over it. Then I went over to my dresser, took out the revolver I had hidden in the folds of my nightdress, and took out the drawer and pulled out the box of cartridges which I kept behind it. I loaded the revolver and put the gun in one pocket and the extra cartridges in the other. Then I went into Frank's room; he was still asleep. I bent over and kissed him on the forehead. He was always so warm when he slept. I went downstairs as if I were going from one world—the familiar one in which I had walked for so long—into another, which closely resembled it, but was, in some indefinable way, utterly different. But now I was in both worlds at once. This, I thought, leaving the house, is how a ghost feels.

It would be Jane Holt who would decide what happened to me. And it seemed right that she should be the one to decide my fate. It was quiet outside, and raining. Most people were just getting up. I went up Bald Hill, took out the gun, and fired four times. I hit the branch at which I was aiming. A man came up and asked who was doing the shooting and I said I was; I was just practicing, but I was finished. He said he had to go back in, but he didn't think I ought to be shooting within the city limits and I said I thought I was far enough away not to bother anyone. I waited a while, looking down at the city, the outline of its houses against the dull, gray sky, and put the gun back in my pocket. I began walking to Cherry Street and the Ludlum house. I must have lost track of time and my destination, because when I got to the house, it was seven-thirty.

I could see figures moving in the kitchen and I knocked at the side door. An old woman opened it and peered up at me. She was still in her red flannel nightgown and her long braid of silver hair hung heavily down her back. "Yes?" she said; "are you the girl from the seamstress's?" "No," I said; "I'm looking for Jane Holt. Is she here?" "She's here," the old woman said; "do you want me to get her?" "Yes, please," I said. The old woman left the room and I looked about me. It was a splendid kitchen, large enough for an inn. The room exuded an air of order, of warmth, of privilege. It must be like this, I thought, at Jane Holt's house, people everywhere, the house humming warmly, everything in the room promising that tomorrow would be no different from today and that these days would never end. Jane was wealthy; she was working for a wealthy family. I was wealthy, too, but I had never felt as if I had a family.

The old woman reappeared in the doorway on the other side of the room. "Do you know her?" she asked someone standing behind her. "No," said the girl; "I'll see what she wants." It was as if someone had shut out all the sound in the world. I saw Jane Holt, a tall, thin girl whose wavy blond hair was pinned up on top of her head, moving toward me. She was wearing a green skirt and a white blouse; she was absolutely clean. I looked at her and tried to imagine her with wet shoes and socks or with unwashed hair, and it was impossible. She was a good, sweet girl, I could see that clearly enough. She was smiling at me. "I'm Agnes Dempster," I said; "I'm a friend of Frank Holt's." "Oh," she said; "of course. I should have known who you were." "If you don't want to talk to her, tell me," the old woman whispered to her. "It's all right," Jane said, motioning her away. Rain was beginning to spatter the windows. "It's raining," said Jane. "Yes, it is," I said; "I didn't come here to talk about the weather." "No," Jane said, "I'm sure you didn't."

"Do you know who I am?" I asked her. "I've seen you," she said; "you've come into the Emporium." "But you don't know who I am?" I asked. "I know that Frank used to go about with you," she said. "He did more than that," I said; "I've been engaged to him for a year and a half. I'm engaged to Frank Holt." Jane went white. "You seem surprised," I said coldly. "He told me," said Jane, "that he broke it off with you last summer when you went back home. That's when we started seeing each other again. He asked me to marry him and I said yes. I've known him a long time. I always wanted to marry him." "He told me he was through with you," I said; "he told me you meant nothing to him. He came home with me to meet my father and told him we were getting married." "Well," Jane said at last, "he can't be engaged to both of us." "No," I said, "he can't. We're supposed to get married and go to New York." She looked at me with widening eyes. "You're the one he carves the statues of," she said. "Yes," I said, "I am. I'm also the one he got into trouble last summer." "Let's go out," Jane said nervously, looking about her; "I don't think this is the place to talk about it." She got her mackintosh and put it on. "Where would you like to go?" I asked her. "To Willow Drive," she said; "I live there." By now it was raining heavily. "It's raining," I said; "I don't have an umbrella." "I have one," she said; "we can share it." She went over to the old woman and said something to her.

"I told her I had to go home for a few minutes," she said; "we can talk at my house. My parents are at the store." "That's fine," I said. We walked until we were almost between Elwood's dump and Juniper Street. "If we cut through this field, won't it be faster?" I asked her. "Our shoes will get wet," she said. "Mine are already wet," I said. "Well, so are mine," she said; "we might as well." We turned off the street into the field and suddenly I stopped walking and turned to face her. "Do you intend to marry Frank Holt?" I asked her. "Yes, I do," she said; "in the spring. We've discussed it with my parents." "He's also discussed marrying me with my father," I reminded her, standing under her umbrella while the raindrops dripped from its rim, falling in small silver streams around us.

"He told me he once wanted to marry you, but he said he didn't any longer," Jane said; "isn't that true?" "No," I said; "it's not true. Last summer, he made me get rid of his baby. He promised me we'd be married before the year was up and now he's talking about marrying you. How can you marry him?" "I trust him," Jane said. "How can you trust him?" I asked her; "don't you believe me?" "It's not that I don't believe you," she said hesitantly; "it's just that I believe him more." "I'm telling you the truth," I said. "I trust Frank," she said; "I love him."

I slipped my hand in my pocket and felt the familiar, warm weight of the gun. I would not have to stand much more of this world. And then I looked up and Jane Holt was not there. Instead, I was watching myself standing opposite me. "Do you love him more than anyone else in the world?" I asked my other self. I was not at all surprised to see her there. "Yes," I said, "I do." "Then you don't want to give him up?" I asked the girl, who was also me. Perhaps, I thought, whoever it was standing there was only impersonating me. "No," I said, "there's no reason for me to give him up." "Even if he got me into trouble?" I asked my other self. "It takes more than one person to get someone into trouble," she said. "I have something to show you," I said, and pretended to rummage in my pocket.

The other girl who so precisely resembled me seemed interested in what I had to show her. I took the gun out of my pocket with my left hand and raised it to her head. "Turn to the side," I said, and she turned her head. Of course she would; I was only talking to myself. I fired once and the bullet entered her temple at her hair line. I watched, fascinated, as she fell slowly toward the ground. There I was, falling through the air, blood pouring from my temple, coming to rest on the snow. And when I looked down at her, I saw her smiling up at me, raising her arms up to me, my double, my shadow self, and I knew that this was the sleep I had always wanted, that this was the embrace I had always been seeking and that no one would ever be able to separate the two of us again, not ever, and I raised the gun again and thrust the barrel into my ear, and it was cold, and I pulled the trigger and I saw myself falling slowly toward my own face which was warm and perfect and unscarred and as wide and welcoming as the earth itself.

On Trial

39

The hired man was widening the path through the snow at the Holt house when he heard the shot. He listened, heard nothing else, and resumed shoveling. Then he heard another shot. He turned and looked toward the fields across the road from the Holt house, but he saw no one. Just before, two girls had passed him, both leaning together under one umbrella, one dressed in black, one wearing a green skirt which looked like Jane's, but he had been too far away to see who they were. Whoever they were, he thought, they must have a lot to talk about to go out walking with rain slicking the snow like this. He went back to work.

Evelina Starr had been walking home from the Emporium and she saw the two girls turn off into the field opposite the dump. She thought one of the girls was Jane Holt, but she wasn't sure. The other girl, who walked closer to the road, was very pretty, but Evelina didn't know who she was. When they turned into the field, she stopped and stared after them. The snow was wet and slushy and she wondered why they were going into it. When they had gone far enough into the field so that they were opposite the Holt house, the girl in black took a gun from her pocket and shot the other girl above the right ear. The girl fell to the ground without uttering a sound. Then the girl in black lifted the gun again and shot herself through the head. Evelina Starr began shouting for help, and the hired man looked up and saw her waving at him and ran over to her.

"She shot her," Evelina babbled; "she shot the girl and she shot herself, too. I saw them fall." People were coming out of the neighboring houses. "What was that shot?" someone called to the hired man, and he called back, "One girl shot another girl." "No, she shot herself, too," Evelina called out. Soon there was a little crowd on the edge of the road across from the

411

field. "Well, who's going?" the hired man asked. "We'll go with you," said the Grayson brothers.

The others watched the three men start across the field. "To the left, to the left!" Evelina Starr called after them. When the men caught sight of something black against the snow, they slowed down. Just then a rising wind filled the open umbrella which had fallen from Jane's hand and sent it spinning down the field of snow. "Come on," said one of the men. The girls were lying in the snow as if they were sound asleep. The girl in the green dress and green plaid mackintosh lay on her back, her face peaceful. The men could see no sign of a wound. The girl in black had fallen across her so that her head rested on the other girl's stomach; she too had fallen on her back and there was a glint like black satin against her breast. The left side of her face was covered with blood which poured from wounds near her eye and behind her ear. "I think they're dead," the hired man said, his voice trembling.

"Isn't that Jane Holt?" asked one of the Grayson brothers. No one wanted to touch them. "It's Jane," said the hired man; "who's the other one?" "I don't know," said a Grayson brother; "I've never seen her." "We better get them back to the Holt house," said the hired man; "maybe the doctor can do something for them." "They look dead to me," one of the brothers said to the other. "You take Jane," they told the hired man, "and we'll take this one. She's blood all over." The hired man picked up Jane Holt, and when he did, he saw the dark pool of blood in the snow; her head had been resting in it. His hand, which had touched the back of her head, was sticky. "Let's put them on the porch," he said; "they're terribly messy." "I think this one's dead," said one of the Graysons. "Jane's awful cold and stiff," said the hired man. "So's the weather." "We've got to get Doctor Salter over here," said one of the other men.

When they came out of the field carrying the two girls, the crowd had swelled considerably; it pushed forward to see who the men were carrying. "Get back, will you?" the hired man said roughly. He didn't want to fall carrying this cold young woman he had known all his life; he didn't want to end up tangled in her arms and legs, bloody in the snow. They went up the steps to the porch. "Put them on the piazza," said the hired man; "I'll get some blankets." He went in and came back with carriage blankets and covered both girls. "Don't cover their faces," someone called; "they won't be able to breathe." The three men on the porch looked at one another. "Someone should send for Doctor Salter,'' one of them said. Evelina Starr grabbed another girl's hand and the two of them ran off down the street.

"What do we do now?'' asked the older Grayson; "wait?'' "I think we better wait for the constable,'' said his brother; "we have the murder weapon here.'' "They may not be dead,'' the hired man said stubbornly. The brothers looked at each other but said nothing.

People were starting to run toward the house. "Is that Mr. Holt?'' the hired man asked. The brothers shook their heads. "There's Mrs. Holt,'' said the hired man. She was running in back of her husband, her hair pulling loose from its pins, streaming in wet strands which the rain plastered to her face. "Oh,'' said the hired man, "my God.'' He put his head in his hands and started to cry. The man sitting next to him reached out and patted him clumsily on the shoulder.

When he got to the porch steps, Mr. Holt stopped and then marched straight over to the girls and stood looking down at them. He turned and looked at his wife. "Is it Jane?'' she whispered. He nodded dumbly. He began to cry, looking at his wife, who slumped down on the steps. "It's Christmas tomorrow,'' she said; "it can't be Jane.'' Mr. Holt was bending over his daughter. Her eyes were open and did not blink. She must be dead. He went over to his wife and lifted her by the elbow. "I think she's dead,'' he whispered to her. "She can't be,'' she said; "it's someone else. No one would kill Jane.'' He led her over to the two girls who were lying side by side on their backs. Mrs. Holt covered her mouth and began sobbing.

"Does anyone know who the other girl is?'' the older Grayson asked; "she must have a family, too.'' "I've seen her,'' Mr. Holt said dully, "in the store. I think she's a friend of Frank Holt.'' A whisper went through the crowd. "Let me look,'' said the large-boned girl who was standing next to Evelina. It was Lilian Bugbee, who worked for Mrs. James. Lilian went up the steps and looked down at the girls. "It's her,'' she said; "I knew it was her.'' "Who?'' asked the hired man; "who is she?'' "Agnes Dempster,'' Lilian said; "she works for Mrs. James. She said she was going to marry Frank Holt and that Jane wasn't going to marry him if she could help it. She comes from North Chittenden. Is she dead? She looks dead.'' "I think she's dead,'' Mr. Holt said, his voice stunned and hollow. He was trying not to look at his wife, who had knelt down beside their daughter and had taken the girl's hand in both her own and was rubbing the dead girl's thumb with her lips and cheek. "Come away from there,'' he said to his wife, but she seemed oblivious to everything but Jane.

Doctor Salter was coming up the steps and in back of him was the ambulance from Whately Hospital, frantically ringing its bells. "All right, Gertrude," the doctor said to Mrs. Holt, "move back a little and let me see to her." Mrs. Holt placed her daughter's hand on her breast, patted it gently, and stood up, leaning against her husband. The doctor saw immediately that the girl was dying, but he remained bent over her until his eyes stopped stinging. "Tom, Gertrude," he said, "I'm sorry. She's dying." "Maybe it's just the loss of blood," said Mrs. Holt; "maybe she'll wake up." "The courts will want her at the hospital anyhow," he said; "if there's anything to be done, they'll do it there." Two men got out of the ambulance carrying a stretcher. "All right, everyone. Go home," Doctor Salter called; "this is nothing to stand around and watch. Go home." No one moved. The doctor advanced on the crowd and the people retreated rapidly before him and began scattering down the street. "You two go inside," he said to the Holts; "I'll go with the ambulance to the hospital. You can come down there later." "I want to go with you," said Mrs. Holt. "No," said the doctor, "it's against the rules."

He waited until the Holts had gone into the house, listened for the scream he knew would come, and then turned back to the attendants. "Don't bother with two stretchers," he said; "one of them's dead or an eyeblink away from it, and if the other one isn't dead, she will be when they get there." The men picked up Jane, laid her in the stretcher and then picked up Agnes and laid her down next to her. "Look at that," one of the attendants said softly. Agnes's arm had fallen across the eyes of the other girl. "Let's get this over with," the other attendant said; "it's awful." "It's a tragedy," said the man at the other end. When they settled the stretcher in back of the ambulance, the three men looked dazed. "Did they say why it happened?" one of the attendants asked the doctor. "An argument over a man," the doctor said, shaking his head; "that's what it sounds like." They turned to look at the two girls and looked back at one another. "Over a man?" one of the attendants said.

When the ambulance reached Whately Hospital, it drove up to the rear entrance. The doctor told the men to carry the girls in behind him, and he spoke to a nurse who told him he could put both girls in a small room which opened onto the entrance area. The men carried the stretcher in. There was only one bed in the room, a narrow bed, its metal frame painted white. They picked up Agnes first because she was on top of the other girl and laid her down on the outer edge of the bed; then they picked up Jane and laid her down against the wall. "She's going to fall off that way," one of the men said, looking at Agnes; "turn her the other way." "But they'll be looking at each other!" the other man said. "They may look, but they won't see," said the first man, flipping Agnes over so that she and Jane lay nose to nose.

A policeman had appeared at the Holt house, had taken the revolver from the Graysons, listened to their accounts of the shooting, made some notes about Frank Holt, stopped to ask if that wasn't an odd thing, that the man the girls fought over had the same name as one of the victims, and the girl's parents said it was just a coincidence, there was no relationship between them, and then he set off to look for City Sheriff Epworth. Everywhere he went, people stopped him to ask him about the girls, how they were, who they were, were they really going to die, was it true one of them had already killed the other in a fit of jealousy and then shot herself; was it true that they had argued over someone named Frank Holt, and who was Frank Holt, and who was the girl?

He was relieved to find the city sheriff and give him the gun. "Do you want me to look for this Frank Holt?" he asked the sheriff, but the sheriff said no, if it was as everyone said, he'd be pretty crushed when he heard the news, at least he would be if he'd intended to marry the Holt girl, the way everyone said he had, so there was no hurry. The policeman was uneasy about leaving Frank Holt on the loose; he had two daughters and he knew men often went around with more than one girl at a time. If he'd been in the sheriff's place, he would have gone right after Frank Holt before he had a chance to make up a story, if he had a story to make up. "Are you going over to look at the girls?" he asked the sheriff. "That's where I'm going," said Epworth; "if they die, I'll be rounding everyone up." "You're sure you don't want me to get this Holt fellow?" the policeman asked him. "No, Delonnay, I don't," the sheriff said, looking at him oddly. "Go over to the Dempster girl's boardinghouse and look through her things. They say she did the shooting. Maybe she left a note." They set off in opposite directions.

Frank had slept late that day and stopped by the Emporium, hoping to see Jane. When he walked in, everyone in the store stopped what they were doing and stared at him. He looked around him, puzzled. "Is Jane here?" he asked. The old lady in back of the candy counter began crying. "What's wrong with everyone?" he said; "where's Mr. and Mrs. Holt?" The girl behind the yard goods counter shook her head at him, her eyes wide. What was the matter with all of them? Frank stood still, watching them. The store was filled with women staring accusingly at him. "They think Jane's dead," the old woman said. "Dead?" said Frank. "A girl shot her," said the old woman. "A girl?" he echoed. "A girl named Agnes," the old woman said; "someone named Lilian came in here and said they fought because of you." "Agnes?" Frank said; he saw her, standing next to him, between himself and her father, at the edge of the field in North Chittendon, firing at targets. "Agnes shot Jane?" he asked. "And then she shot herself," said the old woman; "people think they're both dead." Agnes couldn't be dead, thought Frank. Even when he'd decided to leave her, to marry Jane Holt, he'd always thought of her existing in the world somewhere. She couldn't be dead. "No," Frank said, "Agnes wouldn't hurt someone else. She couldn't kill anybody." In the depths of the store, someone else began sniffling. "We thought you were going to marry Jane," the old woman said reproachfully. "I am," said Frank; "Agnes was just a girl who lived in the same house I did. I didn't love her. She used to be my friend's girl. That's all she was." No one said anything. "I've got to get to work," he said; "I've got to see the Holts." They stared at him, silent.

He turned toward the Holt house. None of it was true. It was all some kind of joke. It was not possible, not Jane and Agnes at once. And, as if Agnes were there, he began talking to her. He asked her how she could do it? How could she shoot herself? How could she shoot Jane? And he could hear her saying that she'd warned him; she'd told him she'd shoot herself. She'd told him he'd never marry Jane. But you never said you'd shoot Jane, he thought, and he could hear Agnes asking him how stupid he could be, because if she was ready to shoot herself, she was ready to shoot anyone, and he thought that he ought to have taken the gun from her, and he could hear Agnes saying that yes, he ought to have taken it. He asked Agnes if she were dead, and she said she was, and he said she could come back and she said she didn't want to. He asked Agnes if Jane were dead, and Agnes said she was dead, too. He asked Agnes how she could do it, he told her it wasn't fair; everyone would blame him for

416

causing the trouble between the two women. But Agnes said they wouldn't; she said they would blame her. She had done the shooting. Frank looked up and saw he was opposite the Holt house. Agnes was not there; they said Jane was not there either. He went up the steps and knocked at the door. The handyman opened it. "Oh, Mr. Holt," he said, "come in."

Mrs. Holt was motionless on the couch and her husband was kneeling near her head. "Where are they?" Frank asked. "They?" asked Mrs. Holt, struggling to sit up. Her husband put his hand behind her back, pushed her forward, and slid a sofa cushion behind her. "The doctor gave her something," he said softly. "What doctor?" asked Frank. "Doctor Salter," said Jane's father; "who told you?" "They told me in the Emporium," Frank said slowly; "I came to find out if it's true." "It's true," said Mr. Holt; "they took the girls off in an unconscious state. Doctor Salter said he thought Jane was dying. He said the other girl wasn't dead, but she soon would be." "Both of them?" asked Frank. "Both," said Mr. Holt.

"Both," Frank repeated again. "Stop saying that!" exclaimed Mrs. Holt; "we don't care about the other one. The murderess!" "You mean Agnes?" Frank asked. There was a mist behind his eyes that would not clear. "The one who used the gun, that's who," said Mrs. Holt; "that's all I want to know about her." "Where were they shot?" asked Frank. Perhaps Agnes had shot at Jane from a great distance; perhaps, for once, she had missed and the girl was only slightly wounded. Perhaps she had not really hurt herself badly. "Jane," began Mr. Holt, starting to cry again, "was shot in the head. Here." He pointed to the space above his right ear. "When we saw her lying there, we thought she was asleep; there wasn't any sign of a wound. But her eyes were open and she never closed them the whole time." "And Agnes?" Frank asked; "the other one?" "One shot through the ear and into the eye," said Mr. Holt, crying; "they don't think she'll live." "I hope she's dead now!" said Mrs. Holt.

Frank looked around the room, confused. It was more than he could take in, more than he could imagine. He wanted to talk to someone about this; he wanted to talk to Agnes, and then he realized that Agnes had been taken to Whately Hospital and everyone said she would not live. "I'm terribly sorry," Frank said; "I wish there was something I could do." Mrs. Holt began sobbing. "Maybe," said Mr. Holt, "you could carve the stone." For both of them? Frank was about to ask, but he realized what Mr. Holt meant and stopped in time. "Maybe I could," he said, "but I don't believe it. I just don't believe it." "You didn't see them," Mrs. Holt said bitterly. "Maybe I should go to the hospital," Frank said. "No," said Mr. Holt, "don't go there. Reporters are coming from all over." "Reporters," Frank said faintly. "They've already been here," Mr. Holt said; "it's going to be all over the front pages soon enough." "Is there anything I can do?" Frank asked. "Just go home!" cried Mrs. Holt; "you've done enough!" "Stop it, Gertrude," said Mr. Holt; "it's his loss, too." Mrs. Holt shook her head and covered her eyes. "I'll go," said Frank softly; "I'll come back tonight."

He walked rapidly down the street and ran after the car to Barre and swung himself on. I've got to talk to Charlie, he thought. The car seemed to creep along. He had never realized how far from town Barre was. It was as if the earth had become more elastic and was stretching away from him. He didn't like thinking that way; he sounded like Agnes. Agnes! His mind closed down and he stared blindly out the window. What would the Holts say if they knew he'd seen Agnes with the gun the night before? If they knew she'd threatened to kill herself? If they knew how well she shot and that he'd known all along how dangerous a gun was in her hands? He didn't want to think about it.

He jumped off the car before it stopped and ran up the hill toward the stone sheds; it was still raining lightly and the ground was slippery and more than once he fell and had to pull himself upright, but he ran faster each time, and finally he was at the back entrance to his shed. "Charlie," he said, grabbing his friend by the arm, "I've got to talk to you. Put your jacket on." "What happened?" Charlie asked; "did anything happen to your father?" "My family's fine," Frank said; "they're the only ones who are. You've got to tell me what to do." Charlie shrugged on his coat and followed Frank outside. "It's raining again," Charlie said, turning up his collar; "this coat smells powerful when it gets wet. Sheepskin. I hate it." "They say Agnes shot Jane," Frank said.

Charlie raised his hand to his hair and smoothed it back. "What?" he asked; "Agnes shot Jane?" "That's what they said," Frank told him. "How's Agnes?" Charlie asked. "Probably dead," he said; "they're pretty sure Jane's dead and they think Agnes is, too." "What happened to Agnes?" Charlie asked. "She shot herself. After she shot Jane," Frank said. "Where are they?" Charlie asked. "At the hospital," Frank said.

"What are you going to do?" Charlie asked; "they probably

already know what was wrong between the girls." "Look, Charlie," Frank said urgently, "if it's true and Agnes is dead, or if she's dying, I'm not going to tell the truth. They'll be after me like a pack of wolves. I'm going to say I was engaged to Jane but I never had anything to do with Agnes." "The last time I talked to Agnes," Charlie said, "she told me you accused her of writing letters to Jane's family." "I did," Frank said. "Well, she said she was going to write *you* some letters," he said, "and if she did, you know what she wrote them about." "You think they're still in her room?" Frank asked. "They might be," Charlie said; "it wouldn't hurt to look, not if you're going to say there was nothing between you." "Why aren't you telling me I deserve whatever I get?" Frank asked him. "You're getting it, aren't you?" Charlie asked, his voice strained; "and if she's dead, she's dead. You're still here." "But you'd trade me for her, wouldn't you?" Frank asked. "Yes," said Charlie, "without thinking twice. She was always worth two of you." Frank's eyes filled and he began crying. "I didn't think you could cry," Charlie said; "well, it's too late now, isn't it?" Frank asked him if he would come back to the boardinghouse with him. He didn't want to go into Agnes's room alone, and Charlie said he would. "But I'm not going to lie for you," he said; "keep the newspapers away from me, and the police."

They went back to the Trowbridge house, said hello to Iris, who had not yet heard the news, and went up to Agnes's room. "I can't find anything," Frank said after a while; he was turning back the mattress and looking beneath it. "I'll look in this," Charlie said, picking up Agnes's photograph album. "This is old," Charlie said, running his fingers along the bottle green velvet of its cover; "the nap's rubbed off where it opens." "It belonged to her grandmother," Frank said. Charlie began leafing through it. "Wait," he said; "this looks like a letter." He unfolded it and began to read. "'Dearest Frank,'" he read aloud, "'Don't blame love-sick girls for they were made thus by loving. Jane is not to blame if she loves you.'" He looked at Frank and read silently. "Listen to this," he said: "'If you listen for it, you will hear the voice of the little soul who went before us calling to us, asking us to come toward him together.'" Frank was crying again.

"If I were you," Charlie said, "I'd burn this. If they show this to Polly, she'll break down and tell them everything and then some." Frank wiped his eyes and took some kindling from the woodbox and threw it into the stove. Then he struck a match and waited for it to take fire. "Put the letter in," he said to Charlie. "No, you do it," Charlie said; "finish what you start for once."

Frank dropped the letter in; it caught fire slowly. Then its edges began to blacken and a narrow border of translucent orange appeared between the black border and the paper, still white, still covered with violet ink. And then the letter was gone. "You don't think she made any more copies?" Charlie asked. "She might have," Frank said; "she locked herself up in here for days after Polly's wedding." "Where would she have put them?" Charlie asked; "there's nothing else in here. Maybe we should look in your room." They got up and started down the hall to Frank's room. When they went inside, Charlie leaned against the door and Frank sank into his chair. "We should be looking," Charlie said. "I know," said Frank. But he was. He was looking around the room for some sign that, since morning, his world had really been forced out of shape. There was no sign of deformity anywhere, but he saw it everywhere, just beyond his line of sight. There was a rap at the door and they both jumped. Charlie moved away from the door and Iris came in, followed by a policeman. "This is Officer Delonnay," Iris said, staring meaningfully at Frank; "he wants to search your room, and Agnes's too." "I just came out of the young lady's room," the policeman said, "and I saw that someone made a fire in her stove. Was that you?" "Yes," Charlie said; "we burned some letters Agnes wrote him." "Why?" asked the policeman. "They'd only hurt people," Charlie said. "It's called destroying evidence," said the officer. "What difference does it make," Charlie asked, "if they're both dead?" "I'll worry about the law," said the officer; "don't burn anything else."

The policeman began going through Frank's drawers, unfolding his clothes, slipping his hand beneath the cut-up feed bags lining his drawers. "Why don't you all stand out in the hall?" the officer asked at last. "I've got to check the floor."

Iris went outside with Charlie and Frank. "Is there anything in there for him to find?" she asked Frank. "I don't think so," he said. Officer Delonnay was down on his knees, working away at a floorboard. "Well, what's this?" he said, lifting the board. He took out a long box and from it removed two ten dollar bills, a box of cartridges, and a rolled up sheet of paper. On the bottom of the box was a single, folded sheet. Charlie looked at Frank and Frank stared ahead stonily. The officer unfolded the single sheet of paper. " 'Don't blame love-sick girls,' " he read, " 'for they were made thus by loving.' " He broke off, looked at Frank, and then turned the page over to check the signature. "It's signed Agnes Dempster," he said, rolling it up again. Charlie shook his head. Frank went back into the room and sat down on the bed. "What's the rest of it?" he asked, looking at the scroll in the policeman's hand. "Don't you know?" the policeman asked, surprised. "I never saw that before," Frank said. Charlie looked at him and saw that he was telling the truth.

The officer untied the ribbon holding the pages together. "It's another letter," he said. "Read it," Frank said. "'The future is a wonderful place and everything in it is wonderful because all horizons are imaginary.'" He stopped, turned some pages, and said that the letter went on for a long time. "'The child I gave back is waiting for us to recreate him and bring him back, and I know that you are the only one who can give him back to me because you created him for me and no one else can make him grow in me but you.'" The policeman stopped reading and looked at Frank. "Can we burn that?" asked Frank. "No. It's evidence," the policeman said. "Will the Holts have to see it?" asked Frank. "I hope not," said the policeman. "Are these the cartridges she used in her gun?" he asked Frank. "No, they're for mine," Frank said. "I'll just take them with me," the policeman said, and he and Iris left and started down the stairs.

"You just couldn't leave her alone, could you?" Charlie burst out as the door closed; "I guess once you carved her, you didn't care what happened to her." "Now you sound like Agnes," Frank said. "Poor Agnes," said Charlie.

At Whately Hospital, the nurses kept coming into the room to look at the two girls lying together on the little metal bed. They had heard the girls were already dead and didn't observe them carefully. Outside, the reporters were waiting for further information. A nurse who had just come on duty went over to the bed and bent over to get a closer look at the girls. She picked up the blond girl's arm and felt no pulse; her flesh was cold. Then she bent to look at the other girl, and let the first girl's arm fall across the second girl's shoulder. She thought she saw the second girl's eyelids quiver. She bent closer. She heard something, a faint, mewling cry. The girl's eyelid was beginning to open. She backed away, horrified, and ran into the hall. "She's not dead," she cried to the people there; "she's alive! One of them is alive!"

In the whitewashed room, in the small metal bed, Agnes's right eye opened slowly and everything slowly swam into focus. What was she looking at? It was white and blurry. It was also yellow. She strained to see more clearly and it seemed to her she was looking into someone else's eyes. They were light blue eyes. She made a tremendous effort and moved her head back a few inches on the pillow. It was another girl and the girl was asleep. She was not very pretty and her skin was terribly white. She didn't know who she was, but she looked familiar. The girl was terribly cold. She wanted to get away from her. A scream formed in her throat and flew like a trapped bird through her skull but she could not make a sound, only the little animal meeps she heard coming from somewhere beyond her. The girl was dead. They had put her in bed with a dead girl. They would bury her with a dead girl. The scream flew through her skull like a flock of ravens. The girl was cold. She had never felt anything so cold. The girl was not human. Her skin felt like the skin of a salamander. She continued staring into the fixed light blue eyes and she continued screaming, silently screaming.

Two orderlies and two doctors surrounded the little bed on which the girls lay. "This one's alive," said one of the doctors; "get this one into another room." The nurse who had seen Agnes's eyelid twitch had come in and tried pulling the dead girl away from her, but could not move her. "Leave that for the attendants," the doctor said; "go with this one. Take her down the hall and clean her off. Stay there with her. If she gets stronger, we may have to go into her head." "Go into her head?" repeated the nurse. "After the bullet," the doctor said; "she can't live if it stays there." "Do you think she'll live?" the nurse whispered. "No," said the doctor. Agnes heard him and smiled inside. None of the muscles in her face would move. I'm going to die, she thought to herself and she fell back into the darkness from which she had just emerged.

"Hurry up!" the doctor was telling the nurse and the attendants; "get her out of that bed. Who did this? Who put them in together?" "We thought she was dead. We thought both of them were," the attendant said miserably. "If you weren't sure, you shouldn't have done it," the doctor said; "even if you were, you shouldn't have done it. How would you like to wake up with a cadaver staring you down?" "I'm sorry," the attendant said. "*Never* do it again!" the doctor said; "put her in next to the operating room, and I'll be there soon." "Calm down," he told the nurse; "at least you noticed she was alive. No one else bothered checking on them." "It was horrible," the girl said; "I'll never forget it." "I doubt if any of us will," said the doctor; "let's try not to mention it in front of the reporters. None of the people close to the girls would ever forget it either, so it's better they don't know about it at all. Just keep quiet." The nurse nodded dumbly.

Then she and the doctor turned back to face the dead girl lying in the bed. "Draw the sheet up over that one's face," he said. "Are we keeping her here?" the nurse asked. "Only long enough for Doctor Salter to take the bullet out of her skull," the doctor said; "the police need it for evidence. Then her family wants her back." "Do they know?" the nurse asked. "Doctor Salter told them he thought she was dying before," said the doctor; "he's going out to tell them now." "Were they out there when I ran out?" asked the nurse; "did they hear me say someone was alive?" The doctor said they weren't there; they were sitting in the front entrance hall and they hadn't heard anything. "I bet they hope she dies," the nurse said thoughtfully; "imagine someone killing you just because you're going to get married." The doctor nodded. "Jealousy is terrible," he said. "We're all jealous," said the little nurse, "but we don't try to kill people. Not even if we want to." "Although we sometimes think about it?" the doctor said, smiling slightly. "Well, thinking about it!" said the girl; "everyone does. It's terrifying, knowing that someone might really kill you just because you have something of your own. I hate her!" "You didn't even know her," said the doctor. "She shouldn't get away with it," said the nurse. "It doesn't look like she got away with much," said the doctor. "She's still alive," said the nurse.

When Officer Delonnay left the Trowbridge house, Iris came back up to Frank's room. For once, she was at a loss for words. "Well, boys," she said. Then she shook her head and sat down in an armchair. "I wonder if I should get her things together," she said, almost to herself. "Packing them up wouldn't be a bad idea," Charlie said; "if she gets better, she'll need them." "She's not going to get better," Frank said; "she's dead." "The man said he didn't know," Iris answered; "he only thought they were dead." "They were unconscious when they were taken off," Frank said; "Mr. Holt's sure his daughter's dead." "Maybe Agnes isn't," Charlie said softly. "If she's not dead," Iris said, looking up, "she'll be put in jail. She shot someone." "Jail," said Charlie. "They hung a woman here two years ago," Iris said, "for shooting her lover." Frank and Charlie exchanged glances. "Who's telling Agnes's father?" Charlie asked. "I don't know," Frank said; "I'm not." "The police will see to it," Iris said. "I'll go," Charlie said. "Maybe you ought to keep out of it," said Iris; "they'll wonder what she meant to you." "Once she meant a lot to me," Charlie said.

40

Frederick Parsons, the state's attorney, was considered a handsome man, and everyone said he looked like Abraham Lincoln from a distance, but up close, he was handsome, if severe. He was one of the ablest prosecutors in the state and had an impressive record of convictions. Soon after Jane Holt was officially pronounced dead, the district attorney came into his office and told him that one young girl had shot another and then tried to kill herself and they didn't know if the girl who had done the shooting would live. There was a lot of talk in the city already, the district attorney said, and he thought if the girl lived, people would be out for blood. Everyone knew the dead girl's family because of the Emporium; he told Frederick Parsons that a crowd had gathered beneath the wounded girl's hospital window.

The district attorney said he thought it was going to be a hard case. He'd asked the hospital guard if the crowd was friendly or hostile and the guard had said he couldn't tell; he heard some people mumbling about hanging "the murderess," and other women stood there, silently weeping. It was, he said, more eerie outside the hospital than in it. Perhaps, said Parsons, the intense interest in the shootings was related to the time of their occurrence: the day before Christmas. But the district attorney said he didn't think the timing of the event had much to do with the crowd's reaction. He didn't know why people should be so interested, or why he himself was so fascinated by the incident he had so often heard described: one girl raising a gun to another's head, the first girl falling silently, the rain slanting down over them, the girl with the gun raising the weapon to her own head and falling, just as silently, on top of her victim in the snow. "Well," said the district attorney, getting up, his knees cracking, "you're going to be the one prosecuting this case. I thought you'd better hear about it right away. It's best to have as much time as you can to think things out." "Yes," said Parsons, "it is." "Merry Christmas," said the district attorney, grimacing slightly. "Merry Christmas," said Parsons.

After the district attorney left, Parsons put his feet up on his desk and stared at the wall. He saw the girls falling; he saw the crowd outside the hospital. He got up and went over to his diplomas, neatly framed, hanging on the wall. He read every word written on them. The district attorney had seemed uneasy about the town's reaction to the case. Was he afraid they would want to lynch the girl? Without knowing why, he got up and set off for Charles Kingsley's house.

Charles Kingsley was almost seventy, and every year brought rumors of his impending retirement from legal practice. But he did not retire and he had become something of a legend as an attorney for the defense. Frederick Parsons often thought that his life would be pleasant if it were not for the existence of Charles Kingsley. The man had an unnatural skill; Parsons had come up against him time after time, and after each case, he was left with the same impression: Kingsley talked to the jurors in words which were somehow inaudible to everyone else in the room. He had become famous as a defender of hopeless cases and Parsons did not like to think of how many "hopeless" cases had walked out of the courtroom free men because of Kingsley's ingenious strategies. There was no end to his resourcefulness. He rang Kingsley's doorbell and waited. Mrs. Kingsley came to the door with a half-filled stocking in one hand. "Oh," she said, "it's you. You're not here on business, are you?" Parsons said he didn't know. "Well, then," she said, "I'll go get Charles."

The two men went into the library. Mr. Kingsley lit a lamp and the room came alive with shadows. The tall bookcases which lined the dark red walls leaned in as if they were considering toppling and burying their students beneath them. "I guess you came to wish me a merry Christmas," Kingsley said. "Not exactly that," said Parsons; "did you happen to hear about the shooting on the edge of town?" Mr. Kingsley said he hadn't. "Well, this is how it was," said Mr. Parsons, and he described the incident to him. As he talked, he again saw one girl falling, then the other, as if he had been there, as if they were falling before his eyes. "Well," he concluded, "there couldn't have been more witnesses. There must have been at least four people I know of who saw the shooting. Someone's already come forward and said he saw one of the girls practicing with a gun earlier in the day, and they found letters in her room addressed to the victim's fiancé. It's an open and shut case. They'll hang her."

"That's all right with me," said Kingsley; "I never had much sympathy for either murder or jealousy." Parsons sighed. "How about a cigar?" Kingsley asked. Parsons took one. "What I don't understand," said Kingsley, once the cigars were lit, "is why you're telling me about the case. If it's open and shut, anyone can handle it. Who's going to prosecute the case?" "I am," said Parsons, "if she lives." "You've gotten so fond of appearing with me in court, you want my company again, is that it?" Kingsley asked; "or did you hear I had a shock last summer and that I'm not quite what I was? My hand shakes but that's all the damage that was done. Read me a page and I can recite it back when you close the book. I'm no worse for wear." "King of the foxes," said Parsons, "that's what they call you in court." Kingsley looked pleased.

"If the girl recovers," said Parsons, "someone has to defend her." "Not me," said Kingsley; "caught in the act, a city full of witnesses, another love-sick girl run wild. Let someone else defend her." "If you don't do it, and if she lives," said Parsons, "she's sure to be convicted." "One way or the other, it sounds as if she's sure to die," Kingsley said; "either a bullet in the head gets her or a verdict from a jury. Let's hope she dies. That seems to be what she wanted."

"If you don't defend her," said Parsons, "you might as well put the rope around her neck yourself." "Stuff!" exclaimed Kingsley; "I'm no magician. The city's full of competent and more than competent defense attorneys." "You're the one who got Dynamite Dan off," Parsons said. "You mean that idiot who tried to blow up the seminary with all that dynamite? Anyone could have gotten him off." "He was convicted in the papers before the trial began," said Parsons; "you got him off." "I bribed the jury," Kingsley said, grinning; "that's what *The Sentinel* reported." "Not in so many words," Parsons said. "Well, two buildings went sky high and they found Dynamite Dan walking around with a stick of dynamite," said Kingsley, "so I can see why they thought the evidence was strongly against him." Parsons shook his head; he still could not account for the acquittal of the young man in question. He ought to be able to; he had been the prosecuting attorney.

"Why do you want to come up against me again?" Kingsley asked; "I keep beating you. You do very well when I'm not around." Parsons got up, looked out the window, came back, and sat down on the edge of the desk. "The law's an adversary process," Parsons said; "I need someone to fight." "No," said Kingsley, "you don't want to be the one to tie the knot around her neck. Or you'll tie it, but you want to make it look good. You want to be reluctant about it. You don't want to drag off a young girl kicking and screaming all the way to the scaffold." "That's right," said Parsons; "I don't. She shot herself through the head. They say she's only seventeen, maybe eighteen. If a noose has to go around her neck, I'd just as soon fasten it there after a struggle. You're a defense lawyer. She needs a defender in the old sense of the word. She needs a knight in shining armor." "It doesn't sound like she's done too well with knights in shining armor so far, does it?" asked Kingsley, puffing on his cigar. "No," said Parsons, "it doesn't."

"What makes you think anyone wants me?" Kingsley asked; "is her family here?" "I don't think they know yet," Parsons said. "Then why are *you* here?" Kingsley asked. "Because when her family arrives," said Parsons, "I'd like to recommend you." "Just so I can make it harder for you?" Kingsley asked him. "There's no possible defense," Parsons said. "I wouldn't say that," Kingsley said; "there's always a defense. Remember the man I got off on a mistrial? I let you make that mistake early on in the trial and then I won on the appeal. There's always a defense." He fell silent, chewing on his cigar. "Would you mind waiting here a minute?" he asked. "Why?" asked Parsons; "are you going to ask your wife's permission?" Kingsley raised his eyebrows. "Something like that," he said. "One of the many things I don't understand," said Parsons, "is why you *want* people to think of you as henpecked." "Ah," said Kingsley, his smile widening into a grin.

Mrs. Kingsley, her three daughters, and several of their friends were decorating the Christmas tree and hanging dried pine boughs from the shelves. The fragrance of the Christmas cookies baking in the stove floated warmly through the air. The fire burned on the hearth like a tamed beast. "Mr. Parsons wants me to take a case," Mr. Kingsley said, and everyone stopped what they were doing and looked at him. "You don't need any more cases," said his wife; "you were invited to teach at Harvard. That's a much more sensible profession for a man your age." "Don't you want to know what case it is?" Mr. Kingsley asked. "No," said Mrs. Kingsley, "we don't." "*I* do, Mother," said his oldest daughter. She was, Mr. Kingsley realized with a shock, over forty herself. He still thought of her as a child.

"It seems there was a shooting today," said Mr. Kingsley. "You mean the two girls?" asked his oldest daughter. "Which two girls?" asked Mr. Kingsley. "You know which ones," his wife said, watching him suspiciously. "One girl shot another and then shot herself," said his youngest daughter; "is that the shooting you mean?" "That's it," said Mr. Kingsley. He watched his daughter's face. She was staring at him, her mouth open. "You wouldn't take that case, would you, Poppa?" she asked, her chin quivering; "that girl shot Jane Holt for no reason at all. She was in love with Jane's fiancé and she shot Jane. She's a monster!" "A monster," said Mr. Kingsley thoughtfully. "I hope you're not thinking about taking that case," said Mrs. Kingsley; "everyone's talking about it. How would we have felt if that girl had shot one of our daughters? The Holts are never going to get over it. I won't have you taking that case!" "That's strong talk, Martha," Kingsley said; "I make up my own mind."

"He's thinking about it," Mrs. Kingsley said, sinking down in a chair; "I see the signs. He wants to see what we make of it." "She killed Jane!" his youngest daughter exclaimed and burst into tears. "I didn't know you knew Jane Holt so well," said Mr. Kingsley. His daughter said she didn't know her well; she only said hello to her on the street. Then, said Mr. Kingsley, she seemed to be taking the talk of defending the girl who shot her pretty personally. "And why shouldn't she?" demanded his wife; "when the very same girl could have shot her if things had been a little bit different and the other girl imagined she was in love with Jim?" "Imagined?" repeated Kingsley. "They say the girl who did the shooting thought Jane's fiancé was in love with her and that's why she killed Jane," his daughter said, starting to cry again. "She thought he was, but he wasn't?" asked Mr. Kingsley. "Will you stop worrying the subject?" Mrs. Kingsley asked; "can't you see you're upsetting the girls?"

"They weren't upset about Dynamite Dan," he said thoughtfully. "Dynamite Dan wasn't after them," his wife said impatiently. "And this girl was?" he asked. He looked at the seven women in the room. They all stared at him with hard, blank eyes. On his wife's face was a familiar expression, as if her face would say what her mouth would not: You're only a man. You can't be expected to understand. You're only a man. "None of you

429

people know why there's a crowd under the girl's hospital window, do you?'' he asked. ''Probably they're friends of Jane's,'' his wife said; ''probably they want to hear that the other one's dead.'' ''Good Christians standing out in the rain on Christmas Eve, hoping someone will die?'' he asked; ''I doubt it.'' ''So do I,'' said one of his daughter's friends; ''I walked by. I saw them. I hoped she didn't die. It could have been any one of us. We could all have done it.'' ''Gotten shot?'' asked Mr. Kingsley. ''Fired the shot,'' the girl said. ''Oh, I don't think so,'' said Mrs. Kingsley; ''you couldn't hurt a fly.'' ''If you'll excuse me,'' said Mr. Kingsley.

He went back into the library. ''What do you think?'' Parsons asked him. ''Well,'' he said, ''my wife doesn't think I should touch the case. One of my daughter's friends seems to think she could have pulled the trigger herself. There's a hung jury in my living room. Facets everywhere. I'm interested enough, I guess. If the girl lives. If her family's interested in paying my fee. I'm too old to take on a case just to get some attention. It's Friday. If the girl's alive Wednesday and if her family wants me, I guess I'll do it. You ought to get a run for your money.'' ''You already have an idea,'' Parsons said. ''It's too late to undo it now,'' said Kingsley, his well-known grin lighting up his face. He thought a moment and then said he didn't want anyone talking to the girl unless he approved of them first, not unless they were police officers. ''That's normal procedure,'' Parsons said; ''we don't want everyone talking to her, either.'' ''All right, then,'' said Kingsley; ''we'll wait and see.''

He walked Mr. Parsons to the door and watched him walk down the path and out of sight. Self-defense was out for this case. Everyone said the dead girl had carried no gun and had made no attempt to harm her companion. But the girls said the other one had shot Jane Holt for no reason at all; she'd imagined Jane Holt's fiancé was in love with her. He thought about the women in the parlor. One of them was crying for the girl who was still alive. Another was crying for the girl who was dead. He thought about the girl who was still alive. A lot would depend on what she was like. If she was the kind who could move the jury's sympathy, the best defense would be insanity. That would give him a chance to keep the girl before the jury and the spectators.

The insanity defense meant expert witnesses. He was impressed with Doctor Train, the supervisor at Highbury. He'd have to wait a while to talk to the girl and see what she was like. In the meantime, he'd go talk to Doctor Train and see what *he* was like. It was all a matter of personalities, of the forces inside them, of which way their emotions ran. The emotions occupied the territory; the intellect marched in and set up garrisons. That was the trouble with Parsons, he thought; he expected the law to be logical and precise when it was actually an accumulation of contradictory edicts which had lived uncomfortably together since the beginning of time. There was such a thing as justice, he thought, although it existed only when human beings were able to manipulate the law, that vast machine which moved, at times, in obedience to the music of the spheres. In court, the law was a machine whose cogs and wheels were the hearts and minds of the humans of the jury.

The mind of the jury. That was a subject he could go on about. He thought of the jury and the spectators behind them as the wolf pack, and the accused was the stray trying to escape exile or death at their hands. And he and the prosecuting attorney fought to lead the pack. Years ago, forty years ago, after he'd won his first important case, he told the prosecuting attorney he thought of the jury as a pack of wolves and the man had been horrified. "They're instructed to make a determination based on the evidence in front of them," he had said; "they're not supposed to be swayed by their emotions." But they were; juries were the great balance wheel of the law. Oh, he knew juries. If you were defending the right client a photographer could bring in life-size pictures of the man strangling his victim and the jury would decide there was something wrong with the pictures and that the man had been bending over the dead man trying to resuscitate him. There were cases which had been handed to him on a plate by juries, acquittals for a husband accused of trying to murder his wife's ex-lover, even though, in the courtroom, in full sight of the jury, the judge, and the press, the man had tried to throw himself once more upon his victim. There was a deep animal wisdom in juries; it was something primitive. He relied on it. And there were times when juries had acquitted clients he himself would have shot, and later he came to believe the jury was right. He disliked the intellectual juries of more sophisticated cities. They confused themselves and everyone else and, after six appeals, the law reached the conclusion a Montpelier jury would have reached in the first place.

Of course, if it was a fine point of legal theory at issue, he didn't want a jury deciding; then he wanted a judge. Juries had no patience with theorizing. But Parsons had said often enough that he, Kingsley, treated the judge as if he were a jury of one and that he could seduce anyone on the bench. Parsons believed Kingsley didn't really know the law at all. He seemed to think Kingsley won his cases by making good use of his theatrical personality and his sly emotional appeals. But Kingsley knew his law. He used it when decisions went against him; then he won on an appeal. But he was never as happy to win a case on a technicality; when the jury acquitted his client, then he felt as if they were all in it together. If the jury went against him, and he saw no grounds for appeal, he gave in. He believed in the mind of the pack. He did. By now, he knew better than to expound upon his theories. They called him a fox. He wasn't a fox. He was a wolf.

He went out to the barn and found the stable boy roasting potatoes in the wood stove. "Get down to Whately," he said, "and see if the doctors think that girl named Dempster is going to live and if anyone asks you where you're going, say you're going to see your sick mother." He went back into the parlor, and before he was through the door, the voices of the women were pecking at him. Well, he thought, this was nothing compared to the cackling the town would indulge in if he took the case.

When he came down to breakfast the next morning, Mrs. Kingsley was waiting for him, brandishing a newspaper. "Have you seen this?" she asked, without handing it to him; "it's a special edition. On Christmas! They never publish a paper on Christmas day." "Let me have it," he said.

A TERRIBLE TRAGEDY

Within The City Limits Yesterday—Crazed By Jealousy A Young Woman Murders An Innocent Girl And Then Attempts To Put An End To Her Own Life—Her Victim Dies A Few Hours Later—The Story In Detail

---

"There it is," said Martha, "right on the front page. Are you going to defend that girl?" "You know, Marty," Mr. Kingsley said, putting down the paper, "every Christmas morning it's the

432

same thing. I wake up at four o'clock ready to rush downstairs and hide behind the closet door so I can see the girls opening their presents and every year I wake up and realize they're not little girls anymore." "Don't Marty me," said his wife; "don't talk about the girls. I want to know what you're going to do about the case." "Well, don't you miss it sometimes?" he asked; "the way Christmas was?" "I miss it," said Mrs. Kingsley; "I used to spend all November and December sewing for the holiday gifts. Are you taking that case?"

"I sent to the hospital last night," he said, "and the doctors there think she's going to die any time." "Well, I hate to hear about anyone dying," said his wife. Mr. Kingsley watched her face. The corners of her mouth were pulled down. She was puzzled. "How old was the girl?" she asked. "Eighteen, I think." "That's right," she said; "that's what it said in the paper. She's just a baby." "A dangerous baby," he said. "Still," said his wife. "Let me read the paper and catch up with you," he said. Mrs. Kingsley sat down opposite him, watching him as he read.

The darkest chapter in the history of Montpelier was written Saturday, and Christmas is shadowed by the most terrible tragedy ever known in the annals of the town. Before eight o'clock Saturday morning word was telephoned to police headquarters by Mr. R. L. Grayson that a shooting affair had occurred just south of his residence on Seminary Hill. Officers and physicians and a large crowd of people hurried to the spot, and as the news of the dreadful occurrence spread, everything else was for the time forgotten. A representative of *The Spectator* was soon on the scene, and from a mass of distorted rumors, was able to glean the following story:

Miss Agnes Dempster, eighteen years of age, daughter of Amon Dempster, a wealthy farmer of North Chittenden, shot Jane Holt, daughter of Thomas P. Holt of East Montpelier, and before anyone could reach the scene of the shooting, turned the revolver on herself and sent a bullet crashing through her own brain. These young women were both in love with Frank Holt. Jane Holt had been engaged to Frank Holt for the past two years and the engagement had been sanctioned by the families of the young people. In spite of the fact that Frank Holt and Jane Holt had the same last name, they were not related. Several months ago, Miss Dempster became enamored of Mr. Holt, although the statement of many people familiar with the facts go to show that this affection was not reciprocated by Mr. Holt. Miss Dempster became insanely jealous of Miss Holt and has recently made threats that she would shoot herself.

Miss Dempster had rooms at the home of Iris Trowbridge on Chapin Street. She and Frank Holt lived on the second floor of the Trowbridge dwelling. Miss Dempster arose at five o'clock Friday morning and went to the top of Bald Hill, where she was seen practicing with a revolver. She went from there directly to the home of L. L. Ludlum on Cherry Street, where Jane Holt was living. Miss Holt had an engagement to go with Frank Holt to Barre on the half past eight train that morning and was to meet him at his home on Chapin Street. While at Mr. Ludlum's the young women had some conversation and Miss Dempster was heard to remark, "Frank Holt can't be engaged to us both."

Mr. Holt, a stone carver at the Barre quarries, was seen Friday night by a *Spectator* reporter and although suffering from intense mental strain, he was willing to talk and answer any questions asked him. He denied most emphatically that he had ever kept company with Miss Dempster or had been intimate with her. He said that she had often tried to thrust herself upon him and to induce him to take her riding or walking, but he was engaged to Miss Holt and did not want anything to do with her. Mrs. Trowbridge, owner of the boardinghouse in which both Miss Dempster and Mr. Holt resided, stated that she had never heard Frank Holt say he intended to marry Agnes Dempster, but that Miss Dempster was evidently very much in love with Mr. Holt.

Mr. Holt is an industrious, temperate man, and so far as can be learned, both from his employers and his associates in the city, he bears a good reputation.

Miss Holt, the victim of the shooting, had a stainless reputation and whatever the circumstances surrounding this case may be, sure it is that she was the innocent victim of cruel and insane jealousy. Her father and mother are prominent, well-to-do residents of East Montpelier, who have raised a large family of children. Miss Holt has worked out at different times but her moral character has always been above reproach.

Miss Dempster's mother died a year and a half ago. Her father has always been most indulgent with her and since she has been in Montpelier has often sent her money, sometimes as much as $50 at a time. She attended North Chittendon School and taught a term in that town, but the pastoral life in that mountain town had no charms for her, and she preferred to come to the city and earn her own living. She had worked in the tailoring shops of Mrs. C. James and was regarded by her employer as somewhat flighty. She had a very nervous temperament and at times was mentally depressed, often declaring she wished she was dead. It is only charitable to believe that the love she bore for the young Holt had turned her brain.

The scene of the shooting was visited, and the pools of blood where the young ladies lay gave mute evidence of the terrible tragedy that had been enacted and made the strongest nerves quiver. The revolver was found on the ground by Policeman Delonnay, in whose possession it is.

After the shooting, Policeman Delonnay visited the room on Chapin Street occupied by Miss Dempster. He found her clothing all packed in a trunk. In the bureau was a broken box of cartridges and a note neatly written in ink and signed Agnes Dempster. This note strengthens the prevalent belief that inordinate and unrequited love for Frank Holt had unbalanced Miss Dempster's mind.

State's Attorney Parsons explains that an autopsy is to be performed upon Miss Holt Monday morning. The family of the deceased has no objections to this unpleasant proceeding, which is deemed necessary by the State's Attorney because of the possibility of future legal proceedings.

On Friday night, Frank Holt, the young man to whom Miss Holt was engaged, sat with the family, and his grief was most pathetic to witness.

Mr. Dempster arrived in Montpelier Friday night, but was unavailable for comment. The doctors at Whately Hospital hold out little hope for Miss Dempster and expect her death hourly. Mr. Dempster is a kind old gentleman and the strain is telling perceptibly on him. A reporter from *The Spectator* will publish an interview with him within the week. He spoke briefly of his daughter and the tears flowed freely. He said she was the first to disgrace the name of Dempster. He repeated several times his belief that she had been driven insane and was, perhaps, as much sinned against as sinning.

_____

"Well," said Mr. Kingsley, looking up from the paper, "they're starting to try her in the tabloids. Nothing unusual in that. It might be useful." "Useful to whom?" Mrs. Kingsley asked; "you don't mean to tell me you think the girl was insane?

435

She was practicing with a gun a few hours before she went and got Jane out of Mrs. Ludlum's house and shot her." "I wonder why Jane went with her," Mr. Kingsley said. "Curiosity," said his wife. "If someone had come to you when we were engaged and told you I was also engaged to her, would you have gone out walking with her?" "No," Mrs. Kingsley said, "I would have gone looking for you and found out what was what." "I wonder why she did go with that girl," said Mr. Kingsley; "maybe she already knew about her. The father of the girl who did the shooting thinks she was driven insane." "It's his daughter who did the shooting," said Mrs. Kingsley; "what else *would* he think?" "What do you think?" Mr. Kingsley asked her; "are you sure the girl killed Jane Holt intentionally?" "Oh, no," said his wife; "you tell me what you think. I'm tired of telling you what I think so that you can sharpen your wits against mine." "Come on, Marty," he said, his face lit by his famous smile; "I don't know what I think until I hear what you think." She folded and unfolded her napkin; she pushed imaginary crumbs back and forth across the tablecloth.

"All right," she said. "I think it's a terrible thing that people can run wild like that and rip through the town killing innocent people. They're like storms. They're deadly and they ought to be shot just the way you'd shoot a mad dog because that's what they're like. Maybe she was jealous for a reason. I don't care. People who shoot other people ought to be shot. That's what I think." She looked up at her husband, who stared down at the table. "The only trouble is," she said, "the girl is eighteen. She shot herself through the head. It will be horrible to wait for her to recover and then wait for them to hang her." "Why?" asked Mr. Kingsley; "you said she ought to be shot." "She's *already* been shot," his wife said. She looked up at him. "Oh, now you've confused me," she said, irritably; "I suppose that's what you wanted. Are you going to tell me what you think?" "I think we don't know the whole story yet," he said.

"What do you think of the girl?" Mrs. Kingsley asked. "How can I think anything about the girl yet?" he asked; "I don't know why she shot the Holt girl. I don't even know whether she's going to live." "You *never* tell me what you think!" his wife said, exasperated. "When I know, I'll tell you," he said. "No, you won't," she said; "you never know what you think until the verdict is in. By that time, I *know* what I think." "True enough," he said, and asked if he might possibly hope for a bit of breakfast.

A few minutes later, the doorbell rang. "Finish your breakfast," said Mrs. Kingsley; "I'll have him wait for you in the parlor." The woman had second sight, her husband thought; she always knew when someone was waiting for him on the other side of the door. "Come in, Mr. Parsons," he heard her say; "come in, gentlemen." She came into the dining room. "Mr. Parsons and two gentlemen are in the parlor," she said; "I suppose this has to do with the Dempster girl." "I'll find out," he said, getting up and going into the parlor.

"This is Agnes Dempster's father, Amon Dempster," said Mr. Parsons, "and this is Charlie Mondell, a friend of Agnes's. They were at Whately Hospital and the doctors told them that they didn't expect Miss Dempster to regain consciousness today and a reporter came up and told Mr. Dempster that he was wasting his time in the hospital when he really ought to go to the police, because if his daughter died, he'd just bury her, but if she didn't, she'd be in real trouble with the law."

"So we went to the sheriff's office," said Charlie Mondell, "and we found Mr. Parsons there and he told us you'd expressed an interest in the case." "He did, did he?" Mr. Kingsley said. "Is it all up with Agnes?" Mr. Dempster asked abruptly; "if she lives, will they hang her? That's what he said. The reporter." "There's always a chance," said Mr. Kingsley. "I know about you," Mr. Dempster said; "I read for the law years ago. I always followed your cases. I want you to take this one." "My fees are high," Mr. Kingsley said. "I'll pay what you ask," Mr. Dempster said; "I'll sell the farm if I have to." "They're not that high," Mr. Kingsley said. He liked Mr. Dempster's looks, tall, silent, strong boned, his sweet manner. There was something lost about him, as if he were an over-sized doll who had been put away for a long time and had just been taken out hastily, brushed off, and put on a train to Montpelier. "Well," said Mr. Parsons, "if you'd like to talk to your client, I'll go home." "I'd like to talk to him," said Mr. Kingsley. "I know my way out," said Mr. Parsons.

"Who told you to go to the police?" asked Mr. Kingsley as soon as Mr. Parsons had gone; "was it a reporter named the Hammerhead?" "The Hammerhead," repeated Mr. Dempster; "I think that's what they called him." "He's a reporter on *The Inquirer*," said Mr. Kingsley; "it sounds like he's taking an interest in this case. That's good to know." "Why?" asked Mr. Dempster. "Later, I'll go hunt him up and tell him everything we want to see in print," said Mr. Kingsley; "I bet Parsons knows the Hammerhead sent you to him. I bet he's kicking himself now for asking me to take the case." "Did he actually ask you to take it?" Mr. Dempster asked him; "isn't that unprofessional?" "He didn't tell me anything I didn't already know from reading the papers," said Mr. Kingsley. "I see," said Mr. Dempster. "We often discuss cases we read about in the papers," said Mr. Kingsley. "Do you?" said Mr. Dempster. "Oh, yes," said Mr. Kingsley, smiling broadly; "it keeps our minds working." Mr. Dempster was dazed, he could see that.

"We don't have any time to lose," he said to Mr. Dempster. "Maybe I'd better go home," Charlie said. "You don't live at Mrs. Trowbridge's also?" Mr. Kingsley asked him. "No, but I did," Charlie said. "Why don't you come back for Mr. Dempster in about an hour?" Mr. Kingsley suggested. Charlie put on his coat and went out, leaving the two men alone.

"Well," said Mr. Kingsley; "we have one chance and only one chance. Insanity. We have to prove that your daughter's insane. Is there any insanity in your family? Anything beyond the normal run of crackpots?" "I don't think so," said Mr. Dempster. "Try to remember," said Mr. Kingsley; "any suicides?" "Suicides," said Mr. Dempster; "oh yes, we've had suicides. My wife's uncle killed himself. My youngest brother killed himself. But that was all long ago." "Two suicides," said Mr. Kingsley; "that's excellent. Well, what about the crackpots? Every family has some of those. We'll dress them up a little." "Well," Mr. Dempster said, "there was my wife's mother. She once moved into the pigpen, and lived in the chicken coop for a while." "Was she crazy?" Mr. Kingsley asked. "Some people thought she was," Mr. Dempster said. "Good," said Mr. Kingsley. "Some people thought Agnes was, too," he said; "she tried to kill herself when she was thirteen." "Why?" Mr. Kingsley asked. "I don't know. When she came around, she said she knew she was dying anyway, so she decided to kill herself and get it over with." "Was there anything wrong with her?" Mr. Kingsley asked. "Not that we ever knew," he said.

"Well, all that's good," said Mr. Kingsley; "is there anything else?" "Her mother. My wife. When she was pregnant with Agnes, our first daughter was scalded to death and she was out of her mind with grief for a long time. When Agnes was born, my wife didn't want any part of her." "That's very good," the attorney said. "My brother died in Highbury years ago," he said; "Agnes doesn't know anything about that. He hung himself. They put him in there because he was always setting fire to the curtains." "Excellent!" said the attorney. "But none of them except my brother were really crazy," said Mr. Dempster. "Let me be the judge of that," said Mr. Kingsley; "you don't have any oddities about you, perchance?" "No," Mr. Dempster said.

"Well, Mr. Dempster, let me put it to you. Would you be willing to go home and get out the family bible, so to speak, and trace insanity back through three generations of your family, and then after you'd found the insanity running back through your ancestry, would you tell the Hammerhead that you come from a family of raving lunatics? Because if you won't do that, she'll hang. There's no question about it." "I'll do whatever I have to," said Mr. Dempster; "for her." "What about Agnes herself?" he asked; "headaches? Fits? Bad dreams?" "She had all those," said her father; "I thought she'd grow out of it. She was pretty happy the last time I saw her. She'd been sick, though. That young man, he hinted it might not have been an ordinary sickness." "An extraordinary sickness?" asked the attorney. "She might have been in trouble," said Mr. Dempster. "In trouble," said Mr. Kingsley; "that would be too good to be true." He pressed the tips of his fingers together and thought.

"Have you seen today's paper?" he asked Mr. Dempster, handing it to him. Mr. Dempster took a pair of small, round black spectacles from his pocket, settled them on his nose, and began reading. "What's all this about Frank Holt?" he asked, throwing the paper down; "he came to North Chittendon with Agnes and he told me he was going to marry her. He told me so himself. I said I'd give them the money they needed to go to New York but he said he wanted to earn his own way. It says here that he didn't even know Agnes!" "I think," said Mr. Kingsley, "that we have a chance of getting her off. Let's go over your story." "My story?" Mr. Dempster asked. "About the insanity in your family," said the attorney.

That Monday, *The Inquirer* published a long, exclusive interview with Mr. Dempster. They quoted him verbatim:

My name is Amon R. Dempster and I have lived in North Chittendon all my adult life. I married a daughter of Edward Saltonstall of North Chittendon. My wife died a year and a half ago and I have not married again. Bill Brown of North Chittendon has always managed my farm. I have had one son and two daughters. The son died in infancy. One of my daughters was scalded to death. The other is here at the hospital. She was eighteen years old this December 17. She went to North Chittendon school and taught there one term but she did not want to be a teacher and did not graduate from high school. I hadn't seen Agnes for some months when she came home to North Chittendon. She was at home then for a few days and we all noticed something was wrong. She was very gloomy and despondent; her eyes looked wild. She was not herself at all. The last letter I received from my daughter was written three weeks ago. In this letter she said everything had gone wrong since she had come to Montpelier, but she thought it would go better when the birds flew over her grave. I think my daughter's mind was crazed and bewildered with love. I am sure that Frank Holt not only paid her attentions but courted her and promised to marry her. He told me so himself.

My wife's grandfather, Agnes's great-grandfather, while in an insane frenzy committed suicide by cutting his throat; his brother was insane. Two of my aunts are insane and James Dempster, who died in the insane asylum at Highbury, was my brother. Agnes' mother died with heart disease. I think it is very strange Agnes was not killed instantly, as the doctor tells me the bullet entered her ear and is now lodged in her brain. He says it may be two or three weeks before he will be able to say whether she will recover or not. He fears an abcess will form. I shall stay with her as long as she needs me.

"That's a good start," thought Mr. Kingsley, laying the paper down with pleasure. But he was less pleased when his wife and youngest daughter came in, handkerchiefs pressed to their eyes. "We went to Jane Holt's funeral," his daughter said, tears streaming down her face. "What were you doing there?" he asked. "The whole town was there," his wife said; "most of the people stood on the lawn. There were so many flowers they had to pile them up on the porch. They took a wagon load down to the hospital for the patients. I don't imagine they'll give any to *that* one." "The whole town was there?" Mr. Kingsley asked. Mrs. Kingsley told him that there were hundreds of people from all over the state, not just from Montpelier, people had come from Sharon and White River, that he should have been there himself, and that Jane was in a white casket and it was almost impossible to see her under the flowers, and when you did, there didn't seem to be anything wrong with her except that she was so white. His daughter said it had been awful; everyone was crying. Frank Holt was there and cried through the whole service; there were people there talking about going down to the hospital and shouting under Agnes Dempster's window. "And what did the Reverend Whittaker have to say about that?" asked Mr. Kingsley.

His wife said that Mr. Whittaker had been so impressive; he had dwelled upon the fact that it was difficult on occasions like this to make mourners believe that God knows best, but he said he could truthfully tell them that the friends of the deceased had no feelings of vengeance or hatred, but only sorrow for the one who had fired the shot; he said it was no time for severity or unkind feelings; he told the bereaved parents that it was sorrow and not sin that needed repair, and in the coming years their sorrow would only bring heaven and earth closer together. "Noble sentiments," said Mr. Kingsley. When his wife cried, he noticed that she was a short, round woman comically devoid of bones.

Mr. Kingsley's daughter told him that the reverend had quoted from "Snow Bound," the very same poem she had memorized for her school recital: "Wher'er her troubled path may be,/The Lord's sweet pity with her go,/ The outward, wayward life we see,/ Its hidden springs we may not know." "He said that about Jane Holt?" asked Mr. Kingsley. The two women were getting on his nerves, standing there like two Niobes. "Not about Jane, Charles!" exclaimed his wife; "he was talking about the young woman who fired the shot." "Oh," he said; "I didn't realize." His daughter was maundering on about Jane Holt and how she would never forget her, how no one in Montpelier ever would. "Forget who?" he asked. "Jane Holt!" said his wife; "you really are going to take that case! I see it. Well, this time you'll have an uphill course. The whole town is mourning for Jane and I don't think anyone has much pity for the girl who shot her, no matter what the reverend says. I know I don't. Inner springs! Uplifting influences in the years to come! My big toe! If I were Mrs. Holt, I'd want my daughter uplifted; that's all I'd want. And as for you, Charles, I know what you're thinking. You think we went to that funeral so we could have a good cry because that's what women like to do: cry. But let me tell you, there were plenty of men there and most of them were crying. It was something to cry about, and there you stand, laughing at us for going!" "I'm not laughing," he said; "I just don't see why everyone was crying." "You would if you stopped by the house and saw the coffin," said his daughter; "it's on view until four o'clock in the afternoon. The burial is private." "*Why* should I go?" asked her father. "It was so uplifting," said his daughter;

"it was so peculiarly impressive. It was, Poppa. I don't know why."

"I've got an appointment this afternoon," Mr. Kingsley said. "With whom?" his wife asked. "A doctor who wants to talk to me," he said, shrugging on his good black coat. "You're not going to Whately to ask about that dreadful girl?" asked his wife. "I am not going to Whately," he said; "Martha, you always think the worst of me."

41

The good black buggy was already in front of Mr. Kingsley's tall brick house. He got in and told the stable boy that he'd drive it himself. He always thought best when he was driving. It was as if the motions of the wheels jogged his brain, which otherwise hibernated like a contented animal, or, if it opened its eyes, was happy to stare about it in wonder and awe. There were times he only thought if something forced him to; something, however, usually did. The air was cold and he thrust his muffler deeper into the neck of his good black coat. Its black velvet collar and lapels were just brushed; his black leather gloves had been oiled by the maid and his boots polished. He was a wealthy man and the people of the town envied him his success, his happy family, his large red brick house which had once been painted white and now glowed rose because the weather had worn off almost all the paint so that only a white dust remained, powdering the definite color of the brick, making his residence look otherworldly.

But when he was alone, especially on a day like this, when the sky was gray and low and the color of thick ice, and when the snow was a dull white which would turn grayish when the sun began dropping in the sky, he did not feel enviable. Alone, under the gray clouds, watched by the cold eye of the December sun, conscious of the weight of the heavy gold watch in his pocket, that watch, his own personal sun, he felt as if some promise in his own life had not been kept. He did not know what it was or what he thought was missing, and if anyone had asked him, he could not have told them what it was. Was it Martha, his wife? He always started there. Would he have been more content had he married differently? But he had fought so to get her. Her parents were so sure he'd amount to nothing, a plain, rude boy from Dummerston. Still, she wasn't the woman he'd married, but how had she changed? She'd grown older. She was fifty years older than she'd been when he first met her. Did he hold that against her? Did he hold it against himself, the passing of time, the slow stiffening into familiar poses and responses, the slow death of surprise, the slow, sure knowledge of oneself so that no emotion ever seemed truly new or capable of taking you by surprise but was greeted as if it were an old friend or enemy, not deadly, not heavenly, but manageable. You turned what you thought was a new corner, and the same old scene was being nailed into position.

But the young were always surprised. Nothing was familiar to them, except, perhaps, the fear of familiarity, of monotony, of the tarnished and the dull. Everything sprang at them like wildcats in trees. This young girl, now. Eighteen years old and shot through the head by her own hand, and for what? Because love had surprised her, turned on her, changed; because the sun had dared to move past its zenith and start its long, slow curve down to the dark. She didn't want to be there to watch what she loved carried off by the strong arms of the darkness and so she had decided to enter the darkness first. He remembered how he had sworn to drown himself if Martha turned him down. He had spent days alone in his room, his books opened and untouched, imagining her walking on the Cape Cod beach with the young men her family found suitable, while he walked through Cambridge alone. But she had accepted his proposal and he had forgotten about drowning himself; later, he had thought about it again, but then he was still young. When he was young, everything was a motive for drowning.

Odd, he thought, driving along the road, looking toward the horizon which had turned hazy, he never thought of shooting himself. Probably because he knew how deadly guns were. He had been a champion swimmer; that must have been why he thought of drowning himself. It had been such a satisfying spectacle to contemplate: the family's sorrow, everyone saying how tragic it was, what an irony, he was such a fine swimmer, and to perish by drowning—it was inconceivable. And then they would realize that such a fine swimmer had not accidentally drowned, but had taken his own life, and they would feel the full force of his anger, the challenge of what he had done: See, you took such pleasure in my swimming. Well, I swam further than anyone else and I hope you're satisfied. It had seemed such a fine thing, to judge the world and find it unworthy, crumple it up, and throw it down as if it were worth nothing. But now if he thought about suicide it was because he feared not being good enough for this world. He was afraid his mind would fail him and he would be left staring, tongueless, at the judge and jury. He was afraid his legs would one day fail to hold him up, or that his hands would swell and no longer close over anything but the arms of a wheelchair. In such circumstances, he thought, watching the neck of the horse bob up and down, he would want to die. And when he thought of dying, he thought of the river, of drowning.

He thought of his wife and daughter's account of the Holt funeral. The daughters of Montpelier visiting the dead member of the tribe. Jane Holt, daughter of the town. Of course, they had brought her flowers and of course they had cried and of course they had been crying for themselves. It was not Jane they saw in the coffin; they saw themselves, lying in satin like Sleeping Beauty waiting for a prince who could never wake her up. The horse trotted along, surefooted on the hard-packed snow. The black trees stood against the sky like so many hieroglyphs. The earth was not shy about revealing its secrets. It was all there. No one ever wanted to look. Oh, his daughter had cried all right; she had seen herself in the coffin and she had seen how little she had accomplished and how little she had of what she wanted. And when she looked down at the dead girl, she saw that the future was not a wide country after all, but had borders which were close and heavily guarded and there was no reason to assume there would be another chance or another day. The hopeful illusions of habit, in which the future was a mirror image of a past, that, in retrospect, seemed endless. Jane Holt, the embodiment of all their fears, lying in the coffin, saying, happy ladies, this too could happen to you. They would be relieved when it was gone, the white coffin, the reminder that all their hopes were mortal. Of course they cried for Jane. But they would also want to forget her. Or so he hoped.

The Highbury State Asylum for the Insane was coming into view. He was always surprised by how lovely a place it was, but then he knew that the doctors believed a pleasant environment was a powerful force in the cure of the mentally unsettled. Although Highbury was set in the middle of the Green Mountains, it was built on many acres of flat land, and when one looked from the buildings to the horizon, only the small, rounded tops of mountains met the eye. The buildings themselves were pleasant to look at. All the large buildings were red brick, and the widely held belief that things of beauty fought against insanity had led the original architects to design two buildings whose northern and southern walls ended in towers, and in the towers were large, curved rooms with many windows, and each of the curved rooms opened onto attached porches on which the poor insane were to sit, surveying the beautiful country around them. Many of the original houses still standing when the state purchased the land were occupied by the staff and were in excellent repair. They were, Mr. Kingsley thought, eccentric little buildings, and scattered here and there as they were, they successfully fought off an institutional air. He was looking for "a modest gray shingled house with one turret."

That morning, he had telephoned Doctor Train from the Montpelier Inn and that was how the doctor had described his house. Mr. Kingsley pondered that description. Either the doctor was an ambitious man, conscious of how unimpressive his dwelling was, or he was accurate in the way doctors were. Mr. Kingsley had liked the sound of the doctor's voice. Voices were important. So were eyes. Therefore, he did not like telephones. Often enough, the voice was reliable, but the eyes were shifty, and then you knew. The telephone took away too much. Moreover, a telephone conversation could be a nuisance in court. Even if someone could testify to one side of a conversation, it was unlikely that someone else could be brought forward to testify as to what the person on the other end of the wire had said. Still it could be done. It was amazing, he thought, how few private conversations there were in this world. When he became a lawyer, he had concluded that the primary purpose of a human being was to spy on all other members of his race. The telephone made that harder. Still, it conveyed information. He wondered, fleetingly, if the Dempster girl had ever seen Frank Holt clearly. That was something else he had learned. No one really saw the people close to them, not with any clarity, not when they were young. There it was, the modest gray house, and there was a shingle announcing the residence of Doctor Paley Train.

A short dark man answered the door. "I'm Doctor Train," he said, holding out his hand. He wore heavy, dark-rimmed spectacles. His eyes, shrunken by the thick lenses, were evidently brown. His face was round and cheerful. It was saved from innocuousness by cheek bones which jutted prominently forward under his eyes. He appeared reserved and yet he exuded affection for everything around him. There was nothing extraordinary in his looks, Mr. Kingsley thought; he was about forty-five, but he had the round face and apple cheeks of a little boy. He looked like every little boy who had ever gone to school in Vermont. A jury might like him. He was one of them, after all. They went into the doctor's study, a large, undecorated room whose walls were painted white. Bookcases of raw wood were piled high with records, and volumes of all sorts lay open to different pages. One large book was open on a shelf, three smaller books open and face down upon it, as if the doctor had set the large book to reading the smaller ones, hoping to save time. "It looks like the office of a busy man," said Mr. Kingsley. "I always intend to set things straight here," said Doctor Train, "but I never get it done. Well, what did you want to see me about?"

"How long have you been superintendent?" Mr. Kingsley asked; "I don't remember your coming." Doctor Train looked about his room and smiled. "It looks like I just moved in," he said, "but I've been here eight years now." "Then you're the one who laid down the rule about uniforms?" Kingsley asked. "It was necessary," the doctor said; "at least now when I come into a ward, if I see someone in light blue striking someone else, I know I ought to remove that one from my staff. Before, I never knew if I ought to fire someone or put him in a seclusion room." "I heard the ruling about uniforms wasn't too popular," Kingsley said. "No, it wasn't," the doctor said; "it still isn't. No one wanted to be bothered ironing special clothing. Then some of the staff argued that it was better to look like the patients because if the uniforms set them apart, the patients wouldn't trust them easily. And they don't like it, walking into Highbury with a group of patients, because as soon as anyone sees the blue uniform, they know they're all from the asylum. Before, it wasn't so clear." "If the uniforms make everyone unhappy," Mr. Kingsley said, "and if they don't do any good, why bother with them?"

The doctor drummed his fingers on the edge of his desk. "I didn't say they did no good. They do a great deal of good. Now *I* can tell the patients from the attendants. Of course, the patients always knew the attendants weren't confined to the asylum; they didn't need a uniform to tell them if a person was crazy or not. But now that the attendants wear uniforms, they have more authority. The patients respect them more. The attendants respect themselves more. And they have to keep cleaner if they stand right out in those blue suits and dresses. If they're uncomfortable walking about in Highbury, that's unfortunate. Some of them were happy when I moved them out of the wards and some of them weren't. It's always that way. The attendants used to live on the floors with the patients. At the end of a year, they were as crazy as the official population. I thought they'd be delighted to have separate staff residences, but some of them had to be dragged out. When you make a decision, that's how it is. Not everyone likes it."

"It doesn't upset you?" Mr. Kingsley asked. "Well," said the doctor, "of course I wish everyone were happy. A man doesn't go in for this line of work unless he wants to see people happy. But there's a right way and a wrong way to do things. I try to find the right way and then follow it. If I make a mistake, I find out soon enough." "So you believe in truth?" asked Mr. Kingsley. "Truth?" said Doctor Train, smiling; "truth to the superintendent of an insane asylum is an elusive thing. I believe in finding what works." "Do you ever come upon it?" asked Kingsley; "truth?" "Sometimes I think I do," said the doctor; "not everyone agrees with me. But a man in my profession is an observer first and foremost. I do my observing and draw my own conclusions, and as long as they hold, I stick to them. A specialist in nervous disorders can't expect much endorsement of his views from his patients. And as far as the staff goes, I'm the enemy, especially when I don't agree with them. It's a lonely profession. Yours is too, I imagine." Kingsley nodded. He had never thought of his profession as a lonely one; he was forever investigating leads, challenging jurors, standing in front of crowds of people, but it was true. In the end, the responsibility was his. Everyone came to him with their troubles and left the problems with him. He wasn't a member of the pack. It was lonely to be on the outskirts, even if you were there by choice. He couldn't imagine why he hadn't seen it before.

"What do you want to talk to me about?" Doctor Train asked; "you haven't said. Or are you already talking to me about whatever it is you want to discuss?" "Well," said Mr. Kingsley hesitantly, "I guess I wanted to know what kind of man you are." "And do you?" asked the doctor. "A faint truth, but good enough for me," said Kingsley. "I came about a case," he said, after a pause; "or a potential case. Agnes Dempster, the girl who shot Jane Holt. Did you read about it?" "Oh," said the doctor, "*that* case. I may know more about it than you do. The wife of one of my ward supervisors has been in here fifteen times about it. She was the girl's closest friend. Polly Southcote. Well, she's Polly Jenness now. She wanted me to go talk to the girl, but I understand she's still unconscious." "Why did she want you to go?" "She said she thought Miss Dempster had gone crazy, or if she hadn't, she would if she woke up and saw herself in a mirror.

I gather the girl used to be very beautiful." "Used to be," Kingsley repeated. "The papers say she shot herself through the ear," the doctor told him; "she must be quite deformed." "I hadn't thought of it," Kingsley said; "they claim the other girl's face wasn't changed." "The other girl was dead. If the musculature was affected, no one would have known. Death relaxes everything."

"Well," Mr. Kingsley said, "I'd like you to examine her if she regains consciousness. We want to know if she was ever pregnant and if, in your judgment, she's sane or insane, and if you think she's insane, we'd like to call you as a witness for the defense." "I see," said the doctor. "Before you decide," said Mr. Kingsley, "I have to warn you what you'd be up against if the girl recovers, if, in your judgment, she's insane, and if you decide to testify. The state will bring in trainloads of expert witnesses. It's a big case. Anyone who testifies for the defense is going to come under pretty heavy fire." The doctor nodded. "I guess that's all right," he said. "Then you'll go to see her?" Kingsley asked. "As soon as she regains consciousness," the doctor said; "if I can see her immediately, I'll have much less trouble talking to her and the court will take it more seriously if I talk to her before everyone else does." "I can arrange that," Mr. Kingsley said. "Of course, if, in your judgment, she is sane, I can't ask you *not* to testify against us." "No," said the doctor, "but I can fail to come to any conclusion." Mr. Kingsley got up and shook the doctor's hand. "I've testified at trials before," the doctor said, "and I know they're not going to let that girl have many visitors. Do you think you could get her friend in to see her? If she's capable of talking to anyone? The Dempster girl seems to mean a lot to Mrs. Jenness." "I'll see what I can do," said Mr. Kingsley. "She was shot Friday. Now it's Tuesday. If she's going to come around," he asked the doctor, "how long do you think it will take?" "I don't know," said the doctor; "she ought to have been awake already. The longer it takes, the worse it is. But you never know with injuries to the brain. There's hope."

She opened her eyes and couldn't see anything. She could hear people moving in the room and loud noises coming from close by, as if someone were hitting something with a hammer over and over again. Why couldn't she see anything? She knew she wasn't dreaming. Perhaps if she turned toward the light. She turned her head and she saw a white wall. She moved her head again and saw she was in a white room and that someone was sitting in a chair across the way. Her sight was poor. The noise resumed and she moved her head again. She was looking at a window, and as her vision cleared, she saw a man standing on a chair. He was nailing wooden bars across her window. She turned her head again; she saw the door. A policeman was standing next to it. She looked at the man in the chair. It was her father. She was beginning to realize that she could not see out of her left eye. She felt as if she were encased in plaster. She tried to move her hand on the blanket and it moved toward her breast. She concentrated, and she raised her hand to her head. Her hand drew back as if burned. She couldn't feel any hair. Her hand crept back to her scalp. She felt along the top of her head. Gauze. Bandages. She was bandaged. She felt her throat. Her throat was swathed in bandages.

She tried to speak. No one looked at her. The man went on with his hammering. Her father was asleep in his chair. The policeman was staring into space. Her tongue seemed loose in her mouth. It kept slipping away from her teeth or sliding between them. What was wrong with her? She imagined saying the word *Father;* she pushed her teeth forward onto her lower lip and tried saying the word. Her head hurt dreadfully. She tried again and this time she made a sound. Her father stirred in his chair and she saw him look toward her. She saw the look of surprise, and how quickly he got up and came over to her bed. She looked up and tried to smile but her face would not obey her. She reached up and tapped the bandages and looked at her father. He smiled. She tapped the bandages again. She pointed to her left eye, which was covered by a thick pad. "Do you know what happened?" her father asked her. "I don't know," she thought; "you have to tell me." "Do you know what happened?" he asked again. She shook her head slowly. "You shot yourself," her father said; "you're in the hospital. Don't you remember?" "No," Agnes thought, "I don't. All I remember is leaving the house. I left the house and I wanted to shoot myself." "You don't remember?" her father asked. She shook her head. "Don't keep moving your head," her father said; "wiggle your fingers once for yes and twice for no." She wiggled the fingers of her right hand once to show she understood.

"You've been unconscious for five days," said her father. Yes, wiggled her fingers; go on. "You shot Jane Holt," he said. She wiggled her fingers twice. No, she had not. "Jane is dead," said her father. "No," said her fingers. Then the room began to fade, as if she were inside a lamp which was slowly dimming in intensity; the objects around her seemed to float. Sounds wobbled and the light failed.

"She's gone under again," Mr. Dempster said sadly. He went out to look for Doctor Salter. "She woke up," he said, "my daughter woke up." The doctor seemed surprised. "How long was she awake?" he asked. "I don't know," Mr. Dempster said; "maybe three minutes." "Could she talk?" the doctor asked. "I think she said my name," Mr. Dempster said, "but whatever she said, it was slurred." "Did she understand you?" "Oh, yes," Mr. Dempster said; "she wiggled her fingers yes and no." "What did you tell her?" the doctor asked. "I told her she shot herself and that she shot Jane Holt," he said, eyes brimming. "What did she say?" "She said she didn't," said Mr. Dempster. "But she did," said the doctor. "I know she did," said her father, going back into the room. His daughter was lying in bed, motionless. He went over to the bed and watched the sheet which covered her. It was rising and falling. She was still alive.

42

"The Case Of The Sleeping Beauty," as the Hammerhead had promptly dubbed it, disappeared from the headlines during the next week. But each day, a paragraph concerning Agnes Dempster's condition appeared in *The Spectator's* "Montpelier's Notes" and *The Inquirer's* "Notes From All Over." Ten days after the shooting, *The Inquirer* reported,

The condition of Miss Agnes Dempster has remained practically unchanged during the past week. She is slowly gaining strength, and her physician says her chances for recovery are good. She still insists that she wants to die, and it is considered necessary to keep a close watch over her. Amon Dempster, her father, went to his home in North Chittendon on Monday, but returned Tuesday. His devotion to his daughter under these trying circumstances is touching to witness. Miss Dempster's condition appeared to take a decided turn for the worse Tuesday afternoon and her death was hourly expected last evening. She is much stronger today.

Six weeks after the shooting, *The Reporter* carried the following information:

Agnes Dempster has so far recovered as to be able to sit up nearly all the time and walk around the hospital ward. No action has been taken as yet toward a preliminary hearing in her case, and there may be no legal action in the matter until the grand jury reconvenes.

Seven weeks later, *The Inquirer* (and the Hammerhead) denounced *The Reporter's* accounts of the Dempster case:

The sensational and shadowy character of the upstreet contemporary "news" is again shown by its item, last week, about Miss Dempster and the razor. "Stories circulating about town" seem to be the contemporary's main reliance for items, but such stories are not news until their truth is validated. Agnes Dempster did not pick up and open a razor in the room of the janitor or anywhere else. She did not steal a march on her attendant and secure an opportunity to kill herself, if she had wished, and then call the attention of her attendant to the fact. There was nothing of the slightest importance in the "story" or the incident that gave rise to it, but the contemporary, always eager to satiate the appetite of its readers, is famous for such freaks of enterprise.

These items pleased Mr. Kingsley immensely, especially since they occurred daily, and he was even more pleased when he came down to breakfast and found the paper open to the column in which they were to be found. He had been afraid that people would lose interest in the case, but the report of the imaginary razor laid those fears to rest. Every day, he came down earlier, and when he saw his wife look up suspiciously, he said he seemed to need less and less sleep; he thought he must be getting older and soon he would be waking up at midnight and begin his day in the dark, six hours ahead of everyone else. But he was really there to listen to his wife and youngest daughter, Mildred, who was still unmarried and still lived with them. He would settle into the tall high-backed oak chair at the head of the long table, look around the room, admire, as he had for thirty years, the deep red velvet draperies, the rich Turkish carpet on the floor, the gleam of polished wood, the jeweled, swordlike light which leaped from the beveled glass of the heavy mirrors on the walls, the flash of the early light as the heavy silver service reflected it and sent it like lightning through the room. He always expected good news in this room and he always got it. Some instinct told him the girl was going to recover, and when he asked himself why he thought so, he told himself it was because he always took the opposing view. Then he thought it over once again and decided it was something deeper; a profound conviction he had not known he held, that the worst must happen if it could. And he was sure that continuing to live was the worst possible fate for the Dempster girl.

So he came down earlier and earlier, and never mentioned Agnes Dempster himself. He wanted to hear what his wife and daughter had to say first. "When did we start taking *The Reporter*?" he asked one morning; "I thought we only took *The Inquirer*." "Oh, well," Martha said, not looking at him, *"The Reporter*'s gotten so much better." Finally, it was the imaginary razor which set them off. "Why does she have to have an attendant?" his daughter asked him as he was buttering his toast. She wore a green plaid dress and its buttons were embossed sterling silver. She looked as her mother had once looked: short, slender, a round, cherubic face, plump cheeks which seemed puffed out by invisible acorns, a frown which made her look like an angry biscuit, and a halo of curly blond hair which defied the discipline of brush and comb. She exuded respectability and kindness; once he had found that combination irresistible. Now he found it touching; there was so little of either in the world, although when he went to trial, he was always surprised by how much kindness could be chipped out of the jurors' flinty breasts. Well, he saw it every day in his wife and daughters, how kindness warred with respectability, that powerful, invaluable urge to uphold the morals of the day.

"Agnes Dempster," his daughter said; "why does she have to have an attendant?" "Didn't the newspapers say she tried to commit suicide?" Mr. Kingsley asked. "One of them said she did and the other said she didn't," answered his wife. "Which one do you believe?" he asked, taking a bite of his toast. "They're both scandal sheets," his wife said. "So you don't believe either of them," he said. "*I* think she tried to kill herself," his daughter said; "maybe not with a razor, but with something." "Well, if she did," said Mr. Kingsley, pouring himself a cup of tea, "that's why she has an attendant." "They're going to a lot of trouble to keep that girl alive," said his wife. "Well," said Mr. Kingsley, "they can't just let her die."

"Why not?" asked his daughter, her cheeks flushing; "why not? She wants to die. She already shot herself. Everyone says it's a miracle she's not already dead. They say she'll never be the same. I saw a statue of her, at least it's supposed to be a statue of her, and she was so beautiful, and they say her face is half-paralyzed and she has trouble speaking and she cries all the time. If she wants to die, it's her business." "I'm surprised at you," said her father; "suicide is against the laws of both God and man." His daughter's lower lip pushed forward. "She's already

454

killed one girl and tried to kill herself, so God will punish her anyway," she said; "I don't see why it's up to us to keep her alive when she doesn't want to be."

"There must be something in her that wants to live," said Mr. Kingsley; "otherwise you don't survive a bullet to the brain. In spite of what she thinks, she wants to live." "*Everything* wants to live?" asked his wife; "is that what you think?" "No," he said; "the appetite for life is stronger in some than in others. From the sound of it, all her appetites were strong." "In her place," said his wife, "I wouldn't want to live." "But you can't put yourself in her place," said Mr. Kingsley; "you're nothing like her." "If you had taken up with someone when I was pregnant with one of the girls, I don't know what I might have done," his wife said. He tried to imagine Martha, pregnant and jealous, wielding a gun, a huge stomach from which two little hands protruded, one of them holding a pistol, and he smiled wickedly. "I know what you're thinking," Martha said; "maybe I wouldn't have used a gun. You know I don't like them. I hate the sight of blood. But poison is quiet and neat. And we were married. I would have had plenty of opportunities." "Did you ever think about poisoning me?" he asked her. "Not seriously," she said; "I never stayed that unhappy for very long." "You don't mean to say you thought about it at all?" he asked, astonished. Of course he believed—theoretically—that everyone was capable of murder, and he had argued that everyone thought murderously at least once a day, but he had never applied this idea to Martha, his own wife. "Naturally, I did," she said; "you can be terribly trying."

"What about you?" he asked Mildred; "have you ever thought about poisoning me?" "You," his daughter said; "I've never thought about poisoning you, but I've thought about doing away with myself. When I was so sick last year, I thought about it all the time. It was comforting to know that things didn't have to go on and on and that you could hold up your hand like a policeman and say 'Stop!' and everything would." "Is everyone in this house a homicidal maniac, then?" he asked. "Charles," said his wife; "stop it. This isn't the court. I haven't changed my mind about the girl. I still think she ought to be shot or hung. If she wants to kill herself, I think they should let her. Of course, we understand her some. That doesn't mean we have sympathy for her."

"I have sympathy for her," said her daughter; "I don't believe she just imagined Frank Holt was in love with her. From

what I hear, they used to walk out together all the time."
"People say that, do they?" said her father. "From what I hear," his daughter said, "she and Holt kept pretty much to themselves, but they used to go together to the Barre quarries and the men there have been telling their wives and daughters they saw them there all the time. They say if he was engaged to Jane Holt, Agnes must have cut her out, at least until she left the city." "Until she left the city?" asked Mr. Kingsley. "Well, she got sick and went home to North Chittendon," his daughter said; "they say that's when Frank Holt took up with Jane again." "Oh," said Mr. Kingsley. Why bother with detectives when he could just take his time over breakfast? "Maybe," he said, "that Holt fellow was only interested in the Dempster girl professionally. You say he carved her." "Some of the men said he told them he would marry her," Mildred said.

Mrs. Kingsley looked startled. "Where did you hear that, Mildred?" she asked; "I hope we haven't been unfair to her." "It sounds like Frank Holt got there first," said her husband. "The one I feel sorry for is the father," said his wife; "imagine what the poor man must think. It's hard to believe that such a good man could produce such an evil child." "I don't think she's evil, Mother," said Mildred; "I feel sorry for her, not Jane. Jane's dead and gone. This one's lost everything and she's still alive."

"How can you say such a thing?" her mother demanded; "would you want us to be feeling sorry for her if she'd shot you, just because you were dead and she was still alive?" "Yes," said her daughter, beginning to cry; "I would."

"Oh, you don't know what you're saying," her mother said, pushing her chair back from the table; "you're out of your head yourself. Your emotions are boiling over and fogging your brain." She felt her husband's eyes on her and went cold. She waited for him to draw an analogy between their daughter's state of mind and the state in whch the Dempster girl had shot Jane Holt, but for once he kept quiet and spared her. When she came back in from the kitchen she heard her husband asking Mildred how the other women in town felt. "A lot of women feel just like me," said his daughter; "and not just the young ones either." She refused to look at her mother. Mrs. Kingsley cleared the table, her lips tightened to a thin, white line, her chin thrust out.

43

She opened her eyes. This time she had no trouble seeing. Her father sat in the chair opposite the bed. The policeman was gone but a young woman dressed in white stood next to the door; she was tall and big breasted and her face was pleasant. There were bars nailed over her window and the sunlight poured into the room in bars, striping the floor. Little motes danced in the bright light. "We thought you were gone a while ago," her father said. "I wish I were," she said. "Don't talk that way, Agnes," he said. He looked older. "Who is she?" she asked her father. "She's your attendant," he said; "she's been assigned to help watch over you. Her name's Margaret Eckroyd." "I don't want an attendant," she said. Her unbandaged eye was restlessly scanning the room. There was nothing useful in it, nothing sharp, and nothing long enough to wrap around the throat. She raised her hand to her head; it felt like a huge, gauze globe. "I shot myself?" she asked her father; "that's what you told me?" He nodded. "I don't remember," she said; "I remember buying the gun and I remember planning to do it, but I don't remember doing it." "Does your head still hurt?" he asked. "It aches," she said, "but not terribly." "They want to talk to you," he said; "the police and the doctors." "I don't want to talk to anyone," she said. "You have to talk to them, Agnes," he said; "you killed someone." "No, I didn't," she said; "I'm still alive." "You killed Jane Holt," he said; "I told you that before." "No," she said, "I didn't." "That's because you don't remember, that's why you say that, but you did. People saw you." "They saw me?" she whispered; "they say I killed her?" "Try to remember," said her father.

"I remember," she said slowly, "getting up early in the morning and it was still dark. I remember getting dressed and taking the gun with me. I remember I had packed my clothes because I was thinking about going home. I remember leaving the house and how the rain felt on my cheek. I don't remember anything else." She was frightened; she saw herself leaving the house and then she didn't see anything. It was as if she came to the edge of the land and beyond it was black water. She couldn't kill anyone. She tried to imagine killing Jane. There Jane was, sitting with Frank, leaning against the statue in the stone shed. Now she was firing at her, she thought, and now she is dead. She couldn't believe it; if she were dead, she no longer existed. She was dead to them, but to her, she was only stopped, like a clock. She stayed as she last saw her, at Frank's feet, leaning against the statue in the stone shed. She stays with him forever, Agnes thought. She began to cry.

"I want to see Frank," she said. "That's out of the question," her father said; "he's an important witness in the case. They can't let you see him." "If they don't let me see him, I'll kill myself," she said, crying. "I'm afraid you can't do that, either," said her father; "Miss Eckroyd can't let you. That's part of her job." "That's why she's here?" Agnes asked. "That's one reason," her father said. "I want a mirror," she said. "Not yet," said her father; "please. They said not to let you see yourself until the doctor talked to you." "What doctor?" she asked. "Doctor Train," said her father; "he's supposed to be very good."

"Doctor Train!" she exclaimed; "he's the superintendent at Highbury!" Her father and Miss Eckroyd exchanged glances. "You have to talk to him, Agnes," her father said; "your lawyer wants you to. If you get better, you'll go on trial for murder. He wants to help you." *I'm tired,* Agnes thought; *I'm tired to death.* "I can't talk to Frank?" she asked; "I can't see him?" "Absolutely not," said her father; "if it was up to me, I'd bring in anyone you wanted to see, even him. You know that. But I can't bring him in. You've got to talk to the police and the doctor." *It will be all right,* Agnes thought, *this panic will kill me. It rises up until it pounds against my skull. The fear will kill me.* "Well?" asked her father. "No," she said; "I won't talk to anyone unless they promise to let me talk to Polly. I'll talk to the police if they let me talk to Polly." "I don't think they're going to let you talk to anyone," he said. "She's married to a ward supervisor at Highbury," Agnes said; "I guess they ought to be able to trust her." "Will you talk to the others if they let you talk to her?" he asked. "I'll talk to the police," Agnes said; "but I won't talk to the doctor. Not unless they let me talk to Polly."

"You're not in a position to make demands," her father said gently. "I don't have to talk," his daughter said; "no one can make me talk." And for the next three days she refused to utter a sound and she sent all food back untouched.

On the fourth day, State's Attorney Parsons came in with Sheriff Gray and Officer Delonnay. "Agnes," asked Mr. Parsons, "can you hear me?" The girl nodded without opening her eye. "If you answer our questions, we'll bring Mrs. Jenness to speak to you." She opened her eye and looked up at him. "Mrs. Jenness?" she said; "you mean Polly?" He nodded. "Will Miss Eckroyd have to stay in the room?" she asked. "I'm afraid she will," he said. "You must be hungry," said Officer Delonnay. "I don't care if I ever eat again," she said; "why can't I have a mirror?" She was terrified; her face felt stiff, unfamiliar. When she dreamed, someone else's face covered her own. Her dreams were dreadful. In them, her body was hastily assembled from bits and pieces of other people, and at the last minute, the face was peeled away from someone else and it came off in one piece like a mask and then the mask was pressed down over her own face and stuck fast and no matter how she tried or how she screamed, she could not get it off. "You can have a mirror," said Mr. Parsons; "if Doctor Train says you can. It's not up to me." *I am so tired*, Agnes thought; *so tired*.

"We want to ask you a few questions about December twenty-fourth, the day of the shooting," Mr. Parsons said; "are you strong enough to answer them?" Agnes felt her heart pounding. It was an insane thing, her heart. All it wanted to do was live; it didn't care how. If I could, she thought, I would tear it out of my body with my bare hands.

They were asking her to describe the events of the twenty-fourth. A smothering exhaustion pressed her down; all she wanted to do was sleep. She never wanted to wake up. She saw the light falling in stripes over her blanketed body. "I got up at five-thirty," she began, "and I took my gun and put it into my pocket." When she was finished, they asked her more questions; was she sure she remembered nothing after leaving the house? Was she sure when she bought the gun she didn't intend to shoot Jane Holt with it? Finally, they thanked her and left.

Her father took up his place in his chair. Miss Eckroyd sat in a chair next to the door. She turned her head so that her good eye was buried in the pillow. "Frank," she whispered, "what am I going to do? You promised not to leave me alone." She was crying steadily and quietly; she did not want to attract anyone's attention. There was no longer such a thing as privacy. Her life did not belong to her. She felt a hand on her shoulder but did not look up. "It's all right," said Miss Eckroyd; "everything will be all right." "No," said Agnes, without lifting her head; "nothing can ever be all right again." "Your friend will be coming tomorrow," the woman said. Agnes went on crying. Why had she thought it was so important to see Polly? Even if she came tomorrow, there would be the endless days rolling toward her like stones until she was buried beneath them.

The next day, several hours before Polly was to visit her at Whately Hospital, Agnes insisted on sitting up in a chair. She swore that she was well enough to do so and told her father and Miss Eckroyd that she had no intention of frightening her friend. Miss Eckroyd consulted with the doctors and they agreed, provided that she promised to tell them if she was too tired to continue. When Agnes heard footsteps approaching her room, she looked up at her father and reminded him that he had promised to leave her alone with Polly, or, she said, looking at Miss Eckroyd, he had promised to leave her as alone as she could get. Mr. Dempster got up and left without a word. Polly stood in the doorway, nervously fingering the second button of her blouse. She didn't know what to expect. They had warned her not to upset Agnes, but of course they did not know Agnes, and what an impossible task they had set for her. She saw a thin young woman sitting in an easy chair near the window, her head bandaged in layers of gauze so that her face appeared to be hatching out of an eggshell. If she had not known that Agnes was in the room, she would not have recognized her.

"Agnes?" she said, coming in; "it's me, Polly." "I know," Agnes said; "I can see you. What's wrong with my face?" Agnes asked her; "it feels all stiff. They won't let me have a mirror. I think it's paralyzed but when I ask them, they won't say." "Smile," Polly said. Agnes tried. "Well, half of your face smiles, anyway," she said. She felt Miss Eckroyd glaring at her. "They told me not to upset you," Polly said, sitting down on the foot of her bed; "but I don't know how not to do that." "You'll upset me if you behave like someone I don't know," Agnes said; "everyone in here treats me like a cracked piece of glass and the only thing they want to talk to me about is the day of the shooting and what I remember." "What do you remember?" asked Polly. "She's not supposed to talk about her case," said Miss Eckroyd. "If you don't let me talk to her about what I want to talk about," Agnes said, "I won't talk to the doctor."

"Well," said Miss Eckroyd, "I don't see that things can get much worse." "I don't remember anything," she told Polly; "I just remember getting up and going out with the gun.

"What are people saying about me?" Agnes said abruptly. "They say you are a very foolish girl," Polly said. "I suppose I am," said Agnes, "but I can't help it." "You could try," Polly said; "you don't have to go on forever with this foolishness." "What foolishness?" "Frank," Polly replied; "forget about Frank. Put yourself in his place. You shot a girl he was—well, a girl he liked very much. He's probably congratulating himself on having escaped with his own life." "I would never have hurt him," said Agnes. "Well, you did," Polly said; "you don't think he's enjoying all this attention he's getting?" "Is he telling people we were engaged?" Agnes asked. Polly looked over at Miss Eckroyd and then bent toward her friend. "No, Agnes, he's not. He says you threw yourself at him. He's afraid if people find out the truth, they'll come after him. I guess they would. Anyway, you're in here and he's out there and he has to live where he is. It's easier for him if people think there was nothing between you. People are pretty upset about what happened to Jane Holt. And to you, too." "But they think it's all my fault?" asked Agnes. "Some do," said Polly. "They're all against me and for him," Agnes said. "You're the one who killed someone," Polly said. "That's the trouble," Agnes said; "I can't get that through my head." "There's no hurry," said Polly; "it will come to you eventually."

"I don't want anything to happen to him," Agnes said softly; "I want him to be happy. But he has to tell people we were engaged! If he doesn't, I'll sue him!" "Suing him is an odd way to make him happy," Polly said. "Oh, please forget I said that," Agnes said, starting to cry; "I didn't mean it." "I *am* upsetting you," Polly said. "You are not upsetting me!" said Agnes; "I'm upset all the time. Most of the time, I sit here thinking of ways to end my life. I know I made a mistake." "A mistake?" asked Polly. "I aimed too high. I shouldn't have used a gun. I should have used real poison. I thought about chloroform but the girls at Mrs. James's said that didn't always work, either." "Is that what you're spending your time thinking about?" asked Polly. "No," said Agnes, "sometimes I think about my dreams. I dream that I'm killing someone or someone's killing me or soldiers are fighting." "Who do you dream you're killing?" asked Polly. "Myself," said Agnes. "So you think about the same thing awake or asleep," Polly said.

"It's because I'm so alone," Agnes said, starting to cry again; "the only person I want to see is Frank and they won't let me see him. They say he's an important witness in the case. Polly, you've got to help me. If I can't see him, I've got to get something of his to keep with me. Anything. A shirt, a handkerchief, anything." "You want me to bring you one of Frank's handkerchiefs?" Polly asked. "Yes," Agnes said; "I have to have something. I wake up in the middle of the night and I forget where I am and I think I'm back in his room at Iris's and I turn over and feel this thing on my head and I'm on the edge of the bed and if there weren't bars on the windows, I'd throw myself right out. I cry all the time, I can't stop, it's as bad as it was before they put me in here; I can't sleep. I have terrible dreams and I wake up and it takes me hours to fall back asleep and when I wake up, I'm still here, and there's nothing I can do about it. That's the worst part. Maybe I should write him a letter."

"Don't write any more letters," Polly said. "Why not?" Agnes asked; "they say they're going to hang me anyway. I might as well write to him. Maybe he'll write to me." "Agnes, he won't," said Polly. "You could talk to Charlie," Agnes said; "he always tries to help me. You could ask him to make Frank write to me. He could threaten Frank. He could say he'd go to the papers and tell them the truth about the engagement. He'd do it. He cares about me." "He does care about you," Polly said, "and that's why he wouldn't do anything of the kind." "Then what I want you to do," Agnes said, leaning forward, "is talk to Frank for me. Tell him if he doesn't change his mind about marrying me, I will sue him when I get out of here and then he'll have to marry me." "What?" Polly asked; "have you gone crazy? You're under arrest yourself. You *can't* sue him." "I can if they let me go," Agnes said. "That's the most ridiculous thing I ever heard of," Polly said; "you said you wouldn't mention it again." "I changed my mind," said Agnes. "Well, I won't tell him," said Polly; "he's had enough trouble already." "He can have more trouble!" Agnes said, tapping her bandaged head; "what do you call this?" "You sound just like Madge," Polly sighed.

"Look, Agnes," she said; "it's terribly sad. I wish it hadn't happened." "If it did happen," Agnes said, "I wish I could remember it. This way, I feel as if they've locked me up in here for no reason at all." "You do have a bullet in your head," Polly said. "I guess," said Agnes; "it's hard to believe that, too."

"I've got your quilt on my bed," Polly said; "it looks beautiful."
"It does?" Agnes asked, smiling. Polly saw that when she
smiled only half of her face moved; the left side seemed frozen
and the left side of her mouth turned down slightly. It was worse
than she thought when she first came in. "What was it like in
New York?" Agnes asked. "I've never seen so many people,"
Polly said, "and crossing the street was the most dangerous
thing I've ever done in my life! You should see the buildings!
It's an amazing place." "We were supposed to go there," Agnes
said, "after we got married." "I know," Polly said. "Polly, are
you going to help me?" Agnes asked; "you're the only friend I
have." "I'm not bringing you a gun, if that's what you have in
mind," Polly said; "I heard you asked your father to bring you
one." "He wouldn't," said Agnes. "Did you think he would?"
asked Polly. "Just get me something of his," Agnes pleaded.

"Agnes," said Polly, "that is all wrong. Frank doesn't care
about you. You have to forget about him." "I can't!" Agnes
cried; "that's the trouble. It's not his fault. It never was his
fault. It was because of the abortion. I wasn't the same after that.
I drove him away. I have to have something of his to keep. Can't
you understand that?" "What?" cried Polly; "that you need a
handkerchief? A shirt? It can't do you any good." "It will do me
good," Agnes said; "I'm the only one who knows what will do
me any good. If you won't help me, no one will." "All right,"
said Polly, "I'll try to get you something. I don't know how, but
I will."

Agnes sat back in the chair and smiled. "You know," she
said, "it's hard to talk. My tongue wants to go all over my
mouth. If I don't concentrate everything comes out slurred. Last
week, I couldn't talk at all. I don't think my left eye works, but I
don't know. It's under this bandage. I look terrible, don't I?"
"You've looked better," Polly said. "I wish you never had to go
home," Agnes said; "I wish you could stay here with me
forever." "I wish I could, too," Polly said; "I hate to leave you
here." "Don't cry," Agnes said softly. "I'm sorry," Polly said;
"I'm supposed to cheer you up." "You are cheering me up,"
Agnes said; "you're making me forget I'm in here. After you
go, I'll think about it over and over again and you'll still be here.
It's terrible to be in a room with no ghosts. That's what this
room is."

"What's going to happen next?" Polly asked; "do they tell
you?" "State prison or hanging, I guess. I don't care which,
except for my father. I wish he weren't here all the time.

463

Sometimes I lie on the bed and look at the walls and nothing seems real. I wouldn't be surprised if the walls started melting, but I try to act cheerful when he's here. I guess I don't do a very good job. I start to say something perfectly ordinary, like 'Look how sunny it is,' and halfway through, I start crying and I can't stop, sometimes for an hour or more. And then someone comes in and says, 'Would you like some tea?' and I start laughing and I can't stop that, and after I've been laughing long enough, I start to cry. I don't know how all this happened," she said; "I thought I was the luckiest, the most fortunate, happiest person in the world. No one ever loved anyone as much as I loved him. And he loved me just as much. He did. We were supposed to be married. I knew it from the minute I saw him. I can't understand it. I go over it and over it. How can something perfect turn into this?" she asked, touching her bandaged head. "I look like a bandaged darning egg, don't I?" Agnes asked, trying to smile. Polly nodded.

"Agnes," she said, "hold on." "I don't want to hold on," Agnes said; "my body wants to hold on. If it weren't for my body, none of this would have happened." Polly said nothing. "That sounds crazy, doesn't it?" Agnes asked. "Yes," said Polly. "It *is* my body's fault, though," Agnes said in a low voice; "it won't die. It does what it wants." "You're just upsetting yourself," Polly said; "later on, you'll be glad you're alive." "When the roots of a tree wrap around me and the birds fly over my grave, then I'll be glad," she said. "Try not to be morbid," Polly said. "It's morbid to stay alive like this," Agnes said, touching her bandaged head.

Polly got up and kissed her good-bye. "Don't forget," Agnes said; "you promised." "I'll try," she said; "you try not to think about him." "I have to," Agnes said; "I have to think that if I get better and go to trial and they don't hang me, he'll be waiting for me. He's all I ever wanted." "Doctor Train's coming to see you tomorrow," Polly said; "I know you don't want to see him, but he's a good man. Talk to him." "I'm tired," Agnes said. "Talk to him," Polly said again; "if you want things to get better, he can make them better." "I don't want things to get better," said Agnes; "I just want them to end." "Talk to him," said Polly.

The next day, Agnes refused to get out of bed. She lay on her side, her good eye buried in the pillow, her face turned away from her father. I'll never see her again, Agnes thought; she'll never come back. She won't bring me the handkerchief. She thinks it's crazy to want such a thing. Then she would begin tracing Frank's initials on her pillow, over and over, and hours passed as seamlessly as they had when she was in a coma.

"I know you don't want to see me, Agnes," said an unfamiliar voice, "but I'm here anyway." She heard someone pull a chair up to the bed. "Go away," she said. "Well, I can't," said the doctor; "I came to talk to you about the bullet that's still lodged in your brain. What do you think of it?" "I don't believe it's there," she said; he had taken her by surprise. "I thought you'd ask what I remembered about the shooting," she said. "I will," he said; "later. Right now I want to know about the bullet. It has to come out. We need your permission to operate." "Operate?" she repeated. "On your brain," he said; "it's a very dangerous operation. You might not live through it." "Then why bother?" she asked. "Well, I think the district attorney's office doesn't want to go to the expense of a trial if you're going to die in the middle, and if they don't get the bullet out, you might. In fact, you probably will. If you live through the operation, then they know you'll live through the trial." "They want me to have the operation so they won't waste money on an unnecessary trial?" Agnes asked. "As far as I can tell, that's it," the doctor said; "of course, from your point of view, the operation is necessary if you want to live. If you don't, you shouldn't have it." "I don't want to live," Agnes said; "how dangerous is the operation?" "Very. The odds are against you." "I'll think about it," Agnes said. "You're not strong enough now in any event. Do you think you might consider sitting up? Or at least turning to me?"

She turned to look at him. He was a short, pleasant man with a mischievous look. "I understand you asked your friend to bring you something of Frank's," he said. She was about to turn away in despair when he said that was all right; he told Polly she could bring in whatever she wanted. He asked her if she felt restless and she said she did. "Is that something new?" he asked. She said no, she supposed she'd always had a restless disposition. And before she knew it, she was talking without prompting, telling him that she'd never been happy, that even before meeting Frank Holt she'd tried to kill herself; she'd done that when she was thirteen, that her mother never loved her, that she could not control her moods, and Frank no longer loved her because she would think things, and without realizing it, would say them aloud. There were times when she thought she was not in her own body, when she thought someone else's face covered hers; she was a wicked girl, that was why she didn't go to church. She didn't deserve to be in church; she had spoiled her own mother's funeral, first crying through the services, and then running all over, laughing hysterically. She had kept her grandmother awake at nights because she saw faces in the ceiling; one minute she was happy and the next despondent; she never knew her own mind; at first, she didn't think she wanted Frank's baby, but then after she'd gotten rid of it, she wanted it back, and after that, she couldn't eat or sleep and her head hurt all the time; she'd never been able to support herself, not really; she couldn't concentrate on her work and when she was upset, she sewed things inside out, like pockets, and she was only happy when she was alone with Frank, and even when they were happy and she thought she was going to marry him, she'd never wanted anyone else around; she would have been happy if the whole world had been destroyed and they'd been the only ones left. That would have made her happiest.

"When you're stronger," said the doctor, "I'd like to make a physical examination; it's important. I have to look for evidence of pregnancy." "That's fine," said Agnes. "What do you think about," he asked her, "when you're alone?" "How to do away with myself," she said; "I'll accomplish it someday." He asked her if she dreamed, and she said lately she had the same dream over and over again. She was in her house in North Chittendon and it was the middle of the winter and the house was surrounded by deep drifts of snow which were so high they covered the first floor windows and darkened the room and then it began to rain because it had grown warmer, but when it turned cold, the rain froze and the drifts of snow were covered over with ice, and whenever she left the house, she could not stand up. She would struggle upright, fall, and struggle to her feet again. And then a man would come up behind her and try to help her by pushing her ahead of him, and instead she lost her balance and he pushed her feet out from beneath her, and she fell, hurting her head. She had the dream whenever she fell asleep for more than a few minutes, and sometimes she knew she had her own face, and at other times, she knew Jane Holt's face covered her own. And she remembered how, when she was younger, her head would hurt and she would lock herself up in her room and when she woke, she would not remember having come into the room and could not remember where she had put the key.

The doctor scribbled frantically, trying to keep up with her. "Why are you writing?" Agnes asked him. "I'm taking notes," he said; "so I don't forget what you said." "I can always remind you," she said; "the only thing I can't remember is the day of the shooting." "Aren't you tired?" he asked her. She sank back against the pillow. She was exhausted. She hadn't realized it. "Do you want to see your friend Polly again?" he asked. She said she did. "I'll see that she comes back," he said. He reached out to shake her hand, and after an instant's hesitation, she shook it. "No one ever shook my hand before," she said. "Well," he said, "I don't know you well enough to kiss you." "No one ever did," she said.

Polly brought Agnes the handkerchief. Agnes spread it out on the blanket and ran her fingers over the initials. "I remember embroidering this," she said softly; "I remember shopping for the album I gave him." "Hmmm," said Polly. When she had gone to Frank's room, the album had not been in its usual place. "What does he say about me?" Agnes asked finally. "He says you ruined his life," said Polly. "That's funny," said Agnes; "Doctor Train asked me if I thought Frank had ruined *my* life." "What did you say?" "I said I guess I thought he had," said Agnes. "Then why don't you tell something like that to the papers?" Polly asked; "don't you get tired of causing yourself trouble?" "Can I cause myself any more?" Agnes asked. "Do they bring you the papers in here?" Polly asked. "No," said Agnes, "but I can have them. I'm not going to testify, so it doesn't matter. If I live, I don't have to get up in front of everyone and answer questions." "That's because you're doing it already," Polly said; "here." She handed her a long clipping, neatly snipped from *The Inquirer*. "Read the underlined parts," she told her. "March twenty-seventh," said Agnes, looking at the date of the clipping; "weeks have gone by." "Read the clipping," Polly said impatiently. "But, Polly, so many weeks," Agnes said; "where is my life going? It seems like a few days." "That's not what you usually say," Polly answered. "Weeks," Agnes said again, beginning to read:

Miss Dempster is gaining strength everyday and is soon to be transferred from the Helmsley Room at Whately Hospital to a room in the County Jail, which will be her new home and she will continue to share her dwelling with her attendant, Margaret Eckroyd. When last seen by this reporter, she appeared quite bright and she conversed quite freely with the hospital physician. She was perfectly conscious of what she had done, and although she expressed no penitence, she expressed regret that the bullet in her own head had not proved fatal. She repeatedly declared that she did not wish to live and then she urged her father to make it plain to everybody that Frank Holt was in no wise to blame for what had been done. This statement from the young woman refutes the stories that had been freely circulated that Holt had been unduly intimate with Miss Dempster and because of his betrayal of her she had made up her mind to these desperate deeds.

She told her father she had left several letters in her room and several in Frank Holt's room, one of which was addressed to Mr. Holt. Mr. Dempster went to the rooms but failed to find the letters. Mr. Dempster consulted with the district attorney's office and is now of the opinion that some persons had visited the rooms and secured the letters but were afraid to make their contents public. He also believes that some of the letters may have been destroyed.

"I'm going to jail?" Agnes asked. "Didn't they tell you?" Polly asked. "I guess I forgot," Agnes said. "Look, Agnes," Polly said, "why do you want to go and paint Frank in glowing colors? Look at what the paper says. There was no 'undue intimacy' between you. You're making it harder for everyone who wants to help you." "I don't want to make things bad for him," Agnes said. "You better look out for yourself from now on," said Polly. "How is he?" asked Agnes. Polly sighed. "He's fine. He looks more fed up with the world than usual, that's all. He's out in the stone sheds every day; he's got all those orders from New York." "Doesn't he ever mention me?" Agnes asked. "Not often, I'm sure," said Polly. "I wonder if he thinks about me," Agnes said. "I'm sure he thinks about you," Polly said; "I'm sure he can't help it. Whenever anyone looks at him, they think about you. You might as well be married to him. People can't think about you separately." "Good," Agnes said. "It's not so good, Agnes; he's pretty bitter. He told Charlie that he was no worse than Charlie was. He said the only difference between them was that his luck was worse. He said you didn't give him time. You wanted things your way, right away. He said you didn't give Jane any time, either. He said Kingsley came to see him and looked at him as if he were some kind of worm, and I told him he couldn't expect Kingsley to admire him, not when he had to come and see you, here in the hospital. He said he'd

468

leave the city right away if he wasn't ordered to stay until the trial. He said he never wanted to see you again. When Charlie told Frank that you would have wanted a baby sooner or later, he said you were in too much of a hurry to wait and see how things would work out. Agnes, he says he never wants to see you again. Never.''

"He'll change his mind," said Agnes. "He won't," said Polly. She got up and put on her cape. "I've got to go back," she said. "They still haven't let me look in a mirror," Agnes said. "Ask Doctor Train about it," she said; "no one else is going to give you permission." "If you see Frank again, will you tell him I still love him?" Agnes asked. "No," said Polly, "I won't. Didn't you hear a word I said?" "Please!" Agnes burst out; "you're the only one I can ask. It means everything to me." "All right," Polly said, "if I see him." "Did he say anything else?" asked Agnes; "when you went to get the handkerchief?" "Good Lord," sighed Polly; "no, Agnes, he didn't. I don't think I left anything out."

Miss Eckroyd followed Polly into the hall just outside the room. "Do you think she wants to hear that?" she asked Polly. "Right now, if he could kill her himself he'd probably consider it," Polly said. "Is that likely?" asked Miss Eckroyd. "No," said Polly; "somehow he never does anything himself. He gets other people to do things for him." "He doesn't think he's done anything wrong, does he?" asked Miss Eckroyd. "No," said Polly, "he doesn't."

The tent caterpillars had been busy since early spring. Now their white, sticky webs hung shroudlike on the branches of the trees, the thick, gauzelike webs so dense that the branches which held them up were hidden from sight. Agnes knew that if she moved closer to the trees, stood under them and looked up, she would see the caterpillars weaving their white webs. They were beautiful caterpillars, not at all frightening, black and furry, their backs colorful as if their fur were filled with tiny Indian beads. She saw one of them on the ground and picked it up, letting it creep to the edge of her hand and then turning her hand so it crept from the palm to the back of her hand. One of them alone was a beautiful thing. It was time to go back to the house. She put the caterpillar down in the twigs and seeds and dried leaves beneath the big tree. Then she saw that the light was strange, milky white, and when she looked about her, she saw that she was

469

inside the webs and that the caterpillars were working furiously and spinning the webs tighter and tighter. But I want to go back, she said. I am not dead yet. I do not want to live inside this white cocoon. But the caterpillars were invisible now, nothing but gusts of wind, and they wove the fog into solid bands around her. The thready bands woven of fog were wrapping around her face. She couldn't breathe. Something was fastening her hands to her sides.

She woke up and found Miss Eckroyd bending over her, holding her by the wrists. "Stop it," Miss Eckroyd said; "you can't take off the bandages yourself." Agnes looked up at her, confused. "I was dreaming," she said, "about tent caterpillars." "They're all over this year," said Miss Eckroyd. Just then, Doctor Train walked in. "She's trying to tear off the bandages," Miss Eckroyd told him. "I didn't know I was doing it," Agnes said; "I was dreaming. I want to see myself in a mirror." "Next week," said Doctor Train; "we have to examine you internally. Is that all right?" "I want a mirror," Agnes said; "is there some reason I can't have it?" "Only that you'll be upset when you see yourself," said the doctor, "and you've been upset enough already." "I want to know now," said Agnes; "it can't be worse than I imagine." "All right," he said; "I'll get the surgical cart." He wheeled in a little cart covered with rolls of bandages, tweezers, and scissors of every description.

"Sit up and sit forward," he said; "I'm going to cut the bandage off. When did they last change it?" "Three days ago," she said; "but they wouldn't let me look. They wouldn't even let me touch my face." "Well, that's all over now," the doctor said. "Tilt your head," he said, and he cut loose the bandages which encircled her neck. "Now this won't hurt you," he said; "I'm slipping one blade of the scissor under the bandage and against your scalp, but the blade doesn't have a point, so it can't stick you." "Go ahead," said Agnes. Portions of the bandage began falling, like chunks of frozen snow, in front of her face and into her lap. "Well," said Doctor Train, standing back and inspecting her, "it's off. I left the gauze pad over the ear in place, but that won't interfere with anything." Agnes raised her hand to her head. Her scalp was prickly. "They shaved my head," she said. "They had to," said the doctor; "they didn't know where you were injured. It's growing back." "Let me see the mirror," she said. "Don't forget that you're much thinner than you were," said Doctor Train.

He gave her a large bentwood mirror. She held tightly to its long, curved handle. "Aren't you going to look in it now that you have it?" he asked. "I'm afraid I won't see myself," she said. "You'll see yourself," he said, "a changed self."

Slowly, she raised the mirror. She stared into it without uttering a sound and then let the mirror drop into her lap. "My God," she said, looking up at the doctor, "it's not my face at all." He sat down on the edge of her bed. "Is it as bad as you thought?" he asked. "Different," she said at last. "You realize that it's only half of your face?" he asked her; "only the left side is affected. When you gain some weight, the right side will look just as it always did. The change isn't as big as you think." "I never want anyone drawing me again," Agnes said violently. "I feel needles stabbing into my head," she said, picking up the mirror again. "That's because the bandages are off; it's from the blood circulating through the numb tissue. The numbness will wear off."

She was staring at herself in the mirror. "My left eye keeps rolling," she said; "it's tearing." "It's the wound," the doctor said. "Its lid trembles," Agnes said; "I can't make it stop." "Don't try," he said; "it's involuntary movement. It's all from the shot. There's some damage." "Permanent damage?" she asked. "Yes," he said. "My mouth doesn't work right," she said; "the left half of it won't move." "There might be some improvement after the operation," he said.

She stared into the mirror. She saw how her tongue tended to protrude on the left side. She tried forcing her lips into an *O* but they would not obey her. She was looking at a death's head. The bones of her face had risen up as if they wanted to be free of the flesh. The rolling of her left eye made her look mad. She touched the left side of her face; it was slightly numb.

"It's me," she said at last; "I always knew I looked like this." "What do you mean, Agnes?" he asked. "They always said how beautiful I was," she said, her lower lip beginning to tremble, "but I knew. I knew it wasn't true. I knew I was deformed." "You felt deformed?" he asked. "No," she said, "I *was*. And they knew I was." After a while, he reached out to take the mirror, but she held tight to it, watching herself in it. "I have to get used to it," she said; "I might as well start now." He nodded.

"If you have to examine me," she asked, "why can't you do it now? Why can't you get it over with at once?" "I can, but I have to have Doctor Chase in the room with me," he said; "he's the doctor for the prosecution's side. They won't take my word alone for findings about possible pregnancies of yours." "Only one pregnancy," she said. "If I can find Doctor Chase, we'll get it over with," he said.

He came back in accompanied by Doctor Chase. "It looks like you're going to have things your own way, Agnes," said Doctor Train; "we'll examine you now." He took out a speculum. "Do you know what this is?" he asked her. "I don't know what it's called," she said; "but it's what the doctor used on me to get rid of the baby." "It's called a speculum," the doctor said; "lie still now." Agnes gasped at the familiar pain. "Does that hurt?" he asked. "Not much," she said; "it just reminds me of before." "You better look," he said to Doctor Chase. "I see it," the other man said, straightening up. He sounded displeased. "There's some scarring," said Doctor Train, "and a rent at the opening of the uterus. It's obvious you were pregnant." "Don't tell anyone," said Agnes. "Why not?" asked Doctor Train. "I don't want to get him in trouble," she said. "One of you in trouble is enough, is that it?" asked Doctor Train. "Yes," she said. "Well," said Doctor Train, "it's not up to me. This examination—your body—it's all evidence. Tell me," he said, sitting down, "I know I asked you this before, but what do you think now? Do you think Frank Holt ruined your life?"

"I guess he did," she said, "but it wasn't his fault, was it? It wasn't his fault I loved him so much. It wasn't him or me; it was loving him like that. When you love someone so much, you can ruin your life. You can burn yourself up. I suppose that's what I did." "Are you sorry you killed Jane?" Doctor Train asked her. "No," she said, "because I don't believe I did it. Oh, everyone tells me I did, and people say they saw me shoot her, but I don't believe it. I'm sorry she's dead. I didn't have anything against her. It is like a fire, isn't it?" she asked, slowly; "she was like the building that stands next to the one that catches on fire and goes up in flames along with it. I wish she'd been somewhere else. I wish she wasn't dead. Are you sure she's dead?" "We're sure," said Doctor Chase; "I took the bullet out of her head."

"Who will be taking the bullet out of my head?" Agnes asked. "I will," Doctor Chase said. "You don't like me, do you?" asked Agnes. "I don't like unnecessary deaths," said Doctor Chase. "When do you want to operate?" Agnes asked. "Within a week," the doctor said, "before an abcess has a chance to form. If an abcess formed, it would be too late to do anything. Do you want to go through with it?" "Doctor Train said that I might die," Agnes said. "The chances of dying are not small," said Doctor Chase; "the brain's a delicate thing. We really don't understand it yet." "Would you be surprised if I died?" she asked. "Not at all," he said. "All right," she said; "schedule the operation whenever you want. I'll sign anything."

In his chair, Agnes's father was crying. She heard him and looked out of the window. Lately, whatever she said set him off. She wished he would leave her alone. If it weren't for him, she would find a way to die. Perhaps this operation was the answer.

She woke up in a dark place. She couldn't see anything and then she remembered she had to turn her head. It was the hospital room. She reached up and touched her head; the egg of bandages was back. She felt tears on her cheek and touched her left eye; it was crying without her knowledge. Her right eye was dry. They had promised her that she would die. Her body went hot with rage, a slow heat beginning in her belly and flooding her body until her head pounded and the soles of her feet were hot. She groped around in the sheets looking for Frank's handkerchief. "Miss Eckroyd?" she said. The woman was bending over her. Had nothing changed in the world? She knew, without asking, that her father was sitting in his usual chair. "I want the handkerchief," she said. "I'll get it," Miss Eckroyd said. She went to the dresser and opened its top drawer. It was not there.

"It's not here," she said. "Look again," Agnes said, her voice cold. "It's not here," Miss Eckroyd said, looking through the other drawers. "You took it," Agnes said; "you put it somewhere." "No," said Miss Eckroyd, "when you were in surgery, the hospital laundry might have taken it off to wash along with everything else." Agnes saw a small glass full of daisies on the table next to her. She reached out and picked it up but when she tried to throw it at Miss Eckroyd, it fell onto her lap and then rolled onto the floor. "Agnes," said her father. She began to cry. "Why can't I die?" she asked; "why don't I die? Why am I alive? They should have killed me on the table. Why can't I die?" she asked her father. "Mother died. Majella died. Grandmother died. Everyone can die but me." "You'll die eventually," said her father. "I don't want to live until old age," Agnes said; "why should I be kept alive so people can stare at me? Why can't I die?'' "All this over a handkerchief,'' her father said, shaking his head. "Do you want them to hang you?'' Miss Eckroyd said; "you know they might.'' "If they'd do it now,'' said Agnes, "I'd put the rope around my neck myself.''

44

OPERATION ON MISS DEMPSTER

SURGEONS REMOVE BULLET FROM HER HEAD

April 25, 1899—Agnes Dempster, still confined in Whately Hospital in Montpelier, was this afternoon operated upon by Doctor Chase of this city and Doctor Paley Train, Superintendent of the State Asylum for the Insane at Highbury. It was a dangerous operation, as it was necessary to cut away a portion of the cheek bone in order to extract the ball.

It was a very delicate operation and the knife was in the hands of Doctor Chase. Miss Dempster was under the influence of ether for more than five hours. When the bullet was finally taken out, it proved to be a shapeless bit of lead, bearing no resemblance to a revolver bullet. This operation was decided to be necessary by the physicians in order to save Miss Dempster's life, as she would surely have died had the bullet remained in her head. She rallied after the operation and is resting comfortably tonight, although it is by no means certain that this operation will not prove fatal.

COURT IN A HOSPITAL

HEARING IN THE AGNES DEMPSTER MURDER CASE YESTERDAY

Unique Proceedings Before Vermont's Supreme Bench

Montpelier, Vt., May 26—The Supreme Court listened to the arguments in the Agnes Dempster murder case at Whately Hospital this morning. The question to be decided is the validity of the indictment. The respondents claim the presence of a stenographer at the grand jury hearing invalidated the findings.

State's Attorney Frederick A. Parsons opened, followed by Charles P. Kingsley. David Deignault spoke briefly and Charles Kingsley closed. The arguments finished just before noon. The hearing was held in the reception room, Miss Dempster lying on a patient's chair outside the door in the hallway leading to her ward. With the court and lawyers, the room was not large enough to have the chair wheeled in. She lay so she could see into the room but did not look but once. She was attended by her nurse and acted, as usual, nonchalant.

This is the first time the Supreme Court has sat at the bedside of the respondent in a murder or any other case. The court went to the hospital at the express request of the attorneys of both sides, who wished to have the question of the indictment's validity settled at once. All the judges were present but Southby and Richter. Judge Southby was averse to sitting on a murder case unless the respondent was present, and would not go outside the Supreme Court chamber. The case came before Judge Richter in the county court and he naturally absented himself.

It is expected that the decision will be given in about three weeks when the court returns here.

Mr. Kingsley came into the kitchen and pulled up his chair. He had had a late-night conference with David Deignault, who, with two other agents of his, was hunting up witnesses who would testify to the fact that they thought various members of the Dempster family were insane. He was having less trouble than he expected; the people of North Chittendon didn't seem to stray very far afield, although it was said that an old servant of Eurydice Saltonstall had taken up residence in Boston. The rest seemed to live in Clayboro, a tiny town identical to North Chittendon, ten miles from it, whose population was evidently composed of offshoots of the main families in North Chittendon. He had asked Mr. Deignault if he thought they'd have enough witnesses to build a case, and he said they'd have so many they would run the risk of boring the jury to death. He went on to say that after this, if he went out to commit murder, he knew what defense he'd use, because everyone evidently thought everyone else was crazy, and was only too happy to be given an excuse to say so.

"They do seem a bit crazier than the normal run, though," he said. "Do you think there's real craziness there?" Mr. Kingsley asked him. "You know me," said Mr. Deignault, "I think everyone's crazy, maybe not crazy enough to be locked up, but crazy all the same. But they're *some* crazier." "Well, then," Mr. Kingsley had said, "keep hunting. Quantity is more important than quality in a case like this." "It usually is," Mr. Deignault had said; "this is costing a fortune." "It's going to cost the state even more," Mr. Kingsley had said; "wait until the papers get ahold of the figures." "The father still stays there with the girl?" Mr. Deignault asked. "He only leaves at night," Mr. Kingsley had said.

He looked up and saw his wife in the doorway. She set a plate of doughnuts and eggs down before him and sat down opposite him, her face stern. "They say the Dempster girl was seen playing croquet on the hospital lawn yesterday," she said. "That's good," he said, chewing; "then she must be getting better. Everything's all set for the trial but her." "They also say she needs an attendant not because she wants to kill herself, but because they're afraid she'll try to escape." "What do you think?" Mr. Kingsley asked; "why don't we have any potatoes?" "Because Gladys didn't come in. She didn't come in because she went to the hospital trying to catch a glimpse of the Dempster girl, and I didn't want to peel potatoes myself, that's why we don't have any." Mr. Kingsley raised his eyebrows. "Why do you think she has an attendant?" he asked again, looking down at his disappointing plate. "If you were afraid she was going to escape, you'd have a policeman there," she said. "In a woman's room?" he asked. "Who's paying for the attendant?" his wife asked. "The state," he said. "Oh, well then," his wife said, "I don't know. Of course, they kept the attendant there when she was far too weak to do any escaping, so they must have been afraid she'd kill herself." "You'd make an excellent juror," said Mr. Kingsley.

"How is the girl?" asked his wife. Yesterday, Mr. Kingsley, in company with Doctor Train, Doctor Chase, and Doctor Field, the State's expert medical witness, had gone to see her. It was now almost two months since she had been operated upon and both sides deemed it necessary to make an adequate estimation of her current mental condition. "You mean physically?" Mr. Kingsley asked; "physically, her condition is good. She wasn't playing croquet this week, though. Maybe last week. This week she won't get out of bed and she won't talk to anyone. If you walk around to the side of the bed so that she has to see you, she turns her head the other way. If people stand on both sides of the bed, she puts the pillow over her head, and then her attendant has to hold up one end of it so she doesn't smother herself. At least the woman who stays with her thinks she has to do that; the doctors say she can't smother herself that way. If you sit there long enough, the girl may say she doesn't want to live. All she has to do is lay eyes on the doctors and she's back under the pillows and she won't even say that much.''

"What's wrong with her now?" his wife asked; "I heard she was very jolly, even after the operation." "Not after the operation," said Mr. Kingsley; "she had a fit when she realized she was alive. She only consented to it in the first place because she thought it would kill her. I told you that." He sighed and took a bite of another doughnut. "These are heavier than usual, aren't they?" he asked her. "No," she said, "they're not. You're in a blue mood, that's all. I wouldn't want to defend someone like that. Small thanks you'll get for it." "I don't need her thanks," Mr. Kingsley said; "her father will thank me."

"Won't she talk to you at all?" his wife asked. "There's something going on about a handkerchief," he mumbled. She stared at him. She had never seen him so miserable over a case. "A handkerchief?" she asked. "Apparently she had a handkerchief, but she lost it. Well, she didn't lose it. When they took her into surgery, she gave it to Miss Eckroyd to watch for her, and when she came back, Miss Eckroyd couldn't find it, and she got so hysterical the doctors were afraid she'd start up a rupture and they filled her full of morphine until she went to sleep. She says if she doesn't get the handkerchief back she wants to die. But they can't find it; they've turned the hospital upside down. Miss Eckroyd says she isn't sure, but she thinks the handkerchief belonged to Frank Holt and that's why it was so important to her. I asked her to find out what was going on." "Couldn't someone get her another handkerchief?" his wife asked; "if it's so important to her?"

"How did she get one of his handkerchiefs in the first place?" asked her husband; "that's a question I'd like the answer to." "If her father didn't get it for her, then her friend did," his wife said; "no one else is allowed in there." "Her friend," repeated Mr. Kingsley. "Yes," said his wife, "her friend. But if it really was his handkerchief, why would he want to give it to her? It could only cause him trouble, helping her. Neither of them behave very sensibly; she tells the papers none of it was his fault and he gives her his handkerchief. It makes you wonder what they were up to. What they *are* up to." "It does, doesn't it?" Mr. Kingsley said. "I wish the trial were over with," his wife said. "Well, it may be delayed until the next session of the court," he said, "because of the plea I entered after the operation. I said the indictment was invalid so now we have to wait for the Supreme Court." "What do you think they'll do?" "Set the exceptions aside and order the trial to begin," he said; "but it gives me time. It creates suspense. Those exceptions bought me four weeks." "You use the law like a toy," said his wife. "I'll take that as a compliment," he said.

The doorbell rang. "I'll get it," said Mr. Kingsley. "Well, Martha," he said, coming back in, "that was Dave Deignault. Dust off your going-to-church dress. The case is going to court Monday. The Supreme Court threw out the exceptions. It goes to the Superior Court of Washington County, Judge Richter presiding." "Monday!" said Mrs. Kingsley; "does the girl know?" "I sent Deignault over there with her friend, Polly. They're supposed to find out what she wants, if she thinks she needs a special chair, if she needs a nurse with her, things like that, and if she's mad because the case is going to trial, she can take it out on Deignault and then I'll have an easier time with her in court." "I don't know why he works for you," said his wife. "Because he wants to learn," said her husband; "when he goes out on his own, he'll do all the same things." "Lawyers," said his wife. "What's the trouble now?" he asked. "After all these years," she said, "you'd think I'd be used to it. It would be different if you really believed that you should save whatever lives could be saved, if you held a religious conviction of some sort. But you don't. It's all a game or a challenge. It doesn't seem right." "Don't you think everyone deserves a defense?" he asked her. "A defense, yes," she said uneasily, "but a reasonable defense. This girl, for example. No one ought to touch her unless the facts go against her. But you're going to fix it so that the facts will all seem in her favor. You're going to fix it so that no one can convict her even if they should." "That's what I'll do if I can," he said. He looked, she thought bitterly, twenty years younger: the old horse hearing the old bugle. "That's not *right*," she said harshly; "that's not truth."

Mr. Kingsley laid his fork down on his plate. "Well, Martha," he said, "that's one thing I've always envied ubout you. You're an intelligent woman but you're never in any doubt about the truth." "Don't start in on me, Charles," she said; "you know what I mean." "Do you know the truth about this girl and Frank Holt?" he asked; "do you know what it was like to see life through her eyes?" "No, I don't," she said; "but that's not what this trial is about. This trial is about whether or not she

479

killed that girl. How she saw life isn't truth; it's understanding."
"Suppose she didn't know she was killing the girl?" he asked.
"And if she didn't," asked his wife, "is that an excuse for
letting her live? She might kill someone else and not know it."
"Not if she's in the Highbury State Asylum for the Insane," he
said.

"And you'd fight to put her in there?" his wife demanded;
"with lunatics, with raving maniacs, an eighteen-year-old girl
who was so madly in love that she killed a girl who stood in her
way? When she couldn't get what she wanted, she fired the gun.
She's a passionate girl who can't control her passions. What will
life be like for her in an asylum where she can't have anything
she wants, ever? It's like burying her alive!" "What choice is
there?" he asked; "it's either that or the rope around her neck."
"If it were one of our daughters, I'd rather see the rope around
her neck," she said. "That's easy to say when it isn't our
daughter," he said; "if they put her in the asylum, she gets
another chance. If she can prove she's sane, they have to let her
out." "*Prove* she's sane!" said his wife; "of course she could!
Anyone can prove anything. Isn't that what you always say? And
then she could walk around shooting people for a week before
they caught her!" "She has to have a defense," he said.

He supposed it was true, that he believed everyone must be
saved who could be saved. His rational mind held no such belief;
it welled up from somewhere deep inside him. It was the reason
he was so good at his job. There were times he wished he didn't
have any such belief, but he did. His wife was right; the actions
of a lifetime proved he was committed to saving any life, no
matter how unworthy, no matter how pernicious. He wondered
why. Whatever it was, it was not something he could escape or
turn from. "The girl will be a part of it," he said to his wife;
"she'll be sitting in the court every day. People will listen to the
witnesses and they'll listen to me, but they'll end up judging her.
Sometimes I think that's how it is. They defend or convict
themselves. Some of them." "Don't try to push the responsibility over onto the criminal," said his wife; "once they get in that
court, it's all your doing." "That's where you've always made
your mistake," he said; "the jury has a mind of its own. Of
course when there's an acquittal I like to take credit for it, but
sometimes it's all a private transaction between the jury and the
defendant. The rest of us might as well stay home."

"You don't really believe that, do you?" his wife asked;
"you're too proud to believe that." "I believe it," he said; "you

watch this case carefully and maybe you will, too. I have a feeling about this one." Martha sat still, inspecting him. "Is this how you do it?" she asked; "is this how you convince them? You keep changing tack and bringing in new ideas until they're confused?" "It isn't that I bring in new ideas at all," he said; "I bring in true ideas, one after the other, and most of them don't go together. You have to pull your own truth out of them and what it will be is anyone's guess." "But if you give them the ideas," Martha said, the corners of her mouth pulling down, "then whatever conclusion they reach is yours. Everything they had to work with came from you." "It's more complicated than that," he said; "you know it is. Everything you give them adds to whatever they already had. And then there's the prosecuting attorney. He gives them plenty to think about." "Oh, I know it works out," she said, "but I don't know how. It would be nice to think that things worked out *right*."

"Right," he repeated; "right, true. Well, think of it this way. Remember when we used to live in White River Junction and we made maple syrup, and while it boiled, someone was always getting a hair in it, a piece of dust, or a piece of dried leaf, and we strained it out with cheesecloth and your mother always complained that you could taste the cloth in the finished syrup? Do you remember?" "I remember," she said. "So we had it all strained and pure but it tasted of the cloth we used, and everyone who had a tongue as sharp as your mother's could tell whose syrup it was. Is that right?" She nodded. "But it was still syrup, wasn't it?" he asked; "it still came from the sugar maples. We couldn't hide that fact." "No," she said. "Even if we didn't know how the trees made the sap, we knew where the syrup came from. We knew it was maple syrup, cheesecloth or no cheesecloth. No matter what we did to the sap, it was still sap. That's what the truth is. It's something irreducible; something you can't boil down any further. Maybe someone else can but you can't. It's truth and you're stuck with it." "No, Charles," she said, "that's not a good example. Trees can't talk or think. Humans have minds, and truth looks different to each of those minds. Truth *can't* come forth naked and shining, not when people's minds create truth. When it comes to people, there's nothing irreducible. You could always take things down further, if you knew how." "*If* you knew how," he said; "but there comes a point when you don't." "And that's truth?" asked his wife; "whatever is temporarily irreducible?"

"Temporarily irreducible," he said, nodding; "I like the

481

sound ot it. I'm glad we agree." "Agree?" said his wife; "I thought we just disagreed." "No," he said; "you started out by saying I distorted the truth and you ended saying no one knew what the truth was and no one ever could, so one temporarily irreducible truth is as good as another. Isn't it?" Martha pushed the skin back and forth over the knuckles of her left hand. "I suppose," she said, "if the truth is so complicated, because people are so complicated, it's best to keep everyone alive until we know what we're doing. Is that what we believe?" "Yes, Martha," he said; "I guess we do. I hadn't thought of it that way before, but I guess we do." "Don't tell me I made you think of something new?" she asked, her eyebrows rising in surprise. "Yes, Martha, you did. That's how a trial works. Of course, you don't always want to know what you find out." "But you always say it's best to know the truth," she said perplexed. "For whom?" he said, getting up; "best for whom? I don't have a good answer to that one, not yet."

"People should just live out their lives," she said; "it's when they stop and think that they get into trouble." "You think the Dempster girl stopped and thought?" he asked, smiling. "Too much," she said, "altogether too much." "That's funny," said Mr. Kingsley; "I would never have thought of it that way." "The passions don't produce this sort of disaster," Mrs. Kingsley said; "if they did, the world would have ended long ago. She thought too much." "Do you know what you mean by that?" he asked, watching her closely. "Not yet," she said. "Let's both work on that," he said. He stood up and rapped the wooden table with his knuckles. "Sometimes you just hit it on the head," he said.

45

AGNES'S FATE

NOW SO SOON TO BE DETERMINED

WAS SHE ACTUALLY INSANE

OR WILLFULLY GUILTY OF THE WORST OF CRIMES?

FRANK HOLT'S POSITION

The Theory Of The State And The Expectations Of The Defense—If Insane Now, What Was Her Mental Condition On The 24th Of December Last? —The Men On Whom Her Fate Depends—A Brief Resume Of The Famous Case

Only a few more days are yet to elapse before the time set for Agnes Dempster to stand before her accusers and answer to the charge of willful murder which the people of the state of Vermont, represented by the prosecuting attorney and the officers of the county court, have preferred against her. What the result can be no man can forecast. It is not yet certain indeed that the trial will ever take place, for she may find some way to take her own life, and thus carry her case directly to a court from whose decision there may be no appeal.

If tried, however, by earthly courts, the outlook is hardly less appalling. If convicted, she must stand upon the gallows, upon which one Washington County woman suffered the death penalty but a few years ago, or she must pass behind prison doors to await a death little less terrible, though longer delayed.

On the other hand, if acquitted, it will be because twelve men, twelve jurors, sworn to do their duty, which they may not avoid, however distasteful, believe that at the time of her crime she was insane and mentally incapable of controlling her physical actions. So decided, she must pass from the hands of the keepers of the county jail to the control of the keepers of the state asylum for the insane, and spend the remainder of her life in narrow confines surrounded by brainless or brain-diseased lunatics.

The case itself is a remarkable one and destined to be memorable. The accused and her victim came from a higher stratum of society than where such cases are usually found. The general interest is great and will be maintained though the trial will be largely a battle of experts. One of the leading causes of interest will be the light thrown on the position of Frank Holt and his relations with Agnes Dempster which drove her to commit the crime. Testimony bearing on this will be eagerly listened to.

Miss Dempster's mental condition has been examined at different times by Doctor Paley Train, superintendent at the state asylum at Highbury, and Doctor Arthur Crane of the Maclean Institute. What opinions they have formed as to her mental condition will of course not be made public until the time of the trial.

Amon Dempster, father of Agnes, although his daughter has been a source of much anxiety to him, has left his affairs at his home in North Chittendon in charge of the farm manager, Mr. William F. Brown, and has remained in this city in almost constant attendance upon his daughter.

Her unhealthy mental condition previous to the shooting is evidenced by the notes found in her room afterwards. One of these notes about "love-sick girls" has been printed in this paper several times previously.

The three accompanying portraits of the principals of this drama are taken from their latest photographs. Those of the two girls have been previously published, but that of Frank Holt, as it appears in *The Spectator*, is the first and only authentic likeness of the man in the case that has yet appeared. He is a little past twenty-one years of age, and is a stonecutter. He came to this city from Quebec a little over two years ago and is a favorite among the men he works with.

The opening of this case is awaited with much interest by the community and its progress will be noted by large audiences day by day. Agnes Dempster will be placed on trial charged with one of the most shocking crimes in the history of the state; it is in fact doubtful if any incident of a similar nature ever had such a startling effect upon the inhabitants of this community or awakened more widespread interest throughout the entire commonwealth. *The Spectator* proposes to give its readers a full and careful report of each day's work, not in any way attempting to make it sensational, but a faithful record of the testimony as it is given in court.

Monday, June 26th, 1899, the day Agnes Dempster's trial began, was a beautiful day. Spring had come late; now the sky was a light, high, powdery blue. There was no trace of the rain which had poured down the day before, so hard and so heavily that everyone began to say they thought the river might flood and the roads to the city would go out and the trial would be held up because all the prospective jurors would not be able to get to the courthouse. But the rain was gone, and in its place was a freshly washed city, gleaming and glowing under the spring sun. The gold dome of the courthouse spilled its radiance back into the already shining air.

Resurrection was all about. The forsythia swayed lightly in the breeze. The robins nested in the old crotches of the lilac bushes. The bluejays were everywhere, chasing the smaller birds from the sudden plenty which had just appeared on the earth beneath their wiry toes. The voices of the birds rose in an underlying, confused chorus of chitterings and chirps, and the land itself was in motion. The hills greened under one's eyes, and by noon would glow green and gold under the newly born sun. Once more, everything on earth appeared imperishable. Once more, everything on earth turned up its face and pushed its way toward the sun.

The yellow daffodils were still blooming in front of Mr. Kingsley's house and the long stemmed red tulips bent in the breeze like exotic women accepting homage. From his dining room, Mr. Kingsley could see the fields on the mountain above, and the herd of black and white cows, slowly dispersing as they climbed into the higher mowings. He stood at the window and watched them move away from each other, into their own grass, until finally they dotted the hills at random. As if they had been thrown down by some gigantic hand. At random. Even cows have their freedom, he thought. It was such a beautiful sight; the herd of cows climbing, then scattering like a heavy, living cloud, then, as night fell, coming together again and going back down into the secure barn. Oh, the reverend often enough compared God to a shepherd or a farmer, but the average farmer did a better job than God. Was this why he defended his clients so ferociously? So that they could continue to see what the earth never tired of spilling forth? But the Dempster girl didn't want to see the summer. When he had visited her yesterday, she had refused to go to the window.

"Why should I look?" she had asked him; "why should I torture myself with what I'm shut away from?" "But you'll be going out tomorrow," he said; "you'll be able to see it for yourself. You'll feel the spring air on your skin. When you're locked up like this, you don't remember how important it is. The crocuses are already gone," he said, watching her. He didn't know why but he was convinced this girl loved life. "The tulips are still up and the daffodils and the irises are starting. The lilac bushes will be thick all over soon. They'll be like thick purple clouds in front of the buildings and when you drive by, the smell blows into the carriage like good news from heaven." "It's not for me to see," Agnes said; "it's someone else's summer." "It's yours, too," he said; "that's why we're fighting for you." "Mr. Kingsley," the girl said, "you're a very good man. But you are not the best man in the world. The best man in the world would let me die."

In the corner of the jail cell she shared with Agnes, Miss Eckroyd sighed. "Agnes," said Mr. Kingsley, "you're only eighteen. A lot happened to you in eighteen years. You could live sixty years more if we get you off. Think how much could happen to you in sixty years." "If I thought about it that way," said the girl, "I'd go into court and tell reporters that I remembered everything and that I killed Jane Holt because I wanted to. Sixty years! I can't live that long! I won't! I don't have a soul. I'm an inanimate thing. I'm not important." "What do you mean, Agnes?" Mr. Kingsley asked. The girl didn't answer. "She says Frank was her soul, and if she loses him, she's lost her soul," Miss Eckroyd said; "she says he destroyed her soul." "You don't believe that, Agnes," Mr. Kingsley said. "I do," said Agnes, "but I can't expect you to understand it." "Did you tell that to the doctor?" he asked. "Yes," said Agnes; "I did." "And what did he say?" asked Mr. Kingsley. "He said it was impossible for one person to destroy another person's soul," answered Agnes. "And you don't believe him?" Mr. Kingsley asked. "No," she said; "why should I? It hasn't happened to him. It's happened to me."

"So you want to hang?" asked Mr. Kingsley. "I guess I don't want to hang," she said; "not yet. If that means I want to live, then I want to live." "Because she knows she'll see that Holt fellow at the trial," Miss Eckroyd put in. "Is that it?" Mr. Kingsley asked. "Is that it?" he asked again more sharply. "I suppose," the girl said; she was sullen. "I can't have outbursts in the court," Mr. Kingsley said; "if you think you're going to try and rush up to him and choke the life out of him or anyone else, I want to know now." "Choke him?" Agnes said; "if I'd wanted to choke him, I wouldn't be here now." "There are going to be a lot of people you haven't seen in a long time in that court," he said; "you have to behave yourself like a good girl." "I don't think you'll have trouble with her," said Miss Eckroyd; "most of the time I can't get her to talk. It's boring for me in here, I tell you. I think she lies there crying, but she won't let me see her face." "Crying's all right," said Mr. Kingsley; "crying's fine."

"Yesterday," said Miss Eckroyd, "when the matron came to spell me, I went out and bought her a wig. I didn't think she'd want to go into court with all those spikes standing up all over her head. I don't know if she'll wear it." "It's up to her," said Mr. Kingsley. "I'll wear it," said Agnes, "and I'll wear the hat and veil she got me, too." "I'd rather you didn't wear a veil," said Mr. Kingsley. "Just let her wear it for the first few days," Miss Eckroyd said.

"Do you think I'm crazy?" Agnes asked him suddenly. "That's going to be my defense," he said. "But do you believe it?" she asked. "I don't know," he said; "I'll wait and see what everyone has to say, just like everyone else, and then I'll decide. I'll keep my decision to myself, of course," he said, "if it goes against me." "Well," she said, sitting up and staring at him, "I think you're crazy. I think I'm crazy for ever having thought life was worth living, and you're a lot older than I am, and you still think so, so you must be stark raving mad." He repressed a shudder. The girl's left eye still teared incessantly because of damage to the lachrymal glands which had not yet healed; the right side of her face contradicted the left side, and at times seemed to defy it. Right now, the right side of her face was furious, the left stiff, calm, and distorted. And her hair stood straight up from her head in thick black needles. He would be relieved to see her in a wig. "Sometimes," Agnes said, lying back, "I think I see people coming to get me through the walls and then I'm frightened. But what comes next is worse. I know they won't ever come and get me, and I start crying. You should get Miss Eckroyd out of here before I drive her crazy. I'll be glad when the trial is over with. My father can't last much longer at this." "Is that why you're going through with it?" asked Mr. Kingsley; "is that why you're not stealing scissors and running at windows?" "For him," said Agnes. "Don't you ever do anything for yourself?" he asked her. "For myself?" she asked; "I'm not worth anything much now and I never was." Mr. Kingsley looked up at the cow which had reached the highest mowing. It didn't worry about its soul. It knew it had worth. That was the birthright of every living thing. Yet the Dempster girl had said she had no right to be in the world. He could not believe her. He would not believe her.

Mrs. Kingsley came into the dining room, went up to where her husband was standing at the window, and slipped her arm around his waist. He bent down and kissed the top of her head. "See the cows?" he asked. "Yes, I see the cows," she said; "in another life, you must have been Little Bo Peep, you spend so much time looking at them." "Little Bo Peep watched her sheep," he said. "It's the same thing," said Martha. "So it is," said her husband. He looked down at his wife, the neat white line which parted her hair down the middle. "What do you want to be when you grow up?" he asked her. It was an old, old game. "I want to be your wife," she said, "but I don't want to be married to a lawyer. I want to be married to a carpenter." "When I grow up," he said, "I want to be a gypsy and eat my meals under a tree." "You've never said that before," Martha replied, startled. "I've thought it often enough," he said; "I've never wanted to do it so much." "The case will turn out all right," said his wife. "If anything can turn out all right for that girl," he said. "Don't start having doubts now," Martha said; "eat your breakfast. It looks bad if the defense attorney is late."

Sheriff Gray came to Agnes's cell in the county jail and found her standing in front of Miss Eckroyd who was trying to hold a mirror still enough for her. "It's hopeless," Agnes said; "the wig keeps slipping over my left ear. I look demented." "You're supposed to look demented," Margaret Eckroyd said. The right corner of Agnes's mouth twitched upward into a smile. "I have an idea," the attendant said; "give me the wig, quick." She told the sheriff she'd be ready in a minute, put a piece of adhesive tape inside the wig, folded the strip back so that part of it would fasten onto her scalp. "There's only one trouble with this," Margaret Eckroyd said; "when we take off the wig later, it's going to pull out some hairs." "Go ahead," said Agnes; "as far as I'm concerned, you could nail it on." "Ladies," said Sheriff Gray uneasily.

He knew there was an enormous crowd waiting in front of the courthouse and he didn't want his charges mobbed. He looked at Agnes. She was thin and pale and dressed in black, and from where he stood, he could see only the right side of her face which had been unaffected by the bullet. Of course, the left eye teared constantly, but he was used to that. He was not used to seeing her dressed, in a black, curly wig, so beautiful that she made you draw in your breath. He had grown quite fond of the girl. Her misery was so palpable he wanted to plunge into it and tear it from her with his own hands, to cast it out the window as if it were some kind of devil he could grab by the heel. He had even grown fond of her strange looks; when she looked straight at you, without her wig, she looked like a newly hatched chick. Now she had suddenly and disconcertingly hatched into a swan, but she was still standing in his jail; she was still on her way to court. And then she turned to face him and the swan was gone, and the tormented face, divided against itself, was back. What could make up for that? His wife and daughters were so very vain. An eruption on the chin was enough to put one of them to bed for a week. Yet this one' was free of vanity. He watched her adjust the black veil over her face. She didn't want to feed the courtroom's curiosity. Well, he could understand that. She was both the deceased and the mourner; he understood that, too. He wished he could think of something to say to her. He knew that if things were different, and he were younger, he could grow accustomed to her appearance, strange as it now was, and that in the end, it wouldn't make any difference. The girl had turned to him. "Ladies," he said, "let's put one over on them. They're dying to see you. Let's start early and get in the back way." "I'm ready," said Agnes. "Lean on my arm," he said.

They went out the service entrance of the jail. A carriage was waiting for them, and it took a circuitous route to the courthouse, finally pulling up to the back entrance. "Did you see all those people out in front?" Margaret Eckroyd asked Agnes; "it's only seven-thirty. You don't think they're going to wait there until they open up the court?" "They'll wait," said Sheriff Gray; "they've been waiting since five-thirty. They want to catch a glimpse of her before it starts. You seem nervous," he said to Agnes. "Do they want to hurt me?" she asked. "They'll have to hurt me first," he said. "I know you want to take care of me," Agnes said; "I don't know why I never fell in love with a man who did." The sheriff blushed. Margaret looked at her, surprised. "I don't think they want to hurt you," Margaret said; "they're curious about you is all. Probably most of them want to blow off the men's heads they live with and they want to see what happens to someone who actually went ahead and did it." "I didn't blow a man's head off," said Agnes. "Well, you blew up what he wanted anyhow," said Margaret.

"I don't know about that," said the sheriff; "I don't know if that's why they're here." Now that the two women were friendlier, their conversation perpetually unnerved him. "Women aren't so bad as that, Miss Eckroyd," he said. "Then why don't they put women on the jury?" she asked. "Because it's said that their intellects are too weak and their emotions too strong," he said. "And are there more women in your jail than men?" asked Margaret; "more women awaiting trials for violent crimes?" "No, Miss Eckroyd," he said patiently; "but I don't make the laws. I just enforce them." "Would you put women on the jury?" Agnes asked. "Good Lord, no," he said; "they'd set everyone free." Agnes and Margaret looked at one another. "Women are harder than men. Don't you think so, Agnes?" Margaret asked. Agnes's hand crept up to the scar behind her left ear. "Yes," she said. Her face had gone white. She had gone in behind her veil. Margaret and the sheriff exchanged glances. Once again, she had left them without warning. "If that isn't craziness, what is?" Margaret whispered to the sheriff. He shook his head.

Agnes was walking up and down the empty courtroom when Judge Richter came in and took up his place on the bench. "I'm glad to see you're up and about," he said to her. "Thank you," she said. Just then, Mr. Kingsley, Mr. Deignault, and their junior partner, Mr. Latch, came in the back door, followed by Mrs. Kingsley. Mrs. Kingsley sat down on one of the chairs in the front row. "Everyone's early," said Mr. Deignault. "Everyone had the same idea," said Judge Richter; "the crowd out there is going to be a nuisance." Mr. Parsons came in with his assistant, Mr. Wright. "Well, is everyone here?" asked Judge Richter. "We're here," said Mr. Kingsley. "We're here," said Mr. Parsons. "And I'm here," said Judge Richter. "Miss Dempster," he said, "I understand you're still in delicate health. Please take your seat. When I ask the bailiff to open the court, the buffalo stampede is going to be on and they'll trample you, believe me." Mr. Kingsley grinned and Mr. Parsons glowered at some papers on his desk. Richter was known for his sternness. Parsons didn't like the considerate tone in which he addressed the Dempster girl.

Agnes sat down and looked around the courtroom. It was a large rectangular room, freshly painted the color of thick cream. The ceiling was very high and the windows were narrow but very high. At their bases, Agnes could see wooden poles whose hooks were used to pull the topmost windows open. In front of the room was the judge's bench, and behind it, an American flag hung from the wall. To the right of the judge's bench, something framed hung on the wall. She knew what it was without having to see it: The Declaration of Independence. The courtroom reminded her of a schoolroom. A little wooden fence divided the judge's bench and the attorneys' tables from the rest of the room. All the wood in the room was highly glossed and the smell of furniture polish was heavy in the air. The domestic smell of the polish seemed out of place; so did the flag. A plain, clean room for transacting business neatly and cleanly. She sighed and sat back in the plush platform rocker which Sheriff Gray had brought in for her the day before. On his visits to her cell, he had seen how she tended to rock back and forth in her straight chair, tilting forward until the back legs lifted from the floor, and then tilting back so that they hit the floor again, and he thought that a rocker would be the best thing for her.

Mr. Kingsley had agreed, but Mr. Parsons objected, saying that a woman in a rocker was bound to inspire sympathy and he would prefer to have her sit in a normally upholstered stationary chair. And so, a week before the court convened, the case of the rocking chair had been brought before Judge Richter. He wanted to know what the girl's doctor thought and Doctor Chase was brought to the court. He told Judge Richter that he believed the girl's recent surgery, which had involved her eye and ear as well as her brain, had affected her sense of balance and that rocking was undoubtedly her way of maintaining a normal sense of herself. Anyone could see how dizzy she became when she had to stand or walk for any length of time. He thought a rocker would be a fine thing for her to have during an ordeal such as the trial promised to be and it would only be humane for her to have it. Moreover, he suggested that they place another chair in front of her so that she could hold on to it if she felt weak. Mr. Parsons, who intended to call Doctor Chase as an expert witness for the prosecution, was furious, but kept quiet. "Of course," said Mr. Kingsley, "we don't have to have the traditional rock-your-baby rocker. We could get her a platform rocker. It looks like a regular, upholstered chair but it rocks back and forth. It doesn't really look like a rocker. Would that suit Mr. Parsons better?" Mr. Parsons said it would. However, when he looked over and saw Agnes, dressed in black, wearing a black veil, sitting in her plush platform rocker, already rocking back and forth, his spirits plummeted. The girl jumped whenever anyone, even Mr. Kingsley, passed her chair. There was something infinitely pitiable in the sight of her, rocking in her chair, wearing that veil. And when she took it off, she would cause a sensation. Everything she did, he foresaw, would cause a sensation. She had already caused one by living this long.

The bailiff had opened the doors and a mad babble of voices spilled forth from the broad throat of the entrance hall, filling the courtroom. The judge was already cracking his gavel, demanding orderly entry. Mr. Parsons turned around in his seat and looked at the crowd pushing in. A herd of women was pushing into the room. Mr. Parsons looked nervously at the judge. Some of the women had umbrellas and were freely poking others near them in an attempt to gain access to the limited number of seats. Judge Richter had thrown down his gavel, stood up, and bellowed that he would empty the courtroom if there were not an orderly entry. The crowd stopped in its tracks. "And I'll keep it closed!" thundered Judge Richter. The women elbowed each other on their way to their seats, but were more circumspect and less violent. Finally, Mr. Parsons saw some men in the crowd squeezing through the doors. Evidently, they were reluctant to push the women who had so unceremoniously thrust them aside. Parsons saw that the room in back of them was filled; the main entranceway, too, was filled by spectators. He looked back at Judge Richter. He had forgotten what an excellent defense attorney the man had been. He knew all the tricks of the defense. Parsons told himself he was just nervous, performing in front of all these people. He had never seen anything like it. There was no reason to believe that the judge was already prejudiced in favor of the defendant. It was, in fact, Richter's old law partner who had presided over the trial of the Washington County woman hung two years before.

Judge Richter was ordering the call of special jurymen whom the court had already summoned. All but two were present. Then the court clerk began calling out the names of the prospective jurors. As each one walked past Agnes's chair to take his place in the jury box, she looked up into each face. There was something both terrified and defiant in her gaze, obscured as it was by the veil. As they passed her, the men did not look at her, but once in the jury box, they seemed incapable of taking their eyes from her, and Judge Richter repeated several questions more than once before he received an answer. He finally instructed the jurors to pay attention to the utterances of the court, since they were to be bound by what they were told. Mr. Parsons saw the fascination the accused held for the jurors; it was, he

492

decided, natural enough. He, too, had been curious enough about an eighteen-year-old girl who had committed a murder.

Finally, Judge Richter asked if any of the men were disqualified by virtue of having served on any other jury in the last two years, and two of the men said they were, and were excused by the court. The jurors were then sworn, and Mr. Parsons stood and made a brief statement regarding the case. Then he began to examine the jurors. He found all of them acceptable. Mr. Kingsley did not. By three-thirty that afternoon, Mr. Kingsley had examined eight of the twelve jurors and had excused two. He claimed they were disqualified because they held prejudicial opinions formed from reading newspaper accounts; evidence alone could not remove such opinions from the minds, and of course the defense could not hope to guess what possible varieties of prejudicial opinions the jurors held, so they could not combat such opinions at all.

Mr. Parsons looked at his watch, sat back, and sighed. No one had left the courtroom and no one would until the court was officially adjourned for the day. He could see that the work of choosing a jury would be as long and tedious as Kingsley could make it and he thought they would be lucky if they got to taking evidence by Wednesday. Something nagged at him like an unscratchable itch. He knew the old fox was up to something. Before finishing with each juror, Kingsley paused, turned his back on the jury box, and asked the man under examination whether or not his judgment would be affected because a woman rather than a man was on trial, and having asked that evidently innocuous question, he turned back to the jury box and waited for the expected answer. "No," said each of the men.

Choosing a jury was even more tedious than Mr. Parsons had imagined. By Tuesday night, eleven men had been chosen, all of whom were farmers and nine of whom were married. But at five o'clock, the state made its last challenge, and there were only eleven jurors, at which point Judge Richter directed that another special panel be drawn so that in the morning the last of the jurors might be chosen. Thirty-three additional jurors were drawn at that time, making a total of one hundred and forty-one, out of which twelve were to be selected. On Tuesday night, the eleven jurors were confined together at the Montpelier Inn, whereupon Mr. Kingsley looked for Judge Richter, but found he had gone to his hotel. He then went to the associate judges and asked them to refuse newspapers to all the jurors. All the papers were now publishing articles about the Dempster case, he said, and those excused had formed prejudicial opinions based on their reading of newspaper articles published before the trial had begun. Mr. Kingsley said he'd hate to throw out the whole jury now that they almost had one intact, and the associate judges agreed it would be unwise to grant the jurors' request for newspapers.

At nine o'clock on Wednesday, the next morning, the process of selecting the last juryman began, and by eleven-thirty, the state had its fourteen jurors, two of whom were to sit with the others in case any of the original twelve fell ill. Mr. Parsons looked at the judge and held his breath. "I declare the jury empaneled," said the judge; "Mr. Parsons, you may begin."

The state introduced a witness who carried in an elaborate plan of the route Agnes had taken to and from the scene of the crime; the plan specified the location of the houses where the events had taken place. This plan, drawn to scale, was shown to the jury, and Parsons identified each place which had been mentioned in newspaper accounts of the case. When he was finished, Mr. Kingsley objected to the plan being introduced as positive evidence of anything at all. He said the plan was not made from the actual knowledge of the man who had drawn it up, and was therefore no better than hearsay evidence. He asked the man who had drawn up the plan if he personally knew what the locations looked like or even where they were, and the witness answered that he personally knew no more about the localities in question than he would have had he lived on the moon. Judge Richter pushed some papers away from him and ordered the plan thrown out and instructed the jury to disregard any ideas they had formed in relation to it. The judge asked Mr. Kingsley if he would have any objection to taking the jurors to the actual sites, so that they could see the locations for themselves, and Mr. Kingsley said he would not. Mr. Parsons, when asked, said he would not object. But he did object. He objected to the jurors marching out to the field where the shooting had taken place; they would see all too plainly how little attempt at concealment the Dempster girl had made. They would see for themselves that she had shot Jane Holt in full view of half the town. But his own witness had been worse than useless. And now Kingsley was before the bench *again*, and the judge was listening to him with furrowed brow, and before Mr. Parsons had a chance to wonder what disaster would occur next, Judge Richter declared a recess to consider a technical question.

Mr. Kingsley had presented a motion to the court. He asked

that all those jurors who, when asked whether or not the fact that the accused was a woman would make any difference in their consideration of the case, had answered in the negative ought to be disqualified from serving in this trial. "But," spluttered Mr. Parsons, "you yourself asked that question of all the jurors!" "So I did," said Mr. Kingsley, "but last night when I was talking to Mrs. Kingsley, it suddenly came to me and I saw the profound depth of my error. Just *because* the accused is a woman, a difference *should* be made by a juryman in the consideration of her case. A juryman *ought* to make as great a distinction in weighing the evidence just as he would make a distinction if the accused were a child. After all, men and women do not react identically in identical situations, and where a life hangs in the balance, the difference between the two sexes may be critical. The one is swayed by emotions more powerfully than the other. Because these jurors fail to recognize the distinction between men and women they should be disqualified to serve in cases of this importance. I'm sure you agree, Mr. Parsons." "I do not," said Mr. Parsons; "they are all well aware a woman is on trial." "But they are not aware that they must judge her as a woman and not as a man, or worse yet, a neuter specimen," said Mr. Kingsley. "I am overruling your motion," said Judge Richter, without a flicker of expression; "however, I will instruct the jury to consider Miss Dempster as a woman, possessed by all of woman's frailties and all of woman's strengths. It is a fine point, Mr. Kingsley," said Judge Richter, "and may yet be tested in the Supreme Court." Mr. Parsons suppressed a groan. "I hope tomorrow we will get on with the evidence," Judge Richter said. "Proper evidence is always a joy to consider," said Mr. Kingsley.

Mr. Parsons turned to look at Agnes. One would suppose, from the indifferent manner in which she swayed to and fro in that damned contraption, that she was a casual visitor to the court and not the accused in this case, not the one whose life hung in the balance. A breeze blew in the open windows and lifted her veil. She raised her hand and held the veil in place. Mr. Parsons looked away. He did not want to see the face under the veil. The presence of the veil comforted him.

Behind him, Mr. Kingsley was earnestly conferring with the Hammerhead while countless other reporters buzzed about the man like flies. Tomorrow the papers would report that the jury probably could not appreciate the problems of a woman since there was not a woman among them; they would hint strongly that a woman always was in peril when she was tried only by men. Kingsley was a monster. Now the reporters were coming toward Mr. Parsons, undoubtedly to discover *how* prejudiced a hearing the jurors would, of necessity, give Agnes Dempster. And Kingsley, he knew, was out on the street, stopping spectators to get their impressions of the case. The man had nerve.

46

"Well," Mr. Kingsley asked his wife as she served supper, "how do you think the case is going?" "I don't know about the case," she said, "but you have Parsons tearing his hair." "What do people make of the girl?" he asked. "They say it's curious, the way she rocks there as if the proceedings had nothing to do with her. Of course, they're dying to see what's underneath that veil of hers. It's hard to get close enough to get a real look at her." "Do they sympathize with her?" "Not yet," she said; "I think they're fascinated. I think they're all waiting for the man in the case, that Holt person, and then they'll make up their minds." "You're probably right," Mr. Kingsley said; "you usually are. No one goes up to her, though. Did you notice that?" "They may. Later," said Mrs. Kingsley; "I think people are afraid to go talk to her; she never stops rocking. After a while, you start to think that if you stopped the rocker, you'd kill her altogether." "She does like that rocker," said Mr. Kingsley.

On Thursday morning the court did not convene. Judge Richter was waiting for the jurors to return from the tour of inspection of Willow Drive, Cherry Street, North Street, the field into which both girls had gone, and Jane Holt's house, on whose porch both girls had been laid. When they returned, they were in time for the noon recess and it was not until one-thirty that the waiting crowd was admitted. Then the courtroom was immediately filled to overflowing with women who occupied nearly all the seats so that when the doors of the main entrance were opened only a few of the large crowd of men waiting could be admitted. And, as the crowd flooded in, Agnes, her veil in place, her hands in her lap, rocked in her platform rocker.

"She looks like she's watching a play," a woman behind her whispered loudly enough for half the courtroom to hear. "Maybe she doesn't know how serious it is," someone else whispered back. "Well, they say she's crazy," said the first. The two women waited for Agnes's reaction, but the rhythm of her rocking did not alter, nor did her head turn toward them. Agnes sat in the same position, oblivious to them, oblivious to the parade of witnesses who testified to the fact that she had bought a revolver in Barre, that she had been seen practicing with it on two occasions on top of Bald Hill, that she came into the kitchen at the Ludlum house and asked to talk to Jane, that one or the other of them said, "Frank Holt can't be engaged to two of us at once," that she and Jane walked outside, evidently intending to go to Jane's house, but entered a field across the way from it, and that in the middle of the field, she raised her gun and shot first Jane and then herself.

On Friday, the crowd was buzzing at the doors as thickly as ever. The parade of witnesses moved quickly on and off the stand and there was an air of expectancy in the room. A Miss Jenny Dougherty testified that she had gone into the field and saw the girls lying on their backs, Miss Dempster lying with her head on Miss Holt's lap, the pistol resting on her breast. She said she could not see anything like a wound on Miss Dempster's body, but she saw the blood issuing from beneath her and drenching the dress of the other girl. She said she saw Officer Delonnay pick up the pistol and he kept it until the girls were taken to the hospital and she did not know what happened to it next.

Then the state called Doctor Salter who testified that he had been called to the Holt house and found the two girls lying on the piazza. People in the court had heard this story before and were stirring in their seats, when suddenly, everyone fell silent and paid attention. The judge, surprised by the absolute silence, looked up. He saw what it was at once. Agnes Dempster had stopped rocking. She was sitting forward in her chair, nervously grasping the chair in front of her, and when she leaned forward, the veil fell away from her face, and the people near her could see the blood coming and going rapidly in her face, her eyes dilated, her manner startled, as if she were seeing the incidents for the first time.

"I examined the Holt girl," said Doctor Salter; "she appeared to be dying, her pulse beating only three times a minute. Then after I treated her wound, some clotted blood and brain matter escaped from the wound and after that her symptoms seemed improved. She was taken off to the hospital by ambulance, and there portions of her broken skull were removed and the wound was dressed to prevent hemorrhaging. When I left her, she was unconscious. When I next saw her, well, I didn't see her, I saw her body, it was three o'clock and she was dead. I later assisted Doctor Chase in performing an autopsy upon her and we found the bullet to be the immediate cause of death. We found the condition of nearly all the vital organs normal.

"Agnes Dempster was unconscious when I first saw her and her pulse was rapid. I was there when they undressed her, and a paper with five cartridges wrapped in it fell out of her pocket. At that time, only her eyelid twitched and I didn't think she would live. Later in the day, a nurse noticed her moving and she called us in and we realized that the Dempster girl was not dying but gaining strength. We originally thought they both were dead upon arrival at the hospital, which is why the attendants put both girls in the same bed. As soon as they saw Miss Dempster was alive and that the other was not, of course we separated them. I doubt if either one of them was aware of the other's presence at any time."

At this, Agnes raised her hand to her throat and was heard to make a strange, choking noise. People were leaning forward, trying to get a better look at her. One woman bent forward so far she fell from her seat and had to be assisted up from the floor. It was clear to everyone that what Agnes was hearing was new to her. Mr. Kingsley looked around and knew what the audience was thinking. Had they really put her in bed with a dead girl? Had she awakened to find herself next to a corpse? Agnes sat forward, gripping the chair in front of her. Then she suddenly let go and fell backward. Everyone could see that she was still weak. "Why does she have to sit here and listen to all this?" a man asked in a low voice. "It's a crime," said the man sitting next to him.

The next witness called to the stand was Charlie Mondell. Agnes, collapsed in her chair, lifted her veil slightly, as if to see him better. He admitted going to Agnes's room and searching for letters and told the court that he and Frank had burned the ones they found. When asked why he had done this, he said Frank was the oldest friend he had and he would do anything within the law to protect him. "Was Mr. Frank Holt intimate with Miss Dempster?" Mr. Kingsley asked. "I was never there when he was," said Charlie, flushing. "Did he have any opportunity to be intimate?" he asked. "I imagine he did," Charlie said; "they roomed in the same house. But I roomed there myself and I was never intimate with Miss Dempster."

"Did Mr. Holt tell you that he had asked Miss Dempster to

marry him?'' asked Mr. Kingsley. Charlie paused, looking at Agnes. "Yes, he did," he said at last; "but I didn't know if he was serious." Then he was asked to identify two letters and was asked if they were the ones he had helped destroy. "Yes," said Charlie, puzzled; "they are." "Apparently," said Mr. Kingsley, turning toward the courtroom, "Miss Dempster had little to do once Mr. Holt finished with her, and she spent her time recopying the letters."

Mr. Parsons was on his feet, objecting, and a buzz began running through the audience, and three blows of the gavel fell before it died down. "I object," said Mr. Parsons; "the defense is assuming Mr. Holt threw Miss Dempster over. We have no proof he did anything of the sort." "Objection sustained," the judge said.

Lilian Bugbee was the last witness of the day, and she testified that Agnes had told her that Frank would never marry Jane Holt because he would marry her. She didn't know, she said, stealing a look at Agnes, whether she meant to threaten Jane Holt, but she didn't think so.

Finally, the court was adjourned. But the sidewalk in front of the courthouse, the surrounding grounds, and several blocks of Maple Street, were jammed with curiosity seekers. "That crowd goes all the way back to the jail," said Sheriff Gray; "it's too much to put up with." He went up to Judge Richter and complained that the people were not content with trying to stare Miss Dempster down, but were now going to try to follow her to the very door of the jail to be sure no expression of weariness or sorrow could escape them. Mr. Kingsley, who had come up to the bench, nodded and told Sheriff Gray he didn't know if he ought to subject Agnes to such an ordeal. "She's knocked out at the end of the day as it is." "Don't worry about it," said Sheriff Gray; "I have no intention of taking her out into that mob. I guess I don't believe in that sort of procedure." "Can you take measures to protect her?" asked the judge. "If you let us wait them out in here," said the sheriff; "surely I can." "Do what you think is best," the judge said.

"Well, Agnes," said the sheriff, "shall we disappoint your admirers?" Agnes nodded and began walking around the courtroom as if she were the only person left in it. "Did you ever see anything like it?" Mr. Parsons said to Mr. Kingsley; "she's not interested in what we're up to." "I guess she has her choice of going underground or sitting there without her skin," said Mr. Kingsley. "Her skin's thick enough," said Parsons; "she killed that girl after all." Agnes continued walking back and forth through the room. The spectators were gone; they were all removed when the court was adjourned. Agnes never looked out the window at the crowd below. "Well, Agnes," Sheriff Gray said after a half hour had passed, "they're going to have a good long wait if they want to see you tonight." "All right," she said, sitting down in her rocker. "Tomorrow," said Sheriff Gray, "I'm bringing a deck of cards." Agnes kept rocking. It was past six o'clock when the crowd diminished to a few determined stragglers and Agnes was quietly taken back to jail.

The second week of the trial opened less clamorously. The familiar crowd still waited outside the courthouse, but it was a smaller one, and the people in it were less frantic to get in. Monday was taken up with handwriting experts, all of whom claimed to be able to identify Agnes's handwriting as the handwriting on the notes written to Jane Holt and Mr. and Mrs. Holt. The visitors to the courtroom had by now made themselves so much at home that many of them no longer brought anything to drink, but made free use of the court's pitcher and glass.

On Tuesday, the defense began to call witnesses, all of whom testified to Agnes's "queernesses." Her friend, Florence, took the stand and said that Agnes was very forgetful in her manner, often sewed things inside out, and stated frequently that she wished she were dead. A young man testified to the fact that whenever he met Agnes with Frank, Frank would say hello, but Agnes would not. Mrs. Trowbridge testified that Agnes often shut herself up in her room for days on end and refused to come out and had once gone three days without eating. She was, in her estimation, a very queer, melancholic girl. And thus the parade continued. Agnes rocked mechanically. The witnesses moved mechanically on and off the stage.

LOOKS LIKE A LONG SIEGE

RESPONDENT STILL MAINTAINS HER APPEARANCE OF INDIFFERENCE— NOT SO MANY WOMEN SPECTATORS TO-DAY

WITNESSES DESCRIBE QUEER ACTIONS OF AGNES

VICTIM OF MELANCHOLIA

Sometimes Sociable And Again Shunned Her Friends—Would Stay In Her Room For Days

Everyone was waiting for Frank Holt.

47

On Wednesday, Mr. Kingsley called Frank Holt to the stand, and as if by some instinct which usually lay dormant, men and women began to gather in unprecedented numbers outside the courthouse. Frank Holt was sworn in, but all eyes turned to Agnes. For the first time, she showed real emotion. Her body trembled as she leaned forward and stared at Frank as if she hoped, somehow, to speak to him through the vast distances which now separated them. Then, as if in an attempt to see him better, she raised both hands to her head and slowly lifted the veil from her face. The audience sitting on her right side gasped; they had not known she was so beautiful. The men and women sitting on her left bent toward her, horrified. They saw the downward pull of her mouth, the stiffness of the face so that, to them, she appeared to be a caricature of a person. Then, as if disappointed in what she saw, she sank back in her chair, falling back against it so that it rocked violently, sobbing so convulsively that her shoulders shook. Her face sank on her breast and she raised her hands to cover her face, but she did not replace the veil.

Frank sat stiffly in the witness box, his cheeks sucked in, his eyebrows slightly raised. He seemed as indifferent to the audience as Agnes was, and contemptuous as well. Mr. Kingsley began his examination. Although his questions were for Frank, he stood facing Agnes, who sat in her chair sobbing, her hands over her eyes. "How long have you lived in Montpelier?" he asked Frank. "Over two years," he said. "You know we can verify that, don't you?" he asked. "Yes, sir," said Frank. "And how long have you known Agnes Dempster?" "A year and a half or thereabouts," said Frank; "I met her at the rooming house where we lived." "And were you intimate with her?" Mr. Kingsley asked. "I was never intimate with her," Frank answered.

"Did Agnes Dempster know of your relationship with Jane Holt?" Mr. Kingsley asked. "Yes, she did," said Frank; "she told me the girls at work had told her of it." "And when did you meet Jane Holt?" asked Mr. Kingsley. "Six months before I met Agnes," said Frank. "And did you ask Jane Holt to marry you?" asked Mr. Kingsley. "I did," said Frank Holt. "And why didn't you marry her during those two years?" "I wanted to save enough money to support us," he said.

"Did you ever tell a gentleman named Tom Greene that you had promised Miss Dempster something you wished you hadn't?" asked Mr. Kingsley. "No, sir," said Frank. "You never loved Agnes, did you?" asked Mr. Kingsley. "I don't know as I did," he said. "Did you ever promise to marry Agnes?" he asked. "No, sir," said Frank. "You knew that she loved you, didn't you?" Mr. Kingsley asked. "I believed what she told me," said Frank. "Weren't you surprised by her declaration of love?" asked Mr. Kingsley. "No," said Frank; "she was young and her head was turned." "Did you tell a Tom Greene that you thought Agnes was in trouble and that you had to find a way out of it?" "No," said Frank. "Did you ask Tom Greene for the name of a doctor to get you out of your trouble?" "No, sir," said Frank. "You knew nothing about Agnes's saying she thought she was in trouble?" "No, sir," said Frank. "In other words," said Mr. Kingsley, "Miss Dempster imagined the existence of a love affair between the two of you?" "Yes, sir," said Frank. Mr. Kingsley excused Frank Holt and reserved the right to recall him to the stand. The prosecution, said Mr. Parsons, did not wish to cross-examine at this time.

The jury's puzzlement was palpable; they had all heard rumors of the affair between Agnes and Frank. Many of them had seen the two of them together before the trial. They had seen them, noted their presence, and forgotten about them until the trial directed their attention back to them once more. Their eyes followed Frank back to his seat, and then everyone turned to Agnes. She was still crying, her hands covering her face. An angry murmuring ran through the court like a hot wind and then died down. People were straining in their seats, trying to catch a glimpse of Frank Holt. Then the defense called Polly Jenness, formerly Polly Southcote.

Polly was wearing her best dark blue dress and in its breast pocket, she had neatly folded one of the handkerchiefs Agnes had embroidered for her. She sat nervously in her chair, smoothing the folds of her skirt over and over, afraid to look up at her friend. "Tell us how you knew Agnes," asked Mr. Kingsley. "We roomed in the same house," said Polly; "we were very good friends, right from the beginning." "Did you ever hear of Agnes being in trouble?" asked Mr. Kingsley. "Oh, I did more than hear about it," she said. "You may go on and tell," said Mr. Kingsley. "Well," said Polly, "I knew that Agnes intended to marry Frank. He told me himself he had asked her. He told me two years ago. They were going to go to New York. In the beginning, they used to walk out together, but later, they slept in his room." "In the same bed?" asked Mr. Kingsley. "Well," said Polly, "it was only a single bed, but they slept in it together. On very cold nights, they slept in her room because she had a stove in her room. I came in once early and they were still in bed. Then Agnes found out she was in trouble and she didn't know what to do. She wanted me to find her a doctor, but I didn't know one, and she said she would ask Frank."

"Why didn't she want the baby?" asked Mr. Kingsley. "Because of Frank," said Polly; "she kept saying that he didn't want children and if she had the baby he wouldn't love her anymore." "If Frank had wanted the baby, would she have had it?" asked Mr. Kingsley. "She always said she would do whatever Frank wanted," said Polly, "and she meant it. She would have had it." "Did Frank find her a doctor?" asked Mr. Kingsley. "He found a beast!" Polly exclaimed, beginning to pick at the folds of her skirt; "I was there. The man promised to come and use the knife on Agnes himself, but then he got there and said she would have to use it because he was afraid of the police and wouldn't do anything. It was horrible. She almost bled to death. Then she nearly died of a fever. She was sick for weeks afterward. We had to burn her mattress, it was so bloody." "You did that yourself, did you?" Mr. Kingsley asked; "burned the mattress?" "Oh, no," said Polly; "it was too heavy for me. Frank helped me with it."

"Who paid the doctor?" asked Mr. Kingsley. "Frank gave me ten dollars to give the man," Polly said; "I didn't want to give it to him because he was supposed to use the knife, but Agnes said she would go through worse than that for Frank, and I guess she has." "So Mr. Holt paid for the abortion?" asked Mr. Kingsley. "Yes, sir," said Polly. "You knew it was wrong, did you not?" asked Mr. Kingsley; "you knew having an abortion was against the law?" "Yes, sir, I did," said Polly. "Then why did you help her?" "Someone had to help her," she said; "besides, I didn't do anything. I just stayed with her. She needed someone to help her. If it had been me, I would have wanted someone to help me." "And where was Frank Holt while all this was going on?" Mr. Kingsley asked. "Agnes asked him to stay with his friend, Charlie," Polly said; "she didn't want to upset him."

"Did Agnes ever regret the decision to have the abortion?" asked Mr. Kingsley. "Yes, she did," said Polly; "she said Frank didn't want children and he would leave her if she had one. But when she came back from North Chittendon—she went home until her strength came back—she told Frank she'd changed her mind and wanted to have his baby after all, but then he told her he was through with her. He had some important commissions and had no time for her. They argued about the terms of the commissions and he used the argument as an excuse to break it off."

"If I read you a passage from a letter written by Miss Dempster, can you tell me what she intended by it?" "I don't know, sir," said Polly. "This passage is from the well-publicized note which begins, 'Don't blame lovesick girls,'" he said; "now, Mrs. Jenness, what could this mean? 'If you listen for it, you will hear the voice of the little soul who went before us calling to us, asking us to come toward him together.' Can you throw any light upon that?" "Oh, yes," said Polly; "she talked that way to me all the time. She's talking about the baby that she lost; that's what she means in the letter. Before the abortion, she kept saying that she had to give the child back." "Give it back?" asked Mr. Kingsley. "I think *she* thought the baby was going back to wherever it came from and she wasn't really killing it," Polly said; "she thought if she got pregnant again, she'd get the same baby back. That's what she used to tell me. That's what she means in the letter." "Did Mr. Holt know that she wanted to get the baby back?" asked Mr. Kingsley. "Oh, I think so," said Polly; "she talked about it all the time. She couldn't get her mind off it."

"Mrs. Jenness," asked Mr. Kingsley, "how often would you say Frank Holt spent the night with Miss Dempster?" "Once they began, every night," she said; "they spent days together as well. She went with him to the quarries. That was why she was fired at Mrs. James's." "To your knowledge, did Miss Dempster ever keep company with any other young man?" "Oh, no," said Polly; "once she met Frank, she had no use for anyone else, not even me. She used to say that the whole world could explode and she wouldn't care as long as she and Frank were left together. She used to say that she wished the whole world *would* explode and leave them alone together.''

"Mrs. Jenness," said Mr. Kingsley, "how would you describe the love Agnes Dempster had for Frank Holt? Was it, would you say, ordinary?" "Oh, no, it wasn't ordinary," said Polly; "she was very proud of how unusual her love for him was. She used to say that she loved a perfect being. She said he was too good for this world. She said there were ideal forms and creatures and sometimes one of them shone forth into this world, and he was one of them." "And did she consider herself perfect as well?" asked Mr. Kingsley. "No," said Polly; "she thought she didn't deserve him. She couldn't see that he had flaws. She said again and again how lucky she was that he loved her at all, that she wasn't good enough for him. She was afraid that one day he'd wake up and realize how useless she was and he'd throw her over because she didn't deserve him." "And did you agree with her?" asked Mr. Kingsley. "No one agreed with her," Polly said; "everyone told her she was too good for him, but she didn't like that. She'd stop speaking to anyone who spoke against Frank." "Do you think Mr. Holt ever loved Agnes?" asked Mr. Kingsley. "Yes, for a while," said Polly; "I never thought he could love anyone much for very long, and he couldn't." Mr. Kingsley thanked her and told her she was excused. Polly got up, paused in front of Agnes, took out her handkerchief and wiped a tear from Agnes's left cheek. Agnes didn't look at her. Polly touched Agnes's head and went back to her seat. She sat quietly, her shoulders shaking. The silence in the court was expectant, and something mournful, like a premonition of wet weather, stirred through the room.

Mr. Kingsley recalled Frank Holt. "Did you hear the testimony of the previous witness?" he asked him. Frank said he did. "Would you say she was lying?" asked Mr. Kingsley. "She told the truth as far as she understood it," Frank said, his face sullen. "But you know it better, don't you?" asked Mr. Kingsley. "Yes, sir," said Frank. "And are you now prepared to tell us the truth?" asked Mr. Kingsley; "you *are* testifying under oath. Miss Dempster did not die and she is here to tell us the truth and we can ask others if what she tells us is true. Mrs. Jenness has already told us a great deal. Are you prepared to answer honestly?" "Yes, sir," said Frank; "I don't have any choice." "No," said Mr. Kingsley, "you don't." Frank sat back in his chair and folded his arms across his chest. "I ask you again," said Mr. Kingsley; "did you know that Agnes Dempster loved you?" "Yes, I did," said Frank. "And did you love her?" he asked. "For a while," said Frank. "Can you tell us what made you stop?" asked Mr. Kingsley. "I never said I stopped," said Frank. "Do you mean to tell us that you still love her?" asked Mr. Kingsley. "I still love her," said Frank; "I told her I still loved her. I told her I couldn't live with her and I didn't want to. She wanted too much from me."

"But you told her you still loved her?" Mr. Kingsley asked. He sounded incredulous. The courtroom behind him was buzzing. "Why did you do that?" he asked; "if you were trying to break things off with her, why did you tell her you still loved her?" "Because it was true," said Frank; "there are lots of people you love. You don't marry them all. You can love a dog and you don't marry it." "A dog," said Mr. Kingsley; "was Miss Dempster like a dog?" "Sometimes she was," said Frank; "the way she followed me around." "You say she followed you around like a dog?" asked Mr. Kingsley. "Well, she wanted to be with me all the time," said Frank. "And you didn't like that," said Mr. Kingsley. "No," said Frank; "I've always been off by myself." "So Miss Dempster loved you too much, is that it?" "Yes," said Frank; "I told her that. I said I could never love her as much as she loved me, but she said I'd learn to love her." "And did you love her?" "For a while," said Frank; "then it got too hard."

"Why did it get too hard?" asked Mr. Kingsley. "She wanted too much!" Frank said; "she said I was perfect and she wanted me to be perfect. She wanted me to go to New York and become a famous sculptor. I didn't care about any of that. She wouldn't leave me in peace. She kept insisting I wasn't ordinary and had to do extraordinary things. I didn't want any part of all that." "But you carved a statue of Miss Dempster, did you not?" asked Mr. Kingsley. "Yes, sir, I did. Agnes was very beautiful. She wanted to pose for me." "And you wanted to carve her, didn't you?" asked Mr. Kingsley; "after you visited her home in North Chittendon, you knew famous sculptors had carved women of her family before?" "Yes, sir, I knew all that," said Frank, "but I wanted to carve her." "And it was your carving of her that attracted the attention of the New York buyers who commissioned the statues you are now working on, was it not?" "Yes, sir, it was," said Frank. "So would it be fair to say that at least part of your interest in Miss Dempster had to do with her value to your career?" "No!" said Frank, flushing; "she was insatiable! She

508

wanted more than I had to give." "And wasn't Jane Holt insatiable?" "No, sir, she wasn't. She didn't want much. I could give her what she wanted." "Especially after Agnes was finished posing for you," said Mr. Kingsley. "Agnes had nothing to do with it, not her posing," said Frank, clutching the arms of his chair. "She wanted children when I didn't. She wanted to have children if I did, and I didn't know what I wanted. I couldn't win no matter what I did. Whatever I did was never enough. I didn't have any trouble with Jane."

"So when you say Jane wasn't insatiable, do you mean that Jane would let you do whatever you wanted?" asked Mr. Kingsley. "You could put it that way," said Frank. "And would it be true?" Mr. Kingsley asked. "Yes," said Frank. "And when did Agnes stop letting you do whatever you wanted? Wasn't it after you received the commissions from the New York buyers? Wasn't it right after that when you discovered it—that she was insatiable?" "Yes," said Frank; "have your own way." "Mr. Holt," said Judge Richter, "this is a court of law." "I'm sorry," said Frank, glaring at Mr. Kingsley. "In other words, Miss Dempster was of great help to your career, was she not?" "Yes," said Frank. He looked down at the floor. "And you found her demands intolerably burdensome after you needed no more help, did you not?" asked Mr. Kingsley. "Yes," said Frank. For the first time, he looked at Agnes. There was reproach in his face, and hatred. "And did she not offer to pay for any expenses you incurred while you studied sculpting in New York?" Mr. Kingsley asked. "I refused to take any of her money," Frank said. "That was very scrupulous of you," Mr. Kingsley said; "I suppose you know she could not use her money until she was twenty-one." Mr. Parsons objected and the judge sustained the objection.

"How often did you draw Miss Dempster?" "Very often," said Frank. "Would it be fair to say she was your favorite subject?" "For a while," said Frank; "she was." "And why did the vogue she enjoyed with you come to an end?" asked Mr. Kingsley. "Look," Frank said, "I see what you're driving at. You want everyone to think I took advantage of her. You want to think I led her on. It wasn't that way. She was after me. She didn't love me. I was the one who was used." Frank said something else, but the noise in the courtroom drowned him out. Judge Richter was wielding his gavel. "I warned you," he said, addressing the court; "another sound and I empty this courtroom." He nodded to Mr. Kingsley, who once again turned to Frank.

"Do you mean to tell this court that Agnes Dempster seduced you?" Mr. Kingsley asked. "Not exactly," Frank said. "Then she misled you in some way?" Mr. Kingsley asked. "She did!" said Frank; "she swore she loved me. She said she loved me before she even knew who I was. She saw me when she was sitting in a sleigh and fell in love with me. Even I know that's not possible. She used to say I was the other half of her soul and she'd been born for me. She would go on and on about how I was her future and her past and how she'd rather be dead than live without me and then she'd turn around and tell me I only loved dead women and that's why I liked statuary. She didn't love me. She only thought she loved me." "But you thought she loved you enough to ask her to marry you?" asked Mr. Kingsley. "Yes," said Frank. "Is it true that while you were engaged to Jane Holt you became engaged to Agnes Dempster?" "Yes, it is," said Frank; "well, not exactly. I broke it off with Jane when I met Agnes. But when Agnes went to North Chittendon, I knew I couldn't go on with her. That's when I went to see Jane and we became engaged again." "But you were still engaged to Miss Dempster?" "I was," said Frank, "but I kept trying to break it off." "But the girl wouldn't let you?" said Mr. Kingsley. "That's right," said Frank bitterly. "You didn't have the strength to say no to her, is that it?" Mr. Kingsley asked. "Something like that," said Frank.

"Did you love Jane Holt?" asked Mr. Kingsley. "I loved her enough," said Frank; "I saw she wouldn't want too much of me. I saw I could marry her and make it all right. I wasn't madly in love with her. I've never been madly in love with anyone." "But girls are always madly in love with you?" asked Mr. Kingsley. "Is that my fault?" asked Frank; "I didn't *ask* Agnes to fall in love with me. One night, she just showed up in my bed." The courtroom began murmuring again; they didn't like the way he was talking about the two girls. Men ought to keep quiet about what went on behind closed doors. "So she seduced you," said Mr. Kingsley. "More or less," said Frank. "More or less," Mr. Kingsley repeated, his back to Frank, facing the jury, his eyebrows raised. "Miss Dempster seduced Mr. Holt here," he said.

"Did you have no regard for the girl's future?" he asked, turning back to Frank. "Agnes was willing and so was I," said Frank. "Yet you told Mr. Wood of *The Spectator* that you had never kept company with Agnes and that you never fancied her, didn't you?" asked Mr. Kingsley. "Yes, I did," said Frank. "At that time you thought Agnes was going to die, didn't you?" he asked. "I guess I did," said Frank; "I guess I thought I should save what I could." "And you thought you could save yourself?" asked Mr. Kingsley. Frank did not answer.

"Did you become aware at any time that Agnes Dempster was in a delicate condition?" he asked. "Yes, sir, she told me," he said. "Did you advise her what action to take?" asked Mr. Kingsley. "I asked her what she was going to do," said Frank. "Did you talk to her about getting rid of it?" asked Mr. Kingsley. "I told her she could keep it or not, as she pleased," said Frank. "You seem to have had little say in any of this," said Mr. Kingsley. "I told her whatever she wanted was fine," Frank said stubbornly. "You knew that you had got her into trouble, did you not?" "I did," said Frank. "Did you ever tell her that if she would yield to your desires that you would not go back on her?" "I don't remember as I did," said Frank.

"Did you promise to marry her?" asked Mr. Kingsley. "I guess I did," said Frank. "Did you not tell Tom Greene that you would just as soon marry Agnes Dempster as Jane Holt if only Agnes was a little easier to live with?" "I don't remember," said Frank. "Did you not promise to marry Agnes Dempster whether or not she had the abortion?" "Yes," said Frank, "I did." "Do you remember Agnes Dempster telling you that she would end her own life if you went back on your promise to marry her?" "Yes sir, I do," said Frank. "Did she ever threaten Jane Holt?" "No, sir." "Is it true you ignored her threats to take her own life?" "Yes, sir," said Frank; "I never believed she would do it." "Isn't it true you knew that she was an excellent shot and that she had bought a gun and was practicing with it?" "Yes, I did," said Frank. "And didn't you think that she might use the gun on herself?" "It never occurred to me," said Frank. "Because you didn't believe she would take her own life?" asked Mr. Kingsley. "Yes," said Frank. "Wouldn't you say that she always believed you?" asked Mr. Kingsley, turning from him to the court. "Witness excused," he said.

In her chair, Agnes was still crying quietly. As Frank walked toward the door of the courtroom, the angry murmuring swelled into a loud roar, and as he approached the door, Frank began walking faster and faster, the noise rolling behind him. The gavel came down and soon the only sound in the court was Agnes, crying steadily, taking deep breaths, and releasing them in long, slow sobs.

And the day was not yet over. Amon Dempster testified concerning his daughter's visit to his home with her fiancé, Frank Holt, and the steady march of witnesses, all testifying to insane behavior in Agnes's ancestors, began.

48

TESTIMONY OF HER LOVE, FRANK HOLT, BRINGS TEARS

SPECTATORS AFFECTED

Holt Admits His Intimacy With The Slayer Of His Alleged Betrothed—Made Love To Her And Promised Marriage

"I think you *are* getting somewhere," said his wife at breakfast the next morning. "We could still be wrecked by the expert witnesses," said her husband. "I don't think so," said his wife; "no, I don't." "It will all depend on Doctor Train and what he's made of," said Mr. Kingsley; "did it ever occur to you that her life is passed from one man's hands to another? First the doctors who operated on her, then me, then the sheriff, then the expert witnesses, then the jury?" "You forgot Frank Holt," said his wife; "no one else will. Not after yesterday." "Women have nothing to do with it," Mr. Kingsley said wonderingly. "I think the men know that," said his wife; "I think it makes their responsibility weigh even more heavily on them." "Ah, Martha," he said. She still surprised him.

The day had opened gray and rainy. Everyone knew the sun was up only because it was not dark. The trees, behind the mist and rain, were a grayish blue, barely visible. As the morning progressed, the skies darkened and promised violence. Mr.

513

Kingsley came into the courtroom early and found Mr. Parsons staring down at the street from the side window. "Look at that," Parsons said. Beneath them was a sea of undulating gray and black umbrellas moving this way and that like enormous, stiff blossoms. "I thought they'd clear off after Holt came into court," Mr. Kingsley said. "They're not going to clear off now," said Parsons; "now they're sorry for her. They're not going to leave her alone now." "You think they've turned against you, do you?" asked Kingsley. "They've turned against him," said Parsons, "and they're going to feel sorry for his victim. There's nothing I can do about it." He looked down at the sea of umbrellas.

"You knew all along, didn't you?" Parsons said; "about this Holt fellow?" Mr. Kingsley motioned vaguely with his hand. "I suppose I did," he said. "How?" asked Parsons. "I knew after meeting the girl," he said; "I knew she hadn't dreamed up a grand passion. She's not given to dreaming up love affairs. I didn't think she could love a great many people at all. She didn't seem susceptible." "So you thought whatever it was had to be real?" asked Parsons. "That's what I thought," said Kingsley. "How does it feel to be right so much of the time?" Parsons asked bitterly. "Cold," said Kingsley; "people don't thank you for being right." "The girl will," said Parsons. "Do you think so?" Kingsley asked, looking at him curiously.

"There's still the expert testimony," Parsons said, as if to himself; "just because they feel sorry for her doesn't mean they'll decide to acquit her." "Of course not," said Kingsley; "anyway, the rest of the trial will be pretty dull from here on in. They'll get tired of sitting in here, tired of being locked up, and they'll blame her. They'll be pretty sympathetic to your arguments." "You're trying to cheer me up, aren't you?" asked Parsons, astonished. "Well, you're a lot more energetic when you're cheered up," said Kingsley.

They heard the door to the judge's room open and Judge Richter took his place on the bench. "To arms, officers of the court," said the judge, his expression grim. The doors to the court swung open, the court officers jumped back, and the crowd flooded in. Within moments, all the seats in the room were filled. Judge Richter surveyed his courtroom and shook his head. It was taking longer for the audience to get settled; they were closing their umbrellas and trying to find places for them, and a hundred small altercations were starting up and dying down all over the court. Suddenly, a woman in the second row got up. She was dressed in black and carried something in her hand. She approached Agnes's chair with determination. The officers of the court intercepted the young woman and two of the men took hold of her arms. All eyes in the courtroom were on her. She said something to two of the men; they looked down at her hands, and one of them went up to Judge Richter. He nodded and the court officer released her.

The young woman flushed deep red, stared straight ahead, and marched up to Agnes, who was, as usual, rocking in her chair. "Miss Dempster?" she asked, her voice trembling. Agnes jumped in her seat. The rocker stopped. She stared up at the young woman. "I brought you something," the young woman said; "they said it was all right." Agnes stared at her, terrified. "Don't be afraid," the young woman said; "it's only a rose. I brought it from my garden." She held out her hand and offered Agnes the rose. Agnes looked from the rose to the woman's face. "It's for you," the young woman said. "For me," said Agnes. The young woman nodded. "Take it," she said. Agnes reached up for it, took it, and raised it slowly to her face. Then she lowered her head as if she wanted to escape into the flower. The young woman who had given her the rose raised her hand to her own face and wiped her eyes and went back to her seat. Everyone bent forward to look at Agnes. She had stopped rocking and she was holding the flower to the left side of her face and staring into the far distance. Mr. Kingsley looked over at Mr. Parsons. The state's attorney looked ready to throw himself out of the courtroom window.

The day began with witnesses from Clayboro, all of whom testified to the aberrant behavior of Eurydice Saltonstall, Agnes's grandmother, how she had become unbalanced when her husband became ill, how, finally taking leave of her senses altogether, she took up residence in a pigsty, how she set up the brass marital bed in front of the shed, insisting that was where it belonged, and until the day she died, the bed remained in front of the shed, and as far as anyone knew, it was there still. One witness testified that Agnes's great-grandmother was very queer, and that for two years she insisted on washing her dishes in one water and her husband's in another, and that they never used the same towel or chair. She would never touch her bare hands to her husband's chair. Another witness testified that Eurydice Saltonstall often deliberately obstructed the path of men who were doing their winter lumbering with bushes and rails. Another witness testified that she heard Eurydice Saltonstall talking to her husband after he had been dead for thirteen years. Meanwhile, the storm which had been threatening since early morning broke over the courthouse. Thunder rocked the building and rain streamed down the windows in unbroken sheets. Every so often, a lightning flash split the sky jaggedly and flickered in the room.

After luncheon recess, Mrs. Parmeter Blanchard of North Chittendon testified that Agnes had worked at the town school for one term, and when she was finished, Agnes spent all of her money on Rose Petal Face Cream and went through the town trying to sell it, but as far as she knew, she didn't sell any. She thought the girl never had any sense and was given to sudden enthusiasms which carried her away. A girl who had worked for the Dempster family testified that Agnes was subject to sudden and drastic changes of mood. She would come into the house in the morning and dance and sing, and in the afternoon she would be despondent. The witness said she had never measured how high Agnes could kick, but she thought she could kick about four feet in the air. She didn't think there was anything immodest in her kicking, but some days, when you asked her to kick, she would say, "I am not a high kicker and never will be," and would start to cry. A Montpelier photographer testified to having taken four pictures of Agnes and said that she was extremely nervous while she was there and seemed depressed. At the time, he said, he thought she was not right. Throughout this testimony, Agnes rocked on, apparently oblivious to what was said, certainly indifferent.

Standing in front of the courtroom, questioning his witnesses, Mr. Kingsley sensed an electricity in the air, as if something of the storm had taken possession of the people within. It was as if something were gathering inside them, and as he talked and the witnesses talked, he felt it building and building. He did not know what it was, but it was something powerful. He looked at the window and saw the lightning fill it. Whatever it was, he wished it would break. The court clerk came in, motioned to Judge Richter, and the questioning stopped. The judge declared a short recess and left the courtroom with the official. Mr. Kingsley sat down next to his client. Within seconds, everyone was whispering, stirring in their seats, stretching, smiling at each other wearily, then beginning to talk. "It must be horrible to have to sit here and let everyone talk about you," he heard one of the women behind him say. Mr. Kingsley looked at Agnes. She seemed not to hear anyone. Her left eye teared continuously but otherwise she was, as she had been every day but yesterday, dry-eyed and indifferent. He sighed and got up and went over to the window. The rain was pouring as heavily as ever; he saw it pouring from the gutters on neighboring buildings, running from the sharp edges of roofs in small waterfalls. Hardly anyone was on the street. In the great elm across the street, a crow was pressed against its trunk, rustling its feathers. "Sometimes it rains on the just," he said, his back to the courtroom. "And sometimes," he said after a long pause, "it rains on the unjust." He kept staring out the window into the street and so he could not see Mr. Parsons, who was glowering at him. "And sometimes," he said, "it just rains." A tide of soft laughter rippled through the room, and when Mr. Kingsley turned around and went back to his seat, he saw everyone smiling at him.

That does it, thought Mr. Parsons; that does it. He's going to win. Everyone loves him now. He does something like this every time.

So that was what it was, thought Mr. Kingsley, a gathering of affection, for him and for the Dempster girl. It was curious, but he could never tell in advance what emotion was growing behind him, whether it was love or hatred; he only knew it was there, behind him, waiting to spring.

The rest of the week and the beginning of the next was occupied by witnesses testifying either to Agnes's strange behavior or that of members of her family. Mrs. Trowbridge testified that she had come into Agnes's room the night before the tragedy and Agnes had sung, "Put away the little dresses that my darling used to wear." She had never heard Agnes sing that song or any other song before. She said that she found her burning some clothes in her stove three days before the shooting, and when she asked her why she was doing so, Agnes said they were some of her old underclothes. Mrs. Trowbridge advised her to take some of them out so that the stove would not smoke so, but Agnes said she could not take them out since they were not fit to be seen. Mrs. Trowbridge thought that they were some of the bloody rags that had not been burned since her sickness; at least, she thought so because of their odor as they burned. She tried to engage Agnes in conversation, and Agnes asked her if she had been happy when she was married, and then said she wished she were married and keeping house. Mrs. Trowbridge said she told Agnes she thought she was too young to marry, but Agnes said that no one was too young to marry if she got the man she wanted. She said she would only marry a stonecutter; no other profession had any attraction for her. She also told Mrs. Trowbridge that one day a fortune-teller had told her that trouble was in store for her and she told the woman she need not have told her that because she had always been in trouble and always expected to be. Mrs. Trowbridge told Agnes that she would feel better if she attended church but since she had come to Montpelier, Agnes said she believed she was too wicked to go there. Mrs. Trowbridge was quite convinced that the girl had not been right from the minute she met Frank Holt. When Mr. Kingsley asked her if she believed that Frank had driven Agnes crazy, she said she supposed she did.

The boredom Mr. Kingsley had predicted did not set in. Instead, the people were again waiting, this time for Doctor Train, who was expected to testify the next day. People in Montpelier knew and liked the doctor, and rumor had it that the girl had trusted him and had spoken to him freely after the shooting. Meanwhile, thought Mr. Kingsley, the signs were good. His wife told him that when Agnes left the courtroom, she was holding the rose the young lady had given her in her hand and by that time, the edges of its petals were all black and drooping. "Really?" said Mr. Kingsley; "I didn't notice." "Well, we were watching," said his wife. "We?" asked Mr. Kingsley; had she taken to using the editorial *we*? The royal *we*? "The other women and I," said Mrs. Kingsley. So they had swarmed together. If only the prosecution didn't have to present its evidence, he would stop the trial now. The jurors would all march obediently into his hive. "I wonder if this rain is going to go on forever," he said. "No," said Martha; "when I get up, only my hip hurts." On such certainties, he thought, did people base their lives.

49

On Thursday of the second week, Doctor Train took the stand. In the street outside, a fine drizzle filtered down, touching the skin like cool powder, and the skies remained gray, but silvery. They had thinned over the sun, which threatened to burst through its filmy gray wrappings. Mr. Kingsley, who had his doubts about the wisdom of his choice of an expert witness—he had chosen a man whose only reputation was for his clinical successes, and that reputation was confined to the east coast—saw the immediate effect of the man on the court, and with his back to the audience, he smiled broadly at him. He had known the man would instantly impress everyone in the courtroom, and he did.

Doctor Train was nervous, but from the moment the court clerk had sworn him in, it was as if another light had gone on in the room. Doctor Train inspired confidence. His dark brown eyes were so dark they seemed black, and the high flush on his cheeks gave him an innocent, vulnerable look. In the end, it was his eyes, seeming to burn like charcoal, which drew everyone's attention. There was something hypnotic about him. Kingsley could sense Parsons behind him, alert now, confident, sure he could take this man apart during cross-examination. And Kingsley felt the old thrill: this was the unexpected land, the unpredictable. So far everything had gone right. He sensed it in the court's attitude toward this man. Yet there might be something in him that he was not aware of, that the man himself was not aware of, and if Parsons set it off, all bets would be off. This man could undo it all.

The doctor testified that he was forty-five years old and had begun practicing medicine in June, 1877 in St. Peter, Minnesota. He had graduated from the University of Vermont and had then returned to Lester, Vermont where he had been in practice for eleven years. And after that he went to the Macdonald Asylum for the Insane, in Springfield, Massachusetts. He was first assistant physician there. While there, he became supervisor of the Institution and remained at Macdonald for a year and a half. He testified that, while there, he observed and determined the treatment of about one hundred twenty insane patients a year.

"Now I understand you to say that some of these people were admitted to the asylum for nervous disorders, but were not insane?" asked Mr. Kingsley. "No, sir," said Doctor Train; "if the patients were not insane, they were referred to other institutions." "So you were in the habit of deciding between insane disorders and nervous disorders?" Mr. Kingsley asked. Doctor Train said he was. "And are you now a specialist?" asked Mr. Kingsley. "I am considered so," said Doctor Train; "a specialist in nervous and mental diseases—troubles." He went on to testify that, as the superintendent at Highbury, about five hundred patients were under his care. On any given day, he was responsible for them all. "Have you been called upon in the course of your professional life to testify in court as an expert in insanity?" asked Mr. Kingsley. "I have," said Doctor Train. "How many times, would you say?" asked Mr. Kingsley. "I don't remember," said the doctor. "More than five times?" asked Mr. Kingsley. "Oh, definitely," said the doctor; "sometimes in Boston and sometimes in the courts outside."

"At some time, Doctor, was your attention directed to the tragedy of December twenty-fourth last, and were you asked to do anything with reference to Agnes Dempster?" "I was called by you to visit her," said the doctor; "it was my intention to determine what her mental condition was, and I went at my earliest opportunity, which was January eleventh." Doctor Train testified that he had taken notes throughout the interview with Agnes Dempster, had asked her what her occupation was, and that she had told him she was very nervous at that time and always had been nervous; she said she could not work because of headaches and did not earn enough money to support herself and she did not know what she did when her head hurt her. She called those times "spells."

The doctor said that he asked her if those spells ever occurred on the occasion of her menstrual period and she said they did not. He then examined her about her menstrual period, which she said began at the age of twelve, and she said she had never suffered any pain and never had occasion to go to bed in consequence of it. "I asked her about her memory on the day of the tragedy," said the doctor, "and she said that she had no recollection of the events at all. She seemed unhappy at discussing the subject, so I asked her whether she was having any attention from any young man, and she said she was, and his name was Frank Holt, and she had become engaged to him. She said that under promise of marriage, she had been seduced by him and that she had become pregnant about six months before the tragedy, but that Frank Holt had been instrumental in finding her a doctor who helped her to get rid of it. She stated that the engagement continued and that she never knew it was broken off, or that Frank Holt was thinking of breaking it off, until after her friend's wedding, and even then she was not sure he meant it. I again asked her about the day of the shooting, and she again said she had no recollection of it.'' Doctor Train stopped and took a black notebook from his vest pocket. "If I could read from my notes," he said, "I would be more accurate and exhaustive in my description of the day's events," he said. Parsons requested that the judge take the notebooks as evidence and allow the prosecution to inspect them after testimony was completed; everyone agreed and Doctor Train began to read from his notes.

"I asked her if she knew that the other girl was shot, and she said she didn't. She said she had been told the other girl was shot, but she said she had no reason to shoot her. I asked her if she was jealous and she said, 'I don't know if I was jealous of her. I was jealous of anything that took Frank away from me. I was jealous of his work. When he went to his room, I was jealous of the furniture in his room because it was with him and I was not, and when he went to work, I was jealous of the other men, the stones, even the ground he was standing on. I presume I was a little jealous of the girl, but I had no reason to kill her any more than I had a reason to kill Frank's friends or the chair he sat on. I didn't have any ill feeling toward her. I only intended to kill myself.'

"I asked her if she thought her jealousy was normal jealousy, and she said she thought it was, that if you truly loved a person, the whole world was your rival; even the sun was, because it took your beloved's attention away from you, and the greater your love, the greater your jealousy of the rest of the world. I asked her if she thought all people who loved were jealous, even of the sun and the moon, and she said she thought they probably were, although they wouldn't want to admit it, and she was such a solitary girl, she had not had an opportunity to talk to many others. I told her that I considered such jealousy excessive, and she smiled at me and said that she felt sorry for me because I had not truly loved anyone yet, but she hoped someday I would."

"And what did you say, Doctor?" asked Mr. Kingsley. "I said I hoped I would never have to pay for love with hatred of the whole world, and she said that she had not hated the whole world."

"Then what did you say, Doctor?" asked Mr. Kingsley. The silence at his back was frightening. He knew he was asking these questions to satisfy his own curiosity, and in so doing, was breaking one of his oldest and most valuable rules: Never ask a question because *you* want to know the answer.

"I said that there was a fine line between jealousy and hatred, and if jealousy continued long enough, it changed either into love or hatred." "What did she say?" asked Mr. Kingsley. "She answered that it was true. She was beginning to hate the world and everything in it, but that she did not hate Jane Holt more than anything else. I then asked her if she did not think that eventually she would hate the world and hate the man who caused her to hate it, and her eyes filled with tears and she said she hoped not, as that would be worse than death. He was the only thing in the world she cared for." "Then what did you ask her?" Mr. Kingsley said. "Then I asked her nothing. She burst out at me and said I did not understand what it was like to give someone else one's soul and trust him to keep it for you and to find that he had not regarded it as worth anything at all, and that when she wanted her soul back, she could no longer take it back from him. And even if she could, she said, even if she could take it back, she could not have it back, because Frank had destroyed it. He had turned her into an empty shell, a body without a soul." "Can you explain what she meant by that, Doctor?" asked Mr. Kingsley. "I think I understood what she meant," said Doctor Train, "but I would be hard put to explain it to the court. Apparently, she felt she had handed herself—not her body, but her soul, her essence—over to Frank Holt. As she talked, I could not help but think of how saints describe how they consecrated their lives to God. The girl seemed to think of Frank Holt in religious terms. He was, as far as I could tell, her savior and he would redeem her and save her from whatever she feared; he would remove all imperfections from her. When he told her he no longer wanted her, she felt as if he were destroying her soul. I asked her if, when she thought of shooting herself, she realized she would be ending her own life, and she said no, she hadn't thought so. Her life had ended when Frank Holt told her he was through with her. He had killed her soul. After that, she said, she was not really alive."

"Did she believe that Frank Holt's soul had been entrusted to her?" asked Mr. Kingsley. "Oh, yes," said the doctor; "she said that without her, he would be lost. He would never carve the statues he was meant to carve. He would die like a mayfly that falls to the sill in the spring. She became quite worked up about how dreadful his fate would be without her to guide him. She said that although they had not been married, theirs was a marriage of souls. When I asked her why such a marriage had come undone, she said she did not know and began to cry inconsolably. Finally, she said she must have done something wrong, but if she only had another chance, she might make matters right yet." "And then?" asked Mr. Kingsley.

"And then I could see that she was agitated by the subject of Frank Holt, and I asked her if she knew how long she had been unconscious and she said about ten days, and during that time she had dreamed that she and Jane Holt were sleeping together in a bed. She said she presumed she had that dream because she was jealous of the other girl and had often thought that she and Jane Holt shared Frank's bed.

"I then took particular notice of her face and found it to be paralyzed on the left side, the mouth drawn down, the tongue protruding a little to the left, and the left eye, in winking, rolled upward. Her pulse was weak and rapid and she said she did not sleep at all. She said her dreams were troubled and they were often of killing somebody, but sometimes it was one person and sometimes another and that she was exceedingly wearied afterward. I asked her what her general thoughts were as she sat there in the chair, and she said she was thinking of ending her life and would accomplish it someday. She said she was watched too closely now and wouldn't use a revolver next time, but something more sure. She was manifesting considerable fatigue, so I brought the examination to a close after about an hour. When I next examined her, some weeks later, I again asked her, as I had asked her before, if she thought her life had been ruined and she said she didn't know. I asked her if she thought life was worth living, and she said no, it wasn't worth living and that she spent all her time thinking of ways to end her life. She did not want to answer questions. This time, interviewing her was like extracting teeth. I asked her if she was of a restless disposition, and she said she thought she was, and that she was a restless sort of girl and had always been dissatisfied and now she always would be. I had to ask many questions twice before she appeared to hear me. She seemed in a state of considerable depression.

"She seemed impatient with me and asked me to get on with my physical examination of her, saying that if it had to be done, she would just as soon have it done then." "And did you do so?" asked Mr. Kingsley. "In the company of Doctor Chase," he answered, "I then made an examination of the uterus. I made a digital examination, and then an examination with the speculum. I found the position of the uterus normal, and by the sense of touch, a slight condition that led me to use the speculum. I found that the opening was elongated and at the right, a slight rent, with some degree of inflammation, but it was not marked. There was also a small amount of whites, or mucus, present." "Now what did all that indicate, Doctor?" asked Mr. Kingsley.

"That she was correct in saying she had been through pregnancy at some time. I also discovered considerable evidence of scarring, no doubt consequent upon an infection following the self-abortion, and Doctor Chase and I concluded later that it would be unlikely that she could ever again bear children, although we did not tell her so at the time." "And do you believe that now?" asked Mr. Kingsley. "I believe she cannot have children," said the doctor; "not with such scarring. But there is no certainty about it." "And why did you not tell Miss Dempster about her condition?" asked Mr. Kingsley; "was it because she had frequently said that she did not want to have children?"

At his back, the courtroom was silent. In her rocker, Agnes ticked slowly, like a clock that could not stop. Mr. Kingsley turned to look at her. She was slowly lowering the veil over her face, but the rhythm of her rocking was unbroken. "Why didn't you tell her?" Mr. Kingsley asked again. "I thought she was quite depressed enough. When she said she did not want children, I did not believe her. She was in a hospital and she was facing either jail or an asylum. It would be too painful to think about having children. Naturally, she would say she wanted no children."

"Then you believe all women want children?" asked Mr. Kingsley. "No sir, I do not," said the doctor; "but I believe this woman wanted them. I asked her if she could do things over again, would she still have the abortion, and she said she would not. She said all she had ever wanted was Frank Holt, and if she couldn't have him, at least she would have had his child. But she believed he would not have thrown her over if she had had the baby. She said he got rid of her because of the abortion and she had been a fool to have it. I reminded her that she had told me that she

524

feared Frank Holt would give her up if she had had the baby, and she said that she still believed that was true. I asked her how both things could be true at once, and she said she didn't know, but she was sure both things were true at once, and that had been the trouble: Whatever she did, she would do something wrong, something to make Frank leave her.

"I asked her if she still loved him and she said yes, she loved him today as ever, although he was unworthy of her love. I then asked her if she truly believed he was unworthy of her and she said no, she did not. She did not think him unworthy at all, but everyone had been saying he was for so long she thought it best to go along with them.

"When I visited her in the jail, she asked me if I had any intelligence of Frank Holt, and I said I did not. I asked her about the handkerchief that was so important to her and she said it was all she had left of Frank." "What handkerchief, Doctor?" asked Mr. Kingsley. "She had persuaded her friend, Polly Jenness, to ask Frank Holt for something she might keep by her, and Polly had secured a handkerchief Agnes had given him a year before the tragedy. She had embroidered his initials on it herself. Mrs. Jenness brought her the handkerchief and I never saw her without it until after the surgery to remove the bullet from her brain."

"And why was she without it then?" asked Mr. Kingsley. "It had been lost," said Doctor Train, "and she was in a most pitiable state. She cried as if she had lost her best friend and nothing would comfort her. She became quite melodramatic and claimed that the last threads of her soul had been woven into that handkerchief, and now she had lost even those. She refused to speak to her attendant, Margaret Eckroyd, or to her father, who stayed with her all day and late into the night. She cried constantly and complained of headaches and the nurses kept the shades drawn. She was angry with everyone and accused her father and Miss Eckroyd of having deliberately taken the handkerchief because they did not want her to have anything she wanted. She said if she could not have Frank, at least she could have this bit of cloth."

"And how was this problem solved?" Mr. Kingsley asked. "Mrs. Jenness procured a second handkerchief," said the doctor. "Was it one of Frank Holt's?" asked Mr. Kingsley. "It was," said the doctor. "And how do you know that?" asked Mr. Kingsley. "It was embroidered exactly as the previous handkerchief had been and Agnes recognized her own handiwork. Also, Mrs. Jenness told us she had gone to Frank and asked him for the handkerchief and he had given it to her and offered her the two remaining ones still in his possession, but she had told him one was enough.''

"And did Agnes's attitude change after she was given the second handkerchief?" asked Mr. Kingsley. "It did," said the doctor; "she began to sit up and once again conversed freely with me. She told me that after the abortion, she used to lie on her floor near the stove, and when I asked her if she did so because she was unwell, she said no, she needed to feel close to something warm and she was afraid the room might tilt and throw her down. I asked her if she meant that she was afraid of becoming dizzy, and she said no, when she put her foot down on the ground, she expected to go right through, as if she were walking on a thin shell, not a floor. I asked her if she had ever suffered from that sensation before, and she said she had, but not since her grandmother died. She said again that she had made a mistake because she hadn't shot high enough when she shot herself and that she should have used chloroform or a rope and she thought she would use a rope next time if she could. I asked her if she thought Frank Holt believed her when she said she was going to shoot herself, and she said she didn't know. She said she told him he would never see her again, but he said he would see her again. She thought he probably did not believe her.''

"Did the operation change her?" he asked. "It did," said the doctor; "she was furious at finding herself alive and said she would never have consented to the operation except that she believed she would die during the surgery." "What did you find during the operation?" asked Mr. Kingsley. "We found that the bone was slightly carious after the suppurative condition that had existed previous—a diseased condition of the bone, and upon the removal of the bone there was less of it than was anticipated. Still, there was some." "And after the operation you again asked her about Jane Holt?"

"Yes," said Doctor Train; "she said she knew Frank would never marry Jane Holt because she knew it would be all right between herself and Frank. They were going to go to New York where he would study sculpting and that he would someday be known the world over. She said that he had once before gotten a girl in trouble, but that was in Canada. I asked her if it ever made her unhappy, the fact that she had relations with Frank Holt although she had been raised to believe such things were wrong, and she said she often felt unhappy about her relations with him, but she had been led to believe it was all right by Holt who said everyone who was engaged did such things. I asked her if she might not have consented to relations with Frank Holt even without an engagement, and she said she would have, because they were spiritually united from the first, and she loved him so much she could not keep anything from him, but she had always known she would marry him. I kept coming back to the shooting and what she remembered, but she never gave any indication of knowing what had happened. I asked her again if she was jealous of other girls, and she laughed and said if she had been, she could easily have put a stop to his seeing Jane. She said that Frank was jealous of her and did not like it when she spoke to other men, even the old man at the boardinghouse, and when she spoke to Charlie Mondell, Frank's oldest friend, Frank would become black as thunder and would not speak to her for hours. She had gone home after the abortion and had considered whether or not she might not be better off without him, but when he had written her many times, she felt her resolve weakening. Then Frank Holt sent Charlie Mondell after her and he tried to persuade her to come back. I asked her if she thought she might have broken off relations with Frank if he had left her alone, and she said she thought she would not. I asked her if she thought she had an affectionate disposition and she said she must be of a more loving disposition than most girls. I told her that was not how other people represented her, and she said other people had never understood her properly. She never claimed to love everyone else. She loved only one person and that was Frank Holt.''

Mr. Kingsley heard his stomach growl. He knew from long experience that luncheon recess was at hand. He looked up at the window. It was a brilliant square of silver light, shimmering into the room. They were curious, the varieties of silence in a courtroom. This courtroom had been absolutely silent ever since the doctor had begun his testimony, but it was a silence utterly unlike the kind which fell while the audience waited for the verdict of a jury. This silence was animal silence, expectant, quivering, unpunctuated even by a nervous cough. Once again, the pack had drawn back into its cave, alarmed by rumors of disaster befalling one of its members, waiting to learn what had actually happened, and what, if anything, it should do or feel and, until it knew, the pack remained silent, ears up and pointed, sniffing the air, sifting it for the mysterious clues that traveled on every breeze, those vibrations in the air on which they would make their decision. That was how they were listening now. When he turned to look at them, he would be surprised to see them in their black dresses, in their human faces, just as, when

527

he looked down at himself, he was surprised to find he was not suited in fur. Of course it was what the doctor was saying that pulled them so. It was hearing that the Dempster girl could have no more children. It was seeing her sitting there, hearing those words for the first time. And it was the man himself.

When the doctor reported the girl's words and actions, they saw her through his eyes; he made them see her as he saw her. While he spoke, whatever image they had of her was erased, obliterated, at least temporarily. Now the doctor was describing the difficulty the staff had in persuading Agnes to wash her face or hair, and how she had told him she cared little for her appearance since it had done nothing but get her in trouble. "And on that occasion," asked Mr. Kingsley, "the examination was conducted mostly by you?" "Entirely," said Doctor Train. "And was anyone present during that interview?" he asked. "Miss Eckroyd and Doctor Chase," he said. "And did not Doctor Chase ask Miss Dempster any questions?" "He did," said Doctor Train, "but she would not answer him." "Why?" "I have no idea," said the doctor. "And by this time," asked Mr. Kingsley, "had you reached any conclusions regarding Miss Dempster's state of mind?" "Yes, I had," said Doctor Train. Mr. Kingsley turned and looked at Agnes. She was rocking, steadily as ever. "And would you tell the court what they were?" asked Mr. Kingsley.

"I am quite convinced that Miss Dempster is insane now and that she was insane at the time of the shooting."

"Can you imagine anything which might change your mind?" asked Mr. Kingsley. "Something might," said the doctor; "that is always possible. But I haven't seen anything to make me consider altering my decision." Mr. Kingsley thanked him and looked up at Judge Richter who promptly declared a luncheon recess until two o'clock.

At two o'clock, Mr. Parsons began cross-examining Doctor Train, and almost from the instant he began questioning the doctor, a restlessness swept through the court. It was as if the audience sensed and wanted to cut off an impending attack on the doctor. Mr. Kingsley sat back. There was always a point in a case when he knew that things would take their own course regardless of what he did.

"With what kind of insanity, Doctor," asked Mr. Parsons, "do you, according to your opinion, say the accused was affected at the time she shot Jane Holt?" "I think," said the doctor, "she was suffering from that kind of insanity dependent

upon hereditary influence, sometimes called constitutional insanity."
The exaggerated politeness of Parsons and the self-effacing
manner of the doctor grated badly together. "Can you give any
better definition of the kind of insanity with which you say she
was affected or troubled than that?" asked Parsons. "No, sir.
Because it is one of those kinds which is exceedingly difficult to
classify, because it partakes of several manifestations which are
also found in other kinds." "But," said Parsons, his voice stern,
"insanity *is* subject to classification, is it not?" "It is," said
Doctor Train, "but the classification is in an extremely chaotic
condition." "But there are certain well-known classes, are there
not?" "There are certain classes," said the doctor; "but I should
be inclined to class hers in a form that is not distinctly classified
in books although it is frequently seen in an asylum." Mr.
Parsons sighed noisily. "Can you describe the accused's form of
insanity *any* more clearly?" he asked at last. Mr. Kingsley
looked about him. The women were glowering at Mr. Parsons. It
was Parsons's arrogant manner. He took refuge in it when he was
confused or when he was crossed. It undid him every time.

"Well," said Doctor Train, "it is a kind of insanity dependent
upon heredity, manifested by depression, by sudden alterations
from depression to abnormal hilarity; in it, the mind is weak and
the judgment is faulty. Its subjects perform causeless acts from
apparently nonexistent motives; they are subject to sudden impulses,
laugh out suddenly for no apparent reason, cry without provocation,
and so on." "Would you class it as dementia?" asked Parsons.
"No, sir," said Doctor Train. "Emotional insanity?" said Parsons.
"No, sir," said the doctor. "Impulsive insanity, then?" "No,
sir." "Compulsive insanity, then?" asked Parsons. "No, sir, I
think not," said the doctor. "Can you tell us of *any* authority,"
asked Mr. Parsons, "*any* textbook, any written article which
describes the form of insanity under which you say Miss Dempster
was laboring when she killed Jane Holt?"

The doctor squirmed in his chair and thrust his head, turtlelike,
toward the prosecuting attorney. "No, sir, but I think upon
studying the matter—not in textbooks, but in life—realizing the
unusual heredity which gave her an unstable, nervous condition—
with a tendency to convulsions, which is the functional expression of insanity in childhood, the hysterical attacks which have
been spoken of, which were succeeded by alternating moods,
with a life that was marked by unwise, unreasonable, and faulty
judgment, by a vacillating purpose in life, by a profound disturbance of her emotions which were always unstable, by reason of

the seduction, fear of dishonor, of shame and grief at betrayal, desperation at desertion, with a brain that was in a disturbed condition—these were the influences that led up to the act and which made her irresponsible. It was a case of hereditary insanity. Excuse me, Mr. Parsons, but I gather that definition is not good enough for you?'' "No, Doctor," Mr. Parsons said; "it is not."

"Then," said Doctor Train, flushing, "if I were to classify it, I should be more likely to say that it was the insanity of a seduced woman." "The insanity of a seduced woman?" Mr. Parsons repeated in astonishment. "Of a seduced woman, yes sir."

A new quality had entered the silence of the courtroom. Mr. Kingsley looked at Agnes. She was leaning forward, holding to the chair in front of her, her face rapt, her eyes shining. She had stopped rocking. He looked through the rows of women sitting with their mackintoshes folded on their laps and their umbrellas resting on the floor at their sides. The same expression was on their faces. All eyes were on the doctor. It was clear enough to them what the doctor meant. It was clear to them he was fighting for them. So you want to disgrace me? the doctor seemed to be asking Parsons; so you want to make me foolish? Then I'll help you do it. I'll tell you what I think is the truth. Kingsley stared at the doctor, dumbfounded. He was inviting professional disgrace. The papers would print his diagnosis: the insanity of a seduced woman. He would be a laughingstock.

Mr. Parsons had regained his composure. Agnes had not resumed rocking. "Where do you find *that* classification, Doctor?" asked Mr. Parsons. "I do not think it is so classed by any author," said Doctor Train. "Is it *your* classification?" Mr. Parsons asked. "No, I cannot take entire credit for it," said Doctor Train; "another man has written an article upon it." "Is it epileptic insanity, then?" asked Mr. Parsons. "He told you what he thought it was," said the judge. "How many cases similar to this have you in your institution at Highbury?" "Well," said Doctor Train, "that is a difficult question to answer just that way, Mr. Parsons, because no two cases of insanity are alike." "Are there any cases of insanity like this in your asylum at Highbury?" asked Mr. Parsons. "Not exactly," said the doctor, "but if she lives long enough, she will resemble some there." "But there are none there now?" asked Mr. Parsons. "No, sir," said the doctor.

"Even if there are no such patients in your institution, and even if you cannot recommend a work to our attention which recognizes your classification—the insanity of a seduced woman—surely you can describe it to us," said Mr. Parsons. "I can try," said the doctor; "the difficulty is in the limitations of our understanding. We know very little about this form of insanity, but we know it exists." "Are you prepared to describe it?" asked Mr. Parsons. "I will attempt to describe it, insofar as I understand it, which is as far as anyone in my profession understands it." "Please go on," said Mr. Parsons.

The doctor pushed himself back in his chair, took his reading glasses out of his pocket, and settled them on his nose. "Pardon me," he said to the judge; "I think better with them on." The audience smiled at him. "Well," began the doctor hesitantly, "there are some natures in which the sexual impulses and what we call the spiritual and intellectual natures are closely fused, far more closely than they are in most people. For such individuals, whichever passion is strongest pulls the other passion along with it. I may not be making myself clear." The doctor stopped and looked at Mr. Parsons. "Well," the doctor continued, "we have no way of knowing what about Frank Holt caused Miss Dempster to see him as the only man in the world she could love, but since she herself says she loved him even before she spoke to him, the strongest impulse pulling her to him seems to have originated in the intellect. Certainly, once she was attached to Mr. Holt, she was utterly attached to him. She seems to have quite literally handed him her life for his safekeeping. She expressed this when she said that she gave Frank Holt her soul and instead of protecting it, he destroyed it. For whatever reasons, she entrusted him with the care of her entire being. She gave him responsibility for her very existence. There seems little question that Mr. Holt knew that this was what Miss Dempster was doing; she told him she had no life of her own, that he was her entire world, that they needed no one but one another, and although he eventually tired of the demands she made upon him, he did not resist them in the beginning. Miss Dempster literally felt as if she lifted her soul from her body and handed it to Mr. Holt. From that point forward, her survival depended on him. When he spurned her, she naturally felt as if she were being destroyed.

"The seduction, the most dangerous of his seductions, involved his encouraging her to believe that he could be everything to her. Her insanity was in letting herself be so deluded. We do not yet know what causes a person to abdicate personal autonomy as Miss Dempster did. We do not know whether the sexual impulses simply take over and overrule the intellect, or whether the intellect takes over and puts the sexual impulses at its service. But we do know that when one person loves another person so intensely that he loses consciousness of the boundary between himself and the rest of the world, that person is potentially insane. If something happens to disrupt the world of such a person, a world which consists of only two people who are now seen as one, then the disruption produces an insane rage. It may be that only those already inclined to insanity enter into human entanglements like the one which led to the tragedy with which we are now concerned. I believe that to be so. Her heredity produced a nervous condition, an unstable mind and she could not survive the disruption of her life with Frank Holt. She described it as a 'tearing apart.' I believe she meant this literally. When her world tore apart, she was not in the world as we know it. That is what we mean by insanity. She was in something like a frenzy which obliterates all awareness of the world. I do not believe she knew she was shooting Jane Holt. She has always said she believed she was shooting herself.''

"I see," Mr. Parsons said, considering. "Well, Doctor," he went on, "could you perhaps be a bit clearer on one point. Earlier you said that, in some individuals, the intellectual passions interweave with the sexual ones and become inseparable, and thereafter—if I understand you right—all the underpinnings of the character are directed at one aim." "That is right," said the doctor. "Would you not say that in Miss Dempster's case, sexual passion drove her toward Frank Holt, that unbridled sexual frenzy led her to attempt to keep him for herself, and that, to accomplish this aim, she shot Jane Holt?" "No, sir," said the doctor; "I would say nothing of the kind. As I said earlier, she fell in love with Frank Holt before she met him. She claimed to have 'known' him before she ever met him. It is my guess that the frenzy which attached her to Frank Holt was a frenzy of the intellect, which the girl calls her soul. Once the sexual passions came to be enlisted in this frenzy, Miss Dempster had no further control over her actions." "If the sexual passions had not been enlisted, would this have happened?" asked Mr. Parsons. "I have no way of knowing what might or might not have happened," answered the doctor. "But you are reasonably sure that hers was an intellectual frenzy?" asked Mr. Parsons. "As sure as anyone can be, given our limited understanding of a case like this," said the doctor. "So you would not describe her as a lascivious girl whose appetites were insatiable?" "I certainly would not," said the doctor, irritated.

"And yet," said Mr. Parsons, "Miss Dempster complained that Frank Holt considered her insatiable." "Of his *time*, sir," said the doctor; "there is a difference. He felt as if she wanted to possess him utterly. The girl herself says that she did. In that sense, she was insatiable. She wanted him entirely for herself. As she saw it, he *was* her *self*. When she was overcome with rage because he would not marry her, she did not turn on him, possibly because that would have been turning on herself as well. It would have been turning on her own soul. In so far as it is possible to enter into a diseased mind, we might conjecture that she believed that killing herself would not kill her soul, since it would live on in Frank Holt exactly as they both would have lived on in a child had they had one."

"And this is what she *thought*, Doctor?" asked Mr. Parsons. "This is the closest I can come to conjecturing about her thoughts," said the doctor; "she is insane. No one knows what she thinks or how she does. We know how the minds of some of the insane work, but we do not yet understand *her* form of insanity. I have said this before."

"Well," said Mr. Parsons, "perhaps you could tell us how one person hands his soul, I think you called it, over to someone else. It is a farfetched idea, is it not?" "Not to a superintendent of an asylum," said the doctor. "The person simply mistakes someone else for himself. He believes the other person is part of him. We see *that* every day at the asylum. We see it in lovers as well. They often say that 'I belong to you,' or 'you belong to me' and nothing is wrong with it. It is the size and nature of the mistake which determines its pathological nature. Lovers still know they are two people. At some point, Miss Dempster lost that knowledge." "And she lost that knowledge because Frank Holt seduced her into losing it?" asked Mr. Parsons. "She lost that knowledge because of the insanity which she inherited from three generations of her family," said the doctor. "Can you explain the term 'insanity of a seduced woman' any further?" Parsons asked. "He already told you he could not," said the judge; "the court is recessed until nine o'clock tomorrow morning."

533

50

HER OWN STORY

AS AGNES TOLD IT TO DR. P.
TRAIN WHO GAVE IT IN COURT

MISS DEMPSTER SUFFERING
FROM THE MADNESS OF A
SEDUCED WOMAN

*The Pitiful Tale Of A Dishonored
And Broken Hearted Girl Who
Loved Too Much—Meant Only
To Kill Herself*

The night after Doctor Train testified, Mr. Kingsley went straight to bed and his wife knew better than to try talking to him. In the morning, she brought him the paper, and he picked it up, read the headlines and dropped it down on the comforter. "What upset you so yesterday?" she asked; "the case is going very well." "He's a brave man," said Mr. Kingsley. "Yes, he is," said his wife; "you should have heard the women afterward. If his wife knows what she's doing, she'll keep him under lock and key." "His wife's dead," Mr. Kingsley said.

"I don't think I could do it," he said, picking up a piece of the cinnamon toast she had brought in and biting into it. "Do what?" she asked. "Risk myself that way," he said; "risk everything I had. And for someone I don't even know." "You do that whenever you go into court," she said. "No, Martha, I don't. If I went into court and insisted that we should let someone off because politeness required it, then I'd be risking my reputation. The insanity of a seduced woman! That's so bold—" He stopped, fingering the coverlet. "He's either insane, himself," Mr. Kingsley said at last, "or tougher than a dog in a dog fight."

His wife got up and walked over to the window. "Sometimes, Charles, you really are cold-blooded," she said; "not to say foolish." "Don't you think he's a fighter?" asked her husband. "Oh, he's a fighter, but he's fighting because he thinks he's right and because he's not fighting for himself. I don't think he could fight so hard for himself. I don't think most of us could. Even the girl. She didn't fight for herself. She fought to keep that man. She thought she was doing the right thing."

"Do you think there's such a thing as the insanity of a seduced woman?" he asked her. "Of course," Martha said, turning back to him; "all women know that. It's the one thing I would murder for, and I wouldn't need the seduction, either. To think about your body touching the body of another woman's and then coming back to mine! It would be worse than a rape. It would be a rape, not just of my body, but of my heart and soul, my life. You have to believe people mean what they promise you. You can't live when someone smashes your dreams one after another. I could kill the man who shattered the whole world around me. Any woman could. The only thing I don't understand is why she tried to kill the girl and not the man." "She didn't *try* to kill the girl, she did kill the girl," Mr. Kingsley said; his voice sounded far-off. He was trying to make sense of what his wife was saying.

"You know," said Martha, "there's one very curious thing. When the case was first reported, it was Jane Holt, Jane Holt, Jane Holt, what a poor thing she was to die so young, how pitiful her fate was, and how tragic, and how pathetic was her funeral, and now, now no one ever thinks about the girl at all. It's as if she never existed. If it weren't necessary to keep asking about what Agnes remembered about the day of the shooting, no one would even mention Jane Holt or her family. It's as if she never existed and never was shot. It's all become a contest between the Dempster girl and Frank Holt." "You mean people don't think of her as a murderess?" asked Mr. Kingsley. "They don't, they think of her as the victim. It's as if Jane Holt were a figment of her imagination. Do *you* ever think about Jane Holt?"

535

"No," he said, "I don't." "What are you thinking about now?" she asked. "How the doctor will hold up under the next round of cross-examination." "He'll hold up," said his wife; "didn't you see what happened when he left yesterday? He was mobbed by women trying to put roses in his lapel." "These people with roses are getting to be a menace," said Mr. Kingsley; "couldn't they find something less thorny? What's wrong with daisies? They last longer." "Oh, Charles," Martha sighed.

On Friday, Mr. Kingsley again questioned Doctor Train, and just as Agnes had rocked rhythmically throughout the trial, she now maintained a rigid, expectant posture. Mr. Kingsley read several letters which Agnes had written to her father and asked him if they altered his opinion as to whether she was sane or insane and he said they did not. "In your opinion," he asked him, "what would be the effect—assuming that the mother of Agnes Dempster had marked mental disturbances—upon the daughter?" "It is very common to have it transmitted," said the doctor. "And do you think it was?" asked Mr. Kingsley. "I think she is insane," he said. Mr. Kingsley then asked how long an amnesia might be produced by a pistol shot such as Miss Dempster had suffered. "It may have abolished all memory of the actual occurrences immediately preceding the tragedy," he said, "but if that was the cause of the amnesia, her memory should have already returned and I am convinced it has not."

"How much of Miss Dempster's mental condition which you have described to us—her instability, depression, poor judgment, loss of memory, suicidal impulses, and so on—how much of this was caused by the injury or the shock from the injury?" "Her present mental condition has nothing to do with the shot," said Doctor Train; "she was in the same state of mind before the shot was fired. Of course, a shot like that, painful as it was, had an effect upon the nervous system, but it did not cause the insanity. The insanity was already fully established."

After that, Mr. Parsons again cross-examined Doctor Train, hinting strongly that his experience in his field was inadequate, and he ought not to be trusted by the jury. However, Parsons saw quickly enough that he was winning no sympathy for his cause, and returned to the question of the doctor's classification of Agnes's illness. "Do all the authors who write on insanity attempt to make a classification of all types?" asked Mr. Parsons. "Oh, they try to," said the doctor; "but no two are alike that I am aware of." "But they do?" asked Parsons. "Oh, yes," said

Doctor Train. "And the writers are men of great ability?" "Certainly," said Doctor Train. "Men who have given their whole lifetime to the study?" asked Mr. Parsons. "Very true," said the doctor. "And they are men who, if anybody, would have the capacity and ability to do it, would they not?" "Yes," said Doctor Train, "but at the same time each man distinguished in his own profession does not accept the qualification of any other man." "Can you say this is not that class of inherited insanity which you call melancholia?" "I wouldn't classify it as so," said Doctor Train. "Is this case distinguished from mania or not?" "It is not mania," said the doctor. "Do you feel sure of that?" asked Mr. Parsons. "Confident of it," said the doctor. "So there are two classes to which you feel sure this patient does not belong. You have heard of those cases of insanity known as states of fixed and limited delusion of persecution and fear, have you not, Doctor?" "I have," said Doctor Train. He bent forward. "Are you examining me on Doctor Cluston?" he asked. "I am asking you a question," said Mr. Parsons. "Doctor Cluston has just published his first book," said the doctor; "he may change his mind by the second."

"He is an expert, is he not?" asked Mr. Parsons. "Certainly," said the doctor. "So you don't think her case falls under any of the standard classifications?" "I do not," said Doctor Train. "You think she is insane *because she is insane*?" asked Mr. Parsons. "Yes, sir," said the doctor. Clearly exasperated, Mr. Parsons ran his hands through his hair.

"You are aware that this is a case of great gravity?" asked Mr. Parsons. "I am," said the doctor. "And you would not think of testifying in a case of this gravity without giving a great deal of attention to the subject?" "I certainly should not, and I should give it honestly," said the doctor. "And yet you said yesterday that you could not refer us to any authority which would throw any light upon this type of insanity?" "That is true," said the doctor. "Then when you framed your opinion as it was given yesterday, you did not have in mind the authority of any writer on insanity?" "No, it was entirely my own." "So that," said Mr. Parsons, "in basing your opinion, you based it entirely upon your own experience, and you supported it, when you gave it yesterday, by no authority on insanity?" "That is true," said the doctor. "And you were not at the time able to refer to any authority on insanity in support of your opinion." "That is true," said the doctor.

"Then may we go into certain points you made yesterday

concerning your definition of Miss Dempster's illness? I believe you called it the insanity of a seduced woman." "Insanity or madness," said the doctor; "it's all the same thing." "Yesterday you mentioned your belief that Miss Dempster was one of those personalities so constituted that she surrendered her soul when she loved." "I believe I said that," said the doctor. "So it would be correct to speak of Miss Dempster losing her soul to Mr. Holt?" asked Mr. Parsons. "According to her view of things, it would," said the doctor. "You are referring to Miss Dempster's immortal soul, are you, Doctor?" "No, I am not," said Doctor Train; "I was speaking entirely in the context of the mental processes. Miss Dempster meant that all those things which set her apart from others, all those things which made her the person she was, all those things which enabled her to recognize *herself* when she—so to speak—looked in her mental mirror, all those things constituted her soul. All her past experiences and what she learned from them and felt about them, all her dreams for the future, all those things constituted her soul. In other words, when she fell in love with Mr. Holt, she was divested of her sense of herself, her sense of who she was; she lost all sense of herself as an inadequate or unhappy being. She has entrusted her soul, in the sense of which we are now using it, to Mr. Holt. When he turned against her, he handed her back her awareness of herself as an unhappy, unsatisfied girl and, not having felt such things for a long time, she was overwhelmed by emotions which had, before she met Mr. Holt, been familiar to her. Now they were no longer familiar. In effect, these emotions were new and they overwhelmed her.

"Let me be clear, Mr. Parsons. She could not have been so overwhelmed had her own heredity not predisposed her to this form of insanity. The affair with Frank Holt was the exciting cause, not the primary one." "Those are pretty fine distinctions," said Mr. Parsons. "Nevertheless," said the doctor, "I believe them to accurately describe the progress of events." "But you can think of no expert who can be quoted to support you?" asked Mr. Parsons. "No," Doctor Train said; "I have said many times I cannot. Because the dark side of the moon is invisible we do not believe the moon has no dark side."

"You say this is your first experience in testifying in a homicide case?" "Yes," said the doctor. "It is admitted, of course, Doctor, is it not, that these standard authorities who have given study to insanity know more about the forms of insanity, their causes, the progress of the disease, than the average physician who gives his time to working among the insane, is it not?'' The doctor sat back in his chair. "Most of the men you speak about," said the doctor, "work among the insane. Most of those men were superintendents of institutions." "Are they not the men best fitted to give opinions or information relating to the insane disease?" "Very true," said the doctor; "but, upon that same ground, why should I not have the same authority?" "If your opinion should clash with Doctor Cluston's or some other authority," asked Mr. Parsons, "would you feel immodest in suggesting that your opinion was the better one?" "Naturally," said the doctor; "I should entertain more respect for his opinion. But if I found a case that he doesn't quite cover, I should be ready to recognize that he does not see all the insane in the world. I should be inclined to read the work of experts with respect, and if I wrote a work, I should hope they might do the same with mine.''

"You think if you should write a work on insanity that Doctor Cluston and others would have the same regard for your opinion as you have for theirs." "Very likely," said the doctor. "Would they tolerate your definition of the girl's difficulty as one of losing her 'soul'?" "They would, if they understood how I was using the term," said the doctor, "and I trust I could make that clear." "So you think, Doctor," asked Mr. Parsons, "that your experience is sufficient to warrant you in classifying yourself with Doctor Cluston and others?" "Not in the way you mean," said Doctor Train, "but it is sufficient to warrant me in having an opinion of my own to which I propose to adhere." "You do?" asked Mr. Parsons, feigning surprise. "Yes," said the doctor, "because I am honest in it and I believe in it."

Mr. Kingsley took a deep breath and exhaled slowly. He looked around him for confirmation and saw it on every face; everyone there felt sympathy for the doctor. As far as Kingsley was concerned, it was over.

But Parsons was not giving up. He had gone back to the question of the experts, and pursued it in the face of the evident displeasure of the judge, the jury, and the audience. Finally, he asked the doctor what he thought the prognosis for Miss Dempster might be. "I expect," said the doctor, "that under the regular life at the hospital, she would get on very well, but I think there would be a tendency to great deterioration, of which we have already seen some evidence, and then sinking down into something we *might* call secondary dementia, a terminal state. It is a form of futility which succeeds all forms of insanity—well, loss of mind." "Describe such a futile person," Mr. Parsons said.

"They are untidy. They have no realization of their position or surroundings. They simply eat and sleep. Their hands are cold and clammy. Their circulation is languid and the skin is often blue. Their hands and feet are cold. They are not pretty pictures to contemplate."

The cross-examination continued. Mr. Kingsley sat back and absently chewed on his cigar while he watched Mr. Parsons. *What* was the man after? Every response he elicited deepened the audience's sympathy for the girl. He must be, Mr. Kingsley decided, on a fishing expedition.

Doctor Train said that he believed the girl had been in a confusional state when she shot the other girl, but he did not think she had confusional insanity. He thought the murderous act was impulsive, but that Agnes was not homicidally insane. "It is the sort of convulsion which will occur suddenly in a person evidently set upon taking her own life," said the doctor; "it was largely an automatic act on her part. She might as easily have shot into the air. If she had intended to shoot Jane Holt, she would have shot her when she first saw her, not gone up to her in a particular spot and then shot her in front of witnesses."

"Is it your opinion," asked Parsons, "that Miss Dempster was conscious of what she was doing any time that day? From the time she left the house with the gun until she regained consciousness in the hospital?" "I think not," said the doctor; "she was so overpowered by the tremendous emotional pressures upon her that she was probably not conscious of anything, and because she was so overpowered, she may have seemed very quiet and in possession of herself." "How is that?" asked Mr. Parsons. "She was so completely overwhelmed by her emotions that she pressed them all down and when she acted, she acted in an automatic way, without consciousness of what she felt. She reverted to old ways of behaving, old habits which she may not even have known she had. If she had been conscious of what she felt, she would not have been able to act at all, but would have been paralyzed, suffered from a fit of depression, and stayed in her room as she had often done before." "Then you think her trip from her house to the scene of the tragedy and the shooting was done in an amnesia state?" Mr. Parsons asked. "Yes," he said, "I do. An amnesia state induced by the unceremonious return of what the girl called her 'soul.'"

It was wonderful, thought Mr. Kingsley, how Mr. Parson's determination was digging him in deeper and deeper. He could barely endure waiting to cross-examine the doctor when Parsons finished with him. Mr. Kingsley began after the two o'clock recess. "Doctor," he said, as usual facing the courtroom, "we have heard a great deal about experts, and our opponent would like us to believe they are always infallible. But you say that the classifications undertaken are entirely arbitrary and not uniform, do you not?" "Entirely arbitrary, and each man has his own," said the doctor. "Is this true in all aspects of medicine?" asked Mr. Kingsley. Doctor Train said it was. "When did you first know of the classification of the disease known as appendicitis?" asked Mr. Kingsley. "Oh, within the last ten years, the last eight to ten years," said the doctor.

"And you have many patients in your asylum whose diseases you cannot classify," said Mr. Kingsley, "but they are nevertheless insane?" "There is no doubt of it," said the doctor. "So a man might know what a disease is and yet not be able to name it?" asked Mr. Kingsley. "Yes," said the doctor; "when I was in medical school, it was called peritonitis, but the doctors meant what we now mean by appendicitis. It was described as an inflammation of the parts about the appendix and the parts involving the peritoneum; but Doctor Fitts was the man who described it clearly and accurately. For a long time, the disease went by both names."

"And you believe that Miss Dempster's disease is hereditary insanity—the insanity of a seduced woman, you call it—although you are willing to believe a better name will be found for her illness?" "I do not doubt but that it will," said the doctor. "And how many times did you visit the accused before you reached your decision?" he asked. "Three times," said the doctor. "Ordinarily," asked Mr. Kingsley, "does it take three examinations to discover whether a person is insane or not?" "No," said the doctor; "but a careful man will always take ample time." "Thank you, Doctor," said Mr. Kingsley; "I am sure we all appreciate the many sacrifices this trial has required from you." The doctor nodded and looked at the judge. "No further questions," said Mr. Parsons. "The witness is excused," said the judge, and the doctor took up his seat in the courtroom. Agnes collapsed backward in her rocker and once again resumed swaying back and forth. Mr. Kingsley turned around and sought his wife's face. When he saw her, he pretended to adjust his tie. It was an old signal. It meant he thought he'd won.

The trial continued but the headlines indicated the restlessness of the audience, and, undoubtedly, of the jurors. "Defense Rests. State Again Takes A Hand in Dempster Trial. Expert Testimony. Agnes Of Sound Mind. Family History Again Discussed.

The Other Side. Witnesses From Agnes's Home In Court. Queer But Sane. Family History Again The Subject—Ugly Disposition, But Sane Mind. The Case Drags. Little Progress Today. South Clayboro And North Chittendon Continue To Supply Witnesses Wholesale. Dempster Trial. State Expert Testimony In Rebuttal. Agnes Not Insane. Weak And Slow Memory But No Indications Of Mental Unsoundness. End Is Coming. Now Expected That Case Will Go To Jury Not Later Than Next Wednesday.

ARE THERE SUCH THINGS AS EXPERT WITNESSES?

Why Trial of Agnes Dempster is Causing a Heavy Expense

August 12. One of the local justices spoke sensibly today when he remarked that there was no knowing where a trial would end or what it would cost when expert witnesses were introduced. It is, to the average observer, to say the least, a red tape affair. It may be essential but it really seems that it could be handled in a manner that would be less expensive and result in giving the jury a more lucid idea of what they are supposed to know in order to decide fairly on the merits of the case. Doctors are doctors and it is not disqualifying their value in the least to say that if their value as medical practitioners was as limited as their testimony is comprehensible to the average jury the entire populace of the world would perish with catnip fits before they could be saved by the aid of the medical fraternity. It is a case of

doctors being doctors whether on or off the stand. When terms are used by such witnesses as baffle the lawyers what sort of a show does the average juryman stand? Since the first of the doctors left the witness stand, it has all been gibberish, and much of the time, he was not too clear either.

IS AGNES DEMPSTER INSANE?

Mr. Kingsley Made Eloquent Attempt To Convince The Jury

August 14. Mr. Kingsley said the jury must determine whether the act of Agnes Dempster was committed with wicked purpose or that she was irresponsible for the reason of insanity.

He further stated that if the jury should determine that the respondent is insane she would not be turned upon the streets as a menace to the public but her safekeeping would be provided for by a wise and judicious court and so the question for the jury to decide was whether the respondent should go to the scaffold or the asylum.

He placed in contrast the happy light-hearted girlhood of the average girl and the despondent condition of Agnes who was attempting to end her life by taking laudanum before she was fifteen years of age.

AGNES AWAITS HER FATE

Her Case Was Given To The Jury This Afternoon

August 15. Court reconvened this morning at 9 o'clock when the last argument was made in the Agnes Dempster case by State's Attorney Parsons. Mr. Parsons consumed the entire morning in his address to the jury which was clear-cut, covering the salient points made in opposition to the interpretation made by Mr. Kingsley for the defense.

Meanwhile, Agnes awaits her fate, and so far as outward appearances are indicative, she does not care which, although it is reported that she has at one time said she would rather go to an asylum than be hanged, but that in any event she never wished to go out in the world again.

On Wednesday, August 16th, an impenetrable crowd of men and women surrounded the courthouse waiting to hear the verdict which was to determine Agnes Dempster's fate. Over their heads, the great elms flickered green, spangled with golden light; on the lawns, the breezes swayed the pink and white apple trees which filled the air with color. It was a perfect day. Only the people, almost all of whom were dressed in black, shadowed the scene. The sky was a soft but brilliant blue, and the sun, though still small, burned hot and golden. Swallows cut sharply through the air. Fat bees flew from lawn to lawn, every now and then flying into the crowd and creating a sudden disturbance, shrieks, waving of hands, and then, the danger gone, the noise subsided and the crowd resumed its quiet vigil.

Many of the men and women carried little bags. They were evidently prepared to wait all day if necessary, but at nine-fifteen a deputy emerged from the courthouse and announced that Judge Richter and the attorneys were ready to report and by nine-thirty the courtroom was filled to capacity. Agnes was not yet there. The judge's door opened, and she walked in, as usual accompanied by Sheriff Gray. She did not look at the jury. She did not look at the audience. Instead, she went to her rocker and engaged in her usual pastime of swinging backward and forward in her rocking chair. "Don't worry," said Mr. Kingsley, bending forward to speak to her, but she only nodded and continued rocking. The jurors came in and took up their seats in the jury box; within minutes, they were followed by the officers of the court. The clerk asked the foreman of the jury if they had agreed upon a verdict and the foreman replied that they had.

"And what did you find?" asked the clerk.

"We find Agnes Dempster not guilty of the crime of killing Jane Holt by reason of insanity."

The tremendous shout that went up in the courtroom shook the walls, and the gavel blows did nothing whatever to quiet it. Mr. Kingsley looked around him, stunned. One woman after another was beginning to cry. He looked at the man in back of him and saw tears streaming down his face. Wherever his wife was, he knew she was crying. The judge was staring down at his hands as if he were afraid to let the audience see his face. Agnes went on rocking. There was a commotion in the back corner of the room, and Mr. Kingsley stood up to see what it was. The women were mobbing Doctor Train, kissing him, pressing flowers and little gifts upon him. *Now,* thought Mr. Kingsley, the doctor looked frightened. But he had won his case as well.

Mr. Kingsley sat down again and listened as Judge Richter ordered that Agnes be retained in custody and excused the jury subject to return upon the receipt of a call from the clerk.

The case had been given to the jury at three o'clock the day before and it was now only ten in the morning. The jury had reached an agreement within hours. It was as he had expected. He sat motionless and collapsed. Judge Richter declared the court adjourned until two o'clock. Mr. Kingsley got up slowly and began moving toward the jurors. It was his custom to thank the jurors whether he won or lost, and over the years, he and Parsons had gotten into the habit of thanking them together.

He saw Parsons next to him; the man's face was distorted as if he were under enormous pressure of a kind he did not understand or had not felt before. Kingsley had seen Parsons lose in the past, and he knew that once a decision was in, he put any bitterness at defeat behind him. It was something else that bothered him now. The jury stood together, a little human clump that had lived together for so long it was reluctant to disperse; it did not quite know how. For a while, each of the jury had belonged to a larger body, a larger psychic entity. He had never seen a jury anxious to lose its identity with the others and this one was no exception. The men were laughing and pounding one another's arms. Near Mr. Kingsley, the Hammerhead was asking the jurors questions and the foreman turned to speak to him.

"My fellows and I," he told the Hammerhead, "are unanimous in our desire to come again for the purpose of hanging Frank Holt. The wrong person was on trial."

"Congratulations," Mr. Parsons said to Mr. Kingsley; "you have good reason to be pleased with yourself." "I don't feel particularly pleased with myself," Mr. Kingsley said; "do you think after this recess, he'll issue the order to commit her to the asylum?" "Oh, yes," said Parsons; "now she passes into the hands of your Doctor Train." "It's fitting enough," Kingsley said; "he's the man who saved her life." "Do you want to get some dinner?" asked Mr. Parsons. "No," said Mr. Kingsley, "I think I'll go for a walk. I'll be back in time for the sentencing."

Before looking for his wife, he thanked David Deignault for the long months spent hunting up the testimony on which they had built the case and then he fought his way through the crowd of congratulators and well-wishers. Agnes would have her father and Miss Eckroyd. By now, the two women had become profoundly attached to one another although they rarely spoke.

51

The day after the jury brought in its verdict, *The Spectator* carried the following editorial:

AN ENEMY OF SOCIETY

The verdict in the Agnes Dempster case was not unexpected. It became clear, in the course of the developments of the trial, that no jury of men, having the common feelings or instincts of humanity, would convict the young woman of murder. The acceptance of the theory of insanity was apparently a convenient way of justifying a verdict contrary to the naked facts of the conception and execution of the purpose to shoot her victim. In the light of these developments, as man is created, and particularly as men who are fathers of daughters or brothers of sisters, are constituted, jurymen would appeal the case from the sole and frigid jurisdiction of the brain to at least the concurrent one of the heart. In the presence of one crucial phase of the testimony, no power or skill of prosecution could have secured a verdict of guilty; no eloquence of defense was needed to procure acquittal. Whatever the weakness, mental or moral, of Agnes Dempster, she was a terribly wronged woman, but the individual who had done her an inexplicable wrong was not the one on whom she wreaked her frenzied justice. The public must be quite unanimous in its judgment that Agnes Dempster shot the wrong person; it must be quite of one mind in its regrets—if indeed, it is true—that there is no adequate legal punishment for the brute guilty of gross crime in his relations with the chief actor in this tragedy, and who must be considered indirectly the murderer in this case. If existing law, in any of its ramifications, cannot reach the person whose devilishness set in motion the vengeful fury of Agnes Dempster, it is a grievous omission that should be remedied. *The Spectator* will not say that a woman seduced and betrayed and placed under the ban of society should have carte blanche to shoot the villain who is the author of her ruin, but a case like the one recently before Washington County Court would go far to reconcile one to this summary manner of punishment, in the absence of cognizance by the state of one of the most heinous offenses a man can commit against woman and society in general.

When Mr. Kingsley finished reading this, he wanted to go speak to Mr. Parsons, but his wife forbade it. He had promised to take her on a picnic after the trial was over, and she was going to have her picnic, even if she had it in her own yard. They took the carriage and drove into the hills above Montpelier, until the town looked like a child's toy. "The God's eye view," said Mr. Kingsley; "no wonder people like it high up in the mountains." "The Dempster girl lived in the mountains, didn't she?" asked Mrs. Kingsley. Her husband nodded and began pulling up blades of grass, one at a time. "Are you sulking because of that editorial?" asked his wife. "No," he said. "Are you thinking about the girl?" she asked. "Not yet," he said; "but I will." "Everyone tried so hard to save her," said his wife. She lay down on the blanket. "By now she must be in Highbury." "Let's talk about something else," said Mr. Kingsley. "Like what, for example?" asked his wife. "Like pickles," said her husband.

That night, after dinner, he walked over to Liberty Street carrying *The Spectator* with him. Mr. Parsons opened the door. "Well, Fred," said Mr. Kingsley. "Come in, Charles," Mr. Parsons said. He was puzzled; that was clear. "Well, I guess you didn't come to gloat," Mr. Parsons said at last. "Did you see the paper?" Mr. Kingsley asked him. "I saw it," said Parsons; "it's nonsense. They weren't there. They didn't sit through the trial day after day. There was a lot more to it than voting to save the life of a seduced woman." "For once," said Mr. Kingsley, "I think the paper's got it right. It's the worst trial I ever went through, I can tell you that. It had its own life. They all do, but this one was different. I had nothing to do with the outcome. Neither did you."

"Don't try to make me feel better," Mr. Parsons said; "I know I drove everyone off when I questioned the doctor." "You couldn't have done anything with the man," said Mr. Kingsley; "you might as well have argued with a stone. It wasn't what he *said*. I don't really understand what he *said*. It was everything he stood for. It was the way everyone sensed him. He was such a good, decent man. That was why I picked him. I knew that a man like that would conclude that anyone who committed the kind of murder the girl committed had to be crazy. I knew he couldn't conceive of a normal person doing such a thing. And if he couldn't, the jury wouldn't be able to, either. He was an expert, and he gave them persmission to let her go when he said she was crazy. He turned out a lot smarter than I thought he was, that's all. Still, it all went according to plan." "*Your* plan," said Parsons with some bitterness. "Only insofar as I could see into the plan of things which were already unfolding," said Mr. Kingsley; "an idiot could have taken my place, someone deaf and dumb. Well, don't you see it, Fred? We were trying a woman whose child was torn from her, whose face was ruined, who was told she'd never be able to have children again—right in front of the whole town—*and* she'd already shot herself through the head and lived. My God! How much more was anyone going to punish her? I couldn't have voted to convict and you couldn't have, either. You *never* did such a bad job as you did with Train, and you know why, don't you? You agreed with him. You wanted him to prevail."

Parsons started to say something and then stopped. "You're right," he said; "I wanted her to win." "Well, she didn't win," said Kingsley; "and neither did we. She's in Highbury and that doctor really believes she's crazy. He'll never let her out." "Good Lord," said Parsons. "That's what was accomplished," said Kingsley: "a life sentence." "Could we have forced it the other way?" asked Parsons; "to a hanging?" "I doubt it," Kingsley said; "it really wasn't in our hands." "It was in someone's hands," Parsons said irritably. "It was in the hands of the instincts, not even the heart: the instincts. The blood was talking, the marrow."

"Go on and say what you mean," said Parsons, sitting down on the edge of his desk. He picked up a decanter and poured some brandy into two glasses; "say what you mean." He handed a glass to Mr. Kingsley. "It was that girl's womb talking to all the other wombs. I don't know how to put it," he said. "Try," said Parsons; "you usually find a way to say anything." "Well, you know I'm full of theories," said Kingsley. "Go ahead," said Parsons; "I want to know what they are." "Well, the brain came last in us," said Kingsley; "before that all the organs of the body developed one at a time. I think each organ of the body has some kind of mind of its own. The strongest mind of them all is supposed to be the human intellect, but it only controls the body when it works with it. I think the womb has a mind of its own. I think the womb's like the queen bee of the woman's body and every part of the female body works to carry out its commands. Men are the same way; they only keep their hold of their minds when their minds serve their sexual organs. So it was that girl's womb talking to all the other wombs. That was why all the women cried: for the desolation of the womb. That's why everyone hated Frank Holt the way they did. He was the violator of the womb. Men are supposed to penetrate the womb, but they're also supposed to guard it. Holt said all that was unimportant. He said she could take care of herself and that *he* needed protection. What man was going to listen to that? His *body* contradicted every word Frank said. There's a kind of biological truth in us, and that Holt fellow flouted it. The girl didn't. They went for her and against him because *he* was the violator of the womb." "Holt," said Parsons, sipping at his brandy.

"It's good brandy," said Kingsley, looking around the room; "you've lived in this house ten years and it's still unfinished. When are you getting married?" "After this trial?" asked Parsons; "never." "Don't say so," said Kingsley; "it's the ones who are afraid, who stray too far from the center, who wind up in trouble." "What do you think will happen to Holt?" asked Parsons. "If he's smart, he's already on a train going back to Canada under an assumed name."

"But what if he wasn't as bad as everyone makes out?" Parsons asked; "certainly he got the girl pregnant. But he didn't knock her unconscious and drag her off. A man's got a right to change his mind. If she was half as peculiar as the doctor said she was, it was his bad luck to get mixed up with her. She said she was jealous of the furniture he sat on. You look at it from that point of view and it's not surprising that he wanted to get away from her." "No one wanted to look at it from that point of view," Kingsley said. "The girl did," said Parsons; "whenever she saw a reporter, she told him it wasn't Holt's fault." "But she also told the doctor he got her pregnant and promised to marry her whether or not she had the abortion, and then he went back on his word."

"But he had a reason!" said Parsons; "she was jealous of the furniture he sat on!" "You keep coming back to that," Kingsley said; "how she was jealous of the furniture. I guess you don't approve of jealousy." "I don't," said Parsons; "I find it frightening." "Well," said Kingsley, "one thing the trial didn't make clear was whether or not she was so jealous before the abortion or only after." "What difference does it make?" asked Parsons; "if she fell to pieces after the abortion, she would have fallen to pieces anyway." "Maybe not," said Kingsley, "maybe if she hadn't gotten pregnant, or if she'd gotten pregnant later, everything would have been fine." "I take people for what they are," said Parsons. "That's fine," said Kingsley; "if you know what they are."

"Do *you* know what they are?" asked Parsons. "At least I give it some thought," Kingsley said. "And?" asked Parsons. "And I see people as bundles of sensory receptors, and some kind of intangible thing wraps around them and gives them a coherence so that when you meet someone you know, you say, I know this person. It is a collection of receptors which has been bent this way and that by its experiences and heredity and you give it a name, Agnes, or Frederick, or Charles. But when it begins to break down because it's sick, and the sensors stop functioning, the personality starts to dissipate and then you see the animal beginnings. The personality burns off, like a morning fog. If you watch someone who's sick long enough, you see the personality burn off altogether. Then what's left are the biological urges and the blind impulses carrying them out.

"Well, in that girl, when biology began pulling on her personality, her self, her soul, whatever you call it, she wasn't strong enough and the fabric ripped. It happens every day. When she tore apart, she committed murder and that's why the whole spectacle came before us. It happens every day. The doctor thought it was a frenzy of the intellect. I don't. I think it was a frenzy of the instincts. It's a miracle every one of us doesn't kill someone in a lifetime. Or in a week. Something as basic as the need to have children, to keep alive one's image—she tried to push that down and the winds came up and tore her apart. And then they tore Jane Holt apart, and before they're through, they're going to tear apart that Holt fellow. You don't think he can lead a normal life after this, do you?" Kingsley asked him.

"If he gets far enough away. If no one knows who he is," said Parsons.

"Do you think he'll ever be normal again?" asked Kingsley; "after watching everything he touched turn stiff and cold? The man must feel like death itself. In his place, I'd feel pretty betrayed by life. I'd feel pretty persecuted myself. He was no fool. He knew what would happen if he went on sleeping with the Dempster girl. He'd gotten another girl into trouble before. He must have wanted children if he didn't learn his lesson after the first time." "I don't know," Parsons said; "maybe you're taking too complicated a view there. Maybe all he wanted was to satisfy his appetites." "Why should one of *her* appetites have been to reproduce herself and his, *only* sexual satisfaction?" Kingsley asked him. "Men want children too. Sometimes more." "I don't know," said Parsons; "I don't know how much men want children." "Whenever I think about how we're too old to have children, it's a grief I can't even begin to describe. It's a death." "But," said Parsons, earnestly, "the worry, the burden, all of that, you must be happy it's over." "No," said Kingsley; "hungers don't go away. I see a woman holding a new baby and I see that melon-shaped head with the veins showing right through the scalp and I want that baby. I want it to soak my best woolen suit with warm, wet urine. That's how it is." "But Martha wouldn't really want another baby," said Parsons; "even if she could have one." "I don't think she'd ever admit it," said Kingsley, "but if one of her children died and she got the grandchildren, she'd think it was a good bargain. For years after her change of life, she'd cry at the sight of a pregnant woman. We're all biological creatures, and the greatest of us know that and work with biology, not against it." "That's what happened to the Dempster girl, according to you?" asked Parsons; "she worked against biology?"

"Oh, she tried," said Kingsley; "and she lost." "That's how I think of it. As if she lost control of a horse. That's when she shot Jane Holt. She was out of control, running wild. And afterward, when she gave in and dressed in black and rocked and put on a veil and came into court like a common mourner, everyone knew what she was mourning for and they mourned with her. But Holt, he kept it up right through the trial, defying the course of nature. You heard the foreman of the jury after it was over. The jury wanted to hang him. And for what? For being unnatural. No, he'll never lead any kind of life after this. He's scarred, just as the doctor said she was."

"But if he doesn't know he's scarred and the others around him don't know it?" Parsons asked; "everyone's scarred in one way or another. He'll do fine." "You want to think that," said Kingsley, "but it's not true. After this, he won't trust anything. He won't be able to. Oh, I know *him*," said Kingsley; "believe me, this trial had three victims and the luckiest one of the three is the one who's dead. Even that Mondell fellow left town after the trial. He didn't do anything, and it was too hot for him here. He couldn't just stay and see what was happening to her and do nothing. He felt guilty, too. He thought he should have prevented it somehow.''

Parsons got up and walked restlessly through the room. ''In court you're always so cheerful,'' he said. ''There,'' said Kingsley, ''I have a measure of control. Not in this last trial, though. It was something someone else set going and all we did was oil it or push it or wind it or kick it, but it went its own way. I told you. We were two shadows on the wall. Don't congratulate me and I won't congratulate you.''

''Why *did* you come?'' asked Parsons. ''Why did you come to me before the trial?'' asked Kingsley; ''we're partners in crime. Between us, we sent that girl to Highbury. We did it together because we couldn't bear to see her die.'' ''At this point,'' said Parsons, ''you usually say that the person in question should have a second chance, a parole or a discharge, whatever.'' ''This time I think I outsmarted myself,'' said Kingsley; ''Doctor Train's not letting her out of there so fast. But there was no one else I could trust to keep her off the gallows.'' ''Maybe there are some people who aren't supposed to have second chances,'' said Parsons. Kingsley looked at him, surprised. ''I think that's true,'' he said; ''I guess Agnes is one of them.'' ''Still,'' said Parsons, ''you never know.'' ''No,'' said Kingsley.

''What are you going to do now?'' asked Parsons. ''Teach,'' said Kingsley; ''I can do less damage in a classroom.'' ''Not true,'' said Parsons. ''I guess not,'' said Kingsley; ''do you want to keep the paper?'' ''No,'' said Parsons; ''you keep it. I have my own copy.''

52

Late Wednesday night, Sheriff Gray, Margaret Eckroyd, and Polly Jenness got in a carriage with Agnes Dempster and drove to the Highbury State Asylum for the Insane. Agnes had quietly packed her few belongings into her leather bag and she didn't object when Sheriff Gray handcuffed her before taking her down to the carriage. When she asked why Miss Eckroyd was coming with her, the young woman said that she had asked Doctor Train if she might continue working with him at the asylum and he said he would be happy to have her. For a while she would share a room with Agnes just as they had shared a room since Agnes had regained consciousness in the hospital.

"They're still afraid I'll kill myself, is that it?" Agnes asked Polly. "That's it," her friend said; "but you'll be glad to have her, anyway." "Yes," Agnes said; "I will." And then she said nothing else.

When they came to the asylum, they helped her out of the carriage, took her into the main building, locked the door behind her, and removed her handcuffs. She was taken to a small isolation chamber, searched, and because of the lateness of the hour, immediately locked in with Miss Eckroyd. The two women slept on the floor.

In the morning, Doctor Train and an attendant came to get them and take them to his office. As they were passing through the halls, a woman came out of her room and blocked their way. Her eyes searched Agnes's face, and finding it unfamiliar or frightening, she cowered against the wall and began shrieking in a high-pitched grating voice more animal than human. Agnes looked at the woman and saw that she was terrified. She held a hand out to her, instinctively, as on the farm she had held out a hand to frightened animals so that they could smell her, watch her move, divine that she meant no harm. But at the sight of

Agnes moving toward her, the woman recoiled as if attacked and began screaming rhythmically, her eyes rolling skyward, and a dark puddle of urine began spreading out in front of her. Horrified, Agnes held out both hands to her, palms up, but the woman screamed louder than ever.

"Don't worry," said the doctor, "she's not really afraid of you. She doesn't even see you. We don't know what she sees." Agnes turned to look at him, and then looked back at the screaming, terrified woman and for the first time seemed to realize what had happened to her. She stood still, her hands outstretched, palms turned up, the sunlight pouring through them and onto the floor, and although she was unaware of it, tears were streaming down her own face.

The screaming woman saw her tears and slowly began moving toward her, gingerly reaching out, edging closer and closer to Agnes, until she touched her face lightly, and then drew her hand back as if burned. But Agnes did not seem to see her. She stood still, the sunlight pouring through her hands, tears streaming down her cheeks, until the doctor led her away from the woman who had been screaming and who was now being led away into another room by one of the attendants.

The woman Doctor Train had watched so carefully day in and day out, who had seemed so at home in the courtroom, seemed utterly disoriented here. She simply stood inside the doorway of his room looking down at the floor, like any dumb beast on its way to the slaughter. Miss Eckroyd, who was standing beside her, was decidedly pale. He was tempted to ask Miss Eckroyd to sit Agnes down in a chair, but he knew from experience that it was a bad business to treat patients as if they were incapable of understanding his requests and complying with them. "Sit down, Agnes," he said. She sat down in the straight folding chair nearest her and stared down at her hands. It was unfortunate, her collision with Mrs. Tarkey in the hall. Still, he had never found a way to gradually and painlessly introduce a patient to Highbury.

"Well, Agnes," he said at last, "you did not hang." "No," she said; "but I wish I had." "You must try and think more brightly," he said; "the court found you irresponsible. If you should recover, you can go back into the world." "I never want to go back into the world," said Agnes. She looked at the doctor and he flushed. "You told the court that I would never recover," she said. "I said that was the probable outcome; there are always exceptions." "Not in my case," she said; "there are never any exceptions for me." He motioned impatiently with his hand.

554

"Don't you consider your acquittal an exception?" he asked her. "Oh, I'm grateful to you," Agnes said; "I know you fought for me even though I'm not worth fighting for. But I know how things are. Even if you decided to let me out tomorrow, I'd have no place to go, not even home. My father's tired of me and he'll die soon, anyway. I was all right when I was sick or dying or in danger of hanging, but he doesn't want me around to remind him I disgraced the name of Dempster." "Well, Agnes," said the doctor, "you don't sound very good-natured or agreeable yourself." "I don't feel very good-natured or agreeable," she said; "anyway, I am thoroughly hardened toward all the world and can endure more heartbreak than ever before or else I should have died years ago."

"Do you really think you are hardened to the world?" the doctor asked. "Yes, I do," Agnes said; "I am." "You weren't hardened to the woman you met in the hall." The girl went pale. "It won't be an easy thing, getting used to being here," he said. He could see the girl's eyes, moving frantically, scurrying, like little animals searching for a place to hide. "What was wrong with her?" Agnes asked. "She sees things," said the doctor. "What things?" asked Agnes. "We don't always know. We know she sometimes sees snakes. We know that when she's in a bad state she doesn't see people for what they are but what she thinks they are. I think she saw you when she touched your face, but it's hard to know. She rarely speaks." "How long has she been here?" "Eight years," said the doctor; "she's gotten a little better. She used to be violent and break up the furniture and we had her in restraint all the time." "How old is she?" Agnes asked. "She's forty-two," said the doctor. "Forty-two!" said Agnes; "she doesn't look twenty." "Well, that happens sometimes," said the doctor; "some patients are impermeable to new experience and their bodies take a lesson from their minds, and everything remains just as it was." "Forty-two," Agnes said again. "More than twice your age," the doctor said, observing her narrowly.

"Is she married?" Agnes asked. "She's married and has three children," the doctor said. "Who takes care of them?" "Her husband and his people," said the doctor. "Do they come to see her?" asked Agnes. "Yes, Agnes," said the doctor; "they do." So the girl was becoming jealous of Mrs. Tarkey. "Then I don't understand," Agnes said; "I don't understand what she has to be crazy about. She was married. She had three children. She ought to have been happy." "It doesn't work out like that," said the doctor. "Wasn't she happy with her husband?" asked Agnes. "They love each other very much," said the doctor. "Even now?" Agnes asked. "Yes," he said. "Then why doesn't he take her home?" "Because she doesn't know what she's doing or whom she's with, and if someone comes in suddenly, and she thinks that person's a snake, she'll go for him with an ax." "But if she loved him and he loved her, why did she go crazy?" Agnes asked. "You thought if you loved someone and someone loved you, you were safe?" the doctor asked. She nodded dumbly. His eyes were distant and his lips tightened.

"It's unfortunate," he said, "that you have to receive an education about human nature here. People are more complicated than you like to think. Mrs. Tarkey was a happy woman all her life, and then one day, her husband came home and found her sitting in front of her three children whom she had tied to kitchen chairs, and brandishing a knife at him, threatening to cut off his nose if he came any closer to her. It took six men to subdue her. To this day, no one knows what went wrong." "Maybe she would talk to me," said Agnes. "Maybe," said the doctor; "maybe not." "When I was on the farm," Agnes said, "I thought the animals talked to me." "If they did, Mrs. Tarkey might talk to you. We think she believes she's some kind of animal." "What kind of animal?" "I have no idea," said the doctor, smiling.

"Do you think it's funny?" Agnes asked. "Yes and no," said the doctor; "a sense of humor has saved more lives than all of medicine. There's nothing wrong with laughing at yourself or other people, either." "I think it's wrong," said Agnes. "You think it's wrong to laugh at people but all right to shoot them?" "Now you're laughing at me," Agnes said indignantly. "Is that so bad?" he asked. "No," she said, watching his face, beginning to smile; "I guess it's not." "It's even fun, isn't it?" he said. "No, it's funny," she said; "it is." "If you found more things funny, you wouldn't be so angry all of the time," he said. "Serious things aren't funny," she said, the smile disappearing from her face. "They're hilarious," he said; "uproarious, comical in the extreme. Didn't people laugh in North Chittendon?" "Not much," said Agnes; "things were always going wrong." "It's something for you to learn," he said. He fell silent, pressed his fingertips together, and studied her over them.

"You know I'm the one whose testimony led them to declare you insane," he said. She nodded. "Your lawyer came by yesterday and he reminded me that I was the only man who

556

could ever let you out of here, assuming that I remain superintendent, of course. I'd have to petition the court to release you if I thought you had become sane and were no longer a threat to yourself and to others, and of course you know I testified that I didn't think that would happen. Your lawyer is afraid that my vanity will blind me to any improvement that may occur in you. Did he speak of it to you?'' She shook her head. ''Well, it weighs on him and it weighs on me,'' said Doctor Train; ''I thought about the trial a great deal. They were after me about the experts, you know, saying I didn't know enough and all the rest of it. So I told your Mr. Kingsley that I would try to get you out of here if I could, but I only knew one honest way to do it, and that was by curing you, and to tell you the truth, I don't think we doctors do very much in the way of curing the insane. The regular environment does that, and the will of the person confined here. You say all you want to do is die.'' ''I do,'' said Agnes; ''I'm very sorry I shot the girl, but I'm not sorry I shot myself. I don't care about living a long time.'' ''If you could see Frank Holt again, would you feel any differently?'' the doctor asked. ''That would depend on what he wanted with me,'' she said.

''He doesn't want anything with you,'' the doctor said; ''he's left Montpelier and no one knows where he's gone, not even that friend of his. He'll never come back. Everyone's sure of that. It's dangerous for him here.'' ''Because of me?'' asked Agnes. ''Yes,'' said the doctor. ''I should have used chloroform,'' said Agnes under her breath. ''As long as you continue to think along those lines,'' said the doctor, ''you must remain here.'' ''Unless I change?'' asked Agnes; ''but I've never been contented. I've always been restless. And I love him as much as ever and I always will and as long as I live, I'll keep his photograph on my mantel or windowsill so that it's the first thing I see in the morning.''

The doctor looked down at a paper on his desk. ''Perhaps its significance will come to change with time,'' he said; ''it will be the same picture, but it won't mean the same thing.'' ''It will always mean the same thing,'' she said. ''What I started to talk to you about before,'' said the doctor, shaking his head slightly as if to clear it, ''was an attempt at treating your illness. It's the newest thing in Austria. It wouldn't hurt you in any way. You would simply come in here and say what came into your mind, and in particular, you would tell me about your dreams.'' ''I don't think I'll have many dreams,'' said Agnes; ''I never do when I don't feel like talking.'' ''Then you can tell me about the

557

dreams you had before," he said; "if you remember them." "Oh, I remember them," she said with a shudder. "What medicines will I have to take?" "There are no medicines," he said, starting to smile; "only the talking." "Are you having fun with me?" Agnes asked. "The idea strikes me as comical," said Doctor Train; "but they say it works. Of course, it can't work if you take to your bed and refuse to get out of it or talk to me or look at the people around you." "Do you think it can work?" Agnes asked. "It might." "Do you think I could be happy?" she asked him; "look at me. I've never been happy. I've always been afraid. If I weren't always afraid, I think I might be happy, even in here. But of course it can't work." "Agnes," he said, "it might work. It might not. Anyway, you can go on loving your Frank Holt and casting aspersions on the rest of the world and you'll still have plenty of time to talk so it shouldn't cost you much." "No," said Agnes bitterly; "all it costs is starting to hope. When I was in the hospital, I swore I'd never get my hopes up again. I don't want to hope." "Then don't," said the doctor.

"Are you married?" she asked him suddenly. "Not anymore," he said. "Why not?" asked Agnes; "is your wife in here somewhere?" "You mean as a patient?" he said; "no. She died two years ago." "Oh," said Agnes. "Well, I'm still alive," said the doctor.

"Look, Agnes," he said, "things could be much worse for you. Everyone here knows I'm taking special interest in your case. It's to be expected. Your friend Polly is here all the time and she has permission to visit you at any hour of the day or night. All you have to do is send for her. I hired Margaret Eckroyd to work here as an attendant and for a while she'll stay with you alone, at least until you get used to things here. Then she'll work on the ward and you'll be part of the ward yourself. I'll do the best I can for you." "Which won't be much," Agnes said. "I told you," he said; "it's your choice. If you give in and start drifting around like the others and find some cloudy sky to drift in where we can't go after you, you'll end up like Mrs. Tarkey. You're only eighteen. You could live sixty more years like the woman you met in the hall. It's up to you." He looked down at his desk and began shuffling papers into a neat stack. "I've told Miss Eckroyd and Polly they're not to worry about upsetting you. They're to talk to you just as they would talk to anyone who wasn't a patient. You have a lot of advantages. But when you walk out of this office, you become part of the asylum. You'll have to learn to take care of yourself, and to do it in here, you have to want to." "Well, I don't," said Agnes; "I've never felt it was up to me, what happened to me." "Well, it is now," said the doctor; "as much as it ever can be." He looked at Miss Eckroyd who stood up and went over to Agnes.

Agnes started to get up, but then sank back down. "When will I see you?" she asked. "Two or three times a week," he said; "depending on my schedule and how many dreams you manage to have. I can't set times because of my schedule here, but you won't be doing anything special." "Where am I going now?" she asked. "For an examination by the hospital physician and for your uniforms." "Uniforms?" Agnes asked. "It's a rule," he said; "too many new patients used to tear their clothes and their families complained. The uniforms are too tough to tear up. After a while, you'll get your clothes back." She nodded at him, blinded by tears.

"Uniforms," Agnes said to Margaret, as they walked down the hall. The walls were painted a sickly yellow, like butter gone rancid. "There are tunnels under all the buildings," Margaret told her, "so that in the winter you can go from one place to another without digging out." "Uniforms," Agnes said again. "Don't make a fuss," Margaret said; "it's not worth it." They went down a narrow flight of wooden steps. "The hospital doctor's down here somewhere," said Margaret. "God," said Agnes; "it's a crypt." "It's not pleasant," said Margaret. "There it is," she said, pointing ahead. They went into a small gray room and sat down and waited while the nurse at the desk stared at Agnes. "Is *she* the one?" the nurse asked Margaret. "Yes," said Margaret. She looked at Agnes. She was staring straight ahead just as she had in the courtroom. "Come in," said the doctor, opening the inner door; "let's get this over with."

HIGHBURY STATE HOSPITAL FOR THE INSANE
Medical Records

AGNES DEMPSTER

Exciting causes: Disappointment in love. Seduction, abortion, and desertion.
Homicidal: yes.   *Suicidal:* yes.
Untidy: no.   *Destructiveness:* no.
Duration of insanity: unknown.
Admitted: August 16, 1899.
Birth Date: December 17, 1880.

Physical Disposition: Left eye rolls up very much. Excessive lachrymal discharge. Left eye has muscle tremor. *Face:* deformed. Left side paralyzed. Left corner of mouth is drooping, and, with effort, is drawn up and does not relax. *Ear:* slight discharge from left auditory canal where bullet was extracted. Right: normal. Still a slight discharge from the pistol ball wound. Ptosis of right eye and absence of movement on the right half of the frontalis—no mystagmus and very slight, if any, anasthesia of the right side. Whole left side, particularly the obicularis, paralyzed, noticeable in framing lips for the word O, attempts at grimacing, etc., and protruding the tongue to the left side and on extreme protrusion, finally getting it onto the median line. Little sensory disturbance. Seems to be purely motor.

Behavior: Well-oriented, cooperative, although has to be treated with extreme consideration. Shows no consciousness of the seriousness of the crime she committed. Threatens suicide and claims she has no wish to live. Refuses to destroy photograph of Frank Holt and will not turn it to the wall, either. Would not look at camera when hospital photographed her.

Was found not guilty of homicide for reason of insanity and was ordered to be placed here by Washington County Court.

When the physical examination was concluded, Agnes was taken into a small cubicle by Miss Eckroyd and there she was handed a uniform and asked to put it on. It was made of a rough green fabric, apparently cotton. "I don't want to wear it," Agnes said, pushing it back. "Put it on," said the nurse, advancing on her. "I'll take care of it," said Miss Eckroyd; "the doctor gave me authority over her." "*I* have authority over the uniforms," said the nurse. "No," said Agnes; "I won't put it on." The nurse raised her hand as if to strike her, and Miss Eckroyd seized her arm. "I'll take care of it," Margaret said. She turned to Agnes, who was standing still, crying. "Put it on," she said in a whisper; "they can lock you up in here alone in the dark if you don't listen." Agnes sank down on the little bench against the wall of the cubicle and began taking off her shoes and then her stockings. "No long stockings here," said the nurse, watching her; "they're dangerous to suicidal patients."

Finally, dressed in her rough, green uniform which fastened in back so that the hands of the patients could not reach the closings and unfasten them, Agnes stood up. The uniform hung on her. Her face had become slightly fuller during the trial, but she still resembled a scarecrow. And Margaret was not used to looking at her straight on. Without realizing it, she usually took up a position to the right of the girl, so that she saw her face without the deformity it presented from the left side or from the front. "You can take her back to her room," said the nurse; "you'll both be in Seclusion Room Two for the next few days. You can come and go whenever you want, but you can't leave the floor. After a while," she said to Agnes, "if you're good, they may let you out on the grounds, and after that, if you're very good, they may let you go into Highbury." "I want some stationery and some stamps," said Agnes. "We'll see about that," said the nurse. Margaret tugged at Agnes's sleeve. "Come on," she said; "don't mind her."

They went back to the tiny room on the second floor of the main building. Its walls were covered with thick mats and the door was five inches of solid oak in which a small, square panel, covered from the outside by a shutter of wood, permitted people to observe the patient in the room from the safety of the hall. "Well, we're here," said Margaret.

Highbury

53

And I was. Standing in the little cubicle, which was just big enough for me to move about in without banging into you, Margaret, walking about, wearing that ugly green uniform, I began to realize what had happened. Margaret, I see I have quite a pile of paper here now, and when I began writing, I was going to write to you as if I were writing a letter because I knew I could talk to you, and as I wrote, I began to tell the story as much to myself as to you, and now that I am coming to the part of my story which you and I figured in together, I want to stop, as I wanted to stop before leaving North Chittendon. Because I know what is coming next. I cannot say I don't want to remember what happened after I entered Highbury, but I am in no hurry to remember. I would rather remember the time I spent with you when I was not there. So if, when I finish this, you are still alive, and you read this letter which has grown into a book, you will, I hope, forgive me for dwelling on this again. It has to be done. Because I am still telling the story, doing my best to remember events as they were, and at that time, you were still strange to me. At that time, I believed myself impermeable to everyone in the world but Frank Holt. But there were people at Highbury who were better and stronger than I was, and you were one of them, and eventually my peculiar eyes, which always focused somewhere beyond the things of this world, came to rest on you and on Doctor Train, too. And as I think of that cell we both shared that first week at Highbury, I wonder how you stood me at all.

Leaning against the padded wall, I felt as if I were coming alive again after the great, long sleep which had been the hospital and the trial. When I closed my eyes against the light pouring in through the barred window of the little room, I saw various scenes from the trial unreeling themselves effortlessly, and I watched the various witnesses climb into the witness box, swear themselves in, and begin testifying. That was what the trial had been like. While I was in the courtroom, my body rocked and my mind floated somewhere in a warm, gray mist. Then, when I returned to my cell at night, I would lie on my bed and the scenes of the day would repeat themselves in front of my eyes and it was as if I were seeing them for the first time. During that time, everyone treated me as if I were a glass beast with a glass mind and a glass heart. No one wanted to say anything that would upset me. The people who testified had upsetting enough things to say but they were not talking to me, not really. The only people who talked to me as if I might resemble other members of the human race were Polly, who I rarely saw, and Doctor Train. I had never met anyone like him before, a person so bluntly honest. Near the end of the trial, you, Margaret, had become freer in your talk, but you were still careful, and I suppose in your place, I would have been the same way.

Now we circled each other in the tiny room as if we were afraid of one another, when really all we were doing was keeping out of one another's way, off each other's toes, elbows out of each other's eyes. And then we got tired, and I sat down in one corner of the room and you sat down in the other, and when we stretched out our legs, we had to maneuver it so that your legs were on top of mine or mine on top of yours. "I'm not sure it was such a good idea," you said, "putting us in such a small room." I said nothing. It was my habit, left over from the trial. Then I fell asleep.

When I woke up, I saw you studying my face. "What *is* it like to commit murder?" you asked. And then I knew the trial was over and that whatever this new life was, it had begun. While I slept, I had slid down onto the floor so that only my head and shoulders rested against the wall. I slid down the rest of the way, propped my head up on an elbow, and faced you. "Well, that's the trouble," I said; "I don't really know. I've thought about it, or tried to think about it, and I can't remember. But I have terrible dreams in which I'm trying to wake someone up and she won't wake up and suddenly I know it's because she's dead and she's dead because I killed her. And in some dreams a dead girl comes alive, and she follows me around and looks the same as she did before I killed her. I don't know. They say I killed her. You change, and everything around you changes, but the dead person stays the way they were when you last saw them. And they keep getting bigger and bigger and more important and you want to start them up again like a watch or something, but you never can. It's so *final*. I didn't realize that. I thought I'd shoot myself and whatever I felt would be the last thing and whatever happened next wouldn't concern me. It never occurred to me that I'd be left standing watch over a battlefield where the corpses were never taken off, where they just lay there, dead and stiff, and no one ever buried them and the smoke in the air from the guns stayed in the air forever. Well, murder. You've done something you can never undo. Life keeps doing things to you that can't be undone, but you're not responsible for what life does. But if you kill someone—it's different. It would be easier for me if I knew for sure," I said; "if I really *felt* as if I killed her, but I don't. I don't remember it at all, so it's impossible. I *can't* really *know* I killed her."

"I was never sure," you said, "whether you really couldn't remember or whether you just *said* you couldn't." "I can't," I said; "I wish I could." "Maybe someday you will," she said. "I don't think I will," I said; "I think that's part of my punishment. Not believing I did what I'm told I did. Because if I really did it, Highbury is what I deserve. Maybe worse. That's how I felt all my life, as if I'd committed a crime and I can't remember it, so it's just as if a nightmare of mine came true. If I killed her, it's just what I deserve." "Oh, I don't know," you said, frowning; "you felt guilty before you ever did anything. What were you being punished for then?" "I don't know," I said; "I never did." I remember sitting near a pond in North Chittendon, watching the ducks swim lazy circles, swimming through the little clouds reflected on the pond's surface, and thinking how beautiful it was and how I did not deserve to see it. And then I was frightened, I had no idea of what, and I went up to my grandmother's cabin and sat on the brass bed in front of her house, and helped her shell peas. And sitting there with her, the peas lying untouched in my skirt while I scratched Sam between his thick ears, his fur warm from the sun, I was happy to be alive again, and again I felt how undeserved it was and I was afraid. "What was I being punished for then?" I repeated; "I don't know. I never did." "But as far as you know, you didn't really do anything wrong?" you asked. "No, nothing," I said. "Then it wasn't fair before, and it isn't fair now," you said. I lay my head down on my outstretched arm.

"Actually," you said, "the way you describe your life before and the way you describe it now sound exactly the same, as if nothing had ever happened to change things." "Maybe nothing did," I said sleepily. "You don't mean that," you said; "what about Frank Holt?" "Frank," I said, seeing him in the dusty, shimmering light of the stone sheds, seeing him turn to me and smile and turn back to his stone, "maybe I dreamed him." "That was quite a dream," you said; "it put you in here." I sat up and looked at you. "Do you think I'll ever see him again?" I asked you. "No," you said; "I don't." "I will," I said; "somehow I will." "What if he's dead?" you asked. "He can't die," I said; "he can't die before me." "Why not?" you asked. "We're meant to stay alive together. We're meant to be together. If we can't be together bodily, our souls will stay together. That's why he can't die before me." "Did you talk to him like that much?" you asked me. "Sometimes," I said. "Well," you said, "I don't know about him, but talk like that makes me nervous." "I always believed that we were specially created for each other, and that there was no one else in the world who could take his place." "That's because you're so young," you said. "How old are you?" I asked. "Twenty-one," you said. "Oh, you're *very* old," I said. "Every year you learn some things," you said.

I stretched and yawned and sat up. "What do you think of that Doctor Train?" I asked you. "He seems like a good man," you said. "Yes," I said; "he does." "It looks like you better do what he says," you told me, "if you ever want to get out of here." "His wife is dead," I said. "I know," you said; "I heard him tell you." "I don't imagine he'll be on the loose long," I said. You looked at me speculatively. "Don't get yourself interested in him," you said; "that's all you need." "Interested?" I said; "he's an old man! He's forty-five! And he's a dwarf." "A dwarf!" you exclaimed; "he's taller than I am, and I'm over five foot seven. Everyone can't be almost six feet tall like Frank Holt. Doctor Train's a fine figure of a man." "Of an old man," I said. "Well, he's a lot older than we are," you said; "that's true." "I wonder what lunch will be like here," I said. "You know," you said, "you don't seem suicidal to me. You don't even seem upset." "Don't tell anyone," I said, "or they'll make you go to work on the ward right away." "You just don't believe you're here yet," you said; "I know how that is."

I leaned back against the wall of the seclusion room and listened to the noises drifting in from outside. Somewhere, a cow was mooing. Then I thought I heard bells and began listening harder. I was sure they were the Montpelier church bells. And then I heard the train whistle at Montpelier Junction, that deep sound of a wounded beast deep in the ocean. Highbury was only eight miles away from Montpelier. "Do you hear the bells?" I asked you. "No," you said, "but I wasn't listening." "We're only eight miles away from Montpelier," I said. "Don't think about escaping," you said; "don't even think about going back. As far as you're concerned, Montpelier's as far away as China." "I might as well be here," I said, "if Frank isn't there." Just then, a brass gong rippled through the halls and into our room. "Lunch," said one of the attendants, sticking her head in.

54

Because it was a warm summer day, the superintendent had set up tables outside, and all of the patients from our building had lunch on the lawn. As we walked up to the tables, I thought how pleasant everything was here, and how it was probably true that I belonged in the lunatic asylum since, so far, at least, I felt more comfortable here than I had ever felt anywhere. And before I had a chance to sit down, Doctor Train stopped me and asked me to come with him to his office. He seemed nervous. I asked him if he was afraid of being alone with me without Margaret, and he said he wasn't afraid at all, but he had something to tell me. "What?" I asked. "Your father died last night," he said; "we just got word. They telephoned the county jail and Sheriff Gray telephoned me." "He's dead?" I asked. "Yes," he said. "You're sure?" I said. "I'm sure," he said, watching me.

He must have been expecting tears, fury, fainting, books hurled through the air. Instead, I felt a remarkable sense of relief, as if an enormous weight had been lifted from the top of my head, a weight which had, all my life, been pressing me down into the earth. Then I was the last of the Dempsters. They were all gone. They could not come after me. "You don't seem upset," said Doctor Train. "I'm not," I said. "Are you relieved?" he asked me. I flushed. "Yes," I said. "Do you know why?" he asked me. "No," I said. "Do you want to go back outside and have lunch?" he asked me. I said I did.

And as I walked back out with him, I thought that I was on my own, at last, and for the first time I felt lonely, lonely in a new way, not as if loneliness were a permanent atmosphere in which I breathed, but as if I finally knew loneliness as the absence of people around me. I thought about my father, sitting in my hospital room day after day, then in the courtroom day in and day out, and decided that he was probably happier to be dead than to be alive. There was no need to feel sorry for him now. He would probably still be alive if I hadn't shot that girl, I thought; if I was going to feel sorry about anything, that's what I should feel sorry about. "Are you sure you want to join the others?" the doctor asked me. I said I was. "I feel like a child again," I said, wonderingly. "Is that good?" he asked. "Yes," I said, "I think it is."

And then I got closer to the patients and saw what they were like and I began walking more and more slowly. One woman at the end of the table sat in front of her filled plate, chewing constantly on her greasy hair. Every now and then, she would shriek, jump back from her plate, and try stabbing at something with the handle of her spoon. I saw that her spoon was wooden and her plate was made of metal. Another woman sat still, her head shaking continuously from side to side. One of the attendants ladled some food onto her plate and she picked up the plate carefully, holding it in both her hands, and emptied it onto her chest. The attendant began to scold her; another attendant came over and scolded the first one, telling her she ought to have known better than to let her feed herself, and now they would have extra work for nothing. Meanwhile, the woman sat still, covered with tomato sauce, grinning fixedly, her head shaking rapidly from side to side. Another woman, so thin her skin seemed barely stretched over her bones, sat in back of her plate, staring at it and crying. As I walked past her, I heard one of the women coaxing her to eat. Another woman was walking down the length of the table, picking up rolls from each plate, and stuffing one after another into her mouth. She was enormous and there seemed to be no end to her appetite. "Insatiable," I thought to myself; "she is insatiable. I wish Frank could see her." And my heart constricted and my eyes burned. When she reached the end of the table, she began her trip again, in reverse, this time picking up all the mugs and draining them of their milk. At the other side of the table, she stopped near the woman who had screamed so when she saw me, and the woman began screaming when she saw her. Mrs. Tarkey. She had touched my face. My hand stole to my left cheek. She was the first person to have touched my face since the shot was fired.

"Do I have to sit down there?" I asked the doctor. Suddenly, my arms and legs were leaden. The color had gone out of the sky. "You have to sit with the rest of them," the doctor said; "you have to get used to it." "But they're wild beasts!" I said. "Margaret," called Doctor Train, and you came over. "She doesn't want to sit with the others,'' he told you. ''Agnes,'' you said, ''it's a lunatic asylum, not a hotel.'' ''I want to sit next to Mrs. Tarkey,'' I said. ''Agnes,'' you said; ''for heaven's sake.'' ''I want to sit next to her,'' I said; ''at least she looks human.'' ''I'll leave her with you,'' said Doctor Train, and he went back into the building.

''Look, Agnes,'' you whispered, ''you can get away with almost anything while I'm here, but the others aren't going to stand for it. Sit down where they tell you to sit down. Listen to them. When they get used to you, then it's time to insist on what you want.'' ''I'll sit next to her,'' I said, and I sat down on the bench next to Mrs. Tarkey. She watched me sitting down and began sliding away down the bench. I sat still, faced front, put my hands on the table and watched her out of the corner of my eye. She was watching me carefully and when she saw I was not going to move off, she began to climb slowly up onto the bench until she was standing on it. It began rocking ominously back and forth. ''Get up, Agnes,'' you said; ''she's going to tip you over.'' ''She can tip me over if she wants to,'' I said, watching Mrs. Tarkey. It was fun; it was like being back in the barn on the farm at home, sneaking in to tame one of the wild horses. Suddenly, Mrs. Tarkey was the most fascinating thing in the world.

And then, without really knowing what I was doing, I began climbing up on the bench myself. It took all of my concentration to maintain my balance, and when I was finally standing, I looked at Mrs. Tarkey, who was staring at me, her eyes wild. And then, her eyes went blank and she stared straight ahead. I decided that, as long as I was standing there, I might as well imitate a rooster and I did. After all, I was supposed to be crazy. ''Agnes!'' you said sharply. I crowed again. Mrs. Tarkey began crowing back. ''Mrs. Tarkey!'' said one of the attendants; ''come down from there!'' Suddenly, the world seemed to have so much space in it. I was exhilarated.

But now we were taking turns crowing and we were well balanced on the swaying bench. I remember thinking that no one could see me now but the sun. The eyes of the people at Highbury didn't count; they couldn't hurt me. I began mooing and waited to see what would happen next. Mrs. Tarkey mooed back. I was beginning to enjoy myself. This was better than taming horses; after all, Mrs. Tarkey was more intelligent than a horse. I neighed like a horse, and Mrs. Tarkey turned toward me, her eyes wide and surprised, and she neighed back, and then the bench turned over and I was falling through the air, and when I fell, I landed on my shoulder and hip. "I hope you're satisfied now," you said. "She's going to be a lot of trouble, that one," said another attendant. "It's only her first day," you said. But I was watching Mrs. Tarkey, who was lying on her stomach, looking at me. I began crawling over to her and she made no attempt to get away. "Why can't we be friends?" I asked her, our noses almost touching; "I can imitate birds. Real birds, not just roosters." Her eyes swiveled inward and she imitated the harsh cry of the blue jay. "They're nice," I said, "but they chase away the other birds." She looked blank and then imitated the sweet, twittery song of the swallow. "Oh, I like swallows," I said; "they used to build nests over our doors at home." She cringed as if I had hit her. "I can imitate a crow," I said; "you do it first." She did.

"What's going on here?" asked Doctor Train, coming up the path. "These two took advantage of the picnic to throw themselves off a bench," one of the attendants said. "Is that true, Agnes?" he asked me. "Yes," I said; "I threw myself off the bench." "Is that why Mrs. Tarkey's on the ground?" he asked me. You started to say something, but I interrupted. "She fell over when I did," I said. Mrs. Tarkey looked at the doctor and cooed like a wood dove.

"They're making animal noises at each other," the attendant said. "Are they?" asked Doctor Train. "Do you want me to stop them?" asked the attendant. "No," he said; "leave them alone. Try and stay on your bench, ladies. Good day, Miss Eckroyd."

"Are you ready to eat, Agnes?" you asked me. I mooed at you. "Don't start that nonsense with me," you said irritably, handing me a plate and a wooden spoon. "But how am I supposed to eat this?" I asked; "I can't cut the meat with a spoon." Mrs. Tarkey burbled like a dove. I looked down at her and saw her pick up a piece of meat, bite into it and tear it into pieces with her hands. I did the same. Eventually, my hands and face were greasy and I looked about me for napkins and realized there were none. At the end of the table, I saw a bucket of water and a portable wooden towel rack. Evidently, we were to finish eating before we washed ourselves off. I watched the mosquitoes circling. There was a green bottle fly circling Mrs. Tarkey. I felt a drop of grease forming on my chin and raised my hand to catch it before it fell onto my uniform. I should have known they would not trust us with knives and forks. We were lucky to have spoons. And then I saw how it would be, or could be, how

573

tearing my meat apart with my hands and teeth would make me less and less human, and how, finally, I wouldn't care how I looked or whether I ever used a knife and fork again.

Already, watching the others eat, they seemed unnecessary things, and in that instant I wanted a knife or fork more than anything else. I put my spoon down and pushed back my plate. I looked down at my lap and saw the rough green weave of the uniform. In the far distance, I could hear the long, sad sound of the train whistle. If I jumped up and ran, would they be able to stop me? I could not get far in my uniform. Everyone in the world knew what I looked like. My picture had been in the papers so often. The green hilltops swelled sweetly around us. Somehow, they had swung into place against me. I knew my eyes were filling. I didn't want to cry. I wanted to convince Doctor Train that I was cheerful, that I was sane, that I deserved to be returned to the world some day. I looked at the women across from me, the woman chewing her hair, the woman shaking her head, the enormously fat woman migrating up and down snatching things from the others, and the ancient terror welled up in me; it had been so long since I had felt it. I forced myself to sit still, not to get up and run, and then I felt a warm hand slowly cover mine, and when I looked down, I saw that Mrs. Tarkey's hand was over mine. I covered her hand with my other hand, and she took her right hand and put it on top of mine, and we sat there, our hands interweaved, until the attendants told us it was time to get up and go back to the building.

When I went back to my little room and took up my place with you, Margaret, I was happy. I was also tired, and after a few minutes of leaning back against the wall, my eyelids, swollen with the sunshine and the sight of the hills and the memory of the insects buzzing like motes in the air, began drooping. Something itched on my right cheek, and when I reached up, I felt a mosquoto bite. So the mosquitoes would be the furies here, I thought; they would be the only furies the asylum let in. I wondered if we would be punished for our adventure on the bench, but I didn't think so. It had been something apocalyptic, standing on the bench like that, making animal and bird noises. I had talked to her. I wondered if I had ever talked to anyone ever before. At least crazy people showed you when they understood. I would have to keep on the good side of the doctor, I could see that. It shouldn't be hard. I wanted to do it. And then I fell asleep.

In the dream, I was back in my house in North Chittendon,

and outside the hollyhocks were standing in front of the house like tall, thin plant people, and I had gone up to my room to take a nap, when I noticed a door near the stove that I had never seen before. I got up to see where it would go. It opened into a narrow passageway, and at the end of the little hall, there was another door, and when I opened that door, I was in a huge, sunny room I had never seen before. It had high, domed trunks scattered all over. Here and there, a fringed lamp cast small, blossomlike shadows on the floor. The walls were not yet plastered and I wondered why the room had never been finished, it was such an interesting room with its magnificent view of the triangular meadow and the many layered mountains beyond. There was another door to the room and I opened it and found myself standing on a beach. I had never been to a real beach before. I had been to the shore of Lake Champlain, but this was an ocean beach. Everything smelled of salt. Huge waves crashed on it and there were strange, convoluted shells everywhere. I picked one up and looked at it. I remembered that once my grandmother had said that somewhere there was a beach of seashells with roses inside them, tiny, black roses, and I turned the shell over. Black sand poured from it. I held the shell to my left ear so that I could listen to the sound of the sea in it, but I could hear nothing. Oh, I thought, that was because I fired the gun using my left hand and so I had damaged my left ear. I picked up more and more shells but there were no more roses inside them. "Sometimes," my grandmother said, "the beach of the seashells with roses inside them is bleached, blasted, and bare."

Then I was in my room in Montpelier and someone had brought me a tall stack of paper and a large inkwell and I was trying to copy out all of a book for the doctor to read. Every time I looked up, there were more people watching me, and as they filled the room, I knew I had to hurry. I wanted to copy the whole book, but people began to come over and pull on my sleeve and I was beginning to make mistakes in my copying. I knew they wanted me to come with them, but I wanted to finish. I went on writing frantically. Finally, some of the men stood up and came over to me, and I gathered up all the pages I had done and hurriedly looked in the box: three hundred and fifty-six pages. Would that be enough? I had wanted to copy more. I was going to take the book I had just made and give it to the doctor. When he saw it was only three hundred and fifty-six pages long, he would not be unhappy. I wished it were twice as long.

I woke up and looked around me happily. You were propped against the wall, Margaret, sleeping with your eyes squeezed shut. I could get up and walk out and you wouldn't know I had gone. But I didn't want to go. I wanted to see the doctor. I was perfectly happy. So this is what justice is, I thought. It's something real. I must be insane or I would not be happy here. And I am going to be happy, I thought.

55

Of course, I was in a new kind of shock, although I did not realize it at the time. For eight months before coming to Highbury, I had been locked in a room with my father or the nurses or you, Margaret; I had been submerged in a kind of silent isolation I did not know existed on this earth. And whenever the routine was interrupted, it was by something terrifying: a medical examination, a head-shaving before anesthesia and surgery, waking in a darkened room, thinking I was blind, feeling my head pound, realizing slowly that the doctors had indeed taken knives to my brain, wondering if, when I tried to talk, I would be able to make any recognizable human sounds, and then when I was sure I was going to breathe and continue breathing, the relief which was torn to pieces by the bitter panic of fear and anger, and after that, the inhuman, white, silent voice with which my whole soul cried out for Frank.

Because when I was in the hospital, and later, when I was on trial, I knew he was there, somewhere in the city, walking around. I never stopped hoping he might suddenly lay down his hammer and chisel, get on the cars, and, without asking himself what he was doing, come in to my room. I knew the nurses had been ordered not to admit him, and I knew my father would try to keep him out, but I saw it again and again: He was in the doorway and he was fighting to reach me.

He never came. And now they said he was no longer in the city and they thought he was living in Canada under an assumed name. In a curious way, I was free. But I still believed I belonged to him. I still thought I was alive so that I could wait for him. But Frank, waiting for Frank, belonging to Frank, all that had rolled up, as if my life were a scroll and I was walking forward on the carpet of paper which was still white, and behind

577

me, what had happened still followed me, but rolled itself under and out of sight. I did not mind. Nothing had been lost.

And then the trial. It was like a storm so thick that everything sank in the encompassing dark and then the lightning flashed, and for a moment, everything was lit up. I remembered Frank appearing in court, taking the stand and looking at me, and it was then that I knew my face was deformed as everyone had been saying it was, and I cried more for myself than for him. Still, I was crying for him, too. I would never have believed he could have made himself so small, that he would lie so. He was better than he seemed, but he would not let the jurors see it. That had humiliated me the most. Of course I seemed crazy, claiming he was the most perfect man on earth when the man who appeared in court seemed so small and mean. Perhaps he *had* become worse; perhaps I had somehow contaminated him. He said I ruined his life. He looked at me as if he hated me. I could not think of him looking at me like that without bursting into tears. At that instant, I wished my heart would stop and never start again. But the heart will not stop easily; it will not let itself be stopped. It chooses its own time.

I remembered the woman who gave me the rose and how she had frightened me just because she was part of the world from which I was excluded. And of course I remembered every expression on Doctor Train's face, every word he said, that I could not have more children, that I would probably never recover, that I had inherited my insanity from my mother and grandmother. None of it had yet penetrated beneath the skin. All Doctor Train's comments, all the testimony of the other witnesses about my mother, my grandmother, about the scalding of my sister, none of it had permeated the skin. What had been said at the trial was still in the air, swarming over me like bees, flying high above my head as I walked, waiting for me to open myself and let them in. I was their queen and for me they would produce my dark honey. Now they flew, secure they would find their place at last. Oh yes, I was still in shock. And because of that, I was happy.

When you woke me up, I told you that I had two dreams, and you looked at me and smiled. I said that I thought I was going to write Doctor Train a note and tell him. "Look, Agnes," you said, your smile fading, "he'll probably want to hear about them. But don't get too used to it, all this attention from him. He's got five hundred other patients. You may be his prize patient, but most of the time you're going to be stuck here with the nurses and the attendants. And he goes on vacations. Try and see things the way they are." I started to laugh. "Why should I?" I asked; "I'm crazy." "That doesn't carry much weight here," you said, but you were smiling. "You know," you said, "that laugh of yours is contagious." "It's the same old laugh." "Well," you said, "I've never heard it before." You asked me if I really wanted to write the doctor a note, because if I did, you would take me down to his office. But you said I ought to think twice before having so much to do with him. After all, he was in charge of the whole asylum. Every decision went through him. He was only human after all, and we all knew *I* was, and what if something should go wrong between the two of us? Then I'd be nailed up in here like someone nailed up alive in a coffin. I said I thought I'd take that chance.

"Don't you think you've taken enough chances?" you asked me irritably. "But he said this was a chance to get well!" I said. "I don't know that I believe there's anything wrong with you, really," you said; "you're moody and you always look on the dark side of things, but half the world's like that." "You don't think I'm crazy?" I asked. "Not really," you said. "Then why did I shoot the girl?" "That's the only part I don't understand."

"Let's go see the doctor," I said, exasperated. I *wanted* to believe I was crazy. If I was crazy, I was not responsible for myself now, and what's more, I never had been. It never occurred to me, not then, to wonder how much responsibility sane people had for their actions. At that time, free will was not a subject I had given much thought. Doctor Train was to change that.

I waited in the hall with you while one of the nurses took my note in to Doctor Train. "Can you come back in half an hour?" she asked you, and then she laughed. "Of course you can," she said. We wandered aimlessly through the halls. "I know what's so strange here," I said. "Tell me," you said; "I'm having trouble putting my finger on all of it at once." "There are no men here." "*That's* what you think is strange? It's an asylum, not a baby factory." I shrugged and looked at the women sitting on the benches lining the side of the hall.

I saw that all the benches were firmly fastened to the walls and floors by enormous metal brackets and screws. "That's ridiculous," I said; "making the fastenings so much stronger than the material the bench's made of. Someone could tear up those benches no matter how big the screws are. They're only soft wood. How tough can wood be?" You asked me if I wanted you to relay my criticisms to the asylum board and I said no, I never knew when I might need a bench. One woman after another sat on the benches, motionless, silent. I stopped in front of one of them. I bent over her and her eyes did not move. Her skin was bluish. I reached out to touch her hand and she did not pull back. Her skin was cold and moist. I stood up and studied her. "She looks like Doctor Train said I would look," I said. "You'll look fine when your hair grows in," you said; "it's coming in now. Little curls. It looks good." "He said I would end up like that," I said, seizing her wrist. You shook your head warningly. I felt the eyes of the ward attendant on us. "You're not going to end up like that," you said; "I wish you'd be more careful about going over to patients here. You don't know what they'll do. Anyway, I'd rather have her around than your Mrs. Tarkey." "*I* like Mrs. Tarkey," I said. "You better watch out for her. That woman is dangerous. You have no sense of personal peril at all. That's your trouble," you told me.

I did not really believe that Doctor Train wanted to hear about my dreams, but in the months that followed, I found I was wrong. When I came in, as I did on that first day to tell him about my dream of the new, undiscovered room and the dream of copying the three hundred and fifty-six page book, he took out a notebook and began scribbling industriously in it. "You take notes without looking at the page," I said. "An old habit left over from medical school," he said.

"Well," I said, when I finished describing the dreams, "are you going to look them up in your dream book and tell me what they mean?" "Dream book?" he asked. "Polly has a book of one thousand dreams," I said. He laughed at me. "*You* have to tell me what the dreams mean," he said. "Me?" I asked; "I don't know. You're supposed to be the doctor." "That's true," he said, "and this is as puzzling to me as it is to you. You're supposed to tell me what you think of when you concentrate on something you saw in the dream." "You mean I should pretend I'm looking into a crystal ball and see something from the dream in it, and tell you what else it makes me see?" "Exactly," he said, sitting back with a sigh of relief. "What should I look at first?" I asked him. "Anything," he said; "it doesn't matter." "You said they do this in Europe?" I asked him. "They're starting," he said; "there's a man named Bleuler there and there are others too." "Europeans are supposed to be very smart," I said. I considered the littered study, the doctor, and the bars on the window behind him. He was as locked in as I was. "All right," I said; "I'm thinking." "About what?" "The book with the three hundred and fifty-six pages." "Oh," he said.

"Well, I suppose I could have meant the book to be all the letters I wrote Frank. I thought one of the letters I did write him was big enough to be a book." "Why would you be giving me Frank's letters?" he asked. "I don't know," I said; "I wouldn't. But some of the letters I wrote . . ." I broke off. "Some of the letters weren't signed," I said, "at least not with my name. I signed them 'More Sinned Against Than Sinning.'" "So the handwriting expert was right," he said; "I always think they're crackpots." "I wish I had the book," I said suddenly, "and could give it to you." "Why would I want to have it?" he asked me. I looked up, stung, but he was regarding me with his usual serious expression. I wanted to tell him that I had never seen a man with such dark eyes, but that had nothing to do with the dream. Only coal was so dark. Or prunes. He would not be flattered if I compared his eyes to prunes. "Because of the number of pages," I said. "The number of pages?" "The same number as in a year," I said; "I think. I can never remember exactly how many days are in a year." "You're a little off," he said; "there are three hundred and sixty-five days in a year." "That's what I meant, then," I said. "You wanted to give me a book with all the days of the year in it?" he said. I nodded. "What year?" he asked.

I stared at him, helpless, my eyes filling with tears. "Last year?" he asked. "Maybe," I said. "Next year?" he asked. "Next year, yes," I said. "You want to give me *your* next year, or do you want to give me another year?" he asked. "Both," I said. Now it was his turn to look puzzled. "Is it a dream about trusting me?" he asked. I said I thought it was. "Is it a dream about someone taking care of you?" he asked; "someone taking care of the story of your life?" I said I thought it was that, too. Doctor Train stopped writing and glanced up at me. "I'll have to give this more thought later," he said. "You mean you want to look it up in your dream book?" I said, smiling painfully. "Something like that," he said; "what about the other dream? The one about the room?"

"Oh," I said; "I don't understand that at all. The room looked just like our attic, but I always knew the attic was there and I was always in it, too. And I don't know what I was doing on a beach. I never saw a real beach. My mother went to Lake Champlain on her honeymoon and my grandmother used to tell me stories about the ocean, but I never went there myself." "Was it a nice beach?" he asked. "Oh, yes," I said, "but it was supposed to have snail shells with roses inside them, and there weren't any. All the shells were empty. She said there would be black roses in the shells." "Black roses," said the doctor. "My grandmother wasn't a very cheerful woman," I said. "Were you happy to find the room?" he asked. "Oh, very," I said; "maybe it was a dream about coming here." "Maybe," he said; "when you were in it, did you think you'd ever been in it before?" "Yes," I said, surprised; "I knew I had." "So you were really going back to some place you'd forgotten about," he said. "I guess," I said. "Maybe," he said, placing the tips of his fingers together as he always did when he concentrated, "you were dreaming about the baby you lost and getting it back." "Oh, that's outlandish!" I said, jumping out of my chair; "there wasn't a baby anywhere in the dream! It was about a room! It had nothing to do with babies!"

"But," said the doctor, "after Frank Holt testified about your relations and about the abortion you suffered, a woman from the audience brought you a dark rose." "It wasn't black!" I cried. I was furious. I felt his eyes on me, those black eyes. "*Your* eyes are black!" I said accusingly. "She gave you the rose to make up for the loss of your baby," he said, "but when you got to the beach, there were no more roses. Maybe it was a dream about not having babies." "It had nothing to do with babies!" I insisted, and then, without warning, I burst into tears which screwed up my face and my eyes squeezed closed and the inside of my nose began to sting. When I finally opened my eyes, I saw the doctor contemplating me from behind his fingers. "Sit down, Agnes," he said. When I could talk again, I asked him if he would hold my outburst against me. "On the contrary," he said. "Well," I said, sniffing, "I wish I knew what I was crying about." "Someday you will," he said. "And will I want to?" I asked him. "I can't say," he replied; "probably you will. Not knowing hasn't gotten you too far up until now."

And so the weeks began to pass. By my nineteenth birthday, Doctor Train asked me if I thought I was ready to go to the ward on the first floor and I said I wasn't. He said I mustn't be afraid of progress, and I said that wasn't it. I was happy where I was. Remember, Margaret, you had been taken off your suicide watch in early November and now worked on the ward as one of the attendants. We still spent a great deal of time together. "If it's Margaret," he said; "if you're afraid of leaving her . . ." I said no, if it was anyone, it was Mrs. Tarkey. And that was the oddity of it. It was plain to everyone that I was becoming more

582

cheerful, less subject to depressed spells, and as I became more cheerful, so did Mrs. Tarkey. When I was on the ward, she followed me everywhere and when I had nothing to do, I followed her. "Why do you follow her?" asked Doctor Train. "I feel comfortable with her," I said. "You know she's dangerous," he said. I made a face. "She is," he said. "That's all right," I said; "she can hurt me if she wants to." "But you don't expect her to, do you?" he asked me. I said I didn't. She wouldn't. She was like one of the animals in the barn. They had never hurt me, either.

"Does she ever say anything?" he asked me. "Well," I said, embarrassed. "You're still mooing at each other then?" he asked. "Mooing and burbling," I said. "A wonderful vocabulary," he said.

It was a ferociously cold winter, and we were often taken through the tunnels to the other building while enough fuel was carried into our building, which was further from the road and always received supplies last. One day as we were going through the tunnel, I felt someone's hand close over my upper arm and looked up to see Mrs. Tarkey. "Snow?" she asked me. "They say about three feet," I said. "So much?" she asked. "Don't worry," I said; "they'll get us out." "I know," she said, and then she burbled at me like a wood dove. That Sunday, when her husband and sons came to visit, she appeared in my doorway with the four men in back of her. She pushed them into my room and then stood in the entrance, smiling at us. "Agnes," she said to them. Her husband turned to her, speechless. In back of him, the boys began to cry. My throat was tightening painfully. "We're friends," I said. "Um," said one of her sons, "does she know who you are?" "I don't know," I said; "I didn't tell her." I turned to Mrs. Tarkey. "I'm Agnes Dempster," I said; "I killed someone. That's why I'm here." She smiled happily. "I think she knows," said her husband; "everyone always knows everything here." "Did you know?" I asked her. She nodded and smiled. Her husband came up to me and took my hands. "I can't say how much this means," he said. I could feel my lower lip beginning to tremble. Mr. Tarkey ushered his wife and sons out and I sat down on the floor and let the wintry sun gather itself in my lap. I had never felt so happy or so virtuous. And I would never have believed that Mrs. Tarkey's behavior would cause my first real argument with Doctor Train.

Early Monday morning, an attendant came for me and took me to his office. "I don't have any new dreams," I said. "I don't want to talk about dreams right now, Agnes," he said; "I want to talk about Mrs. Tarkey." "I know," I said; "it was such a marvelous thing, like spring right in the middle of the winter. I couldn't believe it when she first talked to me." "Why do you think she started to talk?" asked the doctor. "I don't know," I said, "but she thinks we're friends." "So you think she started to talk because of you?" "No," I said, "but she thinks we're friends and she didn't have any friends before and neither did I." "I told you before that she was dangerous," he said, his voice low, tinged with an accent I had never heard before. I saw him, sitting in the witness box, testifying that he had practiced in St. Peter, Minnesota; perhaps that was where the accent came from. "I know you did," I said; "but I don't think she is. Not to me." "If you persist in regarding a dangerous woman, a woman who has attacked attendants over one hundred times with whatever she's been able to lay her hands on, as your own personal possession," said Doctor Train, "then you're still up to your old tricks. You're trying to get yourself killed. You haven't improved in the slightest." I sat stunned, unable to speak. I never wanted to see him again. There was nothing in the world but betrayal. How could I have deceived myself so? "Aren't you going to say anything for yourself?" he asked at last.

"Why should I?" I asked him; "you already know everything about me and what I do and what I think. You can see right through me. Right to the end of my life. To you, I'm no puzzle. You just look through me as if I'm made of glass." "You know that's not true," he said; "you know I'm trying to understand you. That's why we talk about your dreams." "You only want to understand that I'm sick and weak and crazy!" I cried, my voice rising; "you're not interested in the kind of friendship between me and Mrs. Tarkey. You don't want to know anything about it. You're jealous, that's what it is! I know jealousy! I do! You told the court all about how well I know jealousy. You're jealous because after all this time she talked to me and not to you."

"So you think I'm jealous," said Doctor Train. "I don't think you're jealous!" I shouted at him, banging on his desk so that his straight pins jumped in the air like fleas; "I *know* you're jealous! I'd be jealous in your place. It's nothing to be ashamed of," I said sarcastically. "Maybe I am jealous," he said. "What?" I asked. I didn't believe my ears. "Maybe I am jealous," he said again; "I wouldn't dare go into a room with her alone." "It's because she's afraid of you," I said. "Why isn't she afraid of you?" he asked. "Because I can make animal noises," I said. "I'm serious," he said. "So am I." "That's not the only reason," he said; "I could go in there and cluck like a chicken and she'd either climb the wall or try to strangle me." "Well," I said, still refusing to look at him, "I happen to believe that you can talk to someone without words, the way animals talk, and that's how she and I talk to each other. Go ahead and say I'm crazy. I know I'm crazy. That's why I'm here." "I'm not so sure that's crazy," the doctor said. "Then why are you so angry at me?" I demanded; "what did I do?"

"I thought you were treating her like your own private pet," said Doctor Train; "your own private suicide weapon, too. I didn't think it was healthy for either of you." "My own private pet," I repeated, scandalized. "I love her," I said in a whisper. "Yes," said the doctor; "I guess you do. But she's been dangerous in the past. I agree; she seems much better now. But do you have to let her in your room when you're alone? I don't like it." "If I started keeping her out now, what would she think?" I asked; "I'd rather have a bed out on the ward with everyone else." He nodded. And suddenly, I was so terrified I had to hold on to the arms of the chair as if I were afraid it would throw me out and onto the floor in front of the doctor's desk. "What's wrong?" he asked. "I'm frightened," I said. "Because you got so angry," he said; "and because I got so angry. But you see, we're both still here and we're both just as we were." My heart stopped ramming against my breastbone. "Will you still come and talk about dreams?" said the doctor. "Yes," I said. "And I'll listen," he said.

When I got back to the ward, I sat down on my bed. I had been admitted late in August. It was now the end of December. I had been at Highbury for four months. I felt someone sit down on the bed. It was Mrs. Tarkey. She burbled at me and I said the doctor scolded me about something, but it wasn't worth worrying about. She was still frowning. I told her I wasn't leaving the ward and we'd be staying together. She burbled happily. "You know," I said, "Margaret says we can earn money selling our fancywork. If I ever get permission to go into town, it would be nice to have some money. I never want to take any more of my family's money. I know they've left me some but I'm still too young to have it, I think. Even if I had it, I wouldn't know what to do with it. I never thought I'd end up in here," I said; "I should make you something. Would you like that?" She smiled. "What would you like?" I asked her, and then I apologized. I didn't want her to think I was helping the doctors trick her into talking. "Maybe we should make something for your husband," I said; "we could make a smoking jacket, or we could if I could get the material and they'd let me use a pair of scissors. I can get my friend to cut it out for me if they won't. Would you like that?" She nodded. "Will they let me use a needle in here?" I asked. "No," she said. "Maybe they'll let me go out in the pavilion in front of the ward," I said; "they let people sew out there." Mrs. Tarkey looked dubious.

And so the first year went on. Some weeks, I went to the doctor's office three times, other weeks, twice, other weeks every day but Sunday. When I had no new dreams, we talked about my old ones. He was particularly interested in the dream about the bees which, when they swarmed, entered my body through my mouth and nose and eyes, but his favorite dream seemed to be the dream I still continued to have, the dream about the doll's head lying on the white enamel of the kitchen table. "Don't you think it's important," he asked me, after we'd discussed the dream countless times, "that you always dream the same thing? And you always dream that the head is the only thing that matters and that the body's not important?" "It's not that the body's unimportant," I said; "in the dream, I just don't know it's there." "But everyone is telling you it's there," he said. "They see it, I don't," I said; "that's all it means." "Agnes," he said, "when you have a dream, you play all the parts. You read for all the players. All the voices are your voices." "I don't think so," I said; "I think dreams are glimpses of other worlds. They can warn you of what's coming. If you can understand them." "They can also tell you what you're thinking," said Doctor Train; "far down, where you can't really see into yourself." "Then they ought to tell me if I killed that girl." "You know you killed that girl," Doctor Train said irritably. "What is it that's so important about just seeing a doll's head?" I asked; "you can always put a head on a body." "Really?" asked Doctor Train; "has that been your experience in life?"

"Oh, yes it has," I said, losing my temper. "I should bring in my photograph album. There's my head on my grandmother's body, and there it is on my mother's body, and on Majella's body, and finally, they stuck it on mine." "Did you really look so much like them?" he asked. "Yes," I said, "I did. I really did. And everyone said so. Frank took away a picture of my grandmother when he came home to North Chittendon with me because he thought it was a picture of me, not my grandmother.

586

And my grandmother had pictures of Majella mixed in with mine because she couldn't tell us apart except by our clothes, and if we were in family things, like christening gowns, she didn't know which of us was which. My grandmother said the only difference between me and Majella was the color of my hair and my hair was the only thing about me I ever liked."

"But in the dream," said the doctor, "your hair isn't black." "No," I said, "it's not Majella's color, either." "Did you ever really feel as if your head belonged to you?" Doctor Train asked suddenly. "No," I said, "I didn't. It was a borrowed head. Something like a rented house. People had lived in it before and people would live in it afterward." "What people would live in it afterward?" he asked me. I flushed. "Well," I said reluctantly, "if I had children, girls, they would get the same head and have to live in it." "Then their heads wouldn't belong to them, either, would they?" he asked. "No," I said; "they wouldn't." My eyelids were beginning to droop. I had never been so tired. "If your head didn't belong to you," Doctor Train asked, "what did?" "My body," I answered. "Then why don't you have a body in the dream?" he asked me. "It's not me in the dream," I said; "it's a doll." Doctor Train swiveled in his chair and looked out the window.

"If the head doesn't interfere with the body, what happens?" he asked. "Anything can happen," I said in a mechanical voice, from the bottom of the long, deep shaft into which I had fallen. "And will it be the head's fault?" he asked. "Not if the head doesn't know," I said. My voice sounded queer, metallic. "A body could commit murder and the head wouldn't know," he said; "isn't that true?" I nodded groggily. "So there were certain advantages for you in keeping your head and body apart," he said; "your head belonged to them but your body was your own." "And look what it did," I said, my head slipping from my hand, on which it was resting. "It," said Doctor Train; "the body's not an *it*; it's part of you. If you separate the head from the body, you take off the controls. Don't you see that? That's what your bee dream is about." "My bee dream," I said sleepily.

"Are you awake?" he asked suspiciously. "I think so," I said. "Sit up straighter," he said. I made a great effort and pushed myself upright in the chair.

"If you could be any one of the women in your family," he asked me, "which one would you like to be?" "Majella," I said without the slightest hesitation. "Majella was scalded to death when she was only five years old," he said. "But everyone loved her," I said dreamily; "they still do." "Who does?" he asked. "My mother," I said through the gathering dusk which seemed to roll in around me. "Your mother is dead," he said. "No one dies," I said. "Your mother is dead. Majella is dead," he said. I shook my head. "So you were only Majella's head on the wrong body?" he asked. I nodded slowly. "Who do you think you shot when you fired the gun?" he asked. "Myself," I said; "Majella. My mother. My grandmother. All of them. Isn't that right?" It was hard to believe I could be so exhausted, so utterly ennervated, if I was not dying. "Is that right?" I asked again; "did I think I was shooting them?" "I don't know," he said, "but it wouldn't surprise me if you did."

From that day on, I dreamed all the time and it seemed as if the days were not long enough to recite what I had seen while I slept. Doctor Train had taken to giving me books to read and I went back to the ward with a dictionary, St. Augustine's *Confessions,* Sir Thomas Browne's *Hydriotaphia,* novels by Jane Austen, a novel called *Clarissa* about a poor girl who was undone as I had been, but destroyed herself only, books by Mark Twain and Charles Dickens—whatever the man thought would strengthen my mind. He said I had a fine mind but it was in miserable condition; no one would think of staying off a perfectly fine leg for nineteen years and then trying to use it right away, but that was how I had behaved with my mind. And so, when I was not in his office, I was on my bed, under the window, reading a book. When summer came, I was granted ground privileges and took my books outside and read them out there. The world, I was coming to see, was much larger than I had ever dreamed. And the more I read, the less alone I felt. People had gone through all I had and worse. Doctor Train began to give me assignments in Aristotle, and when I said that since I liked Aristotle so much, couldn't I read Plato, he said absolutely not, picked up the book and put it up on his highest shelf.

"What's wrong with Plato?" I asked. "Nothing that's not already wrong with you," he said. So I read Thucydides and Caesar and Plutarch, and one day, Doctor Train came in looking sheepish and handed me copies of *Jane Eyre* and Wuthering Heights. "Well, I don't know about these," he said, handing them over, "but my mother wanted to know what I was doing to a poor nineteen-year-old girl with all those thick books and she said I ought to give you these and if your head was strong enough to hold up under Aristotle, you should be able to weather the wild passions of the Brontes.'' ''The wild passions?'' I asked, looking at him, startled. ''I looked them over,'' he said, flushing; ''they're silly and melodramatic, but my mother loves them and she says you will, too. And I got you this. It's for you to keep.'' He handed me a brand new copy of Rudyard Kipling's *Jungle Book*. I opened it and looked inside. ''It's all about wolves,'' I said, puzzled. ''And about a little boy who's raised by wolves,'' he said; ''I love this book.'' ''I think Mrs. Tarkey would, too,'' I said; ''can she read?'' ''Mrs. Tarkey,'' he sighed; ''I'd transfer you down to the first ward today if it weren't for her.'' ''It's August,'' I said; ''I've been here for a year. Don't you think I'll be ready to leave soon?'' ''We'll see,'' he said. ''Well, I didn't mean today,'' I said. ''Good,'' he said.

In the months that followed, I fell on the Brontes. I read the two books again and again and finally had to ration the time I spent reading them because otherwise I could not finish the other books the doctor gave me. I took my copy of *The Jungle Book* over to Mrs. Tarkey. She looked at the pictures, smiled, and pushed it away. I went back to my bed and began rereading *Wuthering Heights*. Then I picked up *The Jungle Book* and went back to Mrs. Tarkey's bed. Outside, it was pouring and the windows were filled with a poisonous, silvery light. The huge, long room which formed our ward was sinking in shadows. ''I could read this to you,'' I said; ''I haven't read it yet. It's about animals.'' When she didn't object, I began reading the book aloud. After I had read ten pages, I saw that she was beginning to lean over me toward the page and I moved the book toward her. She began running her fingers along the lines and smiling. I grinned happily. ''If I get sick,'' I said, ''you can read to me.'' The familiar cloud darkened her face.

But that was exactly what happened. As if I had called down a curse upon myself, in December I contracted the worst case of influenza in the asylum and I lost my voice altogether. For two days I was out of my head and, from what people said when I woke up, I had been quite hilarious, but when I did awaken, I could not make a sound. Mrs. Tarkey sat on my bed and regarded me sadly. I pointed at my throat and shook my head. I pointed at *The Jungle Book* on the floor and made a little gesture of helplessness with my hands. Mrs. Tarkey bent down and picked it up and I motioned to her to put it back; I couldn't read a word. But she knew that. She opened the book to the chapter where Mother Wolf has to defend Mowgli against Shere Kahn, and she began reading in an odd, rusty voice. When she began, she could not control the volume of her voice, which was either too loud or too soft, and always trembled, but soon she was reading distinctly and was audible throughout the ward. And everyone in the ward sat still as stone and listened to her read.

> Father Wolf looked on amazed. He had almost forgotten the days when he won Mother Wolf in fair fight from other wolves, when she ran in the Pack and was not called The Demon for compliment's sake. Shere Khan might have faced Father Wolf, but he could not stand up against Mother Wolf, for he knew that where he was she had all the advantage of the ground, and would fight to the death.

Just then, Doctor Train came in the far door, saw instantly what was taking place, and walked toward us. I stopped breathing. I didn't know what Mrs. Tarkey would do to him or what he would do to me now that she had started reading aloud, but he waved to me and came and sat down on the edge of my bed, and Mrs. Tarkey, as if she always read sitting on the same bed as the doctor, continued on until the attendants told her it was too dark to go on. She looked at me and I motioned to her, telling her to close the book. Lying in my own bed, the fever almost gone, I thought it was one of the most perfect days of my life. Doctor Train stood up, felt my forehead, and told me to get a good night's sleep.

And then, the next day, when I came in to discuss my dreams, Doctor Train said that he probably should have mentioned it earlier, but he was going on vacation and he would be gone for four weeks. "*Only* four weeks?" I asked sarcastically, as if I had never heard of anyone taking a vacation that lasted longer than three days. "It's partly a working vacation," he said; "I want to go to Germany and talk to some of the doctors there." "Well," I said, as if it were the most natural thing in the world to come out with, "why don't you petition the court to release me so they can decide on it while you're gone?" The silence in the room was absolute. "Petition the court?" he said; "to set you free?" "Yes," I said; "you told me I was much better." "I can't do that, Agnes," he said; "I'm not ready to make that decision." "Why not?" I asked, my voice cold. "Because," he said, "in the course of any disease there are always remissions. More time has to pass before I can be sure you're really better." "Then you won't do it?" I asked. "No," he said, "not yet." "When?" I asked. "I just told you I don't know how long it will take," he said.

"You're angry at me because Mrs. Tarkey was reading," I said. "No," he said; "you know I'm not." I was too furious to say another word.

"You're angry at me," he said. "Because you won't let me go," I said. "Because I'm going on vacation," he said. "I don't care if you go on vacation," I said; "I don't care if you never come back."

"Agnes," he said. I stared at a point above his head. "I'll be back in a month," he said. I didn't answer. I was horrified. He was right, I thought, not about the vacation, but he had made me angry. I hadn't realized how much I'd cared for him. I never wanted to care for anyone—any man—ever again. And now he was going off and leaving me here. I was not going to let him have the satisfaction of seeing how he upset me. "Just because I'm going," he said, "doesn't mean you have to do anything. All you have to do is wait. Waiting does not kill a person." And if he was killed on the trip, I thought? If he changed his mind and decided not to return and the wait never ended? He could be smug and sure. He wasn't locked up within the asylum walls. "I'm not going on vacation just to show you I won't miss you or to remind you who's a prisoner here," he said as if reading my thoughts. "I don't care why you're going," I said. He studied me quietly. "I suppose there's no point in talking to you further today?" he asked. "No," I said. "Your Mrs. Tarkey is making real progress," he said; "you might try holding yourself together for her sake." I left without looking at him.

56

As I walked back to the ward, I saw clearly enough, or thought I
saw, what a fool's paradise I had been living in. The man didn't
care for me. It had all been a pretense, all an attempt to make
himself feel less guilty for having put me in Highbury in the first
place. Outside, the snow was blowing against the windows,
hitting the warm surface of the glass, leaving its wildcat tracks,
melting and snaking down. I sat down and tried to read some of
The Confessions, but the words blurred in front of my eyes.
Perhaps it was only having one eye that worked properly;
perhaps the other one was tired. I picked up *Wuthering Heights*
but could make no sense of it either. Mrs. Tarkey came over and
sat down on my bed. She cawed at me twice. She picked up *The
Jungle Book* and began to read where she always began—at
Mother Wolf's defiance of Shere Kahn. "I don't want to hear
about Mother Wolf or Father Wolf, either," I said, lying down
and burying my good eye in the pillow. And then I began hearing
the story of *Jane Eyre* floating over me. Mrs. Tarkey was reading
about how Jane had left Mr. Rochester and then, far away, heard
his voice calling to her. Mrs. Tarkey's voice, I noticed, had
considerably more expression than before. I sat up, grimly
determined to behave until Doctor Train was out of the asylum.
He thought his presence here was unimportant, did he? He
thought four weeks would fly by? Well, perhaps they would.

But the next day, when you, Margaret, came in and asked me
if I wanted to work on the smoking jacket in the piazza, I said I
thought I'd wait until later. My head hurt. You regarded me
suspiciously, but didn't say anything. In the afternoon, I followed
you out and worked at sewing for half an hour before I had to
retreat from the pounding of my head. You followed me back to
my bed. "I warned you," you said; "I warned you not to get too
attached to that man." "I'm not," I said. "You never got any

headaches or couldn't read until he decided to take a vacation," you said; "and don't think you're the only one. Up and down the asylum, people are going up in smoke." "Who?" I asked. "Everyone. The seclusion rooms are full and we're almost out of restraining camisoles. All the patients depend on him." "If I'm upset," I said, "I'll get over it." "I certainly hope so," you said.

"Margaret," I asked you, "do you remember they promised me I could always call my lawyer and see him even if I was in here?" "I remember. They put a note about that right on your file." "Well," I said, "I want to talk to Mr. Kingsley." "What for?" "I just want to talk to him," I said. "About what?" you asked. "You don't have to know that," I said. "Well, if you don't tell me," you said angrily, "I could just forget to go to the office and tell Doctor Lindstrum you have permission to call your lawyer and I could forget all about telephoning him myself."

"I want him to petition the court," I said, finally; "I want them to let me out." "Agnes!" you said; "after one year!" "A year and four months," I said. "Will you call him?" I asked. You said you would. "It won't do any good," you said; "I know you think Kingsley can do anything, but the only one who can get you out of here is Doctor Train and he's on vacation." "I already asked him," I said. "Oh, Agnes!" you said.

A few days later, one of the attendants came for me and told me I was wanted in the doctor's office. I opened the door, half expecting to see Doctor Train, but instead there was Mr. Kingsley who had made himself comfortable behind the doctor's desk. He got up, beaming, came right over to me and took my two hands in his. "You look transformed," he said; "the doctor told me how much better you were, but I didn't believe it." His thick mane of silver hair caught whatever light there was and scattered it back again like a living star. "Do I really look better?" I asked, suddenly turning shy. "Oh, I know I'll never be what I was, but do I really look better?" "You look like a different person," Mr. Kingsley said; "I wouldn't have recognized you." "How terrible do I look?" I asked; "tell me the truth. It's not that people here don't tell me the truth, but they're so used to looking at me, they don't even see there's anything wrong with me anymore." "That's how it would be outside, too," he said. He studied me. "Well," he said, "it's something to get used to. You can see right away it's not a normal face, it's so stiff on the left side, and the left eye and the right don't really move together, but it's not the kind of face that would frighten anyone.

Maybe make some people nervous, but they wouldn't know why it was that way." "I know I look all right from the right side," I said. "Well, if you try keeping your right side to everyone and hiding the other side, *then* they'll be afraid of you and think you're strange," he said; "it's something you have to live with. Can you?" I said I didn't think my face bothered me much at all. At least now I felt as if my face belonged to me and no one else. Probably because I had created it. I was, I said, my own monster. "No one thinks you're a monster," he said. "They did," I said.

He sat down on the edge of the desk and looked at me. I had forgotten how he filled a room, how he seized hold of the strings which moved you and held you immobile when he wanted you still, and how when he wanted you to move, you moved as he desired. "What is it you want of me?" he asked. I said that Doctor Train had told me he regretted leaving me in an asylum, possibly for the rest of my life, and I was hopeful that he would now petition the court to release me, because, as he could see, I was so very much better. Mr. Kingsley said that if Doctor Train would write a letter in support of the petition, he thought I might have a small chance, but not a good one. It was still too soon after the trial. People still talked about it. I told him that I had asked Doctor Train to petition the court, but he had refused, and I wanted to do so on my own. His face darkened. "That will put you in conflict with Doctor Train," he said; "do you want that?" "I want to be free," I said. "Can't it wait for the doctor's return?" he asked. I shook my head. "I'll do it," he said, "but it's unwise. It won't work. But it will get your hopes up and when the decision is returned against you, you'll be upset. Forget about it." I shook my head again. "All right," he said, taking a paper out of his case; "sign this." ":What is it?" I asked. "The petition to the court," he said; "I knew what you wanted, even before the Eckroyd girl told me."

STATE OF VERMONT

County Court, December, 1900

To the Honorable the County Court next to be held at Montpelier within and for the County of Washington on the 6th day of March A.D., 1901: Agnes Dempster of North Chittendon in the County of Orange and State of Vermont now confined in the State Asylum for the Insane at Highbury, shows and gives this Court to understand and be informed that she was indicted by the Grand Jury of the County of Washington at a term of said Court for the crime of Murder and was duly tried on said charge and acquitted by reason of insanity and that she was ordered by said Court to be confined in The Highbury State Asylum for the Insane, that she is now sane, and asks said Court to order her, said Agnes Dempster, discharged from confinement in the said Highbury Asylum for the Insane and to grant unto her such other and further relief as to law and justice may appertain.

> Agnes Dempster
> Charles P. Kingsley, Attorney

Dated at Highbury State Asylum
December, A.D. 1900

"It looks so official," I murmured. "It's important," Mr. Kingsley said; "the court takes murder seriously."

I sighed and sat back in the chair in front of the doctor's desk; out of habit, I leaned my head on my hand so that it covered the left side of my face. "Does anyone hear anything of Frank Holt?" I asked. "I'm sorry to hear that name," Mr. Kingsley said; "the doctor told me you were getting better." "I am getting better," I said; "I don't think I'll be recovered only when I forget everything that happened to me before I got in here." "The doctor says you've been reading," Mr. Kingsley said. I nodded. "About Frank Holt," I said; "*have* you heard anything of him?" "Only rumors," he said; "rumors that he's gone back to Canada and is drunk most of the time. Not a word about his sculpting or about other women, but a lot of talk about his drinking." I didn't say anything.

"Well," Mr. Kingsley said at last, "I know how you feel there. I feel sorry for him, too." "If only it hadn't happened," I murmured. "But it did," Mr. Kingsley said. "I know it did!" I said angrily; "I don't see why everyone has to remind me of it, as if I'd never been told before!" And after that, we chattered. Mr. Kingsley told me again how much better I looked, and how much better I seemed all together, and he hoped I would continue to improve and perhaps in another year or two, I would be able to take up a life of my own outside the asylum walls. And when I went back to the ward, everything continued as it had before.

Then, two weeks later, I was summoned back to the doctor's office, and by telephone, Mr. Kingsley informed me that the petition had not been granted. It never would be granted, he said, without the doctor's support, and I dropped the phone and ran back to my room.

"Don't run," said an attendant, grabbing me by the arm; "you'll hurt yourself or someone else." "Leave me alone," I said, pulling loose, and ran on down the corridor. "Stop her!" called the attendant, and the two men at the entrance to the ward ran toward me and grabbed my arms. The woman who had first stopped me walked quickly toward me and looked me over. "Just put her back in the ward," she said, her voice tired. They unlocked the ward door and let me in.

I had never noticed how big and empty the room was before, how pathetic it was. Down the center of the room ran a long path created by the footboards of the beds on both sides of it. The beds were arranged in rows on either side of the room, and from where I stood, they looked like cheap headstones. Paupers' graves. All these dark, unpainted metal frames, unpainted because the insane might chew the paint from them and so poison themselves. And, as everyone knew, it was important to keep the insane alive. I went to my own bed and sat down on it. I looked at the little pile of books on the floor next to it. Who cared what they had to say? The lives in those books were as locked in as I was. No one in there could ever changed. The characters in there were all victims of the authors who created them. There was no book in which Cathy was given another chance and lived happily on this earth with Heathcliff. All the books taught one thing: There was only one chance. There was a principle in every life, just as there was in every book, and it ruled more absolutely than any god. Even Aristotle said so. Every being followed its own law. What a fool I had been to try to find a new page, to try to move into a new book.

I was so tired. I pulled back the covers and crawled into bed and when I heard the dinner call, I could not make myself sit up. Mrs. Tarkey bent over me, trying to pull me upright by my arm, and an attendant came over and seized her from behind. "You leave her alone," I said, rousing myself with difficulty; "she was only trying to help me up." "She's sick," Mrs. Tarkey told the attendant, who jumped into the air. She had never heard Mrs. Tarkey speak before. "Is that true?" she asked, turning to me. "No," I said, "but I'm not very hungry." "Get up, Agnes!" Mrs. Tarkey said urgently. It was evident to everyone how much better she was getting. "If you don't eat, they feed you through a tube down your nose," she said. I looked at the attendant. "She's right," she said, her face expressionless. I got up and trailed off to the dining room, dragged there by Mrs. Tarkey's surprisingly firm grip.

57

And of course, I really don't know how it happened. It seems to me now that all important events of my life had their birth in confusion. I remember that after we came back to the ward from the dining room, Mrs. Tarkey came over to my bed and began reading from *The Jungle Book,* and then, for no reason at all, I began making the appropriate animal noises for each of the characters, and we soon had quite a little group around us. I remember the two ward attendants standing there on the edge of the group, smiling, and I remember wondering why I had not seen you all day. Soon the whole collection of us were making animal noises and the smiles flickered on and off the attendants' faces. And then I jumped on my bed and began crowing like a rooster. Mrs. Tarkey put down the book, grinned at me, and climbed up with me and began crowing along. The attendants were still smiling. Cheerful outbreaks were rare.

But then I ran across to the other side of the room, jumped up on another patient's bed, and began mooing like a cow. I looked for Mrs. Tarkey, but she was still standing on my bed, and she was shaking her head. It was an unwritten but inviolable rule in the ward: No one touched another patient's bed without permission. The bed was the only space we could claim absolutely as our own and that was half the threat of being put into the blank cells they called seclusion rooms: We would have to leave our beds behind us. When Mrs. Tarkey shook her head at me, I went wild. I knew she was getting better; she was so much better she would soon be gone, perhaps not next month, or the month after, but soon all the same. And I began leaping from one bed to another, imitating one animal after another. Mrs. Tarkey got up on her own bed and began baaing like a sheep. She didn't want to leave me alone, the center of everyone's disapproving attention.

And still, everything might have been fine if we had not just that day gotten a new patient on the ward, a Mrs. Colomby. From the minute she was admitted, she reminded me of Mrs. Tarkey as I had seen her on my first day and I knew she was terrified of me. Nevertheless, when I came to her bed and saw her lying in it, curled up like a shrimp, I jumped onto the bed and began cawing like a raven. Oh, the result was dramatic enough. I stopped cawing and saw her jump up, stand up on the bed and put out her hands and the next thing I knew, they were closing around my throat and then I saw Mrs. Tarkey, behind her, her arm locking around Mrs. Colomby's throat, and someone was grabbing at Mrs. Tarkey and the noise was deafening. And then everything was silent.

I couldn't have been unconscious for more than a few minutes. When I opened my eyes, I could see people running everywhere; I could hear them screaming, and the ward door was open and attendants were running in from other wards. One of them was advancing on me with a restraining jacket, a "camisole." I tried to get up and run, but I found I could barely get my breath. My throat felt as if it had been crushed.

"She's the one who started it," the ward attendant called to the woman with the jacket, and the two of them came over to me and put it on. Then they dragged me off to the ward seclusion room, pushed me in, and locked the door. I was in the same room I had been put in when I first arrived at Highbury. I knew that I was the only thing in the room. And I knew that, with the doctor gone, the attendants would be in no hurry to let me out even though the doctor instructed them to let patients out for a stroll every three hours. I would be lucky to be out in three days.

I decided to find out how much freedom of motion I had and soon found I had practically none at all. I could roll this way and that through the little room, at least until I was stopped by the wall. The restraining camisole was made of thick canvas and covered me from neck to waist. It looked like a jacket I might have made when I worked, dreaming, for Mrs. James. It did not have a button on it. The sleeves were sewn closed at the ends, and the jacket closed in the back, closed tightly, laced up by thick leather strips. I tried moving my arms in their bags of sleeves and found that the sleeves were tied across each other over my breast so that they lashed my arms into place there. There must be a way out of this, I thought, trying to get to my feet. It was surprisingly hard to stand up with my hands tied. I rolled to the corner of the room and used the wall to help push me up. Finally, I was standing. The little wooden window was closed, and when I went to it and called out, asking someone to open the door, no one answered. I might have known. The walls and door were padded. Sound did not carry from the seclusion rooms.

And then I began to feel an almost unbearable pain. My arms, which were pinned one over the other, were beginning to ache from the shoulders down. Even worse, the fingernails of my left hand were pressing into the soft flesh of my palm. My right hand was trapped so that the thumbnail was cutting into my fourth finger. The pains turned knifelike and began to spread. The left half of my body was on fire, and although I was determined not to cry out, I began to moan and eventually to scream. I thought you would hear me, Margaret, and even if you didn't, you would ask where I was and you would let me out.

But you did not come. No one came for almost twenty-four hours and by that time I was half-mad with pain and hunger and cold. When I breathed out, I could see my breath fogging the air. I had given up hoping that anyone would come, and cried steadily, hoping to die. I rolled backward and forward on the little mattress placed on the bare floor, trying to ease the pain, but the nerves in my body were on fire, and even when I was quiet, they screamed steadily on.

The smell in the room was overpowering. I had always been squeamish about evil smells, and the room was unventilated and the floor was slippery with my urine and the feces I had not been able to contain in my body. Finally, I lay still and when the door opened, I was trying to lose my mind, to go mad altogether, to reach some peaceful place where I was sure the fortunate insane lived, a polar place where everything was white and frozen and nothing ever changed or hurt and where you did not have to choose between a cold, wet floor or a mattress which someone else had drenched with their own fluids and excrement the day before you were put in the room. If I could have torn the skin from my face, I would have. And then the door to the seclusion room opened, and I began to curse at the attendant, and, unbelievably, the door slammed. I rolled back and forth on my mattress. I was losing all sensation in my left arm, but I did not mind. It hurt less that way. Perhaps, I thought, they'll have to amputate it when I get out and then Mr. Kingsley will sue them for me. I tried to sleep, but it was impossible. The pain kept waking me. I had lost all sense of time. I no longer felt hunger.

And then the door swung open and stayed open. "What's going on here?" demanded Doctor Train. "She started a riot on the ward," the attendant said, her voice trembling. "How long has she been in here?" he asked. His eyes were on me, and when I saw them, two black coals, burning as hot as ever, I began to cry softly and could not stop. "Three days," said Mrs. Tarkey; "they didn't let her out at all." "She doesn't know what she's talking about," the attendant said; "she's crazy." "It was three days," Mrs. Tarkey said stubbornly. "I asked them to let her clean herself, but they wouldn't. They didn't bring her any food or water, either."

"Haven't you had any water?" he asked me. I tried to answer but I couldn't speak. I had screamed myself hoarse. "What's wrong with your neck?" he asked, moving toward me. "Did you do this?" he asked the attendant. "What do you take me for?" she asked; "Mrs. Colomby did it." "And where," he asked, "is Mrs. Colomby?" "She's back on the ward," the attendant said; "we had her in isolation for a while." "I want to see you in my office," Doctor Train told the attendant. "Where's Miss Eckroyd?" he asked me, forgetting I could not talk. "She's in the infirmary with influenza," said Mrs. Tarkey. "I see," he said. He told the attendants to clean me up at once and to bring me to his office as soon as they were finished.

I knew what a pitiable sight I was as I sat facing him, and I must have thought his sympathies would work in my favor. Instead, he seemed angry. "So when the cat's away the mice will play?" he asked. I flushed. "You didn't do yourself any good with that performance," he said.

I wanted to tell him that there had been nothing so very terrible in it, that it had come as a shock, realizing I was really locked up in here and could do nothing about it, and that he couldn't and wouldn't help me because he was responsible for me, but I couldn't say a word. I wanted to say that I was sorry I had upset Mrs. Colomby, but that was all I was upset about. I was twenty and I had acted up. They shouldn't have tortured me for three days because of it.

"I guess you'll have something to say about all this?" he asked. I nodded violently. "The attendants said you were getting pretty depressed before you started jumping on the beds," he said; "is that true?" I nodded. "And Mrs. Tarkey dragged you off to supper?" I nodded again. "Mrs. Tarkey is very much better," he said; "it sometimes happens that way in a case like hers. A remission starts up out of nowhere and lasts for years. You know, if she keeps getting better, she can go home?" I nodded. "Is that why you were so upset?" he asked. I shook my head. "Why, then?" I shook my head and pointed at my throat. I had seen myself coming into his office. The long marks on my throat were lilac, purple, green, and yellow. In places, I looked as if I had smeared myself with ink. "Here," he said, handing me a pad and a pencil.

I wrote something and gave it back. "I know I'm here," I wrote; "I know I can't go." "And it comes as a shock?" he asked. I nodded. "I was afraid it might," he said, "but Agnes, you can still win out." I shook my head hopelessly. "You can," he said, "if we keep on with the dreams."

But I knew better. I knew that, for the rest of my life, the familiar black moods would descend on me like rapidly traveling black clouds in a clear blue sky and I would be lost in them until, for no reason, they lifted suddenly, like coffin lids, once again revealing the world. "Will you try?" he asked. I nodded. But I had lost my belief in happiness. Perhaps, I thought, thinking of Mrs. Tarkey, I should settle for usefulness.

I picked up the pad again. "They shouldn't have left me in there," I wrote. "No," he said, "they shouldn't have. But it's harder for them in here than it is for you and sometimes they run wild just the way you do. It's unforgivable but it's understandable." I regarded him dubiously. "I know you were just getting even and acting up," he said; "I saw the petition. I guess you felt you had to do it, didn't you?" I nodded. "And what did you accomplish?" he asked; "you showed yourself that the world is always against you and that you're right to turn on it and attack it whenever you want to. You've got to give it up, that way of arranging life, or you'll never improve." Had I been able to talk, I would have asked to go back to my room. "When you get your voice back," he said, "we'll talk about your dreams."

58

And we did, and the years began to pass, one the same as the other, punctuated by the arrivals or departures of new patients, new incidents, new varieties of outlandish behavior which soon lost their interest and became irritating. But the discussion of the dreams went on. In some of them, I was being attacked by Indians, and then I realized I was an Indian and the others should not be attacking me, and suddenly I caught a glimpse of myself in a jagged piece of glass that served as a mirror, and I saw that someone had marked my back with a cross. And we discussed my profound belief that I had been destined for destruction by the women in my family, and when we finished our discussions, I was still on the ward in Highbury. Although now, five years later, I was on the first ward.

Mrs. Tarkey had recovered less than two years after I arrived, and she was released into the custody of her family. She came to visit me once a month and I cried whenever I saw her, I was so happy. And then she came to visit less often; she saw that her visits were upsetting me because I could not leave as she could. And finally I pleaded with her to keep coming, telling her she was my only hope in the world. She was the only person I knew who had gotten out, and she began to come every two weeks. And then, at the end of my sixth year, I was coming in from the fields and I saw a carriage pull up and Mrs. Tarkey got out and I knew she was not back to visit me. She was on the third ward, the violent ward, and I was soon visiting her with a special guard and when I asked Doctor Train what he thought would happen to her, he changed the subject.

It was, I used to tell her, as I sat by her silent bedside, a new century and we ought to make the best of it. It was 1905. I wanted to ride in an automobile and I wanted her to come with me. I told her you, Margaret, could come with both of us. I rarely saw Polly, although I knew she was on the grounds. To see her was to want to see Frank, and eventually, I found seeing her too painful. By 1905, she had two children of her own and was unlikely to be anywhere near me, although when I walked into the town of Highbury, for I had unrestricted privileges, I had come across her more than once. She was always carrying one child and pushing another. She was happy.

And for long periods, I would be happy, too. I had begun to draw and to paint, as well as to sew, and I did very well at all of it. I sold almost everything I finished. I would read my books, discuss them with Doctor Train, discuss my dreams, talk to Mrs. Tarkey, who was again beginning to improve and who would soon descend to the second ward, and then, without warning, the lethargy would steal over me, and the first sign, the headache, was always the same. Next would come the long arguments with myself over getting out of bed: I had to get up. If I didn't get up now, I wouldn't be dressed in time for breakfast. If I didn't get up soon, they would notice I wasn't getting up. If they did, they would tell the doctor. If I didn't get myself up for breakfast I knew that, by lunch, I would be even worse, even less capable of movement, and during these times, some instinct would wake me a half hour earlier than usual so I had more time to fight myself out of bed.

And then one morning, I would argue and I would not listen to my arguments and I would lie, inert and gray, beyond voices. I understood what everyone said, but I didn't care. And the nurses would shake their heads, pack up my possessions, put most of them away, and I would be transferred up to the second ward. And then, just as suddenly, I would wake one morning, see the sky blue or gray in the window, hear the cowbells from the asylum farm drifting in on the wind, and jump out of bed, and the attendant would take one look at me, go down to the doctor's office, and return with orders to restore me to the first ward. And I might have gone on in that way forever if it had not been for the flood, because Doctor Train showed me my medical records, and every year, when the clerks recorded their summary diagnosis for the year, there was mine, the same each time: unimproved. But in 1907, eight years after I had been committed, the Minawka River and all its tributaries overflowed.

It had been a very rainy October and I rarely went out to walk during the first two weeks of the month. During the last two, I went out all the time, because Mrs. Tarkey, who had again been released, had brought me a mackintosh and a rain hat and I went everywhere, rain or no rain as soon as I persuaded Doctor Train that I would not stand in the middle of an empty field if there was lightning anywhere. By now, I knew that I loved the man hopelessly, but I had also disciplined myself into thinking of him as the father I never had. It was, I often thought, a fragile peace, but it was better than none.

Toward the beginning of November, the weather was beautiful. Overnight, the weather had turned warm, summery, those days when the earth regrets its necessary march forward and protests, stepping back into the last season, and I followed the Minawka River from the asylum into town, and there I saw it had turned into a raging waterfall where it poured in between two cliffs. I looked up and saw the sky was darkening, and since I didn't have my mackintosh with me, started back. I was halfway to the asylum when the heavens opened as if they had been slashed apart and the rain fell as if it were being poured out of enormous iron tubs. The lightning flashed everywhere and the thunder crashed as if it wanted to shatter the earth with its noise. I was already drenched and walked on slowly.

When I went in, I changed into dry clothes and waited for the flood to reach us. I wasn't frightened. Nothing that happened in the world outside the asylum ever frightened me, not in Highbury; we were better taken care of there than any other people on earth. Nothing about us was left to chance. One of the attendants came on duty and said that there were reports of dangerously high water in the village; many of the cellars were filling with water and people were beginning to leave for higher ground. And as she talked, the lights in the ward went off. "I'll go see what happened," I said. I started to go down into the tunnel which connected us to the other building, the one nearer the town, but one of the men stopped me, saying the tunnels were flooding, and the power house was already flooded and they were going to have to cut off the power at once because the pipes for heat and light were in the tunnels.

I went up to the third floor and looked out of the window on the landing. Outside, it was dark, but the lightning lit the landscape every few seconds, and I could see that the earth around us was gone. Our building was standing in the midst of what appeared to be a lake, and little waves broke against the trees, and the currents eddied around them. I thought about the buildings we lived in and decided we were in no danger; the heavy brick buildings of the asylum would not be swept away by a flood. I went back down to the ward.

By six o'clock that night, the staff began moving all the violent patients and all those who were not easily mobile to the fifth floor of the South building, which was our building. And then we heard the wail of a fire siren. It rolled out over the valley and everyone knew what it was. By eight o'clock, we were all rolling out mattresses into bundles and camping out on the upper floors. I went down to the records room to help pack the medical records in cartons and suddenly a man from the town appeared in the doorway and announced that we were to get into a boat he had moored at the doorway to the building, and we were to do so at once. He was afraid, he said, that the foundations of our building might not hold after all, and all the patients were now to be taken out, but he had room for us in his boat, and wanted us to come now. He was on a rescue mission, anyway, he said, and while we were getting ourselves rescued we might as well come along and help.

The office clerk and I got in the wide, awkward rowboat and we began rowing over to the home of one of the farm managers whose house was near the Highbury train crossing. The waters were swirling muddily all around us, and when the lightning flashed, I could see water surrounding all the buildings, and the old asylum cemetery in the forest was covered by the roiling water. As we approached the house of the farm attendant, we saw that his danger was extreme. Time after time, the exits from his house were cut off by the swiftly moving current which seemed to want to tear his house loose and send it spinning off down the river like an enormous top. But it must not have seemed so to him.

From the windows of the house, we could see the man's wife and four of his children. They were hanging out over the windowsills, laughing and waving. The man who had picked us up in the office was shouting the same thing again and again: "It's going to go! Get in! Get in! Grab the rope!" He threw the heavy rope time and again, but it always fell short, and the farm attendant's efforts to reach it were not terribly strenuous. "The water's going to get him," I whispered, unaware I was speaking; "the water's got its hands on the house." "He's got six children in there and his wife," said the man in the boat, throwing the rope again. "He doesn't know what's happening," I whispered. "He thinks he's safe as long as he's in the house," said the man in the boat.

Through the windows and the house's open door, we could see the farm attendant rushing up and down the stairs, trying to carry valuable objects from the first floor upward. "He doesn't think anything can happen to the house!" I said, starting to stand up, but the man in the boat pushed me back down. "We won't be very safe if you tip us over," he said. "Look!" I cried. I could not believe what I saw. The farm attendant, visible to us by the light of the lantern he carried, was trying to push the family cow up a flight of stairs. The cow stared about her, her expression a caricature of bewilderment and surprise.

And then the water had the house and it lifted it up as if it were only a carton filled with human cargo and it carried it off effortlessly, man, children, wife and cow, all gone on a tide of cocoa-colored water. The house sped out of view; there was no going after it. They were gone.

We maneuvered the boat toward another house and heard voices calling for help, but the water was so deep and the currents so strong that we could not get close to them. Later, the lights in their house seemed to be moving away from us and we realized that their house, too, had been swept away. Another man was on the roof of his house, lashing three doors together into a raft, and as we watched, his wife and two children climbed onto it. And then the water took the raft. The man must have decided that the raft was too unstable a craft for his wife to sail alone, and he jumped into the water, held to it, and tried to steer it for the others, but under our eyes, the current tore the raft from his hands, sent it spinning past the asylum buildings, and carried the man off in another direction. We tried to follow him but lost sight of him. Later, when we drifted past the rectory, we found him caught in the upper branches of a tall elm and he caught the rope the man in the boat threw him, freed himself, and climbed down; he fell into the water, and we hauled him into the boat. It was early morning before we were returned to the asylum, and the first thing I saw was the body of the man's wife, the woman who had been on the raft, and nearby, the bodies of her three children.

When I got out of the boat with the file clerk, we knew that the asylum buildings would be safe, and I promised I would go up to the top ward, but I didn't. I could see the water level was falling and that I was in no danger and I went back to my own ward and sat down on my bed. My ward was filled with almost a foot of water, but it never occurred to me to go up higher where it was completely dry. This was where I belonged. And while I sat on my bed, images from the night before kept rising out of the dark waters as out of the darkness of sleep and then sank

607

back again. I saw the immesne wall of debris which had built up between the asylum power house and the auxiliary buildings, crushing a corner of the laundry and then tearing off its north wall altogether. I saw the train which brought supplies to Montpelier stopped on the tracks, and the engineer and conductor climbing from the top of the train up the wire ladder that led up toward the water tower behind the train station. And again and again, I saw the farm attendant in his doomed house, carrying his possessions in his arms, up and down the stairs like an industrious beaver who knew how to build his dam while all the time the water was eating at the very foundation on which everything stood and soon he would be swept away and drowned. And his cow would go with him. The poor cow. That was what happened to animals when they got mixed up with humans. A cow in the fields would have seen the water and started backing away from it and it might have wound up staring at an eagle in its nest on the top of a mountain, but it would not have been swept away. No, only humans were put on earth to turn against nature, to act in defiance of it, either out of stupidity or out of will.

And I thought of the man who had lashed the three doors together to form a raft for his family, and I realized he had dived off hoping to make it more stable for them, hoping to guide it, and I knew that all the people who had died that night had died at their best; there had been nothing selfish about them. Their lives were the negative image of my own. Here I sat, thinking about the flood, and I saw it as a great spectacle, a catastrophe to be sure, but one destined to teach me a lesson: that nothing lasts, not even Highbury, and that I had been foolish to settle for so little when even that little could so easily be taken from me.

But what was I to hope for? My face was ruined. I could not believe a man would ever want me, or that I would ever want a man again. Every morning, I still kissed Frank's photograph and replaced it in my drawer; every night, I kissed it before I went to bed. I still devoutly believed I would see him again. The least I could do was try to be useful. It was the most I could hope for, I had done myself no good and I had done no one else any good, either. Yet I had done much harm.

A man appeared in the doorway. His slicker and rain hat glistened oily black. "You all right?" he asked me. I said I was. He said he was the first of "The Highbury Navy," and that for the next few days, boats would be coming out from the town bringing supplies. He asked me if I didn't want to see the first of the luxury liners which had just docked, and I said I did. I saw a flat-bottomed scow made from six coffins held together by six wooden beams nailed across their tops. "That is impressive," I said. "They'll be getting through from up above pretty soon," he said; "through Copper Notch. Don't worry." I said I wasn't worried.

I went up to see what had become of the second ward. I didn't think any damage had been done there, but I wasn't sure. Upstairs, kerosene lamps had been hung from the walls and their bright yellow light flooded the room. So much had happened in eight years. I was no longer used to the golden glow of the kerosene. I expected the pale radiance of the electric bulb with its funny, wire filaments which glowed dark reddish orange inside the pear-shaped glass. I was accustomed to answering the telephone when I helped in the office. I had even seen Doctor Train mail an article to Vienna in which he described my case, and heard him say that talking about dreams was going to be a common way to cure people someday. And yet I had never used my will, never tried to free myself from the asylum. Not really. I rarely saw Polly. I saw you, Margaret, less and less. You still worked on the wards, but you were married, and I constantly expected you to announce a baby's imminent arrival. You said you thought you would never have them, and although I said I was sure you would, I didn't know. You had been married four years. Occasionally, the doctor gave me permission to stay with you on weekends, but I usually refused to go. I didn't want to intrude upon you. And, as I sat on the bed I had first been given when I came to Highbury, I saw the cow's face, puzzled, confused, amazed in front of me and I thought, I am like that cow, pushed this way and that by anyone who wants to push it. And I thought that the cow permitted itself to be treated so, because, by and large, it was safe and happy with the others. But I had never tried to take control of my own life. Oh, I thought I had when I fell in love with Frank, but really, all I had done was hand the reins to him. And so, eight years after I was committed to Highbury, a flood caused me to realize I had to take my life into my own hands for the first time.

59

Now I never saw Doctor Train without asking him about a release, and he was weakening; I could see it. One day, he said it would be a matter of finding the right person to whom he could release me, but he thought he would be willing to try a parole now, and if it worked out, make it a permanent parole later. Whenever we talked about my desire to leave, he warned me that I would be unprepared for the world outside. It was not that it had changed so much in ten years, he said, but that I had not had to deal with the people in it for a long, long time. I might not know how to behave, or how to defend myself. I might fight back too hard or not enough. But of course I did not listen. All I wanted to do was get out.

Then one day I was walking downtown in Highbury and met Jenny Petty who had once been an attendant at the asylum and I told her I wanted to leave and learn normal life again, and she said she was about to return to Danbury, where she now lived, and she would be glad to take responsibility for me. We went back to Doctor Train's office; he thought it was a fine idea. Mr. Kingsley petitioned the court, and the court approved the petition for a trial parole, stipulating that Mrs. Petty provide weekly reports on my conduct. And the next I knew, I was on a train, sitting next to my suitcase, on my way to Danbury.

It was the middle of July and very hot, and a soft, moist, warm heat permeated everything. Green leaves poured past the train windows. I looked at Mrs. Petty and smiled. She had brought sandwiches and lemonade and I ate happily all the way to Danbury. When we got to the station, I waited for the usual horse and buggy, but instead a high car drove up and stopped. "There's nothing pulling it!" I said, amazed. "You must have seen cars in Highbury," said Mrs. Petty; she sounded annoyed. "Well, yes," I said; "but I never thought I'd get this close to one." As I slid into the front seat of the car and squeezed over to make room for Mrs. Petty, it occurred to me that I did not really know what was expected of me now that I was here. "We'll settle that when we get home," she said.

If I had been unprepared for the car, I was certainly not prepared for the house. It was a tall rectangular house and it was more imposing than any house I had ever seen, even in Montpelier. Its porches were ornamented by carved fretwork. There were porches on the three sides of the house facing the road and one of them was screened in. Above the third floor was an enormous square widow's walk. The house, painted white, resembled a gigantic wedding cake set down on a huge green cloth. Far in back of the house, where the dark green pine woods began, an octagonal gazebo glared brilliantly in the sun. "It's lovely," I said. "Oh, yes," said Mrs. Petty, "you're lucky to be staying here. It's a beautiful house. My husband is very wealthy. Come in." We went in the front door. Light through the little panes of leaded glass patterned the highly polished oak floors. The stained glass windows which glowed at the top of the first floor landing spilled their colors over my toes. The balustrade curved. I had never seen anything so magnificent. "I suppose you want to see your room," Mrs. Petty said, and when I said I did, she told me to follow her. She was a short, extremely plump woman, and by the time we had passed the second floor landing, she was panting for breath and dark patches were showing under the arms of her green traveling suit. "Is it here?" I asked, seeing her pause. "No," she said; "it's on the third floor. It's the only room up there. You'll have plenty of privacy."

She took out her keychain and unlocked a little door and I saw my room was to be what I had taken for the widow's walk. It had windows on four sides, and from it one could see for miles. But in the summer, under the sun, with the heat from the roof seeping down into it, and the heat from the house rising up into it as if it were an iron resting on a stove, everything in it baked and shimmered in front of my eyes. "It's awfully hot," I said timidly. "You can open the windows," she said; "some of them. It cools down at night." I tried to open one of the windows but it would not move. Sweat was pouring down my face and dripping from my chin. "I wouldn't mind something plainer," I said, "if it were cooler."

"Servants always stay here," she said. "Servants," I repeated. The room spun. I had never done well in the heat. "Yes," she said, looking at me, surprised; "surely you know that's why I took you in?'' ''I wasn't sure what my duties were,'' I said. ''Well, come on,'' she said; ''I'll show you.''

And she took me on a tour of the house. It was a grand house and, evidently, I was to clean it all. There were double parlors filled with gleaming mahogany furniture; in one, a grand piano stood, its lid down, covered with a magnificent white silk piano shawl embroidered all over in white roses. I touched it and sighed, thinking of my days at Mrs. James's. The curtains were heavy, green velvet, and the carpets thick and rich, and, I knew, heavy. Everything was polished and scoured. There was no trace of dust anywhere. The whole house shone silver and gold, silver tea things, ornaments, curlicued picture frames, good wood, gold frames, brass platters and candles, and the curtains were tied back with intricate glass flowers. I had never seen such tiebacks before.

''Well,'' Mrs. Petty asked, ''what do you think of it?'' I stood in the second parlor and stared about me. My spatial sense was gone or irrelevant. I was in a room which was utterly filled with objects; there were no spaces between things. Everything in the room seemed to be leaning toward me, ready to fall. This was what Doctor Train had meant, I thought. I was used to the spaces of the asylum, its barrenness, its openness, which I had come to accept as usual, ordinary, *normal*. ''Well, what do you think?'' Mrs. Petty asked again. ''Mrs. Petty,'' I said at last, ''I don't think I can do all this. I'm not used to heavy work. I never did do it.'' ''Well,'' she said, ''that's not all there is to it. There's the laundry, too.'' I didn't say anything. ''Let me tell you something,'' she said; ''I didn't want anyone to help me in the house but my husband insisted I get someone. If you can't do it, that will be fine. You'll just go on back to Highbury and I'll have my own house again.'' But I didn't want to go back. I was determined to try and stay.

Still, from the first supper I ate there, I knew. It had been ten years since I had used a knife or a fork, and when I picked them up, I wasn't sure what to do with them or how to hold them, and when I finally had them in order, I looked down at the table and saw that I had forgotten to put the napkin in my lap and had to put down the knife and fork and begin all over again. I looked up and saw Mrs. Petty staring at me, eyebrows raised, annoyance written all over her. Mr. Petty, a short, round man, with thinning, black hair and a shiny, mottled scalp, mopped his shining brow and smiled at me sympathetically. ''Don't encourage her in her blundering,'' said Mrs. Petty, seeing him smile. The smile sank back down into his face. "Will I be eating with you?" I asked Mrs. Petty. "I don't see any harm in that," she said, looking to her husband for confirmation; "of course, when we finish up, you're to do the dishes." "And after I'm through with the dishes," I asked, "should I go up to my room?" "Yes," she said. I ate little, my old difficulty in swallowing returning to plague me once more. I was conscious of each thing I dropped, of how loudly the knife scraped against the thin porcelain plate when I pressed down on it too hard. I was terrified of carrying the dishes into the kitchen because I might drop them.

Mrs. Petty got up, went into the kitchen, and brought in a cake, bought she said, to celebrate my arrival. My heart sank when I saw she was about to serve it on cake plates and we would eat it with special cake forks. Then she brought out the silver tea service and three coffee cups on beautiful matching saucers. The china was so thin I could see my finger through its shiny skin. I was afraid to pick my cup up, afraid I would hold it too hard and snap it, or not hold it tightly enough and drop it. "Drink your coffee," Mrs. Petty said. I picked up the cup and raised it shakily to my mouth and took a sip. I screamed and dropped the cup in my lap, then jumped up and upset the water goblet in front of me. It fell, spilling its water over the cloth, my dress, and the chair on which I sat.

"*Must* you be so clumsy!" Mrs. Petty exclaimed; "Edward, they told me she was fine!" "I am fine!" I said, my eyes burning; "I'm not used to all these things." "Then you're not fine," she said brusquely, mopping up the water at my place setting, bending down to sop up the water which had spilled onto the rug. "Why don't you both sit down?" Mr. Petty said mildly. "I suppose you're not upset by this?" said his wife, slamming into her seat. She ran the house, that was clear enough. "Eat your cake," she said in a more peaceable voice.

I could see she wanted me to eat the cake, to approve of her largesse, and indeed, I had never seen such a cake. It was a three-layer cake covered in maple icing, and brown swirls decorated every bit of it. More than anything, I wanted to eat that cake, but I knew I would not be able to swallow it. "There are cherries between the layers," she said, mollified by her own generosity. I took a bite of the cake; I couldn't taste it. I might as well have been eating ashes. I forced myself to swallow. "Do you like it?" she asked me. "It's the most delicious cake I've ever seen," I said. "How does it *taste*?" she asked. "Delicious," I said. "She already told you that," said Mr. Petty. I chased the cake around my plate, waiting for them to finish. "Just this once," said Mrs. Petty, "come with us to the parlor before starting on the dishes. After all, it's only your first night." I got up and followed them through the glass doors.

The entire room was furnished in carved pieces upholstered in black horsehair. A dark wine paper covered the walls. From the center of the ceiling hung a huge, crystal chandelier. I could not take my eyes from it. It was like a vision of heaven in the middle of a funeral parlor. "It takes forever to clean," said Mrs. Petty, following my glance; "you have to clean each crystal separately and polish off all your fingerprints. I hope you're not sensitive to ammonia." I said I wasn't. Mr. Petty made some polite comments about the weather, and then, as if at a signal, he fell silent.

"You know, Agnes," Mrs. Petty said, "I remember you when you first came to Highbury. Of course, you look ever so much better how, now that your hair has grown back. I guess it gets in your way when you work." I didn't answer her. How had this happened? The Mrs. Petty I remembered had been a kind, gentle person. What had happened to her? "Where are your children?" I asked suddenly; "visiting their friends?" "I have no children," she said; "this house is my child. It's the only child I need." She was glaring at me with something surprisingly like hatred. "I see," I said. "I doubt it," she said; "I never could have them and now I'm too old. I never had the choice." So that was it, I thought; she was thinking about my abortion. Was everyone in the world destined to be jealous of everyone else?

"You know, Agnes," she went on, "when I was in the asylum, *I* never asked you. I know some of the girls did, but I never did." "Asked me what?" I said; I didn't want to make it easy for her. "During the trial, all the papers said you didn't remember if you shot the girl. Was it true?" "What the papers said?" "No," she said impatiently; "was it true you didn't remember?" "I really don't remember," I said ambiguously. "I don't mean now. I mean then," she said. "I've never been able to remember," I said, "but if it makes you nervous, having a murderess in your house, you should send me back." "Well," she said, looking down at her hands, "there were extenuating circumstances." I sat still, looking at the little cloth-covered button of the love seat on which I sat. I was enraged. I wanted to tear chunks out of her fat, self-satisfied chairs. "But you never acted as if you were aware of how serious a crime you had committed," she said; "when I was there we had to be so *careful* with you or you would get uppity and run to Doctor

Train." "I never complained to Doctor Train about anyone or anything," I said. "Then what were you doing in his office all the time?" she asked. "Talking about my dreams," I said; "he wrote an article about them." "Your dreams," she said, looking at her husband. "You might do some embroidery for me, if you have the time." I looked about me and said I doubted that I would have any time at all.

And I didn't. I had never done such heavy work and I was worn out by it. If there was a way of proceeding that was absolutely ruinous, I was sure to find it. When I was sent into a room to clean off the long white hairs of the angora cat, I used the rags to clean off the hairs and then used the same rags to polish the furniture so that when Mrs. Petty came into the room, the furniture gleamed with furry polish and Mrs. Petty spent the rest of the day undoing my work while I washed the upstairs floors, and when I was finished, their shine was gone and the floors were dull. I had made the water too hot and it had knocked off the gleam of the wax. I knew I couldn't last long, and I told myself that I didn't care, I would find another place, and since it was only a matter of time, I was not to become despondent when the inevitable occurred, as I knew it would.

I had been there three weeks when Mrs. Petty decided that there was nothing that stood upon the floor that I could be trusted with, nothing made of wood which would not splinter in my hands, nothing made of glass that I would not either smear or break. And so she decided that I would do the laundry. She took out a huge cauldron and filled it with water and set it on the stove to boil and then went out and brought in a huge pile of clothes and a long, sturdy wooden cane which she called the stirrer. "I'll put in the soap," she said; "you just drop in the clothes and start stirring them." It all seemed so simple, so easy, so much less work than I had been accustomed to doing. And to my utter surprise, I heard myself saying no.

"What did you say?" asked Mrs. Petty. I said I was sorry, but I couldn't do it. "*Why* can't you do it?" she said, her voice beginning to climb the scale ominously. "I don't know," I said, backing away from the stove; "I just can't." "Are you afraid of the stove?" she asked, advancing on me; "are you?" "Yes!" I cried; "I am afraid!" "You're still crazy as a loon!" she shouted at me; "and you're ungrateful, too. I don't know why I should have expected more from the likes of you, a murderess twice over."

Pure, hot rage, hotter than the water on the stove, welled up in me. The woman's face was coming and going in the fog pouring from the cauldron on the stove, and in terror, I turned and ran out of the kitchen and up the three flights of stairs to my room. I threw myself down on my bed and pounded the pillow with my fists. It was impossible. I could not stay here. After a while, Mrs. Petty came in. "Of course you know you're going back," she said. I said I knew. "And of course you know I've called Doctor Train and told him about your wild and irrational behavior!" "You bitch!" I screamed; "you sterile old bitch!" I picked up a book and threw it at her. She retreated to the safety of the hall, her face white. "And of course I'll tell him about that, too," she said.

And so, by the end of July, I was back at Highbury.

60

And of course Doctor Train wanted to know why I was back. I went through the process of commitment all over again. Again, they took my clothes and issued me the standard green uniform. Again, I was put on the second ward "for observation." As I fell asleep the first night, I looked around me and felt safe and secure. For the first time out, I told myself, I had not done too badly, and even if it had not turned out well, still I had acquired some skills needed for ordinary life. And then I talked to Doctor Train.

"Mrs. Petty described you as deliberately destructive and hostile," he said; "is that true?" "Do you think it is?" I asked him. "I wasn't there," he said. "You weren't there," I repeated; "I've been here for ten years and you've seen me almost every day, and you take that woman's word over mine." "It's not a question of taking anyone's word," he said. I began to rave about how she had made me clean the whole house even though she knew I had never done such work before, and how she never showed me how she wanted things done, so that I was always disappointing her, and worse, disappointing myself, and she made me sleep in a room that was so hot no living thing *could* sleep in it, but when I tried to steal out of the house to sleep on the lawn, she stopped me and sent me back, and if the nights hadn't been cool, I would have perished from heat and exhaustion; as it was, I walked around with a pocketful of rock salt or I was too dizzy to remain upright. She cross-examined me about the day of the murder and what I remembered; she called me names and she as much as told me on the very first day that she hoped I'd go back to Highbury because she wanted the house to herself and had only taken me on because her husband insisted she needed someone, and if he asked me, I thought she'd taken me because she knew I couldn't do the work. No one could, I said, bursting into tears.

"You make yourself out to be quite the martyr," Doctor Train said calmly. "Don't you believe me?" I asked. "Well, I don't know," he said; "when Mrs. Petty was here, she was a much more generous person than the woman you've just described." "The *new* Mrs. Petty," I said bitterly, "is mad at the world because she can't have children." "Perhaps your own experience makes you think that," he said. I stared at him, outraged. "I don't want to discuss it any further," I said; "either you believe me or you don't believe me." "Of course I would like to believe you," he said. "Then believe me," I said. "We'll talk again tomorrow," he said. His voice was tired. I looked at him sadly. He was getting old. Whoever he was, he was not mine. He had no faith in me. I had been wrong to believe he had.

Back on the ward, I laughed and talked with the nurses and attendants. I suppose I didn't really believe I was back, just as, when I first came to Highbury, I didn't realize I was there for as long as they wanted to keep me there. I had returned with my suitcase, and my trunk had not yet been shipped back from Danbury. I felt like a visitor, and in spite of how badly my visit to Danbury had turned out, I had been fascinated by the complex world I found there. Tomorrow, I thought, I would talk to Doctor Train again and he would believe me and then I would try again. And just then, one of the attendants came in carrying my trunk on his back. The minute I saw it, I felt my flesh go cold. "Take it back," I whispered to him. "No, Agnes," he said, "it's yours." "Take it back," I said again. He looked at me suspiciously and I kept quiet. When he put the trunk down, I stared at it and could not take my eyes from it. I didn't dare open it. If I did, I knew what I would see, an empty, black space leading down to a flight of damp steps, the steps proceeding into the earth, endless damp, earthen steps.

"You might as well unpack your trunk, Agnes," one of the attendants said. I remembered the bottle of perfume inside my trunk and decided I had better get ahold of it before anyone became suspicious of me. If the trunk had come back, it meant I was here to stay. How could I have thought it meant anything else? I opened the trunk and found the pink cut-glass bottle of perfume which, under his wife's disapproving eye, Mr. Petty had handed me. I went with it to the head of the bed and pretended to let it slip through my fingers. Then I cried out in disappointment. "I broke my bottle of perfume," I called out to one of the attendants. She made a face, shook her head, and went to get a broom and a dustpan. I took a sharp piece of glass and slipped it into my pocket. When she came back, I helped her clean up the glass on the floor. "Well," she said, standing, "it smells better in here than usual." "I wish I had more bottles to break," I said, and we both laughed.

That night, when everyone was asleep, I slipped the piece of glass out from beneath the pillow case and the mattress and slowly slid my hand up under my gown. I pushed the glass into what I now knew was the birth canal of the vagina. My body cramped against the pain, but my soul, whatever that was, opened petal by petal by petal as the flowers we made in the hospital workroom opened when we dropped them in the water. I took the glass I had used and threw it as far from my bed as I could. And then I felt the warm, steady flow of blood running out between my legs, over my thighs, until I was lying in the warm, welcoming blood. I breathed deeply and felt that when I did the blood flowed faster. I took deep, deep breaths and smiled, knowing the blood was leaving my body. And then I was floating off on a filmy tide and I was asleep.

61

In the morning, I woke up in the hospital infirmary. Something was packed between my legs. Doctor Train was standing over me, pale and frowning. "You suffered a severe hemorrhage last night," he said; "there was clotted blood all over the floor. You almost died. You must have lost over two quarts of blood." I gestured feebly as if I were too weak to speak. "Was it a self-inflicted wound?" asked the doctor. "Can't you tell?" I asked, finding my voice; "you can't trust my answers anyway." "Agnes," he said. "If you want to find out, examine me," I said. "It's too early to examine you," he said; "there's still the danger of infection and further bleeding." "What's everyone doing crowding in here?" I asked him, looking around; "everyone wants to view the menagerie. Let them look at someone else." "Agnes," said Doctor Train, "if you will not tell me whether or not this was a self-inflicted injury, I'll have to tie your hands tonight." "Then tie them," I said.

That night, I was put in a restraining jacket, but one which allowed for considerable movement, and by moving considerably, I managed to rub a band of the jacket against the wound until I succeeded in causing another hemorrhage. When Doctor Train asked me what happened, I refused to answer. That night, I rubbed the band around my wrist back and forth so often and so hard that it cut through the flesh, and in the morning I had to be bandaged. And then Doctor Train called you, Margaret, and we were sent to the third floor, the violent ward, and we were locked up in a seclusion room.

I was not there long. But when I came down, I no longer spoke to Doctor Train. You said you could not understand it, and even I did not know why I had turned so utterly against him. But when he came in, I avoided speaking to him, and if it was necessary to do so, I told the nurses what I had to say, and they relayed my messages to him. For a while, he tried to coax me back into cordiality, but after a month of my inflexible rudeness, he gave up. Soon, my attitude toward the entire medical staff was bitter in the extreme. I was given back all my privileges, but whenever a member of the medical staff attempted to talk to me, I would only say that I would make away with myself should I ever be presented with the opportunity. They soon began to avoid me. I meant what I said, but I also wanted them far from me. I knew they would decide that their influence upon me was not good, and they would leave me alone, and so they did.

And so the years continued to pass. I sketched and painted and sewed. In my twelfth year, you went to live in Oregon where your husband was going to become a tree farmer. You wrote me constantly and I wrote you as often. When I didn't get a letter from you every three days, I would lose my temper and accuse the medical staff of destroying my letters or not mailing the ones I wrote. I no longer had Doctor Train to occupy me. More and more, I thought about Frank and what had become of him and what he would think of me if he saw me now. I began to stop what I was doing and imagine that he could see me as I sat brushing my hair, sewing, lying on my bed, and I tried to imagine what he would think.

And I began to resent other people's visitors, for I had none. When visitors came onto the ward, I would pick up my fancy-work or my sketch pad, and if the seclusion room were empty, sit down on the floor there and work away until they were gone. My father had died the night I had been admitted. I had barely noticed. I had been relieved. Now I was sorry he was dead. I spent more and more time in bed and less and less time on my appearance. And when I had been in the asylum fourteen years, you wrote me and you said you and your husband wanted me to come join you in Oregon, and that was when I began to come alive again. But when I spoke to Doctor Train, he said absolutely not; he would not consider petitioning the court for at least two or three more years. Of course, by then he knew the hemorrhage I had suffered had been self-induced, and in his judgment, I was no longer to be trusted, at least not for a long while.

Doctor Train and I now spoke to one another, but not at length. Occasionally, he would stop me and tell me to come to his office and pick up a book he thought I would like, and I would go get it. I was thirty-four years old. If I had known that it would be six more years before he decided to release me, I would have done away with myself then, but I did not know. I was growing more and more interested in the patients around me, and I was either listening to Mrs. Tarkey's tales of her family, or reading to Mrs. Tarkey on her periodic readmissions to the hospital. When I asked her if she were not bitter at her life which kept bouncing her back and forth between her house and the asylum, she said she wasn't bitter at all. Some people were home all the time but were so sick they never came down from their rooms, and even if they were carried down, they saw nothing worthwhile around them. She did. When the mist lifted, when the bands of the snare relaxed, it was the creation of a new world and she saw it new every time. When she visited, we talked about what she saw when she was admitted, "wild-eyed and raving," which was how she described herself in those states.

"It was just the opposite of what they thought," she told me one December afternoon as the long, thin black shadows stole across the floor; "I wasn't afraid of people *because* they were animals. I wasn't afraid of animals at all, and when I thought people were animals, I wasn't afraid of them. When I started to think someone was a person, not an animal, that's when I got frightened." I asked her if she remembered what she saw when she was "normal" again, and she said she did. It was as if, while she was sick, she saw life two ways at once. She saw the real thing in front of her and she saw her own version of it, and her own was more real. If it wasn't more real, she said, giving it some thought, at least it was more safe. Safer. She said she had liked me because I was the first person who behaved like an animal instead of a person, and what's more, I treated her as if she were an animal. "Animals," I sighed; "we're animals, too." "Deformed animals," she said; "animals with minds." I said I'd always thought the same thing. Without realizing it, I'd reached up to touch the left side of my face. I felt the stiff flesh beneath my fingers. "You know," she said, "I loved *The Jungle Book*. If you hadn't given me that book to read, I don't know if I would have come out of it." "*I* didn't get you that book," I said; "Doctor Train gave it to me."

"Are you talking to him now?" she asked. I said I was. She said I should; he was really a good man, and I didn't understand what it was like to live beneath the burden of responsibility he labored under every day. And from then on, I went to see Doctor Train, and once a week I again discussed my dreams with him.

Finally, the day before my fortieth birthday, he came onto the ward and sat down on my bed. "I've got another letter from

Margaret," he said; "she wants you to come out there before you're both octogenarians." I looked away. "I'm inclined to think it's a good idea," he said. I got up and walked around the bed until I was standing in front of him. "If you're not absolutely serious," I said at last, "I never want you to mention her name again." "See here," he said, "we've known each other for more than twenty years and we've gone through our ups and downs. I think we've done better than we might have considering all the disadvantages I've been laboring under." "What disadvantages?" I asked; "*you've* had all the advantages." "*That's* been my disadvantage," he said, smiling; "all these years, I've had complete power over you and you never liked being told what to do. No wonder you've had trouble with me. You were happy with me when you didn't hang, but then you were angry when I couldn't let you go. In your place, I would have hated me, too." "I never hated you," I said. "Oh, yes you did," he said. "All right," I agreed, "yes. And you've hated me, too." "Sometimes," he said.

"Twenty years," I said; "is my life over?" "That's up to you," he said. "Do you think I'm cured?" "Cured?" he said; "you're as well as anyone else. At least I hope so." "Except for my depressions," I said. "Except for that," he said; "but they're not as violent as they were." "Why now?" I asked him. "A hunch," he said, "that's all." "After all this time, you'll let me go on a hunch?" "Do you want to go?" he asked me. "Will you let me go?" I asked. He nodded. "I want to go more than anything else in the world," I said. "Well, she wants you to come more than anything else in the world," he said.

"What does she want me to do?" I asked. "She doesn't want anything. She just wants you to come." "You know she doesn't have any children?" I asked him. "Don't let it worry you," he said; "Margaret's not like Mrs. Petty. There's only one problem," he said; "we don't know anyone going out to Portland. You'd have to travel out alone—although I'm sure she'd come out here for you, if that's how you'd like it." "No," I said, "I can go alone. Will the court let me go so far?" "On a permanent parole, with a former employee of the asylum, they'd let you go to the moon," he said. I nodded. "You're sure?" he asked. "I'm going to be forty tomorrow," I said; "I better be old enough to get on a train by myself."

"It will take a while," he said, "the petitioning, all of it. She'll have to send the court a written report once a month." "Then it's settled?" I said. "It's settled," he said. "I'll miss you," I said. "I'll miss you, too," he said; "well, we've spent half a lifetime together." "Yes," I said, "half a lifetime. If I had mine to do over, I'd spend my life looking for someone like you." "That's very flattering," he said; "your head's turned by the thought of getting out of here." "That's not it at all," I said, my eyes brimming. "Don't go and get insulted now," he said.

Oregon

62

Although I did not know it at the time, Doctor Train had written in support of my petition, saying that he knew the crime for which I had been committed was an enormous one, and even after twenty years, not easily forgiven, but since I was now forty, I was safely beyond my years of passion and therefore it was highly unlikely that life would once again excite in me such impulses as those which had caused my original troubles. I did not learn that such was his view of things until I arrived in Himalaya, Oregon, where you were living with your husband, Jake Plumly. But you had a copy of the petition and the doctor's letter and you didn't want any secrets between us, and so you showed the letter to me. I said I found it comforting and you said you found it ludicrous.

From the minute your husband's car pulled up in front of your house, I felt I was home. Himalaya, Oregon was actually a good-sized mountain town, and the mountains in which the village nestled reminded me of home. The house in which I now found myself living was a severe, white, high wooden house unadorned by shutters. From a distance, it looked like a child's drawing of a house, perfectly ruled. Inside, the rooms were large and rectangular, and because the village was up so high, and because it was the custom to clear trees from the immediate area around the house, the rooms were very bright. I was given my own room on the second floor, and it opened onto a small balcony which formed the roof over the side door. I put my portrait of Frank Holt up on the mantel, but somehow, once I began living with you and Jake, I began paying less and less attention to it. I was faithful to the picture, but it was the faithfulness of habit.

Jake was working long days at the logging camp and you did volunteer work at the hospital in Portland and I was thinking of joining you there, too. But I was still shy about my face. For a long time, when I went into town, I was sure that everyone was staring at me and that everyone knew how my face had become deformed. Since I did the shopping for the family, I went into town frequently, and I soon realized that people there got used to my face the minute they saw it, and after I was there for a while, I understood why. Men who work in lumber camps lose arms and legs, even noses and ears. I was nothing spectacular. Occasionally, someone would ask me if my eyes gave me any trouble or if the tight muscles on the left side of my face hurt, but they would have asked me about an arthritic knee had I had one. And they were not shy about exhibiting their own injuries. The man who brought the fresh fish hiked up one leg of his trousers to show me the scarring which ran from his ankle to knee. "Burned as a child," he said; "making soap."

And soon I was looking forward to my trips into town. I particularly liked shopping for food; the new methods of packaging were wonderments to me. I loved to buy oatmeal in brightly colored paper cylinders when before, I had scooped up my oatmeal from a huge canvas bag and had transferred it to a smaller bag of my own. And when I first saw loaves of store-bought bread in their bright wrappings I thought they were Christmas presents. Now companies were putting things in cans. I thought of my mother and grandmother, bent low over their cauldrons, cooking in the summer kitchen, stirring the thick fruit slowly turning to jam, pushing their wet hair back with their free hands, and I shook my head. And when I got home, I would begin to cook. When I started in, I must have been a severe trial to you, but within months, you and Jake were complaining about your expanding waistlines and I began dropping various items from the menus I never tired of compiling.

I had been living with the two of you for two years when the butcher shop was sold, and to my surprise, I came in one morning and found myself faced with a large, black-bearded stranger who was sawing up a side of beef. He saw me come in, wiped his hands on his apron, and came over to me. "I guess I look like I've been attacked by Indians," he said. I smiled. "What happened to your face?" he asked me. "Oh," I said, "I should have been more careful, playing with guns." "Well, I guess you should have," he said, inspecting me critically. "It didn't hurt you much, though," he said. "Well," I said, "it did. They had to take the bullet out afterwards and my face was never the same again. I didn't always look like this," I said, and I flushed. I didn't know why I was talking to him about the shot, the operation, or, for that matter, anything else.

"I limp," he said. I said I hadn't noticed. "Well," he said, "I don't walk much in the store." "Why do you limp?" I asked him. "I used to work for the police in San Francisco. I was running down the street after a bank robber and he turned around and shot me in the leg." "Did they catch him?" I asked. "Nah," he said; "I was the only one stupid enough to chase him uphill." "I see," I said. I was smiling.

"Well, what can I do for you?" he asked. "Lamb chops," I said, blushing. "Something about lamb chops that makes you blush?" he asked. "Of course not," I said. "Have you been living here long?" he asked. "Two years," I said; "I live with the Plumlys." "Oh," he said, "they're nice people."

Whenever I came in, we talked in the same way. And then one day he said something about a book he was reading, and I said I was reading my way backward through history, and he proposed that we trade books. They were hard to get hold of, he said, in Himalaya. "Oh, no," I said, "I never lend anyone my books." He nodded as if to say he understood, but I saw that I had hurt his feelings.

Do you remember how I came home and told you about it? It was March and it was unusually warm and we sat out on the front porch inhaling the piny air. "Do you like him as a man?" you asked me. "I suppose," I said; "he's certainly not a woman, not with that beard." "Does he frighten you?" "I don't know why he should," I said. "Just because he's a man," you said. "Oh, well," I said; "men." "You're not still faithful to that Frank Holt, are you? You know he could be long dead." "It's not that," I said. "Then what is it?" you asked; "do you think he'll get blood on your books?" I didn't answer. "I think you can trust yourself," you said; "you're not the same woman you were." "No," I said; "I'm over forty. I'm beyond passion." "That's not it, either," you said; "you're mature. You have some measure of control. That's all any of us have. Anyway, the doctor has a point. Those biological storms you used to worry about so much, they die down a little at forty." "I don't know," I said. "Well, don't start worrying about it now. You have to go into his store almost every day and I'm not ready to consider vegetarianism."

And I found myself coming earlier and earlier, before the other customers, because then I had more time to talk to Mr. Franklin about books, about cuts of meat, about marinating, about more and more, until one day I stopped myself just before mentioning Highbury. And when I did, I realized that I wanted to tell him all about my life before I had come to Himalaya, Oregon, and I went home, frightened, and I was only driven back when we were entirely out of meat and down to the last of our tuna fish and peanut butter. When I finished ordering, he asked me if I would like to go for a walk after church.

I said I didn't even know his first name. If that was the only problem, he said, he'd stop by the Plumlys on Sunday. His first name was Goodrich. "Goodrich?" I asked. "No one ever called me Goodrich," he said. "What did they call you?" "Goody," he said, grinning. I started to laugh; he was such a huge man. He must have been six foot three, and to be named Goody: It was ridiculous. "If you're like everyone else," he said, "you'll go for three months without calling me anything. That's about how long it takes to get used to that name." I said I'd meet him after services and we'd go for a walk. "But I'll bring the food," he said; "I'm a better cook than you are." "How do you know that?" I asked indignantly. "I worked as a cook for years," he said. I said he seemed to have done a lot of things. "Nothing I ever really wanted to do," he said. "Neither did I," I said. "It's different for a woman," he said; "they're not supposed to do anything." "Oh, they are," I said; "certain things." "Well," he said, looking down at the counter, "not everyone manages. There have to be some of us to remind the others of how lucky they are." "Oh, well," I said. He pushed his thick black hair back with his enormous palm and I saw that his eyes were black. "Well," I said awkwardly, "then I'll see you on Sunday."

It was August, still hot, but one of those summer days, which, in a hundred indefinable ways, threatened the loss of the heat and the light, the green canopies fluttering against the roofs, the shedding of the soft, velvety skin of leaves and the return of the black, stark branches against gray skies. The dawn had been pearly gray, streaked with rose, and as the sun sailed up the sky, the goldenrod glowed in the grass as if it had been electrified there. The corn stood, its silken tassels flowing in the breeze, and the cool air touched the skin lightly, cool as a cat's nose. By noon, the light had become the heat of August and everything shimmered in the rippling, golden light. I came out of church, said good-bye to you and Jake, assured you three times that I would see you later, and finally went over to Mr. Franklin.

He was right. I could not bring myself to call him Goody. He asked me if I was a good walker and I said I was. We started on the road which wound above our village and ran along a broad stream. Boats were out on the water, some filled with young girls and their escorts, the girls trying to catch leaves in the water as they sailed by, keeping the boats off balance as girls always did, much to the distress of the rowers, who did not complain but kept rowing. Other boys were fishing, one was paddling about, one angling. The air was warm and soft and the sun only occasionally was concealed by long, thin clouds. We passed a swimming place teeming with small boys; they splashed and shrieked and swam like the others, while the boys on the bank, wearing only their skins and patches of sunshine, ran behind trees and bushes at the sight of us and the boats full of girls.

Once I had been young and now I was not. I had heard other people say that so many times. Usually they asked where the time had gone. But I didn't. I knew where it had gone. I thought I knew *why* it had gone but I wasn't sure. I looked at the boats carrying the girls down the river and shook my head; somehow, it was just that, that innocent happiness, I had been shut away from. "You know," I said, "at home it's very beautiful now." "Isn't it beautiful here?" Goody asked me. "Oh, yes," I said; "it's just that I find myself thinking about home more and more. It's been over twenty years since I've seen it; I don't know why I should be thinking about it now." "It's that time of year," he said. We walked on. He was carrying a large, wicker hamper. "Tired?" he asked me. I said I wasn't. "I come from Nebraska," he said; "I never thought I'd miss it, but sometimes I do. It was so flat. If you found something to climb up on, like a windmill or a water tower, you could pretend you'd see to the end of the earth. I used to work in the wheat fields and keep an eye on the storms moving in. It was beautiful there. A different kind of beauty. When I first saw the sea, it reminded me of Nebraska when the wheat was ripe." I said I'd never been to the ocean; really, I'd never been anywhere. "That's too bad," he said.

We sat down on a flat rock and ate our lunch in the sun. Evidently, we had been walking for a long time; under the cedars, shadows were gathering and bats flew their erratic paths above. The crickets and grasshoppers started up in the grass, and the birds were singing loudly against the setting sun. Down in the valley, the lights of Himalaya were twinkling on one by one. "This is really our supper," Goody said. "I wasn't hungry before," I said. The robin in the tree across the road finished its song and flew off into the dusk. "Margaret and Jake will be worried," I said. "Then let's go back," he said. "It's not that I

want to go back," I said; "it's that I'm not used to freedom."
He looked at me speculatively, but said nothing.

"At home," I said, getting up, "it's all dreaming villages, white steeples in the blue sky, sleeping farms, deep green woods. There are birches there, too. They stand out more in the winter, did you know that? You wouldn't think they would, because their trunks are white and in the winter there's snow and ice everywhere. Right around now," I said, "the ponds start dropping down and there's a wide rim of mud around them. There was a farm I passed on the way to school and it was always reflected in its double ponds. I thought it was such a fine thing, to have a farm with double ponds." "It does sound like a fine thing," Goody said. "All these pebbles in the road," I said, pushing at some with the toe of my shoe.

"You're homesick," he said. "No, I'm not," I said, stung. "That's nothing to be ashamed of," he said; "I think of homesickness as a permanent condition. Everyone always wants back what he first had, whether it was good or bad. First home, first bed, first love, first anything. There's no reason for it. The more time passes, the fancier the frame you put around the picture. Everything that happens to you gets carved into the frame. So the first thing turns out to be simple and beautiful after all. And it doesn't change."

I walked along without saying anything. The moon was full and blue. "Would you live your life over again?" I asked. "You mean if I had to?" he asked. "No," I said; "would you want to live it over again?" "I'd only make the same mistakes," he said. "I don't believe that," I said; "I think some people can learn from their mistakes and not repeat them." "Not me," he said. "You could," I said; "I couldn't."

"No," he said; "I was wild. All I wanted to do was travel. One day, I came home and found my mother standing next to the stove looking at a burned pot and my father was trying to talk her back into cheerfulness—after all, he knew that she could smile when she wanted to—and it just burst over me that when you got married, you were saddled with these vain creatures and all their little worries and all their big ones and if you wanted to have a marriage, you bowed your head until the vertebrae showed in your neck, and the little woman fastened on the yoke, and you had to be a pretty heroic sort of person to take that. I thought I might as well lie down and let a woman put her foot on my throat and crush it because that was how marriage seemed to me. So I traveled all over. I've seen things. Every man I know envies me, or they did envy me. I don't know if they do now. I don't have anything they think is worth having. You only get those things when you lie down and let someone plant her heel right here on the jugular,'' he said, and he tapped his throat. "Hmm," I said. "You're not shocked?" he asked. "By what?" I asked; "by your not wanting to get married? I'm not shocked." "Didn't you want to get married?" he asked me. "Once I did," I said.

You and Jake were up waiting for me in the parlor like the parents of any inexperienced young girl. "Did you like him?" you asked me; "all the men like him." "He seems very nice," I said, taking off my hat and sitting down. "You're not worried about my walking out with a man?" "We think it's wonderful," Jake said. "He reads a lot," I said; "he used to travel and when he was on board ship, he read." "Then you have something in common," Jake said. "Does he know about me?" I asked suddenly. I remember you looked at me, startled. "I'd never tell anyone about you," you said; "if you want to tell anyone anything, that's your business." "I still get gloomy spells," I said thoughtfully. "We all do," Jake said. I smiled, kissed you good-night and ran up the stairs. As I went into my room, I thought I heard you telling Jake it was too good to be true, and I assumed you were talking about what had happened to me. Silly, I thought, getting into bed, to make so much of it.

All through that autumn we continued to walk, and then one night, it was unusually cold and Goody asked me if I wouldn't like to come in and see his house. It wasn't much. It was only a log cabin but it was his and he made good hot coffee with rum. "Rum," I said. "Do you know what it is?" he asked me. "I've heard of it," I said. "Well, come in and smell it, anyhow," he said.

When he closed the door behind us I stood as if I had been nailed to the floor. The walls were covered with stuffed, mounted animal heads. There were bucks and deer, two bears, a boar, and on the floor was a tiger skin. "Well," he said, "what do you think?" "It's like an animal cemetery," I said. "I do a lot of hunting," he said. "I hate hunting," I said; "animals deserve to stay alive as long as they can. If they can." He sat down in a chair whose back was ornamented by two ram's horns. "Sit down," he said. I sat down in a chair whose legs ended in deer feet. "Are those real?" I asked, pointing at them. He said they were. "I used to dream about deer," I said, "trapped in the snow, and when the last one was standing, I had to shoot it."

"It's better than letting them starve," he said. Suddenly, I had nothing to say. I wanted to go home. "I'll go get the coffee," he said. He came back with two mugs.

"What's that funny smell?" I asked him, taking the mug. "Rum," he said; "too much of it and you get drunk." "I'd like to get drunk," I said; "if I knew there was someone around to watch me and see I didn't do anything wrong." "We could try it sometime," he said; "you'd wake up with a rotten headache and your stomach wouldn't settle down for a week, but otherwise you'd be fine." "Still," I said, "I'd like to try it." It was a revelation, that one could do something wild deliberately and not cause any harm.

"Why did you kill all these things?" I asked him. "I don't do it anymore," he said; "only deer for meat. When I was younger, I was a monster. Everything young's monstrous. Maybe I didn't believe they were really alive. I felt good with a gun in my hand. I was the strongest animal on earth. King of the beasts. Haven't you listened to hunters talk? Especially the young ones? Getting back to the natural man? Returning to the primitive ways? They're all the same." "Are you sorry you shot them?" I asked. I couldn't get off the subject. "I'm sorry they died," he said. "So am I," I said; "I was always sorry things had to die. I always wanted a world where nothing died." And so, I thought, sipping my coffee, and choking as it burned my throat, not with its heat but a new kind of burning, the rum, that was what it was, I cared so much about keeping things alive that I had hunted down a young girl and shot her just as he had shot one of these animals. I looked up and found myself gazing into the deep, liquid eyes of a moose.

"I shot someone," I said to Goody; "I killed a girl." "When?" he asked. "More than twenty years ago," I said; "when I was eighteen." "What happened?" he asked. And the next thing I knew, I was telling him everything about it, about the trial, about the asylum, about the parole to Mrs. Petty's, about Doctor Train, about Frank, about everything. And when I finished, he sat still, looking into his cup, refilled our mugs, and brought me another one.

"You've had some bad luck," he said. "None that I didn't make myself," I said. "That's a kind of pride," he said, "taking all the responsibility for your life. It's the other side of saying you don't have any at all."

And then I started telling him about my mother, about how my sister had been scalded to death, how once I had been called one of the Druitt girls, and people had come from all over to draw and sculpt the women in my family, how my grandmother had taken leave of her senses when her husband fell ill and had set up housekeeping in the pigsty, everything. And I began remembering things I had never thought of before, how one day my father had walked out the door saying that he was going into the woods and he would never come back, how I used to sleep in the barn with the cows, what my friend Louise was like, what my school had been like, why I had once thrown a scissor at another girl in my class, and how beautiful the countryside was.

"You always end with that," he said. "It would be a beautiful world," I said, "if it weren't for the people." "The people are such a small part of it," he said. "Except to themselves," I said; "they're never complete alone, the way animals are. They always need someone else." He listened and drank his coffee. "I've always felt like the half-moon," I said, and right then, I felt like it again, like someone floating gently on warm, dark currents; "the half-moon ripped apart from its other half and bleeding into the empty sky, and all the stars..." "All the stars?" he asked. "And all the stars might be the other half of the moon, pulverized and thrown back into the sky." "That's sad," he said. "It's how I've always felt," I said. If he wanted to be rid of me, I wanted him to be rid of me now. "And you?" I asked; "how do you feel? Beneath all of it, the hunting, the butchering, the getting from day to day?" "Sad," he said; "but I don't have the words for it. Not as sad as what you just described, but my life was never as lonely either. Right from the start, there were people around me, and they stayed and were solid. But sad all the same." He started to laugh. "What's so funny?" I asked. "The way you just described my life," he said; "how did I feel between the slaughtering and the butchering and the getting from day to day. You made me sound like Attila the Hun." I smiled and sipped at my coffee. The fire crackled in the fireplace. The flame caught a pocket of sap and sent a sizzle of sparks flying up the chimney.

"I want you to come to bed with me," he said. I put down my mug and stared at him. "But I *told* you," I said, "I told you what trouble it got me into." "You're not the same person now," he said, "and I'm not the same man." "I could still get pregnant," I said. "Please do," he said; "if you don't want the baby, I'll keep it." "You'll keep it?" I repeated. "I'd love to keep it," he said. "Aren't you afraid it would look like me?" I said, my hand sneaking up to my left cheek. "Pistol shots aren't hereditary," he said. "If you got pregnant," he said, "what would you do?" "I'd have the baby," I said. "You're sure?" I said I was. "Would we fight over it?" I asked him. "Why should we fight about it?" he asked; "we'd be having it together." "You don't want to marry me," I said; "not after what I just told you." "I wouldn't mind," he said. "I could never love you as much as I loved—" I broke off, embarrassed. "That's a relief," Goody said. "You wouldn't want me to get an abortion?" I asked; "I don't *think* I can get pregnant, but it could happen." "No abortions," he said. And then I covered my face with my hands and sobbed until my shoulders shook. Goody waited for me to stop. "I'll take you home," he said. "No," I said, "take me to bed."

And I couldn't believe it. It was as if time were spinning back onto its loom, as if, thread by thread, the cocoon in which I had been encased was unweaving, and I was stepping out of it, free and naked and clean and no older than I was before I had entered the asylum. A kerosene lamp hung on the wall and the yellow light of my childhood spilled through the big room. Goody took off all his clothes and lay down on the bed first. I had never seen such a big, hairy body. His chest was covered with thick black fur; his arms and his legs were furry. Hair grew on the back of his fingers. He was like a bear himself. "Don't look," I said, suddenly shy, and I began shedding my clothes where I stood, and then, quivering in the cold, I looked down and saw him in bed and I was quivering, with excitement, with fear, with indecision, with cold, and I couldn't bear it any longer, and I just jumped as if I were jumping into water and landed with my breasts on his chest and my cheek on his. "Well," he said, rolling me onto my side of the bed, "I always say you should build your furniture strong." He reached over and smoothed my hair back from the left side of my face. "I guess they didn't crush the life out of you after all," he said. "They did," I said. "Impossible," he said.

And he began to trace the lines of my body and I could feel myself drawn again on the page of life, once more part of the long, complex story which would end, eventually, in the dark, and I was happy to be alive even if the world was not permanent, even if things would not last forever. "It's not just the face," he said; "there's something beautiful about you. Your nerves are beautiful, that's what it is." And he bent down and kissed me on my triangle of fur.

I discovered that Doctor Train was wrong and that the passions had not burned out. They had been banked all those long, monotonous years and they erupted now. And when I felt him inside me I began to cry the exhausted cry of utter happiness. When had I last felt that way? Not twenty years ago, no. In another incarnation. I wiped my eyes and said I didn't know about his nerves, but everything about him was big, especially his heart. "That's me," he said, "a big, stupid man who likes to cook." I said he wasn't stupid and what's more I loved being there with him; it was like being with a bear in a den and it was a wonderfully safe feeling. I had never known how good it was to feel so safe. "Ah," he said, "better than a grand passion. Safety wins hands down every time." "Safety isn't all I'm happy about," I said. "It's the greatest thing in the world," he said, turning serious, "and you should be happy about it."

After that, we were together constantly. The people of Himalaya took little interest in us, the butcher and the spinster with the paralyzed face. I had worried that you and Jake would write Doctor Train in alarm, telling him that my old troubles had returned and caught me up, but you both said that Doctor Train himself would give his blessing if he saw me with Goody. "Goody," I sighed. "If that name is the greatest cross to bear," you said, "I wouldn't complain." "After all," Jake said, "you can't call him Frank for short." "I never thought of that," I said, surprised. "That's odd," you said, "his last name *is* Franklin."

For five years, he and I went on in that way. I worked in the butcher shop during the day, and at night, I stayed at Goody's. You insisted that my room was to be kept for me in your house unless I married; you wanted me to know I had a place to which I could return. In fact, you said, even if I *did* get married, you would still keep the room for me. You could never tell. We ate dinner with you and you ate dinner with us. When we went to your house, Goody usually came with the main course already prepared. He had taken to baking bread and cakes, and both households were overflowing with food, and on my forty-seventh birthday, you made me a surprise party and invited everyone we knew and I surprised everyone all right; I cried for half an hour.

"You know," you said later, "you might as well be married." "Not yet," I said. "What are you waiting for?" you asked. I said I didn't know; not a child. It was evident I wasn't going to have one. "But you're waiting for something?" you asked, puzzled. I said I was. "He cherishes you," you said softly. "I know," I said. "And you?" you asked. I shook my head and my eyes filled. "Don't scare up trouble everywhere," you said; "everyone's bad luck comes to an end. Everyone has one chance at least once in a lifetime." "I already had mine," I said; "twenty-five years ago." "No," you said, "that was just the opposite of a chance. Now you have a chance."

And I suppose I would have married him if Jake hadn't come home one day, burning with fever. When you called the doctor, he could find nothing wrong with him, and when he was taken to the hospital in Portland, none of the doctors there could find a cause for it. So you brought him back home again, and I watched you watch him begin to die. Then one night I fell asleep and dreamed about the deer, and again they had all strayed into one meadow and the heavily falling snow had cut them off and my father told me we had to shoot them, and we shot at them until only one was standing, and the one who was left was a stag and his antlers were huge and he turned his head and looked at me. "Shoot," said my father, and I said no, I would not shoot, and a shot rang out behind me and the stag fell. My father had shot him. And when I woke up, I was crying and I was desolated beyond comfort. Goody sat on the edge of the bed, waiting for me to stop, but I did not stop. Finally, he got up and got dressed and then came over to the bed, laid me down on it, and covered me. "Get some sleep," he said. I fell asleep, and when I woke up, I didn't get out of bed. When he came home, I was sitting in the chair with the four deer feet. "I'm going back to Margaret's," I said.

He couldn't understand it, and for a while, neither could I. But I could not do otherwise, and as time passed, I saw I could not live with the fear of losing him to illness or accident, to the erasing hands of chance and time, so busy in the world. Perhaps my talks with the doctor had cured me after all, for I no longer suffered from the deep, paralyzing depressions which had haunted me throughout my stay in the asylum, but I had not been cured of my fear of chance, that random principle of chaos loose in the world.

Goody and I had talked and talked, and I had felt the thousand little threads which bound me to the past unraveling, and now, at last, I saw myself as I was, a lovely enough thing, but a thing which had been deeply cracked, something like a beautiful china cup which had been mended so that it appeared to be as good as new but could never really be restored to what it had been. The crack was there. Under pressure, I would split. Or so I thought. I was not certain. But everything in me cowered before the danger. I don't know why. I had my second chance, and some mystery of my character would not let me take it. I could not take the chance that the crack, as real as the fault lines they found in the California coast, would widen and swallow either or both of us.

So I went back to your house. Goody and I continued to talk, even to see each other on occasion, but our meetings were painful, and eventually he decided to move on to another town. And it was curious, how little I minded and how deeply I mourned. Because I knew it was necessary. I knew I could not have what other people took for granted because I could not stand to lose what other people could both hold and surrender, while I, like a claw, could only hold on.

63

And I helped you nurse Jake through his last illness and that took two years, and when he died, I was forty-nine. You were fifty-two. And after Jake's death, the two of us seemed to change places. You were the one who lay in bed, crying, unable to move. I was the one who exhorted you to sit up, to brush your hair; I was the one who read to you, who made you laugh. I developed mad passions to see the Portland Opera House, to go on an escalator or in an elevator, a trolley, anything which would get you out of the house, and, for a while, out of Himalaya. The courts had finally released the money my grandmother had left for me, deducted the cost of keeping me in the state asylum, and the sum left over was still considerable. They sent it to you, who were still considered my conservator, and you handed it over to me, and I spent as much of it on you as I could. You came back to life slowly, and when you did, you were not the same. You were like a leaf left out in the sun to dry.

We sat on the rockers, rocking in our wicker chairs, and we talked about our childhoods. Now, when I talked about my mother and grandmother, I did so to amuse you. They were becoming mythical figures to me, and as I talked to you, I began to invent new adventures for them. We talked about our childlessness and how unhappy we were not to have had children, and I said I probably ought not to have had them; the women in my family had shown no talent for raising anything but vegetables, and you said I was not like them. I would have done a good job. "No," I said; "they wouldn't have been safe with me. They would have been safe with you."

And they would have. You were one of the truly remarkable people of the world; your soul was clear as glass. You saw it and knew what you were. You saw the world, too, and knew what to ask of it. After your husband died, you only asked for what you could have, and what you could have was what you wanted. You had not lost the pure, simple relation of the beast to its world. I loved you.

"You know," I told you one day, "when I was living with Goody, I told him that if I had a baby, and neither of us wanted it, I would have given it to you. At the time," I said, "I thought giving the baby to you was a good enough reason to get pregnant." You started to cry. Once we got together, we seemed to have a great deal to cry about. "I'm coming around to your way of seeing things," I said; "the Fates must have looked kindly on me when they sent you to my hospital room." "They were good to both of us," you said. And so, in the winters, when we did not do volunteer work in the small hospital in Salem, we rocked near the wood stove in the kitchen or sat on the porch, looking at its gray, weathered boards.

It was a warm, simple animal contentment I rocked in, and it went on for a long time. And when I was sixty and you were sixty-three, arthritis began to steal over you, gnarling your hands and feet, settling in your hip joints so that it was harder and harder for you to move, and I looked at you and thought how odd it was, how you had always exuded a calm that partook of the vegetable and the animal at once, and now you looked like a creature slowly turning into a twisted, gnarled tree. And for a long time, you fought against the disease because you wanted to stay with me, but it was getting harder and harder for me to get you in and out of your wheelchair and your bed. And finally, I knew you were tired of the sturggle, and if it weren't for me, you would go into the Portland Retreat for the Aged. Many of the people you had worked with were already there. I was keeping you in Himalaya with me. I knew you would never leave while I stayed.

One day, we were rocking on the porch; we were great rockers, the two of us. "Margaret," I said, "I want to go home. I'm awfully old and I may not have another chance. I'll take you with me." "You know I can't travel, Agnes," you said. A long time passed. "Do you really want to go?" you asked me. I said I did. "I've been thinking about the Portland Retreat," you said. "I don't want to force you into it," I said; "I'd rather die first." "Don't say that," you said; "I want to go. It's too much trouble now." "Do they have room for you?" I asked. "They have an opening now," you said, "but they may not have it for much longer." And then you turned scarlet. "I wouldn't have gone and left you here," you said. I said I knew that, and I wouldn't go home unless you went to the Retreat. And the next week you did, and I was on a train back to Vermont.

The
Upland
Pasture

64

When I got off the train in North Chittendon, I was dressed in black and wore a hat with a veil, just as I had done on the train from Portland. I wanted to see Cloudy Pastures; I wanted to see the hills; I wanted to feel the air of the town, but I didn't want anyone to see me or recognize me. I knew no one would be curious about an elderly woman who wore a hat and veil as so many old ladies still did. I went to the livery stable and asked if they had a carriage and the owner, who I didn't know, said they had long since given up on carriages, but they still kept a few in good repair for nostalgic reasons and because tourists like me loved to take them out on the roads. The stable keeper gave me a map and told me that whoever rented the carriages generally drove them to the highest farm in the area. I asked him what the name of the farm was, and he said that people around the town called it the Brown place; he said three of the Browns ran the enormous farm and they ran it well. They saw the value of tourists and provided little boxes of maple sugar candies for them, cans of maple syrup, and best of all, well-marked trails up the mountains which they kept clear of branches and debris. He congratulated me; I couldn't have found a more beautiful place in all of Vermont to visit.

He told me that the young people who rented the first carriage earlier in the day had driven it out to the Brown farm. They followed the map, the same one he gave me, and he guessed they were still up there. I said I'd take the second carriage. He wanted to know if I could control a horse and I said a horse was one of the few things I knew I could control. I didn't need the map. I got in the carriage and took the road up to Cloudy Pastures. I went up higher and higher and made the hairpin turn and found myself facing the tall white house which glowed under the newly hatched sun. Up above the farm, the meadows soared, one after another, and the black and white cows moved like unmoored ships through the grass. The road was edged with waves of goldenrod and the uncut fields of grass were waves of green tossed back and forth by the gentle wind. A cool breath blew out of the pine woods and over my face. I drove past the house and hitched the carriage in a clearing behind it and began climbing the trail marked "to log cabin." Tourists, I imagined, must climb up to it and rest. I climbed slowly, breathing deeply, and there it was, the cabin, the brass bed, still standing incongruously in front of it. I wondered why they still kept it there. Memories of the trial had long ago faded from people's minds. I thought, leaning against a tree, it was more convenient to keep it there than to make a new bench for people to sit on.

The western breezes swept over the hills and the forests murmured gratefully. In the tilled meadows, the rye and the wheat nodded and the corn rustled, and beneath the trees, the cattle lay at the edges of the fields, and it was noon, and they were content. The crocuses had gone, and the lilacs had followed them, and then the roses, but now the winds blew heavy with the fragrance of honeysuckle and hay, and sweet cut grass. The blackberry bushes were full of thick ruby red berries, and the fat, black ripe ones at which the birds dived, shrieking. The oaks were alive with bluejays and robins flew, and a hummingbird quivered near a wild rose bush and hovered in the air, feeding. A bee flew its beeline back to its hive. From higher up on the mountain came a little corkscrew of black smoke and the smell of wood burning. Someone was making charcoal. The sound of a chain saw cutting wood for the winter woodpile could be heard in the valley below. An engine started up somewhere, chugged into life and fell silent. When I was a child, there had been no electric saws, no automobiles.

I saw a young couple coming out of the cabin and for the first time saw the sign above the door: Gift Shop. I saw them begin walking toward a path in the woods behind the cabin and I began circling through the woods so that I would come up in back of them. Finally, they sat down and I stayed behind them, hidden by a large tree. I knew how to be quiet in the woods. "It's so peaceful here," the young girl said, leaning against a tree and staring up through the trees to the sky; "I could stay here forever." "I wish we could," said the young man. "Maybe someday we will," she said. "Who could ever afford this?" he asked. "Well," said the girl, standing up, brushing off her skirt, "let's go up higher. I'm not tired."

They climbed until the town was spread out beneath them, the two church spires, the twin graveyards, one on each side of the road, guarding the entrance into town, the whitewashed houses with their black shutters, the heavy grapevines on their trellises mere green blurs. The church bells rang out and the sounds spread out in the air. I had climbed up behind them. It was astonishing how easy it was to follow people when they had no reason to suspect the presence of anything that wanted to harm them. "Look at the cows," the girl said, pointing to the meadow below; "they're really very stupid, aren't they?" "I guess they are," he said. "I wonder what they think about?" she asked. "I'm sure they don't think at all," he said. "I don't know," she said. "Only humans think," he said. He grinned. "That's why we're called the lords of creation," he said. He looked around him.

If the trees were whispering, if the water was running over the rocks and into the earth, if the clouds were whispering, saying man knows little of his lordship and less of his subjects and less of himself, he did not hear them. He and the young girl stood up and walked on the earth as if they knew it belonged to them and would always support them, and because they thought that and knew it to be true, it was. They stepped on the ground as if they knew the fabric would never tear and they walked in the golden light and they were golden themselves and the magnificence of North Chittendon and its high upland pasture, its green emerald pond set improbably in the highest mountain peak, was only an appropriate setting for them. And as they drove down the mountain road, the crow would caw his knowing comment, the hawk would swing and sail aloft, and the field mice would scurry back and forth, and the very air would woo them and tell them that the earth had wedded itself to them out of love, the phenomenal love of the earth for its creatures.

I waited until I was sure they were well on the road back to town; from where I stood, I could see their carriage. Their world was not mine. And so I went back to Highbury. No one had recognized me at Cloudy Pastures. How could they have? I behaved like a tourist; I kept on my veil. It was as if I and my family had never lived there at all. Our names were wiped out. We were no longer caught in the wheel.

Highbury

65

Nothing had changed at Highbury. I could see that before the train pulled into the station. The town dreamed under the whitish yellow sun. It was a foggy day and the green leaves were grayed by the mist. A cab driver offered to take me to the asylum, but I asked him to take my bag, paid him, and walked on to the asylum myself. There was Doctor Train's old gray house with its funny turret. The slate roof of his house and all the other houses glistened in the mist and faint light. The brick buildings were warm and solid and familiar. It had now been twenty years since I had left the asylum. I went into the main building. The office was where it had always been.

When I asked for Doctor Train, I was told he wasn't there; the clerk said he must have retired or died or both. "Well," I told the clerk, "I'm an inmate here who's been out on parole and I want to be readmitted." "Why?" asked the clerk; "don't you have any money?" "Actually, I have plenty of money," I said, "but I'm suicidal. I always have been. Look in the records." "What's your name?" he asked. "Agnes Dempster," I said. He got up and went into the records room. "There's a little old lady out there who wants to be committed again," I heard him say; "she doesn't look like she'd hurt a fly." I heard a file drawer open. "Good Lord!" he said. He must have shown my file to the girl inside, because the two of them fell to whispering over something. When he came out, his attitude toward me had changed.

"You're voluntarily committing yourself?" he asked. It was 1940; the insane were beginning to have legal status. I said I was. "You'll have to give up your clothes and spend some time on the observation ward," he said, watching me uneasily. I said that was only what I had expected. And so I was again at Highbury.

After two weeks, I was moved down to the first ward, and after a month, I had full privileges. I wandered everywhere. I was particularly fond of the neighboring farm which had once belonged to the asylum, but which had been sold when families complained about their relatives working on a farm because they were ordered to do so. The families refused to believe the work for which their relatives were not paid was good for them; they no longer had confidence in the old philosophy which held that fresh air and hard work balanced the body and the mind, and so the farm had gone. I would wander here and there, like a cow separated from the herd, and when I got to the farm, I helped out with the chores. And then, when I got too stiff to do much, I would sit under the trees and watch the others work. I felt like a ghost haunting a previous life. It was not an existence everyone would have envied, but I was perfectly happy. Coming home from Oregon, I had cried for six days. I had learned to mourn for my lost ones and so they let me go.

I was becoming older and stiffer and my excursions about the asylum were not as extensive as they had been. In the winter, I tended to remain inside. And so things went on until I was sixty-seven. When I was sixty-seven, they said my mind was beginning to wander and they told me to ask before I went outside because I didn't always have a clear conception of what the weather was like. I said that was nonsense, I had always been aware of the weather, and could even anticipate it before it came.

And then one day I woke up and wanted to climb the hill in back of the asylum and look down on the village. I asked the attendant if I could go, and she said why not? It was spring after all. And so I walked out, through the blossoming trees, the pollen fragrant in the air, up to the top of the hill, and when I got there, I was terribly sleepy, but I was in no hurry to lie down, either. Lately, it took me so long to get back up. And then, suddenly, I was falling slowly through the air, and I looked down, and saw the girl in the grass reaching up to me and I reached out my arms to her and I saw we had the same face and I saw I would never be separated from her again. Never again would I feel like a half-moon torn from itself, bleeding silently and steadily into the cold sky, watched by the impenetrable, brilliant stars. I felt my face against hers and I felt something in my hand and when I raised my hand, I saw it: the doll! The doll and its body! And I pressed the doll to me and squeezed my eyes shut in pure joy and then the other girl and I were tumbling together in one another's arms, laughing, and the doll, its head safe on its body, was safe between us. It was the most wonderful dream I ever had.

HIGHBURY STATE HOSPITAL FOR THE INSANE
Medical Records

AGNES DEMPSTER

1940–47: Behavior good. She helps in the dining room and on the ward. She is particularly helpful with violent patients who take to her and she to them. She sells much of her needlepoint and her artwork. She is often irritable and suspicious and jumps if she suddenly comes upon someone in the hall or someone comes into her room.

1948: Behavior continues good. Her mind, however, is beginning to wander, probably with the onset of senile dementia. She goes out in her uniform thinking it is spring while a snowstorm rages. She still manifests considerable irritability, perhaps because her impaired sight causes her to be taken by surprise; and considerable depression, although nothing very remarkable.

June 2, 1949: Agnes Dempster was discovered in the High Meadow on the grounds of the old asylum farm beneath a tree after a search was made for her when she failed to return to the ward in time for dinner. She had evidently died in her sleep. Cause of death: natural causes. Condition: unimproved. At her previous written request, she was buried in the old asylum cemetery. Town health officials have granted official approval.

"Look at this," one of the attendants said, coming into the office holding a newspaper clipping he had found in the office files. He began to read:

**YOUNG WOMAN MURDERS
AN INNOCENT GIRL
AND THEN ATTEMPTS TO PUT
AN END
TO HER OWN LIFE—
HER VICTIM DIES A FEW HOURS
LATER—
THE STORY IN DETAIL**

The darkest chapter in the history of Montpelier was written Saturday, and Christmas is shadowed by the most terrible tragedy ever known in the annals of the town. . . . A representative of *The Spectator* was soon on the scene and from a mass of distorted rumors, was able to glean the following story:

And he kept on reading, until he had finished the article.

"That old lady?" one of the clerks asked. "The darkest chapter ever written," said another clerk, laughing; "they were so melodramatic then." "Were they?" asked one of the girls. "No one's shocked by murder anymore," one of the men said. "Don't be ridiculous," said one of the girls, turning her back to them. "The poor thing," someone said; "to live so long." "Put the clipping back before we get in trouble," said one of the clerks. "I wonder who Doctor Train was," one of the girls said. "Who knows? Who cares? It's way before our time," said another; "a doctor's a doctor."

The sun, which had been covered by a cloud, suddenly pulled loose and its brilliant golden light flooded the room. It gilded them all.

ABOUT THE AUTHOR

SUSAN FROMBERG SCHAEFFER is the author of four earlier novels, *Falling, Anya, Time in Its Flight,* and *Love,* as well as five collections of poetry and one book of short stories. She was educated at the University of Chicago where she wrote the first doctoral dissertation on Vladimir Nabokov. She has written many scholarly articles and is a frequent book reviewer for the *Chicago Sun-Times*. She is Professor of English at Brooklyn College and a founding member of its Master of Fine Arts Program in Poetry. She lives in Brooklyn and Vermont with her husband and two children.

The Days of Eternity

by
Gordon Glasco

Here is a breathtaking saga of a passionate love so overwhelming that it defies war, betrayal, conscience—and time itself. One Sunday morning, Anna Miceli, a successful American lawyer, sits in church and sees a man—and her heart stands still. At that moment, time melts away. Once again Anna is the innocent girl of an Italian country village. It is wartime, and the time of her first consuming love—for the young German lieutenant who commands the occupying forces. But when he commits an unspeakable act, Anna's world is shattered, her life changed forever. Now, twenty-eight years later, he stands before her—a priest. And now, Anna knows the time has come to face an agonizing choice. For here is the man whose memory has been a cold cinder of hatred inside her, the man she has vowed someday to destroy—and the man her turbulent heart can never surrender.

Read THE DAYS OF ETERNITY, on sale September 1, 1984, wherever Bantam paperbacks are sold, or use the handy coupon below for ordering:

A masterwork of mounting suspense, in the grand tradition of Alfred Hitchcock and Mary Higgins Clark

WOMAN IN THE WINDOW

Dana Clarins

It began on the happiest day of her life. Natalie Rader was on top of the world. Freed from her empty marriage, newly single and loving it, she was celebrating her first million-dollar deal. Now, as night descended on the city, she stood gazing through her third-story office window.

Suddenly, on the street below, a man was running toward a construction site. Natalie saw him clearly, and she saw what he threw over the fence: a gun. As she watched in horror, the man looked up. His eyes locked with hers . . . and Natalie Rader's well-ordered life was about to come apart. . . .

Don't miss WOMAN IN THE WINDOW, on sale July 14, 1984, wherever Bantam Books are sold, or use the handy coupon below for ordering:

SPECIAL
MONEY SAVING
OFFER

Now you can have an up-to-date listing of Bantam's hundreds of titles plus take advantage of our unique and exciting bonus book offer. A special offer which gives you the opportunity to purchase a Bantam book for only 50¢. Here's how!

By ordering any five books at the regular price per order, you can also choose any other single book listed (up to a $4.95 value) for just 50¢. Some restrictions do apply, but for further details why not send for Bantam's listing of titles today!

Just send us your name and address plus 50¢ to defray the postage and handling costs.